Following careers as a film e
Roger M. Kean has written 1≥
under various pseudonyms. Among his non-fiction work he has written the best-selling
*The Complete Chronicle of the Emperors of Rome, Forgotten Power: Byzantium—Bulwark
of Christianity, Exploring Ancient Egypt,* and with Angus Konstam *Pirates: Predators of
the Sea.* He is a member of Goodreads.com and the M/M Romance Group. Kean lives
with his partner in a medieval town in England on the border with Wales.

As Roger M. Kean
Felixitations
Thunderbolt—Torn Enemy of Rome
A Life Apart (Empire Trilogy #1)
Gregory's Story (Empire Trilogy #2
Harry's Great Trek (Empire Trilogy #3)
What's A Boy Supposed to Do

As Zack Fraker
Boys of Vice City
Boys of Disco City
Boys of Two Cities
Boys of the Fast Lane
Boy of the West End
Raw Recruits
Blood and Lust
Desert Studs
The Warrior's Boy
Deadly Circus of Desire (Boys of Imperial Rome #1)
The Satyr of Capri (Boys of Imperial Rome #2)

Under other names
Mississippi Hustler (Gay Pulp Fiction #1 – Rod Bellamy)
Mulholland Meat (Gay Pulp Fiction #2 – Kip Nolan)

In progress
The Wrath of Seth (Boys of Imperial Rome #1)
Mulholland Dreams (Gay Pulp Fiction #3 – Kip Nolan)

Felixitations

Masterful, unforgettable celebration of the human heart expressing itself through its fleshly, sensuous vehicle. It is by far the most powerful thing of beauty I have had the honor to enjoy in recent memory.

I highly recommend this book to anyone who enjoys beautiful, lyrical, challenging writing. — **RJ Scott**

An irresistible force just as Felix is an irresistible character and Felixitations is an irresistible book.

Thunderbolt – Torn Enemy of Rome

If you are a history buff and love sexy scenes thrown in the middle of the discourse, this is the book for you.

A spectacular adventure of a war within a war in this historical rare gem…the best historical romance I have ever read. It has the most real history and the most real love.

A Life Apart

Two unique and memorable characters and the most remarkable book

Love, sex, violence, adventure, seashells, 1884 British military strategy, spitting camels, Fuzzy Wuzzies and Yorkshire pudding. What more could you desire in a historical romance novel? It's a brilliant story of treachery and hate, loyalty and love. **Hearts On Fire Reviews**

A piece of work to be savored at leisure without the indignity of interruption. This is a work of gay literary fiction that transcends the romance genre to give us something lasting.

Superb writing, refreshing, and bang-on history. — **Gerry Burnie**

Gregory's Story

Action, adventure, history, m/m romance...what's not to love? The story is told in page turning fashion.

Boys of Vice City, Boys of Disco City, Boys of Two Cities,
Boys of the Fast Lane

Delightfully homoerotic stories of love and lust… Cassics .

The sense of sexual heat is palpable. Zack's brilliant and explicitly erotic drawings add to the sexual excitement…fun, fast-paced and deliciously lewd.

Fast paced and full of sexual thrills, adventures and misadventures. Both the writing, and Zack's unique drawings deliver a mega-watt erotic charge.

Harry's Great Trek

ROGER M. KEAN

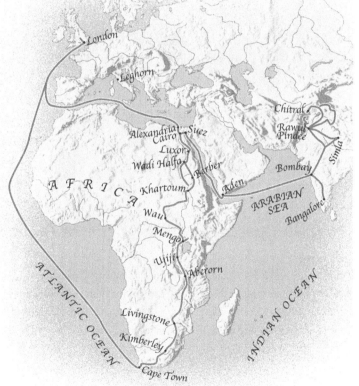

BOOKS

Reckless Books
Shropshire, England
http://recklessbooks.co.uk

Cover illustration and design by Oliver Frey
http://oliverfreyart.com

ISBN-13: 978-1507837788

Author's note

In Britain, the term "public school" means the exact opposite of its meaning in the
United States. A British public school—more often than not with a substantial number
of pupils boarding—is a private, fee-paying establishment, often regarded as elitist and
for the children of well-off parents. Today, many of these establishments have become
coeducational… but not in the time depicted in this story.

This is not just a continuation of the stories in *A Life Apart* and *Gregory's Story*,
it is more than that—it is a wraparound… and it is Harry's own story.

The love that dare not speak its name in this century is such a great affection of an elder for a younger man as there was between David and Jonathan, such as Plato made the very basis of his philosophy, and such as you find in the sonnets of Michelangelo and Shakespeare. It is that deep spiritual affection that is as pure as it is perfect. It dictates and pervades great works of art, like those of Shakespeare and Michelangelo…It is beautiful, it is fine, it is the noblest form of affection. There is nothing unnatural about it. It is intellectual, and it repeatedly exists between an older and a younger man, when the older man has intellect, and the younger man has all the joy, hope and glamor of life before him. That it should be so, the world does not understand. The world mocks at it, and sometimes puts one in the pillory for it.

— Oscar Wilde, May 25, 1895

For all those who inspired Harry's story, you know who you are,
and for Oli, heart and home.

PART ONE

Cast adrift, 1874–1891

"Soldier, soldier come from the wars,
Why don't you march with my true love?"
"We're fresh from off the ship an' 'e's maybe give the slip,
An' you'd best go look for a new love."
New love! True love!
Best go look for a new love,
The dead they cannot rise, an' you'd better dry your eyes,
An' you'd best go look for a new love.

— Rudyard Kipling, "Barrack-room Ballads"

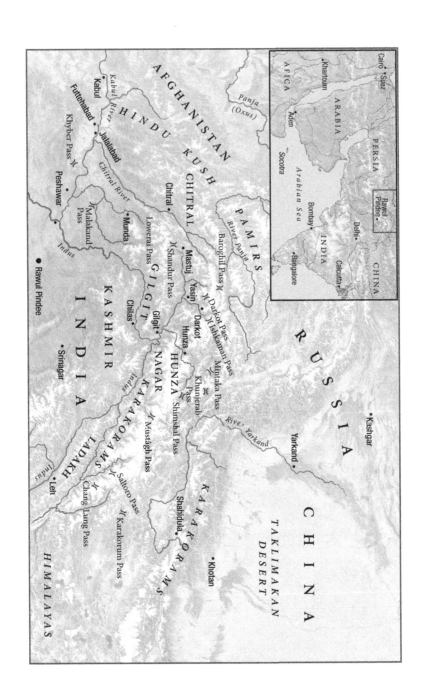

8

CHAPTER 1 | *Suez to Aden, August 1885*

IS IT really only six months since the murdering bastards speared General Gordon?

Harry Smythe-Vane, who insisted on being called simply Vane, bent his gaze between two decks of open porthole shades, white squares against the dark water that creamed along the iron hull twenty feet below. The wake streaming from the stern made a pale tramline etched against a violet sea, and for brief moments marked the steamship's southerly passage. He was forward enough that by leaning out over the rail he could just see the *Malabar*'s ram bow cutting through the dark waters of the Red Sea, the Star of India proudly displayed on either side of the point.

A Peninsular and Oriental or a British-India Steamship Company liner would have been more comfortable than a Royal Navy troopship, but as luck (or otherwise) would have it, H.M.S. *Malabar* docked at Port Said to deliver fresh troops to Egypt at the opportune moment and so Harry's Dragoons regiment, barracked at Cairo but intended for India, entrained for Suez to catch the ship as it left the Canal. From there the vessel was bound for Aden to refuel and reprovision, and then across the Arabian Sea to drop the Dragoons at Bombay, before continuing its long journey around the peninsula to Madras and Calcutta.

"We Guards subalterns are dogsbodies as much as any ranker," William Maplethorpe had remarked sourly when, fresh from London, he joined Harry's detachment of 1st King's Dragoon Guards Regiment a few weeks before their departure from Cairo. The second lieutenant's moan was fair enough, but then, Harry's enveloping depression colored the view of his own station more than the drudgery of barracks life. He'd spent a couple of months' in Cairo fighting off exhaustion after the dispiriting retreat from the Sudan following the failure to relieve Khartoum. And the death of heroic General Charles Gordon there at the hands of Mahdist fanatics had not helped his mood—or indeed that of any other officer or serving soldier.

"How on earth could a bunch of religious crazies have so besmirched our dignity and made fools of British arms?" Maplethorpe had asked; rhetorically, Harry said to himself, since he was only spouting the newspapers' jingoism.

And gone unpunished for it. The further indignity of a retreat almost to the Egyptian border as the Mahdi's Dervish army forced them back from Merawi and Korti to Dongola and then finally to Wadi Halfa did nothing to raise morale—and William Maplethorpe was at that time yet in England so he missed the ignominy. Harry could list some minor victories, though insufficient to hide the fact of defeat.

But languishing in Cairo another wound nagged at Harry's soul. It was the real source of his low spirits: the uncertainty surrounding his friend Richard Rainbow's fate.

Harry's mood did not match the sea's sparkle. He wasn't paying the natural display any attention. In Cairo he'd feared that Richard was as hopelessly lost in the Sudanese wastelands as his "brother" Edward, for whom Richard had gone in search. Now—after Suez—Harry knew better, and the knowledge of both Rainbows' delivery from the Arabs cut like a knife even when he knew he should be delighted for them. The bitterness he couldn't avoid feeling lay as a lump of guilt in his stomach. At moments when he least expected it a dyspeptic sob rose up like a bubble of air desperate to escape.

Richard. It was always Richard. The exhalation became a sigh. He knew it was useless to think of him. The world thought of Richard and Edward Rainbow as twin brothers, an error both men deliberately promoted in order to explain their closeness. Richard's love for Edward eclipsed whatever Richard had felt for Harry and everything they had shared since school. His ever-present guilt rocked Harry whenever he faced the truth of his awful betrayal. When he and Richard learned that Edward had fallen into the hands of the murdering Mahdists, Harry hoped he was indeed dead at the hands of his captors, those tribesmen who had dragged the boy off from Metemma in the dead of night. Harry confessed to Richard something of the darkness in his heart, there in the riverside camp at Abu Kru before the fall of Khartoum. "I grew angry with

Edward, thinking about how selfish he was to run away from you the way he did," he blurted to Richard. "I told myself that whatever the circumstances, no matter how awful, I would never abandon you the way Edward did. But your love for him went deeper than any betrayal and I came to understand that, and finally accept it."

Accept it? No, not really.

"You see," he'd told William Maplethorpe in Cairo, "the first Richard and I knew that Edward was even in the expeditionary force with us to secure the escape of General Gordon from Khartoum was on the Nile near Metemma." Harry waved a hand dismissively. "You see, two years before that there had been some kind of family ruckus and Edward ran away from the school we all attended. He just vanished. Then he turns up there in the Sudan. Not that either of us knew it at the time, since it seems he hid himself from us. It was I who found the wounded sergeant who had taken Edward under his wing and he told us what passed, that they'd both been wounded at Abu Klea—trust me, that was a scrap worth missing—and that Edward had gone to seek help for the sergeant, since his own wound was only slight. Later, we learned of the Dervishes taking him. You can imagine how distraught Richard was to have lost his brother at school and to have almost found him again only to lose him to the enemy.

"It was a dark time. We all knew that captured white men were forced at the point of a blade to recant Christianity and embrace the faith of the Moslem, or face immediate decapitation. It seemed hardly likely that a headstrong boy like Edward would ever consent to apostasy."

"Why did he run away in the first place?"

Maplethorpe's was a reasonable question, but Harry felt unequal to the task of explaining the story of Richard and Edward's births, the mix-up that meant they were not even related, though raised by Colonel Rainbow and his wife as twin brothers. "It was something buried in their past. It must have hit Edward hard for him to run off and hide away, but that's what he did and evidently joined the Hussars as a trumpeter, which is how he found himself on the Nile campaign."

But then we heard that Edward's captors were not Mahdists that they were desert traders who would prefer to keep him alive in slavery. And so Richard hared off on what seemed like a hopeless quest to search for his true love.

A gong sounded, the one-hour alert for dinner. The Dragoons' commanding officer liked to keep to strict regimental orders, even aboard ship. Harry glanced back along the *Malabar*'s almost four hundred-foot upper deck, past the three barque-rigged masts with their spider's web of ropes and the huge belching stack rising from the confusion of superstructure. Time soon to retreat to the stiflingly hot cabin he shared with William Maplethorpe to dress. At least he wasn't crammed sardine-like in a can as were the enlisted ranks, hundreds sharing the new-fangled bunks stacked four high so that to turn around in bed the soldier had to clamber out and then get back in again in his new chosen orientation. A number of the lower ranks had secured accommodation on the open-top troop deck at the bow and stern areas with the advantage of fresh air, and the drawback of having to huddle under the central awning if it rained. It didn't a lot, but it might more on nearing their destination.

A school of flying fish leapt in silvery arches across his vision. Such fleeting moments. *"We've spent so many years, closer even than any brothers, thinking we were twins,"* Richard had said. *"I still feel like he's my brother."* Richard always mixed that latent misplaced guilt of incest with a bad conscience for hurting Harry. Harry knew that as well as he knew himself. *"I think your feelings for each other are as strong as they are because you aren't brothers, even if you didn't know that as you grew up,"* Harry replied. And then, not long after the withdrawal from Korti began, Richard obtained six months' leave of absence, joined a band of Arab traders, and vanished into the trackless dunes with little more than a rudimentary training in Arabic.

No, the subsequent months in Cairo had not been recuperation for Harry, a time only to mope for the loss of Richard's love, perhaps even the loss of Richard himself at the hands of the very sheik who agreed to act as his guide. There had been no guarantee of success, either in finding Edward or even coming back alive from the nest of Dervish vipers. Success, in fact, had hardly seemed a possibility.

The half-hour warning gong sounded and broke his sad reverie. Now he really had to go and clamber into formals for dinner. Full mess folderol in the blistering heat of the Red Sea suggested life in the cantonment of Rawul Pindee could be even worse.

But Harry had a plan, one that would avoid the dreariness of garrison life. He hoped.

ംക്ക

The relief at departing Aden was palpable throughout the *Malabar*. Making a good thirteen knots, with the upper sails catching the following wind, at least provided a deck breeze, even though the sun beating off the copper surface of the Gulf of Aden made it feel as though she sailed across a cauldron of boiling oil. To the northwest the low-lying dun-colored coast of Yemen framed the horizon, rising here and there to a line of purple jagged hills farther inland. The transport's route followed the Arabian coast to the point off exotic Oman before cutting across the Arabian Sea to the Indian subcontinent and Bombay.

At almost twenty years old, the *Malabar* showed her age in small matters, but the officers' accommodation was reasonable, better by far than that provided to the wives of officers and enlisted men alike, who were berthed in a single long cabin. This was the Dovecot, so named for the continual shrill squabbling that poured from its door and added to the squalls of noise from the adjacent nursery. The promiscuous conditions occasioned endless arguments among the women and even some fights between the lowest-born. Harry thanked his stars that he had no such dependents to concern him.

He knew that if he left the shade of the strung awning—which did little to abate the heat—and climbed the great foremast to the top-tree lookout, in the opposite direction he might just make out the hump of Socotra, the island famed for its mushroom-shaped dragon's blood trees. The thought of such an apocryphal climb caused his stomach to heave. He'd been quite unable to face the luncheon buffet in the regimental officers' wardroom.

"It is a great deal finer than the canned meat and hard biscuit of the desert march, so I'm informed."

Harry had managed a wan smile for William Maplethorpe, who in fact had only digested such fare second-hand, since he himself had not been on the Nile campaign. But they all knew the hard-tack rations on officer training exercises back home at Aldershot. Under other circumstances he might have reacted more warmly at the first subtle undertones in the young lieutenant's overtures of friendship, but the specter of Richard in Edward's embrace haunted his waking moments and stunted even an erotic response. His new friend ("For God's sake, Vane, call me Maps, everyone at school did.") had sought Harry out at every opportunity—they were of similar ages, Harry having turned twenty-one in the June past. But comely as he was, Maplethorpe wasn't Richard, and Harry's heart was still closed against anything more than distant friendship.

On the other hand he suffered the natural urges of his youth and Maplethorpe's evident interest in pursuing a more intimate relationship soon beat down Harry's reservations. That—and Harry's naturally polite nature—meant he did not rebuff Maplethorpe, and when it came to shipping out he agreed to share an officers' cabin. Such intimacy threw them into a cozier companionship whenever their varied duties brought them together within its private confines.

"I know I should take advantage of the fresh comestibles," he answered Maplethorpe. "Salted meat will soon be all that's left on the menu, but I fear my delicate constitution won't take this much for luncheon." He offset the effect of the arch words with a slight suggestion of throwing up, and immediately regretted the childish gesture. It made him feel he was back at Benthenham College.

But in fact I never allowed myself to behave in such a manner then.

The fried fish of various kinds, mutton chops running in grease, some kind of game pie (probably rank pigeon from Aden), with a "medley" of sad looking diced vegetables of indeterminate origin was simply too much for his stomach in the heat. His fellow subalterns, including Maplethorpe, second lieutenants, and a scattering of captains made short work of the fare, but Harry stuck to a small portion of fish.

"Anyway," he continued, "I've my books to study."

"Hah, my dear Vane, you will go blind trying to learn the Hindoo."

Harry waved his left hand airily while chasing a forkful of fish around his plate. "The Indian isn't so difficult, it's getting the hang of Pashto that's taxing, though having a basis in Persian is a help. Evan—my brother that is—argued that I should be a diplomatist to make good use of my flair for learning new tongues."

"I've not noticed you breaking into Arabic at every juncture." Maplethorpe ineffectively stifled his grin at Harry's reproving look.

"It is clear that you were not in the Sudan with us, my dear Maps, or you would know. Was there ever an opportunity? I had a friend—the Richard Rainbow I've spoken of—and he had a sound reason to learn to speak it, though he was never as good at languages as his brother. Indeed, Edward Rainbow is the only person I know who exceeded my enjoyment of mastering a new lingo… and he's now for home, his head no doubt filled with the Arabic picked up in captivity."

Maplethorpe raised eyebrows inquisitively. "You were going to tell me what happened to this friend."

Harry realized Maplethorpe wanted detail of how on earth two unrelated boys came to be brothers, let alone that they'd fallen in love with each other. (It hadn't been long after Maplethorpe's posting to Cairo that Harry and he first turned a clapped shoulder into a secret hug and then something more intimate in Harry's bed. That familiarity meant sex between men was not a taboo subject as long as there was no one to overhear them.) But he chose to deflect the evident curiosity. "I don't really know anything yet about Edward's captivity. I think I told you that we all met quite by happenstance in Suez and really only for two minutes due to the *Malabar*'s warning horn sounding."

Harry was unsure why he'd brought up the Rainbows, unless it was like worrying at an aching tooth. But there it was. The recurring images of what happened on that last day in Suez before the *Malabar* departed plagued Harry's every waking hour. The timing, as well as the event, was too cruel. The transport was docked and taking on provisions and fuel for the next leg of her journey to Aden; she was due to depart in hours and shore leave for the troops was over. Officers were expected on board before sunset, so Harry took a last landlubber's stroll on *Terra firma*. The prospect of being trapped on board a navy troopship for the ten days to Aden, with a day's layover for refueling, and then another two-and-a-bit weeks to reach Bombay did not appeal over much, even with the consolation of William's company. He wandered lonely among the garish stalls of the souk, undecided as to whether he really wanted a souvenir of Egypt. In mid-muse, a shout brought him to an abrupt standstill… and his heart lurched painfully.

"Harry!"

He whirled around, hardly daring to believe his ears. "Good God!" He choked over the words and then he was wrapped in Richard's arms, which stifled any further attempt to speak for a moment. The sounds of the teeming bazaar faded, tears pricked at his eyelids, and he breathed in the scent of his lover… his borrowed lover. "Oh, Richard."

"It really is you," said Richard breathlessly

They broke apart, staring wide-eyed in the amazement of meeting.

"You made it… and…" Harry trailed off in wonderment at the interloper approaching. An avatar of a boy grown into a young man, sun-darkened skin, almost absent hair on his shapely head, in ill-fitting army clothes, so familiar yet so changed. "…and Edward."

Edward smiled, almost shyly. At school they had never used Christian names. Harry swallowed uncomfortably. "Sorry… I've known you as Edward for so long now—ever since you—"

"Ran away from Benthenham." Edward laughed easily.

But then he could. He was back with his beloved Richard… brothers in arms. The glimmer of bitterness evaporated in the happiness at the reunion even as his breath hitched at the cruel timing. Harry extended a hand and shook Edward's, and then quite impulsively he leaned forward and gave Edward a long hug. "You must tell me about all your adventures, both of you. But I fear that'll have to wait until I get back to England." It gratified Harry to see a look of disappointment cross Richard's face. "You see I've had a few day's shore leave before going on to India with my regiment and our transport departs in less than an hour now. What a bugger. But we shall catch up soon. It's only a sixth-month tour of duty. And then…"

"You must come visit us, Harry."

Harry held Richard in his gaze for long seconds, and then gave him a tight-lipped smile. He nodded. "Yes, of course, I should like that."

He turned before the risk of another burst of tears unmanned him. The Smythe-Vanes did not make emotional scenes in public. It only occurred to him as he wove his way between the importuning traders that there had been a black-skinned African-Arab boy with the Rainbows, and he briefly wondered what his role with them might be. But the perfidy of finding Richard after so many months and then having to lose him again in such an impossibly abrupt manner swept away any curiosity as to what that might be.

Maplethorpe seemed to sense Harry's reluctance to reveal more of the mysterious Rainbows and changed the subject. "A tale for a cooler day, perhaps. So, is it a language-studying afternoon?"

"I shall retire to our cabin."

"Is it really any cooler two decks down? As this is our first voyage to the Great Peninsula, I am in no position to judge the truth behind the reasons for locating senior officers in cabins of their own on the port side of the ship."

Maplethorpe's comment piqued Harry's interest and took his mind off Richard for a few moments. "And what is this potential truth?"

"As we travel toward India, the port side faces away from the hot afternoon sun and so affords a cooler atmosphere. Were we returning home, the arrangements would be reversed so that, again, senior officers should benefit from being housed on the starboard, as far away from the sun as it is possible to be on a vessel the size of the *Malabar*."

"So in going out, our starboard side cabins are several degrees warmer by the afternoon?"

"So goes the hypothesis." Maplethorpe sighed heavily. "I suppose only on our promotion will we discover its accuracy." He reached out and took a scrubby looking orange from a bowl of fruit.

"I shall leave you to it." Harry swung his legs over the bench and stood. "I don't think I can take any more citrus, and I'm sure the surfeit I've had recently will stave off the scurvy until we reach Bombay."

"Indeed. And thank you for leaving me to it. You know full well how much I enjoy supervising my squadron's drill. I see no good reason why it requires an officer when the sergeant is far more capable than I. Think of me as you relax in the 'chill' of our abode."

Harry threw an ironic wave over his shoulder and briefly acknowledged the salute of the mess orderly who held the door open for him as he stepped through onto the muster deck. The temperature outside was the same as within, but the vessel's speed generated a momentary pleasing draft of heated breeze. As he descended the steep stairs to the lower decks, Harry looked forward to renewing his acquaintance with the languages of Afghanistan. Learning as much as he could was central to his plan.

CHAPTER 2 | *Shottery and Benthenham, 1874–1878*

IN SPITE OF William's skepticism, Harry had convinced himself that their cabin *was* cooler than being on the muster deck—what a passenger liner might more grandly refer to as the promenade. Tiny as it was, the rectangular compartment represented a haven of comfort, even though the Admiralty had designed it for one and the War Office insisted on fitting in two subalterns. He hadn't missed Maplethorpe's envious prod at senior officers having cabins all to themselves. The door—so narrow it obliged Harry to sidle through it—faced the open square port through which he heard the hiss of the sea against the hull, and through which came a damp smell of ozone. Two small cots fitted to the sidewalls left a space two feet wide in between, which allowed a cane table to sit under the porthole.

Harry sat on his cot, too short for his six-foot frame, and thumbed the pages of a book in which were listed common words in Pashto and Tajik. Harry traced a fingertip across the raised gilt letters of the volume's leather cover which spelled the name of its compiler: the intrepid trader-explorer Robert Shaw ignored the rule in force at the time that no Englishman should venture beyond India's frontiers. Seventeen years ago he journeyed north to Yarkand and farther, to the court of the Muslim adventurer Yakub Beg at Kashgar on the westernmost edge of the dread Taklamakan Desert. Shaw's intention was trade, but also to discover the truth that a Russian was already courting Yakub Beg, who controlled a vital section of the fabulous Silk Road from China. Tsar Alexander III's expansionist ministers were forever trying to find routes by which the army might invade British India.

To Harry the book represented more than a useful compendium: each page turned released a scent of the lands Shaw had explored; every column of text freed the acid-excitement of jeopardy; every word conjured the Pathan tribesman in all his violent grandeur. In short, Shaw's book was a passport to an experience far in excess of mere garrison duty. It was very much a part of Harry's plan to join an enterprise in which he hoped to equal Richard's evident achievements in the Sudan as revealed by his success in finding Edward. If he accomplished his ambition to become a "political" it might also give him something more than a broken heart to think about. The trick would be to obtain an attachment to the Indian Political Department, which might as well be described as the Intelligence Department. The IDP recruited most of its agents to the petty states from the officer corps of the British Army in India, and the role of ambassador-spy appealed to Harry's sense of adventure.

What excitement, what endangerment! Robert Shaw spent several months, virtually a prisoner of the wily ruler, before being dispatched back in the role of petitioner to the viceregal authority in Calcutta. Yakub Beg claimed British protection against the grasping Russian militarists (although it seemed clear he was simply playing off one great power against the other). The Viceroy was happy to supply the barest polite minimum, anything to keep overbearing Russian influence at bay and as far away from the borders of India as possible: the Tsar desired the brightest jewel in the Empress Victoria Regina's crown.

As he began to study, a part of Harry's mind reflected on the omnipresent temperature. The heat encountered crossing the Sudanese Bayuda Desert, and in the stone pan at Gakdul wells building two way-forts, was enough to fry the brain. But dry. Out here on the ocean the humidity made the heat more unbearable, so that within minutes every bit of clothing clung to the skin. One trooper described it as like being gripped by an amorous octopus, which seemed odd, considering he was a farmer's son from Shropshire and surely uneducated about the sea's denizens. Carter—Harry and Maplethorpe's on-board soldier-servant—did his best to keep up with their laundry, but the wet atmosphere made short work of the man's best efforts. Harry knew from those who had been stationed in India that he would encounter a drenching humidity until the blessing of the monsoon rains. Likely by the time they actually reached Rawul Pindee, the cooling downpours would have ceased for the year. He swung his legs up and leaned back against the bulkhead and cast his mind back to something cooler… much cooler.

It was a shock to hear the truth behind Edward Rainbow's sudden and out-of-character disappearance from school. As one of the seniors in The Lodge, one of eight boarding houses at elite Benthenham College, Richard Rainbow confided in him what had driven Edward to flee. The ship's thudding engine seemed to drift away as the memories crowded in. Harry had pressed Richard to spend that Christmas vacation of 1882 with him at the Smythe-Vanes' palatial country mansion of Hadlicote rather than mope around brotherless at the Rainbow's Costwolds home. It seemed like such a long time ago, but that was surely because the Nile campaign's stress and distress made it seem so far off; in reality barely three years had elapsed.

"That's really kind..." Richard had said.

"You would be company for me, Rainbow. Someone my own age around." Harry's older brother, Evan Frederick Peverell Smythe-Vane to give the man his full name, was five-going-on-six years Harry's senior and, in the way of aristocratic families, the boys had been raised quite separately. And it wasn't as though Harry had many friends at Benthenham.

It had been like that at Shottery Hall, the preparatory school to which his parents sent him aged eight in the ferociously cold January of 1874. After the comforts of Hadlicote's nursery, Shottery Hall came as a jolt to little Harry's system, all the worse for the extraordinary degree to which he thought headmaster Mr. Bowles's head resembled a skull. Only the lightest covering of gray skin covered the bony protrusions and concavities of his cranium, and its papery thinness blended indistinctly to wisps of cottony-white hair adhering to the sculpted cliffs of his temples. Harry shuddered at every unwelcome contact, particularly when examined under the large magnifying glass Mr. Bowles used to compensate for his strangely damaged eyesight. In the way of claustrophobic boarding schools, there were experts who would tell of how Boggsie, as the boys for some reason called him, could see well upward and downward but had a thick line through the center of his vision, hence the massive loupe. All Harry knew was that it made the man's gimlet eyes bulge to the terrifying proportions of a gargoyle, like one of those on the corners of the family chapel at Hadlicote which confronted arriving worshippers as they rounded the ancient yew from the driveway. The grinning beast so frightened him when he was very young that he hid his face in the folds of his mother's coat. Facing Mr. Bowles, there was nowhere to hide.

"Why do you shiver, boy?"

"It's the cold, please, sir."

"Cold? What cold?" The glass passed in scrutiny over Harry's face. "Your brother never suffered from the cold."

And that was another burden: the constant reminders that Evan had flourished there before him.

"At Shottery Hall, we pride ourselves on preparing our boys perfectly to fit in with the public schools to which they go on. This is achieved through excellence." Mr. Bowles leaned forward and raised his hairy eyebrows. They reminded Harry of the tufty brushes between the horns of Hadlicote's Home-Farm bulls when they tossed their heads. "But even more is achieved through *discipline*." The emphasis lent terror to the word. "Here at Shottery Hall, Smythe-Vane Junior, my demand is all the law there is. Bowles's Law is what you obey, or I shall come down on you with utmost severity. Do I make myself clear?"

"Yes, sir."

The forty-odd boys aged between seven and thirteen shivered through the winters in their simple short pants, shirts, and painfully thin jerseys, struggled to write when the ink in their desk wells froze, and then sweated the summers in reverse discomfort. Boggsie hammered home the intricacies of Latin, Greek, and English, often with a birch cane, while a younger scholar—at least, he wore a gown like one—pummeled them with arithmetic and history… all those monarchs. (*Willy, Willy, Harry, Ste / Harry Dick, John, Harry three / One, two, three Neds, Richard two / Harrys four, five, six—then who?* There were too many King Harrys and in the immutable way boys in an establishment where only surnames are allowed could ferret out the hidden Christian name, every time they were forced to parrot the mnemonic the class underlined each *Harry* with demonic glee. He was only happy no one ever discovered the true nature of the name that his parents gave him at the baptismal font, and which not even the servants at Hadlicote dared ever use.)

There was a part-time teacher, obscurely called Kreutzinger, who took them for geography and physical exercise, which included reciting the capitals of major European countries while swimming in the weed-clogged River Avon. The spartan school stood on a slope above the confluence of Shottery Brook with the Avon, not far from Shakespeare's Stratford. The school was not so far from Hadlicote either, but too far for Harry to run back home in those first horrid weeks when it seemed every hand was turned against him and all too often found satisfaction in slapping or punching him. Mrs. Bowles acted in the capacity of matron, but her buxom bosom did not extend to cuddles for young boys lost and away from home. Quite the opposite, in fact: she was a harridan who charged the boys from their pocket money for any medicine and she had no time at all for "cry-babies."

Harry's happiest moments of the day started the minute he curled up on his uncomfortable paillasse under a scanty blanket. *Alone at last.* He didn't much mind evening *prep* either, the task of sitting for an hour preparing for the next day's lessons, memorizing whole passages of Gaius Aurelius Cotta's tedious orations for recital, and working out the English translation of the Latin. He found a calm in the eye of daily cyclonic activity while conjugating verbs and declining nouns, without reference to anyone else. The boys treated prep as a free-for-all the minute whichever adult on guard duty vanished for a bit of time-out (usually a pipe of tobacco), but Harry's head-down attitude earned him the epithet "dirty swot."

Early on in his life, then, Harry learned to keep his own counsel and hold others at bay through an icy self-control. He was no better born than several of his fellow pupils, but he created a carapace of snooty aristocratic indifference, while ensuring as he grew older a cool respect through an unsuspected skill for boxing. The sport, while held in high regard for gentlemen of a certain type, found no favor with Mr. Bowles. He regarded "pygmachia" as fit only for "lowborn stevedores." However, Herr Kreutzinger regularly arranged bouts in secret. These were held in a makeshift ring in one of the stables, now free of equine pursuits and disused—apart from the occasional storage of sports equipment—since the Hall had fallen on hard times and been sold off as a school.

In a reversal of character young Harry could never work out, his very aloofness made him a fine pugilist, and all the better since—in complete double-contravention of Bowles's Law—Kreutzinger encouraged betting between those selected boys who were allowed to watch the fights. Kreutzinger took twenty per cent of each bet placed, half of which went to the winning boxer of each bout. In this way, Harry augmented his pocket money, although the excess inevitably went straight into Mrs. Bowles's capacious pocket in return for styptic pencils to dab on his bruises. If the woman ever wondered where they came from, she never asked.

Harry never lowered his guard, not even out of the ring, and never allowed his boxing success turn him into a popular figure among his peers, though as he progressed through the years and attained some eminence he could not prevent the hero worship of younger boys. And then, like so many before him, there came the inevitable moment when his age stripped Harry of a senior boy's rare privileges. It came in the transfer from the discomforts (but familiar and understood) of prep school to the unknown and feared horrors of public school.

In his case Harry moved from Shottery Hall at one end of the Costwold Hills to the other… and Benthenham College. He carried his carefully crafted persona with him to this new, terrifying environment. So he was well aware of the way his peers in The Lodge viewed him: stuck-up, haughty, manicured and fashion conscious but conservatively tailored. A swat-snot more interested, for instance, in the work of the rash of ridiculous French daubers who called themselves collectively the Impressionists as making an impression on the rugby field. However, as a well-respected boxer and tennis player few called him "Smarmy"—derived, of course from the homonym of *Vane*—to his face. (Harry banished his double-bareled surname on the first day at Benthenham.) But he knew what they all thought of him. Harry was in fact as lonely a boy as he'd ever been.

So when that fateful Christmas of 1882 after Edward's sudden disappearance he added, "We might even get up to some japes," it came as little surprise that Richard Rainbow responded with amused and possibly mocking astonishment. "Do you actually extend to… jolly *japes*, my dear Vane?"

Japes indeed. Oh how I longed to have japes with Richard. And how little he knew at that moment when he accepted my invitation to spend the festive season at Hadlicote with my family how much I wanted him… every bit of him.

As though it were yesterday, Harry remembered Alfred Winner—Winner the Spinner—holding forth in The Lodge on the Rainbows, who were temporarily absent from the Senior Common Room on some mission of their own. "Like limpets," he said with a shake of the head. "Those brothers are closer to themselves than to anyone else." And Harry resented Edward his intimacy with Richard.

The three had started at Benthenham College in the January of 1878. The Lent term was out of kilter with the normal school year commencement of September, and Harry still shivered at his memory of his thirteen-year-old self standing in the freezing Junior Common Room of The Lodge with a dreadful sense of déjà vu that this was still Shottery, under the keen interest of boys his age and some years older; a gaze Harry was certain contained not a little gleeful hostility. "New Bugs" were always bullied... *Willy, Willy, Harry, Ste...* It would all have been even more awful were it not for a quickly whispered greeting from his fellow *newbies* before they had nervously shuffled in from the hallway. "I'm Richard Rainbow. My brother Edward."

"H–Harry Vane."

It warmed him that the boy had offered their Christian names so simply because there was little else to provide inner heat. But as chill as the Junior Common Room was the flat scrutiny of the three gentlemen who faced them, standing upright, stiff and military, hands tucked behind their backs, was far colder. The room stretched into a wide bay window that housed a table between the arch of a semi-circular window seat, and with chairs at its ends and three facing the window. This, Harry learned was called Prep Table, and after high tea accommodated the house monitor of the day and his favored henchmen of the Junior Common Room to oversee daily prep. Running centrally down the length of the room was Long Table, its venerable surfaces scarred by the penknife-carved names of endless wicked boys. There were wooden benches either side for the rest of the Junior Common Room to sit at their prep. With a shuffle up of the juniors, the seniors could just fit around Long Table for evening prayers and house notices read out by the housemaster, Mr. Tonkins.

All this knowledge was an hour and more in the future as Harry and the two Rainbows faced the dour gentlemen before them. The one who seemed gowned in the more oppressive seniority because of the gold capped swagger stick tucked under the left armpit of his immaculate morning coat spoke in a clipped voice. "Quiet down, please, JCR." The drawn out pronunciation made the letters into *jay-see-eurrr*. He barely raised his voice, but it carried and the room stilled instantly to an occasional shuffle of leather house-shoe soles on bare polished floorboards. He never took his stern eyes off the new boys. "Stand up straight." Another rolled *r*.

"Yessir," the fairer haired of the two other new boys snapped out. That was Richard, Harry noted, and glowed inside at the recognition.

A flicker of distaste passed across Swagger Stick's august visage and he enunciated each word clearly with a gap between them, as though speaking to an imbecile. "Do not call me 'sir,' I am a College prefect, not a master…" He made it sound like *pr-raefect*. His eyes widened in question. "Which are you?"

"Rainbow, sir—"

"You may address me as Eltern. I am The Lodge's head of house and the College's most senior prefect this year. The gentlemen with me are Roberts and Elphinstone, house prefects." He unfolded his right arm and indicated behind at four less exalted boys standing self-importantly apart from the rest of the JCR. "Runsam is senior house monitor. Messers. Jefferies, Woolfe, and Richards are the dormitory monitors, to be obeyed without question at all times. Are you clear on that?"

"Yes, Eltern," the brothers said in smart unison. Harry's mutter mingled with theirs and he was grateful for the unspoken support.

Eltern manipulated the swagger stick with practiced ease as he reached inside his coat and produced a small notebook. He consulted a page, and glanced up at Harry. "Since these two are Rainbows, by subtraction that makes you Smythe-Vane."

Harry nodded.

"Speak up!"

"Yes, Eltern. But j-just Vane will be sufficient."

"You may offer opinion when asked, but not otherwise. I remember your brother referred to himself by the glory of his full appellation. He was head of house when I was new."

The look Harry received was not a comforting one. His heart sank at the thought of the horrors Evan must have put Eltern through, now to be revisited on his young brother with interest.

Roberts and Elphinstone gave the three new boys a final look over with pursed-lip contempt and then turned away to follow Eltern from the crowded room. He held the door connecting to the boarding house's front hallway open for his colleagues to pass through, and with a final glance back said, "Carry on, please, Runsam."

Harry wished the piggy-faced but frighteningly fit looking Runsam with his lizard eyes wasn't the senior house monitor. Harry knew a pugilist when he saw one and he didn't like the way those narrowed eyes took him in, looked him up and down and came again to rest on his middle for a long moment.

"You were no doubt cocks of the walk at your prep schools, but now you are cast down, lowliest of the plebs." Runsam took a step toward them and peered closely at the other two before turning to Harry. "Hmm." He swiveled around and addressed a soft-faced, floppy-haired boy standing among the gathering of curious juniors. "Benson! You are retired from your fagging duties."

Benson's face lit up in gratitude. "Thank you, Runsam!"

Runsam rounded on Harry. "And you will take Benson's place as my fag for this term." He glared at Harry as though daring him to speak. Wisely, Harry kept silent, even though he could feel his feet sinking through the floorboards. Runsam sniffed peremptorily. "Without limitation, subject to my pleasure, you will make my bed every morning, fetch clean bed linen every Wednesday and Saturday from Matron, lay out my nightdress and gown, my clothes for each morning, always ensuring the collars and cuffs are properly starched, and stud and cufflinks are half-inserted.

"You will clean and dust my room twice a week, be available for afternoon tea after going to the tuck shop to purchase toasting bread, teacakes, and buns as well as any other vittles which I might require. Naturally, you will be expert in laying the fire and getting a good blaze going the minute after-sports baths are completed in the afternoon. I insist on a nice strong glow for the toasting fork. I trust you know the difference between a good Darjeeling and a Laspsang Souchong?"

It was clear Harry's answer was taken for granted.

"I shall expect my morning coat to be brushed every day before I get up. Oh, and of course you will be my bed warmer. You others," he said to his fellow monitors, "can fight over the Rainbow brothers. I don't care for the look of spirit in their eyes." Runsam concluded without smiling.

From the corner of his eye Harry saw the relieved Benson laughing behind his hand, and he felt sure it was about the last-mentioned task, which filled him with deep unease and a sense of appalled embarrassment. Why didn't he have some of the spirit Runsam saw in the Rainbows' eyes? To Harry's mind the tousled, darker haired of the two—the one he remembered was Edward—regarded his interlocutors without any expression, but Richard's striking gray eyes exuded confidence. He had an inch in height over his brother and it put him on a level with Runsam, even though Harry supposed he was only just thirteen and Runsam a good sixteen. Harry soon discovered that the Rainbows were younger than him by eight months, which made their brave front even more remarkable in the face of the hostility present in the room. (And it meant they would be in a younger stream in the classrooms of school, which didn't make him feel happy.)

"Are you twins?" the monitor called Jefferies demanded.

Edward spoke up. "We are."

"But one of you must be the elder, even by a minute or two?"

"That'll be my brother," Edward said affably.

Jefferies shouldered Runsam slightly aside and nodded firmly at Richard. "Then I'll have you, Rainbow *Senior*. Runsam was most concise in outlining your duties as a fag, but I hope you know how to toast muffins properly. I prefer them to teacakes." He sniffed at Runsam and then turned on the gathered boys. "Jackson, like Benson you are relieved... but before you get all excited, Elphinstone has asked for you."

Snickers filled the room.

"Shut up!" Runsam glowered at the juniors.

Woolfe proclaimed himself happy with the fag he already had and so Rainbow Junior was handed over to Richards. Harry thought Edward was lucky. Tall, lanky Richards seemed pleasant and unassuming.

I tried hard not to huddle in a corner of the Junior Common Room that first awful day as the house monitors checked us out.

But when it was done and the New Bugs dismissed to the mercies of the rest of the JCR, Harry snuck covert looks at Richard, drawn as though by gravity into his orbit. When Benson swung over, Harry stiffened up for the anticipated assault, but the boy just grinned, though not pleasantly.

"Runsam's not so bad, once he gets used to you, and as long as you do what you're told, and in fact do a lot more you're not told. Anticipation... that's the watchword." He tapped the side of his nose knowingly and smiled slyly. He leaned in confidentially. "Whatever you do, never mix up Earl Grey with Lapsang Souchong, or you'll be up for *tighteners*."

"T- tighteners?"

"Clench up your buttocks before the cane strikes. It hurts a little bit less."

Harry swallowed.

"And don't worry too much about the bed warming bit. Just make sure you're up in his study room a good twenty minutes before he turns up."

"But... what do I do?"

"Get in his bed, silly, under the blanket and quilt and warm up the sheets for him. If he's in a good mood and feeling kindly, he might, when he gets up there himself, get in and warm you up for a bit. If you know what I mean."

Benson suddenly reached out and grabbed Harry's right wrist in a cruel pinch.

"You are right-handed?"

"Of course." *Who isn't?*

"Well, I hope you have a good wrist action, you know, for those evenings when Runsam feels like *It*." He pinched harder until Harry snatched his arm free. Benson grinned devilishly for a second. "Don't worry, he shoots quickly." And then he turned to run out of the noisy room with two other boys, all chortling loudly.

Their reckless humor boded nothing good.

CHAPTER 3 | *Benthenham College, 1878–1880*

BENSON'S THOUGHTLESS cruelty was almost nothing compared to that of the twenty-odd JCR, delighted at the prospect of new prey to devour. For the course of Harry's first year he endured the usual rich mix of torment: Chinese burns; rabbit punches; kidney digs; instep stamps; name-calling (*Smarmy-smarmy-smarmeee...*); wet towel flicking in the echoing bathroom, usually aimed between the legs; apple-pie beds and blanket tossing in the dormitory... but, unlike Harry, the Rainbows had each other, even more so as twins, which made them a mutual support unit—a kindred enfilade against the rest. If rebuffing their attackers with good-natured rowdiness failed, the occasional well-placed physical riposte did the trick. Soon enough everyone wanted to be pals with the brothers, but it was Rainbow Senior, whose very bearing contained such serene purpose, Harry wanted as a friend.

Somehow on that terrible first day, Richard had caught Harry's shy glances. Anticipating a typically indifferent schoolboy cold shoulder, the returned warm smile gratified Harry. Richard astounded him even more when, uncaring of who saw, he reached a friendly arm around Harry's waist and actually hugged him. It was, *really was*, love at first sight.

As for Richard, he was always proper and polite toward Harry and lent a diplomatic hand whenever he could to alleviate the worst of what they all suffered. Of course, after that initial private confidence before entering the Junior Common Room they were Vane and Rainbow to each other, and Harry had to think of him as Rainbow Senior lest he let slip Richard's private name. If a boy's first name leaked out, it was rarely acknowledged, almost as if it were taboo. Harry never heard the nickname the rest of The Lodge gave him slip from Rainbow Senior's lips, but except when playing rugby football there was never another hug.

Richard Rainbow's kindness that first day changed Harry and bolstered his damaged courage to face his peers and seniors with the delicate disdain he'd employed so well at Shottery Hall. He quickly established himself again safely behind the façade which everyone came to know, the boy who in Alfred Winner's words took an age "to fold his clothes without a crease, to scent his hankie, and coif his hair."

Like many of his contemporaries who came from families with a military tradition and who were fully expected to pursue careers as officers and gentlemen, Harry was eager to hear any tales of derring-do out in Britain's widespread Empire. He preferred to read newspaper accounts, but made a secret habit of reading novels like *The March to Coomassie* by G.A. Henty and the just published *Young Buglers, A Tale of the Peninsular War*. As the juniors moved into their second and third years at Benthenham war games were a constant diversion in free time. Returning for the fall term of 1880, Harry found—as he quite expected—everyone full of the electrifying news from Afghanistan: the victory of General Frederick Sleigh Roberts two weeks before on the first of September.

"This is going to be a tough one," Winner, who had become something of a barrack-room lawyer, warned the Junior Common Room. "I bags being Bobs."

"I don't think, Spinner, that your stature is suited to the role of General Bobs," Hammy Harmondsworth objected with noisy disdain and not a little pomposity. "Whereas Smarmy fits the bill perfectly."

Winner's violent snort cut off Harry's quiet intention to defer the role of the hero of Kandahar to someone else. "Vane, no offense intended, but you never want to get your hands mucky, let alone those elegantly garbed legs of yours, so I really can't see you playing a part in this, unless of course you'd offer to be one of the delegates who negotiated with the Pathans after the battle. The ones who sat around in ornate pavilions with fixed smiles on their faces ready for the daguerreotypists."

Harry gave a polite cough. "I think you will find, Winner, that most of the enemy were actually Ghilzais, who have never liked us. Pathan is a general term for—"

"Not interested! Smarmy, you really must look to the Big Picture. Now, who wants to be the villain of the piece?"

No one, it seemed was willing to play Ayub Khan.

"I think Rainbow Senior is the obvious choice for Bobs, though." Harry's firm drawl brought instant silence. Then…

"Here, here!" Rainbow Junior cried out from his perch on the edge of well-worn Long Table. Immediately the common room rang in agreement, apart from a sulky Winner.

"Thank you, Vane, but forgive my ignorance," Rainbow Senior said. "I'm a bit confused as to what happened. Didn't we lose rather poorly at… Maiwand, wasn't it?"

Rainbow Junior jumped down from the edge of Long Table and shook his brother's neck in fond disparagement. "My brother never reads the papers."

"Nothing like a battle well lost," Winner said, rubbing his hands together briskly.

"And then there was the siege," lanky Skiddy Scudamore broke in.

"That's right." Winner strode to Prep Table and leaned on it to point out the window to what appeared to be a small building site across a width of grass. "The new Eton Fives courts will make a perfect Kandahar citadel."

"Bags I play the good native." Harmondsworth bobbed up and down vigorously. "What's his name, Ab-what?"

"Abdur Rahman," the group chorused. "Play him if you like, Hammy, but I think he's a weed," Benson added.

Winner rounded on the others. "Tell you what. If I can't be Bobs I'll be Ayub Khan after all." He thumped his breast aggressively. "From my stronghold of Herat I shall advance on Kandahar and repeat my victory of Maiwand." He pointed a finger at Harmondsworth. "Watch out for yourself, traitorous cousin. I shall wipe the memory of Abdur Rahman from the mountains and valleys of this proud land the Great Alexander gave us, as I shall drive the infidel British back across the Indus, there to cower in their garrisons." His pointing hand swept around the room and the grinning faces. "But I, Ayub Khan, shall then lead my loyal men down through the Khyber Pass and invest Rawul Pindee and hurl the British foe before my warriors. Verily, shall I sweep them from Calcutta into the sea!"

"Winner's energy as a bad fellow is most commendable, if a trifle exhausting," Harry said in aside to Rainbow Senior. "One might almost believe he could alter history."

"Quite. The point I suppose—I'm sure Ed will put me right on this—is that this Ayub fellow lost?"

Harry, who followed developments in the newspapers as assiduously as Rainbow Senior's brother evidently did, quickly enlightened his questioner. "Indeed, and splendidly. They marched from Kabul, the Highlanders with their skirling pipes, the Gurkhas and the Sikhs with their British officers and NCOs, all bearing their Sniders and Martini-Henry rifles. Alas, poor Winner, he must face the loss of a thousand of his brave men, all his artillery, and his encampment at Kandahar. The last I read before setting out on the tediously extended rail journey to this worthy establishment was that Ayub Khan is a fugitive, and his cousin Abdur Rahman is appointed Amir of Afghanistan."

In the event, Winner failed to persuade his fellow boarders to change the real outcome of early September, which was so disastrous to his cause as Ayub Khan, and so he insisted on their first replaying the battle of Maiwand so that he could at least boast a victory. Such was the general buzz of excitement over the outcome of what was now officially referred to as the Second Afghan War that the mid-junior Lodge boys even involved their rivals from Fabian and School House to join in the two planned battles. And since he had proven the most knowledgeable, it fell to Rainbow Junior to act as Greek Chorus for the event. The as yet uncompleted row of Fives courts—their walls raised only a little above waist height—made ideal fortifications. On a bleak autumn afternoon the area around the construction site rang with the bangs and roars of battle as the boys recreated the events of July 27.

Rainbow Junior stood forth; arm raised, and addressed the gathered audience. "Racing from his stronghold of Herat, here to do battle, comes Shere Ali's youngest son, Ayub Khan. He is eager to avenge the defeats of his tribesmen at Masjid, at Kotal, and at fabled Kabul. He has vowed to retrieve the villages taken by the infidel British, especially blessed Kandahar, Dakka, and Jalalabad."

With loud ululations and bloodthirsty war cries, Alfred Winner, exotically garbed as Ayub Khan, led his men onto the field of battle. To indicate the difference in numbers Winner's band amounted to thirty boys compared to Harry's fifteen, though in fact the real disparity had been much worse for the British. Harry was playing the unfortunate British commander, Brigadier-General Burrows. Three boys from the College's Volunteer Corps followed Winner's group. Each carried a Snider rifle borrowed from the school armory and fired blanks (*strictly into the air or otherwise…* the College's Regimental Sergeant-Major Fielding had warned from under bristling mustaches). These mini-explosions stood in for Ayub Khan's artillery batteries, which had really included modern Armstrong guns.

Co-opted referees with coded flags darted around to indicate who had been shot, and once the reluctant victims were persuaded to accept their demise, zealous death throes were enacted all over the battleground. Some even suffered real damage in particularly exuberant eruptions of violence. "None mortal!" cried the referees as they helped the wounded from the field of battle to the infirmary to have grazes and cuts dabbed with iodine (more excruciating than the injury) and bandaged. After an hour's battling, the rough-edged concrete walls of the Fives courts and the area all around were littered with dying and the dead.

When the British left flank collapsed under the overwhelming onslaught, Brigadier-General Burrows began to withdraw with the remnants of his brigade. Rainbow Junior stepped out in front of the spectators from the three participating boarding houses (the seniors had disdained childish play) and placed his right palm dramatically across his left breast.

"As brave Lieutenant Henn and Captain Slade secure the retreat from General Burrows's defeat," he declaimed in a bold voice, "all is terror across the expanse of desert. The camels have thrown their loads. The native coolies have downed their *dhoolies* and left the wounded to the merciless foe. Gun carriages are weighed down with injured men. Horses limp from the agony of desperate wounds. All cry out for water. Horsemen ride down our baggage animals. They cut our men down: Englishmen bold, Gurkha or Sikh, Indiaman or Punjabi. The wild Pathan takes his pleasure and loots…" He paused dramatically. "The small army of two thousand Indians and five hundred British faced ten times as many of Ayub Khan's Afghans. Of these brave men, more than a third perished at the hands of the Pathans, the rest…" he pointed to Harry's reduced huddled group, "…will reach doubtful safety at Kandahar."

Enthusiastic clapping rattled sharply in the air from the young audience like an echo of the Snider gunfire, now silenced. As the dead and wounded began to spring back to their feet, Winner's voice rang out. "Today Maiwand. Tomorrow Kandahar!"

"What the heck is a *dhoolie*?" one junior asked another, who shrugged.

"It's like a palanquin," Harry informed as he walked up to stand beside

Rainbow Senior (temporarily brave Lieutenant Henn of the Royal Engineers until he should turn into even braver General Bobs). "A carrier for wounded men, slung over bearers' shoulders." He finished his explanation, nodded at the younger boy, and then formally shook Rainbow Senior's offered hand, with a mock bow. "I think your brother got a little carried away. I noted his impartial oration became personal toward the end: '…cut *our* men down.' Tut, tut."

Rainbow Senior bridled. "He gets involved, that's all."

Harry wished he had someone who so protected him as did Richard his brother Edward, and vice versa. Winner was correct. The brothers were closer to each other than anyone else. He dipped his head, accepting his admonishment. Rainbow relented and clapped him on the shoulder.

"So that's the end of the war, Vane? I mean the real thing, the news, you know."

"It seems so, but mark my words, Rainbow, it isn't the end of the Russians who keep stirring would-be emirs against our interests. The Russians want India and are determined nothing shall stand in their way."

Rainbow Senior rubbed his hands together in an eager gesture. "I do hope they won't lose interest before we're commissioned. It would be a tragedy if there's nothing to go out there for."

"I shouldn't worry about that. Afghanistan is where we'll be going with College over and officer training finished."

"Ed, I mean Rainbow Junior, insists there is a lot of trouble in the Sudan, where General Gordon has his hands full."

Harry waved a hand in airy dismissal. "No. The Sudan will never be our problem. My brother—when he deigns to speak with me—who sits at the foot of the Whitehall panjandrums after going up from Oxford, says that now the Liberals are back in government Gladstone will have no truck with wasting money on the Khedive of Egypt or his dependencies. Trust me, it will be India, not the Sudan where the real excitement will be." He brushed at a speck of mud from his vest as he glanced shyly at Richard (privately he thought of him as Richard not Rainbow, try hard as he did not to do so). "Meantime, I think you'll make a very elegant and handsome General Bobs in the next round."

The flecks of gold in the otherwise gray irises brightened Richard's expression. Harry would have so liked to brush the side of a finger lightly over the modest smile and capture it for himself.

CHAPTER 4 | *Hadlicote House, Christmas 1882*

AS THE *MALABAR* parted the sea, in Harry's mind the years went by, the boys grew up, became seniors with the younger boys to fag for them, gained responsibilities. Runsam's bed warming slipped away into an unsavory but thankfully hazy memory and Harry went out of his way to be firmly, distantly pleasant to those younger boys who had to perform their slave-like duties for him. In consequence, he attained a level of respect from the juniors that any command he issued was obeyed at once and with a willing attitude that often flummoxed his fellow seniors. On returning to Benthenham after the long summer vacation of 1882 for that fateful Michaelmas term, as he approached the Senior Common Room Harry heard some of his peers talking about him. A smile twitched at the corners of his lips at Winner the Spinner's raised voice.

"It gets my goat when he saunters up as if it were an honor he's turned up, and speaks in that *d-r-a-w-l-i-n-g* way."

"Does it matter if he makes an asshole of himself so long as he plays well in the team?" someone Harry suspected was Harmondsworth muttered.

Winner sounded incredulous. "The words *team* and *Vane* don't go together—there's *nothing* sociable about him."

But by that time—only a few weeks before Edward Rainbow did his amazing disappearing trick—Harry had attained the exalted rank of College prefect, and his top-drawer act had become an ingrained part of his personality. Not that he didn't enjoy putting it on as thick as Winner spread butter on his teatime toast knowing how much it riled the terrier tyke. Funny how close a friendship they formed later in the wastes of the Sudan, Harry Vane the Guards lieutenant, Alfred Winner in his blues as a naval officer.

Yes, it was cold as Richard and I traveled to Hadlicote, the silent ghost of runaway Edward between us.

There was an unusually early fall of snow that Christmas, but the heating on the Great Western train compartment they shared with four other passengers between Paddington and Banbury made it advisable to shed heavy overcoats and tuck them up on the overhead luggage rack with their suitcases. During the journey from Gloucester to London, Harry tried hard to cheer Richard without sounding crass. It was obvious that Edward's abrupt running off from school, friends, and family had come close to unhinging the boy sitting beside him. Lacking any sibling sympathy for Evan, Harry found it difficult to understand what Richard was going through, beyond an academic apprehension that it must be hard if you were close to a brother and a twin, though they were by no means identical.

On the other hand, he knew better than most how close the two were, and it was as if Richard didn't feel quite the same need to hide his filial feelings for Edward from Harry as he did from other Lodgers. *Filial.* Sometimes Harry was sure he sensed much deeper swirls in the currents of the brothers' relationship, something more intense than brotherly love. And he resented it.

Nevertheless, he felt it best to support Richard in his bereavement—for that's what it appeared to be—with a calm non-judgmental naturalness. Besides, not discussing the Edward matter any further—at least until Richard was ready to do so—meant Harry could avoid letting a certain happiness at the other brother's absence creep into his tone of voice. It seemed mean, but there it was… now he had Richard all to himself.

At London's Paddington station, having ascertained the time of their arrival at Banbury, Harry dived into the general telegraph office and sent a telegram to request two carriages to transport them and their baggage home, Banbury being some fifteen miles of winding country lanes from Hadlicote. The Great Western express service to Birmingham's Snow Hill station was busy and all but two of the eight seats of their first-class compartment were taken by the time the train guard's whistle sounded.

Once settled, Harry's musing returned to the brothers' relationship. In his presence neither had kept up the appearance of sibling indifference to which they treated the rest of the boarders, an attitude over which Harry pondered often, perhaps even obsessively. Did their relaxation in his company—little enough as it was—stem from that first day exchange of Christian names? And in those few moments when he felt privileged to see inside the fence of good-fellow-well-met Rainbowness it seemed the boys' relationship verged on the amorous.

Now there's a thrilling thought, taboo and unsettling but sexy nevertheless…

And then there was the heat of Richard's thigh pressed against his own. The portly gentleman seated on their side of the compartment took up more than his fair share of the bench. Squashed in the middle, Richard nevertheless had an inch or two of leeway, whereas squeezed up against the car's wall by the window Harry had no room to maneuver, so when he very gently pressed his left knee against Richard's right, his companion could certainly have edged away enough to put air-space between the pinstripes of their school uniform pants.

But he didn't.

Somewhere a bit after High Wycombe as the locomotive chugged toward the Chiltern escarpment and the Oxford Basin, Harry became convinced that Richard was pressing back. There was nothing more he could do under the circumstances but try to relax in the comfort of that secret touch. Partly to take his mind off the thought of Richard's thigh and as much to engage Richard in a low-voiced conversation that required him to press even more firmly against his side to hear, Harry regaled his companion with ribald tales of Lady Helen Vane-Tempest Stewart, who by some mysterious family connection was an aunt. "We don't talk about her much at home for reasons that have been carefully withheld from my innocent ears," he said in a conspiratorial whisper. "I rather hope she will be coming for the festivities, though. She's fun."

After alighting at Banbury, once more swaddled in greatcoats against the chill—though here the snowfall had been so slight that the roads were clear—there was no more opportunity to exchange any thigh compression on the jouncing trap which carried them to Hadlicote, their belongings following in the dogcart behind. Nor was there any during the first days of the vacation, for as usual Hadlicote—filled with relatives and invited grandees from London to celebrate the festival and Evan's twenty-first birthday a week later—rang with merriment all day and long into the night. And in the daylight hours, or once most revelers had fallen out of bed, been dressed by their valets, partaken of breakfast, and readied themselves for some exertion, Richard and Harry went riding in company.

On the eve of Christmas Eve the guests and members of family assembled in the vast withdrawing room. Some occupied comfortable chairs in their various scattered groups. Others stood around the pianoforte and sang carols lustily if not always in tune while imbibing freely of the champagne that continued to gush in the aftermath of dinner. The occasion was informal, which meant the men wore three-piece lounge suits with matching vests, except for Evan's, Harry noticed with a twinge of irritation, which was of a color and pattern that could only be described as loud: a lime green with slightly paler yellow dots; but then, he was an Oxbridge toff sucking up to any Liberal parliamentarian who came within range.

Richard, ensconced quietly against the edge of the third of the deep bay windows, now shuttered and draped against the wintry views of the expansive lawn outside, looked resplendent in a pale fawn lounge suit. His unbuttoned jacket gave Harry the thrill of seeing the shape of his friend's sex bunched up beneath the well-cut gabardine. How strange, Harry wondered, that a sight familiar enough in school togs or sportswear should seem so altered—so excitingly transformed—in a different context; *on my territory...*

"Oh, Trent, thank you. I'll take two of those."

Harry swept two full champagne saucers from the butler's laden tray.

"Master Harry," Trent began in reproving undertone, "you will have me in trouble with your father—"

"It's almost Christmas, Trent."

"I shall deny all responsibility should you descend to a state of inebriation, Master Harry." Trent sniffed, but failed to hide the smile as he turned away.

Harry bore down on Richard. He felt happy, perhaps a touch light-headed after the previous two glasses of bubbly and two of wine at dinner, which had deadened the twinges of guilt he felt at knowing he was trying to replace Edward in Richard's affection as a way—he defended his position—of lightening Richard's loss. But he was seventeen and allowed a modicum of alcohol. Richard, that bit younger... well, his parents were far away in Nice with Richard's young sister for the holiday period, no doubt mourning the disappearance of prodigal Edward. Perhaps it was the silvery lining of sadness that made Richard appear so delectable, a sleekly suited sylph whose very stance inflamed Harry's passion. He hoped Richard, who had also partaken of a few glasses along the way this evening, would feel equally... free.

Richard looked up and smiled, took the proffered saucer by its short stem and raised it in salutation.

"Cheerio."

Harry turned and stood shoulder to shoulder with his friend. Like an observant audience, they watched the singing, the coming and going of busy conversational groups, as Trent and two maids wafted between them dispensing tea, coffee, more champagne and also brandy for some of the gentlemen.

"Who is the strikingly good looking, knife-edge-straight man of undeniable military bearing over by the edge of the fireplace?"

Harry glanced across the gathering. "Colonel Langrish-Smith, a friend of my father... and maybe even of your father, Richard. His boy Jolyon is my godson, for some obscure reason. The child is attractive enough as tadpoles go when they are the age of... oh, what is he now? Seven, I think... though I have only seen him squalling at his christening and here at Christmas last year. They obviously left the brat behind with his nanny in London this year."

He saw Richard's attention switch to a group of well-set young-bloods and elegant young women standing beyond the piano, all carousing happily to a gay wassail, led by Harry's brother. Richard licked at his lower lip before raising his champagne to take a sip, and the flicker of tongue hit Harry's stomach like a physical punch from a boxing opponent. He was aware of the pleasant effects of the champagne and perhaps it was that which guided his hand under the back of Richard's jacket, where he hooked two fingers into the waistband of his evening pants. To detract from the action, he nodded at his brother. "Evan has set his sights on becoming a great mandarin in the government. Nothing so coarse as a military career for him." He put a little disdain into his tone and kept his gaze fixed firmly on the merrymakers across the room, while gently wiggling those trapped fingers. "Of course, one day he will have to take his place in the Lords, though that won't prevent him being a minister."

"You mean he's glad-handing Gladstone?" Richard swayed slightly in self-appreciation of his wit and Harry's fingers moved with him.

Harry was very aware of Richard's weight against his hip and shoulder, and the pressure of his amused—*aroused?*—scrutiny. "I feel your eyes on me, Richard."

The quiet smile wafted across the corner of Harry's vision, but Richard said nothing. Neither did he reject the guddling fingers at the small of his back, a countryman's way of enticing trout to come to the hand for capture. Harry swallowed. "I'm aware I may, just *may*, please note, have imbibed a few more bubbles than is good for me. So please prepare to forget anything I might say." He emphasized the point by pressing against Richard's spine, just above his coccyx.

"One ear and the other," Richard breathed.

Harry ducked his chin to stifle a small burp and then turned a dreamy gaze on Richard. "You must know that I am not immune to your charms, my dear Richard."

He paused and Richard stared back, the slightest frown marring the perfection of his forehead. Harry was aware of the heat radiating against his hand from the spare flesh of Richard's back.

"Do you know that?" Harry raised the hand holding his champagne, knuckles to his lips to disguise a second unwarranted belch.

Richard shook his head slowly. "I–I didn't… know."

The tone of wonder contained no censure that Harry could detect, if anything, the opposite. His heart soared. They held each other's gaze.

And then Evan crashed the moment. "Young Rainbow," he said brusquely as he marched into their secluded corner. "Will you excuse me? I must whisk Harry off to meet someone. I promise to bring him back."

❧·☆·❧

William Maplethorpe's face drifted across Harry's reminiscing. He couldn't deny the tug at his groin occasioned by thoughts of Richard and the availability of his fellow shipboard lieutenant. How, he wondered, does the pain of loss become an erotic urge? And how long does it take for the fresh and surprising to become familiar and used? Harry wasn't sure. He was barely free of his adolescence, hardly a jade, and yet he was sure nothing could ever again match the edge-of-a-cliff excitement of discovering Richard Rainbow's returned love, even though he came to know that he shared Richard's affections with his… with Edward. But knowing that wasn't enough to dim his love.

Maplethorpe had remarked on the danger they would have been in in years past from their proximity to Socotra, since ancient times a nest of pirates.

Pirates.

Yes, of course. There was Blackbeard.

On the morning of Christmas Eve, waking without the anticipated hangover ("I never suffer such an infliction as long as I remain with the champers," Evan so often claimed, with due smugness), Harry felt emboldened, determined to elicit from Richard that they both shared the same feelings for each other. He dragged Richard out for a "constitutional," after insisting on rugged clothing, so they were similarly attired in warm flannel shirts, Norfolk jackets, and thick cord trousers tucked into vulcanized Wellington boots. A short stroll from the main house brought them to the home farm. Harry led the way between two massive Dutch barns, which he knew were almost fully stocked with sheaves of baled winter hay.

"Is this what you wanted to show me?" Richard asked in an amused, perhaps puzzled, tone.

Harry cleared his throat. It felt parched. Perhaps his constitution was not the same as Evan's after all; perhaps it was the shaky-ready-to-be-filled emptiness he felt at Richard's proximity, their aloneness, and the full knowledge of what he was about to embark upon, come what may. He paused to look sideways. Richard, so unfamiliarly garbed as a gentleman farmer. So used to seeing him clothed either in formal college uniform or kitted out for sports, he had to remind himself that his friend also hailed from a farming community, even if his family, like Harry's own, were straight up-military. "Yes. This was always my special place as a child. Actually, it still is. Here, among the hay, was my Darién, my Porto Bello or Cartagena. I made pirate ships up there and sometimes I was Blackbeard, sometimes the noble Sir Francis Drake burning the Spanish Main. Often, I was the poor ordinary seaman, captured, bound, and stripped naked for the torture."

Harry looked at Richard's surprised expression. He knew his school friend was seeing a new Harry Vane, one he might never have supposed to exist. Harry swallowed, but pressed on. "I usually had to play two parts, sometimes more." He shrugged apologetically. "Older brother, not interested in my games. What's a lonely fellow to do? Here!"

He forced a bright smile, and strode on and then reached up to haul himself over a chest-high ridge of hay retained by low-set boards. "Come on!" Harry clambered up the narrow chute between stacked bales on all fours and hauled himself up the dusty incline of shifting straw. A quick glimpse down between his knees revealed Richard struggling up behind him, half-laughing,

41

half-sneezing against the flying chaff. And then he reached the top, high up in a natural hollow formed of hay bales under the barn's curving arch of corrugated iron. The forage released the sweet smell of summer along with stored warmth into the fragrant atmosphere. As Richard crawled the last few feet and began to stand unsteadily on the uncertain floor, Harry laughed loudly flung his arms wide, spun around like a child, and threw himself flat on his back. *Here goes nothing... oh, sweet Lord, love me.*

As an invitation, it exceeded Harry's expectations. Richard barely paused before hurling himself across the space, arms outstretched, to land on top of Harry. His head fell against Harry's shoulder and he pressed their ears together. Sudden arousal flooded Harry's body and the way it slammed into his brain nearly overwhelmed him.

Richard chuckled against his cheek, hot wet breath bathing Harry's ear. And then came the words. "Now I'm really concerned," he burbled breathlessly. "What simulacrum is this which has replaced the real Harold Smythe-Vane?"

Harold. The deliberate provocation informed Harry better than anything that Richard's feelings for him were more intense than he could have hoped for. It was a tease and of the sort that could only emerge from a true affection, for Richard was being purposely contrary. Years of public schooling had to be thrown aside for the Christmas gathering, and on inviting Richard for the holidays Harry had insisted on using their Christian names,

"If we're to spend time out of school together... Richard. And for God's sake, not Harold. And I'm not a Henry."

Richard might reasonably have asked what kind of Harry he was then, but he accepted the request without comment and allowed Harry to keep his given name as his own secret... at least for the time being. If anyone were to learn it, he would allow Richard to be that person.

His emotions swamped his natural caution. In a moment he enfolded Richard in his arms and rolled him back. Richard didn't resist. Those beautiful smoky eyes flickered left to right and back again to focus on each of Harry's. Time stopped. The quiet in the barn was a physical presence and it only served to concentrate the sounds of their breathing. Harry crushed his lips against Richard's. His tongue broke through the barrier of Richard's teeth and sought his tongue and Richard didn't deny him. After the briefest hiatus, Richard mustered his counter-attack and Harry's mind side-slipped into the amazing petard of Richard's tongue exploding in his mouth, a sensation of such intensity he feared he might faint.

For an eternity, he lost himself in the incredible frisson generated by this sudden onslaught of passion, all coherent thought erased by the wonderful recognition of Richard's ardent response... and as physically. He felt the bone of Richard's hardness push against his stomach and reveled in his own stiffness thrusting back against Richard's thigh. He broke the labial contact and reared up triumphantly above his conquest. "You didn't reject my hand last night."

"We were drunk."

The response might have hinted at evasion, but Harry didn't think so. "Hah! Yes, weren't we? And...?"

"What now?"

The uncertainty in Richard's tone matched the sudden fear of rejection that cut a deep runnel in Harry's hopes. Had he gone too far, too fast? A worm of fear crawled in his gut. *Too serious, too soon.* He desperately hoped Richard was suddenly being cautious because he feared these portents of passion might be misread. But surely not? They had kissed. It was mutual. They both sported erections, and yet the next move to something more overt suddenly loomed like a barrier. He opted for levity to ease any of Richard's concerns.

"Now? I think I'm going to be Blackbeard, which means I'll have to strip you naked and torture you until you give me what I desire."

Richard relaxed under Harry's weight and grinned. "The stripping bit sounds like fun, but pray tell me sire, what might your desires be?"

CHAPTER 5 | *H.M.S. Malabar, 1885*

THE CLATTER OF SILVERWARE on china dimmed the continual throbbing of the *Malabar*'s engine. Scarlet dress coats reflected from the wardroom's mirrors and its polished paneling, and added to the roseate glow of the low sun. Its diminishing light through the windows made rectangles on the opposite walls, which rose and fell with the vessel's slow swoops. Harry rolled his neck inside the starchy high wing-collar. The darned thing trapped his chin and made swallowing so difficult. In Egypt Richard and Alfred Winner teased him endlessly about his "sybaritic" lifestyle, about having to give up starched collars for the drabs of Camel Corps khaki, but oh what he would give for the soft kiss of an undress shirt now.

"What will you take… Harry?"

"My apologies, William. I was miles away for a moment."

They both kept their voices low, still uncertain of using Christian names.

Maplethorpe consulted the handwritten menu. "Thank goodness for service *à la russe*," he murmured, as the few duty orderlies began to lift hot dishes from the buffet and circumnavigated the table in rotation with the selection of *entremets*, vegetable dishes, and the sauce boat.

Harry agreed. His parents still insisted on the outmoded free-for-all of *service à la française* for their formal dinners, in which all the dishes were placed on the table and everyone had to hand them around, or at a crowded table risk eating only what fate landed before them; and servants intervening only added to the general confusion.

"I strongly suspect the Canards à la Rouennaise and the simpler Spring Chicken have the same parent in fact."

"A Yemeni buzzard, you suspect, William?"

"I hope not Coleridge's portentous albatross, but otherwise something of that order." Maplethorpe treated Harry to a bright smile and the madder light showed up the attractive scattering of freckles across the upper curve of his cheeks. His eyes were not gray like Richard's, but an unusual shade of light brown, almost amber in the gloaming, and a match for the hints of red in his luxurious hair. Harry was aware of the warmth of William's thigh, pressed against his own on the crowded bench (individual chairs were too awkward with ship movement). At the contact, his mind slipped back again.

Blackbeard sailed far, far away.

"I loved you that first day at school." He leaned down to brush Richard's lips slowly. "I loved you then. I love you now."

When it started, the undressing was gentle and mutual. And there, in the strange warmth rising from the hay beneath and around them, their youthful limbs entwined. He shouldn't have been surprised that Richard lost any shyness the minute they embraced and held each other's yearning bodies skin to skin. Harry was perfectly aware that many boys in The Lodge indulged in sex with their fellows, though he never had—at least, not in any willing sense. There were the few unsatisfactory times Runsam propositioned him after warming the monitor's bed. He could hardly avoid having to rub Runsam but avoided the other's touch on his own private parts. In truth, neither he nor Richard was very practiced in the ways of sex, and theirs was a simple, tight press of heaving flesh, cocks trapped side-by-side between them, and a huge release. More kissing, slower at first, faster as arousal came again, and a second, fumbling engagement of hard stomachs slicked with spent seed and hay-scented sweat…

"I think we could trust the Compote of Cherries. They must surely come fresh from a can?"

Harry started, and covered his second momentary lapse with a short coughing laugh. "Of course. Cherries it will be," he said over his shoulder to the orderly waiting on them. Harry noticed the man swayed to the ship's movement naturally, which he admired since most of the landlubber soldiers couldn't get the hang of the sailors' rolling gait to compensate for the continuously shifting deck. Fortunately, Harry had never suffered the effects of seasickness that afflicted so many of his colleagues and subordinates. He inclined his shoulder slightly to allow the servant to deposit a dish of dark cherries in front of him.

"Will you take some cream, sir?"

Harry glanced suspiciously at the jug proffered by a second orderly. "Is it Borden's?"

"Certainly, sir, Borden's Condensed Cream. I opened the tin meself not a 'alf 'our ago, fresh from the *h*ice room."

"Cat got the cream, hey?" Maplethorpe gave Harry a sly smile as he slipped the tip of his spoon between his upper lip and tongue. A cherry disappeared, and a thin smear of thick sweetened milk marked its passage across the lower lip. The slick vanished in a quick tongue-lip-smack. A dimple winked at Harry in the maneuver, and again came the pressure on the side of his thigh. Harry's reaction was autonomic, a distinct nudge of muscle against his companion's firm, trousered flesh. A part of him regretted the twitch he'd barely controlled, but he welcomed the definite responding squeeze and settled fatalistically into what would surely follow… a repeat, in fact. Richard had survived the mad Sudanese quest and found his Edward. Richard was gone to Harry now. He had to get over Richard Rainbow, and William Maplethorpe was an attractive proposition. They shared a cabin. They had moved progressively from snatched early fumbling in Cairo to a session of good hard sex the day before, after which William had shyly suggested continuing to use their family names in private would be unnecessary. And now William, idly scratching at the top of his thigh, was also moving his hand accidentally against Harry's leg.

Accidentally?

Barely three months since his twenty-first birthday, prior to last night Harry's only sexual experience—if he discounted occasionally giving way to the vice of Onan and disagreeable rubbings of Runsam's prick—was making love with Richard in those weeks of the Nile campaign. Much discussion in The Lodge dormitories—Harry punctiliously avoided joining them—established that masturbation was no real sin, however many blind Catholic priests there might be around, and in any case, such a crime as it might be was greatly lessened if you got someone else to finish you. This, too, Harry had avoided, truth be known because in his notorious fastidiousness he didn't like the idea of someone else's mess.

Any squeamishness he suffered over the expenditure of another's seed flew away like chaff from the hay that first time with Richard at Hadlicote. It had been the closeness of their bodies, the tactile presence of hands caressing naked flesh, tracing the shape and hard form of youthful sinews, lips squeezing erect nipples, and the sheer sensuousness of their mutual arousal which mattered most. After finding each other again at Korti, far down south and far up the Nile, they graduated to more than finishing each other by hand, to the unexpected joys of fellatio and to fucking, each in turn. When he was really low and felt the need to torture himself, like worrying at a sore tooth, he imagined Edward fucking Richard… or maybe the other way around; imagined them tucked like two opposed commas, bringing each other off with their mouths.

Gentle lovemaking with Richard hadn't prepared Harry for the whirlwind that was William Maplethorpe. When they attained their cabin that evening the veils of staid Victorian probity fell away in an instant. An unaccustomed amount of claret to mark the colonel's birthday lubricated Harry's libido so that his usual reserve collapsed in the face of William's amorous onslaught. Almost three weeks cooped up with the person he claimed to most admire had left William in a desperate state, and it rapidly became clear to Harry on the first occasion, that he was possessed of a great deal more sexual experience than might be drawn (if at all) in the normal course of social interaction. After the first exhausting tryst, Harry put that down to the fact that William didn't brag endlessly about his amorous conquests as did so many of the other young officers, which made him seem ingenuous, especially in the context of his usually innocent mien. But Harry accepted that William's sexual preference probably accounted more for such modesty among his peers. Harry was much the same, but were he otherwise his braggadocio over feminine conquests would be as without foundation as he suspected was the case with most of the young unmarried officers.

There was little innocence on display now. Dress uniforms littered the spare corner at the foot of William's cot and under the angled hanging rail that acted as their only wardrobe. Regulation underwear draped off the end of Harry's cot and the two young men writhed in a tangle of legs and arms on the cool floor in the tight squeeze between the cots, but a close-knit fit was what they wanted. William was like a tiger, all teeth and gripping mouth, biting any flesh in reach until Harry lay gasping, half-laughing, and allowed the attack to roll all over him. In its violence, their intercourse couldn't have been more different from his with Richard, for which divergence he was glad.

The tussle slowed when Harry finally gave way to William's demand, which seemed only fair as their last encounter the day before resulted in Harry taking William. The memory of that feeling, of humping William's tight ass, of the way he gripped Harry and held him in until the bright burst of orgasm flamed through their united flesh now filled Harry with the need to reciprocate.William bore him down on the hard deck plates, barely relieved by the inadequate little rag-weave mat Harry had purchased in Aden, and inserted himself forcefully while biting down on the corded tendons of Harry's neck. With his rampant cock trapped between his belly and the rough texture of the mat, there was little to be done but give way to the friction engendered by William's energetic humping. And then suddenly, wiping out all emotion, Harry was moving forth and back on the lubrication of his own gushing release, while William gasped harshly in his ear, bit down viciously on his neck again, and moaned a gutturally indecipherable expletive as he let fly. Harry felt the pressure deep inside him, where the bulk of William's big cock had him pierced to the core.

Movement slowed, breathing quieted. They fell apart. Actually, that was impossible due to the restriction of space, so it was more of a gentle disengagement and a relaxation of muscles slicked with the sweat of sexual exertion. And an amused huffing in Harry's assaulted ear. "That's some mess you made of your rug. And you so fussy about your things, too."

"Belay it, William." Harry reached around and ruffled his companion's hair. "I'll have to give the damned thing a good wash. Can't have Carter seeing it in this state."

"If you left it he'd probably think you failed in trying to starch it!"

William struggled up between the cots, stepped over to the small basin affixed to the cabin wall behind the narrow door, and poured a little water from the jug kept on the floor underneath. He dampened a towel and came back with it. Kneeling down over Harry, he proceeded to wipe the semen gently from Harry's stomach. "Do you think we will have as much freedom to... well, be ourselves when we reach Rawul Pindee?"

48

The question irritated Harry. Neither of them knew much about the arrangements of the cantonment, of what kind of accommodation there would be or how much sharing between younger officers, so what purpose was there in asking? He sat up and reached for his breeches as William concluded his ministrations. Harry's natural modesty obliged him to cover at least some of his nakedness once the sexual heat dissipated.

"If I answered, it would be the blind leading the poorly sighted. Besides…"

Harry trailed off, unwilling suddenly to enlarge on his hopes of not being confined to the garrison duties all of them knew lay ahead, unless another outbreak of hostilities across the borders of the North-West Frontier Province put men and officers in the field like the uprising General Roberts suppressed. The thought of Bobs brought to mind the games they'd played at Benthenham. But since those cheery days Harry had endured the slog across the Sudan's dreadful Bayuda Desert, the chaos and horrors of Abu Klea when the Mahdist fanatics broke into the square and slaughtered so many good men. And after the grueling trek from there to the Nile, harassed at every step, and following the battles fought as they retreated to Egypt along the way they had come, Harry no longer saw the adventures of war through rose-tinted spectacles. Not that that dented his wish for adventure; real adventure. And should he succeed in his ambition, it would certainly mean leaving William Maplethorpe behind.

Maplethorpe fastened on that "besides." He gave a slight grunt, and got up to sit on his cot. Reaching out, he patted a second small book lying on the cane table between their berths. "I had a quick glance through the pages, you know, so I think I understand what you'd prefer to be doing. Mind, it's a bloody boring thing. Where on earth did you get it?"

"In this little bookshop in Suez, far from the places it describes. It seemed like a good portent to discover writings about Afghanistan, so I bought it. It's a compilation of reports and the opinions of several politicals compiled by a clerk working in India."

"Dryly informative, is what I'd call it. But you know being able to boast a little information about the interior of Afghanistan and Tajikistan isn't going to turn you into a political officer. Those loners must combine a reckless bravado with conciliatory skills to become the kind of freebooter explorer-diplomat-spy Johnnies you so admire."

"And you know me well enough to know I am not that sort of man?"

Maplethorpe grinned amiably at Harry's tetchy tone. "I don't somehow see our top brass setting you free to roam as you please. And that phrase book you study so hard, what's that done for you? I suppose you can order a croissant and chocolate in any of four native tongues, hmm?"

"Mock me as you will, William. I am determined to do my best, and I'm sorry for it that we will be parted as a result of my success." He knew he wasn't sounding very apologetic. He held up a hand to forestall Maplethorpe's response and swallowed down some of the soreness he felt at the unthinking words. "But it will no doubt take time, and in that space I am sure we shall find how to make the best of whatever arrangements there are at the cantonment."

Maplethorpe wrinkled his nose thoughtfully, which made the scatter of freckles dance across his cheeks. "It might not come to bashing the parade ground for very long, Harry, old chap. Don't forget the pesky Ruskies. The 1st Dragoon Guards are just a part of the build up going on. You heard what the colonel said at dinner yesterday. The situation has become very fluid and we need troops, good British troops as well, to counter the threat to the North-West Frontier Province. I can't myself think for a moment that the Russians will come tramping across that wasteland of desert and mountains I read about in your little book there, but I don't trust the jumpy mandarins in Calcutta not to get hot under the collar and imagine a Russian under every rock. Before you know it, we'll be mobilized and moving off as a regiment into Afghanistan double-time."

Harry sighed. That would be preferable to sitting around training and drilling in the garrison, but he wanted to be a loner who went out into the field like the native pundits, the "men who know things," disguised as a Buddhist pilgrim with his rosary of a hundred beads to count his measured paces, and his prayer wheel inside which lay concealed the daily logbook of distance traveled between *daharamasalas*. He craved adventure, to wield the secret geographer's tools: compass hidden in the top of his pilgrim's staff; sextant concealed in the false base of his carry box; mercury for setting an artificial horizon for sextant readings nestled in cowrie shells to be poured into his begging bowl. And if that so happened to help grease the wheels of British civilization and ensure Imperial Russia was kept well out of Afghanistan's affairs, so much the better.

He couldn't help the smile which creased his lips—wild, wiry, terrier Alfred Winner the Skinner would not recognize this Harry Vane at all, willing to face the rigors of tramping rocky hill and muddy dale, faced with raging mountain torrents and the chance of running into Pathan bandits at every turn. In the packet of correspondence and other papers he kept in his saddle wallet there was a special letter. One he hoped would make all the difference when it came to facing the officer who might release him to his imagination.

A last swell carried H.M.S. *Malabar* from the Arabian Sea into the relative calm of Back Bay. All on deck—most of the men and officers with orders to disembark on reaching Bombay—gave a collective sigh of relief at the sight of the palaces and palms stretching around the bay in a serene crescent. On her way to the anchorage the troopship passed close to Government House sited on the northern Malabar Point, its grand arched porticos and windows glinting palely in the sunshine through lush foliage. Two miles away to the south, Harry could just make out the military lines of the British Infantry Barracks, where the Dragoon Guards would be housed for their brief stay in Bombay before taking the train north.

As the ship lost way some hundreds of yards from the Marine Lines, a fuss of small tugs bustled up to take charge. Black smoke from their tall smokestacks curdled the air. Through the haze and on the other side of the pleasant greenery of the English Gymkhana, the extraordinary sight of the new railroad terminus towered above the low-rise government buildings.

"A tropical St. Pancras, Station" Harry said with no little admiration.

"But with distinct Hindoo overtones," Maplethorpe added.

Harry nodded. The scale of the incomplete construction certainly matched the great London station, but while the façade with its ornate turrets and exotic central tower might look comfortable in Brighton it would not in Kings Cross.

So anxious were the officers and men, and not to forget the women and children, to escape the cooped up confines of the ship that skirmishes developed at the head of the two sets of gangway-steps. Below them, numerous lighters began to cluster in their own battle to fill their seats with disembarking passengers. The noise and confusion were indescribable. Boatmen vying for officers because they were presumed to be better payers, flurries of hands to catch flying portmanteaux, curses from those who saw a case end up in the water, the furious and magical disappearance of rupees or English bank notes into leather wallets strung around the boatmen's necks.

"This is madness," Maplethorpe shouted over the din. "It could have been avoided had we docked properly in the harbor."

"That's all for merchantmen and liners," Harry said. "We army men don't get such luxury. After all, we are supposed to travel light between barracks." He grinned at the sight of a major's wife haranguing her two servants who struggled under the weight of several large banded trunks. "They'll need two boats to carry that lot to shore. Besides," he said, continuing with his original line of thought, "the *Malabar* will want to be on her way as soon as possible. It's still a long way to Calcutta."

Maplethorpe and Harry stood back, as more enlisted men pushed to get to the head of the lines. Harry shrugged nonchalantly. "I shall wait until the hubbub dies down. We've waited weeks to be here and I don't suppose another hour will hurt. Though I must say, William, my eyes ache for some greenery after Egyptian and Arabian deserts, and the monotony of a rolling sea."

"I feel sorry for the regiments continuing on."

"Ah, but they will have a lot more room to spread out with our lot gone."

Maplethorpe leaned on the rail and gazed down happily at the chaos below. After a moment, he turned his head up and frowned. "I do hope they have some decent mounts for us up at this Rawul Pindee place. I was peeved, to say the least, to have to leave my mare behind. No doubt you felt the same regret at whatever you had to abandon at, where was it? Wadi Halfa?" he added considerately.

Harry snorted politely. "My dear William, I was almost always mounted on a dirty camel. Trust me, a horse will be a delight, although I hear they also use camels a lot up where we're going."

A wrinkling of William's nose indicated his distaste. "God, I hope not. They spit, don't they?"

"And bite, and groan, and kick… not so different from a bad-tempered nag."

Maplethorpe wiped a hand across his brow. "Is it even more humid here than at sea? Speak for your own, Harry. I spent a deal of time, not to say money, getting my beautiful Guinevere fit and trained. She was coming along very well in the arena."

"Really? I hadn't spotted you as a dressage rider."

The comment stung. Maplethorpe drew himself up as if in reprimand. "And did you spot me for an avid climber of mountains? I may not yet have mounted the heights of the Himalayas, but I have conquered peaks of note in Sardinia, France, and Canada, as much indeed as I have scribed scores in the seven to nine range with my Guinevere in *piaffe*, *passage*, and half-pass, but shortly before the orders to Egypt I had her doing some fine Airs above the ground. At least, we had mastered the *mezair* and *capriole*, and I was working on the *courbette*. I only hope the training master will find her a rider I approve of. I suppose you prefer polo?"

It was meant and spoken as a return dig and Harry laughed easily. He well knew the disdain with which dressage riders held polo players, and the reverse was equally true. "I'm ashamed to say I haven't ever played. At home I rode mostly to hounds, a thoroughly mucky business, at Sandhurst for the cavalry drill training, and since then I have ridden for the necessity of being a Guardsman at Knightsbridge protecting my sovereign." He waved at the nearby shore and the waves in between covered with an assortment of boats, tugs, and lighters ferrying to and fro. "Anyway, your mare would not have thanked you for dragging her all the way to Cairo, and then even farther abroad to the Land of the Raj. I'm sure we're best suited with mounts used to the conditions we'll soon be encountering."

Harry gave Maplethorpe a sidelong look in appraisal. "I hadn't pegged you as a rock climber, it's true, and I'm, impressed, I will say. Envious even, for I rather hope to be placed in the position of having to master some mountaineering skills if I should be so lucky to secure the role of surveyor-political."

"It's been some time since I indulged in hanging from precipice edges, Harry, but I'm confident I haven't lost my head for heights. I'm far more worried about the horses, actually. I've been so long out of the saddle, will I remember how to ride?"

Harry demurred with a slight, humorous shrug, but played along with his friend's whimsy. "Really, William, for one it's hardly been *that* long, and for two I'm reliably informed—having never tried myself though I've seen them in Hyde Park—that it's like riding one of these new Coventry safety bicycles. Once you have, you never forget how. Besides…" He gave Maplethorpe a playful dig in the ribs, "you mounted and rode me the other night without any problem."

CHAPTER 6 | *Rawul Pindee, autumn 1885*

THE DRAGOONS EXCHANGED the monotony of sea travel for that of the Great Indian Peninsula Railway. Harry kept a note in his journal of the tedious journey through Rajasthan and Uttar Pradesh. The train clanked at a slow pace across the wastes of the parched Thar Desert. Even when the late summer monsoon lashed them, the run-off vanished from the surface almost as soon as the rain abruptly ceased. As day followed night, shanty hamlet and town passed by the grimy windows.

From Bori Bunder in Bombay and the builder's yard of the new terminus all around the old station's platforms, the train took them to Tannah. From that short distance of the first-laid rails, the subcontinent stretched away, impossibly huge, measured in stations: Surat; Ankleshwar; Utran; Godhra; Ratlam; Nagda; Kota; Agra and there the line joined the East Indian Railway coming from Calcutta. The British Empire ruled possessions with iron roads.

At the periodic stops, the men clambered down to the dusty station hardstands looking for latrines, refreshment, a chance to stretch legs. They were immediately surrounded by tumultuous humanity in all its forms from persistent traders to char wallahs, beggars to religious fakirs, paan sellers to gobble wallahs. "Quickie mouth relief behind building, sahib," one of these youngsters offered. He was a likely lad, probably not even in his teens, leader of a ragged group of boys all offering the same service in return for a rupee a go. Harry waved them away, but he noticed a couple of younger troopers go off with the boys, only to return after a short while looking well satisfied.

Given his recent acquaintance with the joys of riding camels, Harry was less than happy to see how much use was made in India of the ubiquitous beasts of burden. Their train was no exception in having several wagons packed with camels being transported from one stop to another, and one of the less pleasant aspects of the halts came when the transportation captains made their rounds to see to their charges' welfare. On loading, the camels were kneel-haltered to keep them from standing and risk broken legs with every jolt. In addition, their heads were tethered to rest chin down on the bed of the truck. In spite of this, at least one stupid beast would manage to free itself and lift its head high to stare at the passing landscape in ungulate surprise. Unfortunately, there were many low tunnels on the way, and at each stop the transport captains had to remove any decapitated camels. The heads no doubt ended up in a local's soup pot.

The rest stops were also a time for older hands in other units returning to the front to fill the newcomers with dread tales of Pathan savagery, invariably delivered with gleeful relish. Back on the train, the unsympathetic wooden seats, the clattering wheels, the dust, heat, and biting insects made sleep at nights next to impossible.

Agra, Mathura, Delhi, Umbala, Amritsar, Lahore, and finally through Jhelum to Rawul Pindee in the heart of the Punjab, gateway to Afghanistan and Kashmir. The regiment's arrival at the major British cantonment for the North-West Frontier Province coincided with a terrific thunderstorm of the late monsoon, which left most of the men crowded into the station's long but narrow confines waiting for the downpour to stop. Harry leaned against the side of a brick and stone-faced arch beside William Maplethorpe. They both stared out at the rain, a little mesmerized by its vertical force.

"It will stop as suddenly as it started," Maplethorpe opined above the drumming of the downpour on the roof above. A great web of electrical discharge in the heavens speared the gloom. Harry turned at the tap on his shoulder. He looked along the pointed finger. "I can just make out the tent lines of the cantonment. I hope our accommodations are proofed against this rain."

Travel-grimed and travel-weary, Harry was not disposed to crack much of a smile. "I hope so too, but more I hope Carter got our things safely under cover. Where is the man?"

"Sensibly hiding away with the division, I've no doubt."

Harry blew out a breath of frustration. "Looking on the bright side, at least if the monsoon prevents us moving it will also keep the Russians pinned down… wherever they may be."

At the jab of a finger in his ribs Harry huffed in a mixture of amusement and irritation. "I thought you more astute," Maplethorpe teased, "than to credit stories that the big bad bear is breathing down our necks. Were they not thought to be entrenched somewhere beyond Merv?"

"They took Pandjeh and are now within easy reach of Herat," Harry countered hotly. "I know your sense of geography is hazy, my dear William, but I can assure you that Pandjeh is well this side of Merv." He put up with his friend's affectionate taunts, but Harry had no intention of letting Maplethorpe's ambitions for them to climb the officer ranks as administrators divert him from volunteering as a political. Maplethorpe had used the tedious rail journey to try and surmount Harry's hopes and bend him back to garrison life… and his bed in exchange for a mat on a hard rock somewhere out in "benighted Pashtoon-land."

"The Amir stands in the Bear's way."

"Abdur Rahman is an uncertain principle in a wavering treaty, William. He'd cave as easily to Russian promises as ours… or threats more likely."

"Sir Charles MacGregor has Russian bees in his Scottish bonnet." William sang the words lightly in Harry's ear.

"The Major-General knows more about India and the North-West Frontier than anyone. And you know that perfectly well… when you're not trying to annoy me. As the quartermaster-general, look how much he's done to replace native informers with trained cartographers and improve our knowledge of Afghanistan, of it peoples, and its terrain."

"Oh, piffle! As far as I have seen, we still know sod-all. Look at those peaks out there." He swatted at the flies, which in spite of the downpour continued to plague them under the station's canopy, and then jabbed a finger at the darker silhouette, barely visible through the lessening rainfall. "Well, I never understood why the Army of India employed native agents for the job up in those Pamir Mountains anyway."

"Those are merely the Kashmir hills, William. The Pamirs are some three hundred miles distant from Rawul Pindee… and probably because the pundits know the country?" Harry raised an ironic eyebrow.

"Yes, and how to weave beautiful fabrications to mislead. Witness the problems Roberts had five years ago at Kabul. I can't understand why you want to risk yourself out there, alone but for a servant boy—"

"I shan't be alone if I win a posting with Colonel Lockhart's expedition. As you so accurately point out, we know little of the region in the Pamirs, the Hindu Kush, or the Karakorams, and out there is almost certainly one of MacGregor's five possible routes for the Russians to attack India. Lockhart's for the high passes of the Pamirs and the Hindu Kush and I want to be with him." He emphasized the point by crushing a persistent fly on a stone quoin of the arch and lifted both eyebrows in surprise at his success.

Deep inside, Harry acknowledged that his desire to become accepted as a political was as much because he needed to get away and be alone, as Richard had been in the Sudan when he went in search of Edward. He didn't like to confront the sentiment, but on occasion when he allowed a modicum of truth to creep into his thinking it would also get him away from William and the ever-present disappointment that his shipboard lover was not Richard. He had to grapple with the guilt, of course he did. He felt affection for William, but it wasn't enough, and in the face of that uncertainty—that he knew how much stronger were William's feelings for him—he wanted to be freed of it. *Run away? Yes, in part.* But there was also the undeniable envy he suffered whenever he thought of the excitement of Richard's hopeless quest to criss-cross the Sudan in search of Edward. He needed that challenge, and if coincidentally it got him out of a pleasant entanglement, but one without a future and the inevitable upset that would cause, should he say "No" to be—what? Honorable?

Maplethorpe swatted irritably at the fly that had finally won a beachhead on the bridge of his nose. "Harry, just promise me not to get captured, then. I shudder to think of you staked out for the Pathan women."

And he did shudder. So did Harry.

The peculiar manner of executing some British soldiers who were captured after the disaster at Maiwand made a subject of revolted fascination among troops heading for or entrenched in the cantonments of the North-West Frontier Province. A senior NCO who served under General Roberts at the time treated Harry and William to the gory details as they shared some pipe tobacco during the halt at Lahore. Harry was quite unable to envision what the man described in the same frame as he remembered the noble reenactment they had performed at Benthenham. Nothing could have been more abhorrently at odds from the way the "wounded" boys got back to their feet at the Fives-courts Maiwand, wreathed in satisfied smiles at a game well played.

"See, the Pathan warriors they spreads the injured man out on his back on the ground, y'see, and secures his wrists and ankles to stakes. Then they jam his mouth open by means of a crudely fashioned wooden gag with a hole cut in its middle. And they shoves small bits of stick down between the lips and the gag to prevent the poor soul from swallowing. Then the Pathan women squat above the man and piss into his mouth until he drowns in urine."

Maplethorpe, whose mouth had dropped open in sympathetic horror at this telling, snapped it shut.

"Yes. You can imagine, if you tries. Often, a single woman's bladder is insufficient, so several take their turn over him to accomplish the execution to apparently great joy and happiness, and no doubt some natural relief."

Every fastidious fiber of Harry's body revolted at this awful barbarity and the sergeant's tale threatened to bring up his lunch. It took a snatched lungful of tobacco smoke to calm the vomitory reaction. Harry had looked for a smile, anything that might indicate the NCO spoke in jest, however gruesomely, but his grave expression belied any foolery. Both subalterns were too upset to think to ask whether the sergeant had actually witnessed this loathsome form of killing.

"I will certainly do my best not be captured, William. I promise."

The rain proved Maplethorpe correct when it ceased falling with a similar suddenness to the way it had started. Rickshaws and two-wheeled, horse-drawn *tongas* abruptly appeared as if by magic and soon filled the muddy roadway in front of the station, their owners vying for trade with the officer cadre to transport them to the cantonment.

Harry drew in a deep lungful of rain-damp air in an effort to banish the awful image of squatting Afghan women. "Ah… as the wretched Carter isn't going to I think we'd better battle for one."

In no time at all the senior officers' servants had commandeered all the tongas with their coverings designed to keep the last drops of rain off their fares. Amid the bellowing commands of NCOs, the other ranks began to form up on the station forecourt for the march, and Harry was forced to dodge around one troop as he waded toward a vacant rickshaw before any one else made off with it.

"Harry."

"What?" Harry settled himself in the rocking seat as Maplethorpe clambered up beside him. He twisted his head and saw a look of uncertainty in his friend's expression.

"I know you have pull with the quartermaster's office, so I'm sure you will get what you want. I… I just wanted to you to know that I have become… well, quite attached to you and I hope to see you return. If you get what it is you want, that is."

Harry sighed softly as the rickshaw man bent his thews to the task of getting his vehicle under way through the sticky track. In a splishing of mud from wheels and bare feet, a huffing and puffing in many hoarse throats, one after another, the rickshaws began moving. Harry patted Maplethorpe on the knee gently. "I know, William. I will be back. In the meantime, I'm going nowhere immediately. The minute we have our accommodation allocated and I've managed to cleanse the grime of the Indian railways from me, and the moment I locate Carter and persuade the man to clean the mud from my boots, I'm sure we can find something to do to fill in time before the mess call to dinner."

"Wherever it is in this godforsaken spot."

Perhaps because he was certain he would soon be a free soul, Harry was particularly energetic an hour later in satisfying his companion's desires, first in allowing him to fuck and then, after a bit, in rolling him over, raising his legs, and thrusting into him with an urgency born of equal need and regret—double guilt in fact: for his intention to soon abandon him; and that his own urges felt like a constant betrayal of Richard.

"Sir Henry speaks highly of you, Vane."

It was the third week since the Dragoons arrived in Rawul Pindee. They were anxious weeks as Harry waited for a summons in response to his formal application to the quartermaster. Now he stood at ease before the desk of Major-General Sir Charles Metcalfe MacGregor, quartermaster-general of the Indian Army, a little bemused at being treated to a brief historical treatise.

"I've heard it voiced with some surprise that a quartermaster should also be head of the Intelligence Department, but that simply shows ignorance of a long tradition… or possibly of Latin." He looked up at Harry. "I trust you were studious in your Latin lessons?"

Harry correctly presumed the question to be rhetorical when MacGregor swept on.

"The Roman army quartermasters were the *frumentari*, the collectors of grain. This essential task obliged them to travel widely throughout the empire and so gather intelligence of all the locals' dirty secrets. And their purchasing power gave them great influence to disseminate propaganda or buy loyalty to the regime." He glanced up again from the papers held in his hands and treated Harry to a wry glance. "Not so different from our political agents today."

Harry was more concerned with what MacGregor understood of the missive he was supposed to be reading than in how ancient Romans organized their spies. The letter from Major-General Sir Redvers Henry Buller had come up from Bombay in the diplomatic bag. It was effectively a repetition of the sealed one Harry had handed to the adjutant for MacGregor's perusal a fortnight earlier. Harry knew of the second letter's existence (carrying more weight for its inclusion with the diplomatic mail) but not the contents of either, though he knew Buller had his best interests at heart. Between the overhang of General MacGregor's sweeping mustache and the fulsome beard—which Harry couldn't help but think was more the cut and style of a naval officer's—it was hard to tell if he smiled, but Harry heard it in his voice.

"Redvers was ever a headstrong fellow so I am confident he would only recommend someone of equal impulsiveness and, I trust, reckless bravery, but practical and level headed at the same time." He looked up again from under bushy, encompassing eyebrows, which showed the gray that had turned the hair on his square head to salt-and-pepper. "Are you recklessly brave, Lieutenant Vane?"

Harry had already requested the simplicity of the second half of his name. "Not reckless, I hope, sir, but as brave as needed."

MacGregor chuckled deep in his throat. "Very well, young Harry Vane. You've the impetuousness of youth, Redvers says, clothed in common-sense, two attributes I must say I have never before encountered in a single individual, but I am happy to take his word as he is expert at achieving the correct end by leaping to the wrong conclusion. Colonel Lockhart has already seen this." He waved General Buller's letter. "You'll find him waiting downstairs for you. Good luck."

Harry left in a happy daze from the abrupt conclusion of the successful interview.

Downstairs was on a floor one up from the ground. Everything in India,

Harry had observed, of any consequence occurred at least one floor up so as to avoid the thick clouds of dust or equally glutinous monsoon mud. From a long arcade, it overlooked the surprisingly wide street of the Sudder Bazar. Last night's torrential downpour was but a memory of rutted ground, soon dried out under the relentless sun. Beyond the town the brown plain stretched to the jagged line of the distant Kashmir hills, pale blue in the haze.

After he turned the corner of the building ornate wooden screens in triple-arched windows dimmed the exterior light but did little to cut the noise of the crowds below. One screen, which had its hinged wicket wide open amid the tracery, framed the three crenelated pavilions which rose above the low roofs of the station. In this direction the shanty town's appearance was more marked, evidence of the way it had sprung up at the edge of—and as a result of—the military cantonment. In fact, Harry thought with a wry smile, in exactly the same way a town to service the many needs of soldiers sprang up beside every legionary fort, which the ancient Romans called a *vicus*, General MacGregor.

Harry paused and looked along the length of the hallway. Native orderlies seated at tiny desks outside each of the ten or so office doors appeared to be deeply occupied scribing or shuffling papers.

"Colonel Lockhart's office?"

The third man along shot to his feet and saluted with exaggerated smartness. "Sahib, here please. Are you being Left-tenant Haarivan, please?"

Harry stepped along the arcade and nodded.

"Please, sahib Haarivan sir, you are expectant."

He kept a smile from his lips and followed the orderly into a spacious office, much deeper than it was wide. More screened windows pierced the far wall. An open one revealed the greenery of trees in the enclosed courtyard beyond. In a corner of the long room a punkah-wallah cross-legged on a cushion pulled in desultory fashion on the rope that worked the wide fans above. Their wafting did less to relieve the stifling, damp heat than the shutters did to quiet the outside noise, but as he'd learned, the very movement imparted an impression of coolness.

"It's always like this. Blessed relief from the heat with the rain, and then out comes the sun, burns off the clouds, and down comes the heat again. And with it the accursed flies. Don't worry, Lieutenant, you'll soon get used to them."

If General MacGregor's head was square in profile, William Stephen

Alexander Lockhart's formed a powerful rectangle firmly divided by a long, straight nose. Hair, cut to a sparse fringe, framed a broad and high forehead, while a full mustache cut in German style covered his upper lip and left the lower peeking out and looking rather disapproving. This impression was at odds with the twinkle in the colonel's eyes; and the smoothness of his skin, stretched over jowly jaws, belied an age in the mid-forties and years spent in tropical climes. The impression was one of youthfulness and at the same time world-weary experience. This confluence in his physiognomy reminded Harry of a demonstration he'd seen as a boy of a chromotrope magic lantern in which two slides depicting a man smiling and unsmiling continuously flickered between them. The effect was disconcerting; Lockhart's facial age transformations were slower and conducted more in the onlooker's mind than in reality, but at times unsettling nonetheless.

"The dreadful outcome at Khartoum must have distressed you," he addressed Harry in a clipped tone and indicated the lone chair at the front of the desk. "The loss of Gordon has shaken everyone in India and given the Big Bear a stick to beat us. The Russians hoped the government would withdraw troops from here to Egypt to fight the Mahdists and denude the Indian frontier, but even the Liberals are not so wet."

With his brother Evan a panting Liberal, which made Harry by definition an ardent Conservative, this was a view he did not accept. It was Gladstone's shilly-shallying that fatally delayed the dispatch of troops to lift the siege of Khartoum. It was the Liberal government's tardiness that had led to the collapse of British influence in the Sudan. To Harry, Liberal and "wet" were tied at the waist. Naturally, he kept all this to himself, content that Lockhart had qualified wetness by the word *even*, which meant the colonel thought the Liberals to be at least a little bit damp.

"Are the Russians threatening, sir?"

"As it happens, no. Or not at this time. By past performance, Tsar Alexander prefers conquering 'vacated' possessions to all-out war, but his General Staff like thumping the table. Amir Abdur Rahman's obsession with not having us, or the Russians, trampling all over Afghanistan has resulted in a settlement. I don't suppose you would have heard of it on your travels. Not that the Russians will abide by the treaty, of course. Already their agents, in reality soldiers, are busy mapping and probing well south of the Oxus in that vast no-man's land.

As we speak, they are seeking passage through the mountains into India. Our task is to learn all there is to know about those mysterious heights, the passes, and the natives. The Joint Afghan Boundary Commission might be settling the western borders of Afghanistan, but those with India are open questions. It is in the Crown's interests that the farthest west into Afghanistan it can be drawn the better for India's security, but we're bound to face serious opposition from those tribes who see the entire North-West Frontier Province as their own."

Lockhart paused, and then fixed Harry with an appraising look. "Are you ready to join me, Vane? It won't be a boring jaunt, mapping the high passes around Gilgit and Chitral, you know. They are places as yet largely unknown to us, other than by rumor."

Harry inwardly patted down his immediate instinct to leap up from the hard chair and shout out, "Absolutely, sir." Instead, he took a grip of his emotions, desperate not to come across as some callow youth without a grasp of the importance of what he was being offered, or the potential dangers involved. He allowed a smile to reach his lips and answered calmly. "I'd be honored to go with you, sir, and do whatever I can."

Lockhart nodded, a curt inclination of his abundant forehead. "It's been voiced in the corridors of power back home as to whether there is value for money in pursuing an expedition toward Gilgit. That is, of course, because those who question the proposition sit on their comfortable backsides in Whitehall and not with us on the frontier. What is the importance of Gilgit, they ask."

Harry felt he was about to be told what he already knew from his recent reading.

"Why should we interfere there? The answer is Russia. The Tsar's armies have advanced practically to the Hindu-Kush and it is necessary to see they do not cross it." He allowed a small smile of deprecation. "I think we shall find it an unlikely route for a large army, but smaller groups of infiltrators would cause us havoc, arouse the maliks, the petty rulers, against us, and at the worst tie up troops desperately needed farther to the south where the Great Bear may well attempt to come through from Herat to the south of Kandahar. I note you claim a passing acquaintance with some of the Pathan tongues."

Harry quickly recovered from the abrupt change of subject. "All from books, sir, but I have been studying aboard our transport from Egypt, particularly Pashto and Tajik."

"Tajik may come in useful for its derivation from Persian, of which I gather you have a practicable knowledge." Lockhart shook his head. "Abdur Rahman has fallen back on Persian as the language of his court and government, even as he's forcibly relocated many Pashtoons from the south and east to the Tajik and Uzbek north, particularly those of the Ghilzai tribe. It's not always been a happy situation, the pundits tell me… at least those who returned with heads still intact. The Amir is hell bent on grinding the Ghilzais down, so there is much unrest among them, and don't forget, some of these tribesmen are the same people who helped drive us from Afghanistan in the past. They can be friends one minute and ruthless enemies the next. They are a proud people who have reason to hate us since they see Abdur Rahman both as their oppressor and a puppet of the British. We may well encounter elements of those relocated and resentful tribesmen in the lands through which we must travel."

"I understand, sir. I've read that as long as you stand firm without threat, even Ghilzais can be managed."

For a freezing moment Harry thought he'd overstretched himself. Lockhart's expression could easily be interpreted as contempt for the shallowness of youth. But then a tight smile creased his lips.

"Perhaps you have not heard it, young Vane, but there is a Pashtoon proverb you might always bear in mind. It goes: 'You should always kill an Englishman. First comes one as a hunter, then two to make a map, and then an army to take over the country; so better kill the first one.' We will be the first ones that many Pashtoons and certainly the pagan Kafirs there will have met."

"Sir!"

"We are as likely to encounter great hospitality as we are to have those who would murder us in our beds. The tribes of Khurasan—that fabled region encompassed by Alexander the Great, incidentally the last European to set eyes on much of it—are numerous and varied, and according to the Afghan poet Mirza 'Ata Mohammad, 'The Afghans of Khurasan have an age-old reputation that wherever the lamp of power burns brightly, there like moths they swarm, and wherever the tablecloth of plenty is spread, there like flies they gather.'

"Make sure you use every opportunity to brush up your language skills, but even so you will need a native servant with sufficient English to help you, to look after your things and watch your back as well. We all need a companion of that sort. I've taken the liberty of asking my day-orderly to look someone out for you and he's come up with a suitable lad. Check outside with him before you leave, and look in on the quartermaster's store as well. Sergeant Jackson there will know what you need in the way of kit and survival rations, all that sort of malarkey. We'll be setting out in two days, so be ready."

"Yessir."

Harry left in high fettle and not a little dazzled by Lockhart's poetic display. But the colonel had made up his mind to include him on the mission even before the interview, otherwise why already look him out a servant?

"Yes!" He punched the air.

"Ah, Left-tenant Haarivan, sahib," the orderly said, instinctively ducking Harry's boisterous fist. "I have a boy, he is expectant of your exalted presence. You his chief, so he your *pishkhidmat*, servant to a commander. Very good juwan, good boy. Young is true but can be trained. He look after all things most well. Please follow me, sahib."

Wondering what he was being let in for, Harry followed Lockhart's day-orderly down a set of open-sided stairs into the central courtyard.

There, waiting patiently under the shade of a towering chinar tree, stood a pale-skinned native boy. He might have been twenty, but clean-shaven cheeks and jawline suggested a much younger age. It was hard to tell. He stepped forward as they approached across the cobbles.

"This your new sahib boss-man," the orderly said, waving the boy forward. "He speak little Tajik, little Pashto, too much Persian."

To Harry's ears, the orderly sounded as though he considered the boy's background to be less than wonderful, but the enthusiasm with which he delivered the statement belied his words.

"This Arshan. A very bad Persian juwan, ungrateful boy to his mother and uncles everywhere, but he know Hindu Kush, he say. Nasty places…"

The orderly carried on, but Harry paid him little heed, all his attention fixed on the vision before him. Arshan stood in a sturdy unafraid pose, regarding Harry without the usual cast-down look of the Punjabi camp followers. The frank appraisal took in Harry left to right, top to bottom, and then centered on his face with a slow beaming smile which revealed a flash of sharp white teeth. His unruly mop of dark brown hair, so dark it was almost black in the sunlight, stood in contrast to the almost European hue of his skin, against which strong eyebrows seemed to have been added with the audacity of an artist's brush. Harry felt Arshan as a physical presence, and he knew with a sudden insight that the juwan, the youth, could see straight into his being. The regard simultaneously unsettled and excited him at a visceral level. He switched his attention back to the orderly lest Arshan see in Harry's eyes the admiration brimming in his breast.

Perhaps penetrating the heart of the unexplored Pamir and Hindu Kush mountains was going to be more interesting than Harry had ever thought.

"You say 'Left-tenant Haarivan,' Arshan, and be quick."

Harry extended a hand. Arshan took it in a firm grip and shook once before letting go and stepping back smartly one step to salute.

"Just Harry will do."

Arshan's smile turned shy, but he never looked down. "Yes, Haari sahib. Now we go adventure, yes?"

"Yes."

PART TWO

Of jezails and dancing boys, 1885–1891

*There is a boy across the river with a bottom like a peach
But alas! I cannot swim.*

— 17th-century Pashtun poet Kushal Khan Khattak

CHAPTER 7 | *Roof of the World 1885–86*

"IT'S A BIVALVE MOLLUSC SHELL, *Petricola pholadiformis*," the bright-eyed girl informed Harry. He had been staring at the two conjoined halves of the jet-black seashell on the mantelpiece for some minutes when Madge Rainbow spoke. Fitted together as it would have been when inhabited, the cuttlefish shell resembled a narrow case to house spectacles. Harry had only ever seen one half before, the one belonging to Richard Rainbow. It seemed inconceivable with all Edward had suffered in the Sudan—in the ferocity of all-out war, to be captured and enslaved by Arab raiders—that his half should still exist. There hadn't been time at that all-too-brief happenstance meeting in Suez a year ago to talk about such mundane matters as little boys' keepsakes, yet here it was, reunited. Brothers in arms.

"They picked it up on a beach near Penzance, you know? Where the pirates come from?"

Pirates. Blackbeard…

Harry smiled.

"Are you the very model of a modern Major-General?"

"I certainly have information vegetable, animal, and mineral," Harry responded. Madge made him nervous, which was ridiculous. She was a young girl, at least four or five years his junior, no doubt leading a typically sheltered existence; he an army officer, blooded in conflict against fanatical Dervishes and Chitrali and Kafir warriors. What was there to be nervous of?

"I think *The Slave of Duty*—that's the opera's alternative title you know, is appropriate to my brother Edward, do you not think so?"

Harry professed ignorance of the other title for the Gilbert and Sullivan comic opera, though he knew it perfectly well. In his first nights spent in officers' quarters in London on returning from Bombay friends had dragged him off to the Savoy Theatre to see a production. Nothing could have been farther from the jagged terrain of the Pamir Mountains and the Hindu Kush. And none in genteel London society could possibly imagine the things he had seen.

As if she'd read his mind, Madge said, "I imagine the brutality of stage pirates cannot compare with that of Pathan savages?"

Harry turned his back on the obsidian cuttlefish shell with its disturbing symbolism of partners reunited and looked around at the Rainbows' comfortably appointed withdrawing room, so much cozier than its equivalent at Hadlicote. "The Pashtoons also enjoy theatrical ebullience, Miss Rainbow."

He flinched inwardly at the asinine comparison, but there was little he could say of Afghanistan to this gently raised girl, other than to praise the extraordinary landscape and offer generalities as to the way its inhabitants dressed. Richard had warned him that she knew only the barest essentials of his and Edward's adventures in the Sudan, and only all she needed to know of Yussuf, the black-skinned Arab boy Edward brought with him from there.

Harry was also sure that Madge had developed a crush on him over the few days since he came to visit Richard, which meant walking a fine line between politeness and false encouragement.

❧❦❧

In retrospect, confronting a squadron of Shui Kafirs aiming their jezails was easier on his nerves than riding the Great Western service from Paddington via Oxford to Bourton-on-the-Water. The short words of telegram exchange were a poor preparation for how Harry was to cope with meeting Richard and Edward for the first time since that brief encounter in Suez—and really Edward since Benthenham. The five intervening years since Edward had run off from school yawned as deep as a crevasse, and posed as many perils of falling in. And Richard...? As the train rattled along the rails through the gently mounded Cotswold landscape, its rises and falls coated with the green cotton-candy of aspen, hornbeam, elm, oak, beech, and ash, between sweeping fields of harvest-ready wheat, all so English and different from the jarring valleys and white-topped peaks of Afghanistan, Harry fretted at the mistake he was making. But Richard had been insistent: Harry must spend some days with them. In the event, the greeting he received at Bourton's small station turned out warm enough, even from Edward.

"You had to come now," Richard said as he stowed Harry's modest valise behind the seats. "Edward thought he'd get away with not going to Sandhurst, and he sort of did, thanks to General Wolseley, but the army still insisted on giving my unruly…" He waved at Edward, aware of how silly it was to maintain in front of Harry the fiction that Edward was his twin, "…some training, so we ended up being here longer than hoped for."

"But that's over," Edward butted in enthusiastically. He moved over to make room for Harry. "I've earned my spurs and we are off to join Kitchener next month."

"Where to… or is that a deep secret?"

Edward shook his head. "No. Suakin. He's been brevetted lieutenant-colonel and takes over as Governor of the Red Sea Territory next month."

Richard followed Harry up onto the bench seat. "You'll remember how determined he was after the fall of Khartoum to take back all of the Sudan…" He trailed off and looked sheepish. "Ah, no you wouldn't. You weren't there, of course. We met him just after his promotion to major at Suakin. It was just after I'd found Ed and we'd been chased from the Nile to Kassala and almost to the Red Sea by Mahdists. So this is a start and he and plans to battle that knave Osman Digna to the death."

"Good luck there. That Fuzzy Wuzzy is the shiftiest villain alive."

All three laughed at that.

Richard shook the trap's reins and geed-up the two horses. "It's only a fifteen-minute trot to Rissington Manor." Then he switched back to the subject in hand. "With our Arabic I'm hoping we will be out in the field most of the time. The Dervishes have had it all their own way for too long. But what of you, Harry? You had a promotion. Captain Harry Smythe-Vane. I'm jealous. I'll have a word in the old man's ear when we get to Suakin."

Edward laughed easily. "Kitchener won't prefer you for promotion, Dick, or me for that matter, if he ever hears you call him an old man."

"Then I'll call him Sirdar, that's the Egyptian rank he wants, I know. But enough of our hopes, what of your adventures in the land of the wily Pathan? You've said so little."

Harry smiled. "It's not easy to say much in a telegram and getting a word in edgewise between you two is harder than battering down the door of an Afghan *qala*. And since getting back, what with the summer season under way in town, I haven't had any time to sit down and write."

And so the conversations had begun. He wanted to pour out his heart to Richard, but on the few occasions they found themselves alone or at least separated from the others by the distance of a room, the words failed him. He was rarely so tongue-tied, but this was the first time he'd been so exposed to his friend's feelings for Edward in Edward's presence, and if others of the family couldn't see it, Harry saw clearly in the looks they exchanged their shining love for each other. He saw also their mutual impatience to be away from home again, off to the desert wilderness. He admired the way they managed the brotherly familiarity, almost as if their sister—well, the blood-sibling sister of one of them—and Colonel and Lucy Rainbow had fashioned them as real brothers. (Harry always thought Richard to be the true Rainbow, but in the absence of any proof he kept this opinion to himself.)

Harry's familiarity with Edward's open nature as experienced at Benthenham did not prepare him for the generosity Edward extended to his two guests when it came to the nature of amorous relationships. His fondness for Yussuf (the black-skinned boy he'd seen at Suez that day) was frankly apparent to the point of complete openness with Harry about the sex he enjoyed with his former fellow slave during the time of captivity in Darfur. Disconcertingly, Richard appeared to be comfortable with this, and Edward made it clear that he was entirely familiar with Richard's entanglements with Harry. For his part, Harry was less comfortable about Edward having that knowledge, as much as their sister's embarrassingly open admiration for Harry discomfited him. Yussuf, too, seemed entirely equable about his former lover's engagement to Richard, and in this Harry found for himself a measure of composure.

The four young men were seated on cushioned garden chairs at an ornate round table of pierced metal painted brilliant white. A large parasol sprouted from the table's middle to provide scant shade since the sun had inconveniently moved to another quarter and cast the shadow away from where they reposed. Autumn's colors were yet to tinge the foliage surrounding the lower lawn and the sun's warmth enfolded them, which made the lemonade they were drinking very welcome. The grass, mowed the day before, still smelled sweetly where the gardeners were raking it into the compost heap a way down the garden.

"I missed my godson's twelfth birthday, so when I return to town I anticipate a summons from General Langrish-Smith." Harry glanced at Richard. He took a quick sip and relished the lemonade's sugared tartness. "You may remember you asked me who Colonel—as he was back then—Langrish-Smith was that Christmas at Hadlicote?"

Richard nodded as he refilled his glass from a jug pearled with condensation.

Harry sniffed and gnawed at his lower lip. The others sensed his tension. "He reminded me of something terrible. Not of himself," he hastened to add, "but because of his age. Were he Kafir, Ghilzai, Tajik or one of the numerous Pashtoon tribes it's more than likely young Jolyon would be seized and used as a *bacha bazi*."

The other three asked their unspoken questions at the unfamiliar phrase in individual expressions. The melodious warble of a blackbird broke the silence following Harry's words.

"I should start at the beginning."

"It wasn't an easy matter, parting company with William Maplethorpe. It had rather crept up on me quite how much he had come to mean. But if I am honest, I fear he was the more heartbroken. I had, after all, the adventure of exploring regions—some never before visited by Europeans—to look forward to, he only the drudgery of garrison life. It was a bleak moment of separation.

"The two brave men who had gone before us, at least part of the way, my heroes Robert Shaw and George Hayward—you remember him, from the fuss made after his murder in the Yasin Valley in 1870?—these had persuaded the authorities that the passes leading across the Pamirs, the Hindu Kush, and the Karakorams into northern India were vulnerable. At Calcutta the authorities, as men set at a distance will do, worried that the Russian army would one day come pouring through these high routes. And so the Viceroy of India, Lord Dufferin, commanded Colonel William Lockhart to take a mission to unknown Kafiristan, which sits astride several of these worrying mountain passes. I was thrilled to be picked to go with him—"

"I can see from the light in your eyes that you're still excited, Harry, though the prospect is now in the past." Richard grinned as he broke into the narration.

"Yes! The place gets into the blood. Our task was to survey the region and map the terrain stretching from the princely state of Chitral and its southern dependencies in the west to Hunza in the east, and determine if there was an easy passage south from Chitral into Afghanistan. More importantly, we were to map the northern passes connecting to the valley of the upper Oxus and its feeder rivers, the Panj-Bartang, and Pamir. It was vital to determine once and for all whether these passes represented a threat to the defense of India.

"We set out, Lockhart in command, myself and two other officers, five native pundits—the local 'men of knowledge' and surveyors—a small part-Punjabi, part-Kashmiri escort of sepoys, and several coolies. As an aside, I should say that the upper-caste Dogras, who have ruled Kashmir for hundreds of years, show little regard for Kashmiri villagers such as our carriers, who are impoverished and oppressed. The Dogras refuse to pay coolies, treat them as slaves, and hundreds frequently perish of diarrhoea and dysentery on long trade marches, brought on by overwork and bad food. Lockhart insisted on paying our coolies, but it was always a struggle to get the sepoys and pundits to treat the poor souls in a reasonable manner. Anyway, we white officers also took along our personal servants. Here…"

Harry produced a wallet from the inside pocket of his coat, which lay discarded over the back of his chair. From it he pulled out a stiff card, a little frayed at the edges, and handed it first to Richard, who smiled broadly at the photographic image.

"That is my boy Arshan standing next to me. It was taken as we approached the foothills in Kashmir."

"Very handsome," Richard said and passed the picture to Yussuf and Edward. Yussuf peered with frank interest at this native of an impossibly far-off land.

Harry knew they saw a slightly hazy monochrome image of two proud faces, smiling for the camera box, but whenever he took it out he saw it in all the intense colors of Kashmir—Arshan's pale cheeks, yet unmarked by beard or mustache, rouged with pink from the cold, the deep indigo hues in his brown hair, the green glints in his dark eyes, reflections of the mountain stream they posed beside as it rushed on its way to join the Indus in the valley below.

"What's his age?"

"I can't tell you accurately, Richard. Arshan himself is unsure. He and his young brother were orphaned and some uncle sold them both to… well, I'll come to that story soon enough." He took the photograph back. "This was the last moment of civilization, and breathtakingly beautiful too. I know we fell under the stark allure of the barren Bayuda Desert of the Sudan, but Kashmir's charm is all in its rich greens. Imagine the great valley, shut in by a circular rampart of snowy mountains, majestic and refreshing to the parched desert eye. Fine rivers run through richly cultivated lands, adorned by a chain of lovely lakes, watered by a thousand streams.

"Everywhere, the numerous villages are embowered in every species of fruit tree and the magnificent oriental plane tree, or chinar as they are known there, which Arshan told me the Mughal emperors planted wherever they dwelled for it provides a deep and delicious shade. The road runs below great cliffs clothed with forest, at one time through thickets of lilac, barberry, and hazel, and at another through the forest itself, here composed of magnificent deodars. The many ruins of Buddhist temples—some in a fair state of preservation—bear witness here, as do other remains throughout the Hindu-Kush and northern India, to the widespread power of the creed of which now scarcely a trace remains, except in time-worn stones.

"Everywhere, rice is the most important grain. The Kashmiris are very clever in its cultivation, and they grow it up to an altitude of seven thousand feet. The fields are terraced carefully to hold the irrigation and anxiously weeded, and are incessantly watered by the mountain streams."

"Any peas or beans? I know you are fond of your legumes."

A sour expression answered Richard. "Not to speak of. The mung bean is grudgingly sown in paddies requiring a rest from rice cultivation. I'm not keen on mung beans." He chuckled ruefully. "From this pulseless paradise, our way lay on the winding track ever upward into the Pamirs. Two weeks after leaving Kashmir we traversed the Kamri Pass, thankful for our mounts doing most of the footwork, for at over thirteen thousand feet the air was almost too thin to breathe. The path up was no more than a track worn by men and animals, but it was a delight of grassy slopes covered in miles of flowers, acres of spirea, and dense thickets of roses. That was below the snow line, but our way led still upward. For mile upon mile now the road ran through thick snow until we descended into the valley in which Gilgit is situated almost a month after leaving Rawul Pindee. Here we stayed for some days on hearing from local guides that the streams on the Chitral passage were swollen with melting snow."

Harry leaned forward and spoke quietly as though afraid others beyond their circle might overhear, even though they were a distance from the house one way and the gardeners in the other direction, and the rest of the family had gone up to London for the day. "I know I am among friends who understand, so I shall speak frankly. I have seen sights I never thought to witness. One day Lockhart tasked me to take two pundits and two of our sepoys and go with some natives to a small village the locals called Gilgit-i-ghar. This was situated twelve miles to the north up the Hunza River. I was to investigate it for the record we were building of the regions through which we traveled.

"We think of a village as a scattering of individual dwellings, but with the scarcity of flat land and what there is needed for cultivation, in the Pamirs—as I learned happens in much of Afghanistan as well—a village, or a qala, is a single structure of connecting rooms and hallways, built to act as a fortress within surrounding walls. From the exterior, the result resembles an untidy pile of boxes. It is of the defensible aspect of these hamlets the authorities wished to learn. How much they might hinder any Russian advance, or indeed the actions of our soldiers.

"I had noted these villages sometimes had a large yurt erected without the walls and wondered what its purpose might be. Arshan only looked disconcerted when I questioned him and muttered 'Bacha, Haari.' This is a Persian word, which means child or adolescent. At Gilgit-i-ghar I was to discover for myself the degrading rites enacted inside the yurt. To this point we had not encountered anything other than wary interest from the natives, and the men of this qala—and all the children—who had never left the mountains found me an interesting specimen. But there were a few who had adventured south and were acquainted with the Sikhs and Indians, and so also to a tiny degree with Englishmen. The language of Gilgit is Shina, a relation of Kashmiri Dogra, but there is a smattering of Pashto, which is close to Persian, so between my poor Pashto and Arshan's translation we managed well enough.

"In the later afternoon, as the pundits went about their surveying, some of the village men invited me to join them in the yurt to drink tea and partake of their *narghiles*—a water-pipe like the Egyptian *shisha*. Arshan became agitated, though at the time I didn't know why. He tried to dissuade me, but I feared insulting the elders. After all, our task was expected to take more than a day meaning we would have to stay there for at least one night, so I had no wish to upset our hosts and make the job more difficult."

Harry opened a thin silver case and extracted a cigarette. "Egyptian," he said, placing the open case on the table. Yussuf immediately took up the offer. "Can't get decent Egyptian tobacco in India. Oh, thank you," he added as Edward reached over to refill his glass.

Once he'd struck a vesta, lit Yussuf's cigarette and his own, and extinguished the safety match, Harry continued his narrative. "Several lamps lit the interior and threw bright pools of light on the ground, which had been covered with overlapping rugs of intricate designs in the Persian manner. Around the circumference were piled cushions, many already occupied, the men seated in cross-legged pose. I noticed straight away the looks that some of the men directed at Arshan, and how he kept his eyes lowered and sat close by me when one of the elders gestured me to a cushion. Men soon filled the yurt and it and buzzed with animated conversation. A haze hung in the air from the *narghiles*, cups of tea clattered on metal trays, and other drink was offered, quite potent. Yes, I know these are Moslems, but in this respect they do not follow the precepts of their faith… and not in another respect as well.

"Three young men struck up a slow rhythm with flutes and kettle drums, a plaintive melody. With a sudden flourish, the flaps of the tent parted and two young women rushed in and began to dance. They were barefoot and wore long, brightly colored dresses that reached just below their knees, and narrow trousers cinched at the ankles. Rings and bangles glittered on their arms and wrists; their long hair flared out with the whirling motion they set up and the way they threw their heads sideways with each turn—it was decidedly coquettish. I settled back to enjoy the performance and took an offered pipe to smoke. The tobacco had a heady flavor and I suspected an opiate in its contents.

"After a bit the pace of the music increased, and the girls—in fact I could see as one or the other gyrated close to me that they were very young—began to move in a more lascivious manner. The slightly taller of the two went so far as to bend over and wiggle her rump in a man's face. He reached out to run his hands over what she offered to the great merriment of his fellow villagers. I had grown irritated at Arshan, normally a joyful companion, who sat beside me as rigid as a convicted soldier at his execution. I leaned in and I said, 'It surprises me that their wives put up with their menfolk taking such liberties with young women.' Arshan looked up at me, eyes wide. 'Haari,' he whispered, 'they are *bacha bazi*.' I stared back, unsure of what he meant. 'Boy dancers,' he said. And then it struck me. *Bacheh-baazi* is Persian. It means 'playing with children.' But these were dancing. Where did 'playing' come in?

"I soon found out. Both boys I'd mistaken for girls began to flirt ever more outrageously with the men, stroking their painted nails down bearded cheeks. Instead of the recipient flinching he wrapped arms around the boy and kissed him. The boys raised some of the younger men to their feet to dance with them as do men and women in Europe, and the men wandered their hands over the boys, even between their legs when the dancers raised their skirts unceremoniously to offer their partner their private parts."

Harry stopped. Stubbed out his finished cigarette. For the first time since beginning to relate the events, he took his gaze from the distant trees and looked around at his three companions. He smiled ruefully. "The fellow seated next to me spoke in poor Pashto. He asked me if I would let 'my boy' join the fun. I don't think Arshan could hear over the wailing music, which had reached a fearsome sexual heat. The man didn't seem to want an answer because at that moment one of the *bacha* thrust his bottom in the man's face. In a flash he was fully occupied running his hands over the bare cheeks and demonstrating the lad's evident erection. 'Do you want to fuck with this one?' he suddenly asked me. 'I have your boy, you take this one.'

"I saw things in India which shocked, like the young gobble-wallahs. But they, forced by circumstances to earn money, at least still had choice. As I discovered, the *bacha bazi* are often sold into prostitution by their parents. The boys are trained to play instruments, to dance, and to offer their childish bodies to men. I saw compliance in these boys' eyes, but how should they know any better? Arshan later told me that some masters are kind enough, but most care nothing for the boys and discard them into poverty when they have grown and lost their childish charms for the pederasts.

"I'm still not sure how I managed to extricate myself and poor Arshan from the yurt without entirely throwing over our mission. But I did. Our two sepoys had erected tents on a small patch of almost level ground belonging to the headman of the qala. I made a low obeisance, ducked out of the yurt with Arshan ushered before me, and fled to the tents. I can only surmise that the villagers saw a white man on fire with lust from the *bacha bazi* performance and the clear suggestion of what would undoubtedly follow, rushing his boy to privacy, there to ravish him. And so they forgave my retreat for my hasty need to rut."

Throughout Harry's quiet but insistent tale, Yussuf hung on every word. When Harry paused to drink some more lemonade he spoke up, face alight with excitement. "So, with Arshan you go tent and fuck-fuck-fuck, yes?"

Edward burst into peals of boyish laughter. "His English improves every day," he addressed Harry, "but I think his grasp leaves him missing some of the more subtle undertones." He turned to Yussuf. "Harry was protecting his servant, Yussuf, not doing the... well, you know."

Yussuf did. He flapped the dark shelf of his eyebrows at Edward and laughed happily.

Harry felt Richard's eyes on him, but his friend said nothing. Richard knew him a lot better than Edward and he knew Richard was reading between the lines. *And keeping his thoughts shrouded.*

As the sun began its late summery downward drift, Harry explained that he'd never suspected, never had a reason to suspect, that Arshan had himself been a *bacha bazi*. "Despite what he suggested to me at the time, Lockhart's orderly who recommended Arshan to me for the expedition knew nothing of his background. Recalling the man's words, I questioned Arshan about his 'mother and uncles.' He told me that Tajik bandits murdered his father and in due course his mother was obliged by local custom to marry his father's brother. But this uncle cared nothing for Arshan and his younger brother Firuz, and since Arshan's mother had no say in what happened to them, she could do nothing when the uncle sold them to passing traders. In turn these itinerant merchants made a small profit by selling the boys on to a man I was soon to meet—though I didn't know that then.

"The thought of being dragged back to the life of a dancing sex slave filled the boy with horror. Though he was, he assured me, beyond the age the whoremasters prefer I could see his youthful looks still held him hostage to the sexual greed of his elders. Worse, he confessed that his young brother Firuz still languished in the hands of a brutal master in the Bashgal Valley, from where Arshan had somehow escaped the year before. He had traveled with a caravan to Kashmir and thence into the market at Rawul Pindee.

"In due course, on our return to Kashmir, I learned that Arshan had quickly established himself as a hard working and trustworthy hicarrah, a messenger-wallah, and so came to the attention of the headquarters orderlies. The cantonment is full of natives like that—a mixed lot from many tribes, many far-flung regions—acting in all sorts of semi-official and completely unofficial capacities. When he heard rumors of our proposed expedition, Arshan saw hope of going along and rescuing Firuz, which he did not suggest to me until after the incident at Gilgit-i-ghar. So while my official job was to help explore this mysterious region and map it, I had been allocated—without my prior knowledge—the task of riding to the rescue of a dancing boy."

CHAPTER 8 | *Feet of the Sun 1886*

"WE GAINED USEFUL information about the country in the vicinity of Gilgit. After a stay of eight days following my return we set off on the perilous journey to climb through the valleys and across the high passes of the southern Pamirs and then in a westerly direction into the Hindu Kush. The route lies along the course of the wild Gilgit River to the Shandar Pass, then across ranges of the Hindu Kush in a northward diversion before descending into the valley of the Mastuj River, which in turn runs south to the Chitral River.

"This fabled region almost defeated Alexander and Marco Polo. It was humbling to think we could do better than either of these explorers, but then, we were equipped with modern weapons, tents, surveying instruments, and army emergency rations. And they were all needed. Some of the natives call this land the Roof of the World; others refer to it as the Feet of the Sun, which is appropriate for the inhabitants of Kafiristan, who still worship pagan gods in their large cedar temples.

"But between Gilgit and Chitral we were still within the realms of Islam, and a people fiercely independent and resentful of outside interference in their affairs. Our way took us over roads—no more than vague tracks—often passing around the face of a precipice. In every chasm torrents foamed far below. We lost two mules when they fell over a sharp edge. We could not proceed until we recovered the lost loads. We needed every item. More than once we encountered great crevasses in the path. For men on foot, spanning the chasm with a few logs will make a rickety bridge, but while we might have hazarded such a crossing, our mules could not, so we had to take some higher path over the mountains and so extend our journey.

"A continual avalanche of stones is one of the region's terrors. Ranging from pebbles in size to great rocks, they are loosened from their great heights by the freezing conditions one minute and the unshaded sun the next. I had a near escape when a boulder the size of my head crashed into the shale of the path in front of me. One of the sepoys had his leg snapped clean off by a rock that fell from a great height. I was glad of my pustin, the Afghan sheepskin coat which shelters one from falling stones as well as the cold. We climbed every day, higher into the sky until eventually we reached the Shandar Pass, some twelve thousand feet above the sea. It took our party almost a month to traverse the hundred and fifty miles from Gilgit to Chitral and on several occasions shots rang out from even higher and we were forced to take cover. Lockhart supposed these were either lone bandits or small groups, since they did not materialize or attack us, put off by the return of our gunfire. However, the invisible shooters made us nervous and it was natural that the party was fearful as to what kind of reception we might receive as we approached our second destination."

Shadows lengthened across the lawns of Rissington Manor.

"I hesitate to interrupt you, Harry, but shall we go in, gentlemen?" Richard said. "I'm sure Evans can find us something to drink a little stronger than lemonade, and you…" he placed an arm over Harry's shoulder as they all stood, "…can tell us the rest of your adventures at the Feet of the Sun over a slug of Scotch or a shot of gin."

Edward and Yussuf led the way across the close cropped grass toward the beckoning French doors set into the pale Costwold stone walls of the house. A maid walked across the grass as if she had been poised waiting for an indication they had finished with the lemonade jug and glasses. As their paths crossed, Richard halted and politely thanked her. Harry paused too, and then as they started to stroll on Richard took advantage of the distance that had opened up between them and the other two to speak quietly.

"I feel I must ask if I am misreading what you didn't reveal, but I suspect you had a more intimate relationship with your Arshan than you suggested."

Harry glanced sideways briefly, saw Richard's gentle smile and matched it. "You're right. Beyond your believing in my susceptibility to a handsome face, what did I say that made you think so?"

"Not what you said, how you looked. I know you, Harry, better than any. I saw it in your eyes."

"At Rawul Pindee the cantonment only had brick-built barracks for a few. We newcomer Dragoons had to make do with large tents, three or four subalterns to a unit, although there were interior partitions for some privacy." He paused, but Richard made no comment on the apparent non sequitur. "You see the weight of a communal tent like those on an expedition such as we were about to embark on would have been a severe drawback. So we had small tents barely sufficient to fit two, which gave us a greater measure of privacy after retiring, and naturally the officers had their servants sleep across the closed opening at nights."

"Cozy?"

Harry smiled again. "Intimate. When it grew severely cold it made sense to have one's servant inside to pool body warmth. I'm sure the proprieties were maintained… but. We were only two days out of Kashmir when the attractions Arshan held for me matched his desires. My beautiful Persian boy. The way he used to breathe 'Haaaari' in my ear… Oh."

Richard raised an eyebrow. "What?"

"I feel odd. Talking to you about this. It doesn't seem right, I—"

"Harry. It's all right." They dawdled in silence a moment. Richard lifted his left hand, splayed the fingers, and then closed them up into a fist as though catching a thought. "I am in no position to judge you, not for anything. Truth is, it's me who should be judged. The way I treated you."

"No, you had reason."

Ahead of them, Edward and Yussuf disappeared into the house.

Richard halted again, placed a hand above Harry's elbow, and swung him gently around so they faced each other squarely. "You're being kind, as usual. I think the Sudanese sun burned off my guilt as I searched for Ed, but only to a degree. I always thought of you during that lonely trek. However, finding him overwhelmed my senses… But seeing you again, Harry. It's hard."

"But you love Edward. You always have. 'Closer than limpets,' Alfred Winner used to say. As close as two halves of a cuttlefish shell that fit together perfectly." He sighed, dipped his chin sadly. "We travel different roads, Richard. I think William and Arshan made it possible for me to hold you in my heart and yet extend affection to others. You have completed your trek. I am yet on mine. There is a beautiful herald of spring in Afghanistan, when the purple crown of the istalif iris pushes up through the snow—a symbol of eternal hope. One day

I shall find my iris, what my heart desires, as you have done. And I know you're anxious to be back to the desert… and time to be yourselves."

"Arshan isn't the one?"

The question took Harry aback for a moment. *How strange we are, that an Englishman can ask of another Englishman whether love is possible with a native. Was it like that with Edward and Yussuf?* He thought for a moment, and then shook his head slightly. "I find I am not like so many of my compatriots, who treat natives as something less than themselves, but I have to face facts. I want to love someone I understand and be loved in return by someone who knows my heart. Isn't that truly possible only within the same social group? Perhaps deep down… perhaps it *is* xenophobia, though I don't really think so. More a question of Arshan and I not sharing a culture."

Richard waited silently for Harry to gather his thoughts.

"When I departed Rawul Pindee for Bombay we parted finally in the sense that you never know where the Army will post you next. We both regretted it, but I can't honestly say with a hollow heart. I think you, above all Richard, know that a heart needs a home. Arshan is a wonderful someone who is just visiting. It's easy to make love to a handsome boy like Arshan, but it's less easy to love the mystery that lives inside of him. Bluntly, we're *firangi*… foreigners."

"And you still await a permanent home for your heart," Richard finished. "But how do you think he feels about you?"

"I don't think he wants to spend his life with me. Mostly he wanted help to find his brother and save him from a life he himself knows all too well. If I should be posted back to the North-West Frontier I shall be most happy to see him, but unless I get involved in another political expedition, I doubt there will be any realistic way we can be together as we were in the mountains. And if we should, I shall cherish Arshan as much as I already have and hope he still feels the same way toward me." Harry squeezed Richard's arm. "We'd better go in or the others will wonder what on earth we're up to out here."

"It is my sincerest hope, Harry, that you will find a refuge for your heart. Whoever it may be, will be a very lucky person. Though I fear it won't be Madge."

Harry coughed. "You noticed."

"Not very hard to miss. But don't worry. I'll sort my dear sister out. Couldn't have her marrying a cad like *Haarivan*, could we?"

And laughing easily, they went on arm in arm toward the open French doors.

≈✦≈

"They call the headman the Mirtar (the Kahsmiris render it as Mehtar) or sometimes Badshah. The Mirtar of Chitral, Aman-ul-Mulk, came out to greet us with a large following, including his heir, Nizam ul Mulk. As an aside, I should say I was quite struck with Nizam, a good-looking young man with striking eyes and a well-shaped face. His younger brother Afzal was equally handsome and possessed of a charming character… at least, so we first thought. Anyway, I digress. We were about two miles from the fort when we encountered hundreds of horse and foot lining the opposite bank of the Chitral River on which the town sits. They were ablaze with color. Their chogas—a long-sleeved robe—of gold, green, and blue velvets, gorgeous silks of Bokhara, or brilliant broadcloths, floated loose over bright silk or colored cotton undercoats. Their comical ballooning breeches were tucked into high black boots; some merely had them slipped into the gay-patterned knitted woolen socks which all Chitralis wear.

They were armed to the teeth. All had a long-barreled gun slung over the shoulder, the ubiquitous jezail. Most had a metal or leather shield on the back and nearly all, in addition to a sword, carried a dagger and a pistol stuck in his belt. They waved their jezails and fired off rounds into the air, apparently delighted to see a British party come to visit; a great relief to us. There was much rejoicing, shouting, drumming, and blowing of pipe instruments, as we rode along."

The four were comfortably seated on a sofa and chairs, smoking Egyptian cheroots and sipping a rare single-malt. Harry noted that Yussuf had acquired the habit for alcohol and when he remarked on it, Edward laughed and told him that the Moslem tribesmen he stayed with in Darfur fermented camel milk to quaff happily enough on special occasions. "Tasted disgustingly foul until I got used to it!"

Harry nodded and picked up his story again. "Rain and distant thunder threatened. Where an Englishman might run for shelter, because the monsoon is unpredictable in Chitral and rain essential for the crops, a downpour is taken as a good omen and welcomed with open arms. So the Chitralis accepted us as bringers of good fortune. The Mirtar's age is hard to determine, but perhaps as much as seventy. I might also add that he's a prime suspect to have connived at the treacherous murder of George Hayward in the neighboring valley of Yasin. Lockhart insisted there is no evidence to prove the point, but the Mirtar has sovereignty over Yasin, and Hayward's bones are buried there in Chitral.

"Aman-ul-Mulk stands at about five foot nine, is very broad in figure, with the fists of a prize-fighter. In spite of his advancing years he holds himself royally as befits his ancient lineage. A flourishing beard, mustache, and fulsome sideburns—the beard dyed bright red—hide most of his features, other than an aquiline nose, and his complexion is pale in the Persian mold. To our great amusement, he rode hand-in-hand with Lockhart, which the colonel found very disagreeable. As we passed the fort's mud walls, a humorously sporadic artillery salute greeted our party.

"We were given a mulberry grove in which to pitch our camp, less than half a mile from the Mirtar's fort, which I could glimpse through a majestic copse of chinar trees. It's a fine looking stronghold, square in shape with square towers at each corner. It sits in a fine walled garden containing low structures designed for the relaxation and pleasure of the Mirtar's harem. Against the south-facing garden wall there sits a fine summerhouse, which being outside the private part of the complex is where the Mirtar entertains guests and visitors.

"In the other direction great snow-topped Tirich-Mir, the tallest peak in the Hindu Kush, towers above the steep V-shaped valleys which marched away from us, fading from a bright viridian to a mist-wreathed blue-gray. When the dawning sun strikes and the valley is still in darkness, the mountain appears as a pillar of fire. Burnished like copper, it turns to silver through the day and liquid gold at sunset. Chitral is actually six large villages extending on both sides of the river for about three miles. Here, the narrow valley abruptly widens out and the barren mountains about become thickly wooded with pines.

"As far as we could ascertain, Aman-ul-Mulk holds sway over two hundred thousand souls and claims sovereignty over those who live in the Yasin Valley, some hundred miles to the northeast, and the upper Bashgal Valley, which runs in the opposite direction. I also discovered that he held sway over any free woman he had eyes for, and wherever we went there would be a son or a daughter in his own image. I was told he had as many as eighty children scattered about, in addition to those with legal claim on him from his many official wives.

"And in one way he was not at all like his countrymen—he abhorred what Lockhart referred to as the 'rampant unnatural vices of the country,' by which I took it he meant the bacha bazi. In this respect, as a 'good Mohammedan,' he said, 'My success in defeating all my enemies I attribute to their depravity, against which God's wrath is kindled.' But the Mirtar equally avoids interfering with his subjects' religious or sexual inclinations, and his eldest sons Nizam and Afzal surrounded themselves with flusters of dancing and singing boys all the days we were there.

"After some ten days Lockhart decided we should travel farther on, the short distance to the Dorah Pass, although it was a steep climb to the top at over fourteen thousand feet. From this westerly direction we turned south via the Zedek Pass to meet the Bashgal Valley and Kafiristan, a state inhabited by Chitrali pagans, or Kafirs as the Moslems call the 'unbelievers.' We were the first Europeans to set eyes on Bashgali-Chitrali men and women in their own country. Aman-ul-Mulk furnished information as to the villages in the valley, and we determined to reach at least as far as a place called Shui."

Harry broke his tale for a moment to grin at Richard.

"You know how you all teased me about my comfortable camp bed when we trudged through the desert."

"I'm sure I did not!" Richard protested, which only made Harry smile more broadly. He knew what Richard was thinking; of the times he had praised Harry's campaign bed for being so much broader and more comfortable than his own when they shared it on those nights of passion when circumstances permitted.

"Well, you would have laughed all the louder at my state on that expedition. Arshan always complained at sharing my camp bed. He said it was too cold and too cramped, which was true. He claimed sleeping on the ground to be much better. In fairness, Lockhart first adopted this arrangement for himself. My turn came one evening as we made camp, shortly after departing from Chitral. Arshan went to fetch water so one of the coolies put up the structure without fitting the joints properly, and it smashed irretrievably directly I sat on it. For the next months I slept on the ground, and in cold weather there is no doubt that it is far more comfortable and very much warmer than a bed. We gathered straw whenever possible, or the coolies cut dry grass, and put a foot of it down all over the floor of the tent. We then stretched my tent carpet over the grass, and put down the bedding on top. In real cold, such as one encounters in those regions, this makes the most perfect sleeping place because there is no gale of icy wind blowing under you as is usually the case if you have a bed. Into this warm, flexible nest, Arshan and I rolled together and relished the comfort we gave each other."

When he saw Edward's slight widening of his eyes and a raised eyebrow, Harry realized he'd given away more than he intended, and blushed. But Edward seemed only to be indicating that he had known all along, and understood. Harry covered the slight embarrassment by drinking some Scotch, and clearing his throat.

"But I've digressed again. Where were we? Ah yes, approaching Shui. As we neared the village a band of some fifty Kafir men and boys met us. Arshan shouted out a greeting in Persian, which these people spoke more clearly than the derivative Pashto, and I found I could manage fairly well to understand, though they professed not to understand the way I spoke it. The Kafirs were all on foot but brought with them a tiny pony which the headman insisted Colonel Lockhart mount to ride into the town. Why he had to abandon his own horse for this little thing was unclear, but he had no wish to cause insult, and we all curbed our merriment at the way he had to raise his ankles all the while to prevent his heels dragging on the springy turf. Meanwhile, we dismounted to walk with our strange hosts. The path ran through pleasant woods of deodar, the noble Himalayan cedar, and silver birch, alongside the Basghal, a mountain stream at this point. The Kafirs were extremely curious about the color of we officers' skin and demanded the removal of breeches as well as coats so they could see that the white went all the way up.

"We pitched camp in the village, which comprised individual dwellings within a low wall, built more to keep out wild animals than human predators. Here we may have remained were it not for Arshan. As the village men came down to wave their carved steel and brass daggers and short axes in dance around a large log fire put up earlier for the ceremonial purpose, he told me of Lut-Dih, which means the Great Village. 'There is an important temple there,' he said, loud enough for the colonel to hear it with interest. The headman immediately embarked on a paean to its beauty and importance. As Lockhart absorbed the information, Arshan whispered to me. 'Lut-Dih is magnificent. It is also wicked, for it is there Baktash-al Ghulam Ali holds my brother in thrall to his evil bacha bazi business. You will save him, Haari.' I could hardly refuse him, but there was the problem of Lockhart and what my commanding officer would think."

"I would imagine he wasn't very encouraging, seeing as how far from help you were," Edward said.

"He wasn't at first. But like me—and you, Richard and Edward—Lockhart detests the mundanity of garrison life. This expedition wasn't his first into the wild lands beyond the frontiers, and I've no doubt it won't be his last. So he has sympathy for a plan others would disdain as being reckless. I am sure the decision to move on to Lut-Dih was prompted by the needs of our mission, but I like to think it gained impetus from the notion of adventure. The written record states that we proceeded to Lut-Dih, a large town of some five thousand inhabitants, set in a high valley made pleasant by the abundance of vines, apricot, mulberry, and walnut trees, and that our party remained there but a few days before returning to Chitral with the good wishes of the headman.

"The reality was somewhat different."

"Making the acquaintance of Baktash-al Ghulam Ali proved simple because he was as curious about the strange white men who had come among his people as we were about him. He held a high position in the town because he rented out his harem of boys for parties. Arshan informed me that he partook of their favors on a regular basis, buggering as many as three a night. Baktash also invited selected guests to the lavish revels held in his *haveli*, the name they give in those parts to a courtyard house. His 'palace' turned out to be a sprawl of damp rooms, some on two floors, near the center of the town, and not far from the mighty temple to the pagan gods. None of these Bashgali had ever set eyes on a European before, and Baktash was eager for us to sample his wares.

"It was the first time I heard the colonel mention the dancing boys and he made his disapproval of the custom clear at the same time as he emphasized the requirement for blind eyes and diplomacy. However, at my pressing he saw the point of accepting the invitation to that evening's entertainment. But only the two of us. My officer colleagues wanted nothing to do with such unsavory activity, and Lockhart said he had the morals of the pundits and sepoys to guard." Harry gave a short laugh. "But I saw disappointment in their faces. The Dogra pundits are as partial as the Afghans to a well-rounded boy's bottom it turns out.

"Since arriving in the region, I'd ensured Arshan either remained out of sight or, when that wasn't practical, we disguised his appearance so that there would be no danger of Baktash-al Ghulam Ali or any of the man's servants, of which he appeared to own plenty, recognizing his erstwhile dancing boy. In spite of a natural terror of his former master, Arshan found the dressing up hilarious. He wore pantaloons borrowed from a pundit, into which we stuffed more material about the waistline to pad out his narrow hips and flat tummy. With a liberal coating of ash to his face and an overlarge turban wrapped around his brow, he aged many years in appearance.

"The evening passed in similar fashion to the one I'd attended in Gilgit-i-ghar, except in this case the dances took place outdoors in the secluded courtyard. A wooden peristyle around three sides of the square sheltered the audience in the event of a sharp shower, to which the region is prone. At either corner, attendants looked after blazing braziers, which provided both light and warmth, although the night was not particularly cool.

"Arshan came with the colonel and me as a serving man and his nervousness only added to his adopted age, but I made sure he stayed behind me in the shadows against the back wall. Baktash-al Ghulam Ali possessed a veritable harem of boys, ranging in age from not more than eight—although it's hard sometimes to put an accurate age to Afghan children—to perhaps eighteen, at which point they have almost always lost their allure for the pederasts who eagerly attend these orgies, which masquerade as quasi-religious rites.

"Whatever, our purpose that night was to identify Firuz, if that were possible, and learn something of the layout of Baktash's palace and whatever security he employed.

"In the first we were swiftly successful. The first of the bacha bazi—four very young boys—performed, playing fifes and a stringed instrument as they pranced and pirouetted before being enticed one after the other into voracious arms amid friendly taunts and salacious advice to the successful suitor as what to do with the lad. This lasted no more than a quarter of an hour and then on came two willowy adolescents of surpassing beauty. They performed a dance reminiscent of the Seven Veils nonsense you see in the London variety halls. But this… this was the real thing…"

"I can see how it upset you, Harry." Richard spoke softly into the sudden quiet.

Harry cleared his throat, which had become suddenly dry at remembering the events so recently past. He picked up his tumbler and let the sharp tang of Scottish malt shock his larynx.

"It saddened me to see boys treated so, dressed to be girls, made to dance in the manner of girls and show off feminine wiles. They danced oblivious of our regard. Arshan tapped my back anxiously and whispered in my ear. The shorter of the two was Firuz."

CHAPTER 9 | *A Narrow Escape, 1886*

"AFTER WHAT I judged to be an hour, Colonel Lockhart made satisfactory excuses to our host and proffered trade goods as gifts. Baktash-al Ghulam Ali accepted these graciously and we took our leave, Arshan bowed under the weight of our uniform accessories I had purposely burdened him with. Out in the lane that led through the town's main market square toward where we had our camp Lockhart spoke quietly. 'I observed three jezailchis also armed with curved blades. One stood not far from Baktash. The others were in the hallway, which looks to run from side to side of the place. The men obviously watch the two entrances. From what I was able to glean as we entered, the ground floor is mostly given to store rooms and, by the smell of wood smoke, kitchens.'

"Lockhart remarked that the place was not a fort by any means. In fact, the collective village of Gilgit-i-ghar would have been a great deal tougher nut to crack. I asked Arshan where the bacha bazi were housed and he told us that they had two rooms behind the grain store at the back in a narrow corridor off the main passageway. 'At night we are locked in and one of Baktash-al Ghulam Ali's men keeps a watch outside. But by his snores we know he sleeps every night.'

"What we didn't know was whether there were any more men stationed on the upper floor. Arshan thought there had been in his time, but now…? I determined to come back much later after the townspeople were asleep, and hopefully the household of Baktash-al Ghulam Ali also. Lockhart wanted to go with me, but I persuaded him of the sense in his being able to lay the blame on a hot-headed subaltern, should anything go wrong. Instead, Arshan insisted on going with me, in spite of his evident nervousness, saying that he would be able to speak to Firuz and calm his brother's natural fear.

"At a time approaching three in the morning, suitably disguised in local garb obtained by one of our pundits and with my face and hands stained dark with a berry juice, we set off. I carried my jack knife and my Enfield revolver. I thought a rifle would be of little use in enclosed spaces. I hoped I wouldn't need to use it—you're familiar with the problems of unloading spent cartridges from the Enfield and refilling the cylinder. Arshan had armed himself with a native saber. There was only a new moon, barely a crescent low in the sky and in the streets the night was as black as the depths of a cave, but we could risk no light. The lane to Baktash's palace ran uphill from the square between mean single-story dwellings. I could make out their uneven flat-topped roofs showing as blacker shapes against the stars, the light of which was about sufficient to see where we were going if I looked from the corner of my eyes. But it was hard to avoid treading in the discarded rubbish littering the muddy track.

"Arshan's sight, keener than my own, espied the taller walls of the palace first and he held out an arm to still me. In front of us, I knew from our earlier visit, stood the almost blank wall forming one side of the enclosure where the boys had danced. Small openings well above head height protected by close-set vertical bars presumably let daylight into the storerooms on the other side. To the right of where we stood pressed against the wall of a house, the narrow street was a dead-end against another building adjoining Baktash's palace. I knew we could backtrack around this obstruction to come up on its other side and so to the front door we had entered by earlier, but Arshan tugged my arm. He wanted to go left.

"This alleyway turned sharply at the end of the palace and brought us to a side entrance, which I deduced was opposite the front door. 'Ahead are the stables,' Arshan whispered. 'We have to go over.' He pointed up. This doorway was no more than a gate. Wide gaps between its strakes allowed me to see that it opened onto a small courtyard and not into the bowels of the building. Arshan seemed to have shed the fear he showed when we came to see the dancing boys. In a trice he placed a foot on my bent knee and shinned up and over the timbers. Then he reappeared as a dark form against the stars and reached down a hand to help me make the climb. From the top of the gate it was easy to descend quietly for there were a number of protrusions and declivities in the badly maintained inner wall for foot and handholds.

"I turned and felt over the door behind us. It took a moment to find the balk of wood and the large iron staples hammered into the stones of the wall that secured it across the gate. By sliding one end loose of its staple, it was possible to angle the beam upward, pull it free at the other end, and so secure us a means of rapid escape. It seemed too simple, but I prayed it was just good fortune because we were on the side of the angels.

"From the cramped space, a door offered entry to the main building and the long cross hallway where presumably we would encounter one of Baktash's men on sentry duty. Arshan knew how the door was barred, although it turned out that it wasn't. Clearly, with the outer gate secure, no one thought it necessary to lock the inner door. He pushed quietly in. The flickering light of a taper farther down the hallway showed an empty chair. I'd hoped against hope to find the seat occupied by a snoring watchman, but this absence threw everything out of kilter."

৵৵✦৵৵

"Where can he be?" Harry hissed in Arshan's ear.

The boy shook his head. He raised an expressive eyebrow and made a pissing gesture. "Maybe, Haari?"

"Which way to the harem?"

Arshan pointed. "Down there, two doors at the end. But without keys…?" He shrugged.

"And the man supposed to be on that chair, he has the keys?"

A quick nod.

Harry wished he had Winner the Spinner along. Alfred had a quick brain when it came to tactics. As he was voicing this futile thought to himself, they both started at a dull shuffling noise which sounded from farther down the passage and off to the right, in the direction of the main courtyard.

"Someone's coming," whispered Arshan redundantly.

There were two options, to scuttle back through the doorway they had just entered by, or to dive down the side passage off to the left, which Arshan had said led to the harem. Harry hated to retreat. They ran as silently as church mice into the dark maw of the side passage. It was some fifteen feet deep, with two facing doors either side of the dead end. Halfway along on the left was an opening. As he reached it, Harry realized it was a staircase rising up into the dark. His night-adjusted eyes discerned a glimmer of distant lamp light from somewhere up there, but he heard nothing of people moving about. He slipped into the opening and placed a cautious foot on the first step. Stone. Good. No creaking timbers to give them away. He felt Arshan shove against his ass in a panic to get on up the steps and out of the passageway. The slap of bare feet on stone flags added impetus to the silent scrabble. Harry turned, pressed his back into the corner of the stairwell, and pulled Arshan into a hug against his chest. He slowed his breathing, and felt no more movement from the boy. Under other circumstances the embrace might have been the welcome start of something intimate.

Beyond, out on the main corridor, came the dusty ruffle of loose clothing. A man's silhouette appeared briefly against the dim light and then folded up.

"He sat down." Arshan had the better view. He had to reach up to whisper in Harry's ear, and the warm exhalation sent shivers of arousal through him. It was hardly the time to get an erection, and yet that was what happened. And Arshan felt it pressed against his butt cheek. Harry felt him wriggle a hand back between them to grasp him and squeeze. He also sensed the silent giggle shaking Arshan's frame.

Eros fled at a sudden scraping noise of wood on stone. The watchman was on the move, and his doing so made Harry wonder where his fellow jezailchis might be lingering, always assuming Lockhart was correct in the numbers and that there were still three men on duty through the night. Harry suspected that in this quiet valley of pagans Baktash-al Ghulam Ali felt secure enough to keep a light guard. He hoped so. In the humid night, even more cloying inside, the guard's naked feet made a sucking sound as he lifted each foot in turn and an almost webbed splat sound as he slapped them down on the stone floor. It would have been funny if the noise didn't precede possible peril. The bulky figure loomed dimly in the narrow space. Arshan shrank back into Harry and they both stopped breathing.

And then Harry's stomach rumbled loud enough to be heard. He clenched his gut in a panic to prevent further enteric discord.

The guard paused. He breathed in heavily through his nose and patted his pronounced paunch.

A laugh almost burst from Harry's throat at seeing the jezailchi mistake the noise as emanating from his own belly.

He started forward again and with a rattle of keys stepped past where Arshan and Harry were hidden only feet away. He went to one door, unlocked it, and glanced in for a moment. He gave a faint grunt and shut the door. As the key rattled in the lock, Harry whispered, "When I push, fall down and tangle his legs." He pulled the jack knife free of its shallow scabbard and folded out the blade with its ugly bullnose tip, a close-in combat weapon made for slashing rather than stabbing. He hoped he wouldn't have to use the blade, only the hardened wooden haft as a cosh.

The jezailchi unlocked the second door and repeated his scrutiny, only this time it seemed an age before he gave another grunt and pulled the door shut, locked it. Harry heard the scuff of his feet before his dark form came into view, heading back to his chair. He waited until the man was drawn level with the stairway opening, expecting every second that they would be discovered before he was ready. And then the juncture arrived. He pushed Arshan, who immediately dropped down and rolled forward. He took the guard about the legs in a tackle that would have won him high praise from Alfred Winner as captain of The Lodge rugby team.

A deep intake of breath presaged a startled cry as the man began to fall to his knees, but before he could express the intake of air as a shout, Harry wrapped his left arm around the lowered neck. In the next instant he brought his raised right hand down to dash the handle of his jack knife solidly against the man's temple where it was bare of his turban.

The blow cut off the threatened shout, turned it into a breathless whoop. But Baktash's jezailchi was no pushover, as Harry realized when the man managed to shake one foot free of Arshan's grasp and stamp down. Arshan bit off his own cry of pain. Harry ducked a wild swiping fist, which caught him sharply on the shoulder. Desperate to prevent the man yelling for help, Harry launched himself from the first step on which he stood, and used the height advantage to retake his grip around the guard's head. His weight brought the man down to his knees. He brought his knife hand around, and pressed the sharp edge of the blade across the bobbing Adam's apple. Instantly the jezailchi ceased struggling.

"Arshan! His turban!"

The boy understood. In a moment he had the yards of cloth off, and while Harry kept the blade pressed dangerously hard at the man's throat, grabbed his arms and lashed them tightly.

"Use the rest to secure his ankles to his arms," Harry urged in a low voice.

As soon as Arshan was satisfied their prisoner wouldn't be going anywhere soon, he whipped his own turban off and used it to gag the jezailchi.

Harry slowly lowered the knife and stared hard into the guard's dark eyes. There was hatred there, but also relief that his strange assailants had left him alive.

Arshan took the keys. "Haari, I go. Find Firuz. You stay, or you may afright him."

Harry understood. Nodded sharply. He stepped away from the floored Kafir guard and watched as Arshan unlocked both harem doors and disappeared through the one on the right of the dead end. The wait was nerve-wracking. He expected one of the other guards to appear at any moment. They could come from either end of the main hallway. Perhaps someone would come down the stairs. A rustle announced Arshan's reappearance. He shook his head, and slipped through the other doorway. Harry tried to breathe calmly but found it difficult to prevent hitching with the tension. He felt exposed, and soundlessly urged Arshan to hurry. In spite of his fear of Harry's knife, which he still had exposed in his hand, the man on the stone flags kept making low mewing sounds beneath the gag.

And then they were there. Two boys, peas from the same pod, except the younger looked to have a lighter coloring to his hair. Unlike Arshan, Firuz sported an elegant hairstyle, in keeping, Harry presumed, with his role as a bacha bazi. His clothing, even for a late night, was clearly designed to arouse, though Harry had no use for its femininity. What he most thought was that dressed in that manner Firuz would stand out like a polished pomegranate floating atop a mud bath.

The boy stared at him from huge eyes. Harry wondered if he was drugged in some way, but when Arshan urged him forward, he snapped out of his sudden daze. *It must be a shock to see Arshan, be urged to escape, and run into a European man when he's probably never seen one before.* But there was no time to comfort the lad. Harry couldn't count on their extraordinary luck so far holding for much longer. To this point the false sense of security Baktash-al Ghulam Ali must feel had been their best ally, that or the sheer incompetence of his soldiers.

"What about the other boys?"

Arshan gave one of his eloquent shrugs. "They are afeared to leave, Haari. I have trouble with this one." He shoved Firuz had in the small of the back. "I lock the doors again."

It made sense, but Harry hated the thought of shutting up innocent boys. He shook his head sharply to clear his thoughts. "You're right. We must get out.

Now. There's no time for keys. Throw them down." He pointed at the bound and gagged jezailchi as he stepped across his bent knees and made for the intersection of passageways.

And almost ran headlong into the large man who stepped into the junction. Harry's heart leapt, but the other was the more shocked. His bellow was vast. It sounded like all the hounds of hell barking, and echoed up and down the walls and stone floors. His alarmed surprise was all Harry needed. The time for secrecy ended in the noisy response from other quarters of the building and the thump of distant feet. He pulled the Enfield free and fired.

"As you know, the Enfield is pretty lousy at a distance, but at four feet it took the Bashgali Kafir down and left a smoking hole in his upper chest. In the confined space the noise of the shot deafened me."

By this time, Harry's listeners were sat forward, various expressions on their faces: Richard tensed and frowning; Edward rubbing the forefinger of his left hand back and forth over his eyebrows, a trait Harry recognized from their days at school whenever he was mulling over a problem.

Yussuf simmered with suppressed merriment. "So you escape to tent and go fuck-fuck, now?"

Harry chuckled, a little burble of light relief. "Not exactly, Yussuf. The cry and the gunshot turned the place over like a disturbed hornets' nest. I grabbed Arshan by the shoulder and hurried him and Firuz to the doorway out into the small, enclosed courtyard. As we reached the outer gate, shouts arose from all over. And then came the flat crack of the jezail, maybe three or four, all firing randomly. I'm not even sure that those shooting knew what they were aiming at. The shots came from above, from the roof of the upper floor. My greatest fear was that the enemy would sally out from the other side of the building and cut off our route of retreat down to the square. And my second worst fear was that Lockhart and the soldiers would hesitate to come to our aid for fear of upsetting the overall mission.

"But I needn't have worried on that score. We rounded the corner of Baktash's palace and plunged recklessly down the steep alley. As well we did because a moment later more firing pursued us. Baktash's men poured out from the opposite alleyway, but on the run they were unable to reload their ancient weapons quickly enough, and soon we were down in the open. This should have been a more dangerous position, but the rattle of Henry-Martini rifle-fire rang out and echoed repeatedly off the closed-in walls. Our men were firing over our heads higher up the lane at our pursuers, but Lockhart told me, once we'd calmed down, that he ordered the soldiers to fire over their heads to avoid unnecessary casualties."

Harry paused to take a sip at his drink and Edward took the opportunity to satisfy a point of curiosity.

"How did this youngster, Firuz, take his sudden freedom?"

Harry looked thoughtfully over his friends' heads for a moment. "I'm not sure. I think he was actually somewhat terrified, and not only because of the shooting. Since Arshan had spirited himself away and been forced to leave Firuz behind, the child had known only Baktash, the household, and his fellow dancers. I'm not sure he saw what was happening to him as anything less than frightening, certainly not freedom as we think of it. Having Arshan with him helped the boy, but the sight of sepoys armed to the teeth with daggers, swords, and modern rifles, and other white officers left him bewildered.

"But there was no time for concerns about his welfare. The rescue had stirred up a right swarm of angry hornets, and the pagans wanted blood. If it were not for our small but well armed force of sepoys, I don't think we would have left the valley alive. I can't say Lockhart was entirely pleased at the outcome, but he rallied our men to a sterling defense, which put the villagers of Lut-Dih to flight. Though as it turned out, they were the least of our problems. Baktash-al Ghulam Ali must have roused bands of the Kafirs in all the hills along the valley, for as we made our lengthy return we were attacked day and night by marauding brigands who dashed out of the tamarisk thickets as they would at any lightly guarded caravan. We were, of course, far from defenseless, but it took all our skill and training to remain alive. And I am not at all sure we would have survived if it were not for the Mirtar, who wished to remain on good terms with the Viceroy and sent out a force of warriors to escort us over the pass and back into central Chitral. A month later, we were back at Rawul Pindee and my leave papers were awaiting me."

"Did you accomplish what you wanted?" Edward wanted to know.

Harry shrugged modestly. "We'd mapped formerly unknown regions, marked all the passes. Colonel Lockhart's report left the matter of Russian infiltration an open possibility but expressed the opinion that Russia couldn't easily get a large army through the Hindu-Kush and the Pamirs to attack India. If we establish a resident and a division of sepoys at Gilgit, to call up reinforcements when required, smaller incursions can be met before doing much damage.

"We cemented a friendship with Aman-ul-Mulk, that he should remain neutral in any conflict between neighboring petty states and Afghanistan. In any case, it's clear that Amir Abdur Rahman and his eternal ambitions frighten the Mirtar, and he's therefore thankful that the unconquered Kafirs to his south hate the Pathans and will happily murder any who fall into their clutches. Less happily, we confirmed that via the Dorah Pass a caravan route connects Russian Badakshan via Chitral and then south to Dir and the Swat Valley with India. A weakness Russia might one day exploit. And that makes Chitral the crucial outpost for Britain to maintain and, if necessary, annex."

At Harry's leave taking, Richard alone took him in the two-horse trap to the station. Harry had given thanks to his hosts, Colonel and Mrs. Rainbow, bid his farewells and disentangled himself—he hoped graciously—from Madge's embrace, shaken Yussuf by the hand, and hugged Edward. On the fifteen-minute ride into Bourton the former lovers remained uncharacteristically quiet. Iron-shod hooves and wheels rattled loudly off the stone parapet as they crossed the humped span over the River Windrush, the passage of which no doubt prompted Richard's words.

"A lot of water under the bridge, Harry."

To Harry it sounded like the prologue to a long goodbye, more of an *adieu* than *au revoir* and he didn't wish to follow the reasoning implicit in Richard's words. "I was worried about visiting, you know," he began hesitantly. "About seeing you again. I feared it might unman me, but I'm glad now that I did come."

Richard loosed a grunt, half a laugh. "Because you realized you no longer feel the same way about me?"

"No!" Harry slapped his friend's thigh affectionately. "Never that. You were and always will my first, dear Richard. What I think I fear the most is that you might be my only love, that I never will find another so intense. So important to me. Surely no one for whom I will feel so…" he paused for a second. "As I see you do for Edward."

"I shall always have feelings for you, Harry. After all, you were my first real love too. What passed between Edward and me up to that point at school was little more than brotherly affection and a form of calf love that frightened us really, for obvious reasons at the time… incest, as we innocently thought of it. It was our being so cruelly separated that turned the loss into something stronger."

He fell silent for a moment, staring ahead over the backs of the horses, and then nodded slowly, a smile touching his lips. "You were the first with whom I had intimate relations." He blushed becomingly as he deftly guided the horses toward the station road. "Well, real sex."

"Yesss…" Harry's breath caught in his throat.

Richard turned his attention from the road ahead for a moment to gaze challengingly into Harry's wide eyes. "Am I still the only one outside your family to know your real Christian name?"

"You are."

The answer seemed to please Richard. He nodded firmly and looked ahead again before speaking. "In fact things haven't been easy. It's been difficult with Ed, you know. We had to… we had to find the way because there wasn't anything physical there between us before. Well, just childish stuff really. Oh, Harry. If only things were different. If we hadn't grown up the way we did and I was free. I'd catch the train now and go with you to the ends of the—"

One of the horses stumbled on an unevenness in the road and the trap jinked in response. Harry started and shifted on the seat, aware that he'd been daydreaming. "Sorry, I was miles away. What did you say?"

Richard smiled. "Nothing important." He took a hand from the reins and waved over his shoulder at the river behind them, still visible between the butter-yellow Costwold houses and shops. "I said that there's been a lot of water under the bridge."

"Oh. Yes." *I can't let him see how I feel. It wouldn't be fair. Oh, but it's so hard.* Harry swayed slightly on the sprung bench seat in unison with Richard, who deftly guided the horses toward the station road.

"So will it be back to Rawul Pindee, or will you get a posting elsewhere in the jewel in our crown?"

Harry coughed politely against his fist and used it to mask the hoarseness in his throat. "I shall discover that on my return to London. I suspect my immediate destination is less sure than yours and Edward's. I rather envy you your return to the Sudan. At least you're guaranteed excitement under Kitchener's command. And who knows, if things continue to deteriorate there, I may well find myself posted to Egypt and the Sudan again."

"It appears to me that you are finding plenty of excitement on the North-West Frontier…" Richard turned with a sly grin. "Of all kinds, some even involving military action." The accompanying wink was salacious. "But I should be more than happy if events turn out that you're sent to the desert again. I shall hope for such an outcome, Harry. In the meantime I wish you some happiness with your William Maplethorpe… perhaps with Arshan?"

The trap's iron-shod wheels sounded sharply on the cobblestones of the station's small forecourt and set a murder of crows aloft with noisy cawing from an overhanging oak tree. Impulsively, Harry leaned over and brushed his lips against Richard's neck above the collar and felt the grip of Richard's hand around his waist. "Don't wait with me, please. The train will be along in a few minutes." He looked briefly into Richard's narrowed eyes, saw him fight a sudden rush of tears, and then jumped down, reaching over the back for his travel case at the same time.

At the station's doorway Harry turned for a second and waved with his free hand and then strode through to the London-bound platform. Hooves on cobbles, and Richard was gone, leaving Harry with the dregs of his imaginary conversation.

CHAPTER 10 | *London and Hunza, 1887 to 1889*

"THERE'S A LIEUTENANT FELLOW back from India. About your age, I'd say, young man. Caused quite a stir he has with his tales of crossing China from one side to the other. Odd name. Younghusband. Met the fellow twice now. Only the other day at this new sports place around the corner on Palliser Road. Are you a member?"

Harry deflected the question with raised eyebrows and a slight shake of the head at Major-General Sir Neville Airey Langrish-Smith VC KCMG, who as a lowly subaltern in 1854 won the Victoria Cross for his heroics at the Battle of Inkermann during the Crimean war. The retired soldier had given the godfather of his son Jolyon a warm welcome.

On his return from Rissington Manor, a note waited for Harry at the Albany, as the barracks complex beside Regent's Park was familiarly known, requesting his presence for a "beverage" before dinner. Now he was seated in the Langrish-Smiths' comfortable home in Cadogan Square, feeling that at twenty-two and a veteran of two campaigns no one ought to call him "young" any more. "I'm afraid I am not a member, sir."

"Oh, but you must apply before they fill up the books. It's very exclusive, and a young feller like you must surely enjoy the activities. They host matches of rugby football, proper football, and this new-fangled racquets thing… er, lawn tennis, that's it. All looks a bit dandified to me—though it is more exercising than croquet, and gentlemen of your age seem to enjoy dashing about the court."

"I shall certainly look into it, sir. The name of the establishment?"

"The Queen's Club. Named in honor of Queen Victoria's Golden Jubilee. Opened for business earlier this year. And that's the damnedest thing. This wild man from America, the one calls himself 'Buffalo Bill' Cody, has this Wild West extravaganza. Quite extraordinary, got horsemen from all over the world taking part and doing stunts, including a bunch of savage Red Indians. The Queen was thrilled by a show the man put on for her specially. You should see it before returning to duty, my boy."

Where it came through the sheer drapes covering two large windows in the general's study a weak autumnal sun painted a pastel yellow weave across the pale rug. He insisted on calling this sanctum his den, wherein he might sit behind a large leather-topped desk or retire to the comfort of a sofa and two armchairs around a low table next to the large Adam fire surround. This is where the two men were now seated, enjoying cigars with gin and quinine tonics (Harry's light on the gin, the way he took the drink in the tropics).

Between men who did wild things, Harry was more interested in someone who had crossed China, though he made a mental note to see the Wild West Show. "And it was at the Queen's Club you bumped into Mr. Younghusband?"

"Lieutenant Francis Younghusband, to be precise. Made it from the Chinese Emperor's court all the way to India."

"That's most impressive. And which is his regiment, sir?"

"Yours, my boy, King's 1st Dragoons. That's partly why I mentioned him, and partly because you ought to meet him. With your own experiences in the Hindu Kush and whatnot and his you'll have a lot to chinwag about I've no doubt. For his exploit the man's been elected to the Royal Geographic Society. Youngest member of that elite body, I understand, which given his surname is perfectly apt."

The general burst into a throaty chuckle at his wit, to which Harry added a polite laugh. From outside an irregular racket of hooves and cab wheels, some passing around the square, others stopping to let passengers alight, signaled the comings and goings of the well-to-do who lived in the elegant London suburb of Knightsbridge. The louder rumble of a four-wheeler almost obscured the quiet tap-tap at the door.

"Come!"

The wide paneled door swung inward, accompanied by a faint creak above the muted traffic, to reveal a young boy of outstanding beauty. Jolyon stood framed in the opening, aglow in the low sunlight. He stood stiffly upright, attired in a navy cadet's uniform. Six brass buttons formed a gleaming row down the front of his tunic, a high-waisted, close fitting jacket in deep blue, adorned by bands of gold braid above the wrists and around the high collar, above which poked an Eton-style starched shirt collar. His stark white dress pants bore a vertical blue stripe from the front of each hip to the cuffless bottoms collected on the top of black leather shoes so polished the shine hurt Harry's eyes. He stood at attention: slender shoulders squared, noble head held high but with chin tucked in to that strangulating collar; hands at his sides, fists curled, thumbs to the fore in the correct position. Young Jolyon possessed the grace of a gazelle, lean and agile, slightly tall for his twelve years, and in spite of his army posture, Harry thought he saw worry in the boy's eyes as if he expected to be found wanting.

"You may enter, Jolyon."

The boy's eyes widened fractionally at his father's barked command.

"Come and greet your godfather."

He raised a hand in a smart salute to the visor of his peaked cap with only the barest hint of a smile touching the corners of his mouth. The hand slapped back to his side, bringing the cap with it, which he tucked under his arm. He stepped forward smartly and delivered a neat bow from the waist to his father and then to Harry. He extended his right hand. "How do you so, sir?" he said in a child's voice.

Harry smiled warmly and shook Jolyon's small hand. "Very well indeed, thank you, and I hope to find you in as good health."

"I am well, thank you, sir."

"Now be seated on on the sofa," the general growled, "and pray inform us as to your progress at school,"

It was the first time Harry had seen his godson in some time and the boy's quiet demeanor and polite, even reserved manner charmed him as, for five minutes, Jolyon held the floor and explained in his well modulated treble voice how his first term at Eton had gone. There was pride that he hadn't received any Rips and almost had something Sent up for Good, although his best friend earned a White Ticket after ending up in the Tardy Book for missing too many Divisions and messing up some Hexameters, for which he might have had a Pop-Tanning if it weren't for the fact that he possessed no Old Trousers, which the Pop found hilarious and so let him off.

The bewildering argot left Harry completely bemused (for all that public schools developed their own peculiar language, Benthenham College had been pretty straightforward and he remembered conversations with his fellow boarders in The Lodge as being largely conducted in plain English) but he nodded sagely and made encouraging sounds at appropriate moments. He was also visited by a visceral shock that reminded of what he'd mentioned at Rissington Manor that this delightful, beautifully mannered boy was the same age as Firuz and but for the accident of their births it may have been innocent Jolyon who he dragged from that house of infamy in Lut-Dih.

A gong sounded and the general stood, which concluded Jolyon's recital. Without any word of praise for his son, he ushered them out across the hallway. Beside the open doors to the dining room the butler stood as stiffly at attention as had Jolyon earlier. Waiting inside, Lady Langrish-Smith greeted Harry warmly, asked after his family and their plans for next year's season and generally fussed over seating him.

His father allowed Jolyon to join the grown-ups on this occasion because the general held that Harry was a positive influence. Harry hoped he lived up to it. Jolyon adhered to the rule of being seen but not heard and answered only when spoken to, but during the meal he remained engrossed as Harry regaled his hosts with the excitements of his Hindu Kush trek. Naturally, he made no mention of the dancing boys, confining himself to derring-do, the bravery of the sepoys and officers in the face of wicked hostility, the wonders and splendors of Chitral, and the glory of the mountains, passes, and lakes.

It did Harry's heart good to see how young Jolyon clung to his words, an expression verging on adoration matching the sharp aspirations he blew through slightly parted lips at the most perilous moments of the tale. He also liked the indications of an incisive mind indicated by a narrowed calculating look in the boy's eyes as sometimes he seemed to question the veracity of Harry's claims; and the shine there when he accepted the adventures. At one point, when Lady and General Langrish-Smith were engaged in a private conversation, Harry asked Jolyon if he had also enjoyed Buffalo Bill's Wild West Show. The boy's eyes glowed with childish enthusiasm.

"Oh yes, sir. It was most remarkable, almost as exciting as your stories. Have you been?"

"I have not, but I shall certainly make a point of going to see it, now you have recommended that I should."

Jolyon's smile of pleasure at the implied praise lit up his attractive face. When after the cheese course he was ordered to bed, he stood before Harry to shake hands formally. But then abruptly he leaned forward and gave Harry a tight little hug before dashing off from the dining room in less than perfect military style.

Younghusband's words came back to Harry as he and his party began the steep ascent of the route from Kashmiri Ladakh up into the towering Karakoram Mountains. Harry had met Francis Younghusband after a talk the explorer gave at the Royal Geographic Society, which Harry attended at the general's insistence and through his good offices. A passage regarding the mountains of the North-West Frontier seemed particularly apt.

To those who have struggled with them, the mountains reveal beauties that they will not disclose to those who make no effort. That is the reward the mountains give to effort. And it is because they have so much to give and give it so lavishly to those who will wrestle with them that men love the mountains and go back to them again and again.

Now that those revealed "beauties" again surrounded him, the wooded slopes and their distant views of snow-capped rugged rock, it sometimes seemed to Harry that the encomium was overrated and the struggle hardly worth the effort. An unworthy thought! His mission was vital.

After returning from leave, months of dreary garrison duties with the Dragoons at Rawul Pindee had made Harry long for the open trailway, something that infrequent sightings of Arshan only exacerbated. The Persian boy was busily occupied in a different part of the large cantonment, although Harry managed to spend one evening with him, which went to show neither had lost the enjoyment of the other. William Maplethorpe also enlivened a few weeks of the period when he returned from a secondment at Meerut, where he'd been training enlisted sowars, the native cavalrymen. They quickly fell into a routine of bed-sharing, for Harry a guilty casual benison, for Maplethorpe perhaps something more, although Harry thought he detected a withdrawn attitude, which went some way to calming the disturbance he felt at wanting the physical from his friend but not being able to offer a full emotional commitment in return.

"The wild upper reaches of the Pamirs have made you ethereal, Harry."

"Really?" The thought surprised Harry. He didn't feel in the least bit otherworldly. Indeed, abandoning poor Arshan, as he'd had to do on going back home to England and since on garrison duties, was a rather heavy burden to bear. *More guilt, dammit.*

"I mean by it that you go about with your head in the clouds, somewhere up there."

Harry sighed and tried to stifle Maplethorpe's analysis by closing his mouth with two fingers. He rolled over until their hips were pressed together, semi-hard cocks and balls squashed in sweaty embrace. He leaned close and brushed his own lips over Maplethorpe's. The ploy worked in as much as Maplethorpe kissed back passionately and they both began to writhe eagerly against each other, rapidly reaching a mutual climax that glued their stomachs with their copious release.

"You left your heart in the snowy heights, Harry," Maplethorpe persisted as their breathing slowed.

The sigh was longer, deeper, an affirmation of the truth of the words.

"I know you did. You never made a secret of your ambition to be a political, out with pundits and villagers, mapping, exploring, conquering… running away—"

"What?" Harry sat up abruptly. He glared in uncertainty at the languid, slightly sad face. Maplethorpe smiled gently.

"You have been, Harry. I sensed it when we first met on the *Malabar*. Who hurt you?"

"No one."

"Was it the boy you spoke of once, the one from school; the one who went out to the Sudan with you?

Harry remained silent and outwardly calm, though his heart bumped and his stomach churned evilly and made him wonder whether he might bring up the chicken curry they ate for dinner. He started at the touch of Maplethorpe's hand closing over his.

"It's all right. You needn't answer my impertinence. You long to be away again. If it's all right with you I will enjoy the time we may have together here with a happy heart." Maplethorpe dropped his forehead to lean against Harry's strained supporting arm, and his voice came up muffled. "You're a good man,

Harry Vane and you deserve to find someone to love as much as they love you back. I only hope for you it happens some day."

Harry marveled at how close this was to what Richard had said, but as much that Maplethorpe delivered this small speech without any bitterness and perhaps only a hint of regret. It renewed bad feeling, despair at his inability to return Maplethorpe a scant part of the affection the other showed him.

And then the call came from Simla, headquarters of the British Intelligence Service. Sir Henry Mortimer Durand, the Foreign Secretary for India, enjoying a brief respite from Calcutta's steamy heat at the delightful hill station, had called in Harry's papers. A new mission was afoot. There was time for a last and surprisingly passionate session in his bed with Maplethorpe before scooping up a delighted Arshan from his mundane commissary duties. The two headed off by train southeast to Loodiana, from where road transport was available for the last short stretch.

Simla's fine residences appeared to Harry as a cross between European-Tudor and Swiss-Victorian, though he doubted such classifications existed, but there was studiedly no sign of the ubiquitous Anglo-Indian bungalow familiar in all of the subcontinent's army cantonments.

Sir Mortimer, as he preferred to be known, explained what was on his mind.

"We've a serious problem brewing on the trade route between China and Kashmir, captain. In the last year almost every caravan has suffered bandit attacks. While that's worrying, it's where the raiders are coming from that has me most concerned. Please, be seated, captain."

Harry hitched his dress pants up at the knees and took the chair opposite Sir Mortimer, eager to hear what could be more worrying than banditry.

"The few survivors all agree that their attackers are men of Hunza."

A startled expression crossed Harry's face. "Hunza, sir? How is that possible?"

"Ah, I see you are familiar with the written records of George Hayward?"

"Yes sir, the only man to have explored the Yarkand–Leh trade route."

"Good. Then you will also know that he insisted the mountains to the west of the route are impassable, making it impossible for Hunzakut raiders to reach the caravans. All the Intelligence we have from Gilgit suggests the valley of the upper Hunza is accessible only at its western extremity, from Gilgit."

"So there should be no way out of the valley to the east and the trade route?"

"Exactly. And yet from Hunza come the raiders, it seems. The information, such as it is, comes from Hunzakut traders. So it's suspect. We must get to the bottom of this mystery, Captain Vane. Are traders' reports of Hunzakuts using a secret mountain pass to be believed? You will go north to Leh and then proceed up through the lower passes to the Yarkand River and discover the truth."

Sir Mortimer didn't raise the underlying concern, but Harry knew that his younger brother, Colonel Algernon Durand, the Resident at Gilgit, had forwarded disturbing reports about Russians entering the Hunza Valley. This petty state sat at the point where the three great empires met: Britain, Russia, and China. Mountain-girt Hunza, which lay beyond the British sphere of influence to the northeast of Gilgit, was a worrying hot spot.

On the Indian side of the Panja River three passes gave access to Gilgit, or by a sharp left turn seventy miles to the northeast of Gilgit into the upper valley of the Hunza River. A khan who owed allegiance to the Maharaja of Kashmir, a British vassal, ruled his fiercely independent state, a hundred miles long but not much more than one mile wide between the peaks towering over its depths. However, the Maharaja's influence, Colonel Durand had stated, appeared to be nominal and the treaty with Hunza fragile at the best. Russians in Hunza was a frightening thought.

"The real fear," Harry told Arshan, "is that if this rumored pass truly exists at the eastern end of the supposedly dead-end valley, not only can Hunzakut bandits get through to raid the caravans to and from China but a Russian army can use it too. Think of it, instead of being like an appendix, the Hunza Valley becomes a corridor. The enemy can bypass Gilgit altogether and our troops now stationed in the area. Then from the Yarkand-Leh trail the way down through the Karakoram Mountains to Ladakh and eastern Kashmir in the summer will be pretty easy going. In less than a month after a Russian army has entered Hunza all of India will lie open to the invaders. And the first we'll know of it is when army stations like Umbala, Meerut, and Jullundur fall, thus cutting off the majority of the army stationed in the North-West Frontier Province from the rest of India."

Arshan's delight to be reunited with Harry was in inverse degree to William Maplethorpe's disappointment that he'd had Harry to himself for such a relatively short period of time. But for Harry the call to political duty came as a great relief to the dreariness of garrison duties that William only partly alleviated. For his part, Arshan was excited to join his Haari on another adventure, all the more for knowing that Firuz was safely engaged as a cantonment hiccarrah back in Rawul Pindee.

The party consisted of Arshan, six Gurkhas, a small detachment of Kashmiri Imperial Service sepoys, and four coolies presided over by Kishen Ali, a Ladakhi man hired in Simla to leave Arshan free—as he informed Harry with firm insistence—to be of "greater military and personal assistance" on the expedition. "Kishen Ali," he assured Harry, "will be good guide for he many times travel the passes."

Harry anticipated the truth of this assertion because the Ladakhi had been a member of George Hayward's party that explored the route to Yarkand and Kashgar almost twenty years before in 1869. To think he was following in the footsteps of his hero warmed Harry in spite of the increasing cold. Distantly, he mourned Hayward's murder at Yasin, only the year following the trader-explorer's successful campaign to open up a secure trading route between China and Kashmir. It was also a sobering reminder that in isolated Hunza he might face a similar fate… if he discovered the raiders' secret pass.

Like most of his men, Harry wore a dark blue *goncha*, the traditional long woolen robe Ladakhi men wore, with its colorful sash known as a *skerag*. The hat, a weird kind of top hat of knitted wool, insisted on slumping under any rain into a shapeless muddle against its leather skullcap. Harry was forever struggling to pummel the damned thing into something that looked a bit respectable.

They departed from Ladakh's capital of Leh at the beginning of August 1889. "We must reach the village of Shahidula, Capitan Haarivan sahib," Kishen Ali insisted. "Is there, very high, that many traders live."

"And it is from these men we shall learn of the secret trail?"

"Oh yes, sahib. Surely some men will know valleys Hunza robbers descend from Shimshal Pass."

So the mysterious pass has a name. "Hayward sahib did not know?"

Kishen Ali shrugged eloquently. "Never robbers then, Capitan. Nothing to know."

The party marched southeast along the valley of the Indus to reach a point some twenty miles from Leh where the road turned north up a ravine into the

Chang Chenmo range and crossed the first low pass to reach Tanksee. This poor village, at a distance of about fifty miles from Leh, was the Maharaja of Kashmir's farthest outpost, and the last place before Shahidula where any supplies might be obtained. Kishen Ali bargained for several yaks to carry grain for the horses and mules, and engaged four Bhoots—Ladakhi villagers—as extra coolies.

At nights, Harry slept in the tent on the ground in the manner he'd learned on campaign with Lockhart, with the additional warmth of Arshan at his side. Their love-making was less inhibited than on the Chitral expedition, since there were no other British officers present, and Kishen Ali, the Gurkhas, Kashmiri troops, and certainly the Bhoots seemed to find nothing amiss in a young Persian sharing the sahib's tent at nights. Arshan curled up on the makeshift ground bed to welcome Harry into his arms, and used his considerable wiles to "awake your man," not that any were needed, but Harry enjoyed the pretense of needing to be aroused.

Some nights, their foreplay extended for more than an hour before Arshan rolled onto his side and encouraged Harry to enter him. It wasn't in Harry's nature to be violent and their lovemaking was usually a sensuously gentle matter, though rarely was the outcome so peaceful. As passion and need swelled, Arshan made plain from every movement of his lithe body how desperately he wanted Harry to fill him. In return, Harry sometimes brought Arshan to climax with his hand, sometimes with his mouth, sometimes by reversing roles and guiding Arshan to slip his urgent cock into him. And always there was the kissing in whichever position they found themselves.

For extra comfort, Arshan purchased hanks of sheep's wool from merchants who used the animals to transport salt from the mines of the Chang Thang district down to Leh and Kashmir. As the trail got higher, the wool was a godsend to a night's sleep; and it added an extra bounce to the sex. The only drawback was its greasy smell. By the tenth day of trekking ever upward into the Chang Chenmo range toward the higher Karakorams, everyone smelt equally rank, so it hardly mattered.

Sometimes, when there was a spare moment in camp, Harry removed himself from the harsh mountain scenery and buried himself instead in the foggy streets of London, reading a novel he'd purchased in London, drawn by the fact that its narrator, a certain Dr. Watson, had just returned from Afghanistan—not that the North-West Frontier entered much into the tale of murder most foul and the clever methods of detection the hero employed to nail the murderer. As far as Harry knew *A Study in Scarlet* was Arthur Conan Doyle's first Sherlock Holmes novel and he vowed on his return to London to discover whether the author had written more.

And when he wasn't reading cheap fiction, he worked on the copious notes recording the progress of the expedition in the way he hoped George Hayward would have approved.

"What do you scribe, Haari? Ever scribing."

"It's my field book. I'm putting down today's recordings. I noted the angles of our ascent at different points with my Watkins clinometer and the barometric pressures with Mr. Fortin's mercurial barometer. The two different readings require to be correlated, as well as the height of the pass where we are camped. I need to check it against that made by George Hayward. He measured the temperature of boiling water then as being 178.4° Fahrenheit, whereas my thermometer, which I believe is more accurately calibrated than his could have been back then, measured the water as being 178.6° Fahrenheit, which I shall also show in the French manner as 81.4° Centigrade." Harry consulted a leather-bound notebook with a series of neatly inscribed tables. He ran his finger down columns of figures until he reached what he was looking for. "There, 178.6° Fahrenheit is equivalent to a height of 18,170 feet above sea-level."

"How is that?"

Arshan had watched Harry boil up cans of water and then stick in a long glass instrument, which on pulling it from the steaming water he examined carefully. To that point he'd simply shaken his head in puzzlement at the mad antics of Englishmen. Boiled water was for brewing chai.

Harry smiled and looked up from his writing. "It is a miracle of science, Arshan. At the level where the sea meets the shore, water boils at precisely the temperature of 212 degrees or 100 degrees as the French will have it. But the higher you are, the lower the temperature at which water boils. Some years ago, working from mountains called the Alps, scientists drew a table—like this—to indicate altitude against the boiling point of water. So now we have a result which is only three feet different from that which Hayward recorded for the Karakorum Pass."

Arshan giggled.

"What?"

"I know what height it is by how much you shoot your seed. The higher we go, the harder you fire."

Arshan neatly ducked under the clip aimed at his nearest ear, only to fall against Harry and wrap arms about his waist.

"That, my boy, must wait until I've finished today's notes. If I don't keep the field book up to date and accurate, Sir Mortimer will have my balls for breakfast and my guts for garters."

"This most painful for you, Haari." Arshan grinned conspiratorially. He'd long gotten used to the phrase, and was quite certain the great English *khaarejee* man preferred the new elasticated rings to keep up his socks and putees, and a light mutton curry for his breakfast.

Harry felt the same, but did not want to suffer the Foreign Secretary for India's anger at any failure to record the details of the expedition; there was no Lockhart to hide behind this time. The last thing he wanted was to fall short of expectations and on his return find papers ordering him back to the garrison.

But the real undertaking lurked ahead. Somewhere in the jagged peaks lining the horizon a valley of merciless killers waited.

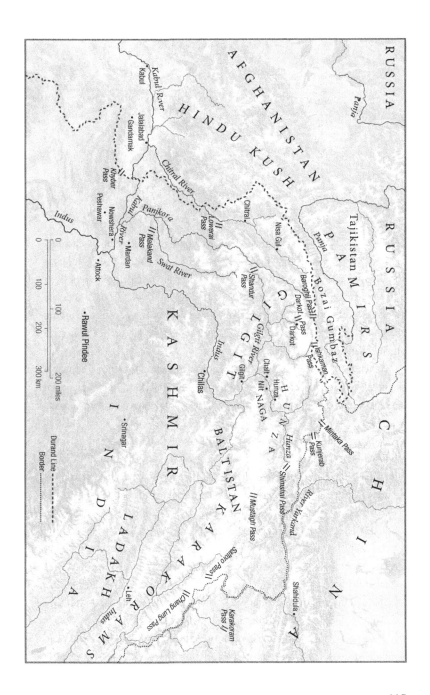

CHAPTER 11 | *Hunza, 1889*

SIXTEEN DAYS after leaving Leh, the British party reached remote Shahidula (189.7° F or 87.6° C, Harry noted, exactly 12,000 feet above sea-level). It was hardly a village. A few scattered nomadic yurts in which the traders lived surrounded a small run-down stone fort. The structure wouldn't have kept any raiders at bay for more than a few minutes. While Harry was occupied in urging the Bhoots to help the Kashmiri contingent get the tents put up in a protective square, Kishen Ali walked across to the fort.

When he came back it was from the nomadic encampment. "The fort is abandoned, Capitan sahib. The headman of the traders say the Panja-bashi and two bands of soldiers plus two of the Yarkand king have been gone many months. So sorry, sahib."

Under Yakub-Beg, the Muslim adventurer-ruler of Kashgar and Yarkand, trade with Kashmir had been brisk, but Harry knew that a Quing army defeated him in battle in 1877, and he took his life rather than fall captive to blood stained Chinese hands. That the Chinese only rated the trail worthy of a sub-officer and a dozen soldiers spoke volumes about how little the Quing dynasty valued the trade that had sustained Kashgar for so many years… and now even that tiny garrison had fled from Hunzakut raiders. Harry's own force was not a great deal bigger, but all equipped with Henry-Martini MK-IV breech-loading lever-actuated rifles. In the hands of a trained and disciplined soldier the rifle was capable of delivering twelve rounds per minute, killer-accurate to 400 yards.

Time to find the secret Shimshal Pass.

Harry now donned his full Dragoons officer's uniform, which had been carefully packed in a weatherproof pannier, the better to impress their hosts of his imperial authority. He accepted the headman's hospitality of a meal of roasted mutton and took Arshan and Kishen Ali with him. As they took their places on rugs placed between braziers for warmth, Harry apologized that he didn't speak the traders' dialect. The headman replied he understood Harry's Persian if he spoke slowly, and so they got along with Kishen Ali translating some of the more obscure words.

"I can show you Shimshal, sagr. It leads west into Hunza."

"Is it easily passable?"

The man nodded slowly. "Yes, sagr, for the passage of men and pack animals, but not for souls, for it is guarded by a fortress from whence issue the raiders who so plague us humble traders. These are wicked men who know nothing of the world beyond their mountainous stronghold but to raid our caravans. They are sent by the Mir of Hunza, who the men say is called Safdar Ali Khan."

The other traders instantly made a sign to ward off the evil eye. Arshan and Kishen Ali copied them hastily.

"You are come to protect us, sagr? We will willingly change our allegiance to your empress from the uncaring Chinese."

Harry explained he was not empowered to do any such thing. "But I can station my Kashmiri troops here in the village and that will curb the raiders' activities." Then he addressed his companions in English. "It may be these Hunzakuts in the fort will allow us passage. Colonel Durand at Gilgit was instructed to send a message advising the ruler of Hunza that we are on the way, but we won't know whether this has reached the raiders, in their stronghold, in time to stay their hands against us… if they would even regard it as pertinent to do so. And then we must consider the opposite. If this Safdar Ali is in cahoots with the bandits, he may be angry to learn of a British expedition discovering his secret pass and then he might well issue instructions to slaughter us all."

"Will he not fear reprisals from Gilgit when khaarejee Durand at Simla learns of our deaths?"

Harry shrugged at Kishen Ali's question. "Who knows the workings of a Hunza mir? Savage kings don't always think things through, and he sounds like a complete barbarian."

After allowing the men and beasts two days to recover from the arduous trek from Leh, the party set out. At least, that was how Harry wrote it up, as though they were embarking on a leisurely day out. In fact, according to the headman the Shimshal lay some two hundred miles to the west and their route would mean crossing the Yarkand river, a precipitous descent into its narrow valley and then an arduous climb back up to follow its course thousands of feet above. Not for the first time, Harry wished he had Richard and the ever-practical Alfred Winner at his side. Even Edward might be accommodated. *How much the "twins" would love this derring-do stuff.* He thought briefly of William Maplethorpe and his claims of being an accomplished mountaineer.

Fairly sure that a beautifully uniformed officer would offer an irresistible target for trigger-happy Hunza warriors who had obviously seen off the Chinese soldiery, Harry was back in his shapeless goncha and stupid hat. And if, as the headman assured, Hunza men had little knowledge of the outside world, the weight of authority a British military uniform was supposed to convey would probably go over their heads anyway. "Better a live ugly native than a handsome Haari dead," as Arshan said with his usual cheeriness.

In the lower reaches they marched through pine forests, making long hairpin diversions around each of the numerous transverse valleys running down into the Yarkand River, so that while miles were made in a day, the actual forward distance might be only a fifth of that. When the trail left the main abyss of the Yarkand and climbed to higher altitudes, the trees gave way to alpine meadows studded with rocks ranging in size from a man's head to a small house. Higher up, the landscape turned to a brownish-gray devoid of any plant life other than dull lichens.

"Ahead lies Shimshal," the headman said on the ninth day since leaving Shahidula.

They set off up the desolate, narrow pass toward the fortress, known to the traders as the "Gateway to Hunza," a portal firmly guarded against intruders.

"Haari, look!"

All eyes swerved up to follow the direction of Arshan's pointing finger. Silhouetted against the clear sky, perched like an eagle's nest on a dramatic spike of rock high above their heads, was the robbers' lair, a zigzag pathway cut into the near vertical cliff the only way to reach it. Hoofmarks in the churned snow at the foot of the path indicated its being wide enough for horses.

"We cannot get up there safely."

Harry was inclined to agree with Arshan's assessment. "Safely? No. We'll have to go bravely. Kishen Ali, get the coolies to make camp here on this side of the stream." He spoke briskly to the Gurkha officer. "I'll take two of your men. You give us covering fire if we need to make a quick withdrawal. If that happens I'll wave my rifle in a wide arc. If you see me wave my skerag, we're all right. You stay here," he added to Arshan.

"No, Haari! Where you go I go. You may need me to help translate Hunza dialect."

"Sinnce when were you proficient in Hunza dialect? I'll cope."

"Speak all dialect… mostly." The expression on the young Persian boy's face brooked no further argument. Harry sighed, and minutes later the four men urged their horses across the river at the bottom of the gorge, which at that altitude was frozen and so afforded an easier passage than had it been in torrent. The beasts slithered on the hard surface but all made it over to the far bank without injury. And then began the climb, which went without incident to the point where Harry began to wonder whether the stronghold was occupied. On nearing the top of the precipitous zigzag path, to his astonishment he saw that the fortress gate stood open.

They rode onto a rocky ledge almost a square of some sixty to seventy yards on a side. A high wall of stones loosely topping a waist-high rock face closed off the way ahead. In its center a short, narrow ramp led to the gate. The Gurkhas rode up to join Arshan and Harry on this stony but reasonably flat maidan and peered with deep suspicion at the loopholed wall and gaping opening. The Gurkha gentling his horse next to Harry whispered, "It's a trap, sahib."

As if the Hunzakuts heard, the gate suddenly slammed shut and a matchlock cracked loudly. Dust spurted up from the plateau a few feet in front of the Gurkha who had spoken. His mount skittered back and both soldiers immediately threw themselves down into a defensive crouch, using their horses as cover, rifles to their shoulders.

"Hold your fire," Harry said quickly as he quieted his own horse. "Those long-barreled jezails are accurate enough at this distance." He unwound the skerag from around his waist, hoping he was correct, and waved it to tell the contingent down in the gorge that they were safe. This was definitely a gamble, for at that moment the wall some twenty feet above came alive with wild humanity, warriors all shouting and pointing their matchlocks threateningly.

Harry thought hard. "Mixed signals, Arshan. Gate open, warning shot, clamor and threatening gesticulation, but no further firing. They're unsure of us. I'll bet you my Breguet they have heard from Safdar Ali about our presence and will hold their fire."

Arshan coveted Harry's pocket watch, so the offer of a bet placed him in a quandary: win the bet and they were almost certainly dead; if Harry were right, he wouldn't get the beautiful watch.

"Tell them to send out one man to parley with me."

Standing high on his stirrups, Arshan drew a breath of freezing mountain air and shouted loudly to be heard above the uproar. "Bi Adam! Bi Adam!"

A tense period followed as the four men awaited the outcome. Though massively outnumbered, the Gurkhas looked prepared to sell their lives dearly if the need arose, and all hoped it would not. After a long interval, the gates creaked open again and two men emerged. As they did so the shouting from the wall quieted. The Hunzakut emissaries crossed the open ground to where Harry and his party waited, and with curt bows asked his business. Their dialect of Tajik was tolerable to Harry's ears.

"I journey to Hunza to see your Mir," he told them.

"My chief has heard of your coming," said the man who was the elder of the two. "You are to enter." He inclined his head slightly in invitation and stretched his arm out behind him at the gate.

"I trust them not." Arshan spoke quietly in English. "They will kill us the minute we enter and are out of sight of our men below."

Harry thought Arshan could well be correct. Certainly the men's appearance didn't foster confidence in their honor. A wilder bunch of ruffians would be hard to imagine. Not even Richard's Blackbeard the Pirate could possibly look as ferocious and mean-hearted. "That is certainly a risk. But I came here on a vital mission, and I can't falter at the first sign of trouble—"

The Gurkha next to him yelled suddenly

Harry reacted sharply and whipped his head around in time to see the younger of the Hunza men seize his bridle. Fearing treachery, he swung around in his saddle so he could lean down and grasp the man by his arm before he could do any damage. Instantly, the shouting from the wall broke out again. With a sharp keening sound the Gurkha brought his wicked kukri from his belt and would have slashed the Hunza across the throat if Harry hadn't shouted a warning.

For his part, the emissary cowered back from the threat but still retained his hold on the head of Harry's horse. "It's all right," Harry called to Arshan, who was in the process of wheeling his mount back to come around to his pishkhidmat's rescue on the side where he was still held captive. "He's curious about something."

The Hunza was staring in a mixture of admiration and terror at the bullets lining the bandolier slung around Harry's neck and under his left arm. As his horse stilled, Harry let the man run a finger over one of the long, sleek .303 metal-jacketed cartridges. "What terrible ball is this?" the man asked in wonder.

It gave Harry an idea. "Call out your chief and I will demonstrate this wonderful weapon." *Now I really wish I had Alfred or Richard here. Both are far better shots on the range than me.* He comforted himself with the thought that in this circumstance an accurate aim was not the point, and in any case at the maximum distance available he shouldn't miss. In English, indicating the two Hunzakuts, he said, "Arshan, will you ask these two to set up a suitable target close by the far edge of this ledge."

As soon as Harry's instructions were understood, an immediate excitement ran around the fortress and within minutes several score of the bandits came out onto their maidan and formed up one side of an imaginary line between where a kind of straw scarecrow was hurriedly set up. The chief of the bandits issued from the gate, dressed in all his finery, which amounted to a gaudy skerag wrapped around a fine wool robe of regal maroon and an eccentrically ornate version of the traditional hat, with its donkey-ear side brims. He and his sub-chiefs took in the preparations and nodded in satisfaction. The British party dismounted. One of the Gurkhas took the bridles while the other maintained a watchful presence.

The gathered caravan raiders watched in fascination as the strange white man went to take station beside an outcrop of rock on the edge of the maidan near to the zigzag path. From there he waved at his servant, who immediately walked to the target, turned, and then made a curious loping return to his master; evidently a ritual, some sort of invocation to a white god perhaps.

"Sixty-five paces, Haari."

Harry nodded and quickly set the Henry-Martini's rear sliding ramp sight for sixty-five yards, and then took the opportunity to reassure the men waiting far below with another wave of his skerag. The distance between firing line and target should pose no problem for the chosen marksman from among the bandits.

A tall Hunzakut stepped from the throng, head held proudly high. He strode to where Harry waited for him, Arshan close by to one side. The two contestants stared at each other for a long moment. The man was a wild apparition, but his clear eyes showed a fiery spirit and a haughty intention to humble this foolish white man.

Harry indicated he should fire first. The Hunzakut took time to prime his jezail carefully with powder, wadding, and push a ball into the muzzle. In the sudden quiet, other than for the light whine of wind through a rocky gap, the ball's rattling passage down the ornately decorated barrel sounded clearly. More wadding was rammed home with the long loading rod. He primed the firing pan, and then he was ready. With steely eye and greasy grin the marksman raised the weapon and leveled it at the distant figure of straw. Silence reigned. A redstart's sudden harsh cry did nothing to disturb the Hunzakut's concentration, the intense application of a mountain sniper sighting on a distant foe.

The firing cap clicked a split-second before the loud crack as the priming powder exploded and hurled the lead ball in an almost flat trajectory toward the target. A rising sigh from the crowd urged it on its way and almost as soon as it had left the muzzle the ball slammed dead center into the straw target's chest. The sigh burned up into a howl of triumph from a hundred and more throats.

"Bull's eye, Haari." Arshan smiled.

Harry smiled back. "Bull's eye," he agreed. "But never mind the quality. Time to feel the breadth. I think I should try to look as fearsome as possible," he said with a teeth-bared grin. In seconds, Harry packed his mouth uncomfortably with five cartridges. His Pirbright armory sergeant would have had a fit at the unorthodox treatment of .303 shells, but Harry felt it was time to act out his Blackbeard character for the audience. He took four more shells, levered open the rifle's breech and inserted one of the cartridges, and then closed his right fist—his lever-trigger hand—around the other three, ready.

The Hunza marksman began the lengthy process of reloading to take a second shot at the target. As he did, Harry stepped up, raised the Henry-Martini to his shoulder, made a brief final check of the front and rear sights, took a nose-wheezy breath, released it, and squeezed the trigger.

Bang! He ejected the cartridge, chambered the next, and fired again… and again… and again. He whipped the bullets from between his lips after firing those in his hand, and worked the rifle's lever in a blur. In just twenty-four seconds he shot eight cartridges—his best rate ever—and watched with satisfaction as the scarecrow came apart in a cloud of shredded straw. Its exposed armature staggered under the onslaught and then flew off the edge of the maidan, to disappear amid shattering reverberation of the shots careening back from the opposite side of the gorge.

It seemed as if the echoes would never end, but fade they did and into the shocked quiet, Harry neatly removed the remaining shell from between his lips and returned it to the bandolier. He swept out a booted foot and scattered the expended brass cartridge cases. None of the brigands missed the gesture, or its implication. Some, made of sterner stuff, remained rigid and scowling, but most stood open-mouthed, slack red lips and yellow teeth gaping between extensive facial hair.

"Point made?"

Arshan grinned. "Point made, Haari."

CHAPTER 12 | *Simla, 1890*

"GOOD LORD ABOVE! It's a pair of Kashmiri bandit kings. I can't believe in a Harry Smythe-Vane with a bushy pundit beard. And who is this strapping jezailchi I see before me?"

William Maplethorpe shook both men's hands vigorously.

Harry grinned broadly. "It's very good to see you William. And pray what are you doing up here, not enough patrol work for cavalrymen along the Kabul River?"

As he usually did, Arshan went all shy in front of another officer, even though he knew Maplethorpe from seeing him frequently in Harry's company at Rawul Pindee.

"The Amir has been keeping several regiments busy with training schedules which then don't materialize." William spread his arms in frustration. "Don't know why we don't just damned well annex Afghanistan and have done with it. We don't, guess who will. And where have you come from?"

"I'll tell you all about it after Arshan and I get cleaned up. You won't recognize him once the face fungus is removed."

"You have sprung up, young man, since last I saw you. What are you now?"

"Haarivan sahib has worked with me to decide, Left-tenant Mappletop, and we think I am currently twenty summers." He shrugged eloquently. "But maybe not, maybe less. I was already old when I can first remember." His engaging smile made the Persian youth look much younger than the facial hair suggested.

"Shall we see you later in the officers' mess, William, when I'm back in a proper uniform?"

"I look forward to it."

Harry suspected from the way Maplethorpe's regard took in the returned travelers that he thought them bedfellows, although their shapeless Ladakhi gonchas would hardly excite the amorous attention of any Englishman.

As they parted company with another round of handshakes, Harry cast his mind back over the long debriefing with Sir Mortimer Durand, and continued to do so as he lounged in a welcome and deep tub of warm water in the Simla officer's hammam. His only action was to call over a bath wallah and request the luxury of a shave while he soaked. Beyond the odd greeting he paid no attention to subalterns as they entered, bathed, chattered casually of important matters such as the inter-regimental polo match, an attractive gobble wallah new to the camp, and whether the Russians were better at fucking than Englishmen (*Doon't forget the Scawts!*), as they ordered and drank their chai or chota pegs, and left.

"After the demonstration of the power of a modern rifle, we and the Hunza brigands became firm friends, even more so after the Gurkhas produced their tobacco and offered it around our hosts. They were two very happy soldiers. As I later found out, their officer had told them not to bother returning if any harm befell me because the honor of the regiment was at stake."

Sir Mortimer stroked the left extension of his long mustache. Its extreme width seemed calculated give balance to his physiognomy, which rose from a determined looking narrow jaw to a broad forehead, made the wider because his hairline had abandoned its forward position and was in retreat to a defensive point father back on his crown. In his mid-forties, born and bred at Sehore, Bhopal, Sir Mortimer was thoroughly steeped in British India's matters, and for two years until 1880 he had been the political officer at Kabul, so he was fully experienced in the byzantine politics of Afghanistan's ruling families. He was fluent too in Persian. "Since the Indian Mutiny, the Gurkhas have been invaluable allies. Good men." He laid his hands in his lap and looked steadily at Harry, unbothered by his wild native appearance and apparently not by the stench of journeying for months in the wild uplands which came off Harry's clothes and body.

Oh, how he longed for a bath!

"Was it as we suspected with the Hunza raiders?"

"Yes sir. That became clear within minutes of sitting to eat, drink, and talk with their chiefs. Thanks to the gift of the Gurkhas' tobacco, they loosened up quickly. Their ruler had told them to expect a British party but Safdar Ali gave no instructions as to how to receive me, hence the initial uncertainty. They were raiding caravans under orders, they claimed, but I detected a sense of dissatisfaction, which I put down to the fact that the raiders took all the risks and Safdar Ali all the profits. I suggested this and as one, the headman and his deputies agreed. 'Why do you do this if that is the case?' I asked. 'If we refused we would be killed,' was his simple answer.

"I told them that my government was angry at the raids, the robbery, murder, and people seized to be sold as slaves, and that I was charged with meeting their ruler to tell him this, but also to discuss with him how the raids might be ended to his great benefit. I pointed out that all my Gurkhas in the gorge below were armed as was I, with the terrifying weapon they had seen demonstrated, and that the Gurkhas were all much better shots than I was."

"Put the fear of God up them?"

"Yes sir. Adequately. The following day we returned down the mountain and set off with seven Hunzakut guides. We'd gone hardly any distance when an emissary from Safdar Ali rode up bearing a letter. In it he gave me the freedom to explore his kingdom as I wished and then attend him at his palace at my convenience. The results of our exploration I gave to your adjutant."

"He's already given me a digest, heights, widths, streams, and—most vitally—there are other means of ingress to Hunza than those we are now aware of. That was well done, Captain. And I have already gleaned that the runner I sent after you found you with the message that the Russian agent Konstantin Golovonov was back in the area."

"He did, sir." Because he felt it reflected poorly on his capabilities as an agent, Harry left out of his report that it was the Russian who found him, sending a messenger with a note inviting Harry to come to his camp. In Harry's report the suggestion was that the intrepid British spy tracked down his quarry and cornered him in his den. Well, either way, the outcome was satisfactory. "Golovonov treated me most courteously and dined me very well. He was open about the rivalry between—as he put it—the Tsar and the Queen-Empress over our Asian interests."

"Was he, indeed! I'll be damned. I expected a close-mouthed Cossack."

"He did have a small escort of seven Cossacks. But I felt his free speech had more to do with a confidence in the beneficial outcome of Russia's ambitions in

India than a naturally pleasant character. 'The Russian army, officers and men, think of nothing but the coming invasion of India,' he said. So confident that he had no problem with my seeing his map on which the 'Pamir gap' was marked in red ink—the very route through Hunza and Shimshal to Ladakh we fear."

"Bloody blackguard."

"Golovonov views it as a tit-for-tat situation because of British interference with Russian interests on the Black Sea and in the Balkans. He even went so far as to say that he couldn't understand our failure to annex Afghanistan to prevent the Tsar getting his hands on the territory and that we should anticipate that happening soon."

"It's plain greed and aggrandizement, is what it is. I'll read the report in detail, don't worry, but for now tell me did he propose how the Russian army will come?"

Harry smiled tightly. "Willingly, sir. He boasted that the plan was for four hundred thousand men to cross the Pamirs using the passes and Hunza."

Sir Mortimer sat back in his chair, both hands placed on the edge of the desk. His eyebrows rose high up the dome of his forehead, the tips of his mustache pointed up in response to the twitch of his mouth. "Four – Hundred – Blooming – Thousand!"

"Yes, sir. That's exactly what he claimed. I'm aware that Sir Charles MacGregor has calculated the maximum number of men who could be deployed in such hostile terrain is a quarter of that, and I said as much and pointed out the huge logistical problem of transport and supply, but Golovonov simply batted it aside. 'The Russian soldier,' said he, 'is not a man to trouble himself about such matters. He does as he's told with utter stoicism and if at the end of a grueling day's marching or fighting he finds no tent, no warmth, no food or water, he just carries on.' He appears quite convinced of this."

"And the man had the damned nerve to request permission to winter in Kashmir before returning with all his Intelligence to his masters in Central Asia. Fortunately, he's obviously a bombastic Ivan who hopefully will come to a very bad end."

"I take it, sir, you denied his request?"

Sir Mortimer's derisive snort was answer enough.

Harry decided he'd had enough of his lazy bath when the water cooled to the point of becoming uncomfortable, which is to say, body temperature, since down on the Kashmir plain the heat was considerable compared to what he had been used to for months. He decided to get dried, dressed in uniform, and head for the mess. First though, he went to see that Arshan was happily ensconced again in the camp followers' quarters (a few rupees in the hands of the havildar commanding the native section of the cantonment secured the boy a place to call home until they returned to Rawul Pindee or received orders to go elsewhere).

❧ ★ ☙

"So tell me of your adventures in Hunzaland, Harry," Maplethorpe demanded. "I'll allow that you bore me with that as long as I may bore you with the dreariness of the Kabul Valley after."

Harry smiled. "Deal. Where shall I start? But remember," he added, tapping the side of his nose, "mess walls have ears, and little Punjabi or Kashmiri birdies might tell tales across the Pamirs."

"I shall not repeat a word."

The two friends were seated in cushioned cane chairs on the veranda of the officers' mess, well away from any other groups. They were pleasantly full of a spicy goat curry and beers fresh from the mess ice house, kept chilled in pouches of soaked straw. Now each sipped brandies in glasses wide enough to accommodate the ice lumps.

"Mir Safdar Ali Khan, was every bit as big a villain as I'd come to expect. Charming, of course. I attired myself in all my uniformed splendor after Arshan's hours-long ministrations to clean the stink of travel from me—"

"Which I rather think you both enjoyed?"

Harry gazed at Maplethorpe over the rim of his glass. "You guessed?"

"Not difficult." Maplethorpe became busy with some imaginary fluff on the cuff of his dress jacket.

"I'm sorry, William. Truly I am. It's not that I don't feel—"

"It's all right." Maplethorpe raised his eyes again. "Really, Harry. I'm over it, which is to say… Well, we never exchanged vows or anything."

"But a native?"

"Arshan doesn't strike me as some lickspittle low-caste peasant, Harry. Are you saying you ought to feel guilty for replacing me with someone so much lesser?"

"No! I don't know. It's not that. I'm not sure I *replaced* you."

"Shall I tell you what it is before you bore me with Tales of Hunzaland?" Maplethorpe said in a light tone that removed any sting his words might have conveyed. He leaned forward in his chair. "I don't wish to put myself on any kind of plinth or even attempt to match myself to... Richard, wasn't it? But being a relatively well off and well educated Englishman speaking in the cultured accents of an upper-class gentleman, I'm disturbingly close enough to Richard to make you feel you are betraying the man you've placed on such a high pedestal. When we have sex, Harry, you feel crippled by guilt... at least afterward. Don't deny it! I've always sensed the disturbance in your soul. With Arshan it's different. He is a person with absolutely no connection to your past affections, your culture, your family, friends, school... background of any kind."

As Maplethorpe paused to take a sip of brandy, Harry was appalled at the unexpected torrent of words. His friend was not given much to long speeches, much less to analysis—oddly, quite like Richard Rainbow. The words cut deep and must have showed on his face.

"I'm sorry. I'm not much good at saying these kinds of things, Harry. Now you think I mean you're treating Arshan like some cheap native whore, and I don't really mean that—"

"Not 'really,' but almost?"

"No! You're a kind person, Harry. In fact too damned kind for your own good. That stiff, haughty, aristocratic veneer you hide under sometimes... well, look at you returning from adventures in the mountains. Nothing very haughty there. But..." he hesitated until Harry reluctantly nodded him on. "But your Richard must have done something quite extraordinary...?"

Harry felt unable to talk about Richard with Maplethorpe, or say anything more about him than the very little he already had on the *Malabar*. Instead he simply dipped his head in a form of mute acknowledgment.

They both sipped at their brandies. "So," Maplethorpe began in a brighter voice. "Hunza?

"Where was I?"

"Attired in all your scarlet and polished brass and silver military splendor."

"Yes indeed, and arrived at a village called Gulmit where the mountain potentate had erected a vast pavilion and fired a thirteen-gun salute in my honor, would you believe. In fact the marquee was a gift from our government via the Maharaja of Kashmir, given Mir Safdar Ali Khan at an earlier time and part of a presentation to persuade him not to deal with the Russians. And my principal diplomatic task was to remind him of who his real friends are.

"I thought we got off to a good start, since Safdar Ali emerged from his grand pavilion to greet me. He is of average height with an unremarkable Moghul face, sparse mustache above small lips, and flowing bifurcated beard touched with henna. For much of the time, he peered out from almost closed eyes, curiously of an upturned curve to match arched eyebrows. But it is a crafty face from which poke disturbing little signs of cruelty. The laughter lines radiating from the corners of his eyes and an almost perpetual half smile make him look as benevolent as my grandfather."

"I'm guessing your grandfather is, and Safdar Ali isn't?"

"No, he's not, and it's those narrowed, calculating eyes give him away. The instigator of the murderous raids on the Yarkand–Leh trail secured the throne by slaughtering his father and mother. Two brothers he had hurled from a cliff into an abyss. Of course, none of these sins amounted to anything as bad as intriguing with the Russians."

"Of course not."

"Quite. After a bit of power maneuvering with who sat where and on what—I was supposed to kneel as a supplicant, but I had Kishen Ali bring in my camp chair and place it beside Safdar Ali's throne—we got down to business. He happily admitted to the caravan raiding and justified it on the grounds that it was *rahdari*, which he would call a rightful toll for using 'his' road, but which under these circumstances I would call protection money. Since Hunza is poor, his state has no other way of earning a living, he says. He is prepared to stop the raids if the British government gives him subsidies in return for his lost rahdari so his people have something to eat."

William laughed uproariously. "What a scoundrel. How did you respond?"

"In the only way possible. I said our Queen does not give way to blackmail. Besides, I told him sternly that there are now troops stationed at Shahidula so go ahead and try another raid through the Shimshal Pass and see how badly your men will fare against modern weapons and strict British discipline."

"Did it work?"

"Time will tell, I suppose, but my feeling is not. I feel in my bones that we will have to face him down again… and soon, probably. The trouble is that this ignorant king thinks the powers surrounding him are no more than other local khans all out for his support, so he'll continue to intrigue with Russia. He just won't be raiding much after receiving a bloody nose near Shahidula. No, with the message delivered and—thanks to the Mir allowing me to roam his narrow realm before meeting him—my job of mapping the valley and the district leading east to the Yarkand River done, we returned to deliver the findings and report."

Maplethorpe waved at one of the native orderlies and ordered another round of brandies. "Now it's back to the usual rigmarole of training, drilling, patrolling, officers' mess balls, avoiding the machinations of the unmarried ladies."

"Thank you, William. To be honest, I shall be grateful for some quiet in the warmth of Rawul Pindee."

"Hah, I find that difficult to believe, Harry. When you say that, I'm reminded of those cheap romances where the hero claims he wishes for nothing more than to put his slippered feet up at the hearth, tea at his side, and a pipeful of tobacco, and then the author writes, 'Little did he know that…'!"

CHAPTER 13 | *Pamirs and Hunza, August to December 1891*

IT WAS A particularly wretched couple of weeks that dropped temperatures low enough to freeze water in the basins in the men's tents in spite of it being mid-summer. But high in the Pamirs, summer is a relative term, Harry reflected. Maplethorpe's facetious prediction had proven accurate. Urgent messages from London about a rumored Russian incursion through the Pamir gap into the eastward poking tongue of Afghanistan known as Bozai Gumbaz had Sir Mortimer Durand directing Harry's feet toward Gilgit and beyond with a degree of urgency matched only by the battle of diplomatic exchanges between London and St. Petersburgh.

In the inhospitable region hovering between China to the East, India to the South, the bulk of Afghanistan to the West, and Russia to the north, it suddenly became of enormous importance to the British to discover if the small and scattered nomadic tribes owed allegiance to any power.

"No sepoys in support, this time, Captain. Don't want to antagonize any of these touchy headmen," Sir Mortimer told Harry. "An envoy from one of the more powerful warlords has brought a message from his master that he will readily come to meet the British Ambassador for discussions." He shook Harry's hand firmly. "Good luck!"

And so they camped and waited, while Harry reflected on the nature of a warlord's punctuality, knowing that *readily* could mean anything from a day to a month.

"I don't envy Russian troops sent to occupy this region for any length of time," he said to Arshan. They and the small body of lightly armed servants suffered badly from physical weakness and lassitude brought on by the extreme altitude. "A garrison will be tempted to head south in search of a warmer climate after only a short exposure to this unkind place," he added ominously.

He had known moments of such severe heat in the deserts of Sudan that neither he nor Richard could contemplate the exertion of lovemaking, for the very act of fleshy contact was too uncomfortable; on top of the world Arshan and Harry craved shared body warmth, but after the shattering cold of the march setting up camp leached too much of their energy to take amorous advantage of their proximity.

On August 13, London's worst fears were realized and the lie put to the Tsar's denials of interference in British affairs when Harry ran into the invading Russians. He woke from a fitful sleep, aware of Arshan's absence from their bed and a sibilant hiss.

"Haari. Haari!"

He rolled to all fours and peered past Arshan, who knelt in the tent's doorway and shivered from more than the bitter chill. Harry stared balefully at some thirty Cossacks and a handful of officers riding past the encampment in a fine haze of the rainbowed ice crystals thrown up by their passage. They continued on their way, having shown the Russian flag, and set up camp half a mile away. He grunted part in irritation and part in satisfaction at the contact. "Hah, the vanguard of Golovonov's four hundred thousand. Now we shall find out what they are up to, since they don't seem compelled to violence."

They didn't have long to wait. Shortly after establishing their tents and pony lines, four officers rode up. The senior man introduced himself in polite English as Colonel Piotr Yazov. "In the interests of harmonious relations, I bring food and drink to share," he said as he swung down from his shaggy mount and extended a hand.

Harry took it and they shook firmly. The other officers also dismounted and busied themselves with distributing provisions to Arshan's servants, who quickly set to building up a good fire, eager to taste some of the remarkably fine meat and vegetables the Russians had brought with them.

"I am happy to meet you, Colonel Yazov, for now you may put my masters' unnecessary alarms to rest," Harry said. He treated Yazov to a diplomatically pleasant smile. "They are all ajitter over native rumors—no doubt baseless—that you Russians are annexing the entire of the Pamir region."

Yazov returned an equally broad, pleasant smile that twitched his mustaches into a straight line under his broad nose. For answer he produced a map and showed Harry the area marked in a thick red line. "This is what I have claimed in the name of Tsar Alexander, Captain Vane."

Harry felt his heart go as cold as the snow underfoot. Yazov's pencil enclosed an area stretching south 150 miles from the Russian border to include Bozai Gumbaz and the "Indian watershed." Yazov's next words were truly alarming. "The Pamir region is just the beginning," he said expansively. "You see us not on our way to somewhere but on our return. We have been into Chitral and Hunza territory by one pass and returned by way of another, see… here and here." He pointed on the map to the area near Mastuj to the north of Chitral town and eastward to the Yasin Valley, which gave easy access to Gilgit and Hunza.

"But this territory falls exclusively under the sphere of British influence."

Yazov looked genuinely surprised. "If it is of such strategic importance, how it is that you have no representative of any kind in Chitral?

Harry had no answer to this because he had no intention of sharing with the Russian his government's lamentable reluctance to finance the whims of yet another petty ruler. Perhaps this situation would change the minute his report from Gilgit hit Calcutta and the telegraph wire to London began to burn.

Considering the circumstances, the meal was convivial, and in the morning the Russians moved on. The party continued to wait for the promised meeting with the Kirghiz chieftain, and then on the third day, the Cossacks returned. Colonel Yazov offered his regrets but told Harry he'd received instructions to expel him and his party from territory now claimed by Russia.

Harry remonstrated, arguing that this was Afghanistan territory and he had every right to be there. "What if I refuse to go?"

Yazov looked uncomfortable, but remained adamant. "I should greatly regret it, but I would have to remove you by force."

Harry's mission was one of enquiry. Only he and Arshan were armed with anything capable of taking on an equal number of enemies, but thirty Cossacks…? "Then I shall bow to force and leave, but under the strongest protest," he said, mouth set in a grim line. He agreed to go east into China and not return directly to Gilgit. "The good colonel doesn't want me reporting his presence before he's ready, evidently," he said toArshan.

"Nothing 'good' about that fucking Russian," Arshan spat. With his Persian background, he had little love for anything Russian and an undesirable liking for common British Tommy-speak. "What we going to do in China? Go to Kashgar or Yarkand, Haari?"

"Neither. We'll cut across the great bend in the Panja, and when we reach its southernmost point, head south at speed for the Darkot Pass. That's the way Yazov came north and he won't be revisiting it this soon."

Forced by circumstance to use the deceitful detour, it took Harry's party the better part of a month to reach Gilgit, bathed in late summer warmth in comparison to the high Pamirs. At his dispatch a diplomatic row erupted with the roar of a volcano long shuddering to release its pent-up magma. But it was journalists' lurid reports of a brave officer's ejection from Empire territory that led to the British press excoriating the Russians. At fever pitch of public anger, Harry had to laugh when he read the Liberal peer Lord Rosebery's description of Bozai Gumbaz as "the Gibraltar of the Hindu Kush." But it was no exaggeration that a division of the Indian Army had been put on a war footing at Quetta, a base from where it could strike northwest through Afghanistan to Herat, Merv, and into Russia. A terrible famine had much of Russia in a grip and the resulting widespread unrest meant the Tsar was in no position to take Britain on. Russia withdrew its troops from the Pamirs. For the time being.

"You're the only Englishman to have met Mir Safdar Ali, Captain Vane." Colonel Algernon Durand, the political officer at Gilgit, knew of Harry's expedition across the Shimshal Pass into the Hunza Valley. "That makes you our only expert on him, and you're familiar with the terrain up there."

That was six weeks ago when Harry and Arshan emerged from Bozai Gumbaz. At the command of his brother Sir Mortimer Durand—relaying the Viceroy's orders—Durand had in the greatest secrecy assembled a force of Gurkhas and Kashmiri Imperial Service troops to nip in the bud any Hunza affection for the Tsar. With the Russians' back-down, everyone drew a breath of relief, but by his actions it was clear that Safdar Ali remained convinced his Russian friends would come to his assistance. Harry's prediction that the Mir would cause more trouble was borne out by renewed raids on the Yarkand–Leh trade caravans the moment winter's onset forced the Kashmiri garrison stationed at Shahidula to withdraw before the snows trapped them.

"London has determined to remove any potential Russian allies, and so Safdar Ali's days are numbered," Durand informed Harry at the briefing. "While you were up in the Pamirs, inspired by your Colonel Yazov the wretch has even had the brazen effrontery to try and seize the Kashmiri fort at Chalt. Reinforcements I sent thwarted the attempt, but now he's persuaded the ruler of neighboring Nagar to join his cause against the 'meddlesome British.' Another raid can't be far off as long as the savage thinks the Russians will support him. Find out what you can of his immediate plans."

Which is why Harry—dressed in Kashmiri garb, and with Arshan, a Kashmiri jemadar called Birbal Dhar, and three of his Imperial Service sepoys—was crouched in cover at the edge of a precarious path cut into the shoulder of a steep slope, warding off snowflakes on an early November night some miles east of Chalt. A little behind them the stone roof of a small snow hut—typical of the refuges constructed at regular intervals to shelter travelers from the frequent winter blizzards—broke the bleak lines of the barely visible landscape.

The party waited for the predicted return of a man Birbal Dhar had recognized trailing a small trade caravan bound for Gilgit. Durand rightly feared that Safdar Ali would send spies to discover what the British Resident was up to. It was the third day since Birbal Dhar convinced Harry that the man he'd seen was a Hunzakut spy. If he were right, the man would soon head back east to his master. They waited and waited until impatience drove Harry to order them deeper into the Hunza Valley. But before they could gather their belongings and saddle up the mules, Birbal Dhar hissed for silence. They all dived for cover again.

"Is it he? The same man?"

"I think so, sahib."

A hunched over figure emerged from the light snowfall, and Harry told the jemadar to stop and search him.

"Halt! You must show me—"

The man broke into a run before Birbal Dhar could shout another word.

"Arshan!" Harry cried out.

The Persian boy leapt from cover and hurtled down the slight slope to the pathway, cutting across at an angle to the runaway's limited options of direction, where he curled up and fell in a bundle immediately in front of the fleeing man. In full flight, unable to avoid the obstacle, the Hunzakut tripped over Arshan and sprawled forward. Harry, hard on Arshan's heels, was waiting and used the man's momentum to land a hefty punch to his stomach. Hot steam whooshed from the spy's mouth in the frigid air. He doubled up and was quickly overpowered by the Kashmiris, all thought of pulling his wicked curved knife driven from his mind by Harry's blow.

"I'm a poor trader," the Hunzakut wailed once they had him safely ensconced in the snow hut.

"Not with a blade such as you carry," Birbal Dhar said. The jemadar crouched down, beard and mustaches bristling with suppressed humor. He stroked the tip of the confiscated kukri along the man's hairy jawline. He glanced up at Harry. "Shall I loosen his tongue with his own knife, sahib?" He fingered the sharp edge of the blade suggestively and flicked his tongue across his upper lip.

Harry signaled him to be patient. "Your name?"

The spy wriggled for a second. "Rustam."

"So, Rustam, you can answer my questions and be sent to Gilgit, safe from Safdar Ali's anger, or you can refuse, anger my man here even more, and go to Gilgit in small pieces." Harry glanced at the jemadar, the gesture not missed by Rustam. The man remained stubbornly silent. After a minute, Harry nodded curtly at Birbal Dhar. "Don't cut… yet." He took Arshan by the arm and stooped out under the low lintel into the steadily falling snow. Behind them the spy's grunt of pain cut through the otherwise quiet valley.

"I hate the necessity."

Arshan sniffed dismissively. "Is necessary, Haari. He fucking spy. Would do worse to you if position back to front." He spat, and the gobbet burned a hole at his feet in the thin covering of fresh snow lying on compacted earlier falls.

A few more cries of pain followed the first, but after a short wait Birbal Dhar stuck his head out. "Pah! The Hunza-filth is a woman. No stamina."

Harry heard the bitter disappointment in the jemadar's tone at the lost opportunity for some bloody fun. Rustam was ready to spill all he knew, which was more than his task of estimating numbers of the Kashmiri and Ghurkha force Durand was gathering in Gilgit. By the good fortune of his master's boastful nature, Harry learned that Safdar Ali planned to surprise the garrison at Chalt by sending men disguised as Gilgit coolies laden with burdens on their backs but in reality filled with weapons. Once inside, they were to fall on the unsuspecting guard and open the gates to Safdar Ali's waiting troops.

"By which plan," Harry said grimly, "he has sealed his fate."

I declare Chalt to be more precious to us than the strings of our wives' pajamas and demand the fort be handed to us. Be aware that should the Durand dare to enter our land of Hunza and Nagar he will face three nations—Hunza, Russia, and China; and know that the manly Russians have promised to come to our assistance. We have given orders to our loyal servants to bring the Durand's head to us on a platter should he so dare to enter our lands.

"The royal 'We' is a nice touch, don't you think?" With his head firmly in place, Colonel Durand advanced with his force of a thousand regular troops, Gurkhas and Kashmiris, several hundred Pathan road-construction troops, a battery of mountain artillery, seven engineers, and sixteen British officers, including William Maplethorpe.

"Thanks for yanking me out of the tedium of Rawul Pindee," Maplethorpe had said when he arrived posthaste in Gilgit at the summons.

"I recalled you boasting of your mountaineering skills, William, and recommended them to Colonel Durand. From experience—that is, viewed from a distance—I'm aware there are hills and sheer rock faces ahead of us."

William chuckled at Harry's dry tone and gazed at the towering mountain corridor in which flowed the Hunza River.

Durand's engineers bridged the river below Chalt and the British force crossed to the southern bank on December 1 to begin a slow, torturous march to the east and Safdar Ali's fortress-capital. On the northern side of the torrent, the precipitous mountains made passage impossible. The force encountered a first major obstacle at Nilt. The ruler of Naga boasted that his fortress was impregnable, and the British seven-pounders made little impression against the stones of its massive walls, while marksmen were unable to hit the enemy hidden behind narrow loopholes. The gates looked like the only weak point, as long as explosives could be laid against them.

Harry, a lieutenant, Birbal Dhar, and a hundred Gurkha sappers led by Captain Aylmer rushed the gate, carrying charges of guncotton. A heavy covering fire helped keep the defenders' heads down on the wall, and those behind the gate back from the loopholes. Aylmer ordered the Gurkhas to take cover where they could and wait for the gate's destruction. Then he, Harry, and Birbal Dhar made the final dash to the wall, zigzagging to throw off the enemy's sporadic aim. Amazingly, none were struck, and then they were right up against the wall, as close to the gate as could be managed. The wall provided shelter from the enemy's weapons because anyone wanting to fire down had to lean right out and so expose himself to accurate British fire from the main force as well as the Gurkha sappers in cover.

Aylmer and Harry fired their revolvers point-blank into the loopholes piercing the thick wall just above head height and then took advantage of the confusion this caused locally to reach the gate. This necessitated sprinting around a buttress, which put Aylmer and Harry back under the field of fire from the top of the wall as they ran out into the open. The jezailchis risked British rifles when the danger to the gates became apparent. Musket balls thunked into the ground about their feet. One struck Aylmer in the leg. Harry grabbed the man's arm and hauled him hard up against the timbers, just in time to miss being struck down by a hail of rocks thrown over the parapet.

In spite of his wound, Aylmer laid the guncotton charges and lit the fuse. He hobbled back around the buttress with Harry's help.

"By all that's—!"

The captain swore loudly. Harry saw the spark fizzle out.

"I'll go!"

"No, Vane. My job."

Again, Aylmer hobbled around the projecting buttress as best he could. Harry saw jezail lead shred the cloth of his tunic at the corner of his shoulder and blood spurted up. A withering rejoinder from the British rifles quelled the worst of the enemy shooting. The fuse relit, Aylmer staggered back to shelter behind the buttress. A moment later a great explosion of flame and smoke erupted, accompanied by a deafening roar. Lethal shards of timber flew in every direction.

"At them!" Aylmer yelled in parade-ground voice, and led the way through the settling debris of the former gate, Harry at his heels, both their revolvers blazing. The Gurkhas were only seconds behind, all shouting their war cries as they swarmed through the gate and spread out. They shot and bayoneted the enemy indiscriminately. Harry rushed up a narrow street with Birbal Dhar and a score of men behind him. A spate of musketry originating from the roofs ahead forced the British troops to seek hasty cover in barred doorways.

Harry took in the situation at a glance. He signaled the Nepalese officer crouched in a recess opposite. He jabbed a finger up, then straightened his palm twice to indicate ten men, and waved in the direction of the snipers on the roofs. The man nodded, shouted orders, and in seconds half his men dropped their weapons, clasped hands together, and helped heave the rest up onto the low roofs. Continuous volleys answered the scattered fire of the Naga-Hunza snipers' ancient muzzle-loaders. As Harry moved out with the ten men still on the street, he realized that behind the cartridge powder grime and rock dust one of them was a grinning Arshan.

"What the—? Get back!"

Before he got the last word out, a musket ball struck the toe of Harry's boot with a fat thwack and almost upended him. In a flash, Arshan was across the street and being yanked into the doorway.

"Is it all right, Haari?"

Arshan's eyes were wide in fright.

"Yes, damn it. Darned thing bounced off the leather under the toecap. Stings like hell, though. Well now you're here risking your hide," Harry added ungraciously, "we might as well finish the job. C'mon."

In minutes the entire British force followed the hundred Gurkhas into the fortress-town. After furious hand-to-hand fighting, discipline and modern weaponry soon told. Overwhelmed, the defenders fled as best they could. And so impregnable Nilt fell with the loss of six British lives, but more than eighty of the enemy lay dead. Among the injured, Captain Aylmer had taken no less than four jezail balls, yet remained cheerfully alive, and Harry received a sore big toe and a nasty though not serious arm wound caused by rock shrapnel from a shot that just missed him. "Don't fuss," he begged Arshan, busy washing and bandaging the laceration.

"My middle name is Fuss, Haari," Arshan replied. The humor of the few Tommies brought in to stiffen the resolve of native troops was rubbing off on him. In spite of his protests, while it didn't incapacitate him from normal duties, the injury continued to trouble Harry for several weeks.

For a further week, the column fought its way along the steep-sided, winding valley toward Safdar Ali's Hunza capital. The enemy contested every step, harassing the troops from sangars built on the bare rock, and their defiance cost Durand more valuable troops. Two days from Nilt, engineers constructed a bridge so the troops could cross back over the river—cliffs falling almost sheer into the torrent made the southern side impassable. The river's northern bank was not a great deal easier. Progress resumed at a slow pace. Forward scouts brought dismal news. Ahead, where a tributary joined the Hunza at a sharp dogleg bend, the enemy had turned the entire mountainside guarding the confluence at Haiderabad into a stronghold.

The stream, which might have been fordable near its mouth in summer months of low water, was now a foaming spate. Sappers quickly established that the force would need to march along its right bank almost a mile upstream to cross where it narrowed, and then come down the left bank to rejoin the Hunza. In so doing, they would be at the mercy of an estimated four thousand Hunzakut warriors. Innumerable sangars commanded the formidable heights above the valley along which the British must pass, twelve hundred feet below.

"We can't advance without first driving the enemy from their positions," Durand told the gathered officers. "That appears to be an impossible task. Yet I refuse to turn back in failure."

After the discouraging briefing Harry lay in his tent in a half-doze, half-awake state, aware of the warmth of Arshan asleep beside him. There was satisfaction in knowing that a handsome young Pathan Arshan had befriended for the purpose was almost certainly warming William Maplethorpe in similar fashion. Sleep was about to overtake him when there came an urgent scratching at the tent flap.

"Capitan sahib," Birbal Dhar whispered.

Harry stuck his head out the door flap into the chill night air. "What is it?"

"There is a path up the mountain. I have near the top been, and unseen by our foes." The jemadar paused to catch his breath, and went on in a calmer but more urgent voice. "So sheer is it in places, the defenders they cannot well see down or shoot at climbers. Skilled mountain men can go this way."

"Looks like a mission for a cragsman, William," Harry said after the morning briefing had set in motion the crazily hazardous plan to scale the tall cliff. "I'll go with you—"

"Not with that arm," Maplethorpe and Arshan said in unison.

Birbal Dhar helped to choose fifty Ghurkhas and fifty Kashmiris to make up the raiding party. The road-builder Pathans were ordered to pack the camp to make it appear to the Hunzakuts that the entire force was about to withdraw (Birbal Dhar and Arshan had urged the deception, fearing that some among the locally hired coolies might slip away and warn of the real undertaking). To support the climbing team, the best marksmen took up a protected position on the southwestern flank of the hillside across the tributary from the enemy stronghold. Beside them were placed the seven-pounder mountain guns. This was done in great secrecy under the cover of darkness before moonrise. From across the cascading stream were heard the raised voices of the Hunzakuts, who had fortunately chosen the night for one of their periodic celebrations, and their rowdiness helped cover the sounds of troop movements.

"Happily, they may also enjoy severe headaches, come morning," Harry said to Arshan with a grim smile.

It was the night of December 18/19.

"Good luck, William." The two shook hands in dawn's pale light. "I wish I were going with you."

"Well out of it old chap. Promise me something…?"

Harry was aware that, as they all did, Maplethorpe had written his possibly final letters to family in far off England and that the missives were entrusted to the reliable military postal system. He inclined his head in question.

"If I shouldn't return from this little party, take my Guinevere and look after her?"

It took Harry a moment to recall the name of Maplethorpe's beloved dressage mare. "Of course I would, but there won't be any need, William. I'll see you presently."

Arshan and Harry found themselves a sheltered spot beside the marksmen where they had a good view of the mountain. The perilous pathway that Birbal Dhar, Maplethorpe, and the native troops followed was quite invisible to the enemy across the stream. To the anxious watchers the men climbing first left, then doubling back right, then again left, looked like a scattered line of ants picking their way up a rugged vertical wall. The wait became unbearable, and then…

"Something's wrong," whispered Harry, his voice husky with alarm.

The mountaineer force had stalled. To the anxious watchers it was clear that the cliff above the men was utterly inaccessible. A swift semaphoring from Maplethorpe explained that a wrong turn had been taken and there was nothing for it but to return to that point and seek a new way up.

"Two hours gone to waste."

"Yet still the fucking Hunzakuts are ignorant," said Arshan with a grim smile.

A fresh start was made. Another hour passed. Tension mounted. It came as relief when the marksmen were passed the order to commence a dropping fire to distract the enemy from their approaching doom. Maplethorpe attained the top of the cliff along with a few of the best climbers, among them resolute Birbal Dhar. Shots rang out.

"The men in the nearest sangar have spotted them," Harry cried out.

Immediately, the British fire settled to a disciplined rapid rate and the seven-pounders barked. The gunners directed their shells as close as they dared to where the scaling party scrambled over the higher ledges behind the sangars. More of the enemy ran forward from cover to hurl heavy rocks down on the Gurkhas and Kashmiri soldiers still climbing. Some were struck and injured, though miraculously none fell to their deaths. Then their comrades already on top started firing on the defenders who had exposed themselves. The Gurkhas and Kashmiris, kukris and bayonets glinting brightly in the sunlight, formed up rapidly into small groups and began to move from sangar to sangar, slaughtering their occupants, the enemy's defenses now turned into his grave.

In less than ten minutes from Maplethorpe first reaching the higher ledges, the battle was over. Hunza warriors started to slip away from sangars farthest from the action, and then wholesale panic took over. The fugitives made easy targets for the scaling party, and for the marksmen across the stream who picked them off like ducks at a fairground shoot. Corpses soon littered the mountainside.

The Hunza capital was devoid of life apart from a few elderly souls. Hurriedly emptied coffers shattered the troops' anticipation of rich booty plundered from a hundred caravans.

"The five days since we stormed Haiderabad gave Safdar Ali time enough to make good his escape." Harry, Maplethorpe, and Arshan wandered through hallways and chambers that echoed to the footfalls of disappointed Gurkhas.

One of the Nepalese officers hurried up. "Sahibs! Come quick!"

As one they turned and strode after the Gurkha to a place where some of his men had broken down a wall, a false one by its thinness. Within the space lay a secret cache of Russian-made rifles, ammunition, and more household goods. Harry's eyes took in samovars, furniture, and a large portrait of Tsar Alexander III.

"Hmm, he left behind Yazov's gifts," Harry murmured. "The wily bird has flown and with five days' head start I doubt the horsemen sent in pursuit will catch him. Safdar Ali knows these mountains better than we."

Maplethorpe kicked at a samovar. It returned a hollow boom. "Where will he go?"

"China, I imagine. We stand in his way to Russia, and anyway he must feel betrayed. His 'manly' friends abandoned him."

"Well, he won't be returning, that's for sure."

Harry and Maplethorpe saluted their commanding officer.

Durand acknowledged with a brief nod. "It turns out that Safdar Ali left behind a young brother, one very anxious to placate the wrath of the great white Empress, so I'll put him on the erstwhile ruler's throne. That will save a lot of palaver with the locals. And to make sure he toes the line, a small garrison of Imperial Service troops will be stationed here to keep order and refuse entry to unwanted visitors, like your Colonel Piotr Yazov."

Harry wished he'd stop referring to the Russian as being "his."

"You, Captain Vane, have a different destination. Not one I'm sure I envy you, but orders from Sir Mortimer arrived this morning."

Harry smiled inwardly at Durand's strictly correct manner of referring to his brother.

"We are to take the Russians' visit to Chitral with every seriousness. To this date we have been content with a treaty on paper, but there is no longer confidence that this arrangement with Mirtar Aman-ul-Mulk will survive under pressure from the Russians. I am now appointed its political officer, but I have too much to do at Gilgit to be there, so you are to be my deputy on the spot. I believe you know Aman-ul-Mulk and his family, as well as the district."

"Yes, sir."

"Good. You will patrol the heights and valleys to apprise me and our masters in Simla of any developments to pass on to Calcutta."

"This will look good on your record, Harry," Maplethorpe told him later, a sly smirk on his lips. "After all, as I recall years ago on the old *Malabar*, this was exactly what you craved."

"I had hoped for some leave."

Arshan wove a hand between Harry's arms and waist. "But it means I stay with you, Haari… maybe many years."

PART THREE

Heroes and Aesthetes, 1892–1896

"You will always be fond of me. I represent to you all the sins you never had the courage to commit."

— Oscar Wilde, *The Picture of Dorian Gray*

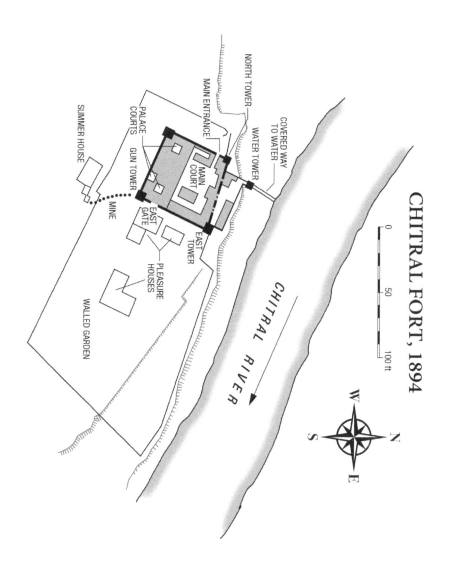

CHITRAL FORT, 1894

SUMMER HOUSE

PALACE COURTS

GUN TOWER

MAIN ENTRANCE

NORTH TOWER

WATER TOWER

COVERED WAY TO WATER

MINE

MAIN COURT

EAST GATE

EAST TOWER

PLEASURE HOUSES

WALLED GARDEN

CHITRAL RIVER

0   50   100 ft

N
W   E
S

CHAPTER 14 | *Chitral, 1892–95 and London*

HUNTING SAVED Nizam-ul-Mulk's life; restraint brought about his downfall.

Harry's appointment as Durand's man-on-the-spot at Chitral didn't mean he spent all his time in the town or even in the valley since his role was a roving one. He kept an ear to the ground while doling out British opinion—the *proper-gander*, as Arshan called it—to the Mirtar's extended family. As it happened, when Aman-ul-Mulk passed away at the end of August 1892 after thirty-five stable years on the Chitrali throne, Harry was at Gilgit with his hopelessly small contingent of three Gurkhas and Arshan. The Mirtar's death threw into jeopardy all British plans to use Chitral as a bulwark against the Russians.

The disturbing news arrived at Gilgit with Aman-ul-Mulk's eldest son Nizam. He'd been away hunting in the Yasin district, which was as well for his health because his ruthless brother Afzal-ul-Mulk had advanced plans in place for Nizam's death. In the event he sent assassins to Yasin to find his brother and seized the throne while he waited on news of Nizam's murder. Before that happened, loyal runners found the heir-apparent and the prince fled the easy distance to Gilgit in search of sanctuary.

"Treacherous man, that Afzal," Arshan said.

Harry agreed. "Under that surface of generosity and bonhomie he has the heart of a pure savage. He's all charm and arms-open honesty which in reality cloaks his naked ambition and treachery."

"What a Pathan would call a mix of monkey and tiger, Haari."

Discord on the Chitrali throne was the last thing the Viceroy needed and Durand soon received instructions from Calcutta to support Nizam "with everything at your hand."

"Basically, Arshan, that's us for the time being," Harry muttered when he conveyed this news to his small unit. But in truth, now in his twenty-seventh year, Harry Smythe-Vane could ally experience beyond his years to the fitness and strength of a lean athlete. The prospect of handling the situation in Chitral thrilled his very being. Some six years his junior, the time they'd spent together had matured Arshan into a fine warrior to stand at Harry's side. He too was fired by excitement at the danger ahead.

A trickle of Chitralis fleeing Afzal's brutal rule soon turned to a flood as the new Mirtar killed off as many of his numerous brothers and half-brothers as he could lay hands on. He feared they might try to unseat him (and almost certainly would if opportunity had arisen before their lives were stripped from them). But before the British-sponsored intervention could set out, agents appeared with information that the former Mirtar's brother Sher Afzul Khan had brought a force up from the south through the Swat Valley. Sher had long been exiled to Kabul for conspiring against Aman-ul-Mulk and now returned with the blessing of Amir Abdur Rahman, who wanted to see his own puppet on the throne of Chitral.

By some sleight of hand, Sher lured Afzal out of the fortress and shot him. The Chitralis switched their allegiance to Sher, but when weeks later, on hearing of his brother's death, Nizam began to march west to wrest his birthright from his uncle, many of Sher Afzul Khan's followers abandoned his cause. So it was that Harry returned to Chitral at the head of a small army of Nizam's followers, swollen by twelve hundred of Sher's turncoat troops.

Sher had no stomach for a proper fight, Harry wrote Durand. *He upped sticks and fled back to Kabul and the hopefully less than welcoming arms of our ally, the Amir Abdur Rahman Khan. Nizam-ul-Mulk has speedily restored order and stability and is happy to parade me about to wave the Union flag and distribute the good wishes of the Queen-Empress among the townspeople and those inhabitants of all the valleys hereabouts. I can happily report that we have again slammed shut the door leading to India in Russia's face.*

"I should have known that I spoke too soon."

Alfred Winner raised a pale eyebrow in question.

It was the first days of February 1895 and Harry was returned to England for his overdue leave… and as an invalid. Following a short convalescence at

Hadlicote, he had removed himself to rooms at the Albany Barracks to be in London. By the time of his long overdue leave, he had been acting as deputy-political for almost two years, and in that time the upheavals in Chitral had kept him fully occupied. He and Alfred were comfortably seated at an out of the way table in the Grill Room of the Café Royal in Regent Street. Harry was perhaps less comfortable than his old school chum and fellow Sudan campaigner due to his healing hip and thigh wounds, but enjoying the exchange of his army uniform for civilian clothing. Alfred was also enjoying some weeks' leave in town from the Royal Navy and his sprightly mood made a bright contrast to the appallingly cold February weather.

"In less than a year Nizam lay dead, assassinated by his adolescent brother Amir while they were on a hunting trip together. I blame myself, Alfred." Harry paused to shake his head sadly.

"How should it be your fault?"

"Nizam confided in me that he intended the removal of Amir before the youth could make trouble, which might well be the middle name of all Chitralis of noble birth. As he pointed out, the elimination of younger siblings is virtually a tradition among them. I prevailed on him to do no such thing, and persuaded him that the British authorities would not look favorably on his disposing of his brother. And Nizam paid heavily for listening to me and for his forbearance."

Harry broke off when a waiter deposited on the small table between them a large silver tray laden with the apparatus of afternoon tea: fragrant Darjeeling steaming from a teapot, milk jug, bowl and tongs for the sugar lumps, cups, saucers; small plates and silverware; a selection of tiny sandwiches and another of small fancy cakes. Alfred extinguished his Egyptian cigarette in the gilt ashtray. "Shall I be mother?" With typical Winneresque efficacy he picked up the milk jug without waiting for an answer and poured a small amount into each cup before taking the teapot and filling the cups. "One lump or two?"

"Don't you remember?" Harry smiled.

"Of course I do. I only wondered whether you had abandoned your irritating abstemiousness." He handed over the sugarless tea.

"Thank you, Alfred."

"So Nizam dead and…?" He raised the cup, took a sip, and made a noise of appreciation. "We have such dreadful stuff on board when we're at sea."

"Amir was impetuous and careless, not a happy combination. He expected me to send word to Gilgit seeking British approval of his bloody act, but I told him pretty sternly not to expect much sympathy. He was Chitral's fourth ruler in little more than two years and I was certain that Calcutta wouldn't tolerate the situation any longer. I had to keep him sweet, though, so I told him that the Viceroy so far away needed time to seek advice from his Empress to make such an important decision, when in fact I'd written warning Gilgit to expect serious trouble."

"Of the Russian kind?"

"Indeed, Alfred. I'd called him *kumbukht*—silly idiot—but Amir turned out to be a modicum more intelligent than I'd credited him. He suspected he might not receive recognition from the Viceroy, in fact possibly even retribution for his murderous act. I thought he'd appeal to the Russians for help but in fact he surprised us all by requesting aid from the ruler of Swat, Umra Khan. Amir never considered that his new ally was marching with three thousand Pathans and the intention of annexing Chitral to his own fiefdom. It was never an easy posting, but I now realized my own peril. I wrote to Gilgit where Major George Robertson had replaced Durand as the political. He might be an army doctor but he wasted no time in setting out with all the men he could muster, about four hundred troops. When he arrived in Chitral he removed Amir and replaced him by his twelve-year-old brother Shaja al-Mulk."

"So young?"

Harry took a swallow of his tea and gestured with the cup. "But a clever lad, so not such a bad move. But commandeering the fortress and moving his troops in there was an unfortunate decision on Robertson's part. I tried to dissuade him, although clearly it made strategic sense with the imminent threat of a siege, but it greatly offended the Chitralis. You see, to them the stronghold served as the royal palace, harem, and treasury and they viewed having European officers and their Sikh and Kashmiri troops running all over it as a deep humiliation. So we lost their support. Worse, many of them turned coat to aid the advancing enemy. I was blessed in my *pishkhidmat* Arshan who had the locals' ear and kept me abreast of their feelings."

"What's a pish-thing?"

"Ah… it's a personal servant to a chief or commander, and Arshan always held me to be his chief. I don't know what I would have done without his services." Harry did not enlarge for Alfred's benefit the extent of Arshan's personal services. Unlike Richard and Edward, Alfred remained innocent of his friends' sexual inclinations and his interruption of Harry's narrative made clear what he might have said had he known of them. A look of distaste crossed his narrow features. Harry swung his head around to follow Alfred's suddenly alert gaze.

"You wouldn't know Londoners are dying like flies from the effects of this wicked freeze when you see over-privileged dissolute youths like that, parading their haughty airs and prurient wit—humor, as they name it—in this place to be seen and that place to be heard. Really."

Alfred Winner's burst of indignation amused Harry as he sought to put names to the fashionably attired men making their way to a table halfway down the ornate Grill Room. "I think I recognize the older gentleman, he's the writer Oscar Wilde isn't he? But the others…"

"You're correct about Wilde, wearing the carnation in his buttonhole—his adoration of the bloom gives him away, as well as his towering size. I imagine he's all pumped up with boastful pride for the opening of his newest play next week."

"Ah yes, a long-standing acquaintance—you might remember him from boxing matches at school, John Douglas-Scott-Montagu?—has invited me to join his party for the opening night."

Alfred's shrug showed the name didn't register. "Bully for you, Harry, but I never pegged you as an aficionado of low comedy. Now the bumptious young dandy preceding Mr. Wilde is Max Beerbohm, a rising star of lampoonery and journalism, I understand." Alfred's sneering tone made these skills sound little better than those of a newspaper peddler. "At Wilde's side—and those who claim to know say always there like a limpet—is his little university friend Bosie." He gave a shudder. "Actually to my shame my namesake, Lord *Alfred* Douglas. In the train behind is the effete draughtsman Aubrey Beardsley. His drawings for *The Yellow Book* are as decadent as the corrupt vehicle in which they appear."

"With which, I take it, you are familiar?" Harry's grin teased as much as his words.

Alfred tensed and returned the look of fierce asperity so familiar to Harry from their days at The Lodge. Then he relaxed into a wry smile. "Well, I might admit to having had a browse, once. You know me well enough, Harry, that I'm not one to condemn something of which I have no knowledge."

"And well enough to remember how pompous you can sound—"

Alfred sniffed.

"—though I know you are not."

"Quite. In fact I confess I like his style. It's in what cultured people are calling Art Nouveau. You can tell they're cultured because they use French to describe a style that could be so much more simply stated as 'New Art.' Anyway, given time—Beardsley is so very young—he might even become a great artist, though one has to wonder, since he always appears to be fashionably at death's door. At his side, and looking like the image of the man he apes, even down to the velvet smoking jackets in unusual colors, is another writer, poet, and contributor to *The Yellow Book*, who also uses French words to describe himself, Richard Le Gallienne. Oh, and there is a face I saw only the other day, the rather thuggish looking adolescent is Aleister Crowley. He's an aspiring poet apparently, struggling to gain some acceptance, which is no doubt why he's trailing after Wilde, looking to pick up crumbs of wisdom."

Alfred's tone again left Harry in no doubt at all as to what he thought of Wilde, his acolytes, and his wisdom, but he barely took the words in because his eyes had alighted on a tall, slender youth almost hidden from view behind the bulk of Crowley's substantial shoulder. Recognition ran as a shiver right through to his extremities. It was surely Jolyon, who would be...? He calculated for a second. Nineteen. Might he be misled as to the youth's identity? Jo was only twelve the last time Harry had seen him and seven years makes a tremendous difference in a growing lad, not to mention the effect the awful loss of his parents must have wrought. But his ethereal beauty caught at Harry's breast and he was sure it was Jolyon. His heart went out to the boy.

General and Lady Langrish-Smith perished in the terrible cholera epidemic of '93 while he was obscured in the depths of the North-West Frontier Province. Harry only received the upsetting news in Chitral months later when a courier placed a letter in his hand from an aunt of Jolyon's. At such a distance there was nothing he could possibly do to help. He'd meant to write but somehow never gotten around to it, what with all the native unrest which seethed about the British at Chitral, as he'd been recounting to Alfred.

"Are they such bad fellows?"

Alfred returned his attention to the cake tray and selected a sticky looking confection. The creamy morsel disappeared in a single bite. He cleared his throat. "They're a bunch of degenerates, if you want my opinion, and Mr. Wilde's lifestyle has been attracting unwelcome attention of late—particularly from the father of young Bosie. Mind, I think the man's a total cad, so I suppose some of it must have rubbed off on his simpering son. Didn't you used to talk about him, Queensberry, when you were boxing?"

Harry nodded. Alfred's words aroused discomfort, although more in what he hadn't said than what he had. He determined to go over and make his introduction in the hope of having a word with Jolyon. He was certain it was Jolyon. In the meantime as much to cover his confusion at what Alfred seemed to be implying about Wilde's morals as to bring his friend up to date, Harry continued his story.

"Not only did Umra Khan ignore Robertson's demand to return to his own country, wily old Sher Afzul Khan reappeared as his ally. Whatever promises to share the spoils they made to each other, they would be bound to break after victory, but this didn't concern us, so much as the threat their substantial army now posed. We were promised that a British force was being mobilized to march north through Umra Khan's Pathan domains of Peshawar and boot his ass, but we had no clear picture of when it would reach us. The reconnaissance party of Kashmiris commanded by a captain sent out to assess Sher's position and strength was driven back with severe casualties and twenty-three dead. It was a terrible blow to morale.

"The siege began in earnest. Frankly, we were in a pickle. Including Roberts we were six British officers, a little less than four hundred native troops, and more than a hundred non-combatants, all to be fed. Fortunately, with the fortress hard against the river our water supply was assured. We constructed a covered walkway between the water tower and the bank to shield carriers from enemy attack. But we had food for a month at best, even on half rations, and we soon fished out the shir maheh, a sort of river trout. Further, the ammunition supply was low because the small contingent bringing ammunition and explosives from Gilgit, commanded by lieutenants Fowler and Evans, had fallen into Sher's hands. As a result of this disaster we had less than three hundred rounds per man.

"Although our stronghold was stout, copses of tall trees surrounded us and on the other side of the river the heights were ideal for snipers to fire down on us. It would have been prudent to demolish the mud-brick buildings which stood close to the fortress walls inside the pleasure garden because they gave cover to the enemy and made it hard for us to fire back at them. In particular, we were to have reason to lament not having destroyed the lovely summerhouse where once in another lifetime Mirtar Aman-ul-Mulk received Lockhart and his contingent, including me.

"After the first month, Umra Khan's force arrived and soon direct assaults began from sangars their sappers dug under cover of the mud buildings. There were several incendiary attacks, one so serious it almost brought down the gun tower nearest the summerhouse. I don't know why it was called that. You could never have placed a decent piece of artillery on its largely wooden flooring, and it was that of course which blazed up so merrily in the assault. Thanks to our plentiful water supply, we managed to douse the flames before the heat could bring down the stone walls. That would have left us entirely vulnerable. And then four nights later something odd began happening."

"In what way odd?"

"Revelry. From the summerhouse. The enemy began beating drums and playing pipes at full tilt, dancing and screaming. They kept up this din for several nights. And then a havildar—a native non-commissioned officer—swore he'd heard noises coming from under the earth. That's when the penny dropped and we realized what the bastards were up to."

べ☆゜

"A mine?"

"Yes, sahib. It must be." The Kashmiri havildar was insistent.

"They're hoping to distract from the sound of their digging with all that carousing," Harry offered.

"Of course." Major Robertson looked seriously alarmed through the grime and weariness, which they all shared. "And the Pathans have the means of bringing down the wall, Lieutenant. The Gilgit resupply column they captured was carrying explosives."

None of those precariously present atop the damaged gun tower needed him to elaborate. They stood in glum silence among the charred timbers. In the morning suspicion became certainty. By reaching down with long bamboo poles pressed to the ground it was possible to hear the scurrying and the sounds of a pick at work. "About twelve feet from the wall now, sahibs," a sepoy snapped out to the officers gathered anxiously on the walkway out of sight of the besiegers' snipers.

Robertson turned his eyes heavenward as if to read in the clouds the solution to this new horror. "I understand the usual measure is to dig a counter-mine. How long will that take?"

One of the subalterns coughed politely. "I don't think we can, sir. The enemy tunnel is too close to the wall. They would hear us digging. Wouldn't that force their hand? They'd bring up the explosives. Even at four yards the force of the blast so close would surely make a breach?"

"Captain Vane, you're looking thoughtful. You know this place best. Do you have a better idea?"

Harry was peering through a narrow loophole at the summerhouse, some twenty-five to thirty yards away. "That's where they're coming from," he said as much to himself as to the other officers. He straightened up and faced Robertson. "There's not a moment to lose in case they realize we've detected them and they blow up the mine in the hope they can bring down the wall from where they've reached. Really sir, there's nothing else for it. We must send out a party as soon as we can get organized, storm the summerhouse, and destroy the tunnel."

A stunned silence met Harry's words. And then, slowly, Robertson nodded his head.

When Arshan heard the plan on Harry's return to his cramped quarters his eyes took on an excited glint. "I knew we volunteer to command the attack, Haari."

Looking up from his preparations, Harry barked a laugh of denial. "You're not going along. It's a job for soldiers."

The Persian boy's expression turned from excitement to flashing anger in a second. "You will not leave me behind. Have I not already proved a warrior? Was I a mere desert djin at Lut-Dih?" The anger ebbed as suddenly as it blew up. Arshan cast his eyes down. "You need me with you, Haari."

"Dammit to Bombay and back, Arshan." Harry took him in his arms. "*I* volunteered to lead the sortie and so did the soldiers going with me. But *you* didn't volunteer—"

"You are pishkhidmat. I have to be at your side. You volunteer, I volunteer.

You know I fire a rifle well, Haari. You don't want me go, you should not volunteer as leader."

Arshan's practiced pout was usually guaranteed to win any argument, even more so when, with his head slightly lowered, he looked up demurely from under impossibly long, black eyelashes and dared flutter them.

"Imp!" Harry sighed. "I don't want to get you hurt, but…" He held up a hand to forestall further discussion. "I know better than to deny you what you will only go and do anyway." He straightened the arm still holding Arshan about the waist so he could look him in the eyes. "But this won't be easy. Some will die."

"As long as it is the Khan's filthy fucker Pathans and Kafirs." Arshan's eyes glittered with all the fiery spirit of his people and a hatred of those who abused him when he was a child and had done so with his brother Firuz.

At four o'clock that afternoon, with the shadows lengthening in advance of dusk, Harry mustered his not inconsiderable force at the stronghold's eastern gate: forty Sikhs and sixty Kashmiri soldiers, armed with Martini-Henry rifles. (Requests for some of the newest Lee-Metford .303 riles had fallen on deaf ears. It seemed the marvellous bolt-action weapon with eight- or ten-round magazines for extraordinarily rapid fire were needed at more crucial junctures of the Empire.) "Anyway, we will win this day with bayonets, not bullets," Harry told his men. The havildars carried their preferred pistols and sabers, as did Harry, although for when out riding he'd managed to obtain a cavalry carbine version of the Martini-Henry, its shorter length more useful in close combat. He kept Arshan close at his side as the gates were opened. The hinges, generously greased earlier, made no sound. Only the timbers creaked, but no louder than the honking of bar-headed geese, marbled teal, and tufted ducks on the river, the twittering of woodcocks and the haunting calls of snow pigeons settling to roost in the garden trees for the night.

A peace we shall soon shatter.

The plan called for no complicated tactics. The assault force sallied out, raced around the corner of the gun tower, and made straight across the narrowest part of the pleasure garden for the summerhouse. The low, enclosing garden wall posed no problem since several decorative openings pierced its length, allowing entry and egress. In the lead, Harry concentrated on reaching the nearest gap and getting through it before the enemy knew they were under attack. He was aware of Arshan's presence at his side as if an umbilical cord joined them, but then he put aside worries for the boy. There was no time for sentiment or fear for another's safety.

At the last second before they reached the summerhouse a jezailchi flung open a small window just above head height and fired. The weapon's bark was stunningly loud at such close range and it heralded a fusillade of shots. A Sikh running beside Harry stumbled and fell under the onslaught of primitive musketry. And then the troops divided, Sikhs to the front, Kashmiris to the rear of the house. Within seconds of leaving the shelter of the fort, the assault party was inside the building.

Harry loosed two shots from his carbine and the noise crashed through the confines. At close quarters, the long jezail barrels were a hindrance to the Pathans, and once discharged, they were little more use as clubs. A great milling of the enemy, terrified by the surprise attack, tried to flee out the back. Sikh bayonets carved a murderous path through those jammed in the rear hallway. Pathans fell bloodily and those who made it outside died on the kukris and bayonets of the waiting Kashmiris. The occupants trapped inside perished with their backs in ribbons, those fleeing out at the rear took the flashing blades in chest and stomach, and the shouts and screams rang off mud wall and tree trunk.

"Havildar Ranjit! Take twenty men and position yourselves to fight off any counter-attack." Harry thrust out his arm in the direction farther along the riverbank where Sher and Umra Khan had their encampments. As soon as he had seen Ranjit relay his orders and gather his small defensive force, Harry and the others began frantically searching for the mine's entrance. Arshan spotted it first, and laughed, a harsh and humorless sound.

"Haari, we near fell into it."

He was right. The dig started just outside the garden wall. With rifles all pointed down at the darkness like the strakes of a yet to be woven wicker basket, the Sikhs immediately circled its ragged opening. The screams and sound of gunfire must have alarmed the tunnelers. Abruptly, like burrowing creatures frightened into the open with the devil at their heels, several dirty-faced men began to struggle up, blinking at the late daylight. As they emerged, one after the other in a panic, the eager Sikhs bayoneted them to death.

"Stop!" Harry piled into the yelling Sikhs, with Arshan repeating his orders, in a desperate attempt to stop the killing. "Save these two."

And two of the twenty odd were all that was left of the subterranean moles. With evident reluctance, the Sikh havildar ordered his men to bind the two petrified survivors. "They deserve the steel, sahib."

"That they do, but Major Robertson wants some prisoners taken back for interrogation."

"Now he's happy." Arshan smiled. "He will have more enjoyment in the torture than in the bayoneting."

The Kashmiri officer ran up. "Left-tenant Haarivan sahib. We find the splosiff fulminant. All safe, sahib."

A short line of soldiers ran out from the summerhouse carrying wooden boxes bearing familiar British markings in their arms. In moments the tunnel mouth was packed, a fuse train laid, and fire set to it. The victorious assault party stood around like children at a fireworks show. The resulting detonation was so violent it not only collapsed the mine workings, it made the garden wall above sag and fall apart. The force of the blast bowled Harry over. He had been stood to one side but the lash of flame singed the Sikhs' beards and the turbans of those in its path.

Harry looked around and found Arshan lying some feet away, dazed, his pale skin blackened, but otherwise unharmed and inclined to a degree of mirth that suggested a possible concussion. Harry didn't feel at all like laughing. They'd accomplished the easy part. Now the troops faced a return to the fortress surely in the teeth of fierce resistance from Pathan warriors with vengence on their minds.

Even as he shouted out a recall-and-concentrate order, the enemy opened up with a withering fire from the protection of the forest behind, from the pleasure buildings in the garden, and the sangars which zigzagged between them. More men ran around the far west corner of the fort and quickly took up position on the flank. Fortunately, covering fire from up on the walls largely neutralized this threat, but the British soldiers still had to run the gauntlet through a storm of lead coming from the east through the gardens.

The Sikhs and Kashmiris ran as a single compact unit, firing their rifles from the hip. They made for the East Gate from whence only minutes ago they had issued. Harry heard Arshan's panting breath and then his sharp yell. The boy's feet faltered.

"Arshan!"

Harry wheeled and fell out of the formation. Arshan lay on the ground, rifle outflung. Harry saw blood gushing from an ugly wound on his upper arm, which instantly stained his blouse in carmine. In a second, Harry knelt down beside him.

"Here, let me take your weight." He thought the boy more bewildered by the force of the bullet's strike than incapacitated by his injury. He slid one arm under Arshan's and raised him up to a sitting position. Immediately, Arshan struggled to help himself to his feet. Which was when a shard of Pathan lead sliced clean through Harry's left shoulder.

"Oh fuck!"

He felt the impact as one punch but he knew the exit wound had opened up the back of his shirt and battle dress tunic. Instantly, Arshan switched positions so they could both help each other. Harry, senses beginning to swim, took some comfort from seeing the last of his men scurrying through the gate ahead, their retreat covered by continuous volleys from the wall and ruined gun tower. But wounded and in the face of unyielding musket fire, the distance looked too much to cover. Already, blood-lusting Pathans were closing in to cut off their path to safety.

"Haari, we must go back to the summerhouse."

"No! That way is certain death." He raised the carbine in his uninjured arm—thank God his right—and aimed loosely at the oncoming foe. It was painful work to chamber subsequent bullets, but even wounded he could outgun the ancient jezails of the Pathans, which needed the better part of half a minute to reload. He fired off two more shots, aware that he would not have the strength or dexterity to reload again, and his pistol was still in its buttoned down holster. It might as well have been on the moon.

"Come, Arshan. Now!"

Each holding the other, tottering like a pair of drunks after graduation and the passing out parade at Sandhurst, they staggered toward the gate. Harry could see fear on the faces of the two soldiers keeping it open. They shouted encouragement. Then a figure ran out between the men. The fulminating Kashmiri havildar—finder of splosiffs—raced across the grass toward them. He jinked left and right to throw off the enemy's aim.

"Come, sahib!"

With his help, Harry and Arshan made their way to the fortress, a painfully slow step at a time. Harry could feel the slick, warm blood running down his chest and back from the shoulder wound. His vision blurred and his mind swam from the loss, so he hardly felt the impact of a second shot. Its force would have thrown him to the ground were it not for Arshan, himself in a bad way, on his right and the havildar on the left holding him at the waist to avoid the injured shoulder. In seconds, blood bloomed just in front of the havildar's grip, swiftly soaking the area around Harry's left hip where the ball had struck.

Five more wobbly steps. The damned grass gripped his boots. It held him back. The world blazed with rifle fire.

And then everything went black.

CHAPTER 15 | *Café Royal, London, February 1895*

"TO CUT THROUGH a long story, I led a force of men out and we took the summerhouse, discovered the tunnel entrance, and used the captured explosives to destroy it. Of the hundred men, we lost eight in exchange for forty or more of our foemen."

Alfred Winner signaled a waiter. "Why do I think you're being just a tiny bit modest, Harry?"

"I was only doing my job."

"I will take a good malt. You, Harry?"

"The same. Thank you, Alfred."

As the waiter departed on his mission, encumbered by the tea things, Alfred smiled, a pursed lip affair that suggested he didn't entirely believe Harry. "I saw in the Army Gazette that no less a personage than Colonel John French mentioned your exploits. Not bad to have the Army's Assistant Adjutant-General praising you—did you actually meet the man in India?"

"Not out there, and only at a distance when he was with us as Commander of Cavalry on the march across the Bayuda Desert for Khartoum in '85. And he was Commander of Cavalry in India while I was on my travels, so I suppose he must have known of me, but anyway—"

"And I saw a newspaper headline which described you as The Hero of Chitral," Alfred swept on, undeterred by Harry's embarrassed modesty. "Another one used the word 'Savior,' although I confess I never thought much of your ability to walk on water, and indeed I recall in the Bayuda you had a low opinion of it apart from its usefulness in washing—"

"Oh that's all utter rot. Rubbish. Newspapermen are never to be trusted, as you well know. The real heroes were Colonel Kelly coming to our relief from Gilgit and General Low who forced the Malakand Pass and approached up the Swat Valley in Umra Khan's rear.

"But your wounds?"

"Were of less consequence than first supposed."

Harry glanced anxiously across at Oscar Wilde's companions, fearing that during his recital they might have decided to go on elsewhere—he didn't want to miss the opportunity to speak with Jolyon—but they seemed settled in for the time being and were well into several bottles of champagne.

Their waiter sashayed between the crowded tables, balancing on his tray two Edinburgh Stewart crystal tumblers and a mid-sized decanter of pale gold single-malt whisky. Harry waited until he had poured them a generous measure each before continuing his tale. "Of course, trapped as we were, we didn't know what progress the two British forces racing to our relief from the south and from the east were making."

"The race made headlines like the ones when we were tearing up the Nile to the relief of Khartoum. I read several newspaper reports when my ship docked at Gibraltar. Everyone was screaming at the government not to allow another Khartoum through dilatoriness. Gordon's murder there in the Sudan was the ill wind which blew you some good."

"I suppose. I know how Gordon must have felt at the end. We were very low in Chitral, reduced by sniper fire and next to no food. And of course, after getting stupidly shot I was no more use to anyone than a blunt sickle in a wheat field. But then, you know what it's like. You suffered more on the Nile because your arm was shattered. The bullet that struck my shoulder took a chunk out of the upper arm bone but missed my collarbone. Similarly, the ball that struck my hip chipped the edge of my pelvis, but did more damage to the flesh. An inch this way or that with either and I would have been a complete mess. It was painful and I lost a lot of blood, but our brave doctor had hoarded his medicines—"

"When we met out on Regent Street," Alfred broke in, "I noticed you were still limping, so I suspect the injuries were more severe than you're letting on. Damned toff! I fail to understand how that upper lip of yours doesn't suffer from cramp from being so stiff."

Harry grinned amiably. "Arshan, my boy, recovered from his injury much more quickly with the strength of youth, and looked after me like a mother hen. And then quite suddenly it was over. Kelly's troops braved hostile terrain and several forces of heavily armed Pathans. Their relief march from Gilgit was truly epic. Umra Khan could see the writing on the wall of his ambition. With Kelly to the east and Low with Younghusband coming up behind him, and fearing to be caught in a British pincer movement, Umra Khan retreated. He made a stand with some twelve thousand Pathan warriors at the Malakand Pass, which leads into the Swat valley and the route to Chitral. But Khan faced some of our best infantry. Hundreds of his men were slaughtered. The man himself escaped into Afghanistan.

"He was honorable in one respect, though. He freed the two subalterns he'd captured along with all that ammo and explosives. It seems he held Fowler and Evans in relative comfort at his fort at Barwa in the Panjkora Valley. Sher was less lucky. In his wretched life he'd made many enemies among his own kind and when some foes caught him they handed him over to us… well, not us in Chitral, and he was exiled to India. He's still there, bitterly accusing Umra Khan of having misled and cheated him before fleeing the field.

"As I was being shipped home I heard about the arguments as to whether we should annex Chitral as we did Hunza and have a permanent garrison there in case the Russians decided to try their luck again, as well as keeping the local tribes under the thumb."

"Did I read only the other day a decision has been taken?"

"In the sense that a road will be built from Peshawar to Chitral and as a safeguard for the Resident and small garrison stationed there, a fort is to be built at the Malakand Pass to safeguard the Swat route, and another fort eight miles up the valley at Chakdara on the crossing-point of the Swat River. Anyway, enough of that. Now I am here, at least for some months of leave to recuperate."

"And what of your, what did you call him, your pishkhidmat?"

Harry faced Alfred with a neutral expression, but inwardly the probing question left him feeling sad. He shrugged in an unconcerned manner. "Oh, these youngsters find a new officer to serve easily enough. Plenty of choice at Rawul Pindee. Arshan's probably already found a new master."

No point mourning for a loss that can't be helped. At least I persuaded General MacGregor to take him under his Intelligence wing as a pundit.

๛๚๛

Alfred Winner left for a date with some lady friend: drinks before a theater performance; a supper at Rules in Maiden Lane to follow, very much what Harry anticipated in a few days when he joined friends for the opening night of Mr. Oscar Wilde's latest offering. They parted company with promises to catch up again. Alfred happily accepted an open invitation to Hadlicote the minute the extreme weather broke and a promise of spring clothed the trees in pale buds.

With a degree of nervousness not becoming the Hero of Chitral, Harry strolled as nonchalantly as his limp allowed between boisterous groups of Café Royal patrons to the table where Alfred's dissolute debauchees were polishing off yet another jeroboam of Reims' finest Champagne Hau & Co. "More for the delightful frivolity of its label," chimed Oscar Wilde on Harry's introducing himself to the party. He waved the bottle to display the label's design, which Harry considered to be more of the Pre-Raphaelite school than the *haute moderne* Art Nouveau. Unlike Alfred, Harry had no fear of French usage. The big bottle was too heavy for Wilde to keep aloft for more than a second and he thumped it down with sufficient force to shake the others' glasses.

"Bosie, dear boy, pour our hero a glass… well then get a waiter to bring one. Good heavens. Youth, wasted you know on the young. I am acquainted with your elder sibling, my dear Smythe-Vane… may I call you Harry? We do so try to avoid stuffiness. I recall a delightful evening in his company when it must be said we consumed freely. He mentioned his young sibling, but I'm sure he called you by another first name than Harry…"

Tea and malt rose into Harry's gorge, appalled that his stupid brother had let slip his real given name, the appellation no one outside immediate family knew, and which even they dared not call him or risk his rare temper. Was Wilde about to reveal it?

"Hmm, in any case, I must say, Harry, that of the two *frères* you are by far the most comely."

"Er, thank you, Mr. Wilde."

"No stuffiness! Oscar, dear boy, please. I am so sorry I'm unable to introduce the most interesting of my happy band, but Richard Le Gallienne had to dash to some affair—"

"Of the heart," Beerbohm quipped.

"—a reading of his English Poems, I believe, Max. Have you read his *Robert Louis Stevenson: An Elegy and Other Poems*?" Wilde asked Harry.

"With a title so long, has anyone?" Bosie's sulky tone of voice immediately put Harry's back out of joint… or perhaps his hip was hurting him.

"I… no, I'm afraid I haven't. I shall certainly look out his work." Harry took a chair, still feeling weak from the ridiculous phobia of almost having his name revealed in public.

He accepted the greetings of the others around the table. When it came to Jolyon's turn to be introduced, the boy didn't acknowledge him, which curbed Harry's intent to say how delighted he was to see him again, and so they exchanged a cursory greeting and the handshake of strangers. But then, were they not strangers?

Jolyon was still a slender, well-formed young man of enormous attractiveness, but he no longer resembled the boy-cadet who knocked at his father's den door and stood so correctly to attention, and definitely not the youngster who so unaffectedly hugged his (admittedly hopeless) godfather. He was folded carelessly but elegantly into the curves of his chair, one long leg draped across the armrest. Overlong fair hair fell artfully across his tall brow and seemed to float a fraction of a second after each slight head movement. Harry suspected he pomaded it. And Harry did not approve of the affected way he held his long cigarette holder. Neither did he like his somewhat flushed appearance, presumably from the quantity of alcohol he'd already consumed.

He was seated across the table from Harry, next to the decorous Lord Alfred Douglas, who offered a handshake so limp it amounted to a studied insult. Beardsley, with his fashionable center-parted hair cut in an oddly feminine fringe, his long face, long nose, and even longer, narrow hands, looked like a fidgety cadaver. Harry recognized the symptoms of consumption and equally that his presence at the table made Beardsley uneasy, though he knew not why. Crowley acted supremely uninterested and—other than Oscar Wilde—only Max Beerbohm with his clever eyes expressed any enthusiasm to engage Harry in conversation.

"I think it supremely cruel of you," he drawled, "not to sport your medal."

"Oh, Max. You mustn't tease the gallant… captain, isn't it?" Wilde lowered the shelf of his brow at Beerbohm in gentle reproof. "I'm sure we should all be dazzled at the 'Defense of Chitral' gong…" he included Harry in his roving gaze, "so very few to receive such a high honor, but true heroes do not need to parade baubles."

165

"What was it for?" Lord Douglas looked supremely uninterested in the answer and Harry felt no need, nor whish, to educate him.

A waiter placed a champagne saucer in front of Harry and filled it to the foaming brim. Harry raised the bowl to salute the table. "To the opening of your new play, sir," he said to Wilde, who dipped his head graciously.

"We're most *earnest* in our anticipation of the opening night," Lord Douglas drawled. Harry disliked the way he smirked at his own pun and the way Jolyon reached across the small gap between their seats to pat Douglas on his shoulder and chortle quietly at the unfunny joke. Even more, he hated the irritable manner in which Douglas threw off the importuning hand with a faint hiss, which Jolyon reflected in mute embarrassment and a curling up of his arms and legs. Harry guessed there wasn't much love lost there, reinforced whenever Wilde said something nice to Jolyon and Douglas added a faint scowl to the already sullen set of his face. He was a picture of spoiled brat. Harry couldn't decide whether he was a callow youth attempting the airs of someone much older or a roué trying to shed years to keep in with a younger set.

"I had a dream," Douglas announced. "I dreamed that some drunken lout in the audience threw something at you, Oscar." He lifted himself slightly from the back of his chair and raised his voice in a pained cadence. "On taking your righteous bow as well."

If the taunt was intended to rile Wilde, it failed and his voice boomed out loudly enough for several tables to hear. "How apt, dear boy. Shall I stand there, unafraid before my public and declaim: 'Our revels now are ended. These our actors, as I foretold you, were all spirits, and are melted into air, into thin air: and like the baseless fabric of this vision, the cloud-cappéd towers, the gorgeous palaces, the solemn temples, the great globe itself, yea, all which it inherit, shall dissolve, and, like this insubstantial pageant faded, leave not a rack behind. We are such stuff as dreams are made on; and our little life is rounded with a sleep'?"

Max Beerbohm slow-hand clapped. "Bravo, Oscar. You would make a fine Prospero if ever you learned to pace your prose."

"Why on earth should I wish to do that? I am a weaver of chimera, not a speaker of the words I place in the mouths of players. And a dreamer is one who can only find his way by moonlight, and his punishment is that he sees the dawn before the rest of the world."

"I don't know, Oscar, that seeing the sun rise is your only forfeiture," Beerbohm came back snappily. "I know no man of genius who hasn't paid, in some affliction or defect either physical or spiritual, for what the gods have given him."

"I'm delighted that you consider me a genius, Max. Pray inform his lordship." Wilde waved a lazy hand at Douglas. "I have nothing to display but my genius, but by dawn Bosie hears whatever I say only as plain words."

"That's because I need my sleep Oscar," Douglas said in a lackadaisical voice. "The older you get the less sleep you need, but we young panther cubs, we need our slumber... unless," and he turned a sneer in Jolyon's direction, "you're like Langrish-Smith; just really too enthusiastically energetic at all hours."

Harry didn't understand the barb, but he did see Jolyon flinch at Douglas's poison. Jolyon regarded Harry with guarded eyes, warning him off saying anything in response.

Douglas turned to Harry and ostentatiously folded one leg over the other, smoothing the material of his Oxford bags as he did so. "Jolly is a Langrish-Smith and you are a Smythe-Vane... Smith and Smythe, Smythe and Smith. Are you chaps related by any chance?"

Harry ignored the alarmed glance Jolyon gave him from under his long lashes. "No, Lord Alfred. We are not related," he answered honestly, and saw Jo settle back with a faint look of relief in his eyes. *Why is he denying me? Perhaps he's ashamed of a "hero" among these... friends.*

Beardsley placed a long etiolated hand in front of his mouth and yawned theatrically. "Well I am determined to make an early night of it for once," he said, continuing the previous thread of the conversation.

"Not before you show Captain Smythe-Vane your latest sketch, Aubrey." Aleister Crowley was leaning forward rather in the manner of an eager bull terrier to address the artist, who seemed suddenly even more ill at ease.

"Are you sure the Café Royal is ready for the epiphany of the yellowest of *jaune* imagery?" Beerbohm twinkled all around.

"It's only a rough sketch at the moment. I have yet to accomplish the line work."

"Don't be shy Aubrey," Wilde intoned jocularly. "Modesty doesn't become you, and I am quite tumescent to see again your sketch." He smiled broadly at Harry. "While you have been defending the Empress's frontiers against ruminant Russian bears and punacious Pathans I am afraid we have been playing here in London. So you will have missed seeing Aubrey's magnificent drawings for the English folio of my tragedy, *Salome*. They are quite wonderful, but more restrained than the drawings Aubrey has been toiling at recently."

Beardsley reached down beside his seat and brought up a small portfolio, which he proceeded to unfasten. He laid it on the table and swiveled it around so Harry had a clear view of the pencil drawing lying on top of several sheets of cartridge paper. Harry was aware of the company's eyes on him. An expectant hush fell over them.

"It's the Lacedaemonian Ambassadors," Beardsley said quietly into the silence.

Harry stared, wondering whether he'd been lured into being the butt of a sophisticate's joke. The drawing depicted three naked men, one in front less than half the height of the two behind. They were shown as if walking from right to left and they sported massive foreskin-retracted erections. The dwarf figure's monumental phallus was so enormous he held it under the bulbous crown in outstretched hands with his nose pushed against the tip as though testing the scent of a giant plum. The other figures boasted endowments of more modest scale. The thinner man's was proportionately slender, though it extended upward sufficiently to reach the underside of his pectoral muscles, while the larger man's was brutally thick in girth and reached halfway to his chest. The dwarf went barefoot and wore an elaborate Turkic headdress; the middle figure had the piled up ringlets of a Regency dandy; the third man's hairstyle resembled that of an ancient Greek, which seemed to a stunned Harry to be the only thing that suggested Lacedaemonia. The feet of the two men at the rear were tucked into frilly-fancy boots. The drawing was at once brutal, decadently elegant, grotesquely masculine, utterly effeminate.

"It… they… are impressive."

Harry's words provoked an explosion of mirth from Lord Douglas and the Crowley creature, to which Jolyon joined in, to Harry's disappointment. It seemed whatever Douglas did, Jo would follow, only to receive a put-down, which promptly occurred.

"What are you laughing at, Langrish-Smith? You're too young to understand the perspicacious humor of our Captain Harry, Hero of Chitral."

"Bosie, be nice," Wilde gently scolded Douglas. "Harry is our guest and

Jolyon has many fine qualities, almost as many as you, but a coarse sense of humor is not among them, I'm pleased to say."

Jolyon's expression mirrored Wilde's words, flattered at fine qualities, soured at not having as many as Douglas, pleased again at not being found rude.

Good god! The poor boy is completely smitten by Oscar Wilde. Harry recalled Alfred Winner's comments about Oscar and Bosie, the underlying disapproval at their close relationship, and suddenly understood Douglas's attitude toward Jolyon. *He's jealous!*

Oscar leaned across and spoke to Harry in an aside. "It gives me pleasure to be with those who are young, bright, happy, careless, and free. I do not like the sensible and I do not like the old… but the young can be so wearing at times." He simpered indulgently at Bosie and Jolyon.

Shortly after the revelation of Beardsley's Ambassadors the party broke up: Oscar Wilde and Lord Alfred Douglas to the theater to attend a dress rehearsal of *Importance*, as they referred to the new play; Beardsley to some arcane function, to which Crowley wanted to accompany the draughtsman. When Jolyon made to leave with Wilde, the great man gently disentangled him. "Do you join us for supper at the Florence Restaurant in Rupert Street, dear boy?" And he swept off with Douglas clamped to his side. The catamite's glance back held a sour look for Jolyon.

They stood awkwardly. Harry suddenly felt both sensible and old. Perhaps it was the setback of his injuries, but his twenty-nine years sat heavily on his shoulders as he looked at Jolyon, almost ten years younger, and from a different world it now seemed. What should he say? Jolyon shuffled his feet, but he didn't immediately leave.

"Could we have a little chat? Perhaps you can tell me why you pretended not to know me?"

The boy wrinkled his nose at an imaginary smell. "What's to say? You weren't around when my mater and pater passed away. I would've kicked the proverbial bucket too, only I was at Eton and the air out at Windsor is fresher than in London."

"I… I was trapped in India, Jo. I couldn't desert my post."

"And that's it. You're Army. You don't fit with my friends. They are cultured—"

"They are leading you astray."

"You don't understand. I knew the minute I saw you walk over that you'd never understand. You only know war and killing and brutal things. Philistine things. You can't know how beautiful Oscar is."

"Jo, you're acting like a child—"

It was a mistake to say it, and Harry knew so the second the words slipped out.

"Jo, please. Come back."

But Jolyon strode off toward the front hall and Regent Street.

Harry stared after his retreating figure and thought by his hunched shoulders that he seemed forlorn. No, that's how *he* felt. Jolyon was still a minor, at least for another year, but he was under the legal jurisdiction of his aunt. It looked like the little boy who had adored him had grown into something quite different.

Dissolute, Alfred said.

CHAPTER 16 | *London, February 14, 1895*

VALENTINE'S DAY fell on a Thursday, perhaps a portentous day for the opening night of a new Oscar Wilde play. It was also far too cold to be waiting for a hansom cab, so Harry arranged for Corporal Timms, the Albany Street gate duty porter that night, to hail one. When the weather turned foul before Christmas Harry thanked his foresight in having purchased a heavy-duty ankle-length greatcoat with a thick fur collar and a matching dark gray top hat. He bemoaned that evening fashion forbade the wearing of a country-style deerstalker with ear muffs and took scant comfort in thinking that temperatures on the heights of the Hindu Kush were far worse. He felt about as warm as was possible when the trooper the corporal sent to his rooms informed him his cab waited at the main gate.

A quietly spitting brazier in a corner made the guardhouse feel cozy. "What's the temperature, Timms?"

The corporal glanced through the frosty window and squinted at a large thermometer hanging from the nearest brick pillar of the gateway. "Hmm, cold enough to freeze the balls off a brass monkey, sir."

"That's not particularly helpful, Corporal Timms," Harry pointed out with a smile.

"It's reading minus seven, sir."

Harry worked it out. "My God, that's almost forty degrees of frost."

"Very fresh sir. What our French friends would call minus twenty-two degrees centigrade," Timms added with a touch of pride in his knowledge. "But last Friday was worse, near on fifty degrees of frost. Is it true the edges of the Thames have frozen, sir?"

"So I've heard, and thousands have been skating in Hyde Park on The Serpentine. I keep asking myself why the cold in England is so much worse in feeling than it is in the Hindu Kush, where believe me it gets far colder than this. Still, it isn't so much the cold as the fact we've had this freezing weather for almost two months now. I pity the poor without any means of keeping warm, dying by the hundreds every week."

"I'm not much for postings abroad, meself, but right now Egypt or India sounds right welcoming." Timms rubbed his hands briskly. "Well, sir, if I might dare to say, you do look the right toff tonight, and that's a very fancy swagger stick."

Harry raised the dark ebony cane so its golden head glowed in the brazier's light. "Thank you. I found it in the market on Sudder Street in Rawul Pindee. The Punjabi who sold it to me for a frightening price assured me the head was made for Mirtar Saif-ul-Mulk Nasir, the ruler of Chitral."

"Very grand, I'm sure, sir."

"No, not really, Corporal. It's a complete fake actually. You see I know the prince quite well, and he's far too young to be wielding a cane, but it pricked my funny bone, so I paid the… princely sum."

"Well, sir, your conveyance awaits out there on the street, sir. Got a nice thick rug the cabbie has, I seen, to keep your knees warm. And I'm sure the theater will be well heated."

"I do hope so, Timms. Well, I'll be off."

Harry acknowledged the corporal's nod—no salute since Harry was not in uniform—by lifting the brim of his top hat with the cane, or swagger stick as Timms preferred. He left the guardhouse like a train pulling out of Paddington station in a great puff of steam from his breath on the frozen air.

"Colder than a whore's heart, it is, sir," the cab driver greeted him cheerily. He held one of the doors for him and Harry stepped up to settle on the narrow seat. The cabbie held up the advertised blanket. Harry knew well enough how smelly the travelers' rugs offered to passengers in hansom cabs could be, but he accepted it and just hoped the severe cold would mitigate its effusions, which would hardly endear himself to his fellow theatergoers if the odor transferred to his clothing.

The driver lowered the door and went back to his Arctic post on the rear step-seat. The vehicle dipped on its springs when he climbed up. "Giddyup!" he called to the horse, and they were off. Harry's breath soon clouded the front and side windows so he used the cuff of his coat to clear a patch, stared out idly at the passing houses and thought about the evening ahead. Thanks to parental-stroke-military-stroke-school connections, Harry was an invited guest of a friend who'd been endowed with a ridiculously long string of names: John Walter Edward Douglas-Scott-Montagu. Monty, as his close friends called him, had taken a private box in the St. James's Theatre's dress circle to celebrate his election to Parliament for the New Forest constituency. One day Monty would succeed his father as the 2nd Baron Montagu of Beaulieu and be forced from the House of Commons to take his place in the House of Lords.

The cab ran quickly down Albany Street and crossed Marylebone Road onto Great Portland Street. The driver wheeled to the right onto Mortimer Street and two minutes later they were in the evening theater traffic, every vehicle headed south on Regent Street. Harry cleared his patch on the glass again in time to see the Café Royal's portal slide past his view.

Will Jo be there tonight? Bound to be, surely…

The cab joined the chaos of Piccadilly Circus. He took out his watch and saw there was plenty of time. After much twisting and turning, the driver disentangled them from the Circus and gained a walking speed down Lower Regent Street. A right onto Charles Street and around the edge of St. James's Square brought them onto King Street. In the narrow confines all was a confusion of hansoms, four-wheelers, and jostling pedestrians.

At the overhead knock, Harry twisted his head to look up. The driver raised the panel to shout down over the riot of noise. "Best if I let you out here, sir. It looks like the bloomin' Siege of Khartoum down there."

Harry peered through the front panel window, wiped a spot clean. The man was right. The theater was only just visible above the throng. He handed up the fare and a good tip, thanked the driver, pushed the blanket aside and the door up, and alighted. He thought the cabbie's reference to Khartoum quite apt. Duke Street opposite St. James's Theatre looked like a Dervish redoubt packed with screaming fanatics. He even fancied the faces pressed at the front resembled those of crazed Baqqara preparing to assault a zareba, only without Dervish matchlocks. Noise of an indescribable volume pulsated in the confined junction of streets. The policemen struggling to keep the excited crowd back appeared utterly harassed. They formed a line, arms locked, so the crush of elegant broughams and closed-top landaus could drop their owners and families without interference, and the theatergoers arriving on foot could reach their destination. The façade of St. James's Theatre—identifiable by its six Roman-Ionic columns and the name of George Alexander, the famous actor-manager, emblazoned across its marquee—acted like a beacon under the glare of several lens-focused electrical lights. It glowed white-yellow against the star-swept indigo sky.

Harry made his way along the sidewalk. He was unsure whether trudging through the mire of sludge made by thousands of feet tramping the ice was better than risking what earlier in the day would surely have been a lethal skating rink. After much persistent entreaty he reached through the crowd to the steps. All of the front doors stood open and packed. Members of the great and good—secretaries of state, parliamentarians, peers of the realm, senior ecclesiastics—jostled shoulders with actors, writers, academics, dramaturgists, critics, enthusiasts, and Harry Smythe-Vane.

"My, but there are enough fantods on show tonight to warm Hades!" one lady in the press of people filling the entrances remarked in brittle irritation.

Montagu's telegram had advised Harry to use the two central doorways for the boxes, which was fortunate, since he could see the left and right entrances for the upper galleries and stalls were jammed solid.

Inside the elaborate foyer a large painting of Venus emerging from a shell occupied a large section of wall opposite the ticket box (closed, since all first-night tickets were by prior subscription). This edifice resembled an elegant cabinet decorated with blue and white ornaments that matched the gorgeously costumed footmen, who politely checked invitations, handed out program playbills, and directed patrons over rich and costly rugs toward the upper level.

The grand staircase of Sienna marble set between brass standards on either side of the bannisters was itself covered by thick-pile Indian carpet, which helped to mute the cacophony of hundreds of conversations to a comfortable burble. At the top, printed tapestries draped on the walls of the crush bar did their work to keep echoes down. To the left of the staircase several valets took overcoats from the thronging patrons. Harry stood in the line and when he reached the counter he thanked the young man who relieved him of his heavy greatcoat, top hat, and exotic cane. In return, the liveried man handed him a small round token inscribed with a number. He pocketed it and pushed his way into the main area of the crush bar, resplendent with mirrors reflecting the flushed faces of London's elite, expectant of an evening's entertainment and abuzz with excitement at the prospect of the play which "those in the know" claimed to be Mr. Wilde's masterpiece. He looked around in hopes of spotting his host and almost immediately saw him and his party gathered beside a heavily brocaded curtain partially concealing a well-lit passage behind.

"Harry."

"Monty."

Montagu took Harry's hand and smiled broadly. "I'm happy to see you walking about so much more freely than a fortnight ago."

"I'm well on the mend, thank you."

"But it's so cold out that not even a politician dare to touch it." The joke, at his own expense, reflected his status as a new parliamentarian. "But you really do seem hale enough. Mind, getting through that scrabble down there would warm up anyone. So I am pleased that you managed to fight your way through without too many casualties and found us. Your first time at St. James's?"

"It is."

Montagu inclined his head to indicate the passage behind them. "This is about the best place for rendezvous. That leads around to a suite and box fitted up specially for the Prince of Wales." He lowered his voice conspiratorially. "And where Bertie can entertain his latest amour away from his mother and Alexandra's disapproval. La Bernhardt perhaps, who it is said showed Lillie Langtry the scullery door."

"Heavens, Monty, I let you out of my sight to go and win a war for a few months and you turn into a proficient London gossipmonger. Is this what being elected to the House of Commons does for you?"

Harry smiled fondly at his friend. At twenty-eight Montagu was six months Harry's junior and—sudden penchant for society tittle-tattle apart—a refreshingly straightforward man. As Harry knew, after Oxford he went to work for a year in the sheds of the London and South Western Railway to become a practical engineer. He had the peachy-florid complexion often associated with English country gentlemen who are out in the fresh air a lot and a no-nonsense attitude to go with it. His father Henry Douglas-Scott-Montagu (as a boy Montagu boasted that he had a round half-dozen names to his father's meager four) was a friend of Harry's father, and so they had known each other since childhood. But it was partaking in boxing and cricket matches between rivals Eton College, where Montagu was educated, and Harry's Benthenham College which cemented their friendship, though this in itself was of the very British kind which continued more through mutual absence than from intimacy or regularity of meeting.

Harry had just finished making or renewing his acquaintance with the several ladies and gentlemen of Montagu's jovial gathering when a sudden rise in the hubbub announced the celebrated playwright's immanence. Oscar Wilde appeared from the top of the grand staircase like a rising colossus amid his entourage, an oversize hothouse rose between several sharply dressed thorns. Harry immediately saw Jolyon but not, strangely, Lord Alfred Douglas. He later learned that the spoiled aristo-brat was vacationing in Algiers, almost certainly funded from Wilde's capacious pocket, even though he thought it must surely be a decided snub to be absent for the opening night.

Harry prayed that Jolyon was a replacement adornment and not Wilde's catamite, for it seemed that in the absence of his favorite, Wilde had promoted young Jo to be at his side, which itself was a tall cliff of deep purple velvet with intricately decorated lapels and a clashing green-dyed carnation butonnière. He swept through the gathered theatergoers, pausing only briefly to clasp an arm, nod a gracious hello, kiss an extended hand, and in passing the Montagu party to breathe at Harry, "My dear boy, so pleasing to see you again… And now we must sweep up the royal passageway." And he was off through the curtained opening toward the Prince of Wales's private box. Harry tried catching Jolyon's attention as he walked by, but the boy ignored him entirely.

Wilde having made his entry, the crush bar began to empty as chattering groups made their way to their boxes. Montagu insisted that Harry take the seat next to his own close to the crimson, plush cushioned front edge of the commodious box, one of fourteen in the dress circle. Situated slightly to the right of the auditorium's center, it had an excellent view around the curve to the Prince of Wales's box adjoining the proscenium, in which Harry now spied Jolyon settling down in pride of place beside Wilde. Gossip suggested Prince Edward was present as well, but if so Bertie—as his confidants called him—was keeping out of sight toward the rear of the box.

"The Importance of Being Earnest, A Trivial Comedy for Serious People," Montagu intoned with capital letters. He read it from the playbill. "Were it not for the need to be seen I'd rather be comfortably seated in front of my parlor fire reading a story from *The Memoirs of Sherlock Holmes*. That Doyle fellow is dashed clever. Perhaps you don't approve of low fiction?"

"Oh, but I do, Monty. I have read several of his books. *A Study in Scarlet* even sustained me through some freezing cold nights in the Karakoram Mountains…," which immediately brought Arshan's comforting warmth to mind, "though I found his most recent, *The Stark Munro Letters*, somewhat dry. Autobiographical, I sense."

"I'm delighted to discover you don't find my taste in literature entirely frivolous, Harry, for in spite of your cruel allusion to my being a trader in cheap innuendo, I count myself as a relatively serious person, as indeed I do you, and I'm not sure I'm ready for an overlong helping of Mr. Wilde's wit. But I was assured I should be missed by those who count in society were I to abstain."

"I remain to be persuaded, but I shall at least enjoy witnessing the performance of Allan Aynesworth, who I see from the playbill takes the part of Algernon Moncrieff. He's been a casual acquaintance ever since I saw him play in an amateur production in his home town of Sandhurst."

"Ah, when you attended the Royal Military College?"

"That's right. I've forgotten exactly why, but we ended up in a pub after the play and I found him witty and good company." Being of much the same age, Harry had also found it hard to resist the aspiring actor's boyish charm and the long yearning looks Allan kept giving him. That was during Harry's first months at Sandhurst and Harry was drawn to the flame of sexual heat. The affair was a whirlwind one and over when Richard Rainbow's commencement at officer training overlapped with Harry's last months at the academy. Richard's reappearance in his life swept all else aside, and anyway Allan departed for prosceniums new. Allan had recently married and Harry had no intention of renewing a fleeting amorous dalliance with, by all accounts, a happily wedded man. Not, he knew, that Monty would be interested in knowing any of that.

He smiled and said, "I'm familiar with the fact that Mr. Wilde calls himself a writer but I'm not yet acquainted with anything he's written, so I'd be interested in the precise nature of his wit for which you say you're so unready."

Montagu looked as if he was about to elaborate when there came a disturbance behind them and they both turned to see a gentleman holding apart the portière to peer in. It was evident that the intruder and Montagu were acquainted for he immediately stood up with a quick apology to Harry and stepped to the entryway. The two men exchanged a few words and when Montagu returned to his seat he seemed both amused and disturbed about whatever the other had revealed. Harry dragged his eyes away from the sight of Jolyon in animated conversation with Wilde not more than thirty feet away around the auditorium's horseshoe curve.

"Do you know Mr. George Alexander, manager of this establishment?"

"Of course I know the name, but not the gentleman himself."

"He takes the part of John Worthing—or Jack as he's referred to in the play—and as the curtain will shortly rise he's in a rush to put on his make-up. But he has been much exercised by information Mr. Oscar Wilde brought to him yesterday. It involves the Marquess of Queensbury. There's little secret in society that he is insensate with anger at his son's relationship with Mr. Wilde. Queensberry has denounced it as 'unnatural' and demands Lord Alfred Douglas abandon 'the abomination.' If there is anything to it, I'm unsure as to which in their dalliance is Romeo and which Juliet. I find it difficult to take seriously any grown man—well, almost grown—who sticks to using an infantile nickname like Bosie, given him as child by his mother."

"I'm inclined to agree," Harry said with some feeling.

"However, Lord Alfred is a stubborn young wretch and refuses to do anything which might be agreeable to his father. They are not on good terms, not anyway since Lord Alfred accused Queensberry of driving his elder son to shoot himself dead in desperation at the man's violent behavior. In any event, Mr. Wilde discovered that the Marquess has planned to disrupt this evening's proceedings by throwing a bouquet of rotten vegetables at him when he takes his bow after the final curtain, presuming of course that the play meets with the audience's approval. Alexander had the presence of mind to cancel Queensberry's ticket and arranged for policemen to bar his entrance to the theater if he should try to gain access."

Harry drew his brows into a frown. *How strange. That breaks across the dream Bosie claimed to have had. Unless it wasn't a dream and he knew something of his father's plot and has chosen to make himself absent, the coward.* Privately, Harry thought he might take sides with the Marquess were it not for his vestigial interest in boxing at which he had excelled at Benthenham College— Queensberry had lent his name to the official set of rules for the sport—and so

Harry was acquainted with the man's odious reputation. Apart from the effete Bosie with his aesthetic pretensions, the whole boorish family was comprised of overwrought big-game hunters, adventurers, and pugilists. It was all too easy to understand that a sensitive adolescent might rebel against a philistine like his intemperate father by flaunting his sexual insecurity, although Harry was not sure that Lord Alfred Douglas was any more sensitive than his obdurate parent. From his little personal knowledge of the family, Harry would need to toss a coin to determine which he detested the more: father or son. But he was sure of his responsibility as godfather to the young man in his sights across the curvature of the dress circle. It concerned him deeply to see Jolyon aping the insolent manners of Bosie and kowtowing to overbearing sophisticates like Wilde. Sadly, Harry was less sure that Jolyon would any longer bow to his godfatherly authority, which in any case was an illusory one.

The buzz of twelve hundred people, from the stalls to the fourth-floor balcony, which some nicknamed *the gods* since from up there it was like seeing the stage action from Mount Olympus, died away in anticipation of the drop curtain rising. And suddenly in the expectant hush the first scene of the first act plunged the audience into the morning room of Algernon Moncrieff's flat in Half-Moon Street, with its luxurious and artistic furnishings. The sound of a piano, invisible in the wings, rang out. The butler busied himself arranging tea. The music stopped and Allan Aynesworth playing Algernon entered the stage through a door at the side of the scenery. "Did you hear what I was playing, Lane?"

"I didn't think it polite to listen, sir."

Quiet titters rose from the stalls.

"I'm sorry for that, for your sake. I don't play accurately—anyone can play accurately—but I play with wonderful expression. As far as the piano is concerned, sentiment is my forte."

The titters swelled into laughter and the actors paused to let it bubble around the auditorium. Harry saw Jolyon convulsed with laughter and overdoing it, while Wilde patted the large beacon of his forehead with a bright pink frilly handkerchief.

Montagu pressed his shoulder against Harry's. "This," he said lugubriously, "is going to be very tedious, I fear."

∾✿∾

179

Lady Bracknell [to John "Jack" Worthing]: "My nephew, you seem to be displaying signs of triviality."

Jack: "On the contrary, Aunt Augusta…" George Alexander made a grand sweeping gesture with his outstretched arm that gathered in the audience. "…I've now realized for the first time in my life the vital Importance of Being Earnest."

The entire theater roared its delight at the pun of the closing line. Shining faces glowed everywhere, applauding in the stalls, hanging like jolly suicides over the dress and upper circle balconies, waving down from the Gods.

"Looks like Mr. Wilde has a success on his hands," Montagu said dryly, and Harry had to agree. In his final analysis the play had not been tedious. It had in fact been most amusing. The cast took several curtain calls, and then Oscar Wilde stepped out from the wing onto the stage. As one, the entire audience stood to deliver a standing ovation. A veritable meadow of flowers showered the stage, thrown from every corner. Harry looked across at Jolyon who leaned out as far as he could, arms outstretched as if begging Wilde into his embrace. The proximity of the Prince of Wales's box to the corner of the stage meant that if the great man walked over and extended his hand up, the two could have almost touched fingertips—Jolyon's Adam to Wilde's Sistine God. The image soured Harry's feelings about the play he'd just witnessed, and Wilde's self-serving arrogance in thanking the audience for being so perceptive in acclaiming his play's cleverness just plain irritated him. Buried half way to his knees in the festoon of blossoms, Oscar Wilde's moonface shone in the spotlights with more than bloated self-esteem. He mopped at the perspiration with yet another florid handkerchief—turquoise this time—and bowed for the fifth time.

"No rotten vegetables," Montagu observed with a wry grin.

It took the best part of twenty minutes to empty the auditorium of its festive playgoers. Harry made his excuses. "Monty. Do you mind if I take a half hour to have a word with someone I saw farther around the dress circle? Please go ahead and I will be along to join all of you at Rules before you've even had time to place any orders." He didn't say with whom he craved a word, but since no one had yet emerged from the Prince of Wales's box he hoped to intercept Jolyon when Wilde's party came out.

"Don't be too long, Harry, please. We have a lot to catch up on." Montagu gripped Harry's arm briefly and started to usher his friends toward the stairs.

In a few minutes Harry was alone in the crush bar apart from the cloakroom valets, who were already getting ready to close down the counter. He strode over to recover his outerwear. With the coat across his arm, top hat held by its brim, and cane tucked under his arm, he paced up and down for a bit until he began to feel self-conscious up there all alone.

When two women came up the grand staircase laden with buckets, mops, brooms, and other arcane weaponry of cleansing, he decided it was time to do something practical. He rubbed his chin thoughtfully, and then stepped into the narrow passage that curved around the rear of the boxes to open into a luxuriously appointed chamber. The royal suite appeared deserted; all the jeroboams depleted, the stubs of Havanas extinguished amid crumpled yellow Turkish cigarettes.

He pulled aside the portière and glanced into the royal box. It too was as empty as the champagne bottles. Harry let the drape fall back and looked around. Then he espied another door opposite the one by which he had entered. Examination revealed a steep, narrow staircase down to the stage. He descended with care for his mending hip to emerge just behind the proscenium arch.

Here, hidden from the auditorium by the thick drop curtain, he heard the clamor of excited voices floating on the dusty air from behind one of the large flats. He recognized the structure as the extreme right end of Woolton Manor House's drawing room. Discarded behind it, the piano played at the start of the first scene by someone—if it hadn't been Allan—stood forlornly abandoned. From this perspective, and with so much of the stage lighting extinguished, the set looked unconvincing. But the magic of theatrical illusion was not in the forefront of Harry's mind. He peered across the large, dimly lit, empty space running behind the stage.

On the wall between two sets of rickety looking stairways up into the darkness overhead a placard read STAGE DOOR, with an arrow to the right, and DRESSING ROOMS, with an arrow to the left. It was from this last direction the sounds of exhilaration came, accompanied by clinking glassware and the laughter of people content with a job well done. As Harry stood hesitating between advancing on the back-stage party and returning the way he'd come, two figures ran out from an opening at the far end of the stage area. A man and woman, fashionably dressed, holding hands, and laughing uproariously while waving to those out of sight behind them.

"Why, if it isn't Harry Vane!" the man cried out as he and the pretty young woman hanging on his arm came into the light of a low-hanging house lamp.

"Allan—"

"Have you come back to congratulate Oscar?" Allan Aynesworth closed the distance in a rush and grabbed Harry up in a bear hug. "We're all on our way to the Savoy to celebrate the stunning opening of the greatest play of all time: dramatis personae, miracle workers of maquillage, our wizards of electrical trickery, manager, stage manager, prompt, setmen, props, painters, and stagehands. Name it, they're all invited. Bertie and Sarah—" He halted dramatically and slapped a gloved hand across his mouth, eyes wide in faux tactlessness. "Whoops! My big mouth will yet lead me to the gallows, I swear. Anyway he's gone ahead to slip past the crowds incognito… hahaha. You must join us. Oscar will be following shortly as soon as he comes down from the empyrean… which may never happen."

Allan turned to the woman on his arm. "Oh, how remiss of me. My dear, please meet my old friend Harry Vane, and Harry, allow me to introduce the very beautiful Irene Vanbrugh. Harry is a fine officer in the… what is it now?"

"Dragoons," Harry said faintly, a little taken aback at the actor's blast of no doubt champagne- and audience-adulation-fueled words. He recognized the actress who had taken the part of Gwendolen Fairfax.

Irene disentangled herself from Allan, laid a gloved hand on Harry's wrist, and enveloped him in the fragrance of her perfume. "Is it true that that awful man the Marquess of Queensberry was prevented by the police from entering the theater to shoot poor Oscar?" Her eyes were wide with alarm, which Harry rather uncharitably thought might be a thespian wile.

"I understand he intended to throw rotten vegetables, Miss Vanbrugh, though knowing his propensity for firearms and impulsive temper, he might have preferred a spray of bullets."

"After his escapades in the Wild West among all those roughhouse cowboys, I shouldn't think a mere pistol would alarm Oscar," Aynesworth said with a breathy laugh.

Irene shuddered. "Don't be reductive, Allan darling. Poor Oscar, to be terrorized by such a brute. But I do so wish that awful son of his would leave Oscar alone."

"Boy's an absolute wretch," Aynesworth added forcibly, "but fortunately also absent on a holiday in Egypt."

"I thought he'd gone to Algeria?"

"North Africa, isn't it all the same? Ah, though you would probably pull me up there. You were in Egypt, were you not Harry?"

"I was and—"

"Was it very terrible?" Irene fluttered long eyelashes.

Harry never got the chance to tell her that failing to rescue General Charles Gordon had indeed been very terrible because he was interrupted by an eructation of bustling humanity from the opening through which Aynesworth and Irene Vanbrugh had popped a minute ago. Driven like corks from a bottle by Wilde's cannonade of a voice, the procession made its way toward the stage door.

"Come, my children! George, bring me my bow of burning gold; Allan dear… where are you? Ah, over there: my arrows of desire; Irene my spear; O clouds unfold… where is Jolyon? There, my boy, bring me my chariot of fire! Indeed all our chariots await yonder the door and Blake be damned!"

Aynesworth swept Harry up and urged him into the current of actors and technicians who trailed in Wilde's wake like the children of Hamelin damned forever to dance to the Pied Piper's narcotic tune. Before the door, a natural bottleneck trapped all the corks and allowed Harry to catch up to Jolyon, who continued to act as though he hadn't seen him. At the hand on his elbow, the boy turned and immediately lost his bright array of brittle smiles.

"Jo, we must talk."

"Why?" Jolyon looked around but saw that for the time being he was stuck behind several of the company going in single file through the doorway. He turned a petulant face on Harry. "Captain Smythe-Vane," he hissed *sotto voce* as though ashamed at admitting in the presence of others that he actually knew who he was addressing, "Oscar needs me at his side now."

"You mean you're taking advantage of Lord Alfred Douglas being absent."

"No!"

"Jo, please listen to me. This company is not good for you—"

Jolyon's face crumpled for a second and then the expression reformed in snarling anger as he interrupted Harry. "What do you know? You're just like my father was, a soldier. You don't know how Oscar is liberating me from the ranks of timeserving philistine soldiers like you. Now, let me go."

He wrenched his arm free and pushed through the door, leaving Harry nonplussed and distressed.

He's very fond of the word philistine. *Damn! I didn't handle it right again.*

By the time he made it through the stage door, with a pause at the top to put on his greatcoat, and down the short flight of steps into Rose and Crown Yard, Jolyon was back beside Wilde and climbing into a brougham between a line of policemen still struggling to keep the baying crowd back from the alley. When Aynesworth repeated his offer that Harry should join them at the Savoy, he declined, offering up his prior engagement for supper as the reason. And seeing the hopelessness of ever getting a cab of any kind out on King Street, he went in the other direction away from the theater to Pall Mall, where he was lucky enough to hail a passing hackney cab. Typically, it looked down at heel (which matched his sad demeanor over his mishandling of Jolyon), but it would get him across Trafalgar Square and up the Strand to Maiden Lane and Rules to sup with John Douglas-Scott-Montagu and his party.

Diners crammed London's oldest restaurant tighter than a new-fangled can of sardines; the company was warm, the conversation convivial and appreciative of the Hero of Chitral's presence among them; the food as usual tasted excellent, yet Harry only picked fitfully at his *truite aux amandes*. By the time his fellow diners began gathering their coats, gloves, scarves, and hats, Harry had come to a decision.

Jolyon—for whatever real reasons of his own—might reject me, but it's my sworn duty to General Langrish-Smith to ensure the boy's future wellbeing, and no matter how long that might take, no matter how much humiliation—which God knows a man barely out of childhood can heap on someone who cares for him— might lie in my path, I will stand by him. I will see him safely to adulthood… so he may find love with a good woman. So help me God.

But Harry had the distinct impression that nothing could possibly be so simple.

CHAPTER 17 | *London, late May to July 1895*

CAPT. R. RAINBOW
c/o Army H.Q., Suakin
British Red Sea Territories
July 28

My dear Richard,

I cannot know when this will reach you and for all that I know you and Edward may be prowling the wastes of the Sudanese deserts on missions of utmost importance and will therefore not read my words for an age. And since news travels slowly to our outposts, I shall assume that you do not know of the extraordinary events of the past two months.

I have witnessed a modern Greek tragedy and, as you will see, one with passing relevance to our circumstances. You may think only superficially so in respect of the players in the drama, and yet the outcome is a sobering one to reflect on. The events that have occurred between February and this date have a personal aspect to them. You may recall me mentioning once when you stayed at Hadlicote that I was made godfather to Jolyon, the young son of General Sir Neville Airey Langrish-Smith (though he was a colonel then). The General and Lady Langrish-Smith fell victim of the cholera a little over two years past, and since Jolyon is still a minor he has been under the guardianship of an aunt. I know this lady, of course, though our acquaintance is slight in reality. But I know her enough to see she is not equipped to handle a boy with the mettle of Jolyon, especially since he concluded his education at Eton and now hovers in the gap between desire for university and the fear of having to work for his future.

In short, Jolyon fell into bad company, which in his callow eyes he thought to provide him with the experience of life, of advanced culture and sensibility, of new art. On my return to England to recover from my injuries I fear young Jolyon came to look on my recuperation as a damned nuisance—my persistent presence in London a thorn in his side or, as he preferred a different metaphor, a fly in his ointment, a "dampener on his intellectual engine."

(Before you worry yourself, I am pleased to say I am fully recovered from the wounds, unless you count a persistent twitch in my upper arm whenever it rains. Chadwick, my physician, assures me this will fade in time.)

I know you are aware of the work and style of the self-proclaimed genius with the exotic name of Oscar Fingal O'Flahertie Wills Wilde for you commented in your last letter on his fiction *The Picture of Dorian Gray*, which you had read, and the cloying sense of decadence that rose from its pages like the dust from Miss Havisham's trousseau; "unclean, poisonous and heavy with the mephitic odors of moral and spiritual putrefaction," as *The Daily Chronicle*'s reviewer labeled the story.

After that publication, Wilde descended even further into the depths of depravity hinted at in *Dorian Gray*. Oddly, it was our friend Alfred Winner who first pointed me toward an understanding of Wilde's character… and the nature of his friendships. Alfred, after all, is so straight-laced, puritanical, and no-nonsense in attitude, it surprised me that he should be quite so well acquainted with the loose morals of the Yellow Aesthetic movement. And I must be careful; I do not wish to paint myself as a moralizer, certainly not to you, Richard, who knows my inner life so very well. But I like to think I conduct myself with the decorum becoming of an officer in Her Majesty's armed forces.

And so, Richard, to tragedy…

Apart from a handful of Oscar Wilde's more reputable acquaintances, London society was not present at the trial, unless Harry counted himself (and he was there for Jolyon, not in support of the two defendants, although Jolyon—who he hadn't seen since the opening night of *The Importance of Being Earnest*—pointedly avoided sitting anywhere near Harry in the public gallery). Sensational stories of sodomy had filled the newspapers, facilitated by the young keeper of a "house of ill repute" called Alfred Taylor, who procured young working-class men to satisfy Wilde's "unnatural vices." A team of private detectives had compiled a dossier on his association with young grooms, messenger boys, blackmailers and male prostitutes, cross-dressers, and "queer" brothels. The salacious details titillated society while at the same time frightening off the majority who did not wish to appear drawn to the looming scandal about to engulf one who aspired to be one of their social standing. The packed public seats, therefore, buzzed with the prurient speculation of the lower classes.

"Quiet! All stand for my lord."

The clerk of court's stentorian voice quieted the eager spectators as Justice Wills swept in. He wasted no time in addressing the two defendants who had been found guilty as charged by the jury.

"Oscar Wilde and Alfred Taylor, the crime of which you have been convicted is so bad that one has to put stern restraint upon one's self to prevent one's self from describing, in language which I would rather not use, the sentiments which must rise in the breast of every man of honor who has heard the details of these two horrible trials. That the jury has arrived at a correct verdict in this case I cannot persuade myself to entertain a shadow of a doubt.

"It is no use for me to address you. People who can do these things must be dead to all sense of shame, and one cannot hope to produce any effect upon them. It is the worst case I have ever tried. That you, Taylor, kept a kind of male brothel it is impossible to doubt. And that you, Wilde, have been the center of a circle of extensive corruption of the most hideous kind among young men, it is equally impossible to doubt.

"I shall, under the circumstances, be expected to pass the severest sentence that the law allows. In my judgment it is totally inadequate for a case such as this. The sentence of the Court is that each of you be imprisoned and kept to hard labor for two years."

Harry had eyes only for Jolyon and saw the look of utter shock on his finely featured face. The poor boy was not prepared for this judgment, had not the wit to see it coming in spite of two trials and their outcome being everyday tittle tattle in the press and on the street. Wilde's voice was heard above the hubbub questioning the judge whether he had the right to say anything, but hisses and cries of "Shame!" from the gallery drowned him out.

As I wrote you, Richard, *The Importance of Being Earnest* was a runaway success, and yet how quickly are the great fallen, the public idols cast down from their pedestals and smashed. Mr. Wilde has suffered badly from latter-day iconoclasts, though I'm sure there are many—myself included—more inclined to look to the ancient Greeks, of whom he is so fond, for an explanation: nothing less than hubris. Wilde had for some time pursued forbidden relationships with working-class youths in the sordid dens that cater to London's nancy elite. Oscar called his sexual acts with male prostitutes "feasting with panthers," a phrase that in typical Wildean metaphor clothes sordidness in glamor.

His primary paramour, the callow Lord Alfred Douglas, or Bosie to his effete companions, was equally to blame, though thanks to his being a lord he avoided the courtroom scandal. Indeed, it is widely believed that it was he who introduced Wilde to Taylor in the first place, himself partial to sampling the dubious charms of telegraphic messenger boys, some quite young indeed. Bosie is twenty-four but acts like a spiteful, spoilt, petulant child. I am afraid to say that Jolyon—an immature eighteen when he first fell into the aesthetes' circle—chose to model himself on this privileged monster.

Harry stopped writing for a moment as he reconsidered again the events which followed on the heels of the trial.

Lord Alfred Douglas, hidden under a hat pulled down low over his brow, muffled in a voluminous scarf, shouldered past the gawping onlookers outside the Central Criminal Court on Old Bailey and was almost immediately lost in the sea of Londoners forcing their way into the road's narrow confines from Fleet Street. His disguise hadn't fooled Harry. The press of ghoulish spectators reminded him of the opening night for *The Importance of Being Earnest* only now those gathering wanted Wilde's blood. "Hanging's too good for the *prevert*!" Harry heard one man cry out.

Women shouting "Shame!" at the top of their voices jostled him, but Harry had been determined to wait for Jolyon to emerge from the Court's gloomy precincts no matter how difficult the mob made it to maintain a position close to the entry steps.

"Dunno what all these twats are doin' 'ere."

Harry could only agree with the one sane voice in the cacophony. Wilde and Taylor would be taken away in a closed carriage from an exit far away from the grand entrance on Old Bailey. When he at last saw Jolyon's etiolated figure appear in the crowded arch, Harry pushed forward. He saw immediately that the boy was lost and he called out to him. "Jo!"

A blank stare was the only response, and a hoarse but limp cry. "Go away."

"Jolyon. It's me, Harry. Come, let me get you away from here."

"Leave me be—"

"Oy! You! Ent 'e one of them nancy boys of—"

"'E needs castrating!"

A glimmer of panic lit up Jolyon's eyes and for a moment he seemed to recognize Harry. His normally sensuous lips, thinned now into a tense, twisted line, twitched uncertainly, unhappily.

Harry threw an arm around his thin shoulders, ignored the faint mew of protest, and dragged him away from the grand entrance, keeping close to the stonework where the press of bodies seemed to be lessened. The baying cries of mob vengeance dropped away as those converging on the Criminal Court doorway by their sheer bulk shielded Harry from the invective. In their insensate desire to express disgust at the crimes of those sentenced, Harry was convinced that many on Old Bailey that day would tear apart any youth who might—rightly or wrongly—be accused of complicity. Lord Alfred Douglas and his guilty cronies were already fled, but that only made the mob's desire for a sacrificial victim all the more potent. Harry was determined they should not lay hands on Jolyon.

Although the situation looked calmer out on the wider thoroughfare of Fleet Street, Harry was frantic to hail a cab, worried that if Jolyon were given the chance to collect his thoughts he might run off. He was sure the boy was in no condition to be on his own. Time seemed to telescope… or did it expand? He had no idea how long it took to reach the Albany, but he was thankful that Jolyon remained virtually catatonic during the ride.

"I can make some tea, if you'd like."

At the tentative offer, Jolyon threw himself down onto the threadbare sofa and buried his head in his hands. Harry thought it best to leave him be, and went to fill his kettle. When he came back, the regular heaves of Jolyon's back told its story. Harry sat on the edge of the sofa and laid a hand gently on a shuddering shoulder.

I think, Richard, that was the first time I felt something, a stirring… but of what kind? I know my throat became constricted at the sight of poor Jo. He looked so broken. Everything he had come to admire, to aspire to, swept away in such a terrible bonfire of the vanities. And he told me shortly after, that Lord Douglas had made it clear that Oscar in his troubles needed only himself, that Langrish-Smith could—he said—fuck off and die. So Jolyon didn't even have the dubious comfort of the Yellow Aesthetes. He felt everyone had turned his back on him.

But in that moment I sternly told myself I must not show any pity. I was sure he would balk at even the slightest compassion… even more so from me who, since my reappearance in his life, he had utterly rejected. But I felt the need to hold him, to look after him. Was the agitation I felt in my breast the faintest hint of something more than natural affection? I wasn't sure then. I'm not now. Besides, love is a two-way street. I am in no position to give my heart to a void. But there is another feeling as well. I know of no one I could say this to, but you, my dear Richard. You know me too well for me to deny what that turmoil was. Touching Jolyon's shoulder sent a thrill through me that was purely sexual. It went straight to my loins and I was hard. And I felt unclean. This is my godson, I told myself; I the adult, he the child, for in this wretched state he seems so. But I am confessing to you Richard a feeling I must surely reject. In fact, even writing of it is making me short of breath at the failure of my morals and the sheer excitement Jolyon's presence generates in my—

Harry paused. He read the last two paragraphs, which filled a single sheet, and considered what he had written. His past relationship with Richard was sacrosanct and he suddenly accepted that he did not wish to color it with a sentiment that had nothing to do with what they had enjoyed, and now lost… at least Richard haad mislaid it; Harry lost it. He crumpled the sheet and tossed it at the wastebasket. After a pause for thought, he dipped the nib in the inkpot and put pen to paper again.

How did these things come to pass? In part, Wilde's fall from grace was due to his own personality, which is the same as his character—florid, overbearing, and full of his own prodigious talent. Unfortunately for the great writer, he believed himself to be above the draconian laws of our land—either because of his class or because of his assumed brilliance—and dressed up his relationship with the nasty Bosie as something noble, Platonic, and beautiful… "the love that dare not speak its name," he said at the first criminal court case against him. He was quoting some piece of Lord Alfred's poetry, I believe. When Bosie's father the Marquess of Queensberry (yes, he of the pugilists' rules) published a note that referred to Oscar Wilde "posing as a sondomite" (the man's an illiterate boor), Wilde unwisely sued him for libel, driven by Douglas who by his actions seems determined to ruin his hated father.

But Wilde's counsel was unable to convince the court of Queensberry's slander. Worse, Queensberry's counsel announced he had located several working-class youths willing to testify that Wilde had used them for sex. I wonder how much that testimony cost Queensberry's lawyers? I assume that one who prostitutes his body for money is equally willing to sell his honor. Anyway, the case against the Marquess collapsed, and in so doing, pointed the finger directly at Oscar Wilde. The brilliant man of letters was immediately pilloried in the press, which loves nothing more than to drag through the mire a man it previously hailed a genius.

Even with this disaster, Wilde could have availed himself of an exile in sympathetic France, as others have done before him. But he stayed and was back in court in late April, which resulted in an undecided jury, and again a month later. This time the outcome was inevitable. Everything was against the man. Only his very closest friends remained at his side, until he began his two-year sentence.

Were it not for his unmitigated self-regard I suppose I could find some sympathy in my heart for Wilde. In the final analysis he was only following his previously suppressed natural inclinations. Well, the balloon now is surely pricked and he is not alone in suffering punishment for it. Think of the damage this affair has done to his suffering wife and children, and also to the young man I must, bearing in mind my oath given to his parents so long ago, consider my charge: Jolyon.

It has taken me a month to bring myself to write this, Richard. I hope it finds you in good health, and Edward too, and that you are enjoying the freedom of the wastelands.

Ever your friend, Harry

CHAPTER 18 | *London, late 1895 to August 1896*

HARRY CROSSED THE GRASSY open space where, before riding out to royal household duties, the cavalry squadrons mustered for inspection. It separated the buildings fronting Albany Street from those at "the back" of the sprawling barracks complex where it overlooked the trench in which the rail tracks ran north from the nearby Euston terminus. He was a few minutes early for an appointment with Major John Chadwick, Surgeon General to the barracks, but within the squat, two-story structure known to Albany's inhabitants as Sawbone's Compound, the wall clock pronounced him three minutes late.

Following a quarter hour of leg and torso bending, prodding, and poking, Chadwick asked Harry to take a seat again and slid behind his cluttered desk. He selected a paper from the top of a pile and waved it about with a scowl. The growl matched. "This business with the War Office and our status in the Army Medical Service. Damned silly, the whole thing. Both the British Medical Association and the Royal College of Physicians have been bearding the Secretary of State for War for years, but…" he peered down at the paper and quoted, "…'while medical officers may not have actual military rank, the Secretary is cognizant of their enjoying advantages corresponding to *relative* military rank and, in the same, the choice of quarters, lodging rates, servants, fuel and light, allowances on account of injuries received in action, and pensions and allowances to widows and families, and…' blah, blah." He treated Harry to a grim smile. "So, Captain Vane, I am *Relative* Major Chadwick. It's all nonsense. Lucky to recruit any doctors these days the way they go on. Young medical students want equality within the armed forces. It's only fair and right. But it's going to change. We will be incorporated in the proposed Royal Army Medical

Corps. I feel it in my bones. And, rant concluded, your bruised bones seem in fine condition. I think you'll be free to return to active service very soon."

"Thank you, sir. I will be happy to do so."

"Mind, there isn't much doing right now. Are you coping on reserve pay?"

Harry said he was, but as Chadwick began writing notes on Harry's medical record the doctor's next remark startled him.

"I hear you have a patient of your own." He didn't look up from scratching away.

"He is my godson," Harry answered shortly. Should he be alarmed or even amused that the presence of Jo staying in his rooms had reached as far as the Sawbone's Compound? He was uncomfortably aware that his response was not an answer to the implied question of why a young man was staying with an older officer in his quarters. And he was not prepared to go into a lengthy explanation that it had taken all his powers of persuasion to get Jolyon to remain with him so that he could keep an eye on him; not that he needed much looking after. For most days Jolyon simply sat by the window and stared out at… nothing. For the rest he never left the bed Harry had secured from stores for him and made up in the apartment's tiny box room.

Chadwick paused in his writing and glanced up from under bushy eyebrows. "Ah, the son of General Langrish-Smith, I believe." He solved the mystery of how the knowledge of Jolyon's presence had reached as far as the Surgeon General's rooms. "It appears that your orderly is cousin to my man. I understand the boy is in a wan state, and lies abed most of the day. Are you concerned for his health? I should be happy to see the lad. Anything for the Hero of Inkermann's son."

Harry didn't relish the idea of Chadwick examining Jolyon; that might open too many awkward closets whose warped doors would then refuse to shut again. He had managed to deflect those few newspaper hounds who scented a possible scandal over Jolyon's acquaintanceship with Wilde, Bosie, or any of the *Yellow Book* adherents, now viewed as deviants in the public eye. He didn't want a helpful doctor prising from Jolyon the real reasons for his near-catatonic condition, especially at a moment when it seemed he was beginning to emerge from his fugue state.

"There is nothing physically wrong with Langrish-Smith, sir." He managed a firm but unconcerned tone. "It is more… a sickness of the heart. He never quite recovered from the unfortunate deaths of his parents two years ago, and his guardian aunt is frequently indisposed and so unable to provide the companionship he needs. It is a deep melancholy that assailed him after leaving Eton of the type to which I believe young men sometimes fall prey if they are uncertain of their future."

"Hmm, he'd do well to secure a commission, then. Army always sorts out those who have no inclination for the civil service or the Indian service and no talent for a respectable profession. In the meantime I see that the presence of an ailing aunt is hardly the prescription for a youngster." He lowered the pen and sat back, regarding Harry thoughtfully. "It is, however, unusual for a younger and an older man to share rooms in barracks."

There was the implied suggestion of possible impropriety again. He didn't want to hang for a crime as yet uncommitted—if it ever would be. Harry cleared his throat carefully. "Perhaps I am unusual, doctor, but I take my duties very seriously, and those include fulfilling the sacred oath to General and Lady Langrish-Smith I took over the font at their son's baptism."

If Chadwick noticed that Harry dropped the *sir* for *doctor* as a way of emphasizing that *relatively* speaking he was senior in rank and that pushing too hard for information would not be welcomed, Chadwick made no mention of it. "You must have been young to accept such a responsibility?"

"He received baptism a little later than usual, some inconvenience of a foreign posting perhaps, when he was two, and I was twelve. It was the ardent wishes of my parents and the Langrish-Smiths, so…" Harry shrugged and smiled. "I was a very religious child."

The doctor's slight upward tilt of his chin asked the unspoken question.

Harry gave a short, rueful laugh. "No, not any longer. The rigors of school chapel shook the trappings of doctrine from me, but that hasn't shaken me from my duty to General Langrish-Smith's son."

"Of course," Chadwick said shortly. With a final flourish he signed off on Harry's notes and stood to shake hands across the desk. "Well, if there is ever anything you need, let me know. I shall place you back on the active list in two weeks."

At the halfway mark on his return, Harry glanced up at a window he knew to be one of two in his accommodation that looked out onto the muster square. The mullions and transoms framed a pale oval in a pane of glass. Jolyon. An involuntary sigh broke from his lips. He had to find a way through that false carapace of sophistication with which the Wildean aesthetes had coated the lovable child Harry remembered. Considering their poor start at the Café Royal last February, it was no simple matter to gain Jo's confidence, but he felt constrained to try. The disaster of the Wilde trial and the fallout from it had shattered Jolyon at levels beyond those Harry could determine: the damage to his self-esteem; the tragedy of seeing an idol pilloried; the distress at seeing a lifestyle that had been portrayed as something ethereal abruptly revealed to be a sham; no doubt the horror at seeing the awful Queensberry's stance validated, all these must have contributed to his retreat from life.

But Harry couldn't help assuage what was tearing Jolyon apart at a deeper level because he refused to open up. Harry's greatest fear was that—having been rudely awakened from his teenage crush on sophistication—Jo was so ashamed of acts he had committed that he might never recover. With a darkness of his soul, Harry suspected that Jolyon had participated in some of the more lurid activities the trial revealed, that perhaps Jolyon allowed Wilde's feasting panthers to sodomize him. But Harry knew that his questioning Jolyon on the recent past or of his sounding in any way judgmental would be fatal. If a cure were to be effected, he was convinced it would be through his providing Jolyon with a solid, reliable, and steady support. And that he was determined to do.

The time spent recovering from his injuries in England brought about some subtle changes for Harry—not least, his having turned thirty the previous June, a figure that seemed to weigh on him more than he liked to pretend. He thought of Richard and Edward, getting on with their lives while his seemed to have stalled. His family, as distantly aristocratic as ever (happily), nevertheless evinced some surprise at his continued bachelor status. His father hinted that a wife would be a welcome addition to the family (and sons, as a subtext). This step Harry had no inclination to take. Besides, he argued with himself, his brother Evan was happily producing sufficient quantities of male heirs to the Smythe-Vane line to satisfy their father.

The long military leave he'd been given to allow his Chitral injuries time to completely heal also allowed him to join many of the London Season's amusements, which commenced early at the end of April with the opening of *The Geisha* at Daley's Theatre, a two-act operetta that its fans argued outdid Gilbert and Sullivan's *Mikado*. The book, which sizzled with the kind of light froth so popular with London's theatergoers, told of the love of a naval officer and a geisha girl at the Tea House of Ten Thousand Joys. Sidney Jones' light, breezy score did much to lighten Harry's mood.

He attended glittering parties and balls that "comprised all the elements which made a gay and splendid social circle in close relation to the business of Parliament, the hierarchies of the Army and Navy, and the policy of the State," as a sprightly young man said to him at one such event. Winston Leonard Spencer-Churchill was about the same age as Harry's godson Jolyon, but of a very different demeanor. For one thing, he was shorter of stature, for another he showed a natural flair for words; and he was quite unabashed by the near decade difference in their ages. Churchill entertained Harry with his adventures in Cuba, where a war for independence from Spain had been fought since the previous year. "I was shot at!" he happily told Harry, as though that was an accomplishment of a high order. "But everyone who aimed their matchlock or pistol at me missed, you know."

"It's a great skill," Harry agreed, "to be missed."

"The real skill is to take necessary risks and survive," Churchill retorted cheerfully. "Though I don't suppose I'm for great age. My father died young, you know."

Harry did; who didn't? The death of high-flying Tory statesman Lord Randolph Spencer-Churchill, third son of the Duke of Marlborough, who passed away early in 1895 at the age of forty-five, had shocked many.

"Almost all my family die very young, carried off by plague or internal weakness, and I have no hope of being any different. So I don't have time to waste and how much better, then, if I have to go to do it in some glory rather than in the sweat of a sickbed." Churchill delivered this little homily with equal cheer, as though the prospect of imminent erasure held less fear for him than the failure to pack in as much as possible into his predictably short lifespan.

"But Vane, the experience I gained out there in Cuba, of combining a military role with that of a newspaper correspondent, has shown me the way. You see… well, perhaps you don't since you come from a well-heeled family, but for me as a gentleman from the impoverished branch of a ridiculously noble house, my options for earning a decent living are limited. My social standing forbids me trade, commerce, even the Stock Exchange. Touch any and I shall never get on later in life. I don't know about you, but my time spent at Harrow School was largely wasted in the academic sense because my father enrolled me in the Army Class, so I lack the qualifications to go to the Bar and become a wealthy barrister. Of the other options—the Church, for which I have no calling anyway, the Army or the Navy—well, none of these is financially rewarding."

"So where does journalism come in?"

"That's it! I'm happy to take the Queen's shilling as long as I can take a newspaper proprietor's dollars in return for eyewitness dispatches from the front. Problem is, Vane, getting to the front or wherever the action is. Everything is so damnably quiet at the moment."

"What about Egypt? Things are warming up out there."

Churchill's face fell. "Kitchener! He won't take me. Even my mother's considerable influence at the War Office has failed to catch his ear. I hate Wednesdays. I always receive my rejections on Wednesdays. Kitchener refused me on a Wednesday… several of them, in fact."

Harry wished Churchill the best of luck in finding his war. Mention of Kitchener made him think of Richard. For the better part of two years, since becoming Sirdar, Commander-in-Chief of the Anglo-Egyptian Army, Kitchener was ready to capitalize on his decade of careful preparation to avenge General Charles Gordon, the martyr of Khartoum, and return the Sudan to British hegemony. Richard Rainbow was at the Brigadier's side, and Harry envied his friend the opportunity the coming war offered.

For Harry, London's social whirl soon palled and as soon as he could he pressed for active army service. This turned out to be as an instructor at Aldershot, which wasn't exactly active but for which his experiences in the Sudan and the North-West Frontier qualified him. It was also useful to his getting the appointment that the General Officer Commanding was Redvers Buller. Even so, his life was not all duty. In fact he was required to spend less time in Aldershot than in London. Evan, whose governmental position kept him in the capital until the annual closure of Parliament, suggested Harry give up the spartan barracks life at the Albany and move into the family's London house in Mayfair. At first Harry rejected this proposal for the simple reason that at the Albany he was not overlooked by relatives, while in Mayfair he would be hard put to explain to Evan and his brood why Jolyon was a regular visitor.

That would be, of course, if Jolyon were in fact a frequent caller, which was far from certain. However, not long after Harry's talk with *Relative*-Major John Chadwick, Jolyon finally began to stir himself. He took to walking on his own in Regent's Park and adjacent Primrose Hill or along the towpath of the Regent's Canal, and to reply when Harry spoke to him over the simple meals he procured from the mess or whenever they ate out (when they did, the West End where people might recognize Jolyon was avoided). Jolyon remained coolly distant, but occasional sparks of his old humor suggested a gradual thaw that warmed Harry.

A less than welcome intrusion occurred with the sudden appearance of the painter Lawrence Alma-Tadema. Harry knew him to be only a peripheral member of the Aesthetic Movement, more for his hobby-interest in stage design than for any deeper leanings toward the fly-by-night denizens of Wildean society, but the slight connection disturbed Harry on Jolyon's behalf. Jolyon, however, seemed pleased to be remembered from some past soirée and happy to accompany the famous painter to visit the home of ailing Lord Leighton, an artist whose bombastic output Harry could never get on with. And something occurred on that visit that occasioned a weather change in Jolyon's demeanor, one Harry could not put his finger on precisely. Jolyon never elucidated, never suggested that he felt in any way different, and yet his attitude toward Harry *felt* less distant from that day on.

When the Aldershot posting came through, Jolyon announced it was time he spent more time at his aunt's house, but promised not to be a stranger.

Harry mulled over Evan's offer. He'd originally rejected it on grounds of being too wrapped up by family, but the more he considered it the better it sounded. There were pros and cons, greater comfort being one of the former; the potential for creating familial unease were Jolyon to start visiting—more so if he should stay for more than a day—one of the latter. But as far as Evan was concerned, Harry had the genuine excuse that he was the young man's godfather. He could argue his spiritual responsibility toward Jo as he'd done with Chadwick. There was also the fact to take into account that the five floors of the Vane-Smythe residence in fashionable South Street promised him a degree of privacy lacking at the Albany. His parents were rarely in town these days, preferring to socialize at Hadlicote; Evan's aloof wife Frannie spent more time out visiting than at home entertaining, and their children were either already safely locked up in boarding schools or in the charge of a Nanny. They were, in other words, pretty much out of the way of the substantial and self-contained suite Evan offered.

So Harry gave up his Albany rooms and, when he was in London, resided at South Street, from where he sallied forth in the attempt to be a regular beau abroad in society's bosom. It was from South Street that he faced a change in his life that was not so subtle—Jolyon Langrish-Smith, who would turn twenty-one before the end of the year, and so become his own man. The sun slowly emerged from behind the cloud of Jolyon's dull despair. Like a mid-summer blossom unfurling its petals, he opened up to Harry's non-judgmental support and they made great progress in the short space of a few weeks.

From the occasional meal out in an unfashionable part of London, Harry began to reintroduce his charge to more social spots and charge became friend, responsibility graduated to genuine enjoyment (it seemed on both sides), a fragile relationship emerged, and Jolyon did become a frequent visitor to South Street. He often slept on the comfortable sofa under a spare blanket. Some nights, Harry slipped into the sitting room and crossed to his tiny kitchen for a glass of water, and the sight of Jolyon's face caught in the pale glow from Harry's part-open bedroom door took his breath away. Freed from care by slumber, Jolyon possessed the perfectly modeled face of an angel.

Then a burning anger at what the *sondomites* had tried to turn Jolyon into threatened to overwhelm Harry, albeit the visions of depravity were not fueled by any evidence, for Jolyon had never spoken of those months nor even hinted at any impropriety toward him or on his part. Nevertheless Harry knew exactly how it would feel to have Lord Alfred Douglas by the neck while he punched him repeatedly in his snide, surly, depraved face, until blood covered his bunched and aching fist. A cleansing, righteous anger.

"That means you will miss my birthday. Surely that's deeply remiss of a godfather, not to be present for his godson's coming of age? You're the only person now who is entitled to present me with the key to the door."

Harry was at his happiest when Jolyon managed a smile for him, and upward turns of his lips had become more frequent in the past weeks. He stared out across the expanse of the Serpentine as he strolled along its shore under welcome July sunshine with Jolyon at his side. They were both dressed casually and wore straw boaters whose broad brims shaded their eyes.

"Will you send up your papers?"

It would have been evident to any passer-by that the discussion about Jolyon's enrolling at the Royal Military Academy was on old and unwelcome one by the sour expression that settled on his face.

"It was what your father wanted for you—"

"As yours wants to know when you are marrying."

"It's not the same thing."

"I'll make up my mind by the time you get back from India."

"By then you will be too old!" Harry used a wry chuckle to cover his exasperation. Jolyon was already older than most candidates, having misspent the three years since leaving Eton. But the general improvement in his attitude pleased Harry. It suggested that he was trying to put the recent past aside, but as yet he didn't show much inclination to actually get on with life… with anything. So far, the best outcome was his willingness to be with Harry and talk things over, as long as the subject of Oscar Wilde was not raised, or of intimacy in general. In the intervening months since those dreadful dark days in the previous year, Jolyon seemed to have attached himself to Harry, no longer as godson to godfather, but as a companion. Certainly, he seemed content to spend most of Harry's free time from Aldershot with him and showed no inclination to make friends nearer his own age… perhaps a natural reaction to Bosie and his disreputable hangers-on. And to Harry this fledgling, still fragile relationship meant a lot more than he even admitted to himself. In the past few weeks, Jo's presence had become an essential ingredient in his life without his even noticing how that had happened. He realized with a frisson of shock that he hadn't thought of Richard in quite a while, and now that he did it didn't come attended with the usual melancholy.

He decided to drop the subject of an army career for the time being and returned to missing the birthday. "I'm truly sorry, Jo. A posting back to India was inevitable and I'm surprised the War Office has left me to wallow this long." He knocked their elbows lightly together. "At any rate, you'll be free of your aunt's grip and in control of your inheritance."

"Which isn't actually very much beyond the value of Cadogan Square," Jolyon murmured, referring to the home where he had grown up.

"I'm no expert on the value of London estates, but I'm sure a residence in Knightsbridge must be worth something on the market. Besides, how many times do I have to tell you I can afford to give you some help?"

Jolyon snorted in thin amusement. "On an *army* captain's earnings?" He sneered at the word, but humorously twisted lips countered the effect.

"Don't be so dismissive. What the army pays me is barely sufficient to keep me in the style expected of my status, and it costs a fortune to run a horse, even some rotten Army nag, and keep several uniforms in good order, and pay exorbitant mess bills. Which is precisely why my father settled a generous allowance on me. And apart from the necessary expense of keeping up appearances for London society, I'm not a spendthrift."

"I've noticed." Jolyon managed another slight smile. He pulled at the back brim of his boater so the front tilted up cheekily to reveal an ironically raised eyebrow. "Christ, Harry, at least Oscar was generous to a fault."

The statement, so lightly thrown out, startled Harry, as much for the proximity to his thoughts of a few moments ago that Wilde was a taboo subject, as to Jo bringing up the man's name. He managed to keep surprise from his expression and refused to take umbrage at the unfair implication of the facile remark but was still stung enough to snap back, "Yes, Oscar was generous in all his faults."

The furrowed brow presaged a dark look in Jolyon's eyes.

Harry instantly regretted his words.

"I shall manage, Harry," Jolyon said with a shake of his head that settled the boater back into place.

The laughter of children throwing chunks of bread to quacking ducks filled the awkward silence. A governess fluttered around them as if they were the ducklings that so excited them.

"We're walking along the banks of Tyburn Brook, you know," Harry began, as much to fill the hiatus as for any particular reason. He waved an arm back in the direction of Marble Arch. "And back there at the site of Tyburn village, is where they used to hang convicted criminals." He glanced sideways, relieved to see the faintest twitch of a grin in Jolyon's expression.

"You aren't a criminal, Harry."

"Neither is Oscar," Harry said, eager to make redress for his put down. "Not really. Only in the eyes of a narrow-minded society." He sighed and came to a halt.

Jolyon stopped and turned to face him. For a moment he gazed at Harry, and then unexpectedly flung his arms around Harry's waist and hugged him. The nanny ushering her charges away from duck dinner gave them a disapproving look as she strode past on the pathway. Jolyon chuckled playfully against Harry's chest. Harry couldn't stop himself from combing fingers through the fine blond hair, cherishing the elegant shape of the skull beneath. It felt as if an unspoken pact had been formulated. As suddenly as he initiated the hug, Jolyon broke free, his features set in a hard-to-read expression.

"Give me time, Harry." He turned to look out over the lake. "You said this was a brook. What happened to it?"

The abrupt change of subject took Harry aback, but he warned himself for the umpteenth time to go with Jolyon's jinking thought processes. "I… I suppose it just got filled in last century when they began developing Mayfair and the old brook turned into a lake. Perhaps it still exists underground at either end, flowing as a subterranean stream." They started walking again.

"It's a fine metaphor, subterranean stream…" In another swift shift, which afterward Harry thought might not have been such a change of direction, Jolyon said, "There is love in me, you know." He sounded sad. "At least, I think there used to be." He turned back to look at Harry. "I had a huge crush on you when I was a child." He glanced down shyly and kicked at a stone lying half in the verge of the pathway. "I think I may still do."

The words were softly spoken, but Harry heard them well enough. He wanted to reach out and take Jolyon in his arms, return that impulsive hug with something more meaningful, but a sense that it wasn't yet the time held him back. Inappropriately perhaps, a line from Wilde's *The Picture of Dorian Gray* leapt into Harry's scrabbling thoughts: *The world is changed because you are made of ivory and gold; the curves of your lips rewrite history.*

As if Jolyon read his mind, he took Harry's arm, pulled them both to a halt, and smiled… almost warmly. "I will miss you, you know."

"Really?"

Jolyon nodded his graceful head and the bangs of stylishly cut hair, no longer effete in appearance though, dropped across his eyes as if to hide what he was feeling. "Yes. Really, Harry. After all, who will I have to irritate, especially as I won't have to pretend I'm living under my aunt's eaves any longer?"

Harry grunted, part-amusement, part-irritation.

"I make you a promise. I'll examine my options as to which branch of the military I might opt for. I've always had a yen for the sea, you know. And I'll write and let you know my decision so you can scold me from afar."

Harry gave a resigned nod of the head and then reached his arms around Jolyon's slight frame and hugged him again. To his delighted surprise, he didn't pull away. In fact he wrapped his arms around Harry and gripped hard for the second time in as many minutes.

"Try not to be away too long, Harry. Please."

PART FOUR

Envious eyes, green with covetousness, 1896–1899

Over all is a bright blue sky and powerful sun.
Such is the scenery of the theatre of war.

— Winston S. Churchill, *The Story of the Malakand Field Force*

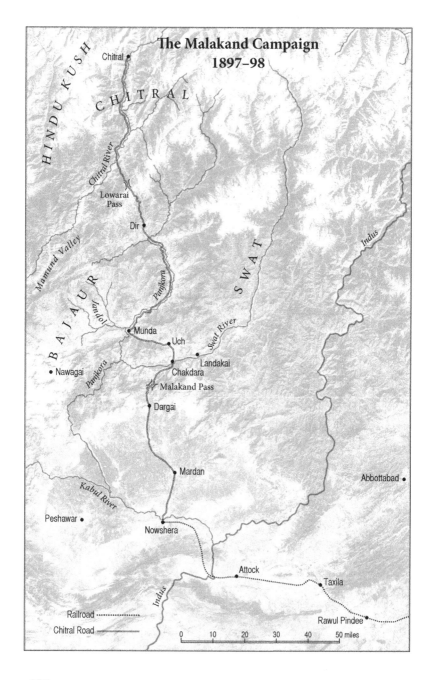

The Malakand Campaign
1897–98

HINDU KUSH

Chitral

CHITRAL

Chitral River

Lowarai
Pass

Dir

SWAT

Indus

Mamund Valley

BAJAUR

Jandol

Panjkora

Munda

Uch

Swat River

Landakai

Nawagai

Panjkora

Chakdara

Malakand Pass

Dargai

Mardan

Abbottabad

Kabul River

Peshawar

Nowshera

Attock

Taxila

Indus

Railroad ············
Chitral Road ──────

Rawul Pindee

0   10   20   30   40   50 miles

CHAPTER 19 | *India, 1896 to 1898*

NOW IN HIS THIRTIES, Harry recognized that it was time to take stock of his amatory inclinations. The first of his loves was pure and untarnished by expectation, the glow of falling for Richard Rainbow a part of something gloriously perfect. With the adamancy of youth he'd sworn that there would never be another. Yet the very enjoyment of physical relations with Richard at Hadlicote, at Sandhurst, and through the burning Bayuda Desert watered the seeds of his vow's destruction. Virtuous Harry Smythe-Vane succumbed to the natural and normal urges of any young man. In England, he curbed his appetite for sex—what point in pining for what was not readily available? (And he'd witnessed what happened to those like Wilde who strayed beyond society's pale.) But he did miss the comfort of lying with William or Arshan, and so it was time to admit that what he perceived in Jolyon was a lot more than a legitimate affection for someone placed spiritually in his care. Jolyon was handsome, lithe, and a natural flirt. Harry could not deny how much in their last few weeks together he wanted to take Jolyon to his bed.

His words to Richard at Rissington Manor haunted like revenants: *We travel different roads, Richard. I think William and Arshan made it possible for me to hold you in my heart and yet extend affection to others. You have completed your trek. I am yet on mine.*

"Bangalore! I tell you, Harry, this is not at all what I had in mind. I've been dealt a poor hand by Damnéd Fate, which is the politest name I can think of for the bloody War Office."

"Winston, there isn't any point moaning about it."

The two were stood on deck, relieved to have left the sweltering Red Sea behind. Churchill stared belligerently through the eyepiece of his powerful telescope, which had been much in demand among the other young officers to scan the coasts of Arabia to port and Africa to starboard. They had sailed for Bombay on September 11, Winston as a cornet with the Queen's 4th Hussars, who were relieving the 19th Hussars, Harry to join the Dorsetshire Regiment 1st Battalion for an unspecified period of time.

"Knowing you, I'll bet your cards will change soon and fate, or the War Office perhaps, will deliver you to the blood and guts you desire so much."

"I crave only action I can turn into high excitement for the armchair generals back home, Harry. I'm happy to leave the gore to you older professionals. But for crying out loud… Bangalore! The action is on the North-West Frontier, not in buggering Bangalore—"

"Think of it as a kind of vacation rest-home for weary soldiers."

Harry's humor did not mollify Churchill. His eyes took on a far away look and then he peered critically through the telescope at the far horizon of the Arabian Sea. "It's all right for older men like you. You've had your moment of glory." He took his eye away, looked sideways at Harry, and turned on one of his charm-assault smiles. "Hero of Chitral."

"That's enough of the 'old,' Winston, thank you. Nine years your senior doesn't exactly qualify me for a walking stick, yet. And I rather hope I have a little more glory in me before my day is done."

Salacious thoughts of Jolyon melded with the presence of his companion. He had been reminded often enough on the month-long sea voyage of Winston Churchill's attractiveness in appearance and character. There were those, he knew, who found Churchill "bumptious," but to Harry his companion's self-assertion (possibly due to being half-American) made a refreshing change from the stuffiness of the typical officers' mess. Apart from anything else, he shared with Harry a preference for hiding away with a book rather than joining the high jinks in the mess wardroom, an eremitic habit that Churchill's fellow subalterns called unsocial (as a captain, Harry was expected to be more reserved).

Achingly—and in so many ways—he resembled Richard Rainbow at that age, though Churchill was shorter in stature. A slight, delicate looking boy, although in fact extremely strong (as Harry knew from losing arm-wrestling matches to him) with blue eyes, many freckles, and short hair, always of a tidy appearance, which threatened to be a decided red, young Churchill's rounded face had enough angularity in the jaw to prevent him seeming pretty. From finely drawn lips, his manner of speaking was nervous, eager, explosive, to match his impulsive nature. This manifested itself toward Harry in a readiness to be physically close in one-to-one conversation, to reach out, touch, and hold for emphasis in making a point.

Harry found his libido becoming engaged. Not for the first time, he wished he were ten years younger and had attended Sandhurst with Winston… but also with Richard, as he indeed had. In a dreamy way, he put them together and drew mental images of himself in bed with Richard-Winston. An unbidden wave of lust washed through his body like a shock of hot-cold water and the image of a naked Jolyon tormented him. Fantasy of course. He'd never seen Jo without his clothes. Even in the intimacy of the Albany or South Street, modesty prevailed.

Bangalore was not what Harry had hoped for on his recall to overseas duty either. For one it meant no reunion with Arshan, no reunion with William Maplethorpe, always assuming both were still stationed at Rawul Pindee and not out in the wilderness guarding the Swat at the Malakand Pass, or farther to the north in Chitral where tribal unrest threatened again. For another, by all reports, delightful as it might be, Bangalore was a colonial backwater.

"Do you know what Bangalore means?" Winston said with an emphatic collapse of his telescope.

This was another intriguing aspect of the man, Churchill's extraordinary kleptomania in general knowledge, unusual in one who professed no academic abilities whatsoever.

"The southern regions of India are not my strong point," Harry said, gracing the comment with a mocking frown.

Churchill squeezed out one of his impish grins. "The Indian name is Bengaluru. Did you know that? I thought not, hardly anyone does who doesn't hail from Mysore. It means Town of Boiled Beans." He added the last sentence with the kind of triumphant rabbit-from-a-top-hat flourish that demanded astonishment from his listener.

Duly, Harry stepped back in surprise. "Boiled beans?"

"Yes! There is a legend that a woman once cooked some beans for a lost king and in thanks for her saving him from starving, he named the place accordingly."

Harry laughed. "I do hope, Winston, much as I love my legumes, that there will be more than boiled pulses to charm the palate when we get there."

The landing in Bombay went much as it had when Harry arrived with William Maplethorpe in '85… eleven years. It seemed like only yesterday. He'd been almost twenty months younger then than Winston was now.

There was one incident, however. In his boyish enthusiasm to get off the ship and into a lighter, Churchill mistimed his swing from hull ladder to boat and dislocated a shoulder in the process, and so arrived on the shore swearing as only a good Harrovian could, supported by Harry and another cornet. "Don't tell me, I know, it's a bloody Wednesday. Typical! I hate Wednesdays."

After a few day's rest at Poona, officers and men traveled by train to Bangalore. The cantonment could not have been more of a contrast to Rawul Pindee: if buff-and-yellow described the northern town, every hue of green clothed Bangalore. From widespread compounds shaded by numerous trees and shrubs, well-established bungalows peeked out shyly from behind their neatly trimmed hedges. Officers' accommodation boasted every comfort, with many spacious rooms, even for those junior officers obliged to muck in two or three to a bungalow. Churchill shared with two other cornets, but on Harry's first visit he showed off the three big rooms which were all his own.

My property is mine alone and comes complete with a butler and a "dressing boy," Harry wrote to Jolyon. I share with my next-door neighbor two gardeners, three water carriers, three washermen (they call them *dhobies*) and a watchman. The cantonment, sited on the edge of the old town, is vast. It covers almost thirteen square miles. A massive parade ground sits at the heart of what is effectively a self-contained city. We have our own stores, bars, restaurants, theater, a hospital, and—would you believe it—a cathedral! We are three thousand feet above sea level here, high on the central plateau. In consequence Bangalore enjoys a pleasantly warm but not over-hot climate, the opposite of Rawul Pindee, and there is sufficient rainfall to justify its title of Garden City without being subjected to an annually compressed and vicious monsoon.

Once he was settled in, Harry's day varied little from that of his fellow officers, except in his duties, which were concerned with instructing non-commissioned officers on the nature of the North-West Frontier, in particular the region around Chitral, where it was anticipated the Dorsetshires would be eventually stationed. As he wrote to Jolyon two months into his tour: We live a privileged life here in the Mysore station. The Madras Presidency has been peaceful since its subjugation in the time of the Duke of Wellington, plain Arthur Wellesley then. Not even the great mutiny, which so shook up the north of the subcontinent, touched sleepy Madras. So you might imagine that we officers are spoilt by too much time on our hands and fret that any real action is taking place a thousand miles away on the edge of Afghanistan.

I rise early, a little after five, for a first breakfast. The others attend parade at six (I'm only expected to do so once a week), which is followed by a second breakfast and a bath. Then for an hour I prepare my instructions for the infantrymen, who "crave" my experience of the Pathan. Between eight and nine I spend time in the stables. In truth, an army of *syces*, as they call stable grooms here, does the work of looking after the horses and ponies. (My fellow officers are there primarily to ensure their precious polo ponies are in good condition, including Winston Churchill, who plays like a Bengal tiger in spite of still suffering from the shoulder he damaged disembarking in Bombay. As you know, I find *Equus ferus* practical but by no means a hobby.) After that duty I'm free until about four every day except for Monday, Wednesday, and Friday, when there are polo matches to attend. I'm a spectator. I won't play no matter how much Winston badgers me to do so. I have kept up with my boxing and tennis, though.

On occasion I go off in a group to hunt game in the verdant jungles. Pig sticking is the replacement sport for fox hunting in these parts, although there is little comparison for foxes don't usually fight back, whereas a wild boar can be excessively dangerous when cornered. For this reason, dogs are rarely employed. Instead, a cadre of natives acts as beaters to flush out the boars. I dislike the sport as much as I disapproved chasing foxes at Hadlicote, but I go along for the exercise.

My dear Jo (I risk the station censor taking me to task for inappropriate behavior—though so little occurs here I believe the censor's office is fast asleep and doesn't bother with the inner workings of our letters, so damn it), I want to say how much I think of you every day and wish we could repeat the last moments of our walk beside the Serpentine. I'm confident you know what I mean. On a more prosaic note, I am greatly pleased to receive your letter and learn of your decision to think seriously of a career in the Army. Don't go near the Navy. All you will get to see is the sea.

જ⭒ક

"Tell me you are glad we came, Harry."

"It makes a change from being cooped up in barracks."

The driver brought their huge mount to a huffing, snuffling halt and a native dashed forward with a ladder to help the white sahibs down from the howdah on the large bull elephant's back. Churchill dismounted with his usual verve. Harry followed despondently and wondered how he had survived the day. It was not hunting tigers from the back of an elephant that caused his distress; it was his stupidity.

He had managed to turn a delightful break from Bangalore into a train wreck of a disaster. How had it happened?

In viceregal India, hunting tiger and cheetah in the foothills of the Himalayas was the classic sport of the White Raj. It was also an extremely expensive amusement, unless the hunters had influence with one of the Indian princes, which as it turned out Harry did. Maharaja Nripendra Narayan, ruler of the princely state of Koch Bihar in western Bengal, boasted an education at Shottery Hall and Benthenham. Three years Harry's senior, the Maharaja was a near contemporary of Harry's brother Evan, and those two continued a long-distance friendship in the frequent exchange of letters, a connection the prince happily extended to Evan's younger brother. *Be so good as to allow me to provide for your every need*, Nripendra had written, a*nd leave behind Mysore's humidity for a month in our cool Bengali hills.*

It pleased Harry to accept the invitation when young Churchill obtained a period of leave to coincide. In truth, this was not a great achievement in Mysore. "You know, Harry," he said, "the tax-payer's money is ill-spent on us in this sleepy military station. We officers are frankly under-employed."

In the past months Churchill had become a regular visitor to Harry's bungalow in the quiet hours after luncheon and sometimes in the evenings. On occasion, if they took a little too much to drink, Churchill bunked down in one of Harry's spare bedrooms rather than face the sweaty walk across the lines to his own regimental area. At such times, he unselfconsciously stripped off naked in front of Harry, just as if they were same-age pupils at a boarding school. There was such innocence in the action, and yet Harry could never shake off the innervation that he was being led into temptation, an allurement he would be happy to follow, if only… it were more obvious what his friend really wanted.

"Now and then I really need to escape our rowdy regimental mess. Are infantrymen as loud as cavalrymen?" Churchill's question—thrown out on one such evening of companionable reading—was almost certainly rhetorical.

"I don't think you'd see much difference. Senior officers bolt off to play rubbers of bridge and then the youngsters take over."

"I didn't think you were very partial to the cards."

"I don't have your luck." Harry laughed in deprecation of his modesty. He thought of the card table Churchill had his mother send out from England. "Oh, I do play, as you well know. It's a vital social grace, after all. But I prefer the quietude of my little garden-palace to a gin-soaked evening partnering hoary captains and majors, and occasionally having to play a weak hand so the colonel might take the honors." He raised a finger. "You're no different, Winston."

"It's true that I find great solace from my reading and writing. It's tiresome having to adhere to the strict dress code in the mess, with all the standards and etiquette you see observed in the best London clubs, only to have some idiot start a food-throwing contest the minute the senior officers depart for their clubs. It's as well we have three dhobies attached to my quarters to keep our uniforms in a spick and span state."

"I have one-and-a-half, and he's full time washing, starching, and pressing."

"You'll remember next time you receive an invitation from me to dine in our mess to wear your second- or even your third-best uniform. It must have been the boredom of last Thursday, but once dinner was eaten and all above the rank of lieutenant had left for their further—and sober—divertissement, our well-trained servants flocked in to remove all the breakable furniture and replace it with a special set of chairs and tables made to smash to pieces. Astonishing fun was had by all.

"And next week, we're promised a real live gymkhana, with two little bazaar ponies to jump the tables... No, Harry, I much prefer sorting through my growing butterfly collection—I have some spectacular Purple Emperors, White Admirals, and even some pretty Swallowtails—and pottering like a septuagenarian gent among my roses. Next time you pop in for a chota peg or cup of chai you must pay your respects to the Gloire de Dijon with its blush pink-orange center and white corona, the La France with its tight pink, primly coiled secrets, and particularly the spectacular sunburst blossoms of Maréchal Niel."

It seemed to Harry that the only enthusiasm he did not share was Churchill's love of polo—"the emperor of games." Harry enjoyed being on horseback for the pleasure of it, and kept his eye in on the tennis courts when came the time for exercise. In everything else, Churchill appeared to enjoy Harry's company above that of any other, and in his unaffected way gripped Harry by the elbow, the arm, or shoulder, and always fixed him directly with his steady gaze. It seemed, as the weeks and months passed, those blue eyes radiated the message Harry hoped for and its significance drew him deeper in until a day without some sight of his friend was a day lost. The two shared another attribute uncommon among the lusty young officer corps: they did not frequent the Bangalore brothels, and while that might simply mean his friend was abstemious when it came to his natural urges, Harry naturally hoped it meant Churchill rejected the fairer sex for the same reason Harry did. Churchill's eager desire to join him on the long rail trip north to Bengal (something Harry wouldn't have wished to do on his own) seemed to seal an unspoken pact.

Among the exotic splendors of the Koch Bihar court, with its lazy days interspersed with bursts of leisurely hunting, its lengthy feasts and slumberous siestas, perhaps most of all the amatory atmosphere which pervaded the elegant chambers of the palace, Harry's usually well-attuned sensitivity slipped. The concupiscent perfumes of nautch girls with their tinkling ankle and wrist bells at evening banquets subsumed Harry's senses. A heightened sensuousness suffused his whole being. Disaster struck toward the end of a particularly long day at the start of the second week.

The hunt for a cheetah fizzled out in a blur of feline limbs escaping through the cordon of beaters as they drove the big cat toward Harry, Churchill, and Nripendra hidden among thick undergrowth beneath sparse oaks and conifers. With the final bag of the day lost, the frustrated hunters returned to their mounts and rode back to the palace, tired out.

"I'm for a long lounge in the hot baths," Churchill said as he half fell from his mount. He weaved around the syces who rushed up to lead the horses away. "How about you?" He gave Harry a heavily lidded look, full of unspoken beckoning.

"Absolutely."

An hour later they lounged quietly side-by-side against the edge of the deep hot-pool, wreathed in steam and the scent of costly oils. Their host had exited the water and, after being dried by his body servant, led away swathed in towels to the ministrations of his team of masseuses. The Englishmen exchanged wry grins. Nripendra was partial to more than the technical ministrations of his nautch girls, now equipped with little more than flimsy panties and breast coverings. It seemed to Harry that seeing the Maharaja herded to his private massage room and the undoubted delights it held prompted Churchill's thoughts into words.

"I hate to pry," he said softly, and twisted his head sideways against the damp towels softening the marbled edge of the huge bath to look at Harry. "We've spoken of many things: of horses; of native soldiery and their discipline; a great deal of the North-West Frontier, which is where we should be stationed, keeping the Russian at bay; of which chai wallah makes the best tea; of roses and butterflies… yet I know almost nothing of your domestic arrangements at home." He smiled engagingly, one corner of his mobile mouth upturned, the opposed eyebrow raised in question.

The spry expression encouraged Harry, who felt they had finally arrived at that fulcrum in a relationship where it is *almost* safe to take the crucial step. The one from which there is no return—the step that divides a burgeoning relationship on one side from the upland of sexual fulfilment on the other. Under the steaming surface of the water, Harry wandered his hand, as if it floated there of its own thoughtless will, fingers stretched out, until they made contact with the skin of Churchill's adjacent thigh. A single silken stroke…

Misread signals. There was no other way to say it. He'd projected his inner wishes to form the reciprocal desire he thought he perceived in his companion. It was not hunting tigers from the back of an elephant that caused Harry's distress but his fatuity. As the returning hunting party stepped up from the grounds into the shade of the long arcaded veranda, Harry strode ahead to put himself apart, intending to hasten straight to his suite and hide away until the inevitability of the evening feast.

The deep shame he felt, laced with an unreasonable animosity toward Churchill for "misleading him," was mixed with bemusement at Churchill's reaction to his sexual advance: not the vicious rejection of shocked indignation, nor protestations of not being "like that, and how dare you!" Instead, he'd simply reached back over the edge of the bath for one of the big fluffy towels piled up, a movement which, as he half-turned, caused Harry's trailing fingers to rub right over Churchill's genitals. He snatched back his errant hand in sudden alarm, but his companion quietly stood and turned halfway toward where Harry lay pinioned by his own uncertainty. As if nothing untoward had occurred Churchill stood and wrapped the towel around his middle.

At dinner that night, Churchill entertained the company with tales of his Cuban adventures and included Harry without any sign of tension. But the next day, squeezed together in the rocking howdah hunting tiger, Harry would have given his right arm to be free of his companion's imperturbable manner. He felt accused by Churchill's inaction. Getting down from the howdah, he almost fled.

On reaching his suite, he sent his valet-wallah away, insisting he could look after himself for once, stripped off the khaki pants, safari jacket, and stepped to the small bathroom with its tub. Half an hour later, bathed and spread out listlessly on the bed, covered by a light dressing gown, a quiet tap at the far door heralded a visitor. Harry sat partway up and stared in silence at Churchill, who crossed the sitting room to the bedroom doorway. A cheery smile brightened his puckish features. Harry moved himself into a more comfortable (and defensive) position with his back against the elaborate bedhead. Without invitation Churchill dragged one of the light cane chairs across toward the bed, spun it around, and sat astride it. He rested his arms on the near-chin-height back and opened the conversation directly.

"I perceive you are distressed, my dear Harry, in a way I've never before seen. And really, I can't think why. It was, after all, simply one of those little accidents men are well aware of, and can't be avoided. We've both been in the changing rooms of the school gym, or the baths, or even the communal house bathrooms, and these brushes happen. Really, you mustn't worry about it."

He's letting me off the hook. How can that be? He knows what really happened yesterday.

Churchill tipped his round head back to stare up at the intricate stucco of the ceiling, and spoke in musing tone. "There was a chap at Harrow was very soft on me. It was most terribly flattering, but a dreadful inconvenience. Fortunately, I knew how to deal with the bullies one always finds in such establishments—after all, we're not short of them now down in Bangalore when you'd think they'd have grown out of such childishness. You see, I'd read my accounts of Byron's life there, of the 'bum and buggery' sessions senior men inflicted on poor juniors, so I was prepared to overcome all adversity on that score. Having a fellow crushing on one as obviously as I endured (I'm unfair, he was fine fellow, really, just inconvenient) is tantamount to having a Cupid firing arrows at you, a signpost pointing the finger so that even the most thick-headed of boors knows to pick on one."

He punched the air in a curiously boyish gesture, which made Harry crack a wan smile.

"Ah! Better. Much better. A smile even, for Winston. What am I gassing on about? Well, I suppose I'm saying friendship counts for a great deal more than spoiled or missed opportunities, my dear Harry. And you are my friend, and I greatly hope will remain so. Will you be dining?"

The quick change of subject took Harry by surprise, but he quickly rallied, feeling that their roles in age had been reversed, he the callow boy, Winston the teacher. "Will you mind terribly if I don't? I'm sure my valet-wallah will fetch me something. I feel as if the elephant's gait has left me feeling a little seasick, which is odd, because I never am seasick, as you know."

Churchill accepted the excuse gamely. He got up and replaced the chair. "Nripendra has a relaxing day planned for tomorrow, so there'll be time to recoup your landlubber's legs." As he reached the door, he turned briefly. "Do have an enjoyable night, Harry."

Churchill crossed the sitting room and let himself out. Harry sat on the edge of his bed, puzzled by the emphasis of that last remark.

❦✻❦

The valet brought some cold cuts and a cool mango sherbet. When he came to clear the plates he spoke quietly. "Sahib, the shampooer is here for you."

Harry frowned. "I didn't ask for a… shampooer?"

"Oh yes, sahib. Is very delightful and relaxation for you."

It seemed he was not to be put off, and a minute later a young man entered, wearing only a tightly wound loincloth. His golden body, oiled, glistened in the lamplight. If the notion of being shampooed intrigued Harry, the fact that a bath had little to do with it surprised him greatly. His lithe and handsome shampooer expressed delight that his client was dressed only in a light gown, which the boy—for he was, Harry thought, no older than Arshan was when they first met—promptly removed. He didn't give his customer time to express alarm at this unexpected disrobing and bade Harry, "Be comfortable, sahib." He plumped the pillows and arranged Harry carefully on the bed. Then he dipped into the small raffia basket he'd brought with him to remove some small vials. Emptying the contents of two into his palms, he rubbed them together and then began to massage Harry's calves and knees.

The sensation was instantly relaxing and at the same time arousing. So was the boy's low-voiced, mesmerizing drone as he worked and explained everything that followed.

"I embrace the rule of Vatsayayana in the performance of Auparishtaka, a ritual most enobling of man." In a light tenor voice he almost sang the words. "I press the thighs now and draw myself up closer, to touch the joints of the thighs I am shampooing, and now the jaghana, the central portions of your body. Aahh, so it is. I find your lingam stands proud…"

The boy held and squeezed Harry's erection, a state he'd not even realized he'd reached until the insistent touch.

"Tsk, tsk, you should not be in this condition, naughty sahib. What should I now do? No! I cannot do that, no matter how you beg it of me. This is the order of the things I cannot perform for you, sahib, in the rite of Auparishtaka. But as you force me to it, I shall tell you of the first state, though I will not perform any farther, no matter how much you beg it of me.

"First, I hold you by the lingam…"

Harry lay supine, enraptured. The shampoo boy lowered his head and placed his lips around Harry's foreskin, working it gently to and fro and slowly exposing the plum-shaped glans. He spoke around his work.

"This is called the Nominal Congress, so now to the Outside Pressing, when I press the end of the lingam with closed lips, kissing it as if to draw it out." He stopped speaking in order to perform the act, which left Harry pressing his head back into the pillows in a growing ecstasy.

"Now I cover the end of the lingam with my fingers collected together like the bud of a flower and press the sides of it with my lips and gentle pressing of teeth. This is Biting the Sides. And now I must not proceed any farther—"

Harry gasped. "Don't, please… don't stop."

"You are most insistent, sahib. I must obey your command, for I am only a lowly shampooer. Now I take your lingam deeper into my mouth…" which he did. "I press with my lips and it is called the Inside Pressing. And now I hold the lingam firmly in my hand and kiss all around, which is called the Kissing."

Through closed lids, Harry perceived the red glow of lamplight. He tried to control his breathing, but he'd never before felt waves of sensation so powerful as this boy aroused in every nerve of his body. Each delicate touch, feather-light to insistent, provoked his cock and balls and built a heat that radiated out to his toes and his crawling scalp. The shampooer proceeded to the next position, which he called the Rubbing. His busy tongue seemed to be everywhere, up and down, around the head, over the sensitive tip, and lower down, a flittering, wet, wonderful feeling. And then Harry gasped out loud as fully half of his rampant shaft vanished between the boy's pursed lips.

"Sucking a Mango Fruit," the shampooer mumbled. "And now, finally, we do the Great Swallowing, and…"

He ceased speaking. His head fell down. He took Harry's entire length almost as if inhaling him. On the screen of his closed eyes Harry saw Jolyon's sweet face, grinning in anticipation, parting his lips and then stretching them wide to fit Harry's bulky girth between them. The fluctuant throat muscles, in tandem with a powerful tongue, squeezed shaft against ribbed palate. The combination worked a miracle, and succumbing to the all-consuming sensation, Harry began to ejaculate in completion of Auparishtaka.

For an eternity of orgasm Harry left himself. He floated free, saw his body prone on the bed, limbs splayed in an X-shape. A black-haired succubus with bobbing head bent over the fork of his frame obscured his middle.

The warm mouth eased his passion, relinquished its fleshy grip, finished him with gentle licking, abandoned him.

It took minutes to recover from the extraordinary effect, while the shampooer tidied away his wares in the small basket.

"May I ask… someone sent you to me. But who? Was it…?" he didn't like to think of his host being so in tune with his guest's sexual predilection, even if the ritual was commonplace in this palace. "Was it the Maharaja?"

The shampooer looked surprised. "Oh no, sahib. It was other sahib."

What other sahib?

The boy left, and in a state of the greatest lethargy induced by the astonishing force of his climax Harry drifted into a deep sleep, the puzzle of who had ordered the shampooer—

He shot bolt upright, eyes staring.

Do have an enjoyable night, Harry…

CHAPTER 20 | *Bangalore and Afghanistan, 1897*

BANGALORE, JULY 25

My dearest Jo, this might be my last epistle to you, though I pray not. Mortality seems uppermost in my thinking today. There in England, you may already know of my father's death last month, but the news reached me only yesterday. I'm sure mother is more saddened by the event than her letter informs. On the other hand, they were ever the "proper" English patriarch and matriarch; the wearing of hearts on sleeves something to be avoided at all cost. No doubt I shall have to visit Hadlicote on my next leave. That's always supposing I survive what's to come. But let's be bright. The Pathans didn't get me at Chitral and I shall remain confident in the belief that they will fail again at Malakand.

Tomorrow I depart for the North-West Frontier Province to a fort vital to our interests, where substantial rumors tell of tribesmen preparing to take up arms against the British position at the Malakand Pass, which guards the road to Chitral, our distant bulwark against Russia. On a light note, yesterday I received a hastily scrawled note from Winston Churchill—his handwriting is execrable—to say: 1) how excited he is at hearing of the uprising; and 2): what a "buggering nuisance" it is that he might miss out on "the fun." What was desirable in getting away from India for leave in London to petition anyone of influence at the War Office to post him to the field of battle now turns out to be entirely inopportune to his purpose of achieving glory in action.

From the Swat to Chitral, the tribesmen grow restive, driven by charlatans among them to a manufactured frustration. These religious fanatics play on the typical superstition of mountain dwellers, which exposes them to the ranting of a complex priesthood—the Akhundzada, Mullahs, and Sahbzadas to name a few of these *malang*, or wandering fakirs. From the time I spent in Chitral, worst in my opinion among these are the itinerant monks called Talib-ul-ilms. It surely isn't possible to find more wretched, filthy, and immoral men than these religious incendiaries, but the natives they sponge off hold them in high regard, even when the rogues demand sexual favors of their womenfolk.

In one respect our interference has provided a fuse for the mullahs to light, and that is the Durand Line. Named after Sir Mortimer Durand, who was commissioned to form a boundary between British India and Amir Abdur Rahman's Afghanistan, it causes much upheaval. The two authorities approved the boundary two years before the Chitral uprising. Sadly, mapmaker, surveyor, and pundit took no account of what an arbitrary division of ancestral Pashtoon tribal lands would mean to those affected, who were never consulted. The many tribesmen who woke one morning to find their homes fell under British rule while their grazing was stuck out of reach in Afghanistan have been ever unhappy.

And it doesn't take much to excite the Pathan to battle. Among the mountain tribes blood feuds lasting for generations are commonplace. I have heard that Canadian Eskimos have more than twenty words to describe snow. I assure you that Pashtoons have many more to define different kinds of feud. There is even one to describe revenge between cousins! Such a people, you can imagine, do not take kindly to foreigners dividing their possessions or foreign armies trampling through their lands. They make friendly allies one minute, deadly foemen the next.

Earlier this year, reports from the forts at Malakand and nearby Chakdara indicated trouble brewing among the Swati tribes, a sullenness among their soldiers serving in the Army as well as an uncooperative attitude from village headmen. The military road to Chitral, constructed in the wake of the '85 uprising, has only increased tribal unease. The intent is that we can move troops and materiel swiftly to the front when the Russians invade, as seems sure. But many Pashtoons view this development with great suspicion. Not only can the petty chiefs no longer charge rahdari, the traditional toll—though they are paid compensation—they believe its true purpose is to help in their subjugation.

The Talibs preach jihad against the infidel. It's tiresome to face obdurate, religious fanaticism again, as I did in the Sudan. There it was the deluded Mahdi. Here in Afghanistan it is a Talib who calls himself Mullah Sadullah, who has seduced the tribesmen into believing all kinds of incredible things of his powers. He has persuaded the Swatis that British bullets cannot harm them as they turn like rain to water the soil and that our gun barrels will melt. The British troops stationed at Malakand have named him the Mad Mullah. In the Sudan we called the Mahdi mad but it didn't stop him being lethal.

I must attend to my final packing, ready for the wearying train journey to Rawul Pindee and thence to the railhead at Nowshera. So to duty, but know this, Jo—I cannot wait to be in London, where I yearn to walk the *Serpentine* with you again.

On the following day, July 26, even as Harry prepared to leave his comfortable Bangalore residence, warriors of the Mohmand and Bunerwal tribes of the Swat Valley attacked the Malakand and Chakdara forts.

The British officers of the scattered parts of what was loosely called the Malakand Fort had finished a game of polo. One of their number, Lieutenant Haldane Rattray, set out to ride the eight miles to his command, the small fort and signal tower above the River Swat at Chakdara. He was two miles from his objective when he encountered two cavalry troopers galloping in the opposite direction. They had seen the advancing tribal army. Knowing he was closer to Chakdara than Malakand, with extraordinary courage Rattray put spurs to his horse and rode right through the tribesmen. On reaching the fort he sent a signal to the political officer at Malakand, Major Harold Deane, who in turn alerted the Corps of Guides at Mardan, thirty-two miles to the south, and requested immediate reinforcements. It was barely in time. Minutes after Deane sent the telegram advancing tribesmen cut the Chakdara–Malakand and Malakand–Mardan telegraph lines and burned the poles.

At Mardan, Colonel Adams, commanding the Guides, put his troopers to their boast of instant readiness, and within three hours they were on their way.

At Bangalore, General Sir Charles Thomas van Straubenzee, commanding the Dorsetshires, ordered Harry to stand down until matters a thousand miles to the north became clearer.

The siege of Malakand was actually two separate actions. At Chakdara a force of only two hundred men—a handful of British junior officers and Indian sepoys—faced twelve thousand foes. The situation looked hopeless, but Rattray had one lifeline left and one serious advantage over his opponents. Although the telegraph line was down, Chakdara could still communicate with Malakand by heliograph and—with greater difficulty and only sporadically—Malakand with Mardan and so beg for reinforcements. And the fort possessed two of the latest Maxim machine guns, which went some way to equalize the disparity in numbers.

The Pashtoons attacked endlessly throughout the day, and used noise and threatened attacks to wear down the tiny garrison at night. Yet the British beat back each assault, leaving piles of corpses below the walls. By the sixth day, with ammunition and water running low, it seemed as if the plucky little garrison must be overwhelmed. As the fighting reached crisis point the cavalry of the relieving Corps of Guides appeared on a nearby ridge. The enemy turned and ran.

When he finally made it to Malakand in September Harry heard how the cavalry pursued the disordered rout of tribesmen for over three miles, dashed in among the panicked warriors "doing splendid execution by sword and lance."

At Malakand the Mad Mullah led the assault on the fort, and as many of the enemy attacked as had done at Chakdara. For days they threw themselves against the walls in a suicidal screaming frenzy, only to fall in their scores before superior weaponry. On the first day Mullah Sadullah showed his contempt of those he commanded by hiding behind a shield formed of young teenaged boys, all of whom were slaughtered instantly in the sleet of lead poured from British rifles and machine guns.

Stalled at Bangalore and fretting as much as the man stuck in England he corresponded with, Harry wrote: "For once the authorities act with dispatch, Winston. Barely does the war begin and a special 'Malakand Field Force' is formed, commanded by Brigadier-General Sir Bindon Blood, who has recently arrived from England. However, he is a veteran of Afghanistan, South Africa, Egypt, and India. He doesn't waste time, either—he received a telegram on July 28 appointing him to his command, and three days later he was at Nowshera, a thousand miles away, marshaling his troops. Urged by heliographed cries for help, he set out from Mardan at 3 am on August 1 and force-marched to Malakand, reaching there by noon. In the ensuing fight Sadullah was slain and the fight went out of the tribesmen. The Malakand Field Force broke through the enemy's lines and ended the siege on August 2."

Sir Bindon Blood's appointment excited Winston, already preparing a hurried departure for India. "Lacking as yet any commission to the frontier, I am on my way to buggering Bangalore under my own steam. My mother and other close acquaintances have some sway over Sir Bindon, so I am sure he will let me join this splendid sounding Malakand Field Force."

Harry generously ignored the probably malicious gossip reaching ears in Bangalore that while Sir Bindon-Blood was still in London Lady Randolph Churchill exercised her feminine wiles in the general's bed to persuade him to look favorably on her son's request for a posting to the war front. For his own part Harry was less thrilled at the prospect of renewing his acquaintance with Churchill. It was one thing to communicate in written form, another to face the young man with whom he'd attempted to commence an affair. On returning to the cantonment of Bangalore in the immediate aftermath of the incident, Churchill's insouciant and unspoken acceptance of what occurred in Koch Bihar unnerved Harry. Now he wondered whether, with more time away from the environment to think about it, Churchill's feelings might have undergone a weather-change. He couldn't help but worry that Churchill must naturally harbor resentment at a blithe assumption that their sexual inclinations coincided. And with a guilty conscience he twice started to write Jolyon intending to explain, and twice ripped up the unfinished letter. Jo might "miss him" and want him to "hurry back," but that didn't mean he'd be jealous at the thought of Harry seeking an erotic involvement with another man. While he worried that Jo *might* be jealous, he was more frightened of uncovering Jolyon's possible indifference.

In the event he need not have worried. On his breathless return to Bangalore, Churchill's only interest was to secure the support of his long-suffering commanding officer to be given leave from his Bangalore duties the moment he heard from Sir Bindon Blood. Toward Harry, he was nothing less than an excited and at times frustrated friend, until a communication at the end of August granted him all he desired. "Sir Bindon writes that I should proceed immediately and come as a press correspondent, and when I get there he promises to put me on the strength at the first opportunity."

"What good news, Winston. And here I am, delayed by a month of indecision still waiting to hear whether or not my experience is required. Have you secured a press commission?"

"Finally, yes. I'm less than happy to be representing the *Daily Telegraph* but *The Times* has already signed up that vainglorious, medal-seeking Viscount Fincastle, and the popinjay is already fighting on the front covering himself with glory as well as earning the stipend that should have been mine. Still, the *Telegraph* has come along, I suppose, and I have just heard that I have an arrangement to write also for the *Allahabad Pioneer*... that's Rudyard Kipling's old rag you know," he added redundantly. Harry did know. Everyone knew. And Harry knew of Churchill's admiration for Kipling, and that to write for the *Pioneer* would add to his glow of satisfaction. He also hid a smile at hearing Churchill's pot calling Fincastle's kettle black.

Harry's papers came through a day later and when he showed Churchill his marching orders he was reticent at first of suggesting they share the journey, but gave in before Churchill's boisterous insistence.

"Harry, it will be too tedious without some company. I know I've been beastly about getting up there, but I'm sure the Pathan and my glory can stand to wait one more day while you gather your stuff ready. Now just get on with it!"

The reestablished telegraph provided quantities of information, refreshed at every halt on the lengthy rail journey, about the situation in the North-West Frontier Province, which gave them plenty to discuss. "A surprise, followed by a sustained attack, has been resisted, Harry. The troops will now assume the offensive, and the hour of reprisals will come."

Harry wasn't very happy at the idea of reprisal. "We are formed to be punitive raiders in recognition that the entire frontier is now in peril, I understand. Yet I hope a more reasonable attitude will prevail."

"While the religious fanatics scurry about garnering kudos for themselves and acting as the grit in an oyster to make a pearl, the simple Pathan will rise to the occasion of jihad."

"A pearl seems an inappropriate metaphor for jihad, Winston. Besides, the bigger part of this picture is the Russian threat." Harry had observed that his friend seemed oddly unmoved about the Russians, and had sometimes gone as far as to declare that they were all bluster and no determination. They would never be a threat, he argued. Harry countered this ill-founded claim vigorously. "If we cannot protect Chitral, so close across an unmarked border with Russian Tajikistan, the Bear who only waits poised with sheathed claws to see the outcome of Pashtoon rebellion will be ready to seize advantage. Never before in our lifetime has India been in such peril."

It had to be stated, but Harry also heard the ring of pompousness in his pronouncement.

Churchill shrugged off this opinion. The topic that most exercised him was the journalist-cum-officer Alexander Edward Murray, 8th Earl of Dunmore, but widely known as Viscount Fincastle, who was attached to the Corps of Guides cavalry. Churchill's egregious rival had joined the first punitive strike against the tribesmen who assaulted Malakand and Chakdara while Harry and Churchill traveled the extent of the subcontinent in a series of clattering trains. As they learned at Poona, Sir Bindon Blood had taken two brigades—about 3,500 British and native soldiers and eighteen field guns—into the upper Swat Valley, a country that had not seen a white man since "Alexander sent an army that way when he invaded India," the general later wrote.

At Bhopal, in the middle of nowhere, Churchill hopped down from the sweltering carriage yet again and dashed to the telegraph office, waving his commission, while Harry waited patiently under the shade of the station awning to hear what developments the wire might reveal. When he returned clutching two thin sheets of telegraph paper to where Harry had slipped into a doze, Churchill looked extremely vexed.

"We can lay to rest the rumors of the Mad Mullah's death in the final days at Malakand. He thrives and has roused the Pashtoons in Swat and there has been the very devil of a fight at Landakai up the valley." He cast feverish eyes up and down the purloined communication. "The enemy held a strong position on a high ridge overlooking a bend of the river. But they did not reckon on the heavy guns, which helped drive them off as the 1st Battalion Royal West Kents attacked up the ridge and our native levies moved in on their flank."

Harry stretched his legs. "What were the casualties like?"

Churchill scanned the flimsy to the bottom. "Very light, considering. None killed, eleven wounded compared to several hundred of the enemy slain or wounded."

"So why do I think something has annoyed you, Winston?"

"During the mopping up operation, bloody Fincastle joined in a cavalry charge against some fleeing tribesmen. Headstrong and heedless of danger, they dashed across muddy rice fields to catch the foe before they could reach the hills and escape. It seems a lieutenant... where is it? Robert Greaves. I know his name. He is... was... a correspondent for the *Times of India*. He became cut off from the others in their silly haste. He was shot, fell from his mount to be instantly surrounded by tribesmen bent on hacking him to pieces. Then

Fincastle dashed to his rescue. His horse was shot out from under him, but still he ran on toward fallen Greaves, while some Guides rallied around and tried to help Fincastle get the fallen man on a horse. In the subsequent melee, Greaves was hit again and died instantly and another subaltern, Maclean, was shot through both thighs…" Churchill glanced up. "He also died. And yet under the constant fire raining down on them, Fincastle managed to extricate himself, his few men, the two bodies of Greaves and Maclean, as well as two other wounded officers, and bring them to safety."

"Who wrote the dispatch?"

"Who do you think! The last section is by the man himself." Churchill slapped the papers against his thigh. "Dammit all, Harry. The blasted man promotes himself to his own newspaper. Fincastle will surely get a VC for this. And I haven't even got to Malakand yet!"

"I don't think the Pashtoons will give up so easily, Winston. There will be still time for glory."

The pursed-lip scowl slipped and Churchill turned a rueful grin on Harry. "Still, it was bravely done. Fincastle's is the spirit that loses the Empire many lives, but in compensation it gains many battles."

On the sixth day the train pulled into Rawul Pindee, a familiar sight for Harry but it left Churchill unimpressed. Two days later on the road for Nowshera he said of the place, "Dusty roads, burnt-up grass, intense heat, and deserted barracks. I am unable, Harry, to recommend it as a resting place for either the sybarite, the invalid, or the artist."

"When I was stationed here, it was lively enough, and a bit green after the monsoon, but now the tent lines are quiet because so many are either up in Swat or at Tirah confronting the Afridi uprising. You ask me, it was the Afridis that sparked the Mohmand and Bunerwal Pashtoons in the Swat Valley to rebel."

At Rawul Pindee Churchill had obtained a proper roof over his head from a friend serving with the 4th Dragoon Guards, while Harry went in fruitless search of… he knew he would not find William Maplethorpe. Their old Hussar regiment had rotated back to England some months before. So did he wish to meet Arshan?

Can the past be brought back as it was? And what of my feelings for Jolyon? It troubled him that his motive in wanting to find Arshan was not really clear in his mind—a natural wish to acknowledge a friendship forged in hardship, a natural inclination to meet an acquaintance on arriving in a place where the person might be expoected to be… or more? *I must be superficial if it's so simple to find comfort elsewhere… anywhere.*

He made his way to the Sudder Bazar and turned into the headquarters building where he had come to see Lockhart, now General Sir William Lockhart and commanding the Punjab Army Corps in the Tirah Valley where the Afridi and Orakzai tribes were up in arms. Eventually, he came across the orderly in service to Lockhart back when Harry first arrived in India, who told him that Arshan was "possible in Simla, possible Meerut, possible here, sahib."

To Harry's mind, the man sounded purposefully obscure, and his last possibility turned out to be a probability. It was Arshan who recognized Harry. Two years had wrought sufficient change in the boy, now so smartly dressed as an official army orderly-wallah and filled out in physique, that Harry wouldn't have known him at a distance. But up close the laughing eyes with their often-unnerving direct gaze were unmistakeable.

"Haari! It *is* you!"

They retreated from the afternoon's heat to a small teahouse outside the confines of the cantonment. Without restraint, Arshan grabbed Harry's hands in his own as they sat on rattan chairs on the same side of a small table. The chai-wallah, evidently familiar with Arshan, waved an acknowledgment from across the airy room and without further orders brought a tray containing a chased bronze hot water pot over a small charcoal heater, sprinkled whole oolong leaves onto the steaming surface of the water, and stirred them gently for a minute. Then he left Arshan to pour the tea into two small china cups. As he did so, he chattered on as if they had not been parted for many months; about life in the garrison, how the cavalry units at Meerut under their new commander, a certain Kernel Ba-doonpowl, were anxious to get into the action in the Swat.

In his turn, Harry filled him in on his movements, but he made no move to close the physical gap between them. Arshan eventually broached the subject of the length of Harry's stay in Rawul Pindee and where was he staying, and did he want for company? Arshan saw the hesitation. His ready smile faltered.

"I shan't be here long, you see. I'm supposed to be at Malakand as soon as possible."

"You don't like me any more?"

"It's not that—"

"I think so. Like the bacha bazi, Haari. I grow too old for you."

"No, Arshan. No! It isn't so. I…" He sighed deeply and gripped Arshan's hand. "I don't care about that, about your age. Anyway, you grew beyond bacha bazi age some time ago! You are still handsome, and I would be lying if I said I'm not drawn to you, Arshan… but…"

Arshan pulled his broad mouth into a tight purse and raised one heavy eyebrow in question.

"There is someone at home. In England."

Understanding dawned. "A wife. You are to be married, Haari?"

An embarrassed laugh escaped along with the shake of his head. "No, not a wife. Not marriage. Another man."

"Of course." Arshan looked closely at Harry. "A white man." A dip of Harry's head set Arshan nodding as well, a gesture of acknowledgment. "He is your lover?"

The hesitation came again. Harry had no wish to lie, but the thought of having to explain feelings he wasn't yet clear about, let alone attempt to describe what Jolyon might think about their relationship was too complicated. Whatever expression he wore, it seemed to satisfy Arshan. He squeezed Harry's hand.

"It is good. Anyone Haarivan sahib likes must be good." He gave a sunny smile that never quite reached his eyes. They remained wide, brown pools of sadness.

Outside, Harry impulsively pulled Arshan to him and hugged his firm body, surprised that he hadn't noticed how the Persian boy could now rest his chin on Harry's shoulder without straining up. Arshan returned the pressure and they held each other for a long time, careless of distant passersby.

"You're happy?" Harry ground out and then could have kicked himself for such an insensitive question under the circumstances, but the muffled voice came back with an increased pressure on his shoulder blade.

"Is all good, Haari. I must go."

A lump in his esophagus threatened Harry's breathing and with it came a terrible sense of loss he couldn't understand. Arshan had been out of his life for quite some time. They had both made different arrangements in their lives, so why did he feel this emptiness in his gut as his once-upon-a-time Persian boy rounded a corner and disappeared without looking back? Perhaps because he could not be at all sure what Jolyon meant to him yet, or more likely that he didn't really know what Jolyon's feelings were for him. *More a question of Arshan and I not sharing a culture*, he'd said to Richard long ago at Rissington. *A heart needs a home and Arshan is just visiting. Bluntly, we're foreigners.*

❧ ★ ❧

As a form of expiation, Harry wrote at some length to Jolyon.

I'm pleased to hear that you find lessons at the military crammer school at least in part enjoyable and I'm sure the result will be a good pass in the examinations and a place at Woolwich. That will be my reward in return for paying the exorbitant fee old Colonel Higgins demands in return for his tutoring. (I jest. It will be well worth it.)

There was no time to post the letter, and Harry left it open to add to as he moved on to the front.

The last stretch of rails carried Churchill and Harry the six hours to Nowshera, the base from which all the operations of the Malakand Field Force were conducted. Two cavalry regiments—one British, one native—and a native infantry battalion normally occupied the place, but as these were now at the front, the barracks had become a large hospital. A small garrison under Base Commandant Colonel Schalch guarded the transport and military stores. It was he who informed them of what lay ahead.

"The pass and Malakand encampment is forty-seven miles away, in normal circumstances a journey of six hours with the excellent tonga service." He frowned and passed a weary hand across his sweaty brow. "I'm afraid the road has been badly churned up by all the frantic traffic and the tonga ponies have been reduced to a terrible condition, so you'll be lucky to make it in anything less than twelve hours."

After leaving Nowshera, the road crossed the Kabul River and ran in a northerly direction fifteen miles to Mardan, the permanent station of the Corps of Guides, though they were now up at Malakand. Thereafter, the landscape became barren and arid. The quality of the road deteriorated and they were driven in a pall of dust thrown up by the ponies and the tonga wheels. When an occasional breeze cleared the cloying stuff for a brief moment, Harry caught a glimpse of the distant mountains ranged like dragon's teeth hemming in the vast plain.

A sizeable encampment surrounded the small mud fort that guarded the crossing of a tributary of the Kabul River. Here they changed ponies, although the fresh ones seemed hardly better off than those led away by the syces.

The road here is so degraded by the traffic that it is nothing more than a white streak that stretches toward the mountains he continued his letter to Jolyon. Sweltering heat and choking dust envelopes us continuously. You would think such conditions would keep the biting insects that plague the area at bay, but that isn't the case. All around us the country is red-to-biscuit, sterile, burnt up. In front of our creaking convoy the great wall of hills rises dark and ominous. After some hours—I lost track of time, literally, because for once I'd forgotten to wind my piece—we reached Dargai at the foot of the pass. It's another mud fort, swelled during the operations into an entrenched camp, and surrounded by a network of barbed wire like a Sudanese zareba. At this point the Malakand Pass appears as a great cleft in the line of mountains—and far up the gorge the outline of the fort that guards it is visible.

In spite of the damage the campaign has caused to the road, it's possible here to see the skill of the sappers who made it. The long ascent from Dargai to the top of the pass is finely graded. It winds up with many double-backs. The drivers flog the wretched, sore-backed ponies without thought for their misery. At last we reached the summit. I looked back at the wide expanse of open country behind and far below under the rippling heat haze. Though we have traversed many low humps and hillocks, from up here it looks smooth, level, stretching away to the dim horizon. The tonga turns the corner and we enter a very different world. As far as I can see, on either side, the terrain is wild and rugged. Innumerable valleys are sandwiched between unfriendly, jagged ridges, peaks and spurs, one after another, marching away to become one dark gray wall. It is as though a vengeful god took the land and crushed it between his mighty hands.

A single step into this broken ground has taken us from India to the mountains, from civilization to savagery.

CHAPTER 21 | *Malakand and Simla, August–October 1897*

SIR BINDON BLOOD was still engaged with mopping up operations in the Swat Valley when Captain Harry Smythe-Vane and Lieutenant Winston Leonard Spencer-Churchill arrived at Malakand. Harry's orders attached him to a division of the 21st Punjab infantry, but on Blood's return from operations in the Swat Valley toward the end of August the general preferred to keep him close at his side to act as a rotating aide de camp, while still having a responsibility within the native battalion. If Harry harbored a suspicion that his friend's bumptious certainty of a favorable reception might have been exaggeration, Blood's reaction shamed him.

"Ah, my young friend Winston Churchill of the 4th Queen's Own Hussars ," he cried with gusto. "You're to join me as an extra ADC—and a right good one you will be!" He clapped both men on the shoulder. "Arrived just in time for the next big party. We're off on a jaunt into the valleys of the Bajaur region, where the Mohmands are buzzing like a hive overturned."

As the general bustled off to his command center, Churchill looked to Harry for enlightenment, since in his dash to reach India lest he miss "joining the fiun" he'd not had the luxury of time for proper research.

"Another Pashtoon tribe with a grievance over the Durand Line's division of their lands. They claim to have settled in these mountains long before Alexander came galloping through and a few British Tommies and Indian lackeys will not lord it over them."

"Thank you, Harry. I must master the local tribes and their bewildering network of alliances and feuds in order to write with authority. All I can see that they have in common is their Moslem faith and an opposition to British control."

Attached as they were to Blood's staff, Churchill and Harry had the freedom of movement within the entire area of operations, a privilege denied to other officers, and ideal from the news hound's point of view. The force set out before dawn on September 5 and two days later made the perilous crossing of the Panjkora River and into the Bajaur district where the Mohmands occupied the valleys. For several days, Blood disposed of his forces, all eager to take battle to the Mohmands, while the political officers under orders from Calcutta attempted to find peace through diplomatic means. For Harry one visit stood out when, with a detachment of the 11th Bengal Lancers, he and Churchill went to the head of Jandol Valley and Barwa Sagar, the stronghold of Umra Khan, whose army he'd fought at Chitral. Here he was shown the rather fine room where the subalterns Fowler and Evans were held after they and the ammunition and explosives desperately needed at Chitral fell into the hands of Sher Azful Khan.

On September 14 Blood moved his divisional headquarters west to Nawagai with the 3rd Brigade, sending Brigadier-General Patrick Jeffreys in the other direction up the Mohmand Valley with the 2nd Brigade to burn crops, destroy reservoirs, and blow up the fortified qala villages. The valley, six miles wide at its broadest point was entered through a narrow gorge. Beyond the rocky gateway the country was unexplored territory. Almost immediately, Jeffreys ran into spirited organized resistance and when the news reached Blood he suggested Churchill ride that way so that he might see a little fighting.

"I'm off, Harry." The warrior-journalist's cheeks glowed with excitement. "At last, an opportunity to show myself on the field of battle!"

Harry nodded. "Be careful what you wish for, Winston. And for God's sake keep your head down. That gray charger of yours stands out a mile. Every Pashtoon in the region will be taking a bead on you."

"I'm quite certain they will miss. I think I once told you I'm not long for life, so I'd rather live it to the full while I can, and a Mohmand bullet is not destined to cut it shorter than my medical inheritance. I'll be back in a day, you'll see."

In this he almost kept his promise, but he returned chastened from a near disaster and a closer meeting with the grim reaper than his cocksure certainties had predicted. The experience he endured on September 16 was of the kind that most men preferred not to recount, but Churchill was present as a journalist as well as a young man seeking glory in order to be noticed by the electorate at home he hoped to woo in order to get into Parliament. Harry pressed a good shot of whisky in his hand. He looked up from his kitbag perch and nodded thanks and began to rehearse the article he would soon commit, as he said, "… to the telegraph for *The Telegraph*."

"It was pretty bloody, Harry. We were about a thousand strong, split into three columns. I went with Colonel Thomas Goldney's center column of six companies of 1st Battalion East Kent Regiment (the Buffs), six companies 35th Sikhs, a half-company of sappers, four guns of No.8 Mountain Battery, and a squadron of the 11th Bengal Lancers—those are the same with who I rode out from Nawagai. Our task was to destroy the village of Shahi-Tangi at the far end of the valley. Goldeney decided to send the Buffs to attack a second nearby village of Badelai to the right, while I went with some eighty-five of the Sikhs ordered to advance up a rocky spur to Shahi-Tangi.

"Another detachment of Sikhs was to take a hill situated between the two villages on which we could see a gathering of tribesmen. Our hill was too steep for any but mountain goats so I had to dismount for the climb, and it was a hard one. When we got there Shahi-Tangi was deserted. We set about firing what would burn and prepared to return. It was careless planning, but none had realized until it was too late that the village was out of range of our artillery support. As we began to retire, the enemy materialized from every cranny around us and attacked in force. Only the spur up which we had toiled to reach the village offered any hope of escape.

"The mountainside sprang to life. Swords flashed in the sunlight behind every rock, bright flags waved, and from far up the hillsides men came running swiftly down, dropping from ledge to ledge like monkeys rushing down trees."

He smiled at Harry. "I must remember all this when it comes to writing my newspaper dispatches!

"Our route lay along a series of three descending knolls interconnected by thin necks vulnerable to fire on both flanks. A group of eight Sikhs under Lieutenant Cassells acted as rearguard in the village and provided covering fire as the rest of us withdrew from the village to the first knoll, and then across the neck to the second. A soon as we reached the slight shelter afforded by the rise of the knoll we cried out to Cassells and he dashed down to the first knoll we had abandoned.

"When we tried to repeat the ploy we came under heavy fire from Pashtoons who had already seized the first knoll behind us and had clear lines of sight. Cassells was shot as he rose to make the dash. Two Sepoys immediately caught hold of him. One took a shot through the leg and fell. A Sikh who had continued firing sprang into the air from the force of the lead hitting him. He too fell and began to bleed rapidly from his mouth and chest. Another turned on his back, kicking and twisting. A fourth lay quite still."

The tenor of Churchill's voice sank down almost to a whisper so Harry had to lean forward to hear.

"The native subedar and four sepoys ran back from the second knoll to help in carrying the wounded. Two fell before reaching it. The subedar seized Cassells, who could barely stand, and they retreated to the screams of the injured dragged by the frantic sepoys over the sharp, unforgiving ground. I, together with the other uninjured soldiers, tried to pull the wounded back to safety, but we no longer had any covering fire. It was a shambles, Harry. The regiment adjutant, Lieutenant Hughes, rushed up with more sepoys to help us recover the wounded and dead, but he was shot and died on the spot. Several more men fell. Colonel Bradshaw ordered four sepoys to carry Hughes off, as the subedar brought Cassells down. I saw a scattered crowd of tribesmen rush over the crest of the hill. Several of the wounded were dropped. Half a dozen Pashtoon swordsmen, hurling great stones, attacked the men helping Hughes, who dropped him and fled. The subedar stuck to Cassells, and it is to his bravery the lieutenant owes his life."

Churchill paused a moment, his eyes wide at the recollection. Harry said nothing. He knew the horror of seeing men killed at his side.

"Hughes's body sprawled on the ground. As I looked on in my impotence, a tall man ran down with a long curved sword, intending to mutilate the corpse. The bullets were flying from all directions, but I was overcome with a desire to kill this man, this desecrator. I told you, I think, that I won the Public Schools fencing medal. I intended to take him down with cold steel. He rushed at me and threw a huge stone. I thought better of a sword duel and instead pulled out my revolver and shot him." He gave Harry a crooked grin. "I'm obviously a better swordsman than fusileer. I fired three times but he ran away. I took steps forward, Harry, I swear I did, to reach Hughes. At that, emboldened by sheer numbers, the Pashtoons closed, firing wildly, but all at me. I was suddenly appallingly aware that I was now on my own. All the others had fled on down the hillside to safety. Bullets sucked through the air above my head and threw up dirt at my feet. So I did the same, turned and ran downhill as fast as I could."

He fell silent.

Harry refilled their cups. "Well, you have certainly made an impact, I'm sure."

"I'm not happy with myself, Harry."

"You couldn't have done more for poor Hughes, Winston. No one could have done more, but for what you did surely there will be a medal—mentions in dispatches at the least, which will be an aid to your future ambitions to gain a seat at Westminster." He raised the cup in a toast.

Churchill matched the gesture wearily and the rims made an unsatisfactory clunk as they met.

The punitive expedition against the Mohmand tribesmen continued. Among its several important objectives was confiscation of all the Martini-Henry breech-loading rifles the Pashtoons had taken in recent skirmishes. While not a match for the new bolt-action Lee-Metfords issued to the British infantry, they were still deadly in the hands of snipers.

Toward the end of September Sir Bindon Blood received a well-respected visitor who like Churchill craved the excitement of the frontier war. It was Arshan's Kernel Ba-doonpowl.

At forty, Colonel Robert Stephenson Smyth Baden-Powell was the youngest colonel in the British Army. He had recently transferred from Rhodesia to India and commanded the 5th Dragoon Guards stationed at Meerut. After the Commander-in-Chief refused his request for the Dragoons to shake some sense into Pashtoon heads at Malakand, Baden-Powell obtained leave to travel on his own, and Blood welcomed him. For Harry this was a treat. As he told Churchill, "The man is completely unorthodox. When you think on it, it's hard to see how he has come through the ranks so fast. I read that in the Matabele campaign he took guerrilla war to the Africans, happy to track the enemy through the night with only two or three scout companions. He reminds me of my old school friends, out on their own, living by their wits, gathering intelligence for General Kitchener in Egypt and the Red Sea Territory."

The treat gained promise when Blood asked Harry to look after the visitor during his short stay. "And with a bit of luck we'll give him some action to take back to Meerut."

Which happened.

"I have set cats among pigeons, young Harry," Baden-Powell said as they rode side by side. It had taken but minutes of acquaintance before the colonel insisted on informality.

The 21st Punjab infantry battalion was on deployment toward a small village targeted for destruction. It amused Harry to be referred to as young. Stephe, as Baden-Powell preferred his easily made acquaintances to call him, was only eight years older. As he'd pointed out on introduction, they were a mere *e* apart in one of their names, and he supposed if they took the trouble to investigate they would discover a blood connection somewhere down the line. "The Dragoons, I decided, spend far too much time on parades and drill and being smartly turned out. My officers frowned at having someone with more experience of traipsing around the African bush than of parade-ground ceremonial placed over them. Well, I didn't wish to disappoint their prejudices, so I immediately reduced all drill and ceremonial folderol." He burst into joyous laughter, but cut it short to glance sideways at Harry. "I do hope I don't shock you?"

"Not at all," Harry hastened to assure him.

"Good. You see I like to be approachable to my men. Anyone. I'm still working to break the silly old custom that a subaltern may never address anyone above the rank of the senior lieutenant unless first spoken to. You see, Harry, I've witnessed at first hand the danger of having lower ranks remain silent for fear of breaking convention when had they spoken out disaster might have been avoided." He sighed. "I have no doubt some of my staff officers will raise a complaint to Wolseley at the War Office, but I don't like kid-gloved high-collared officers and I'm not keen on highly trained staff officers who are stick in the muds with the rule book either. It's better for a man to fall in with the ways of the country where he is, and be ready to cast off the War Office's Red Books— I say! What's that?"

The familiar bark of Martini-Henry rifles shattered the quiet of the valley up which the column marched.

"Form lines by company," Harry snapped at a lieutenant.

The orders rang out, subedar to jemadar, and the sepoys deployed rapidly with precision to meet the enemy fire suddenly pouring down from the crags.

"Impressive!" Baden-Powell said. "The gun battery is most proficient."

Within minutes the artillery began shelling the heights. Bombardment of the ridge continued unabated for several minutes until the rocky edge became indistinct from the battery's drifting smoke, hillside explosions, and the sharper blue of rifle and jezail fire. Harry narrowed his eyes to a squint. "I thought I saw a movement... over there. Yes, look!"

All heads turned as one in the direction of Harry's pointing index finger. Astonishingly, a solitary Afghan tribesman blossomed into dark shape as he came charging down the sharp slope, making his own cloud of dust.

"Christ!" a British NCO in the front firing line shouted. "He's attacking us all on his own."

"Good Lord," Baden-Powell said. "This is foolhardy in the extreme."

The corporal raised his rifle and fired at the oncoming warrior, setting an example for the rest of the battalion. In a second every rifle was barking in a continuous rolling thunder.

He came on, a flap of dark blue clothes blowing out behind him. Spurts of dust and shattered rock jumped up all around him, but they did not deter him.

"Bloomin' heck, look at the daft bastard. He's only got a sword!"

Astonishment gave way to anxiety, for nothing seemed to stop the Mohmand from his crazy dash. He careened down the slope in a barely controlled skid, his mouth a gaping gash from which he screamed what were assuredly obscenities. Suddenly he stumbled and fell.

"Oh goodness me, he's hit," one sepoy cried exultantly.

It seemed so to Harry, but the man just started binding up a wound in his leg. Then he got up. He brandished his glittering sword and shook it at his foes. He came on again, limping now, but determined to reach the line.

"Extraordinary," Baden-Powel murmured with what Harry thought was undoubted admiration.

Harry agreed. It was a grand sight to see this plucky tribesman, reckless of his own life, taking on an entire crowd of men shooting at him. It didn't seem right. Harry raised his voice against the racket of clattering bolts and bullets being chambered. "Cease firing!"

He wondered whether they would obey, even hear his shout, but as one, the men ceased their execution. Gun barrels were lowered all along the line. A minute later the man slowed and suddenly tumbled forward and rolled over once and lay huddled in a heap, dead, a dark slash of blue on gray. When the artillery stopped its bombardment and the battalion went on up to take the heights, Harry passed him where he lay, pleased to see that some of the Indian troops had, out admiration for the Mohmand tribesman's bravery, laid him out straight and decently covered his corpse.

"I think that's the bravest thing I have ever seen. Although…" Stephe twisted his neck and grinned at Harry, riding at his side as their mounts picked a way carefully through the loose scree. "I don't believe you were commanding the battalion, yet you gave the orders."

A sheepish grin matched Baden-Powell's. "No one seemed willing to decide what to do."

"Good man. I like decisive soldiers. You were at Chitral, weren't you? Only soldiers who have found themselves in tight spots and come through know the trade of soldiering."

A week later, with the campaign winding down and Baden-Powell preparing to return to his command, he took Harry aside. "Captain, I'd be delighted for you to break your tedious journey to Bangalore as my guest at the hill station. It's a pleasant relief from Meerut cantonment for me and I'm sure you will find many listeners anxious to hear of your escapades."

So as Churchill went back to Bangalore because his regiment felt he'd done more than enough glory seeking and should buckle down to proper duties, Harry obtained a short leave to once again visit Simla.

Baden-Powel hadn't been entirely honest, as it turned out. He was in fact himself a guest of the Inspector-General of Cavalry in India, General Edward Locke Elliot, but fortunately for them both, Elliot was acquainted with Harry's expeditions with Lockhart and to Hunza and more than happy to accommodate Stephen's "young friend."

Among the widely spaced, elegant residences set in manicured grounds of the hill station, the Elliots' home was large enough to be a first-class hotel, though the general defended its size on grounds of hosting frequent house parties. The frontage on the Mall extended to imposing three-story towers connected by two-story bays of whitewashed roughcast cladding over the brick. The end towers were square and the center tower's wider face contained the grand doorway. Wide horizontal bands of red brick separated each floor, and a shallow spire topped each tower, which lent the building an oddly ecclesiastical appearance. Behind the towers, the rest of the house stretched back to form a square of the whole, broken on each face by curious battlemented oriel windows. All around, the choppy, forested slopes of Simla reminded Harry immediately of Kashmir but also of Switzerland, for where Kashmir's hills were sparsely inhabited, the grand summertime abodes of India's white Raj dotted Simla's hills; and after the heat of Malakand and the Mohmand Valley the temperature was blissfully alpine.

Elliot had recently married and his summer residence still exhibited all the signs of bachelorhood. Harry couldn't imagine his wife putting up with the hunting trophies adorning the white-painted walls for much longer. They ranged from African long-horned antelope heads to a tusker boar; on the polished floorboards a bear rug, complete with claws and head, competed for space and in brightness with a tiger rug, while a proud panther stood in a corner, a triumph of the taxidermist's art. Care was required in crossing the floor to avoid tripping and sprawling headlong over snarling ursine or feline heads.

As he idled away an hour before going to wash and change for dinner, Harry riffled through the library bookshelves, interested in what the varied volumes said about his genial host. He fingered a few military tracts, including Jean Joseph Marie Amiot's French translation of Sun Tzu's *The Art of War*, but found more personal interest on a lower shelf, a selection that pointed to Elliott possessing an eclectic taste in fiction. Among other titles, Hardy's *Jude the Obscure*, Kipling's *The Second Jungle Book*, *The Time Machine* by H.G. Wells, and Jules Verne's *Propeller Island* stood out. The oddest pairing was *The History of the Decline and Fall of the Roman Empire* by Edward Gibbon in several volumes and stuck in between it a handsomely illustrated edition of Richard Burton's translation of the *Karma Sutra*. Harry presumed Mrs. Elliott either didn't read or simply hadn't gotten around to checking out her new husband's taste in literature.

With a quick wary glance over the shoulder, Harry eased the *Kama Sutra* out and flipped hurriedly through the charming Indian-style paintings depicting various positions of sensual pleasure. He turned page after page, and then stopped with a start. The word "Auparishtaka" caught his eye. He lowered his eyes to the illustration, which showed a kneeling young man bowed over the middle of a Maharaja, who reclined in a state of elegant undress. The Maharaja's stiff penis rose from a representation of pubic hair to disappear between the young man's pursed lips.

"Shockingly free in their sport, what?"

Harry almost died on the spot, though some sense of preservation prevented him from slamming the book shut, which would only have compounded his guilt and embarrassment. He'd been so absorbed he never heard Stephe's approach. He took some comfort from the twinkle in Baden-Powell's eyes.

"Hah, yes, indeed. So it seems. I've heard of this, of course, but never seen…"

"And you'd got as far as the 'shampoo' section. Quite shocking."

He didn't sound at all shocked.

"Quite." Harry took the opportunity to insouciantly flip through a few more pages and then replace the book in its secure nook between collapsing Rome.

"Burton was a bit of a rogue, I'd say, though a fine explorer. Man who acted in a way suited to wherever he found himself. Might I recommend something?"

Harry held a hand out in a go-ahead gesture and Baden-Powell reached out to a shelf.

"I was surprised to find this in Elliot's collection, but it is an interesting divertissement." He offered the book to Harry.

The title, *If I Were God*, meant nothing apart from its blasphemous shock potential, but the author's name flipped over hard in his memory. Richard Le Gallienne. Harry was aware of Baden-Powell's intense regard, watching for any reaction. He struggled to find a measure of his usual equipoise and say something sensible. "Judging by this, our host is plainly a man of intellectual discrimination."

A generalization that makes it sound as if I've read the book… I hope.

A broad smile broke out like a sunrise on Baden-Powell's face. "Indeed. Brave too, if you think that most army men wouldn't touch anything by a writer like Richard Le Gallienne. After all, it's a bare two years since the downfall of his muse. Good British soldiers and the decadent *fin-de-siècle* followers of Oscar Wilde don't really mix, do they?"

"I met him."

"Le Gallienne?"

"No, he had to go somewhere. Wilde."

"A strange man. He rather upset the apple-cart, didn't he?"

Harry was unsure what Stephe meant by this oblique remark, but the colonel seemed to want to expand on it.

"He opened Pandora's Box and narrow minds felt free to misinterpret what is innate in fine young men. His words were an eye-opener to many who are not well up in the psychology of the boy or what goes on in a public school today. People instead should have listened to the words of a man whose soul—like mine—soars at the noble sight of young sporting men. Have you read the works of Reverend Edward Lefroy?" Baden-Powell's enthusiasm rendered an answer redundant, as he swept on, sparing Harry the necessity of saying that he had indeed read some of the priestly muscular poems. "A man after my own heart, he says—I paraphrase—'I have inborn admiration for the beauty of form and figure. It amounts almost to a passion and in most football teams I can find one Antinous.' That's a fine phrase! Lefroy declares that many would call it sentimentalism to admire any but feminine flesh and says of it that 'it only proves how base is the carnality, which is now reckoned the only legitimate form. But the other is far nobler and Platonic passion in any relationship is better than animalism.' Now Harry, is that not why the marvellous paintings by Henry Tuke are so popular at the Royal Academy every year? Along with many, I stand lost in admiration for the noble depiction of youth in all its glory, sporting in the water."

Harry nodded, fascinated by this exposition of his co-host's beliefs. Indeed, he reflected, Wilde's trial and conviction had altered the public's perception of the love that dare not speak its name. Before, most would surely have been happily ignorant of the kind of male mutual attraction that led to Oscar's downfall and would now categorize Baden-Powell and Reverend Lefroy's more innocent interests in a similarly degraded light—and his own…

"The carnality of which Lefroy speaks is a burden placed on my shoulders almost daily among the men of the Meerut garrison. Young soldiers, barely advanced from their childhood, suddenly alone, need a firm hand. I have reversed the practice of adopting brothels and placed them off limits, Harry. It's quite necessary to lecture my charges and warn them against the dangers of letting their thoughts run on dirty things or risk becoming dirty beasts. Boys are prone to acts of beastliness in the rutting season—and that lasts from crossing the frontier of adolescence until marching past the threshold of maturity in their mid-twenties. That is the period when adolescent males are attracted to women.

It were better they expend emotional energies in contesting with their peers in physical activity, so I strive to protect my youthful soldiers by counteracting the dangers of 'girlitis' with hard hiking, in athletic enterprise, tracking, woodcraft, and other safe activities in the companionship of other young males."

He suddenly consulted his pocket timepiece. "Heavens, I must hasten to change for dinner. Elliot has the gong sounded at eight sharp. I shall look forward to continuing this little chat after dining." And with that he strode briskly from the library with a cheery over-the-shoulder wave.

Harry wondered whether the schoolmasterly lecture hid more than it attempted to explain. There was a dichotomy at the heart of Stephe's arguments. On one hand he seemed to almost approve of Oscar Wilde's attraction to intellectual "sentimentalism," while on the other praising athletic prowess and reviling effete aestheticism. The sharply exhaled breath rang in his ears, a sigh for lost innocence. He doubted that Stephe would have read *Sexual Inversion* by Havelock Ellis because the Englishman's book was only available in a German translation (a limited release in English having resulted in the bookseller's prosecution), but mostly because Harry didn't think a cold, medical treatise on same-sex attraction, what people were beginning to call homosexuality, would appeal to a latter-day gymnastic Plato. Baden-Powell couldn't see that his evident aversion to women and adoration of lean, muscular, sporty men—a perfectly normal attraction before Oscar Wilde's trials—would today be viewed with deep suspicion. Havelock Ellis had given a name to that which Wilde said could not speak it. Once opened, none of the demons could be locked back inside Pandora's box

"Many envious eyes, green with covetousness, feast on British prowess. The Spanish and Portuguese may have fallen by the colonial wayside, but we must watch out for France and keep eagle eyes upon Germany." Stephe was in full loquacious flow as the Simla Amateur Dramatic Club's company prepared to take the stage. Harry was helping him into his costume as a Chinaman. "*The Origin of the Species* spells it out, clear as the nose on Wun-Hi's face. If you apply Darwin's disturbing findings to human beings, it can be seen that only the strongest nations will survive in the conditions of strife. While we sit here guarding our India against the might of Russia, perfidious France and duplicitous Germany take advantage of our preoccupation to steal a march in other areas rightfully within the sphere of British influence. Mark my words, Harry, the French want all of Africa. Thank goodness we have a man like Cecil Rhodes in South Africa guarding British interests, indeed advancing them vigorously. There. I think I am ready."

The house was full, anticipation bubbling for the opening of the S.A.D.C.'s production of the operetta *The Geisha*, which in London was still playing after a year's run. Stephe was playing Wun-Hi, the Chinese owner of the Tea House of Ten Thousand Joys, and Harry was keen to see what a crack he made of the part played by Huntley Wright at Daley's Theatre. Before he went to take his seat, Stephe pulled him aside and in character whispered, "I may do this because I rove pray acting, Hally, but I am a welly wullied Chinky. It's the women, you see."

Harry didn't.

"There aw nefawious attempts afoot to get me mallied off to one of the sevelal singurl women in the cast and clew. I won't say who is behind this dastawdry pran, but I have my suspicions. Keep you eyes on young Miss Erren Tuwner." He gave Harry a final evil grin from under his long theatrical mustaches and wrinkled the fake high forehead.

Ellen Turner played Molly, an English girl who, for the mischievous thrill of it, becomes a geisha at the teahouse and is pursued by a selfish and ruthless Japanese nobleman. The story tells of her rescue from the consequences of her thoughtlessness by naval Lieutenant Reginald Fairfax and at they end they get married. Wun-Hi provided the humor and Baden-Powell's pidgin English had the audience in paroxysms of laughter, particularly his inarticulate sobbing whenever misfortune befell him, which was frequently. His performance impressed Harry and he was sincere when he congratulated Stephe and declared him superior to the professional thespian Mr. Wright.

Two days following the performance a telegram found him. "I'm to return direct to Bombay and take the first steamer home," he told Stephe. "That's dashed awkward. I'll have to arrange for my things at Bangalore to be sent on."

"What's the cause of the summons and the hurry?"

"It seems my previous experience of the delightful deserts of the Sudan have caught up with me. General Kitchener—well, his adjutant—has requested the pleasure of my company for the next dance."

CHAPTER 22 | *London, December 1897 and Sudan, January 1898*

THE DOOR TO HARRY'S SUITE of rooms at South Street burst open to admit a hurricane. It banged against the wall and rebounded to almost shut itself. He barely had the time to swivel around on the chair he'd drawn up to the small writing table before he was engulfed in the full force of arms and legs as Jolyon cannoned into him. A second later Jolyon's wiry-thin form was seated on Harry's lap, arms wrapped around him. Kisses fell in torrents on his cheeks, eyes, forehead, neck, lips. "Oh Harry. I thought I wouldn't see you for months yet. I was so happy to receive your note. And I have good news. I thought I'd have to write of it, but now I can deliver it straight into your… *mmmm*, ear."

Jo's voice came muffled through the amorous onslaught. Harry felt himself stiffening and feared the boy would feel his arousal, but if he did Jolyon showed no sign of disapproval or any intent of removing himself. Instead, he snuggled closer and breathed into Harry's ear.

"I passed."

"What?"

"The military examinations." He drew back indignantly. "What else did you think?" And then he saw Harry's broad grin.

"That's wonderful, Jo! You'll be able to start with the winter term."

"I know. Officer Cadet Jolyon Langrish-Smith of the Royal Military Academy, Woolwich, attached to the Royal Arsenal and the Royal Artillery! And thanks to you, Harry, I did it on my own merit, not because I'm the son of a red-capped staff officer who can afford to buy my commission."

"It won't be a featherbed, you know. At Sandhurst we had it cushy by comparison, and trust me, the regime at Sandhurst was spartan."

"It's where General Kitchener went to military school, and he got through. So shall I."

"Good for you."

Jo furrowed his brow as he considered Harry for a second, and then moved in again to nuzzle his neck. "I'm not complaining, but how come you're back home before I expected you from your last rather dry letter?"

Harry wasn't complaining either, but Jolyon's ebullient amorousness was startling since there had been no suggestion in his equally "dry" occasional missives that anything had changed between them from when they last parted. But he certainly wasn't going to complain about it. Laughing, he managed to push Jolyon back just far enough to speak. "I was lucky. I was about to leave Simla for Bangalore when the powers that be dispatched me forthwith to England. I was lucky to catch a fast naval packet in Egypt bound for Leghorn and the train journey is—"

Jo wasn't listening. "I passed whatshername... Frannie? on the stairs coming up. I think she was going out."

"She'll be attending one of her ladies' tea parties, no doubt, and then joining Evan for some parliamentary shindig—"

"Oh good! So she won't hear us going at it."

"What?"

Jolyon sat back at arms' length, firmly gripping Harry by the shoulders, so he could look piercingly into his eyes. Harry detected a tone of uncertainty under the mock reproach. "You are going to take me to your bed and do me, are you not?"

The thump in his chest was surely his heart coming to a juddering halt. "This... is... all very sudden."

"I told you I needed time. Well, I've had time, plenty of it, and I am twenty-two for goodness sake! I thought I would have to wait so much longer to find out. But here you are, ahead of schedule. And if you are unwilling, I'm more than happy to have a go at doing you." As quickly as he had jumped on Harry, Jolyon climbed off to stand looking down, hands on his narrow hips. The insecure expression won out over brashness. "You do still like me, Harry? It was love you thought of when I last saw you. Not that I would have known from your beastly letters, all full of technical stuff."

"I mentioned the Serpentine and... I told you—the censor. I didn't—"

"No, you didn't. I thought you cared more for that Winston Churchill fellow than for me."

Harry stood up and grabbed Jo by his coat lapels and pulled him in tight, stung by the closeness of his words to a reality that might have been. "I didn't want to write you into a corner, Jo. The way we left it, you were still uncertain of anything. I wasn't even sure you liked me much, *umnnff!*"

The kiss lasted long seconds and did much to restart the beating of Harry's heart, though at an uncomfortably fast pace. Jolyon's tongue pressed against Harry's lips, sought entry and won through. Tongue against tongue, noses sliding against each other, Harry slid his arms around Jo even as he ran his long hands under Harry's coat to grip the muscles of his back. With eyes closed, the room shrank to this ardent clinch, firm young muscles under the sheath of fashionable vest, shirt, undershirt… just too much clothing. As he pressed in even closer, his erection brushed hard against a reciprocal rigidity. Jo dropped his left hand to grip Harry's buttock, urging him to squeeze their pelvises harder together.

Eventually, they broke the kiss. Jolyon leaned back in Harry's embrace. His face glowed with pleasure, eyes crinkled in affectionate amusement. "You're not going to tell me I have misinterpreted all those Serpentine references are you? How much do you think I like you now?"

"You aren't bothered about the difference in our ages?"

Jo disentangled himself, but only so he could start taking off his jacket. The vest followed. He snapped his suspenders down and tugged shirttails free of his trousers. He laughed happily. "Harry, Harry. You are *so* romantic! I throw myself at you and you get all technical."

"Oh come here." Harry grabbed Jo about the waist and slipped both hands under the loosened undershirt to fondle the smooth skin beneath, reaching up high enough to cup the shelves of Jo's hard breasts and squeeze his nipples. "I want to be sure, that's all."

Jo wriggled in his grasp delightedly, leaned forward and breathed in Harry's ear. "Take me to bed."

It was almost like déjà vu, only this time the image of a naked Jolyon lying in his arms was made of flesh and a rapidly beating heart, all that and a very hard cock. Everything about Jo was eager and they made love with an abandon all the more delicious for the time it had taken to arrive at this place of combining loving bodies, minds, and spirits. Twice, Harry entered a willing Jolyon, who clearly required no tuition in how to satisfy his partner. At the point of reaching his second orgasm, Harry felt joined with Jolyon in a way he hadn't truly known since he and Richard made love.

It felt like he might be coming home.

The light outside gradually faded in the late autumnal haze. London would be plagued with another thick fog as the evening wore on. Comfortable under the covers, warmed by Jo's proximity, Harry's lassitude raised a lazy smile. He moved his feet and wriggled his toes against Jolyon's.

"So, how long?"

Harry grinned. "Several inches, I'd say. Ow!" He tensed for another jab in the ribs.

"How long will it be before you're off again?"

"I'm not sure yet. Not long, I'm afraid. I got leave to come home so as to familiarize myself with a new regiment and receive my promotion." Harry twisted his head around so that their noses touched at the tips. "You're looking at a major in the British Army now. The telegram met me at our brief Aden stop, but Wolseley wanted it gazetted properly in England."

Jolyon propped himself on his arm, while idly stroking Harry's chest muscles. "What outfit are you joining?"

"The Seaforth Highlanders."

Jolyon stiffened. "That means you'll be going to Egypt. I read it the other day. They say General Kitchener is determined to wipe out the Mahdist Dervishes once and for all and capture the Khalifa. There will be bad fighting, Harry."

In a way, Jo's evident concern for his welfare warmed Harry every bit as much as the sex had. He shook his head where it lay on the pillow. "That's what the army's for, Jo. We go out as we're ordered and take our lives in our hands."

"Then I shall do so too. With you. Oh, not immediately. I know better than that, but I've thought about it lots while you were dealing out death in Afghanistan. It inspired me to cram like a madman under Colonel Higgins. Woolwich will be good for me. I really do want to be an artilleryman. I think I shall enjoy explosions. Also…" He leaned down so the fringe of his hair tickled Harry's neck. "I think I'd prefer to fire guns at an enemy I can't really see.

Bayonets and bullets at close range… well, I wouldn't want to look the man in the eyes I am killing. Or he me."

Jolyon suddenly clamped his lips on Harry's nearest nipple and sucked at it. Sharp teeth nipped painfully until Harry yipped and swayed his chest away from the attack with a breathless chuckle, though lying flat on the bed rendered the maneuver useless. Jolyon kept up his attack and his words came as burbles, wet with spit.

"It will be like the Theban Band. You and me, I mean, out on the field of battle, lovers in arms, back to back, fighting our foemen like tigers."

Harry chuckled. "I don't think the ancient Greeks knew of tigers."

Jolyon relinquished Harry's nub with a plopping sound. He raised his head and looked quizzical. Something occurred to him. "The Seaforths? But you are a cavalryman."

"True. The Blues, Camel Corps, Hussars, Dragoons, but you know I think the cavalry might have had its day. There isn't really a place for it in modern battles, somewhat depending on terrain of course. Camels were of more use to us than horses in Egypt and the Sudan. Horses were of use in reconnaissance work and for mopping up after the infantry had done its execution of the enemy. The Dragoons, like the regiment I was attached to at Rawul Pindee, for instance, are really mounted infantry. And at Malakand, the Guides Corps are acting more as mounted infantry than cavalry in the old fashioned sense. You'll see that Kitchener wants footmen more than cavalrymen, even though the enemy are mostly mounted, and fearsome riders too. But in the end, cavalry cannot win battles. You need Tommies on the ground for that. Besides, I seem to have been around the Seaforths before. They were instrumental in rescuing us at Chitral—"

"Where you were a hero."

"You scorned me for that."

"The grown up me didn't really know you."

"That's because you were hardly grown up. The Seaforths were the heroes then."

"Haven't they already shipped out to Egypt?"

"Some divisions are at Malta. I'll join them with the rest at Alexandria before they push on to Cairo and the desert railroad."

Jolyon's pout was almost audible in its extent. "So you'll be going *very* soon."

Harry nodded. "But not before we have a bit more time to explore closer to home."

Jo broke into a sunny smile, his mood as changeable as an English summer. "Has anyone ever told you that you have a very wicked grin, Harry Smythe-Vane?" He leaned down and kissed it.

Harry was so overwhelmed with love he did something he'd only ever done once before, for Richard Rainbow. "Jo, my name. I'm not really a Harry but I prefer it to my given name, which in fact I loathe. But to you I grant the dubious pleasure of knowing it."

"Not Harry?"

"Always Harry, but not really, no. I was christened Haldane. Haldane Smythe-Vane. But it always sounded so…"

"Pompous?"

The cuff around the ear Jo received was more of a love tap. "But you're right. So I prefer to be called Harry Vane. And now you're only the second person on the planet to know it, other than my immediate family, and they never dare to use it. *Apart from the time Evan spilled it to Oscar Wilde.* Oh, hey…" He reached out to gently wipe the tears that had suddenly sprung from Jo's eyes.

Jolyon flung himself down on top of Harry. "I've decided I love you, Harry Vane. Now don't you dare let one of those awful Fuzzy Wuzzies get you, and come back to me in one piece, not like at shitty Chitral."

"I was in once piece after that."

"Yes, but with damaged bits…" The grin returned. "Not, I'm pleased to report, the really important bits."

By the third week of January, 1898, The 1st Battalion Seaforth Highlanders were in Aswan and Harry was already well reacquainted with the hot, dry Nubian temperature, so different from Afghanistan where the occasional cool breeze might ease the sweaty brow and where the climate was as often controlled by vertical height as by season, changing rapidly from searing plain to freezing mountain. On the banks of the Nile, there were only the heat and the flies.

He was lucky to break the tedious journey at Luxor for a few days. On several occasions he joined a group of officers interested in the ancient Egyptian remains—matters of supreme uninterest to the mass of troops—and trailed about behind turbaned guardians who muttered in barely understandable English. And then it was back to the endless troop trains. Because military engineers were in the process of hastily upgrading the last stretch to Aswan, there were many hold-ups while native laborers under supervision tore out old track and laid new rails.

Harry had said to Jolyon that General Kitchener, had requested his presence in theater, an exaggeration that did not take into account that the summons had emanated from the War Office. He had no idea if the general really knew who he was. Their paths in India never crossed, and since the man had spent his time recently in Egypt and the Sudan there was no reason to suppose that he knew of Harry's exploits, or indeed of his existence.

Ahead of Harry and behind him, Kitchener's vast military campaign rolled inexorably along the rails: Alexandria to Cairo to Aswan, where the contorted nature of the valley and the serenity of the river made waterborne transport more feasible than by rail. At the top of the First Cataract a fleet of steamers waited to take the troops and all the materiel of war the 230 miles to Wadi Halfa, terminus of the Desert Railway. From there the rails so hurriedly laid in the previous months crossed the sandy wastes of the Manasir Desert to Abu Hamed, where a battle had ousted the Dervishes only the previous August, and so to Berber. Train after train carried men from Cairo to the advancing front, along with arms, armaments, munitions, spare clothing, food supplies, medicines, construction materials, kit-form amphibious vessels… and newspaper reporters from far off Cairo. The Seaforths reached the desert entrepôt in early February.

Berber raised no enthusiasm from rail-weary troops. Out of the dust-streaked window of his "first-class" compartment Harry stared out at what appeared to be an astonishingly long couple of streets filled in with single-story slum dwellings. It seemed to take an age from the northern outskirts to reach the station. Back in '85 when Harry was with the Camel Corps' expedition to rescue Gordon of Khartoum they cut across the Bayuda Desert, avoiding the great bight of the Nile and so avoiding the important trading center altogether. But Berber looked no different from any other of the Nileside towns he'd seen back then and worse for wear after its occupation by Mahdist troops for so long.

The desert's buff-gray hues dominated, since the houses were built of the local riverine mud, and by far the majority in the north of the town were in disrepair, exhibiting all the signs of fiercely exchanged gunfire. The hastily erected halt had no right to be called a station—sections of palm boles laid lengthways and strapped together three high, formed a rough platform, behind which engineers had packed sandbags against the timber wall and topped them with compacted soil. It was a halt in the middle of nowhere and only the serried ranks of army tent lines stretching away from the miserable buildings against the river provided any element of order in the drear landscape. Regimental standards breaking out in the slight wind provided the only cheeriness amid dun-colored palms.

A small army of Ja'alin natives was gathered beyond the perimeter of the station compound, ready to descend on the officer cadre to offer their services as servants, all crying out the word: "*Geneigh*, pound, pound, please pound!" Harry waded in, briskly snapped his fingers at the least discomposed looking Arab boy, and indicated his things with one hand while holding out a ten-piastre coin. The boy hefted the two worn valises and was struggling with Harry's kitbag, which was almost his own height, when a tall, brown-skinned Arab in flowing *jibba* and black-white checked *keffiyeh* strode up with design and grabbed the straps from the boy.

"Let me take that," the Arab said in a pure English accent.

Through glare-squinted eyes, Harry took in the apparition and gasped.

CHAPTER 23 | *Berber January to March 1898*

"RICHARD!"

The Arab grasped Harry's hand and then planted a traditional double kiss, one to each cheek. "Harry, *is salām 'alaykum*. I'm overjoyed to see you again."

The friends pulled apart to look at each other. Choking back any amount of return greetings he could think of, Harry opted for a wry grin. "In disguise again, I see."

"You are referring to my daily uniform, although now it is incomplete. I wear dark brown tinted contact lenses in the field to hide—"

"Your beautiful pale gray eyes. I remember." He stared, lost in a welter of emotions. "Is this coincidence or did you receive the message I fired off at the Abu Hamed telegraph office? I had to pull rank to send it, but I didn't know whether it would ever find you."

Richard hefted the kitbag over his broad shoulder as though it weighed nothing. "One advantage of fighting a Nile war is that while the country's extent north to south is vast, its breadth is confined to the river's banks and a simple single telegraph line, so the chances of a telegram reaching the intended recipient is fairly good. Anyway, I'm headed to my quarters to change into drabs the minute I've got you settled in. Camp commanders don't take kindly to strange Arabs strolling about the place like they own it. In faith it's luck your telegram found me here at this time, because I've been up and down the river non-stop. Now there's a pause while the Kitchener gathers his foot soldiers… and here you are with your merry Scottish infantrymen, ready to drive the Khalifa and his Dervish horde from Atbara and Metemma to Omdurman and beyond."

He stood back to take in Harry's uniform in which all the dust of travel lurked in every crease of khaki. "*Major* Harry Vane. The rank suits your social station at last."

"As does yours, *Major* Richard Rainbow."

"Everyone's a major out here, or have you forgotten that junior white officers are given the Egyptian honorary rank of bimbashi to place them above any native commissioned officer?"

Harry admitted it had slipped his mind. "So this is temporary home?"

Richard laughed happily. "You're right to scowl, but Berber is not quite as horrid as it first appears, at least in the encampment. Kitchener is most particular to provide at least the basic creature comforts, you'll be delighted to hear, although the sartorial elegance you're accustomed to is hard to come by."

Harry returned the laughter. "You hold a poor opinion of me, Richard, if you think I've traveled the wastes of the Hindu Kush, the Pamirs, and the Swat Valley like some latter day Beau Brummell on heat for a nicely starched and ironed shirt."

Richard snapped out some instructions in Arabic to Harry's adopted serving boy, and they set off to push through the milling throng of kilted Seaforths who were slowly coming to order at the constant bellowing of sergeants.

"Where is Edward? How is he?"

Richard led the way across a wide track that resembled a real road from the sprayed coating of asphalt on its surface. A sign announced it as being Gunnery Way No.3. On the other side a pathway lined by the familiar white-painted stones led into the depths of the massive camp. Richard's jaunty stride echoed his tone."Ed? Off somewhere. Our Intelligence masters keep us on our toes, so sometimes I can hail him riding north on the left bank as I ride south on the right, and we shout to each other from opposite sides of the river."

Harry lengthened his pace to keep up. "And just how wide is the Nile at these moments of moving filial exchange?"

Bared teeth glowed white against Richard's tanned face. "Hah! Moving indeed! Sometimes quite narrow, at others, oh several miles wide if you include the numerous islands. And your Arshan? Did you see him while on your Malakand adventures? You made no mention in your last letter from Bangalore, and that was months ago."

"No, I didn't," Harry lied, uncomfortable at feeling it necessary to do so, but unwilling to explain the confusion of his feelings. "He was elsewhere, and… well, perhaps for the best for him, I think."

The Ja'alin boy staggering alongside under the burden of Harry's cases almost cannoned into Richard when he abruptly halted. "And how's that Jolyon character you wrote me about, your godson?" He rounded on Harry with narrowed eyes and an expression of uncertainty, as if he were expecting something, a revelation perhaps.

Richard knew him too well. The speech he'd rehearsed whiling away dreary hours on the train journey fell apart, and the words drained away. Of course Richard knew of Jolyon from Harry's letter, but he'd thrown out the page he'd written confessing his muddled feelings for Jo. But why couldn't he bring himself to say something of it now? Was it because he worried about Jolyon's avowed commitment, that two years spent at Woolwich might alter everything between them? Or more that he simply felt shy of exposing his feelings to the one other person he truly loved… had loved and lost.

"I sense you are on the verge of saying something, and yet have decided better of it?"

Damn Richard!

"You know I should be so happy to hear that you have found someone to receive your affection, my dear Harry. Someone who will return it as you most surely deserve."

He adored Jolyon, he was sure of that, so why not say something that Richard wanted to hear. But there it was… *As he most surely deserved.* And Harry wasn't yet sure that was absolutely how Jo felt. They had given freely of their bodies, and yet sex could be little more than gratification, the relief of a need, mutually explored but meaning little more than the release. What would happen if—his passion free to express itself again—Jolyon met someone in the intervening months? The lingering doubt that Jo would really return his love made him cautious, even to his best friend.

"If I'm preserved from Dervish musketry or sword, I shall return to London and see what transpires."

He hoped Richard would settle for the unsatisfactorily ambiguous statement. It seemed he did. Richard took both Harry's hands in his own. "Oh, I do hope so for you. Now, we must get on. After you have shaken off the dust of the Manasir and Nubian wastes, I shall take you to the finest *kahwa* in town and we can catch up properly over the best arabica coffee in Berber and a shisha."

❧✺❧

The *kahwah*'s low lintel obliged Richard to stoop to push through a curtain of bright chain links intended to keep flies out and in so doing offered Harry a glimpse of his firm and now properly uniformed bottom. He drew in a sharp breath at the treasured memories the sight aroused and bent low to follow Richard through the doorway. The coffee house's small frontage didn't prepare Harry for the expansive room beyond the entryway's narrow throat. The place stretched a ways back and widened out considerably the farther it went. Randomly placed cold-blast hurricane lanterns threw splashes of light around and candles stuck in the necks of beer bottles dotted around on squat chased-metal tables added to the comfortably low-level illumination, and the torrid atmosphere.

On either side, conversation's insistent buzz filled the smoky *kahwa* to mingle with the watery burble of innumerable shisha pipes. They found a space toward the back, settled cross-legged on thick cushions, and immediately a serving boy bustled over to take their order.

"Your Arabic is fluent, Richard. I remember you sailing up and down the river with that lad... what was his name?"

"Ibrahim."

"And you starting to learn the lingo."

"I've had much practice since then and help not only from Edward but also from from young Gregory Hilliard, who is a master of several dialects, including Ja'alin and Baqqara. I'm sure I mentioned him to you in a previous missive. Brought up in Cairo, so an odd and rather endearing mix of English gentleman and Cairo street Arab."

Harry nodded in acquiescence, but his mind was fixed not on the offspring of some local expatriate Englishman but on another young man, far away in London, hopefully already engaged in securing his military future in the Academy term just commenced. He found that thinking of Jolyon made it bearable to be alone with Richard—the one countered the other.

The coffee house was busy, full of officers and a few of the more senior NCOs, but wrapped in its crepuscular heat and insulated by the rumbles of discussion all around, the two friends might as well have been locked away in a room on their own. There was sadness to the feeling that he might have moved beyond the heartache of missing Richard's touch, but also some comfort from the thought. It meant that Jo had really taken root in his breast, and while his love for Richard would never fade, at least it would no longer disconcert him in the way that used to leave him short of breath and heartsick. His maudlin thoughts prompted an inwardly wry smile.

"Talk of the devil."

Harry realized he hadn't been listening. "Sorry?" Richard was peering through half-closed eyes toward the entrance and Harry turned to see what or who had caught his attention. Silhouetted against the scattered light sources he saw what looked like an adolescent boy making his way between the tables in the company of a striking looking black Arab. The fleeting concern in Richard's expression at the two approaching figures unsettled Harry. It almost looked as if he didn't want to be seen by them. And there was a hesitation in the boy that suggested he might be thinking better of his course through the crowded room. And then Richard beckoned the pair over.

"Harry, meet Bimbashi Gregory Hilliard."

Harry raised himself up in a half-crouch from the low cushion and extended his hand.

"Gregory, this is… my friend, Harry Vane. I told you about him? He's with the Seaforths."

"Major Vane." The accent was strange and the boy polite. He was absurdly young for his rank of Egyptian Army major, which in theory placed him on a level with Harry, although as Richard had reminded him bimbashi was only an honorary field appointment. Kitchener did not want any native officer outranking even the most junior white subaltern, which this Gregory was. He returned Harry's shake firmly. And there it was: not aggression by any means, but a certain independence of spirit that Harry felt was too presumptuous for his age. For all his modest air, he was a bit full of himself and it showed in the confidence with which he introduced his companion Zaki. He was deferential but not in the least cowed by being in company with senior British Army officers and men considerably older. He turned aside and spoke softly in Arabic to the serving boy who had come up and leaned down to hear the order.

Uncharacteristically, Richard drummed nervous fingers on the brass table's curled edge as he told Harry about Hilliard's relationship with the Arab boy, an explanation that evidently did not discomfit Hilliard for its simple frankness. Harry offered his hand to the native, who grinned brightly and shook it. Harry smiled back as warmly as he could and retook his seat on the cushion. He tried hard for a relaxed, pleasant, and easy manner, but it was difficult to achieve. His uneasiness stemmed from that *I told you about him* of Richard's to Hilliard, which left wide open how much intimate detail about their joint past had been offered to the boy. And he had no real clue as to Hilliard's background, beyond the little Richard had mentioned in passing. How much did the boy understand? *I told you about him.* He felt at a disadvantage that this mere slip of a lad, an Egyptian-raised whelp, might know more about him and his past relationship with Richard than he should. Harry tried to shake off his disquiet. Surely Richard would have been discreet about their past sexual relationship?

"You are indeed young, Mr. Hilliard. Richard mentioned your being here and working with him, but he gave me no hint as to your age."

Hilliard's eyes narrowed in possible irritation and the passage of a frown darkened his brow momentarily. "I've been in uniform almost two years, and I'm now eighteen."

It wasn't quite a snap, but Harry understood immediately. *The boy is sensitive about his lack of years.*

"Boys grow up fast out here, Harry, as you should know from personal experience."

Harry accepted Richard's intervention with a faint smile, and he smoothly covered over his possible faux pas. "You remind me of Edward when he was younger." Richard's nod encouraged him to continue, and he did in spite of the fact that it was the younger Richard he was really reminded of. "Not so much the looks but the bearing and the same fire in the eyes. Which school did you attend?"

He meant the words to mollify, but the question clearly confused Hilliard, who looked to Richard questioningly as if at a non sequitur that had no relevance.

"I haven't told Harry that much about you, Gregory. Hardly anything really."

Well, that's certainly true. Harry couldn't understand what was going on here. He felt there was an undertone, a subtext he was not party to.

Hilliard returned his cool gaze to Harry and his chin lifted with a touch of belligerence. "I was born in Alexandria and raised in Cairo, sir. I certainly haven't attended a school such as you must have done in England."

He took the implied rebuke without comment and instead concentrated his attention on the handsome Ja'alin boy Zaki, who was undeniably madly in love with Hilliard. An odd couple: white not-quite-an-Englishman, jet-black riparian Arab, and yet clearly thoroughly in tune within their relationship. Obscurely (and the fact irritated him), Harry felt excluded by Zaki and Hilliard's closeness and held at arm's length by Richard's evident affinity for Hilliard… and that inescapable sense that through Richard, Hilliard knew all about their earlier affair. Had Richard regretted saying too much to the boy, perhaps lied about knowing of Harry's being in the Sudan, and that's why he was disturbed that Hilliard had caught him out in Harry's presence here in Berber?

And in any case, what's it all mean?

The Gregory factor, Harry discovered some days later, extended to Commander Alfred Winner, captain of the steamer gunboat *Trinkitat*. Since Alfred's visit to Hadlicote in the spring of '85, when Harry took a brief break away from Jolyon's care, he hadn't given Alfred's postings much thought, truth be known, so it came as a pleasant surprise to learn from Richard that their old school chum was in fact now serving on the Nile.

"The *Trinkitat*'s just docked after a mission upriver. Let's go say hello," Richard suggested, to which Harry happily agreed.

After hearty handshakes and greetings in the steamer's tiny wardroom, Alfred settled them down with measures of navy rum and spring water ("Whatever you do, Harry, do not touch unboiled river water… gosh, what am I saying? You're an old hand!") Winner brought Harry up to date on his recent commands, and Harry expounded on what he considered a failed campaign in Afghanistan. "They'd be better off in Calcutta sending diplomats to the tribes instead of bullets."

"Have you bumped into Richard and Edward's protégé yet?"

Harry tipped his head sideways in question.

"He means Gregory Hilliard," Richard interjected. "And yes, I introduced Harry to Gregory the other day."

"The lad's journeyed with me on a few occasions as far as Shendi and Metemma and showed a great fortitude that flies in the face of his tender years and unfortunate upbringing."

"Unfortunate?" Harry looked at Alfred over his glass.

"Oh, come on, Alfred!" Richard shook his head, but laughed at Winner's attitude.

"Well, it's true. I don't want to put the boy down, far from it, especially after hearing what he did for General Hunter, but he's hardly had the advantage of a proper English education."

"What was it he did for General Hunter?"

Richard made as if to explain, but Alfred got in first and waved a hand airily.

"Oh not a lot, just trekked across the Bayuda with nothing more than his servant boy, what's his name…?"

"Zaki."

"Thank you, Richard. Disguised as a Baqqara or some such, marched straight into Mahmud's huge camp at Metemma bright as a button and discovered the Khalifa's son's plans, and brought them back so Kitchener had the comfort of knowing he could send a flying column all the way to Abu Hamed and thus secure the entire section of the Nile along which we now patrol."

Harry took a sip of rum and smiled at Alfred's airy delivery. "I can hear that you're impressed."

With a matching smile, Alfred relented. "Mind, he's pretty headstrong, so you'd better keep a good watch over him, Richard… or Edward, whenever he's around."

"As I have a strong feeling Colonel Wingate's plans may well have Gregory and Zaki foisted upon your decks again before long, Alfred, I'll extend your warning to yourself!"

Harry stared into the amber stain at the base of his glass. *They're all besotted with the boy. He must almost be of an age with Jolyon. I would that it were Jo here now, receiving praise for his headstrong bravery. Oh… Jolyon…*

CHAPTER 24 | *The Sudan, spring to fall, 1898*

ATBARA FORT, APRIL 19

Dearest Jo,

I trust this finds you well. I am excited that you progress well at Woolwich. Have you fired any guns yet or do you learn the composition of the latest explosives? The Sirdar—everyone uses the Egyptian title for Commander-in-Chief of the Anglo-Egyptian Army given General Kitchener by the Khedive—is anxious to equip the Nile gunboats with the new Lyddite shells. Perhaps you have fired some? I hope the rigors of the academy are not too disagreeable. At least you get to have six weeks' break before the second term starting in June and then another six weeks over Christmas, when, God willing, we will have smashed the Khalifa's forces and I might even be back in London to share the season with you, the prospect of which I hope raises your interest as much as it excites me.

The Expeditionary Force is in summer quarters. The Seaforths are quartered in reasonable comfort close to the new Atbara Fort, which sits in the fork where the Nile and its tributary the Atbara meet. For my part I have again denied the Fates, and those patron saints of soldiers—George, Demetrius, Theodore the General, and Theo the Recruit—have preserved me. And no, before you enquire, I have not taken to religion, but before any battle there is surely no harm in having everything possible on your side?

It's annoying that I can only write now about the great Battle of Atbara when you will have read all about it in the newspapers. Perhaps, however, I might impart something of the atmosphere that I doubt a journalist will convey (unless he be Winston Churchill, who hasn't bamboozled his way out here… yet).

When you are in the thick of things, it's impossible to say whether what you are engaged in is a jolly good old fight to be remembered by the history books—the sort of combat that will make the pages of an adventure story by G.A. Henty to thrill the souls of little schoolboys—or whether it's just a fizzle in the footnotes. This one, though, will live on, I reckon.

As you must know, Emir Mahmud, a son of the Khalifa, had marched his army down the Nile hoping to attack across the mouth of the Atbara in the low-water season and then recapture Berber. But the Atbara Fort and concentration of troops there confounded his plan, and he was forced farther to the east in an attempt to outflank us. The Sirdar's plan was simple: sally out and meet him in open battle.

The marching and preparation are of little interest to the public, yet they took far longer than the event itself, which happened on April 8 on the banks of the Atbara. It's laughably called a river, and perhaps in spate it might resemble one, but in the low water season there is nothing to refresh sight or soul as, say, the Serpentine can do to arouse emotion. All we saw were stagnant pools of muddy water isolated in a wide and braided trench—the riverbed.

I commanded a division of the 1st Battalion Seaforth Highlanders, attired in drab khaki (over kilts for the troops), which is nothing new to a seasoned Indian hand, but quite a novelty to some of the other battalions (the khaki, that is, not the kilts). The British Brigade, commanded by Major-General Gatacre, comprised our battalion, with the 1st Battalions of Cameron Highlanders, Lincolnshires, and six companies of the Royal Warwickshires. General Hunter, a veteran of this country, commanded the three brigades of Egyptian and Sudanese foot, Colonel Broadwood the eight squadrons of cavalry, Major Tudway the Camel Corps (and glad I was not to be riding one of those brutes again!), while Colonel Long commanded the artillery batteries. Spies told us that Mahmud and that cowardly rogue Osman Digna were ensconced behind the thorn walls of a large zareba with an estimated 12,000 foot and 3,000 mounted Baqqara.

On the evening before the fight, we set out from Umbadia to traverse the twelve miles to the enemy camp in a direction south of east, roughly in parallel to the Atbara. How strange to see in this wasteland some gazelles in search of water, disturbed by our marching, trotting off into the dusky haze, ignorant of the bellicose matters of men. The four infantry regiments moved forward in brigade squares into the twilight. Soldiers dislike night marches, especially in battle formation. Nothing at night any longer resembles what it does in daylight. The darkness sparks irrational fears, and even in close formation the brain begins to fancy that each soul is alone in the wilderness. At the slightest unexpected sound—startled fowl for instance—panic can set in and throw discipline out. But the Sirdar's plan was for a dawn attack, and so we slowly, slowly advanced. For more than two hours we marched across smooth swells of sand broken by rocks and scattered small bushes. Several shallow *khors* traversed the route, and these rocky ditches delayed the brigades until our pace was hardly two miles an hour.

The Sirdar decided the army had made sufficient progress toward the objective to rest the brigades a little after nine o'clock. Canned meat was handed out, and so cool was the air that even that dreadful fare was welcome, while transport animals were taken in groups the mile and a half to the Atbara to replenish water bottles with foully brackish water from the stilled ponds. The men slept until one o'clock when the march was resumed to arrive in battle position before first light, the brigades now stretched out in a long bow-shaped line, there to sit and await the dawn.

My old school friends Richard and Edward Rainbow, who were not with us, have always advertised the genius of their boss, the Sirdar, from when he was Captain Kitchener in the Intelligence Department under General Wolseley back in '85. In reality his foremost accomplishments are in the realm of engineering and in my view he is a strategist who prefers to rely on overwhelming firepower to win the day. At Atbara he unleashed what I believe is a startling exhibition of artillery. You would have been in your element, gleefully pulling lanyards to unleash shell after shell. A battery of Krupps on the right of the Cameron Highlanders opened fire first. Then the two Maxim-Nordenfelt batteries came into action. It was a quarter-past six. The zareba was formed in a ragged circle about a thousand yards across, its rear wall anchored on the arid riverbank. The range for our artillery was perfect.

Guns fired from all four of the heavy batteries; explosion followed explosion, the cannonade grew louder and merged into a continuous roll of thunder. We had with us two rocket detachments. I think their missiles are more use in terrifying the enemy with their hair-raising squeals. When their crews fired them the rockets shot from the launchers with screams worse than those of a dying horse, and left erratic trails of smoke and sparks in their wakes. In the air above the zareba shell after shell flashed into brilliant bursts of blinding light to strike the ground beneath with deadly showers of lead shrapnel, to then disperse into the haze of smoke that hung like a gray shroud over the Dervish encampment. For the first few minutes of this awful bombardment the soldiers stood up on tiptoe to look at the spectacle, but it went relentlessly on so that even this astonishing sight began to loose its novelty. The busy gunners multiplied the projectiles until so many were flying through the air at once that nothing could any longer be resolved or above the racket discussed. Gradually even the strange sight became monotonous. The men sat down again. Some even fell asleep!

So began the battle. But by half-past seven it was time for the infantry to make the assault, and the line advanced on the partly damaged wall of thorn bush. Like my fellow officers, I dismounted to join my company in the double fighting line. War is no fine thing, Jo, but there is something to stir even the most cynical of minds at the sight of sunlight gleaming from thousands of bayonets raised at point, the snapping standards proudly displaying the Colors, the thrilling skirl of Highlanders' bagpipes, English drums and fifes, and the wild exotic trilling of the Sudanese bands. As the advance commenced, the gun batteries were run forward to support the attack. The deployed battalions opened a crushing fire on the zareba and marched inexorably forward at the pace of a slow march.

At some three hundred yards, the strangely unattended entrenchment sprang to awful life and in another fifty yards we began to take losses. Throughout the bombardment the Arab infantry had lain hidden and relatively safe in dugouts while the Baqqara cavalry made an escape from the rear of the zareba. Fearing an outflanking maneuver, the British cavalry rode to confront the mounted Arabs, but the enemy withdrew to be lost to our sight behind the clouds of dust thrown up by so many hooves. Two men only feet to my side were spun completely around from the force of explosive bullets. One company across from my line, Captain Baillie took a mortal wound as we broke through the enclosure. On the other side the works hidden behind became apparent. After the zareba perimeter was a secondary stockade, and beyond that the Mahdists had dug a treble trench. The whole interior was honeycombed with pits and holes. From these there now sprang thousands of Dervishes, all firing desperately to bring the attack to a halt. The unfortunately named Lieutenant Gore, a young officer fresh from Sandhurst, took a ball smack in the forehead that splashed his brains and blood over me. He fell instantly dead between the thorn fence and the stockade.

To one side, I could just make out through the blue-gray of cordite smoke a line of trees that had been truncated some way above head height, to which it seemed naked figures were roped, for the world like the victims of primitive sacrifice. I could not understand their significance, and there was no time to ponder the mystery.

The British brigade struck the north front of the zareba, and swept the entire eastern face with concentrated rifle fire from end to end until it was no longer possible to see the ground for the corpses strewn about, sometimes three deep. Now, because the long initial assault line had converged, there was not room for more than half the force to deploy. Yet the brigades pushed on and further management of the attack passed to the company commanders. But in truth it turned increasingly into a free-for-all, with the whole force—companies, battalions, even brigades—mixed up together. As a single dense, ragged, but victorious line, we tramped on unchecked toward the riverbed and drove our foes in hopeless confusion before us by bullet and bayonet.

Never think the Arab fighter a shirker. Although the Dervishes were unable to withstand the attack, they refused to turn tail and run from the awful slaughter. Many hundreds held their ground and fired their rifles valiantly until the end. And when ammunition failed or overheated weapons refused to fire, they charged with spear and sword. The greater part retired in skirmishing order, jumping over the numerous pits, walking across the open spaces, and repeatedly turning around to shoot.

Forty minutes after the advance was sounded, at about twenty minutes past eight, we reached the bank of the Atbara, having marched right through the Mahdist position. The Seaforths on the left arrived first, though many men were now entangled with divisions of other battalions. I saw hundreds of Dervishes struggling to retire across the dry bed of the river, hoping to hide their retreat in the scrub on the opposite side. It would have been a kindness to let them escape, but for what? Only to regroup at the Nile and join the Khalifa's enormous army? The order was given and the leading companies of the Seaforths and Lincolns, with odd groups of Camerons, opened a murderous fire. I watched in some horror at the fleeing men struggling through deep sand, with the dust knocked up into clouds by the bullets striking all around them. Very few escaped, and the bodies of the killed lay thickly dotting the riverbed.

Behind us in the encampment, there were worse sights. The dead and dying choked the pits. The ghastly effects of the shelling lay everywhere: heaps of mangled camels and donkeys; human remains ripped apart, decapitated trunks, some missing limbs, the heads lying feet away; women and little children killed by the bombardment or praying in wild terror for mercy; black slaves bound in their trenches, slaughtered in their chains. Of their leader Emir Mahmud, he was captured alive, saved from the murderous fury of the Sudanese by English officers who recognized him in time. It's hard to blame the Sudanese soldiers who have suffered endless indignities under Dervish rule.

Blood covered my hands and face, bits of torn flesh smeared my uniform, yet I had come through unscathed apart from a few skin grazes. I have no idea where I earned them or when. But with the roll call British losses were apparent, as I'm sure you have already read. In a battle of less than an hour's extent we lost eighteen British and sixteen native officers and 525 men were killed or wounded. On the other hand, of the powerful force of 12,000 Mahmud had gathered at Metemma and transported across the Nile to seize Atbara and then Berber, it is estimated that barely 4,000 escaped in the direction of Gedaref, among them the Baqqara horse who fled with Osman Digna. At Gedaref we understand they have joined the garrison of Ahmed Fadil, another of the Khalifa's supporters. No doubt the Sirdar will formulate plans to remove even these as a future threat.

It is a terrible thing, battle, dreadful for the loss of life, terrible for the pointlessness of death in the face of overweening ambition. Yet while men bow before the imperatives of selfish rulers or the straints of religious diktats mankind will continue to fight. Looked at in a political light the battle has been a splendid piece of propaganda, for it has shown the oppressed tribes that the Mahdist fanatics can be sent reeling, even destroyed, and this has raised local morale inestimably.

There is one singular thing that popped up, and it concerns the young Hilliard boy Richard introduced me to at Berber, who I mentioned in my last letter. I assess him to be some five years your junior. His is an unfortunate life. His parents came to Egypt before he was born. Then his father marched with the doomed Hicks Paşa punitive expedition in '83 and was presumed killed in action. He was raised on the streets of Cairo without, apparently, much connection to the English expatriates there and rather more to the natives. Then his mother died when he was but sixteen and now he's a lowly interpreter for the Egyptian Army. And yet he has a self-confident bearing at odds with his under-educated upbringing. I'm not sure why, but I found his company quite unsettling.

Anyway, back to the singularity. I have ascertained that somehow he fell into Mahmud's hands some weeks ago but was not executed on the spot. In the aftermath of the battle a colonel of the Seaforths I know slightly called Lyons, came to me and told me an incredible story. He saw this white boy, virtually naked, streaked in gore and dust, fighting like a maniac alongside his men in the zareba. In the quiet after the battle he questioned him. This is what Lyons told me: "The boy blinked and seemed in a daze and then he spoke. 'If Major Vane is all right, he'll vouch for me. I'm Lieutenant Hilliard, sir, attached to General Hunter's staff.' I said to him, 'I am happy to say that Major Vane is quite well.' And then I said that it gave us quite a surprise when a strange white man suddenly joined in the scrap. I pointed to where he would find General Hunter with the Sudanese. I asked what on earth he was doing here. He seemed confused, but said, 'I've been a captive of the Dervishes. I realize I'm hardly dressed appropriately but… they had me tied to the stump of a tree as a target for your bullets. Others—captured deserters—were also tied up. I think most died, as I would have done, if it hadn't been for my…' At that point, Vane, he cussed obscenely and said something that sounded like Zaki. 'He was wearing the Mahdists' patches. I must go,' he added. Apologized insincerely and ran off as if the Devil were on his heels. Extraordinary!"

What do you think of that, Jo? The amazing tricks of war. He must have been one of those figures I spotted through the smoke tied to tree stumps, and I never knew. Since he seems to be thick with Richard and Edward, I suppose I will get to the bottom of this particular mystery.

It was a late afternoon at the start of the second week of August. A confusion of hulls and sails filled the basin formed where the Nile and Atbara met. Harry enjoyed his regular strolls along the newly constructed wharfs lining the perimeter of Atbara Fort where—in spite of the naval activity in loading the

Sudanese regiments aboard barges for the advance upriver to the Sixth Cataract at Shabluka—young boys were using every trick in their armory to con strolling soldiers into taking a sail in their feluccas.

That's when he ran into the reporter for the *Morning Post*. The familiar figure appeared to be under attack from a horde of felucca boys who were demanding his attention with menaces.

"Winston!"

"My God, Harry! Well met."

Harry threw out some words in Arabic, all spoken with a broad smile, and the young boatmen moved back. Churchill brushed his coat down as if recovering from a fight.

"I just got in after a mad dash from Southampton to Alexandria. Barely saw Cairo whiz by, but at least I managed a breather at Luxor… They don't take 'No' for an answer, do they?"

Harry laughed. "They don't."

Churchill noticed how one of the youngest, surely a lad of not above sixteen years, tried to hang onto Harry's coat tails. "Looks like that one's lost his head for your undoubted charms. But somehow I doubt shampoo has ever passed his hands."

Harry froze. He batted the boys aside and glared out at the liquid gold of the setting sun reflecting off the Nile. He flinched at Winston's touch.

"Sorry, old chap. I didn't intend anything mean. Thought you were thicker-skinned than that."

Harry was undecided on how to react. The incident under Maharaja Nripendra Narayan's roof remained one unspoken of between them. To say more would be to accept that Winston knew of Harry's preferences in bed; which of course he did, but if the matter remained *sub rosa* it could be ignored with typically good British manners. He felt abashed at the subject being touched on so immediately after bumping into Churchill. In the end, he settled for deflection and good cheer. "Once again, a little less of the 'old,' if you don't mind Winston." He turned his face from the sunset and smiled tightly.

Churchill patted his coat side pockets and produced a Turkish cigarette. "You could at least inform this callow youth you see before you what is Harry Vane doing in this fly-infested spot. By the way, I haven't forgiven you for diverting to Simla while I toiled on at Banagalore."

Harry declined the offer of a smoke. "But you had your moment of glory."

"No, actually, I didn't. Oh, we all got a campaign medal, but no decorations. You see the fighting at Shahi-Tangi was not part of the main campaign undertaken by Jeffreys, and so it didn't receive official recognition. Typical! It was a Wednesday as well, so that explains it." He stamped a booted foot on the ground, which caused a further withdrawal of felucca boys to a safe distance. "Worse, that bounder Fincastle, when he wrote his piece, didn't even mention me. In fact he devoted no more than a short paragraph to the action. No, Harry, it was my misfortune that all who counted were engaged with Jeffreys elsewhere in the Mohmand Valley, and that there was no gallery of senior officers to observe my courage under fire."

"Wasn't the action at Shahi-Tangi on a Thursday, unless I'm mistaken?"

Churchill glanced up from setting a vesta to his cigarette. "Was it? Felt like a Wednesday."

"I'm sorry. Not about the days, about the lack of a proper medal. I know you deserved recognition of what you did. Perhaps what we'll be facing upriver will offer a better opportunity for you to shine, Winston, though for my part I'll be happy to avoid too much adventure." Harry explained his attachment to the Seaforths.

Churchill in turn said that he was attached as journalist-subaltern to the 21st Lancers, "though God only knows what use they'll be in the desert. Knowing my luck, we'll sit around making tea all day and curry-combing the horses."

"There is that. I can't see a detachment of Lancers doing much, but you never know. There may be glory in it."

"I do hope so. It's been a damned hard fight enough to get out here. The Sirdar kept sidelining my requests. That's why I missed out at Atbara. He hasn't made my life easy. Something I wrote once, apparently."

"Criticism of the War Office, perhaps, or the senior staff officers?" Harry gave a mirthful twist of his mouth.

"No more than they deserve, Harry. But General Kitchener sees me as a jumped up wastrel of the vacuous class, but I managed to wangle it... well, my mother Lady Randolph did really. Just hope we don't ever have to meet face to face, or he might remember what it is I wrote that so gave him moral indigestion... unless he hates me for being descended from the 1st Duke of

Marlborough. Is it my fault that my glorious ancestor happens to be the most successful general of all time, the man whose half-score of victories turned our island-nation into *the* major world power and was given the damnedest biggest palace in the country for it?"

"It might, of course," Harry said slyly, "be your other side, the American blood he dislikes."

"Oh, piffle, I say. I give him too much credit. The man's an engineer. What's he know of history? Speaking of which did you manage some time in Luxor?"

Harry drew his brows together at the sudden shift, although it quickly transpired it was a change only in emphasis rather than subject. "Yes. Why?"

"I don't know about you, but I found Luxor Temple inspirational. I'd taken some time to study Professor Maspero's excavation records. According to the cartouches, the magnificent monument was erected to ancient Egyptian deities by Amenhotep III, Ramses II, some minor official called Tutankhamun, and embellished by a certain Macedonian upstart named Alexander." Churchill blew out a stream of blue smoke. "And then the Romans trampled all over it." He waved at the wide river. "Never got as far south as this though, eh? Our Empire…"

Harry recalled the stark line of the temple's colonnade, standing like stone bones against the sky. "They watch over us from so very long ago," he said quietly. "Makes you think, doesn't it?"

"You felt it too, Harry." Not a question.

"I did… do. It puts into perspective our concerns, our battles, our petty existence."

"Nonsense, dear boy."

Churchill flicked his cigarette stub over the dockside edge into the Nile and Harry reflected with wry amusement and not a little condescended-to irritation on how his young friend made him *old man* one minute and the *dear boy* the next.

"Everything takes its place in history and neither denigrates what comes after nor aggrandizes what went before." Churchill raised both eyebrows in emphasis. "We all make our own history, and while I will never belittle it, I will never let it overwhelm me with the majesty of its years, decades, eons. Besides, five years is a lot. An event that far back is already history. Twenty years is the horizon to most people. Fifty years is antiquity."

The sentiment sounded rehearsed. Harry gave an ironic bow. "Then I wish you glory of your Lancers, Winston, that you may indeed be written into the histories. For my part, I aim to get through what's to come with a safe skin so I might return to London and... my future history."

Churchill narrowed his eyes inquisitively. "You have someone to return to, I deduce from the manner, and that is a great deal more than I have to look forward to. I have not been successful in matters of the heart and in which case, dear Harry, *bon voyage* and the best of luck."

❧ ✦ ❧

Omdurman Camp, September 10, 1898

My dearest Jo,

It saddened me that the circumstances of war—in which neither the Khalifa obliged us a final set battle ahead of schedule nor Kitchener be driven to advance faster than his careful plan—meant I was not home in London for your six-week summer vacation from Woolwich. And the intervening months have been spent in places ill-equipped with postal or telegraphic systems for regular correspondence. So here I am camped opposite Khartoum at Omdurman, the capital of the Khalifa's detested fanaticism. It might interest you to know that the first use of Lyddite shells proved most effective in destroying the tomb of the Mahdi, the madman who began all this.

The telegraph has just reached here but is commandeered for matters of State and battle-hardened newshound-heroes, which is a company of one: My young friend Winston Glory-or-Die Spencer-Churchill. How hard he tries, and on this occasion he will undoubtedly sail into the history books, particularly since he will be writing the book himself. He had the luck—as he would see the terrifying event—to take part in the dashing charge of the 21st Lancers. They were scouting ahead of the British brigades. I'd seen Winston briefly, looking splendid in his uniform, face agog with excitement, his .445-inch 1892 Webley-Wilkinson revolver in hand (a polo injury damaged the shoulder he banged up disembarking in Bombay, so he couldn't possibly hold a lance) shortly before the squadrons rode out to look for any enemies lurking behind the dome of a hill called Surgham.

About half a mile south of the hill they spied a small party of Dervish cavalry and some infantry trying to hide in what looked like a shallow khor. There are several of these dry watercourses traversing the plain across which we infantry had to advance. The four squadrons cantered forward and then, sabers drawn, kicked their horses into a gallop. "The reports of brisk musketry fire didn't worry us," Winston said. But as they neared the scattered enemy position they found that the depression was much wider than it appeared. They'd estimated that it might hold as many as a hundred and fifty foes, but shockingly some fifteen hundred Dervishes lay concealed in the depression.

Too late to pull up, with a desperate cheer the cavalry rode down into the midst of their adversaries like the foolhardy Light Brigade all over again. Their mounts are trained to rear up and strike down with iron-shod forefeet on the enemy. The sheer suddenness of the onslaught dismayed the Dervishes, but they quickly rallied.

A fierce fight broke out, lance against spear, saber against sword, butt-end of a rifle or the deadly knife. Some Lancers cut their way through unscathed. Others were surrounded and cut off. Those who carried right over the khor wheeled their horses and returned to rescue officers and comrades. Once across, the survivors gathered at a point where their fire commanded the watercourse. Dismounting, they speedily drove the Dervishes from it, leaving sixty dead among the rocks. Between the squadrons, the Lancers lost twenty-two officers and men killed, and fifty suffered sword and spear injuries. But not Winston. He had the gore of his enemies' blood on him, but mostly he was covered in glory.

It is eight days since the monumental battle. I am pleased to have been present at the Khalifa's overthrow and the ruin of his Mahdist government that has stripped this poor suffering land bare, but the fanatics' death toll is appalling. It is heartrending to see the futile courage of men no better armed than were the Crusaders face massed modern weapons. The Seaforths acquitted themselves well, but then you know it from the newspaper reports. Yet the Khalifa escaped with some thousand of his Baqqara horse, ready to rally the desert tribes to fight another day. Normally I would be champing at the bit to join the chase to bring justice to this evil despot and his desperate minions like the cowardly Osman Digna, but this time I am thankful that won't be my problem because it means I can return and see you.

The War Office wants me back. I suppose it will mean training duties again or going on the reserve, which will mean being on half-pay. There are rumors that trouble is brewing again with the Boers in South Africa, so perhaps I can lobby for an attachment down there, and who knows, if timing is sweet, maybe we will indeed become the Theban Band, only facing down a laager of boring Boers.

So no telegraph facilities for functionary soldiers, it's ink and paper for the likes of a mere major. I'll stick four Army stamps on the envelope instead of the required one so the postal system will perceive its urgency and speed it to your hand. The Seaforths are first to be shipped home. The minute my feet touch land at Southampton I shall send a telegram so you know when to expect me.

In the greatest affection, your Serpentine Theban, Harry

P.S. An odd thing. Some weeks back at a layover in Wadi Hamed I joined a group of officers relaxing over some wine. Edward Rainbow was with them and we had some silly discussion about an ass called Hartley who was also present. He expects to come into the estates of the Earl of Langdale. And then along came young Gregory Hilliard. Rainbow insisted he sit with us. Hartley was extremely rude and dismissive of Hilliard, whose restraint I found admirable, and ended up receiving a verbal riposte of some strength from Edward, who clearly holds the same high view of the Cairene street urchin as Richard.

CHAPTER 25 | *London, December 1898–January 1899*

A THICK COVERING of snow muted any sounds from the street. Noisier than absent hooves and wheels, only the occasional pair of booted feet might be heard with the characteristic squeaky crunch of compacted fresh snow on South Street below Harry's window. Winter had come earlier than usual, dressing the dirty gray city in a sparkling white robe by the middle of December.

For a long while neither spoke a word to break the extraordinary peace. Harry felt he should close the drapes and shut out the London night, but the sight of drifting snow flakes caught momentarily in the glow from the window pleased him. And besides, he didn't want to waste energy in getting up from the bed when he could expend his stamina in so many better ways—like undressing Jolyon and then himself. Up on the third floor where his suite of rooms were situated no one could see in from the street, and though the trees were in winter's undress, the branches still clustered thickly enough to block sight of the houses across the street.

"Are you happy?"

"Mmm… you?"

Harry sighed. "This is the best run-up to Christmas I can remember since…"

Jolyon raised his head. "Since when?" He ran a long finger down the side of Harry's nose.

When Richard and I declared our love for each other.

"Since the one when I ran into the nursery to see the rocking horse I so wanted."

"Were there tears of joy?" Jolyon teased.

Oh, God, there were tears indeed, of great joy, and floods of release and… It's in the past. This is my future now.

Harry turned an unbidden sob into a choky laugh. "You know me too well. I couldn't wait to mount him—it was a stallion rocking horse—"

"Of course it was!" Jolyon's chortles rang out.

Harry tried kissing Jo's bright eyes shut and partly succeeded.

The giggles subsided and Jolyon turned serious. "I try not to be jealous, but you have so much more experience. I know you do. It stands to reason, so good looking, so much…"

"Older?"

"Experienced."

The claim made Harry lift his eyebrows. "And *feasting with panthers…*?" He smiled to remove the sting in the words.

"Of love, Harry. I never loved before and I was certainly not loved."

The inward breath caught in Harry's throat. It was the first hint Jolyon had let slip that under Bosie's evil tutelage he might have experienced more than decadent sexual suggestion. He looked at the face lying beside him and thought it was the most beautiful image he'd ever set eyes on. The low light of a gas mantle almost hidden on the wall behind the bulk of a wardrobe caught the sharp-edged cushions of Jo's cheeks in a faint glow and made bright shards glint in his dark eyes.

"Listen…"

Harry cocked an ear and smiled slowly.

"What can you hear?"

"Nothing but the hiss of the gas fire…"

They both breathed out at the same instant.

Harry began to divest himself of his confining garments, suddenly too eager to carry out his threat of disrobing Jolyon first, but he was only seconds ahead before impatience won and Jolyon almost ripped the buttons off his shirt in his haste to snuggle up naked. Both were instantly hard and their erections poked at the other's belly. Their lips touched and parted to make way for tongues to invade in turn and revolve slowly together. Jolyon raised his head and traced a line down Harry's neck to his shoulder, then across the clavicle to the hollow below his Adam's apple. Harry sighed with pleasure and stretched his limbs as Jo licked over and down to the far nipple and teased it between sharp teeth.

For some seconds Jo contented himself with licking and brushing saliva-slicked lips over warm flesh, but then he swiveled half around and headed south. Harry pushed his ass up off the bed covering to meet the delicious assault. He gasped again when Jo took his cock in his warm, saliva-lubricated mouth, slurped around the crown and sucked him in, deep down, and then back. Harry snaked his hand between their clinging bodies and took Jo's surging cock in hand. The shampoo boy had been extraordinary, but nonetheless mechanical, devoid of emotion. What Jolyon was doing brought Harry's heart to his mouth at the adoration in his lover's eyes and the sucking was bringing him too quickly toward a climax. Too soon.

"Slow down, Jo. Here…" He brought Jolyon's head up with his free hand. Slightly freed from the weight, he wriggled sufficiently to part his legs and bring his heels up to press against his buttocks. In the yellow-white gaslight Jo's eyes drank him in, faint puzzlement gradually becoming a smile of understanding. He cocked his head sideways, asking for confirmation of what Harry might be offering.

"Do me, Jo. Take me as you have let me have at you."

He felt Jo's hand rub the sensitive flesh of his inner thigh, fingers gently stroking as they reached up to tickle under his tense balls, and then down to meet in the cleft of his ass. Gently, he shuffled to position himself between Harry's spread legs, raised them by lifting under his knees and pressing them back toward the trembling ribcage. He spat copiously on the fingers of his left hand and rubbed them around and into Harry's clenching hole, smiled happily at Harry's rumbling groan of pleasure. He dipped his head and allowed a second stream of saliva to fall down and coat his cock as he brought the exposed crown to bear and felt his way.

Harry's breathing speed increased dramatically.

"Relax, Harry."

"It's all right. Go on."

Jo reared up slightly, excitingly lithe, slender, yet suddenly certain and forceful. He pushed himself past the ring of muscle. Harry drew in a breath sharply at an intrusion he hadn't experienced since that time on the *Malabar* with William, but the more Jo pressed into him, the easier it seemed to feel. He was filled. Jolyon was deep inside him. Tears sprang to his eyes… of joy. Jolyon set up a surprisingly gentle motion at first, pushing in, pulling almost out. But no matter how suddenly wonderful that felt, the best was when Jo strained forward and brought his mouth crushing down on Harry's and their tongues lashed as hard as Jo fucked him. With each inward thrust Jo hit the spot that made Harry explode with sheer ecstasy, and his flesh responded in a way it never had with William's vigorous attack—sharp jabs of intense pleasure.

He knew Jo was on the verge of climaxing, his puffing breath forced into Harry's gaping mouth, their bodies slick with sweat, bones and muscles grinding together, Jo's hand now gripping Harry's cock and masturbating it to the frenzied rhythm of his fucking—all this set up a fluid friction that took them to a height of orgasm. Paused at the very edge of the delicious abyss, Jo gasped...*uh, uh, uh*... and Harry felt the rush of hot seed burst and then flower deep inside him. Jo's release and his heartfelt groans tipped Harry over the edge, and they both flew through the ether like entangled angels. Harry dived headfirst into orgasm in Jo's firm rubbing grip. The intense spasms of mutual pleasure caused them to jerk one against the other until the flood slowed, over-taut muscles slowly relaxed and allowed the drawing out of the joy for long minutes until they rolled sideways in contented exhaustion.

Eventually, Jolyon rolled his head to gaze at Harry. "Thank you, my hero and savior," he said simply.

Harry leaned toward him and pressed the available ear between his lips, savoring the lobe's velvety feel. "I'm happy you are here with me. I've never known such... oh such happiness, Jo."

"I wasn't exaggerating. You *did* save me, Harry. I was harsh, I know, cruel even, but now my feelings for you... rob me of sensible speech."

Harry never did find the energy to close out the night. He was drifting off to sleep, holding Jolyon in his arms, loving the feel of neatly cut hair against his cheek, his own satiated loins pushed against naked ass cleft, buttocks lean... and all his to have and to hold. The snow-bound city slumbered all around, and his last thought before sleep took him away held a murmur of concern.

Our ages... the difference. Is it enough or he will soon tire of me?

"Hallo." For a moment Harry thought the young man he was addressing didn't know who was accosting him, so he smiled politely and tried again. "I beg pardon, my Lord, for my intruding on your thoughts."

The light dawned. "Oh, I'm sorry, sir. I didn't recognize you in civilian clothes!"

Harry laughed. "You have no need to call me sir… if I may call you by your name?"

The young man—barely more than a boy—blushed, which only added to his evident discomfiture. This, Harry thought, came from Hilliard—no, Hartley's—still being unused to the stiff formal attire of social London. The way he kept glancing down at the floor and scuffing his fashionable two-tone shoes was a distinctly boyish trait. "Ah, you've heard that I have almost come into my… er, title, estates, and money?"

"There isn't a soul in London who matters who isn't aware of the downfall of your frightful Hartley cousin and your attaining your rightful position as Gregory Hilliard Hartley, Earl of Langdale."

"Really?"

"Really, Hartley."

"It's so… embarrassing." The frustrated shrug subsided and a cautious smile replaced the frown. "And please, call me Gregory. I'm still not used to such formality. Besides, I've been Hilliard all my life and I'm just not used to being a Hartley. Well, not yet. Anyway, I still await their Lordships' decision on my claim, due at the start of business in January."

"Have no doubt, Gregory. Your claim is sound and the House of Lords is only placing an inked rubber stamp on a certainty. I should know, for my brother Evan is one of the great and good in the Upper House and aware of all its currents. So take my word for it, you're already the Earl, the best New Year's present you could wish for. In anticipation, may I offer you a glass of bubbly?"

It was the evening following Harry and Jolyon's consummation of their relationship—he thought of it like that for letting Jolyon expend his seed inside him instead of he fucking Jo. In search of comedic diversion they went out to the West End and proceeded to the Smythe-Vane family's reserved private box, one of twelve at Wyndham's Theatre on Charing Cross Road. Evan Smythe-Vane was one of Charles Wyndham's patrons and thus a contributor to the funds used to purchase the land and construct the actor-manager's own auditorium, which had recently opened. Mr. T.W. Robertson's comedy *David Garrick* was playing yet again to a full house, an appreciative audience of some seven hundred.

When the interval arrived, Jolyon opted to remain in the quiet of the box. The days when he enjoyed the gaiety and press of theatergoers seemed to have passed with the destruction of his adolescent life. And so it was Harry alone who descended to the foyer with its elaborate Louis XVI period décor in turquoise and cream, a combination he found over fussy. His gamble that the foyer bar would be less crowded than the upper gallery crush bars paid out, and there he had spotted Gregory, looking lonely and rather lost.

He organized glasses of champagne for them and raised his. "Cheerio!"

Gregory clicked the rim of his saucer against Harry's with a reserved nod of the head. But then he said, "It's good to see a familiar face. I feel a bit like an imposter, really, standing here trying to be elegant in London instead of being happy at home. Whoever would have thought I might think kindly of the Sudanese desert!"

"But this is your home now… although, I don't know, have you moved into the palatial Langdale mansion yet? I mean the main London residence in Hanover Square."

"Lord no. That wouldn't do, my solicitor Mr. Tufton says. Not until after the papers are stamped, apparently. I've been hopping between rooms at the Cannon Street Hotel and my two aunts' home in Tavistock, which is in the county of Devon."

He delivered the last in the confidence that Harry would have no idea where Tavistock might be. Harry did not correct his assumption.

"Anyway, I'm dreading it. Great pile. Tufton took me there to have a look over the place. It's got to be three times the size of the Governor General's Cairo Residency, and the butler fellow called me 'milord,' which is just so…"

"Embarrassing?" Harry laughed and for the first time since the brief encounters in Berber and later at Wadi Hamed, he warmed to Gregory, acutely aware of how the extraordinary change in his circumstance must be affecting him. And all that on top his ordeal in Mahmud's camp at Atbara. He certainly was resilient, and if he'd come into great prosperity, his fortitude was surely the greater wealth.

For a moment, the forlorn expression melted into something approaching a smile. "Exactly! I suppose I shall grow into it," though he sounded doubtful about the prospects of that. A look of mild gloom settled on Gregory's features and for a while it seemed he was lost somewhere far away.

It's not all bewilderment at London's whirligig—he's pining for his Ja'alin companion. And Harry understood all to well what that felt like.

The bell sounded a warning of the curtain's rise in five minutes.

Harry asked, "Where do you sit?"

"Oh, er, you know. I have a seat in the stalls."

"Then bring your champagne with you and accompany me to my box. We have six places, all empty but for two."

Gregory welcomed the invitation with the broadest smile he had so far managed and was suitably astonished at the electrically operated lift provided to whisk members of the audience seated in the Royal Circle, Grand Circle, and Balcony up to those empyrean heights. Jolyon was lying back deep in his seat when they pushed through the portiére. The elegant cut of his pinstriped pants emphasized his long, slender outstretched legs. His neatly booted feet were propped up on the brass rail that ran around the edge of the box some inches from the thickly carpeted floor. He glanced up as Harry came through the entrance and, on seeing Gregory, treated him to a frank appraisal that reminded Harry of his attitude from the Wildean days.

"Gregory, the slouch lounging in the middle chair is Jolyon Langrish-Smith. Jo, please meet Mr. Hartley, a friend of mine from Egypt."

Was there a hint of jealousy in Jo's slightly narrowed eyes or just the plain suspicion of two young bucks meeting for the first time? Harry wasn't quite sure why he didn't remind Jolyon of the mentions of he'd made of Gregory in his letters. And as if he took his cue from Harry, Jolyon feigned ignorance. He didn't bother getting up so Gregory reached down to shake hands. Jolyon waved him to the seat on his right and Harry arranged himself beside his lover on the other side.

"When Harry says 'from Egypt' does he mean you soldier out there or that you are in point of fact Egyptian?"

Harry leaned forward enough to see around Jolyon's slumped form so he could assess Gregory's reaction. Jolyon wore the enigmatic half-smile that usually followed his barbed jests, and Harry's sharp bang of his knee against Jolyon's failed to dislodge the moue from his lips. Gregory looked faintly flustered, no doubt unsure if Jolyon was genuinely curious or making fun of him. Harry dived in to save any further embarrassment. "Gregory was born in Egypt and lived there all his life, Jo. So no teasing."

At that, Jolyon folded up his legs and sat forward, his tone more mellowed. "I say, does that mean you speak Arabic, or something?"

Harry was surprised that Jolyon didn't remember his mentioning Gregory being an interpreter... or was it another tease? The question seemed to leave Gregory nonplussed and Harry was about to intervene again when he spoke up.

"I do. Arabic in Egyptian and Sudanese style, as well as the Nubian dialects."

"And your English ain't that bad, either," Jolyon said with a chuckle.

At the risk of piling more awkwardness on Gregory's bashful shoulders Harry decided it was time to put Jolyon in his place. He patted his knee. "Careful, you are talking to the man who may well soon be the fifteenth Earl of Langdale."

Jolyon's fine eyebrows shot up in recognition. "*That* Gregory Hilliard Hartley. Of course you are."

This time Harry was as unsure as Gregory must be as to whether Jolyon's tone conveyed admiration or plain jealousy, and if it were the latter was he was covetous of Gregory's unexpected fortune or was it that he perceived a rival in the boy and wrongly thought Harry was flirting? From his expression Jolyon clearly expected a response from Gregory, but Harry changed the subject as abruptly as Jolyon was wont to do. Even as he did so he realized he was playing with potential fire, but too late. The others had seen him lean against the balcony rail and incline his head.

Jolyon and Gregory followed Harry's discreet indication. In a box sufficiently around the curve of the Royal Gallery to be easily visible from their position there sat an extraordinarily handsome young adolescent boy with flowing locks. He was chatting animatedly with a woman in whose face could be seen a resemblance of the boy's.

Jolyon dipped his head at the sight and smiled knowingly. "Who is the pretty boy, since it is he is who I presume you are pointing out?"

"Why, Jo, Gregory, that young man with his mother is Cyril Holland."

Gregory frowned his incomprehension, which matched Jolyon's, and suddenly Harry was uncertain whether he should continue. Jolyon's behavior toward Gregory irritated him for the implicit suggestion in his tone that Harry was flirting with Gregory, but was it right to rub old history in his face?

"And he would be...?"

Too late for regrets, he could hardly pull back, now. "The son of someone I think you knew rather well... at one time."

Jolyon furrowed his brow in puzzlement. "Holland? Did I ever know a Holland?" Confusion turned to suspicion.

"I probably shouldn't have brought it up, but he is no less than the son of Oscar Wilde; one of them."

A shadow passed across Jolyon's face and his posture froze.

"I believe the boy has started his studies at Radley College and must be enjoying a spell of freedom from school," Harry added lamely.

Gregory's frown deepened. "Is this Mr. Wild a well known writer of theater drama? I have scrutinized the newspapers since getting here, but I don't think I recollect a play by anyone called Wild."

It was easy to hear how Gregory spoke the name. Harry leaned around stiff Jolyon. "That's Wilde with an *e* on the end, and no, you won't have. Even his most sparkling offerings have been expunged from the record, and it reflects on why his two sons bear the name of his mother's family. The voluminously named Oscar Fingal O'Flahertie Wills Wilde was released from prison not quite two years ago and has fled in exile to the Continent."

"For what was he imprisoned?"

"Sodomy," Jolyon said shortly.

Gregory looked as if Jolyon had slapped his face. Harry imagined he was thinking of his friend… Zaki, wasn't it? But he also wondered if the boy's thoughts included Richard and Harry's history. Did he also know about Richard *and* Edward? All of them out there in the desert, swapping stories, and never for a moment imagining that someone might be incarcerated in prison for doing what he and Zaki did… if they did. He tried finding consolation in the paintings following the style of Boucher which adorned the auditorium ceiling, but their frivolity mocked him. He felt the need to ameliorate the situation and reassure Gregory.

"It was a travesty of justice—"

Jolyon cut Harry off. "He was… what was the phrase…?" Staring defiantly at Harry.

You know full well, Jo.

"…Feasting with panthers, and rather a lot, Harry. Cheap rent boys," he explained to Gregory.

If he'd been puzzled before, Gregory looked completely dumbfounded by the term, but they were saved from explaining the nature and institution of male prostitution in London's seedier neighborhoods when the clusters of electric lights in their cream silk shades adhering to the edges of the galleries dimmed. The auditorium buzz stilled.

Oh God, we just had our first argument. I'm so stupid…

In the dark, carefully shielded from Gregory's sight, Harry slipped his hand against Jolyon's and held his breath, only letting it out when Jo relented and entwined their fingers together.

CHAPTER 26 | *London, January and April 1899*

GETTING JOLYON BACK to R.M.A. Woolwich for the start of his second year in the last dark days of January proved harder than Harry envisaged, for several reasons: his own emotions cried out at the separation; Jolyon was utterly miserable on the same account, though Harry was sure it was tempered by his insecurity over Gregory: and then there was the harsh regime. To a young man, with all his life before him, incarceration within the confines of the Royal Military Academy for the better part of two years felt like a life sentence. As a gentleman cadet at Sandhurst, Harry had suffered similar indignities to his self-esteem and person, but Jolyon insisted that Harry couldn't possibly understand. "The state of affairs is so much worse than in your day," he insisted.

The impending leave taking was not improved any when Jolyon faced the abandonment of sartorial elegance for the rough, badly tailored uniforms of everyday life at the Shop, as inmates called Woolwich because it had been founded in one of the Royal Arsenal's converted workshops. The hated hairy uniform and robust underwear, socks, gaiters, boots, and other military paraphernalia were packed in a trunk and waiting in the hall three floors below.

"I wish I could wear the beautiful uniform you gave me for Christmas."

"Don't torture yourself. You know you're not allowed a gunner's dress uniform until you pass out of the Academy. That's just for us when we want to go somewhere and dress sharply, and even then it's a risk if some staff officer attends the same function. You look wonderful in the daguerreotype." Jolyon was not to be mollified so easily. Harry stifled a smirk. "I'll stand it beside my bed always to keep you in my mind and heart at all times."

Jolyon snorted his irritation and rightly waved aside Harry's heartfelt but silly sentiment. He fumed quietly for a second, and then burst out anew. "It's bad enough that nothing really fits, but the material is scratchy on sensitive skin and it doesn't help me to appreciate getting up from the hard paillasse at some godforsaken hour in the morning."

"I know what it's like—"

"Six-thirty! That's when some hellhound sounds Reveille. Then there's extra drill for the idiots undergoing punishment—"

"Which never affects you."

Jolyon looked glum. "Not me that often, but some silly asses just won't learn. At least we're allowed to smoke these days. That used to be forbidden."

"It was at Sandhurst."

A hand went up, fingers straight out for counting off, a process which involved both sets of fingers before Jolyon was done. "Seven-thirty: prayers and breakfast…" he paused to glare at Harry over the fan of fingers. "Religion does not aid digestion, you know. At least we can choose between tea, coffee, or cocoa, and there are always bread and butter to go with either meat or fish. Eight till eleven it's first study period, followed by drills until just before lunch at twelve-thirty, which is usually a sandwich or cold meat and bread and cheese." More fingers counted off. "One until three is second study, and at three-fifteen it's dinner. I ask you Harry, for a soul used to dining late, or having supper after the theater, dinner in the afternoon is just… *unspeakable*. I never digest."

"Like breakfast, spoiled by prayer?"

"Exactly! At a time when civilized persons are taking tea with thin cucumber sandwiches, we're scoffing down hot meat and vegetables, followed by stodgy puddings or sometimes a—I admit—reasonable fruit tart. No wine, either, and any beer has to be purchased out of the meager pay we receive." His tenor voice rose to a squeak. "It's positively barbarian! And then from six until eight there's a third study period, everyone belching and farting from over-eating."

Harry smiled. "I don't think anyone would accuse you of that."

"What, farting?"

"No, over-eating."

"Hmm! Still, I don't mind the study too much."

"After Eton you're pretty proficient in French and German."

"Yes, and not too rotten at practical geography and topography, though I am looking forward to getting down to some practicalities on combustibles and explosives. It's only with swot I fall down—that's mathematics."

"I know what swot is, Jo, I've been through it all as well, except being cavalry we had lots more riding than you and we didn't make big bangs with field artillery. And, of course, things were *soo* much better in my day," he added sardonically.

"Anyway, at eight there are more prayers to sit through while the men with iron constitutions and extra pocket money might purchase cold meat or eggs to go with their bread and tea. Ten, it's roll call and lights out at ten-thirty."

"So there are two whole hours, well, a bit less after prayers, of free time. And what do you do with yourself then?"

Jolyon gave Harry a somewhat shifty look. "Nothing much. Read. Play billiards. Sometimes I go with a few fellows out to Plumstead and a pub there, but it's risky. If you get caught beyond Shop boundaries…"

"Extra drill for the idiots undergoing punishment?"

Jolyon nodded, the corner of his mouth turned up ruefully.

"It's not for much longer. It will all be worthwhile. Promise. Try to behave."

"You're only my godfather, Harry, not my parent. And what about you, gentleman of leisure? How will you fill your time?"

There was a depth of possible hurt trying to hide in Jolyon's suddenly unguarded expression, which made him seem young, vulnerable, and wanting reassurance. Harry took him in his arms and gripped tightly. "I'm hardly a gentleman of leisure. There may not be much need for surplus majors right now, but trouble's brewing in the Cape, and Kitchener hasn't yet brought the Khalifa and his reduced army to book, so I'm sure to find respectable employment soon. Meantime, I don't call having to be at Aldershot on alternate months very leisurely—lecturing subalterns on the means by which we keep Her Majesty's subject peoples in check but smiling happily."

Harry knew his going on about it was to deflect from the obvious fact that every other month he would be in London and fancy-free, albeit on reserve half-pay, which was not a problem with his private allowance and free accommodation here at South Street.

"Do you want me to come with you to Woolwich?"

Jolyon disengaged himself briskly, stood tall, and braced his shoulders. "Certainly not!"

Harry grinned. "You're afraid I'll show you up and embarrass you in front of your returning friends."

"They are acquaintances, and no, I'm not afraid of that. I'm terrified of it. Somebody found out that my father was a hero of the Crimea and my godfather is the Hero of Chitral. Fortunately, like Peter I denied you thrice and managed to convince them that I know nothing of you. Do any of them know theirs?"

"Probably not," Harry said with a smile. "I'm certain that many of your *acquaintances* turn up with their doting parents to drop off their darling offspring in the bosom of Woolwich. But then, I'm not old enough to be your father, I know, so I suppose that would raise some eyebrows as to who we are to each other. We don't exactly match as brothers."

"No, and in point of fact, sadly, your face isn't forgotten from the newspaper pictures either."

"I can see how much of a mixed blessing that is for your nonchalant reputation, Jo, but all I can say is that I wish the older generation in the War Office recognized me as easily." Harry looked around at the sound of a cab pulling up outside with a clatter of wheels, a snorting nag, and the jingle of traces and brass. "That's you."

"You didn't have to get a cab, you know. I'm not too proud to take the Underground railway and an omnibus."

Another laugh bubbled up in Harry's throat and passed the lump there that saying goodbye had caused to rise up. "It's all right, Jo. I shan't be offended— anyway I won't be there to know—if you drop the cab off a mile from the Academy and go the rest of the way on foot to save you the discomfiture of having someone afford you a touch of unbecoming luxury."

Jolyon stood in the doorway to check that no other members of the Smythe-Vane family were present to witness his departure. Harry kept telling him that doing so made him seem more suspicious than simply acting like a normal godchild visiting his moral advisor—an admonishment that always caused Jolyon great ironic merriment. He turned, a forlorn look quickly banished. "I'll miss you terribly, Harry."

"You'll be too busy. You'd better be, my Theban-in-training. Go and learn to blow things up this year. I'm going to keep the rest of your life very busy." Harry gulped down the sudden rush of emotion that threatened to choke him.

Jolyon gave a quick wave and closed the door after him. Harry listened to the clatter of metal-segged army boots fade down the grand staircase, the front door open and shut. He felt empty.

Uncertainty clouded Harry's thoughts. He had just come from an uncomfortable discussion with Evan at South Street as to why he had again applied for and been given rooms at the Albany, and indeed already moved in. His reasons were not exactly clear, but with Jolyon now ensconced in the Academy at Woolwich he felt he should also be "roughing" it, although the Regent's Park barracks officer accommodations were comfortable enough. That wasn't the only—the real—reason. Over the six-week Michaelmas vacation, and on the rare free weekends, Jolyon's visits and the inevitable overnight stays at South Street had occasioned more than one enquiring remark from Evan. There was only so far he could play the godfather-godson card to obfuscate the real nature of their developing relationship and so it seemed simpler for Harry to head it off by vacating his suite in the family home.

And now he was headed toward another meeting about which he was unclear of the desired outcome. He was unsure about the mission Richard Rainbow had charged him with and that now took him to Hanover Square in its execution. Frankly, Harry was unsure where he stood with young Gregory Hilliard Hartley. On the three occasions of their meeting he gained the impression that young Lord Langdale was out of his depth in London. But then, Gregory was always tightly composed and unfailingly polite in the manner of someone determined to give no offense for being unaware of social manners in a world that would—he recognized—terrify Harry were he not born and educated to it. So perhaps it was this reserve in company that made him appear slightly lost on an almost continuous basis.

On the other hand did the absent look hide some deeper feeling toward Harry, the reserve a natural reaction to Jolyon's presence over the festive season? The third encounter at a social event to which both were invited, though neither anticipated meeting there, happened in March. Jolyon was back at Woolwich and in his absence Gregory caused an itch in Harry's mental skein because he suddenly seemed much more approachable and more open to suggestion and conversation. He wasn't sure, but had they not agreed to meet again at some point? Is that what he, Harry, wanted—something of a... an erotic nature? He shifted uncomfortably on the hansom cab seat. How could that be? He had Jolyon now and needed no one else in his emotional life, did he?

Looking farther back in time, the brief meetings at Berber and upriver before Omdurman had left Harry with mixed impressions. Hilliard—as he was then—was undeniably well set, good-looking in a youthful way, and appeared to be possessed of an attractive nature, but something in his character jarred with Harry. He hoped he wasn't projecting his own inherent snobbishness. (He had worked hard to eradicate what he considered a less than noble trait in the presence of natives, that's why he had hit it off with Arshan so well, but when it came to his own people… well… leopards and spots and all…)

Harry accepted that Gregory's education seemed to have been well conducted—at least, as well as might be expected in an outpost like Cairo—but in Harry's eyes there was a great deal more to learning than being shown facts and figures and remembering them. It was a question of background: of being exposed to proper and upright role models; to the correct opinions, attitudes, and social mores. Gregory's colonial upbringing in Egypt showed its raw edges—a way of speaking, perhaps a lack of respect for breeding… In spite of his impeccable politeness, Gregory never acted in an entirely deferential manner, as if at some level he always knew his destiny lay among his betters, in spite of his evident lack of social etiquette and a slightly odd accented English.

Or is it only me that sees this?

There it was again, the snobbery, an uncomfortable feeling. Had he not accepted the charms of Arshan in India without categorizing the Persian boy as something lesser than a well-born Englishman? Or was it a simple matter: Arshan the native accepted for being better than his kind; Gregory an Englishman who should know and behave better for being one?

Even as these unwelcome feelings flowed across the arid plain of his thinking, Harry reminded himself that though Gregory wasn't top-drawer, Richard and Edward Rainbow thought highly of the boy. Mind, the Rainbows' social standing was not of the highest order, military family though they were. But in fact, as Harry recognized with a wry smile, now that Gregory was a Hartley and Earl of Langdale, his drawer pulled out far above that of even the Smythe-Vanes. Sometimes, Harry acknowledged, first impressions lingered to color more mature reflection. The few recent evenings had mellowed his attitude to Gregory (in part due to feeling sympathy for him at Jolyon's attitude that night at Wyndham's), but he could never shift that first moment of unease at Berber when Gregory had fixed him with his serious but guarded gaze, his chin lifted with a touch of belligerence. *I was born in Alexandria and raised in Cairo, sir. I certainly haven't attended a school such as you must have done in England.*

Even now after more than a year Harry felt the rebuke in the words and how easily Hilliard put him in his place. But then there was that second meeting at Wadi Hamed, when he'd been sitting with Edward and a few others finishing up a supply of wine one of the fellows had procured from somewhere. When Hilliard walked past, Edward asked him to join them. Harry felt differently on that occasion, probably because of that insufferable toff Lieutenant Lionel Hartley with his airs and graces, and the way he tried to put Hilliard down by inferring he was a "native." Perhaps Harry suffered a stab of guilt for having looked at Gregory as a lesser person at Berber and perversely made amends at Wadi Hamed. Whatever, although Harry thought of himself as the scion of an aristocratic house he fervently hoped he never came across as detestably as "Hatters." He'd felt for Hilliard, who looked genuinely cut by Hartley's haughtily disinterested attitude, and he took pleasure in explaining to Hilliard the complexities of Hartley's ambitions to inherit an earldom and all the lands and wealth it entailed. What a laugh that turned out to be. The obnoxious Hartley had no idea—how could he then?—that the youngster he so effortlessly derided would deny him the hoped for inheritance. Rags to riches.

Harry's own words came back to him.

"You see at the death of the late earl—who only enjoyed the title for two years—the heir was missing; his younger brother, I believe. He disappeared some years before, and no one's heard of him since in spite of the lawyers placing advertisements all over the newspapers. If he left any children, they would inherit." Harry explained that Hartley's father applied to be declared the inheritor, but the Law Lords ruled that twelve years must elapse before they would consider such an application. "Sadly for Hatters Senior, he popped off five years ago, which leaves his fine son here the one to inherit in about two years' time."

Indeed, how were any of them to know that the missing but widely sought after son was Gregory Hilliard's deceased father and that they were now seated with the future Earl of Langdale? But as fate would have it everything became clear and Gregory was returned his proper name of Hartley, his peerage in the House of Lords, and his massive Langdale inheritance. Not even Charles Dickens could have created a more convoluted and satisfying plot.

In the rattling seclusion of the hansom Harry smiled at the memory as the cabbie drove him from South Street toward the massive pile in Hanover Square, just one of the properties—and not the largest—young Gregory had inherited. The brief happiness faded as he thought again of his own conflicting reasons for making this short journey in the middle of this particular spring afternoon. Was it really the lack of Jolyon, embroiled in his military studies and—having rashly used up his free weekend passes—was now locked up for an age? Was he seeking consolation of some sort? Affection perhaps? Maybe something more physical? Just two occasions Jolyon and Gregory were in each other's company and always that rivalry between them, though it was ever Jolyon who offered the verbal jousting that sadly reminded Harry of the way Lord Alfred Douglas used to treat Jo.

Am I just projecting my wishful thinking, that Gregory might harbor an interest in me beyond the bounds of social politesse? And if that is the case, should I even consider putting a match to the touchpaper of such feelings? Perhaps I'm hedging my bets in case Jo soon tires of me. I so miss his physical presence.

Harry felt his mental processes had never been in such a muddle. The cab bounced badly over a hole in the road. The jolt shook him up and he brightened. He put jumbled thoughts out of mind. There was a more prosaic, though no less urgent, reason for the unannounced visit, and one yet connected to matters amorous.

"I belabor you on behalf of Edward, my dear Harry," Richard had written. "He is concerned at reading in a recent copy of *The Egyptian Gazette* some regurgitated chatter from London newspapers suggesting young Gregory Hilliard Hartley is engaged to be married…"

Harry recalled seeing something of the sort in one rag's gossip columns. It connected Gregory's very recent nineteenth birthday with an announcement of forthcoming nuptials to be expected any moment. Harry dismissed it as the usual claptrap nonsense, another concoction from a fervid imagination with column-inches to fill. He agreed with Richard's opinion that it didn't fit the boy's inclinations. Nevertheless, in the past week rumors had reached his ears, and these suggested there might be a nugget of truth behind the buzz, that

Gregory's indomitable guardian-aunts had his immediate future mapped out, and wedlock was almost certainly a part of their plans.

Harry accepted Richard's mission to probe. But as his conveyance clattered from Brook Street into Hanover Square, Harry wondered whether he might even be too late. He saw a footman helping a familiar figure into an elegant and liveried carriage. It pulled away and rounded the top of the square into Princes Street, no doubt returning Lady Emily-Rose Henrietta Watford to her father's establishment overlooking Regent's Park.

CHAPTER 27 | *London, April 1899*

THE FOOTMAN took Harry's card and dipped his head politely without comment. Harry had anticipated an expression signifying disapproval at the lack of forewarning of a visit from someone who had only called once before and that amid a party of visitors, so hardly a welcome regular. But he stood aside for Harry to enter the great vestibule, offered to take his overcoat, and indicated he should take a seat. A few minutes later the butler came down the main staircase.

"Good afternoon, Reed," Harry greeted the servant.

"Mr. Smythe-Vane, his lordship is happy to… ah…"

Reed turned his back on Harry and they both looked up at the rattle of footsteps running down the wide stone staircase.

"Harry! How pleasant to see you." Gregory skittered to a halt, hand outstretched. "Thank you, Reed. That will be all. I think we'll take a turn in the garden, if that suits?"

Harry laughed at Gregory's evident pleasure at seeing him, so unlike his normal restrained demeanor. "I should enjoy that."

"Will I get you an overcoat, milord? It's still chilly—"

"Oh no, thank you, Reed. I've been looking out from up there, and it looks perfectly warm enough. Come through this way Harry."

Harry puzzled over what lay behind Gregory's evident desire to get out of the house for some "fresh air," and wondered whether it had anything to do with his previous visitor.

Birdsong filled the wide space of the enclosed garden. Spared the cool breeze by the walls of the surrounding house, in the spring sunshine the air was indeed warm enough.

"You're becoming used to the climate."

Gregory rubbed the arms of his jacket. "I'm not sure about that! After Egypt, the Sudan, India, and other points east, don't you find it too cold here? I know I'd give anything to go back and get warm again."

To Harry's ear, this did not sound like the sentiments of a man about to become engaged to his heart's desire. "You're homesick."

Gregory looked around sharply, but he didn't respond.

"Was that the young Lady Watford I saw leaving as my hansom pulled up?"

"Yes. My aunts, bless their souls, have me marrying her soon. Yesterday, if they had their way."

The words came out lightly enough, but the underlying anxiety did not escape Harry. He laughed, a short cough at the back of his throat, and tried for a supporting sympathy. "So far, I have successfully managed to avoid such a fate. Mostly thanks to my being abroad so much and belonging to a family with a blessedly sangfroid attitude to the institution, especially since my father's passing the year before last. And, of course, an older brother who is spewing out male sprogs by the dozen to inherit the peerage from him in due course."

Gregory reached up as he passed under an overhanging branch and brushed at the pink blossom, which showered down on his head. "I didn't know about your father, I'm sorry."

"It will be two years in June. He was seventy-one, a little young for a Smythe-Vane perhaps. I was fond of him as one is of a parent rarely seen, but we weren't really close enough for me to have felt more."

Gregory pulled a sympathetic face. "I know what that's like." Then he brightened again and gave Harry a sly grin. "But you're here in London now. Are you not in risk of nuptial capture?"

"Not for much longer—I hope. I envy Richard and Edward, who may work for Intelligence, but are really under the wing of Kitchener. I need a Guardian-General of my own because I want to get out to this new ruckus in South Africa. I've been bucking for it at the War Office for weeks. The attitude is that it will blow over, but even a blind fool can see that conflict between our interests there and the Boers' is inevitable. There is a man who would look kindly on my request. If only they decide to send Redvers Buller out there I'll be in with a chance."

"Is it war you love, or escaping the clutches of society ladies?"

Gregory scuffed his feet in an oddly childish gesture, but his question carried a weight of meaning. The boy obviously knew something. Harry stared at him and the way he was now avoiding Harry's eyes.

Time for it to be out in the open...

"Richard told you about our history, didn't he?"

They reached the end of the garden. The pathway turned at a right angle along the back wall. Fallen fruit-tree blossom lay strewn like confetti. The sight must have sparked the simile in Gregory's mind too. He shivered. "It must have been awful for you... you know, when Edward showed up again." Gregory turned to face Harry, no longer smiling. His grave expression suggested a greater maturity than Harry credited to his barely nineteen years.

At the statement Harry's breathing hitched. He saw his young companion in a new light. Pink flowers decorated his tousled hair and reminded Harry of *The Roses of Heliogablaus*, the masterpiece by Sir Lawrence Alma Tadema he'd seen the week before displayed in the Royal Academy, where it was on loan from Sir John Aird (it was whispered that the Member of Parliament paid a staggering £4,000 for it). In the painting, the wicked boy-emperor showers his dinner guests with a super-abundance of the petals thrown down from the ceiling. The reference given beside the frame ended: *...sic ut animam aliqui efflaverint, cum erepere ad summum non possent*: "so that some of them expired when they could not crawl out to the surface."

He felt similarly trapped, suffocating from a sudden bloom of guilt. A Gregory transfigured in this vision battled in Harry's affections with the image of glorious Jolyon, but in human matters invariably existence precedes essence. In his garlanded earnestness, Gregory made Harry feel younger, and the longing it engendered threatened to eclipse his feelings for Jolyon—at least temporarily. He struggled for reason in the face of an overwhelming force of nature and tried to find it in the humor of comparing Gregory to Heliogabalus. Gregory, Jolyon, Arshan, William... Richard. These were the pathways carved in his heart, and he realized the organ's fibrillating had everything to do with the past and less to do with the moment.

Yet it made the present glow. The past was elsewhere, and when he could touch reality, that which he could not physically grasp had a diminished presence. And Gregory stood before him... expectant of an answer.

"Yes and no," Harry answered eventually. "I had already steeled myself for that possibility…" *Even while hoping Edward would not be found, for which uncharitable thought I have ever been punished.* "I had no blindfold over my eyes. I knew for a long while before he confessed that Richard adored Edward in a way he would never love another. It's funny…" He gave Gregory a sidelong glance. "You remind me very much of Richard when we were all your age."

Was that true? Or was it simply a yearning for the past and what could never be? The young Lord Langdale looked so elegant, dressed to deceive Rose.

Gregory inclined his head slightly and frowned. "I thought I reminded you of Edward?"

The words took Harry aback.

"In the coffee house in Berber. Remember?"

Harry blushed at the recollection. "I did say that, didn't I? But I meant… well, Richard was there and I didn't want to embarrass him."

Gregory's next question took Harry by surprise.

"Did you ever feel anything for Edward?"

Does he ask because I had compared him to Edward? Harry's expression clouded as he considered how to answer. "Who knows what I might have felt if things had turned out differently?" They had started this conversation as friendly acquaintances, but now it had turned personal. Harry's own reticence— especially in connection with anything of a sexual nature—was being tested, but Gregory's unusually forward manner hinted at something more. A frisson ran through Harry and he couldn't deny its sexual heat. And Jolyon *had* been absent for so long…

He decided to be frank in return. "Richard and I were thrown together by circumstance, but I'd already lost my heart to him the first moment I set eyes on him at school. I just hid it well until much later. Hmm… hiding it well. That's the trick, isn't it? When you know what to look for it's obvious in the eyes, the way two people look at each other."

He came to a halt. Gregory stopped and slowly turned toward Harry. They locked eyes. Gregory's frank disregard for English manners set him apart as the product of a different upbringing. His appraisal pierced Harry to the core, but he refused to break away from it. What did Gregory read there? He wanted to force Gregory's feelings into greater transparency, get him to open up so he might understand what lay between him and his Arab friend. After all, this was surely Edward's concern and why he'd gotten Richard to write: that society was bullying young Lord Langdale in his new position into being someone he wasn't. To Edward—perhaps to Richard—the Ja'alin boy was important, the Watford girl was not. But Harry was a poor spy. He knew he was mixing up the mission with his own confused desires. In bringing up the subject, he hoped by sublimation to divert Gregory's affections toward him. He knew he was doing it, despised himself for it, and couldn't stop it.

"You mentioned the coffee shop at Berber. That's where I saw that look in your eyes. The way you looked at your Ja'alin friend… Zaki? I don't see that look in your eyes, Gregory, at the mention of Emily-Rose Watford."

Gregory aimed a kick at a small stone lying on the edge of the pathway and bit his lower lip. A breath of wind blew blossom petals from his head like small Punjabi prayers.

In the cab they said little. It was as though speaking the name had been enough to make apparent their mutual interest. No Zaki, no Jolyon, just Gregory and Harry. The embrace that followed Harry's statement felt entirely natural. It was warm, encompassing, and there was sexual heat. Any disquiet Harry might have entertained that he would be rebuffed melted at the feel of the hardness in the front of Gregory's trousers and the easy way in which he agreed to accompany Harry back to his new Albany apartment. Their needs seemed to match, and that filled the hansom's interior to the exclusion of needless conversation.

Anticipation at what was to happen made Harry feel like he was floating above the thin rug that covered his small sitting room. Thankfulness that this was not the same set of rooms where he had so long ago comforted Jolyon after the disaster of Oscar Wilde's conviction might have briefly flicked into conscious thought before being swept away by the immediacy of Gregory. Instead realization that in moments he would be running his hands over the lithe body he knew lay secreted beneath the covering of Victorian modesty filled his mind to exclusion of anything else. It was like a delirium, a beautiful madness this desire to see and hold what even in the Sudanese heat remained unrevealed below khaki drabs or the greater fulsomeness of Arab dress.

He longed to run two fingers under the wave of brown hair flowing over Gregory's broad forehead almost to his left eyebrow, lift it, and there place the first, light brush of his mouth. Mounded nipples, aroused to firm nubs of hot flesh by practiced teeth, a tongue, and lips, Harry's to taste before nuzzling the concavities of neck and armpit, belly button and—turned over—the velvety valley opening out from spine to balls…

They barely made it past the recently refurbished armchair and sofa in the sitting room to the bedroom, outdoor coats flung aside, before falling into an intimate embrace. And the minute he felt Gregory's arms around him, he knew it to be wrong; and he felt Gregory stiffen in uncertainty too. A bolt of lightning sizzling from door to window couldn't have been more electrifying. And in the consequent thunderclap realization was cruelly born—they weren't alone in Harry's bedchamber. Two elephants shared the space with them (and they were not those carved one from wood and the other from ivory which he'd picked up in Bombay).

One sat in an elegant frame on Harry's bedside bureau, the daguerreotyped face bearing a familiar smile of enigmatic humor, which hovered between finding something funny and genuine curiosity at what he looked out at. The fine features now stared out above the deftly tailored gunner's dress uniform Harry purchased at Christmas to satisfy a vanity which still required suppression for the better part of a year. It was cut to show the wearer to manly perfection.

The other, Harry was sure—elegant, handsome, buoyant, and black of skin—remained somewhere in the Sudan.

The creak and clatter of a passing cab prompted Gregory to roll slightly apart from Harry's embrace. He let his arms drop and freed Gregory with a deep sigh. "You're right," was all he said.

They both understood it as acknowledgment of a mutual mistake so nearly committed.

Gregory picked up the framed daguerreotype and nodded at it, as if the image had spoken to him. Harry went and sat on the edge of his bed, suddenly feeling old and foolish. Gregory seemed to make up his mind. He ducked his head at what he held. "I was wondering about Mr. Jolyon Langrish-Smith with who you go to the theater. Quite often, I think." After a pause, he added, "And hold hands."

A huffed exhalation stood in for Harry's laugh, a public admittance of the embarrassment he should feel, but didn't quite. "You saw?"

"It wasn't quite dark at Wyndham's, you know, and the desert taught me to have eyes in the back of my head. And I think *your* eyes are for him."

"Ah, Jolyon. Yes. I haven't seen him these past few weeks, stuck as he is at the Royal Military Academy. He wants to become a fine artilleryman." He spoke the words without thinking that Gregory almost certainly already knew this.

Gregory put the framed picture down and went to lean on the wall by the doorway.

"Jolyon likes explosive situations."

Gregory frowned in a questioning way, head cocked to one side, seeking an explanation. Harry spoke at length about he and Jolyon, of Oscar Wilde and the deleterious effect he and the awful Bosie had on an impressionable youngster; of how Jolyon reacted to Harry's attempts to prise him from an unhealthy life with dismissive politeness… well, in all honesty, downright rudeness, until the disgrace of the playwright almost unbalanced the lad. As he recounted the painful events, he was aware of running a hand in agitation through his hair.

"That explains his odd behavior at the theater when you pointed out Wilde's wife and son," Gregory said softly.

When Harry looked up the ruin of his normally carefully arranged locks reflected in a mirror across the room the sight startled him a little. "I have recovered, you know, from losing Richard, and found fulfilment with Jo." He reached for a comb and began to repair the damage.

"Have you told him about Richard?"

The comb caught in a tangle. Harry shook his head slowly. "I never found the right moment." He knew it was an inadequate response.

Rolling his shoulder slowly against the wall, Gregory kept silent and gently bit at his lower lip. He nodded in understanding, his gaze fixed on Harry as though fascinated at the sight of another man tidying his coiffure. *And that's probably right. I don't suppose Zaki ever needs to order those tight coils.*

"Oh, for me there was an attraction there. I'd known Jo since he was a child."

"You had?" Gregory broke his silence in some surprise.

"I'm Jolyon's godfather—"

"Hah!"

"Yes, I know. I should be setting a far finer moral example."

Gregory straightened up. "It was just a surprise, that's all. I'm sure you can't help with whom you fall in love. Besides, it's not like he's a real son, any more than Edward and Richard are real brothers."

Harry nodded and discovered an interesting relationship of patterns in his bedside rug he'd never noticed before. "It was very one-sided at first, but in time

Jo came to return my feelings. I sponsored him for the military exams and got him through—no, that's not fair. I wasn't even here for him, stuck out on India. No, he got through the exams all on his own, and he's grown to be a fine man."

"He seems… very pleasant. I'm happy for you."

"There's the age difference of course—"

"That's not so much! I was born in 1880, so Jolyon's what, six years older than me?"

"Five, in that case."

"That's not much of a difference, then."

"Perhaps not. But it's the usual damned story. When we can be together because of his commitments or mine, it's so often in public, or at the family home in Mayfair, which is limiting. I'm sure you understand."

"Hmm." Gregory suddenly looked unhappy again. He took the four paces across the room that brought him to the bed, and sat down. To Harry it felt normal to place an arm around the boy's shoulder. He was troubled and needed comfort. The gesture was companionable and the half-smile Gregory turned on Harry showed he knew that. Harry wasn't any longer trying to seduce him.

"That's why I want to get out to South Africa. Jo will follow soon after and together in the night on the veldt we can roar with the lions as we make love, and blast the Boers with Jo's field gun in the days."

For almost a minute only the ticking of a clock broke the silence.

"You wanted me because I remind you of Richard as you remember him," Gregory began, and then trailed off.

Harry tightened his grip. "Yes, I suppose I did. For a moment of delusion, at any rate. But I'm not yours, and you are not mine. We each have our own. You made me see that again when, for a moment, I almost forgot what I do have." He took Gregory's chin in a gentle grip and twisted his face around until their eyes locked. "And you are not young Emily-Rose Watford's, either."

They sat quietly. Gregory was in what Evan would have called a "brown study," and Harry was almost certain he knew what was going through his mind. He smiled and Gregory turned against his shoulder to catch the expression.

"What?"

"You don't belong here, Gregory Hilliard Hartley, my Lord Langdale. You just don't, do you? Your essence is planted in a hot soil watered by the Nile. You're a son of the Great River, and you have given your heart to it." He felt no need to add *and to Zaki.* The name hovered in the air between them, the other elephant in the room that had stopped them both making a mistake, which while no doubt pleasant, would have been a disaster in the long run.

"Yes." Gregory breathed the word. He looked back into Harry's gaze. "Thank you." He broke into a broad smile. "You've given me back my life." And then he leapt from the bed and started to laugh with joy.

A new calmness settled over Harry and warmed his heart. It should be he thanking Gregory. His mission for Richard on behalf of Edward that had so nearly run off the rails must have succeeded.

"I've no time, Harry! I must rush to make the arrangements." The whirl suddenly stopped. "Oh blow it! What do I do about the blooming House of Lords?"

Harry joined with his gaiety and laughed brightly. At the soirée they both attended, Gregory confessed that on the two occasions he'd managed to attend the House he hadn't understood a thing. "You know, there is no harm in your being an absentee peer. Why, some lords have never attended in all their lives! But if you feel so inclined you can appoint a proxy, one you approve of, and leave it at that. He can say 'Content' or 'Not Content' on your behalf up to the point that a challenge to the headcount forces a division. Annoyingly, since… oh about thirty years ago, proxies have been discontinued in divisional votes, but that's hardly going to bother you. I'm sure I could persuade Evan to take on the duty."

"I thought you said he's a government minister?"

"He is, but—as a peer like you—he can't vote in the Commons, so I'm sure he'd love another vote in the upper chamber." *In fact I know he absolutely will!*

Gregory finished pulling on his overcoat and rushed to the door, where he paused and looked back. "Thanks again."

"For what? I just told you what you needed to hear. And Gregory…?"

"Yes?"

"Give my love to Richard."

∽✻∾

For a period of time, which might have amounted to an hour after Gregory bustled off toward his future, Harry sat in the growing darkness of early evening, adrift in contemplation. It was a good question: why hadn't he spoken of Richard in a meaningful way to Jolyon? A less worthy part of his mind said it wasn't Jolyon's business, but he knew that for an absurdity. The truth was more likely that he was as yet unconfident of Jolyon's innermost feelings. Would he ever be? He sighed deeply. When he was then would come the time to speak of it, but not yet. In the meantime he needed to clear his head of what had taken place this afternoon and evening. Finally, he came to a decision, one that involved the imponderables of a mountain and Mohammed.

At the bell captain's lodge, the duty man stood to attention. "Good afternoon sir, or should I say evening."

"Evening, Lance-Corporal Jenks. I should be most obliged to you if you would hail a cab for me."

"I can certainly do that, Major. And where would this putative cab be going, if I might enquire?"

"To Woolwich, Jenks. I need to see a man about a gun, and since he can't come to see me I must go to the Arsenal."

"A gun, sir. I'm sure you do, sir. I'm sure you do."

PART FIVE

O, bitter victory, 1899–1900

Don't you hear the tramp of feet, Dolly Gray
Sounding through the village street, Dolly Gray
'Tis the tramp of soldiers' feet in their uniforms so neat
So goodbye until we meet, Dolly Gray.

Goodbye Dolly I must leave you, though it breaks my heart to go
Something tells me I am needed at the front to fight the foe
See, the boys so neat are marching and I can no longer stay
Hark, I hear the bugle calling, Goodbye Dolly Gray.

"Goodbye Dolly Gray," a Boer War anthem, written by Will D. Cobb (lyrics)
and Paul Barnes (music).

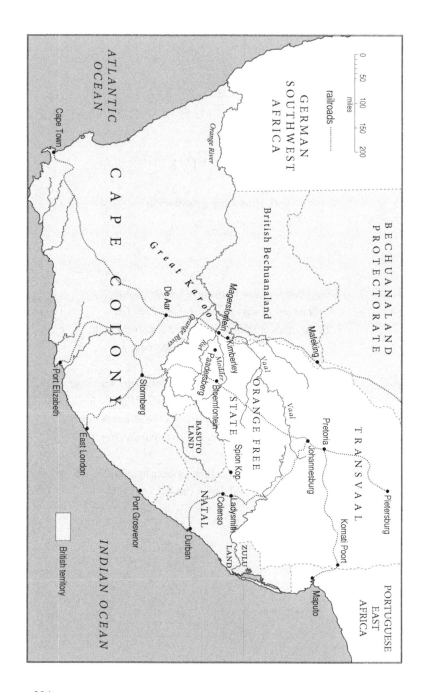

ATLANTIC OCEAN

GERMAN SOUTHWEST AFRICA

railroads ------

0 50 100 150 200
miles

Orange River

Cape Town

C A P E   C O L O N Y

Great Karoo

De Aar

Orange River

British Bechuanaland

BECHUANALAND PROTECTORATE

Magersfontein

Mafeking

Stormberg

Port Elizabeth

East London

Modder

Kimberley
Paardesberg
Bloemfontein

ORANGE FREE STATE

Vaal

Vaal

Pretoria
Johannesburg

T R A N S V A A L

Pietersburg

Port Grosvenor

BASUTO LAND

Spion Kop

Ladysmith
Colenso

NATAL

ZULU LAND

Komati Poort

Durban

Maputo

INDIAN OCEAN

PORTUGUESE EAST AFRICA

British territory

304

CHAPTER 28 | *London, August to September 1899*

"WHY DON'T YOU go and ask Kitchener yourself?" Jolyon said with the exasperation in his voice almost concealed by the depths of an ancient armchair. "Don't waste the opportunity of his being here in London on leave. There's no guarantee as to how long he'll be here. I'm sure he he'll look well on your petition."

"He's not a king," Harry grumbled.

"He *is* the Sirdar, same thing."

They were comfortably slumped facing each other in two deep, overstuffed armchairs in Harry's Albany apartment. Harry's turning up unannounced at the Academy that night four months ago had the happy result of cementing his seesaw feelings and at the same time laying to rest Jolyon's fears that Gregory Hartley had succeeded in stealing Harry away. He confessed to the brink of the abyss on which they had both stood, but that the very danger of falling over the edge in fact had the opposite effect, that it had clarified his own feelings "once and forever."

"This time when I say it, I mean it quite seriously, Jo. All my past is now properly behind me."

Of course, it was still dishonest. The right moment to tell Jolyon that his affection for Richard Rainbow once exceeded the bounds of school and Sandhurst friendship still hadn't materialized, but when he said it he genuinely meant to roll that old passion up in the statement. But then, true honesty needed to be a two-way street and Harry was disappointed that in making plain his own failing Jolyon wasn't moved to finally open up and talk about his experiences while under the influence of Oscar Wilde, Lord Alfred Douglas, and vile men like Alfred Taylor. The time, it seemed, was still unripe for such confidences, but at least Harry was now prepared to wait until Jolyon felt ready. And with Gregory returned to Egypt, there was no longer the threat to Jolyon's equilibrium, which Harry was at pains to insist should never really have been upset. Of course, he felt somewhat hypocritical in saying this, considering what had so nearly taken place, but Jolyon accepted it.

The summer heat forced a regime of casual dress. They wore only undershirts and slacks, no shoes or socks, bare feet idly playing big-toe-tag. Jolyon was on his summer break before his final term at the Shop and London was alive with indignation at what the Boers were up to in South Africa. There was much warlike talk abroad… had been for some time. Jolyon caught the headline fever, even though he appeared quite muddled as to the politics of it all.

Harry sighed. "The Sirdar may know my friends Richard and Edward, but he certainly hasn't stumbled over me, or if he has seen paperwork, it hasn't made much impression. If my father were alive, even yours, they might put in a word on my behalf."

Jolyon suddenly snapped finger against thumb. "Here's another thought. Didn't you serve under Sir Garnet Wolseley when he commanded the Nile campaign to wrest Khartoum from the Mahdi?"

Jolyon's enthusiasm on Harry's behalf was as endearing as it was misplaced. "For crying out loud, Jo, that was fourteen years ago! And we were trying to stop the madman from getting into Khartoum. Anyway I'm only a lowly major."

"You've been mentioned in dispatches several times, been given the odd medal or two."

"So have hundreds of officers. But let's just fantasize for a moment that I did march into Wolseley's office, he would never appoint me to a post behind the backs of top brass like General Kitchener or Field-Marshal Roberts who may well command. It just isn't done. But I'd never reach that far. Not even colonels get to stroll in on the Commander-in-Chief of the Army and demand a posting. Actually, probably not even Kitchener can do that with impunity."

Jolyon pouted prettily. "I bet *he* didn't ask Wolseley if he could take a couple of months off from chasing the Khalifa. And that's a point. Who's looking after the Sudan? The Khalifa's still running loose. Cadet Hambleton says the Mahdists are growing in strength again, enough to march on Omdurman soon."

Harry smiled to himself at yet another abrupt change of direction.

"Richard was guarded in his last letter about the Khalifa and his Dervish army's movements, but the Mahdists seem to be still buried away in the south, so I don't know where Cadet Hambleton gets his sure-fire information."

Jolyon shrugged in a carefree manner and examined the toes of his burnished gunnery boots, which he'd reached over the stuffed arm of his chair to snatch up off the floor.

"I've no doubt Colonel Wingate is up to the task. Richard reports directly to the man, and has remarked more than once on the Colonel's competence. Besides, Kitchener has an extremely loud voice and I'm sure he can be heard even from London."

"And of course he has the invaluable help of Lord Langdale."

"Sarcasm doesn't become you, Jo."

"I know. I'm out of practice since my Oscar days."

The puff of exasperation made Jolyon smile. Harry relented. He was happy to hear Jolyon making light of all that nonsense now. Surely it wouldn't be much longer before he felt free to open up about it? "You have no need to be rude about Gregory," he grumbled. "At least he's back in the Sudan, doing what he wants."

"Wait! Don't you have some relative who's attached to Kitchener? Couldn't she exercise some influence?"

Harry raised his eyes to the ceiling. "My dear Jo, you really must keep up with the goings-on of high-born socialites… even if I prefer to avoid the most of them. It is true that the good General has trotted Lady Helen Vane-Tempest Stewart—to whom I presume you refer and who is in fact some sort of aunt— around Rotten Row on several occasions, but alas on the presentation of his suit, she turned him down flat. She's a notorious flirt. I don't think he needs reminding of yet another Vane. Damn it! You've reminded me. I'm now in a similar position with respect to Kitchener as was Winston Churchill. In his case it was something he said or wrote, I'm not sure which; in my case it's being attached, however remotely, to a relative. Sadly for my plaint, I doubt the lady will do the decent thing and take herself off to a nunnery as used to be the case once upon a time, after which we'd be able to pretend she didn't exist. Anyway, it's not said that Kitchener will be the one appointed to command down there if it comes to open war."

"Oh, come on, Harry." Jolyon sat forward, elbows on suddenly drawn up knees and pointy chin in his hands. "It's an open secret that he's been to see Field-Marshal Roberts, and everyone knows the War Office won't want someone so experienced to rot away as Commander-in-Chief of Ireland. Good old Bobs is bound to lead the expeditionary force to the Cape, and Kitchener will be his second in command. Bound to happen."

They fell silent for a few minutes and then Harry said, "I might have managed something with Baden-Powell, if I'd been in time, but he was dispatched to the Cape early last month as part of Special Services, tasked with raising a militia to cause the Boer kommandos trouble should Kruger's government in Pretoria go on the offensive. He wrote me a short note saying he had requested me, but for some reason the powers that be in both the War Office and the Cape Colony government won't let him have any officers of his choice."

"You'd love to be doing the Special Services thing, hey?"

Harry nodded. "Stephe's a much happier man out from behind a desk doing his tracking and scouting and at thirty-four I'm not sure I'm any longer cut out for the spit and polish brigade either." He gave Jolyon a threatening glare. "And should you ever meet my good friend Alfred Winner, never, ever repeat that."

"Cross my heart and hope to die. Anyway, I don't know who Mr. Winnow is." After another pause Jolyon said, "I'm not sure what all the Boer fuss is about anyway. All we learn about is math, geometry, topography, greasing gun parts, and explosive compounds. They don't think politics are relevant, least of all what's got a bunch of Dutch settlers all riled up."

"There's been bad feeling between the Dutch farmers and the British Cape Colony government for the better part of a hundred years," Harry began, settling back in his chair and stretching out his legs so he could tangle his toes again with Jolyon's. "It's what drove the Boers to trek out into the wild veldt decades ago and found Boer republics across the Orange and Vaal rivers. We had a go at annexing Transvaal— um… twelve years ago, I think it was, but it didn't go well because no matter what people think of them, the Boers aren't a bunch of ill-disciplined natives. They turned out to be well-armed, dedicated, and very tough fighters who brought things to a stalemate. So we declared it a victory at home and treaties were signed."

"So it was a covering up of the reality?"

"It was. In fact Evan, who's been working for the past three years alongside Joseph Chamberlain, the Secretary of State for the Colonies, is busy undermining the pretense that we're all friends. Anyway, then came the discovery of gold at Witwatersrand in Transvaal, lots and lots of the stuff, and that really upset the apple cart. The Boers didn't have the manpower to mine all the gold and they couldn't stop the influx of prospectors and miners—Uitlanders the Dutchmen call them, mostly British—until there are now more British in Transvaal than Boers. So, as you can imagine, there have been squabbles over ownership, taxes, and murders, and accusations, and Britain has been arguing that it's time the Orange Free State and Transvaal were brought to book and came under the Union flag at last. Well done, Evan! Naturally, the Boers disagree."

"Well the Boers need a good kicking then. If it's our enterprise pulling all that gold out of the ground a bunch of Dutch farmers haven't the right to go lording it over our miners."

"Spoken like a true son of Albion. And talking of kickings, Stephe mentioned something a bit worrying. He said one Boer outfit he'd come across actually showed off a light one-pounder gun, which they boasted would give them superiority in the field if it came to outright war. Have we anything like that?"

Jolyon, who had fallen back in the armchair, sat forward again, a look of enthusiasm on his face. "That must be the Maxim-Nordenfelt QF 1-Pounder—Quick Firing gun" he said, showing off. "It's called the pom-pom gun by the lads at the Arsenal because of the noise it makes when it's fired on auto. We've been training on a pair of them. It's a scaled up Maxim machine gun manufactured now by Vickers. But how come the Boers have them?"

"Ah, that makes sense. Stephe says the Boers have been buying up-to-date Vickers weaponry through the French and ammo from the Germans."

"I don't know if it's true—at least, Cadet Hambleton says it's the case—"

"So it must be true," Harry said in a sardonic tone.

"—that the War Office has rejected the gun after trials saying it's too big to use against personnel and too small to be useful against defenses."

"You approve of it, I can tell."

"Oh yes. It comes to bits to make it portable on a small gun carriage, so two can work it, and you should hear it go when it's fired. It can do three hundred rounds a minute… ah, and that's the other problem for the War Office Red Caps. They say at six shillings a shell, it's far too expensive."

"Phew! Why, that's ninety pounds a minute."

A wistful expression crossed Jolyon's features. "I'd love to be out there with you and a pom-pom between us, and if the Boers have the things, our troops should have them too and then we can give those veldt peasants the kicking they deserve. Now, it's a beautiful Sunday afternoon, so why don't we go out into the sunshine?"

Used to Jolyon's rapid changes of subject, Harry adapted as swiftly. "And where in the sunshine would you like to go?"

"Primrose Hill."

❧ ✿ ☙

The sunny afternoon had brought out many strollers. Harry led the way through to the Regent's Park Outer Circle. They walked around a quarter of the park's perimeter, crossed the canal on The Boardwalk, and sauntered along Prince Albert Road until access to Primrose Hill was afforded. Better off laboring families from the newly built houses of neighboring Chalk Farm crowded the lower slopes, taking their Sunday ease stretched out on spread rugs. Some of the men still wore flat caps in spite of the heat, but most protected their pates with a handkerchief knotted at the four corners. On the flat area of grass near the Zoo entrance a bunch of working-class lads played football. Reflected sunlight glistened off sweat-slicked bare chests. Harry noticed Jolyon's eyes drinking in the young players and they exchanged a surreptitious grin. Drawn by the promise of a splendid view, Jolyon broke into a run to reach the summit. From the top all of London to the south made a diorama against which closer structures stood out. Hackney Marshes and the bulk of Blackheath guarding the Kent border in the east to the soft rise in the west of the South Downs lay spread out in a gray-green swathe.

"It's so clear." Jolyon whirled around exuberantly.

Summer's warmth had blessedly banished the sulphurous shroud of smoke from a million hearths and hundreds of manufactory chimneys that blighted the city for nine months of the year. Almost straight ahead the tumescent breast of St. Paul's dome thrust up from the low skyline. Much closer, two figures made midgets by the distance guarded goals formed of dumped top clothes, while in between twenty young men battled over their ball at the base of the hill where it merged with the greenery of Regent's Park.

Jolyon cupped an ear theatrically. "Can you hear?"

Harry didn't have to strain. The slight breeze blowing in a northerly direction brought clear on its wings above the muted footballers' cries the sound of a hooting elephant from the London Zoo. The haunting call acted like an *aide mémoire* to bring back the Koch Bihar hunting expedition and the embarrassing events associated with Winston Churchill there. Not something he'd confessed to Jolyon.

"Elephants."

Jolyon frowned. "Elephants? No, I meant…" and he pointed at the figures of two youngsters sat on the grass under a tree a way down the hillside at a distance which rendered them as silhouettes against the bright sky. "I meant the bugle."

And then Harry heard the unmistakable squawk of a cavalry trumpet. One of the boys blew some off-key notes that he supposed might be reveille or as easily a fire call. "The *infantry* have bugles, Jo. Cavalrymen obey the commands of *trumpets*, and that looks like a lad from the Blues teaching some tyro the calls." He thought of Edward Rainbow, who had hidden himself from sight as Trumpeter Smith in the Hussars. Perhaps, like the boy over there, Edward had blown his first brassy notes up here.

"They'll drive everyone away with that cacophony," Jolyon said with a brisk laugh. And then he pointed out over London. "What is it way over there that's catching the sun so brightly?"

Harry stole the opportunity to hold Jolyon close as he bent his head to look along the outstretched arm as though along a rifle barrel's sights. He saw a flash of brilliance close to the lumpy far horizon and straightened up. "I believe that is the Crystal Palace on Sydenham Hill. It was moved there from Hyde Park after the Great Exhibition."

"Did you go?" The snicker in his voice gave Jolyon away.

"No, you cheeky bugger. I'm not that ancient. That was fifteen years before I was born."

A young couple strolling along a lower pathway across Harry's line of sight caught his attention. The lady, fashionably dressed in a narrow-waisted, full-length silky dress of cream with startling red trimmings, rested her gloved hand lightly on her beau's elegant arm. In her other hand she held a delicate parasol raised against the sun's rays and the feather plume in her wide hat kept catching on its rim as she laughed. The tinkly sound reached up, abruptly cut off as the couple paused and turned to look at each other. Impulsively, her young man bent his head and kissed her cheek, which gave rise to another silvery laugh. Public displays of affection were not customary, and at the sight a stabbing pain caught Harry in the belly and rose to his throat as a choking bubble of deep regret. Even were it seemly, he could never make such a simple, loving gesture to Jolyon out here in the open. Away from civilization in the Pamirs his native escort never remarked on his kissing Arshan or taking his hand; to them such things were natural expressions of affection to be expected. There it was possible to be free. He thought of Richard and Edward, also free to be what they wanted, out in the desert.

Even on his fifth reading the telegram refused to give up its secret. Harry wondered what it really meant.

FRI. 1 SEP. + GENERAL SIR REDVERS HENRY BULLER, VC, GCB, G.O.C. ALDERSHOT TO MAJOR H. SMYTHE-VANE + REPORT HEAD QUARTERS, ALDERSHOT, AT CONVENIENCE BETWEEN 2:30 AND 5:00 PM, MON. 4 SEP. TO WED. 6 SEP., INST. + ADVISE ADJUTANT PRECISE DAY, TIME.

But in the end it was only a summons.

Perhaps Jo's correct. The old man always had a soft spot for me. But what's the adjutant-general running Aldershot want me for this time? Not more instructional duties, I hope.

Thinking of Jolyon put Harry into a daydream that became erotic with the regular rattle of the train's bogeys over the rail joints. With Jolyon back at the Academy, Harry missed their nights spent enjoying each other's company and bedtimes (when they even got as far as that before...) and the pounding wheels on the track matched the rhythm of his heart and groin. The London & South Western train was running to schedule, which was appropriate for the Waterloo–Aldershot route that carried soldiers and officers to and fro between the capital and the British Army's home. The train was well past Surbiton and already slowing for Pirbright. At the brief halt the doors clattered and banged back against the side of the cars as several bedraggled looking Tommies fell down onto the platform, dragging kit bags behind. They were returning to their divisional exercises on Pirbright's blasted army heath, evidently the worse for wear after a night on the town.

Twelve years, most of it spent behind a desk in Aldershot had changed General Redvers Buller. The dashing cavalryman's figure looked resigned to later middle age; his stocky figure now more barrel-chested, and the development of a second chin softened the square-jaw and ensured his face merged seamlessly with his bull's neck (which, along with his brisk pushy nature and surname, meant the men of every rank knew him as the Bull). The African sun-squinted eyes, however, had lost none of their mischievous sparkle, Harry was happy to see. Neither had increasing years and pen pushing reduced the general's brevity or desire to get to the point immediately. His adjutant showed Harry in and typically there was none of the red-capped staff officers' shuffle through important papers while the interviewee stood patiently at attention.

"Be comfortable, my boy," Buller growled even before Harry could salute and remove his cap. The blue eyes narrowed, amused as he continued in typical spat-out phrases. "Bored, hey? Course you are. Spirited feller. Just coming into your age. Prime of life. No right to be kicking heels on reserve pay. So what do you say to South Africa?" The lines radiating from the corner of his eyes creased in impish humor at delivering the bombshell.

After a second's hesitation to gather his thoughts, Harry answered crisply. "Been thinking about it pretty much non-stop since I returned from the Sudan, sir."

"What would you say if I told you the Field Marshal has asked me to be Commander-in-Chief of British forces down there?"

Buller was referring to the Commander-in-Chief of the Forces, Viscount Garnet Wolseley, their joint-boss on the 1884–85 expedition sent to rescue Gordon of Khartoum. Considering what he'd wished for, nothing could have been better and Harry masterfully disguised both his glee and—he thought—his surprise. "Hmm, I would say there are a lot of officers will lose their bets. Not Roberts? Not Kitchener?"

"No, Harry. Me. I admit surprise. See you do too, don't hide it. Thought old Bobs would get it, hey? Oh, Wolseley's fine. I've been one of the 'Garnet Ring' since I was a wet-eared subaltern. With him in West Africa in '73. Trudged through jungles to discipline the Ashanti. We get on well enough after clearing up that little squabble we had back in '85, but Lord Landsdowne… Rotten rat! Less said soonest mended. Hah!"

His loathing of the Secretary of State for War sometimes even made the newspapers and Harry remained silent on the matter of the general's famed short fuse that often led to arguments with senior officers. Harry sometimes thought the Bull and Churchill ought get on well, except common sense told him they absolutely would not.

"Want men I can trust. Not going to be easy." He paused a moment and looked almost shy. "I haven't seen active service for quite a while, you know."

"Like riding a horse, sir."

"Hmmm, as may be. But what about the High Commissioner for Southern Africa and Governor of Cape Colony, hey?" He made the title sound like an obscene curse. "The politicos fête Alfred Milner as a diplomat." He snorted in disgust. "Plenipotentiary powers, *pah*—man will be listened to whatever nonsense he spouts, while the military commander will go unheard. Always happens. Turned down every one of Colonel Baden-Powell's requests. All reasonable. Only wanted suitable field pieces and some trained, regular soldiers. God save us from panjandrums."

Buller sighed heavily and brushed the ends of his mustache. "Want you out there with me, Harry Vane. Not exactly *with me*. Special Forces. On your own. Baden-Powell wanted you. War Office turned him down. Landsdowne again. Wouldn't let him pick his own staff, damned fools. I'd have given Wolseley a piece of my mind if I'd been around. Anyway, last heard he recruited a motley crew of locals. Headed off for Transvaal, Mafeking, to be a nuisance to the Boers. There's something similar for you, Harry. What do you say?"

"When do we leave, sir?"

CHAPTER 29 | *Southampton, October 1899*

WAR DECLARED! BOERS COMMENCE HOSTILITIES!

On the dockside the newspaper vendors shouted out the headline of Saturday October 14, 1899. Harry thought it ironic that he should be departing for the war that everyone had been anticipating for months on the very day the late editions reported it had become an actuality. "But how 'actual'?" Harry wondered aloud. For weeks a whirlpool of rumors had put London into a frenzy: terrible disasters occurred only to be contradicted; great battles raged and remained unconfirmed; and yet beneath the fog of credulous uncertainty Harry felt the tide of war really was flowing.

Only a few of the thousands who came to watch the departure from Southampton of R.M.S. *Dunottar Castle* were allowed inside the dock shed. Nearly all those inside the gate were wives and children and sweethearts of soldiers who had managed to wangle passes for them. Among them was Jolyon, who had begged one of his rare free days off from Woolwich to be there. His presence put Harry in half a mind as to whether a swift parting at Waterloo station might have been easier than the prolonged process of boarding the Castle Line's fastest ship, requisitioned by the army for that reason.

"I read it in the mercantile gazette," Jolyon said on the train journey. "The *Dunottar Castle* is famous for cutting the sailing time from England to Cape Town from forty-two days to just fourteen, plus two days at Madeira," he informed enthusiastically. He dropped a coin in the hand of an urchin newsvendor and snatched a broadsheet. "Paul Kruger, President of the Republic of the Transvaal, having received no answer to his ultimatum that British forces should withdraw from the border, declared that a state of war now exists…" He trailed off and looked up from his reading. "That was three days ago, and it says here that since then Boer kommandos have invaded Cape Colony at a place called Kraaipan and also crossed the border into our Colony of Natal."

Harry nodded. They were standing under the edge of an awning sheltered from the occasional light drizzle and outside the hurriedly raised barriers to separate the civilians from the area of the dock where the troops slowly shuffled toward the embarkation point. Fifteen yards away, at the edge of the wharf, the gray side of the ship towered up. Amid the crush and jostle, it was possible to hold hands under cover of the cape Harry had thrown around his shoulders more to ensure his uniform brasses and braid didn't get soiled than to keep out the autumn chill. At intervals of about half an hour detachments were marched in and formed up at one end of the shed, where they left their bundles and heavy kit. Then they marched in single file up the gangway of the ship. All the troops were in khaki, which made them easily distinguishable from the dark-colored mass of civilians.

"I had no idea there would be so many here," Jolyon said, "but I suppose it's natural to want to say goodbye." He squeezed Harry's hand.

They turned as one at hearing the tramp of boots on concrete as yet more Royal Berkshires came in at the door, marching four deep. The calls of corporals and sergeants rose harshly above the hubbub. Well-wishers formed on each side of the khaki column, and those who had friends in the detachment tried to push to the front of the crowd to attract the attention of the soldiers as they passed.

The men were marching easily, and those lucky enough to see their loved ones had time for a few words, a kiss, or a hand-clasp before they were moved on. Harry heard one young wife anxiously tell the woman next to her, "I'd not the chance to get to barracks, y'see, and say good-bye to my Jake, and I must see the last of him."

The tenor of her voice caught at Harry's throat and seemed to sum up everyone's feelings, so much so that, holding Jolyon's hand in a tight grip, he began scanning the passing soldiers' faces as eagerly as she.

"I managed a message," she carried on, "that I would be here and near enough for a parting kiss…"

Her soul was in her wide eyes.

"There he is!" she cried. "Here, Jake, I'm here!"

Harry tensed, peered around an interposed head, and saw where she was looking. Her young man's fine, honest face bore a look no less intense than hers.

"He's looking on the wrong side," Jolyon said, sounding as worried as Harry felt.

The men marched on, farewells given here and there and, by a cruel trick of fate, he never saw her nor heard her voice above the cheers of the people and the blare of the band. She was fast wedged in the crowd. Someone ran after the man and told him where she was, but too late. His company had been drawn up in rank and file and his sergeant would not let him fall out. Harry willed the poor girl to thrust her way through the press so at least she might shout at her Jake, but long before she got clear of the tightly packed throng he had passed on to the ship, where she could not follow him.

"It's almost too much to bear," Harry said quietly.

Jolyon gave him a look of surprise. "That it is, but surely you're used to the awfulness of partings? You have taken leave on a troop ship before with scenes like these?"

"Not like this, Jo. Mostly I've been with other officers going to a new posting or returning, and to Egypt with the Blues. There was no distress, no families being torn apart. It was not like this. Then, the men were going out as a normal part of their duties abroad. Yes, we knew there was strife in the desert and we were going to rescue General Gordon, but we all—men and officers—believed the Arabs would be dispersed at the first shot. Churchill once said something striking to me. He said war is full of fascinating thrills. The chance of being killed is only a sporting element in a splendid game. In a way he was right. No one went in fear for his life. But these… we're headed for a real war with a very real European-style enemy. The Boers are not ignorant savages. Many who depart this day will never return."

The thought evidently dispirited Jolyon and disregarding any propriety he pressed hard against Harry's side. To feel the familiar body, even through layers of clothing, comforted him.

An old man who had been telling all who would listen that he was looking out for his boy, nudged him and—as though carrying on a conversation with an acquaintance—explained what a fine lad his son was, how keen a soldier. "It's near done break my heart that my boy should leave me and go to war," he said to Harry, "but I'm right proud and it'll do him good, make a man out of him."

The Berkshires passed on into the depths of the shed, and then in their wake came two soldiers half-carrying and half-dragging between them a young man who was so drunk that he could neither stand nor walk. His helmet was jammed over his eyes, but as the men dragged him past where Harry and Jolyon stood it fell off and rolled to the old man's feet. He drew in a sharp breath and his face flushed in mute horror. He muttered something, but loud enough for the person on the other side from Harry to understand. Suddenly all the people nearby began to point and say, "That's his son there, him that's being carried."

Harry felt his throat constrict as some—*God forgive them*—laughed and joked at the old man. Pity choked Harry's gorge and threatened to overwhelm his senses as the man who had a moment ago filled their ears with the praises of his boy gazed after him with a look of bitter amazement and then faded silently away. Harry gave vent to a cleansing sigh and turned to Jolyon. Suddenly he wanted to get away, not from Jolyon, and yet in a way he did, away from the agony of this parting, which he could only console himself by saying it was for a few months, not forever.

Aim for proper British nonchalance, Harry, and show the stiff upper lip Alfred accuses me of owning.

"I suppose I must soon report." He spoke with a calm his heart and rebellious lungs didn't share.

That's the way. Keep it light, Harry old lad.

"General Buller will be along soon and the moment he's boarded he'll beard the captain in his day cabin to weigh anchor and be off, tides, tugs, and God not willing." Harry shivered and laughed at the same time. He felt sick at the thought of the imminent severance.

As if he felt the same, Jolyon murmured in a sad voice, "That looks like the last of them." The shed behind was empty of soldiers and crowd. As the last Tommies made their way up the incline of the gangway, families were allowed onto the space of the quay, other than in the immediate vicinity of the embarking troops, and instant shouted conversations were struck up between soldiers pressed against the ship's deck rail and the civilians below. On the dockside some officers still lingered with their wives and families. Behind them, stevedores separated the mess of kitbags from heavier items and formed a chain gang to load them through a side door in the hull. The larger items were gathered up in rope nets to be craned up by the *Dunottar Castle*'s derricks over the deck to the holds.

"You'd best go, Harry. Your man's got all your things on?" Jolyon referred to Private Wryland, the soldier-orderly appointed to look after Harry for the voyage at least.

"He came down with everything yesterday. Don't hang around, Jo. Once I'm on board I shan't be leaning over the rail waving, so you pack yourself off back to Woolwich. I don't want you reporting in late."

The outraged whinnies of horses broke in on Harry. Eight chargers belonging to officers of the two regiments were objecting strenuously to being enclosed in narrow boxes and swung in mid-air.

"Is that magnificent gray yours?" Jolyon's grin eased the tension.

Harry snorted. "In Afghanistan I heard a colonel ask, 'Who's the bloody fool on a gray?' 'Someone who wants to be noticed,' an officer said. 'Hah! He'll be noticed all right—some Pathan will blow his bloody head off.' And the fool was Winston Churchill."

"He survived, though."

"True. The moral of the story is don't take unnecessary risks. I ride chestnuts or dark bays to blend in, and I'd rather take a mount that knows the country, so it will be a local purchase for me, Jo, and I shall avoid anything that looks even vaguely 'magnificent,' thanks."

The gray in question, belonging to the colonel of the East Surrey Regiment, gave any amount of trouble. It took her groom ten minutes to coax her into the box, and as soon as it began to move upward she snorted and trembled with fear, and finally sat down on her haunches, with her neck hanging over the door. The mare was almost beside herself with terror as she swung in mid-air, moaning piteously. The colonel, who was standing near, spoke reassuring words: "Woa, Bunny! Steady, old girl!" Although the beast could not see him, she suddenly quieted at hearing his voice.

Those on the dock were too preoccupied in craning their necks up at those on board to take any notice of Jolyon and Harry, and to the soldiers lining the ship's rail the two young men hugging on the stone slabs below were obviously close brothers saying their fond farewells. For Harry the clasp could have lasted forever and he didn't care who saw it. "I already have your name down with the general. The moment you pass out from Woolwich you'll be on your way," he assured Jolyon.

"It can't be soon enough for me, Harry. I promise I'll pass with flying colors…" His words failed in a low choking.

"It will be a matter of a few months—"

Jolyon's tears dampened Harry's cheek.

"I can't bear it."

"But you can, and must, my dearest, dearest Jo. You're a soldier now. Brace up and don't make it any harder for me… for us both."

The rumble of the general's brougham arriving forced them apart. Harry straightened in time to salute the passing carriage as it came to a halt at the foot of the gangway. To everyone's amusement, the lead mare neighed in startlement on seeing one her kind swinging in the air above her arched head. Buller got down amid a flurry of red-capped staff officers and without ceremony strode off up the gangway. Harry raised the first and second fingers of his right hand to his lips and then pressed the tips against Jolyon's mouth. He turned smartly and strode away without looking back, returned the salute of the subaltern standing guard at the foot of the gangway, and climbed up the incline after the line of staff officers.

There remained only the naval embarkation officers' inspection, an interval for the crowd of half an hour, which the band on the quay did its best to pass agreeably. At the conclusion of the third rendition of *Auld Lang Syne* the ship's mooring lines were released and thrown over the side of the dock. Fore and aft, sailors rapidly hauled them in. As promised, Harry took to his allotted cabin, where Private Wryland had made a decent job of laying everything out, but because it gave him a view of the dockside a force stronger than his will pulled him to the porthole and he saw immediately that Jolyon had disobeyed him. Down there Jolyon's eyes unerringly sought out Harry's framed face amid the array of portholes. A loud blast from the ship's horn announced the departure and the first pull of the tugs. The *Dunottar Castle* eased away from the quay. Jolyon raised a hand, a forlorn wave in lieu of steadfastly avoiding a mawkish warning to his lover to take care and be alive for when he too landed at the Cape.

When he thought they were safely far enough from the dock to prevent another sight of Jolyon unsettling him, Harry emerged on deck. There was jubilation mixed with the melancholy of leave-taking. Among the younger men there was much backslapping and laughter, boasting, and claims of future prowess.

"No man should shut his eyes to grave possibilities, but they are too young to know."

Harry turned on his heel at the familiar voice and cracked a smile of pleased greeting. "Winston!"

"Well met, Harry. I should have known wherever trouble brewed there would be a Vane to meet it head on."

They shook hands. "Are you ready for the Great Karoo, the Lesser Karoo, and the high veldt?"

"Hah! I see you've been doing your research this time. Yes, I think I have everything I'll need in my cabin, including sufficient funds to purchase mount, horse tackle, and extra weaponry if the local armory is lacking. So, this time is it *The Times*?" Harry grinned at Churchill's glower.

"The *Morning Post*, again, but at least they're paying £250 a month this time. I feel in my bones that *The Times* will regret not hiring me. Look at it!"

Harry turned back to watch the crowd cheering wildly along a mile of pier and promontory.

"I fear they won't be as cheery when the hospital ships begin to pull in. I did spot you on the dockside," Churchill went on hesitantly. "But I did not want to interrupt your goodbye with the young man."

"My godson. He is about your age."

"Ah, so that was Langrish-Smith."

"He's at Woolwich and can't wait to come out to South Africa as soon as he can." Harry hoped he didn't sound as defensive as he felt, but he sensed Churchill already had the relationship in perspective.

"We may be of similar ages, Harry, but I feel I'm a deal older in experience, so I hope you have apprised him that war is no fun—"

"You don't seem to have a problem with it."

"That's because I am a shallow newshound and glory seeker," Churchill said with an expression of mock smugness. "I do not believe the Gods would create so potent a being as myself for so prosaic an ending as a bullet. Besides, as you are aware, my appointment with fate will be one of inherited medical complications and not a Boer round. As far as health goes, I may not even last out this voyage, which is going to be every bit as tedious as I predicted it would be."

"I'm sure Jolyon will treat what is to come more seriously than this lot," Harry said with a sad shake of his head.

The younger men at one end of the ship were still making a great commotion. One held up a flag, which according to the crudely worked slogan painted on it he proposed to plant on "Krooger's Hill." The men—boys barely out of adolescence and recruits for the most part, exhibiting all the inadequacies of a poor British diet and lack of training, all gangling arms and legs and poor complexions—in their blissful ignorance made a joyful noise about the war to which they were bravely sailing, but the reservists and old hands looked grave and sad, and hardly joined in the singing or cheering.

They were thinking.

CHAPTER 30 | *Cape Colony, October to December 1899*

THE GREAT KAROO: a bare and miserable land of stone and scattered foot-high scrub, broken by large mounds of crumbling rock. Fashioned by the rains into the most curious and unexpected shapes, these kopjes as the Afrikaaners called them rose from the gloomy desert of the plain. Yet a drenching shower transformed the Karoo as instantly as the Fairy God-Mother caused Cinderella to blossom: endless stretches of scarlet-purple and yellow-orange flowers burst into carpets to cover the drab, low rolling hills. Purely from the veldt's peaceful appearance it was hard to believe that a bitter conflict raged to the north where lay besieged Mafeking on the Transvaal border and that its violence might erupt at any moment to dispel the countryside's tranquillity.

"Scrutinize and record the Boer lines," commanded General Buller of Vane's Horse.

The surrounding impression of peace was in appearance only. The ears suggested something else: the dull, rolling booming of large field guns reached the four riders who came into sight up a wide *donga*, one of many dry ditches crossing the land—waterless in the summer unless a thunderstorm brought driving rain and flash floods. The men looked indistinguishable from the terrain in their grubby dull-khaki and mounted on dusty bay horses.

November was drawing to a close. There had been little to celebrate in the month, Harry mused. The day after declaring war on October 11, the Transvaal's President Kruger launched Boer kommando units against Kimberley and Mafeking, and the towns were immediately besieged, even as Harry sailed on the *Dunottar Castle*. At Mafeking—or Mahikeng as the local Barolong tribesmen knew it—faced with overwhelming numbers, Colonel Baden-Powell abandoned any hope of fulfilling his guerrilla mission and fell back on the town, which is where all his supplies were kept. At first the Boer siege lines were thin and young boys of the Barolong tribe kept Baden-Powell supplied with information on the Boers' movements, but in time, as General Piet Cronjé tightened the noose, it became ever more dangerous for native spies to slip in and out. Harry had learned subsequently that at this stage the inhabitants of Mafeking were not at risk of starving. The cowherd Barolong replenished their cattle by raiding the Boers' herds. As a result of these depredations tribesmen and Boers had little love for each other, and the Barolongs were happy to divert many head of cattle, spoils of their raids, into the township.

Vane's Horse, as Sergeant Travis immediately dubbed them, cantered up from the shallowing ditch, Harry in company with three British irregular volunteers from the Cape: Travis (brevetted sergeant) was a Cape Colonist, a tough man in this thirties whose farmland near Kraaipan had been overrun on October 12 in the first push of Boers across the border from the Orange Free State into British territory; Stevens was a young merchant seaman who jumped ship at the port of East London in search of a better life on land and now found himself wrapped up in the war; Norris, a Cockney who gave the lie to the common belief that his kind were cheerful, had been one of many adventurers who grabbed a place aboard the *Dunottar Castle* in the undoubtedly mistaken belief that gold would line his pocket once Kimberley was relieved. A mixed bunch, but they had proved useful and tough in a fight.

It was over a week since he had given the order to withdraw with their painfully gathered information from the hills above Mafeking. There had been a few skirmishes with isolated elements of the enemy, shots exchanged in and out between anthills and kopjes, and chases on horseback. None they encountered survived. On one horrid occasion they surprised two Boer watchmen. Seeing they were outnumbered, they surrendered, which left Harry with a moral dilemma: He hated the idea of killing the two—mere boys it turned out—in cold blood. But after lulling the small camp into a false sense of their honor as captives, in concert they attacked Stevens on watch with knives secreted in their boots. Some sixth sense saved Stevens. He whirled out of the way of one blade and suffered a skin deep cut from the other. Harry shot one boy with his revolver and Travis took the other out with his rifle, a killing bullet. Harry's man collapsed, crying out for his mother.

Norris resolved Harry's conflict. "Them or us, chief," the Cockney spat out, and before Harry could stop him, whipped out his Bowie knife and slashed it across the wounded boy's throat. Stevens turned and threw up around his protest. Harry sighed. He never asked, but Norris clearly came from a tough background.

No, there had been little to celebrate, except they had the Intelligence the Bull needed, which oddly included detail on the locomotives in Boer hands—it turned out Stevens was a keen train spotter. What they had discovered would be cold comfort to the men, women, and children trapped in Mafeking. By all appearance and from what local natives supplied, the town could survive for weeks, if necessary—and would almost certainly have to. On the credit side of the balance sheet the siege would tie up increasing numbers of Boer troops and so gain precious weeks for Buller to concentrate on other more urgent matters than Baden-Powell and Mafeking. It was also clear that Kimberley, far to the south of Mafeking, would be the first town the British must relieve, if only to stop the fulminations of Cecil Rhodes who was trapped there.

Now Vane's Horse was headed south. The Horse might be surprised at any moment, so Harry kept a wary watch all around in spite of his musing. Since his arrival in the Cape there had been British victories, but few and marred by costly loss of life. It was quickly apparent to officers and men that the Boers were far better armed, an advantage they pressed by invading Natal and surrounding the colony's main town of Ladysmith on November 2, before Vane's Horse had set out on the scouting mission.

In the great harmonious silence there were natural disturbances. Locusts danced in the sun, little meerkats stood and watched the passing riders for a moment and then scampered into their holes, a thousand scattered gothic sandcastles, evidence of toiling ants, rose grotesquely from the scrub, and stone-covered kopjes stood out like larger anthills. Apart from the mounted men the country looked unoccupied by humans. Harry knew this was a false impression—there was at the very least the fifth member of their party lurking somewhere ahead of their route. In short order Harry had acquired a different kind of sixth sense to that learned in Afghanistan or Egypt, an edge honed by facing the clever and determined Boer, buoyed up by the absolute certainty of having God on his side and the conviction that his Bible affirmed it was so.

Not quite a month in South Africa—or the edge of British Bechuanaland, as they were—Britain seemed a world away. Only images of Jolyon made a link with home, which Harry refreshed every evening by looking at the two tiny photographs he carried with him. Denied any news since leaving Southampton, Buller and his expeditionary reinforcements had arrived at Cape Town ready to roll up the Boers in a swiftly completed campaign.

That was before hearing of the disasters.

๙☆๖

R.M.S. *Dunottar Castle* made landfall on October 30, passing close by the low hump of Robben Island—"a barren spot inhabited by lepers, poisonous serpents, and dogs undergoing quarantine," Churchill told Harry. He'd been reading up his background to "add color to my dispatches." The ship steamed into Table Bay at ten o'clock and anchored for the night.

The morning dawned a fine clear blue, but aboard ship the mood was somber. That was the fault of the Cape Town pilot and accompanying military attachés who brought General Buller, officers, the troops, correspondents, and general hangers-on up to date. To universal frustration, no news had reached Madeira by cable and during the days of sailing the war had moved at a pace— in every sense in the wrong direction. At army corps headquarters, situated in the Mount Nelson Hotel, chaos reigned. Two key towns in Cape Colony were besieged within days of the Boer invasion: Mafeking, close to the border with Transvaal, on October 13; Kimberley, on the border with the Orange Free State, the following day. The defeat of Boer forces at Talana Hill on October 20 only underlined the problem Buller now faced, for General William Penn Symons' victory came at a high cost in lives, his own from a mortal wound included, and—in removing the Boers from a commanding position—he had not pushed them back into Transvaal.

These dismal facts became clear at the first gathering of staff officers, along with the assessment that five-sixths of the British troops stationed in South Africa were now being corralled into Ladysmith. The 1,500 troops just off *Dunottar Castle* were insufficient in strength to be immediately useful, other than as scattered garrisons to keep the Cape townships quiet.

"Month at least. That's what it will take," Buller raged. "A month before the main Expeditionary Force being gathered or already on the sea will be ready. Can't take the field until they're ready." In an irate aside to Harry, he complained of the Governor, Sir Alfred Milner. "Damned fellow insists we defend the Cape

Peninsula. 'Of paramount importance,' he says. Damn stuffed-shirt idiot! It's an area of a few thousand square miles." He turned ferocious brows on Harry as though the Governor's lack of comprehension was his fault. "D'you know? How far the front is from Cape Town. Do you?"

Harry did, pretty well, but decided to let Buller inform him.

"Bloody well as far away as Marseilles is from Berlin! If we're going to fear the Boers reaching here we might as well all go home now."

The War Office and the Foreign Office had hoped that in contrast to firebrand Kruger in Transvaal, the Orange Free State's President Steyn would hold his hand, but it was apparent that he had left behind his scruples along with his earlier peace overtures and sent Free State kommando units across the Orange River into Cape Colony at Bethulie and Norval's Pont.

"Milner might have one thing right," Buller conceded gruffly. "Last thing we need is disaffected colonials getting restive. Damn Dutchmen residing in the Cape Colony could be fifth columnists. Better leave some Tommies for garrison duty down here. Damn it!" Buller stamped around the hotel hallway that acted as his temporary command center. "If Ladysmith falls—which I'm bound to say seems probable at any moment—Natal will be open from the Tugela River to the Indian Ocean. I telegraphed Lord Lansdowne. Told him in no uncertain terms. The situation is one of extreme gravity. Told him: send a lot more men and materiel. Hah! We need a lot more than those pen-pushing idiots in their Whitehall wedding-cake castle would like."

Buller faced the reality in as practical manner as he could. With Kimberley and Mafeking under siege and Ladysmith on the point of falling, his cherished campaign plan of driving up the central (or Midland) railway line through Bloemfontein to Pretoria and thus ending the war at a stroke by taking both Boer capitals was in a shambles.

"I'm splitting the army corps into three detachments, gentlemen," he announced to his gathered staff officers after a day spent poring over maps, many of which contained distressingly blank regions. "General Methuen, you have 1st Division—Guards Brigade, the 9th Infantry Brigade, and the Naval Brigade. Up the western railway you go. Relieve Kimberley and Mafeking.

"General Gatacre you get the 3rd Division. Push north to the vital rail junction at Stormberg. Secure the Cape Midlands district from any Boer Raids and suppress any rebellions by Boer inhabitants.

"I'm for Durban. Take command of the 2nd Division. Then we march to the relief of Ladysmith."

On the following day a thrilled Churchill caught up with Harry (who was battling for time with the General to get his final orders sorted and losing out in the process to imperious colonels). "I've learned that my esteemed colleague Mr. Rudyard Kipling has been a visitor in the Cape and is expected to turn up here at any time."

Harry suppressed the desire to tease Churchill for his effrontery in placing himself on a level with the great writer, who was almost Harry's age; but then, he supposed they had both written for *The Pioneer* in India. But his friend's bubbly enthusiasm redeemed him since it verged on hero worship and the thought that their paths might cross in Cape Town evidently had him in a high fever of excitement.

"He and his wife stay in The Woolsack, which is a house on Groote Schuur." When Harry looked blankly at this, Churchill added, "You haven't the ferret soul of a newspaperman. The estate of Cecil Rhodes. It's a few miles south of Cape Town. But with all this going on, he's bound to spend time in town."

"Mr. Rhodes?"

"Kipling!" Churchill snapped. "Rhodes is stuck in Kimberley, I'm informed."

"I'm sure he will be thrilled to meet you, Winston."

Churchill frowned. "Harry, I think you're condescending to me. Anyway, the problem is that I don't have the time. I must be on the train carrying General Buller to East London from where we sail for Durban and thence to join the Natal Field Force. You see that's where all the thrills will be. Can you imagine how exciting my dispatches from the relieved township will be? So I've written a short note for you to deliver to Mr. Kipling the minute you see him."

Harry tried to point out the problems with this plan, that there was no reason for the writer to entertain his delivery and in any case he was sure he'd receive his orders to depart at any moment and so miss Kipling altogether. Churchill wasn't listening. The glint of glory triumphed over common sense.

A small figure, no more than a black shadow, detached from the shape of a towering, many-turreted anthill. Harry waved his companions to a walk. The scout, a young Barolong boy of about fourteen years—at least, he thought he might be fourteen—who went by the conveniently short name of Neo, knew the local terrain well. He'd been one of Baden-Powell's young scouts until he could no longer risk the perils of creeping through enemy lines to report in. He had approached Vane's Horse five days back bearing a chit as a reference from Baden-Powell that assured "whomsoever it may concern" that Neo was a hard-working, trustworthy boy. He owned every reason to detest the Boers; they had recently killed his father and two elder brothers during a cattle raid. He gestured the riders to halt and made a sign they'd all come to know: hidden enemy ahead.

His warning was a bit late.

Something sang in the sunny air above Harry's head, and he flicked with his whip to drive the locust away. Almost at the same time a sharp *zzing* accompanied splinters of rock flying up from the side of the donga a few feet beyond where they were halted. Immediately afterward came the sharp double knock of a Mauser heard at a distance, followed quickly by another, and after that again the shrill moan of a flying bullet. This time a plume of sand flicked into existence about two hundred yards away to the left, to disperse like spray from a fountain. Everyone ducked instinctively. The natural thing to do was to drop to the ground and take cover, but Harry knew that out in the open if whoever had spotted them had snipers with them they would be pinned down and might well lose their horses to the enemy rifle fire. However, the poor aim puzzled him. Boer riflemen hit their intended targets even from horseback. A possible answer presented itself in a burst of rising dust as a small herd of springbok raced away across the plain, showing their dainty heels in panic.

"They can't have the range but they soon will," Travis hissed.

"I think they're hunting meat, not us, but they'll catch sight of us soon if we stay here. To the left." Harry pointed at a kopje some two hundred yards away. "Here!" At the command Neo reached out both hands and Harry yanked the boy up behind him and then set spurs to flank. All four rode at the best speed of their horses to put more distance between themselves and the still invisible picket. Fortunately, the light veldt breeze blew dust from the hooves in the opposite direction to the approaching Boers.

"Damn Dutchmen and their trenches. Dig the buggers all over the place," Travis, who was slightly in the lead, shouted to the wind as he cleared a narrow irrigation ditch. "Must be a farm somewhere nearby."

"Probably abandoned," Harry shouted back.

There were a few more shots, and always the shrill moan of a 7.65 mm round-nosed bullet, but Harry had a niggling feeling that the gazelles were the targets. It was as if the Boers were shooting for fun more than intention. In two minutes Vane's Horse were tucked under the little hill's shelter. Harry climbed up its steep side, lay on his front, and peered over the flat lip. He scanned the landscape through his field glasses. The image was fuzzy through the coating of saliva-wetted dust applied to the lenses to prevent sunlight reflecting off them and giving away his position. *Nothing.* A puzzled frown creased his grimy brow. No outlying enemy picket, then. He glanced down at the others, huddled in the lee of the kopje and signaled to keep silent and still.

After a further few minutes three Boers mounted on ponies came out from behind the shoulder of a hill and began to walk leisurely across to the next kopje. If they were out hunting game they weren't that bothered about it. At the distance, their black silhouettes wavered against the evening glare. Harry couldn't understand their unwary attitude, but it backed up his supposition that they hadn't actually been firing at Vane's Horse, unless at a mirage (which in the heat of afternoon could fool easily), in which case the Boers hadn't seen their flight to hide behind the hill on which he was now spread-eagled. *If they were shooting at us, they must think they scared us off.* Immediately in front of his position another and smaller kopje reared up, which looked as if it might be useful. Eyes firmly fixed on the three specks crossing the field, he waved Travis up. "Sergeant, take Stevens with you down to that kopje, and see if you can't get a shot at the fellows."

"Yessir!"

Some time elapsed before the men reached the hillock, and still the three Boers moved slowly and unsuspectingly across Harry's view. He saw Travis and Stevens take a bead on the riders with their Lee-Enfields. With a shocking suddenness, the rifles cracked out, one after another. Harry saw the spent .303 cartridge cases ejected as golden flickers and at the same time the Boers seemed to fly instead of to crawl. Through his glasses Harry saw the rearmost man pitch backward from his horse, which still fled, riderless, beside the others, who were soon out of range.

"Now we have to move," Harry snapped as he scrambled down and took the reins of his horse from Neo. "Those Dutchmen are almost certainly part of a kommando and they're bound to be back if our shots haven't already alerted them." On regaining his seat he patted Neo's shoulder. "Well spotted. At first I thought they were already on top of us."

Neo gave a broad, white-toothed smile of pleasure. "Too close they get and I use this." He waved a nasty looking curved blade.

The minute Travis and Stevens returned, the group continued to ride deeper into the northern plains of the Karoo away from the putative border with the Free State where the Boers commanded the western railway line all the way south to the Orange River. Harry gambled on the Boers anticipating British interference only coming from the southeast, from Natal, and from the Orange River, where General Methuen was gathering his forces ready to advance against Cronjé's army. With their attention so engaged they should not expect to encounter any enemy moving through territory the Boers supposed to be secure on their right flank.

The sun descended toward the western horizon and the land rose gently. As the light began to fail they rode on at a slow walk, letting the horses pick their way through the thorny scrub plants.

"Let's bivouac here. Sergeant, we can risk a small fire in that donga for tea and soup, but I think we'll camp without further light up on the low hill. I prefer the height for sleeping." He grinned at Travis and addressed the others. "Smokes only in the donga. Don't want to glow like a firefly up there and let a sniper get a bead on you."

As the men busied themselves quietly and efficiently setting up a simple camp in the declining half-light, Harry took stock. Over the past two weeks they had harried small detachments of Boers by reversing the enemy's own hit-and-run tactics. In fact his orders were to avoid contact, but if that proved impossible, to ensure none of the Dutchmen they encountered should live to give away the presence of British operating so far to the north. He was annoyed that in the last—and as it turned out, unnecessary—encounter two of the Boer hunters had escaped. General Buller wanted Intelligence on movements, numbers, types of artillery, and anything else that might prove useful to General Methuen, tasked with recovering Kimberley and Mafeking. He did not want the enemy to suspect there were flying columns operating to his rear or flank. The most vital part of their mission, to establish the extent of the Boer encirclement of Mafeking, was accomplished. Baden-Powell was well and truly cooped up in the town and it was going to stay that way until Methuen swept away Cronjé's Boer army from the Riet, Modder, and Vaal rivers.

As the men settled down, with Stevens taking the first watch, Harry loosened his shirt to scratch his back. He longed for a long soak in a bathtub, at least a wash in a river, and a proper shave. They would have to wait. He wondered what was happening in other theaters of this strange war. Getting up to date information wasn't easy in their outlying position, though the Barolong scouts were pretty speedy, and what they knew didn't sound very good.

Mild November nights posed no hardship to sleepers out in the open. Harry lay back and gazed up at the starry sky. A familiar ache suffused his being. He missed Jolyon terribly—the photographs only made his longing the worse. Every time he took them out to examine the beloved face he swore it would be better to abstain—which he did not. With Christmas looming he hoped to get back to Cape Town in time to meet Jolyon off whichever troopship he would be on. And there was the problem. He couldn't cable Jolyon if he were already on the high seas, and how was he to know if he was or if he was still in England, waiting to board a troopship? The sooner he could reach the Cape the better. At least he'd had the foresight to send a telegram at the first opportunity after docking in Cape Town, which gave Jolyon instructions on how to wire him care of the Mount Nelson Hotel.

He wanted Jolyon by his side, together again. The Bull had promised him a free hand in officer selection from among the newly arriving troops. A sigh escaped his lips while his right hand found the burning lump in the front of his pants. Masturbating over a mental image of Jo never brought the satisfaction he yearned for, but it did at least ease the pain of separation. He rolled onto his side, away from any of the others (and Neo, who insisted on sticking as close as possible to him at nights and who he was convinced was similarly giving himself teenage relief, judging by the harshly suppressed breaths and occasional elbow jogged against his back). Fixed on those beloved eyes, climax through gaping fly never took long, and Harry spread his seed on the Great Karoo.

Rolling onto his back, he tipped his Highland bush hat down over his eyes. The brim resting on his nose smelled of dust and sweat. A military pith helmet was just too hot and unwieldy out here and he'd rather approved of the headgear the Seaforth Highlanders preferred when not actually in battle or ceremonial. He slept.

The small party was awake before dawn, the horses tacked up, saddlebags repacked. A first edge of pale light showed above the rim of the horizon made faintly ragged by the distant Witwatersrand Mountains. Harry swung Neo up in front of him, the boy's slight form hardly in the way. He caught a long look from Norris, whose sudden grin looked sickly in the yellow half-light.

"You takin' good care o' him, sir." He dipped his brow at Neo, who gave the Cockney a cold stare.

"Ride on, Norris, and keep your voice down. No need to let the foe know we're here."

Norris raised a finger to the brim of his hat and wheeled his horse around to follow Travis.

Harry waved Stevens on, happy to let Travis take point for a change, so that he might consider their options. He had all he needed to report the situation around Mafeking. His problem was getting to a post where he could use the telegraph and all of the Orange Free State stood between him just this side of the Bechuanaland border and General Buller, somewhere in Natal. Keeping to the valleys as much as possible, Vane's Horse rode through knee-high grassland and across rockier outcrops of tableland. Two days brought them to the cattle township of Stella where the British settlers were in a state of deep unease. One hoary rancher explained that there was sporadic gunfire to the south. "Over Vryburg way," he said.

Harry listened out. "I can't hear anything."

"Hah! You ride a nudge west of south and you'll run into trouble!"

It was the direction they needed, and if there were gunfire, it pointed to British troops engaging the Boers. Hopefully, the troops would be in communication with Durban, Cape Town, or one of the other railheads not yet in enemy hands. They watered the horses and soon set off, Harry with Neo on the back of his saddle. It wasn't long before the dull thumps of distant guns came across the flat plain. After two miles the terrain became lumpier and rows of low kopjes made a straight path impossible. As Harry cantered around the flank of one outcrop a man in a British uniform appeared. He raised his rifle with a loud oath and barred the only way forward between the sides of a narrow ditch. Harry reined in sharply enough that Neo behind almost lost his grip. The rest of the troop pulled up in a cloud of dust.

"Who goes there?"

"Vane, Special Services unit. Who are you?"

"Lance Corporal Hastings…" The soldier caught himself and spoke more sternly. "Do you have the watchword of the day, sir?"

Harry relaxed back in the saddle as he heard Travis chuckling. Not a pleasant sound.

"The major asked you your regiment, idiot! Stand to atten-*hut*!" Travis swung down from his horse in a vapor of dust and buzzing flies, at which he flicked irritably and ineffectually. He strode up to the startled sentry, who came to a semblance of parade ground attention. "You silly little man. We're Special Services, out in the wilds back there. How in hell and tarnation's name are we supposed to know what password your commander's given you? What regiment?" The last was shouted into the terrified lance corporal's face.

"A d-detachment of the th-third and fourth companies of 1st Battalion King's Royal Rifles, sir. There's some of Dublin Fusileers with us, 2nd Battalion, sir."

"And what's the watchword of the day?" Travis barked out.

"Dunedin, sir!" the soldier snapped out, and then blushed.

"Dunedin, it is." Harry smiled through the dirt coating his itchy beard.

"You may pass, sir." The lance corporal saluted.

With an ironic tip of his bush hat's brim, Harry urged his horse forward. "Where can I find your commanding officer?"

"Carry on down the donga, sir. He'll be somewhere around at the bottom after it opens out. But I'd keep your head down if I was you, sir. Them Boers shoot anything they see moving." He made them sound like "burrs."

Travis remounted and they proceeded warily down the donga. It twisted left and right as it dropped with the lie of the land. Harry scanned the striations on its sides, which spoke of violent flash flooding in the rainy season. Presently there came a dull report, and the sand rose in a column before the kopjes half a mile away across the lower plain.

"Naval gun, sir," Travis said. "A 4.7 by the sound of it. And that'd be right. Wouldn't want the Tommies to have anything decent to fight back with, would we."

"Unfortunately, Travis, your well-placed sarcasm won't speed up delivery of something more appropriate," Harry said drily. "Had that been the case, Mafeking might even now be a free, open town."

In the confines of the ditch it was hard to tell from where the gun had fired.

He glanced up, twisting in the saddle to look over his shoulder and felt Neo grip his belt's webbing to keep his seat. Again the invisible gun boomed, the weird, prolonged *whirtle* went over their heads. After a wait of perhaps fifteen seconds another cloud of hideous smoke burst right on top of a distant kopje. The report of the exploding shell followed after three seconds   .

Moments later the crackle of returning Mauser rifle fire answered the gun. Dirt spurted up from the sides of the donga, causing all the party to lie flat as possible on their horses' necks. Bullets and ricochets *whinged* off the higher rocks. All urged their horses to a cautious canter, wary of debris in the donga which might trip a hoof, but anxious to get to lower cover. Harry raised his head but failed to see any telltale muzzle smoke from the Boer rifles. The naval gun fired again. Harry spurred his mount on and they emerged onto a rocky level area protected from the south by a low ridge. He suspected it was a naturally formed farm tank for watering cattle, abandoned now because of the war. A line of British Tommies populated the rim, mostly keeping their heads down. A lieutenant turned in surprise at their approach. Harry slid down and in a few words explained who he was and what he needed.

Harry approved of the young officer's apparent calmness even though everything about him shouted fresh out of Sandhurst. He called two men over and ordered them to get Vane's Horse safely behind an outcrop of rock in the opposite direction from the donga down which they had arrived. Then he looked enviously at the rifle with its ten-shot magazine in Harry's hands. "You've got your hands on Lee-Enfields, sir. My lads were issued with Metfords, not enough Enfields to go around apparently," he added bitterly.

"I'm confident that will soon change. General Buller put in requisitions ages ago. Bound to be Lee-Enfields arriving on the troop ships every week."

The lieutenant pointed behind him at where Travis, Stevens, Norris, and Neo were taking shelter behind the jutting rocky buttress. "That's our way out. Behind, there's a narrow path up onto the higher ground," he explained, and then continued in the same breath. "We've no communications here, sir, not even any heliograph contact. Any friendly units are too far away. In fact if you'd turned up any later, we wouldn't be here. We're facing at least two kommandos of Free Staters out there. They must be a splinter of the army driven back by General Methuen at Enslin, which lies a few miles south of Vryburg. I'm not sure of the outcome, but the action was set for last Saturday."

Harry narrowed his eyes in calculation. "The 25th?"

"Yes, sir. It makes sense that we must have had some sort of success otherwise I can't think why the Boers pushed this way. They hold Vryburg now. In the case that General Methuen kicked the Boers occupying Enslin out, our job was to pin down any force retreating this way and prevent them circling around north while the General moves against Belmont and the Modder River. But we didn't anticipate so many coming this way. They're concentrated on our center but the scouts have seen movement to left and right to outflank our position here. So we're about to fall back while we can. The gun up there should give us cover, but…"

As he trailed off, a strange barrage started up from the collection of kopjes occupied by the Boers.

"That's their damned one-pounder quick-firing gun. Ineffective, we were told back home, but I can tell you this, Major, the damned Boers have taken down plenty of good men with it."

To Harry's ears it made a noise closer to *ppm-ppm-ppm*, a curiously unthreatening sound, but the thought of one-pound shells flying through the air about his head was an uncomfortable one indeed. *So that's why Jo said they called it a pom-pom.* "The War Office won't be purchasing any. They say it's too big to use against personnel and too small to be useful against defenses."

Almost instantly, splinters of rock began flying up all around, keeping a hideous rhythm with the distant weapon. As if to underline the lieutenant's bitter statement a corporal of the Dublin Fusileers running in a crouch from the defensive ridge took a hit. One moment he was pumping his feet, the next a shell took off his head. It simply came apart in a blossom of speeding gore following the shell's low trajectory. His torso staggered two more paces as his motor responses caught up with the sudden lack of control and his corpse fell to the dust still with enough forward momentum to carom through the red-gray remains of his head as it did so. The pom-pom shell rebounded off the ground a foot ahead of the man it had slain and lammed into the rock face thirty yards from where Vane's Horse were huddled. The force of the small explosion wrapped a hot, cordite-smoky blanket over them. A score more shells slammed into the ground and rising rear cliff of the tank in a tattoo of death. And then the gun fell silent, either because the gunner saw no targets or perhaps a jam had stopped it.

"Where the hell is the gun?" Harry demanded.

"That's it! We can't see it, or their rifles," the lieutenant said sourly. "They're using smokeless powder. They tricked us the other day. I thought we had a small contingent pinned down to our left as we patrolled toward Vryburg because the muzzle smoke from the rifles gave away their position. But it was a cunning trap. As we moved to flank them at least a hundred rifles opened up from a grassy rise on our right, but they were invisible. Smokeless powder, you see. They used the old black powder to gull us into the ambush. It was a shocking mess. Ten men down in the first minute."

Harry could see tears sparkle in the lieutenant's eyes. He was reminded of his first taste of real action in the Sudan at Abu Klea and how Dervish fury turned the glamor of war to ashes in less than five minutes. The noise of fabric violently frayed by a musket ball a split-second before the sickeningly wet thunk of flesh exploding lived with him still. "You're right. Best to fall back and get out of here to fight another day. I doubt they will pursue us. Their task is to circle around to the north and reinforce the Modder River crossings. Ours is to get to a railhead that's still functioning."

The gully leading away from the temporary redoubt in the tank proffered scant protection from the endless shelling of the pom-pom gun, but in an orderly manner the two rifles detachments made it to safety, with medical orderlies carrying the wounded in makeshift dhoolies. The dead had to be left where they had fallen. There was no time for burial details, and in any case the Boers had already taken terrain where those who had been shot in the first encounter lay. The naval gun fired its last shell and silence fell on the ground of conflict. Shortly after, the thud of hooves and heavy wheels announced the British gun carriage closing fast on the column.

Harry was proved correct. The Boers did not pursue them. But he realized he was wrong in what he'd told Jolyon about the days of cavalry being over. The Boers moved freely and at such speed because they were all mounted. The kommandos ran rings around the foot-bound Tommies, even with their heavier artillery and siege guns, towed behind trains of powerful horseflesh. And the damned pom-pom…

"We have to have the pom-pom," he said aloud.

"I'm sure you're right, sir," Travis said as he rode alongside with Neo clinging to his broad back, giving Harry's horse a rest from the extra weight.

"It's a very sad irony that a weapon developed by the British should now be creating such devastation among our men in the hands of the enemy."

I wonder if Jo can bring a battery of them with him…?

Harry smiled at his own wishful thought. The War Office and the Ministry were always fifty years behind the times.

CHAPTER 31 | *Cape Town, New Year 1900*

WITH THE ARRIVAL of each troopship the disembarking battalions swelled Cape Town's population of 70,000 dramatically. The troops were to repair the fortunes shattered during one short week, "Black Week," as everyone designated it. While those disasters were much on Harry's mind, the approaching H.M.H.S. *Braemar Castle*, its tall funnel, masts, and sharp bow parting the waters of the outer harbor reaches was foremost. For the thousandth time he fingered the creased flimsy in his uniform pants pocket. His worries had been needless: Jolyon had shown particular determination in finding him telegraphically before he'd left Southampton. The cable had reached Harry at De Aar Junction, where Vane's Horse settled in for recuperation over the Christmas period while he headed on to Cape Town. He'd no need to read the telegram; its few words were branded in his memory.

PASSED TOP-FLIGHT GUNNY SHOEBURYNESS + POMPOM SECTION ASSURED WITH RFA 14TH + ARRIVE CAPE HOPE N.Y. 1900 BRAEMAR C. + JO

It signaled Jolyon's success in passing his final gunnery examinations at the Royal Artillery School of Gunnery at Shoeburyness in Essex. It was not an establishment Harry knew at first hand, but Jolyon had described it from his earliest session there as being "a windswept slab of river mud on the northern side of the Thames Estuary." He was assigned to the Royal Field Artillery 14th Battery, pom-pom section, the first of the desperately needed guns presumably loaded on the incoming ship.

The first thing Harry did after climbing down from the battle-scarred train in Cape Town in the last days of December was to stride down Adderley Street to Foreshore and the harbor master's offices. There he checked on *Braemar*

Castle's estimated arrival date. Jolyon's telegram suggested New Year's Day, and it turned out he was correct. "If she holds speed as she did to Madeira, she should dock shortly after dawn," the harbor master's assistant claimed.

His second act was to check with a real estate agent, who arranged some temporary accommodation, a small cottage with a northerly ocean view in the lee of Table Mountain above Three Anchor Bay; *Drieankerbaai*, as the Afrikaaners originally named it.

The *Braemar Castle*, which was barely off the builders' slipway before being pressed into service as a troop carrier on the way south and hospital ship on the return to Southampton, came alongside the outer wharf. Immediately, the organized chaos of getting men and materiel off as speedily as possible commenced. The wounded survivors of Black Week were already marshaled on the dockside. Harry came across one of them—a man who looked as strong as a horse—explaining to an admiring group how he came to be alive at all.

"A bullet passes right through the rim of me helmet, so 'elp me Gawd. It enters me left temple, passes behind the back of me nose, and then through the roof of me mouf, and out through the lower part of me right cheek. Lookee here!" First he showed off the dent in his temple, and then described with many faux-medical words in ever more gruesome detail the shell's passage. "And it came out of me blooming cheek, can you believe it!" His audience did because he tipped his head back to reveal the dent in the flesh, and then passed his helmet around like a conjurer expecting some coins for his magic.

By what irony had the authorities permitted a hoarding advertising Horlick's Malted Milk on the wharf above the lines of wounded? Under a drawing of a single-funnel steamer plowing through the waves a short stanza proclaimed:

Here is the famous hospital ship,
The steamer "Maine" on her outward trip.
And MALTED MILK, by one accord,
They voted the main thing there on board.

It seemed few cared one way or the other for the cheery news that they could look forward to a comforting hot drink on the way home. Most of the injured—laid out on downed cacolets or crouched miserably on kitbags, huddled under blankets—looked tired and serious, lacking interest in anything but their own afflictions. Harry thought it almost a pity that the people back home would never witness such scenes. The appetite for "kicking the cruel Boer," eater of babies, rapist of innocent settler women, only made Harry uneasy. Sadly, the public was in need of having even the most elementary fruits of war brought home to it. The would-be-kicked had kicked back cruelly hard.

After a few minor successful engagements, little more than skirmishes, at an alarming speed everything turned upside down in December. While Harry was falling back with Vane's Horse and the infantry detachment from the Stella-Vryburg district, three calamities reversed all hopes for a speedy conclusion to the war. "Black Week" started on December 10 when General Gatacre's division was driven back at Stormberg with the loss of 135 killed, 600 captured and two guns. The following day at Magersfontein General Methuen's 14,000 troops blundered into a labyrinth of Boer trenches. The loss of 120 killed and 690 seriously wounded left Kimberley and Mafeking still securely besieged and the British advance totally bogged down at the Modder River. And then to cap it all, on December 15, at Colenso on the Tugela River in Natal (the gateway to nearby besieged Ladysmith), General Buller was forced into a full retreat. The debacle left 145 dead and 1,200 missing or wounded. Whole units were cut off and the Boers captured ten field guns to add to their considerable arsenal.

When Buller telegraphed Lord Landsdowne to inform him that he would abandon the attempt to relieve Ladysmith—for which he had no real alternative—and managed to get a message through to General George White urging him to surrender the Ladysmith garrison, the Secretary of State for War relieved Buller of his overall command of the stalemated war.

For Harry on the waterfront, all thoughts of conflict fled at the first glimpse of the young officer descending the gangway. He might have been in a line of subalterns striding down to the dockside—tall, short, of medium height, broad of shoulder, narrow or wider of waist—but the color and cut of the hair, the shape of the noble head under the pillbox forage cap, neat ears and perfect Greek *kouros* profile could only be Second Lieutenant Jolyon Langrish-Smith. The breath caught in Harry's throat. There were moments out there on the veldt when that damned pom-pom gun pumped death that he believed he would never see that lovely face again, flushed with youth yet becoming the man. And now here was, on dry land and beginning to look around, confused at the strangeness of it all: the open wharf, the confusion of unloading, and the ordering of troops, unaware of Harry observing him.

At the barrier, officers with stars and crowns on their shoulder straps addressed the arrivals with clipboards and instructions, separating try-their-luck volunteers from accredited journalists and enlisted soldiers. The War Office, realizing too late as usual that there was a desperate need for more men, had encouraged all-comers. Now the Cape headquarters staff were obliged to cope, and do so in the usual manner of army men: the nobodies who had come out in the hope of getting commissions were turned away like tramps and told that there was nothing for them.

At last, Jolyon was passed through, chitted with the bare minimum of information to find his way to the artillery park where R.F.A. 14th Battery was to assemble. Harry saw his head lift, as all did, struck by the extraordinary sight of Table Mountain catching the early sunlight and then dipping their heads from the sun's direct glare. Jolyon's scrutiny lowered as he continued walking ahead, his back held straight and proud to hide the nervousness of any young man in unaccustomed surroundings, the uncertainty of what to expect... and then...

"H-Harry."

The lump in Harry's throat threatened to suffocate him. There were just too many people about to do what he wanted, to sweep Jolyon into his arms, hug and never let him go. Suddenly he was overcome with a terrible fear. Jolyon looked so slender so easily breakable, so vulnerable to the terrors of the open veldt and the corpse-choked rivers of the Free State. Jolyon was so very handsome, so elegant, so... he was lost for words.

Instead, as eager arrivals pushed past them, they shook hands, smiles of greeting standing in for anything more affectionate. Stuck for anything to say, Harry blurted out the first thing that came to mind.

"Did you bring your pom-pom with you?" The words felt pathetically inadequate, but they made Jolyon crack a broad smile and then a stifled laugh.

"Vickers is making them and the shells as fast as they can, and there are a few coming out on the following troopship."

Harry shook his head in wonder. "Sea travel must agree with you. You shine!"

"It was, in fact, completely agreeable, apart from the accommodations." Jolyon gave a theatrical shudder. "The ship is built for some luxury, but the army has undone it all and crammed us three to a stateroom, and that halved with a partition to fit six into a space designed for two in comfort, with a battle at our conjoined doorway."

"I think you'll find it paradise compared to what awaits upcountry."

"And what does?"

"I'll fill you in as we walk."

At that moment a lance corporal in a gunner's uniform came puffing up with what Harry presumed were Jolyon's belongings; commendably few. Even so the fellow was making hard work of it.

"Right fuckin' battle, excuse my fuckin' French, sir, gettin' this out o' the 'old. You'da think you was carrying the bleedin' Crown Jools in here the way the naval hofficer commanding dis-barkation were actin'."

Jolyon raised his eyebrows and grinned at Harry. "How far is it to the artillery park headquarters, Harry? I can't have poor Wilmslow here expiring—"

"An' bleedin' hot it is too."

Wilmslow! Harry mouthed in amusement. "You're not going there, Jo. I've a place of our own about a mile away around the lower hill over there."

They set off, followed by a grumbling Wilmslow. "Should've 'ad a bleedin' private doin' all this carryin'."

Harry kept Jolyon in the corner of his vision when he wasn't actually looking straight at him. An image of the twelve-year-old hovered in his mind: *standing stiffly upright in a navy cadet's uniform, brass buttons forming a gleaming row down the front of his tunic, a high-waisted, close-fitting jacket in deep blue, adorned by bands of gold braid above the wrists and around the high collar, above which pokes an Eton-style starched shirt collar. His stark white dress pants bear a vertical blue stripe from the front of each hip...*

He shook his head and smiled, amused at the strange sight they made; he in his drab undress khakis that barely resembled an official uniform and would have had Alfred Winner schoolboy chortling with unholy glee, Jolyon neat as a pin in his field artilleryman's uniform of form-fitting waisted frock-coat in dark blue (including the collar, which would be scarlet and gold for the mess), matching breeches with scarlet side stripes, brown boots, gaiters, Sam Browne belt, and gloves. On his sleeve, the plain gold cord "Austrian" knot device marked Jolyon out as a junior officer, the badge of his rank and identification as belonging the Western Division of the Royal Artillery were sewn on the gold, plaited shoulder cords. His sword (to be worn on all parades and duties except on board ship, at mess, or on stable duty) he had in hand and fiddled with attaching it to the belt as they walked. The gold-braided pillbox forage cap sat at a jaunty angle on his head, a hint of his former aesthete's languid casualness. The waisted coat ended just above the bulge in his crotch, which the tight trousers showed off to perfection.

Jolyon's eyes narrowed and a naughty smile creased his lips when he saw the center of Harry's interest. "A place of our own, hey?"

Wilmslow dismissed to find his own billet, Harry took Jolyon in his arms. The hug was returned. Harry pulled his head back only far enough to brush his lips over Jolyon's freshly shaved cheek and then found his parted lips. Their tongues touched, sidled around each other like wrestlers seeking an advantage and then took turns to invade, probe, and slide along teeth.

"Do you want to take a shower?"

Jolyon leaned his head back, a question writ large on his features. "A what? It doesn't look like rain."

A stifled laugh broke from Harry, delighted at the surprise he'd sprung. "This used to be a French naval captain's cottage and he had the device installed. The French army have used them, apparently for some years, but they have to cycle the water through a pump, whereas the pressure of water coming down from up there," he waved vaguely at where Table Mountain loomed over the hillside, "is sufficient to keep it running all the while. Of course, it's not hot, but it does warm in the surface pipes and the summer heat here makes it pleasant. I'm not sure I'd advocate installing them at Hadlicote, though. Too cold." He shivered. "And, you know, it's not a bad idea to take off all those clothes before getting under the water."

The slow smile was reward enough.

As if the Cape Water Company wanted to welcome its newest second lieutenant, the temperature of the shower was just above body heat, although the heat they were generating took some beating. If Harry was famished, Jolyon was ardent. They felt each other's bodies with the hunger of explorers opening new vistas. Pressed together, kissing deeply, swaying under the downpour, the clinch turned to humping. Sometimes Jolyon threw his head far back in ecstasy, the cords of his long neck standing out and tempting Harry to sink his teeth into that enticing throat. In the next second, his own teeth were anointing the side of Harry's neck in a way that would raise a love bite. "Release with me,"

Harry gasped in Jolyon's ear, and their combined movement turned frenzied as the mutual orgasm bonded them together.

Later, dried off, and lying on the bed, a gentle, salty breeze wafting through the open window, the sound of the Atlantic waves threshing on the rocks at the foot of the hillside, they made love more slowly. "We best make up for lost time quickly, Jo. It won't be so easy when we go upcountry in a day or so."

Jolyon rolled over onto his side, head propped on hand and elbow. "So, tell me. No more mystery. You have something up this sleeve you aren't wearing…" he pinched the nearest forearm with his free hand. "Haven't you?"

"Ouch!" Harry ruffled Jolyon's short hair. "General Kitchener extended the freedom to operate that Revers Buller granted me. He arrived on the *Dunottar Castle* as Chief of Staff to Field Marshal Roberts just before Christmas. Bobs has taken over command of the army from Redvers Buller, who is now charged only with the relief of Ladysmith."

"Hah!" Jolyon crowed. "So I was right about Bobs *and* Kitchener!"

A kiss stifled the triumph, and a laugh. "So it seems, O seer. And it turns out I was unfair about Kitchener. He must have heard I was in Cape Town because he summoned me, glared with those frightening eyes of his, bristled his mustache, told me I was recommended on the grounds of my experience in India and because two of his trusted Intelligence officers in the Sudan said he should make use of me."

"Your Richard and Edward?"

"I sent a telegram to Richard telling him what fun I was having out here." He paused, staring into Jolyon's eyes.

"Were you… having fun?"

Harry's expression turned serious. "It's what we're expected to say." And then he brightened again. "But not as much as I would have had if you had been here with me. And now I do have you."

Jolyon made to ask a question, which Harry knew must be on his mind, his having been kidnapped by Harry and told almost nothing about the future, which should have commenced by reporting in to his battery commander. Harry forestalled him by quickly explaining the dreadful events of the past month, including his own experiences up along the Transvaal and Free State borders. "So I have this small roving Special Services command of my own sitting on its collective backside at a tiny railhead called De Aar. Before Kitchener departed for the Natal front he told me to recruit a handful more men and secure enough mules to act as a light gun train and ammunition line for a…"

Jolyon's eyebrows arched up expectantly.

"… one of your pop-pop pom-pom guns."

The eyebrows widened and a look of anxious hope filled Jolyon's bright eyes. "You'd need a lieutenant gunner who could train a crew, if you don't already have all that?"

"Hmmm, I suppose you're right," Harry teased. Then he ruffled Jolyon's hair again, who batted him off irritably, though he chuckled. "I was given written orders and the General informed Colonel Long commanding the 1st Brigade about it, so Major Wincanton—your battery chief—is already apprised that Lieutenant Jolyon Langrish-Smith is now attached to Special Forces Commando Group 28, otherwise dubbed Vane's Horse. And I have the chit to requisition one Vickers Q.F. 1-Pounder, when they arrive, and two gunnies. They'll be down to you to choose, though it would be diplomatic to seek the advice of Major Wincanton. He seems an amiable enough fellow. So, for what it's worth, welcome to Vane's Horse… I know, but I couldn't stop the men naming it so." He gave a self-deprecating huff of a laugh and then an irritable tremor ran through his body. "Damn, but I hate all this hanging about. Now you're here I wish we could just get on, but Kitchener was insistent I remain in Cape Town until he sends orders through as to where best we'll deploy… and anyway we'll need to wait until we can requisition a pom-pom."

Jolyon wasn't listening to the gripe. He rolled onto his back with a heartfelt sigh. After a moment he sucked in another breath until his ribcage creaked and then let it all out in a loud whoop. He sat up. "Harry, you don't know how many times I've dreamed of being with you, stretched out on a blanket under the stars, making the ground shudder with our ecstasy, as the lions roar at the heavens."

Harry laughed happily. "Oh, if only it would be like that! Sadly, we'll be in close contact with my bunch: Sergeant Travis, Stevens, and Norris, not forgetting little Neo, plus whosoever else we drag into this crazy little side war of ours. You won't be able to wash for weeks on end, or shave properly. If you thought the facilities at Woolwich were primitive when it came to relieving yourelf you will think back with fond memories of having had at least the minimum requirement for undertaking the natural bodily tasks in a minimum of dignity. At least we are equipped with packs of Gayetty's medicated paper, but the collective wisdom is that it's better used as hand towels after cleaning up with water from a river or brook… if available. Speaking of which, the water we drink will be brackish and you'll think that tastes sweet compared to the sewage in the war-fouled rivers."

"I won't mind. I'll be with you."

"You might change your mind when I start to stink because I haven't changed clothes for weeks on end—"

"Then I'll smell as badly, so it won't matter. Who's this Neo?"

"A boy of the Barolong tribe. Picked him up outside of Mafeking. He acts as our forward eyes and ears, and he knows which of the veldt plants are edible and which deadly." He took Jolyon's face in his hands and regarded the familiar contours with a serious expression. "It's not much fun really, Jo."

"But we'll be together. If we are, I don't mind what happens."

Harry sighed, and hoped the simplicity of Jolyon's hopes and his trust would survive the horrors he knew with a certainty lay ahead. He managed a tight-lipped smile. "Yes, at least we will have each other—"

"As often as possible, I hope!"

CHAPTER 32 | *Cape Town, January 1900*

"YOU HAD NO NEWS of what's been occurring here since leaving Southampton, I suppose?" They were seated on the front porch and due to the steeply rising hillside enjoyed a view over the roof of the house across the street down to the sea. A light lunch of cold sausage, bread, and beer was following a second shower, which had taken love from bed to bathroom. Neither Harry nor Jolyon wore much of anything in the South African summer heat. Harry had on a pair of knee-length cotton bush shorts and Jolyon shuffled on the bench in a borrowed pair.

Mouth stuffed with sausage, Jolyon answered the question in the only way he could by shaking his head.

"So you won't have heard about Winston Churchill?"

Jolyon gave another quick shake. In spite of the quizzical look that crossed his features, Harry could see he wasn't very interested in the antics of a contemporary he didn't know other than from Harry's letters.

"The Boers captured him. It was a Wednesday as well; November 15."

The day's significance passed Jolyon by. He swallowed a mouthful of chewed sausage meat with an audible gulp. "Why do these bangers taste funny? Not unpleasant," he hastened to add, "just odd."

"They have some curry in them, I think. He was with an armored train making a reconnaissance from Estcourt toward Colenso to discover the Boer movements toward Durban from laagers around Ladysmith."

"Who?"

Harry sighed and smiled with slight indulgence. "Winston."

"In uniform?"

"Not really. Out there, away from regimental nonsense, it's hard to tell one side from another or a journalist from a combatant the way everyone dresses. No he's out here as a civilian reporter. Anyway, he went on this train sortie with two companies of fusileers under Captain Haldane's command and—"

"Haldane!" Jolyon crowed. He sat forward and grinned at Harry. "*He* can't be ashamed of his real name."

"*I* am not ashamed, Jo. I just never *liked* it. Nice fellow, Haldane. He happened to be with us at Malakand, by the way" he added, as if it explained something about their sharing a name. "*Anyway*… the train was ambushed and most of the men aboard captured. There were wounded and dead. As it happens the engine, a couple of the armored cars, and a handful of soldiers managed to get away, so we know more or less what occurred."

Jolyon drank off the last of his beer and put the glass down with an expression of increased interest. "So what did happen?"

Harry shook himself internally. It was hard to believe this handsome man was the youth who such a short time ago had sneered at *army philistinism*. "Somewhat short of Chievely, south of Colenso, they ran into Boers in some strength moving to attack our positions at Estcourt and came under heavy rifle and artillery fire. Haldane ordered the driver to halt and start to reverse. What they could not know is that once the train had passed their concealed position the Boers went and placed a large boulder on the rails around a sharp bend and on a downward slope. With the enemy fire sharpening, the driver urged his steed to greater effort and so crashed into the obstruction at some considerable speed.

"The three trucks in front of the locomotive were derailed. The first was thrown right over, killing those onboard. The third jammed against the second and blocked the line. It seems that while Haldane was instrumental in encouraging a response to the heavy fire our intrepid reporter went to help organize men to attempt to clear the blockage of stone and damaged trucks. The train's only small naval gun was soon put out of action. The Boers had several modern artillery pieces as well as machine guns and Mauser rifles.

"There followed a furious hour's exchange of fire until most of our men were captured or surrendered, including poor Haldane. According to a note the Boer command sent to H.Q. here, Winston was captured while trying to escape up the escarpment. He was unarmed because he'd left his revolver on the locomotive footplate while encouraging the civilian driver to shove aside the truck blocking their path to freedom."

"What bad luck. Do you think he'll be looked after all right?"

Harry laughed. "Oh he's fine. He escaped. Of course, you wouldn't have heard the news on the high seas. It made all the major newspapers, something I'm sure Winston loved, to *be* the news rather than merely reporting it. He's a genuine hero now. He was imprisoned in Pretoria but jumped over a wall on December 12 and somehow got himself across country to Lourenco Marques in Portuguese Mozambique. From there he took ship to Durban and so back to join the Natal Field Force again. Even now I imagine he's champing at the bit to be the first newshound into Ladysmith when the Bull breaks the siege."

"I hope when it comes to it, we have his luck."

"I'd rather have the luck of not being captured in the first place, Jo. The Boer authorities must have been angered at his loss. There's no doubt they knew they were holding the son of Lord Randolph Churchill, a grandson of the 7th Duke of Marlborough. What a bargaining chip he'd have made."

Harry stood, brushed crumbs from his navel, and coughed to clear his throat. "Vicissitudes of conflict, Jo. Ah well... Before I attempt another break-in at headquarters to see if some firm orders have finally come down the wire I have an appointment made a few days ago with a rather well known man. I had this duty to discharge on behalf of Mr. ex-P.O.W. Churchill. Before he dashed off to Durban with General Buller he handed me a note he'd penned especially to this man and begged me to ensure its delivery—a name I'm sure you know?"

An inclined head and go-on look met the question.

"Mr. Rudyard Kipling?"

Jolyon's eyebrows shot up almost to his tidy hairline. "He's here?"

"He is. Dress in something respectable. He's due soon to take us out."

On returning to Cape Town, Harry had gone to see Mr. Kipling. He seriously doubted that his friend's claim of a dubious connection through *The Pioneer* would much impress the great man. After all, they had worked on the venerable Indian newspaper at completely different times. But thanks to Churchill's new fame the author happily accepted the envelope and then engaged him in conversation, enquiring after his experiences in India, the Sudan, and on the South African veldt. Having requested Harry's company on a tour of the main infantry camp in a few days, he took Churchill's letter to read with evident amusement and pleasure.

As prearranged, within the hour Kipling walked up to Harry's cottage and after introductions, the three strolled the half mile to the camp at Sea Point, which Kipling wished to record for future use in articles and stories. As they neared where they thought the camp was located they overtook a private carrying in his hand a large pair of boots. Kipling asked the man if they were on the right road.

"Yes, sir. Are you goin' there? Then you can take these boots," the cheeky soldier said in a strong London Cockney accent. "I 'ave ter get the train at two o'clock, and I ain't goin' ter miss it for no bleedin' boots. 'Ere, take 'old," he went on and thrust the boots into the surprised writer's hand. "You give 'em to Private Dickson, B Company."

When Harry (who forgot he wasn't in uniform and neither was Jolyon) made to reprimand the soldier for his effrontery, Kipling waved him back. He laughed and in singsong voice quoted a stanza of his own poem, *Tommy*:

"I went into a public-'ouse to get a pint o' beer,

The publican 'e up an' sez, 'We serve no red-coats here.'

The girls be'ind the bar they laughed an' giggled fit to die,

I outs into the street again an' to myself sez I:

O it's Tommy this, an' Tommy that, an' 'Tommy, go away;'

But it's 'Thank you, Mister Atkins,' when the band begins to play,

The band begins to play, my boys, the band begins to play,

O it's 'Thank you, Mister Atkins,' when the band begins to play."

He removed his spectacles, cleaned them smartly with a large and spotless handkerchief, and then settled them back on the bridge of his nose while the soldier, Harry, and Jolyon watched the performance in some fascination. "I'm always happy to allow honest Tommy Atkins some leeway, Major Vane," he said gravely.

And to Harry's amazement, Cockney "Tommy Atkins" went and grabbed it. Before he turned to walk off he issued a final command. "And mind, if you cawn't find 'im, Dickson that is, jest take 'em back ter Williams, opposite the White 'Orse."

"I promise I will," Kipling said with a broad smile. "Here." He took out his writing pad from a leather shoulder bag, hastily scribbled a receipt for the boots, and with a grin as cheeky as the soldier's, signed it and handed over the torn-off scrap of paper.

At the sight of the famous man's signature Harry expected to see the penny drop, but the soldier did not notice the name.

"My friend," Kipling said, "you'll get your head knocked off when you get back to the guard-room."

"What for?" the man asked in blissful ignorance as he departed.

Laughing, Harry, Jolyon, and Kipling continued their way toward the camp. But as it turned out the private with boots to give away wasn't the only soldier who failed to recognize the author the private soldiers called their "brother and father." No sooner were they inside the railings than a young and consequently officious military policeman accosted Kipling, who was in the lead.

"Oi! What are you doing here? You must get out of here, you know, sharp!"

"I'm taking these boots to Private Dickson," Kipling said in a genial tone of voice.

"Well, you ought to take them to the guard tent and not go wandering about the camp like this. Hoppit! Out of it, now!"

As Harry already knew, Kipling had a pass from the Commander-in-Chief to go wherever he pleased in South Africa, so the situation amused him. Jolyon, torn between outrage and chuckles, tugged at Harry's sleeve to urge him to intervene. Just then a police sergeant rode up and addressed Kipling with reverence. "Please, sir, I lived ten years with the man as you get your tobacco from in Brighton. Anything I can do for you?"

Kipling aimed a sly wink at his two companions. "Oh, yes," he said, lifting a finger at the hapless policeman. "I want this man taken away and killed!"

"Absolutely, Mr. Kipling, sir." The sergeant turned smartly in his saddle and snapped out, "Jameson! Off you go, smartish, lad, and get yourself killed immediately!"

The youth looked more confused than alarmed because he had done his duty.

"I forgive you, son," Kipling told him with a warm smile. "I give you a stay of execution."

So Private Dickson had his boots, Jameson lived to see another day, and when the story got out minutes later there was great mirth and loud cheering about the tents of B Company.

"It's interesting, is it not, the close protection of the camps by police?" Kipling said as they continued to explore. "I have learned in the short time I've moved among headquarters personnel that the army and civilian authorities are dreadfully exercised about Boer spies."

"Even here, sir, in the heart of British territory?" Jolyon looked horrified at the thought.

"That's so. The Boer spy is feared. He is thought to be the servant of an agency hardly less invisible and powerful than the Indian thugee. We are told that his machinations are as patent as his secrecy is perfect." Kipling waved at a line of painted iron railings they were passing. "One morning a section of railings surrounding picketed horses is found demolished; on another the whole milk supply of a camp is infected by some poisonous bacillus. It seems almost incredible, but it is true that all these mishaps are attributed to Boer treachery." The twinkle in his eyes suggested amusement at the folly of humanity. "In the popular imagination the Boer agent moves undiscovered and stealthily amid the daily life of Cape Town—at noon in the busy street, in the club smoke-room, in the hotel dining-room—perhaps a woman this time, arrayed in frocks from Paris, and keeping a table charmed by her conversation. All fine material for a novel of sleuthing such as my colleague Arthur Conan Doyle might write. (He's around here somewhere as well, by the way.) And yet the objects of this superstitious dread are allowed to possess qualities that make some of our officers dislike this business of warring against them. Have you yet met a Boer Major Vane?"

Harry dodged the question on the grounds that he hadn't actually *known* any Boers and he had no inclination to bring up the matter of those two boys they'd shot. "The only ones I've so far encountered fired on me from a great distance. "I have spoken with some of the Cape colonists—"

"Ah, so have I, many times previously, but they do not a Boer make. An English officer of slight acquaintance told me that he loves the Boers even though he is fighting them. Perhaps understandably his peers find this a bit shocking. His father, however, was a colonist and the neighboring Boers were like brothers of his. I think many families out here are more divided by the war than our government realizes. This officer had been in houses where he knew there were guns stored for the enemy—whosoever that might be and almost certainly the British at some point again—and where the sons would probably be fighting him in the field. And yet, he said, the people almost cried when he went away. 'People here say they're like

353

animals,' he said. 'At least they're like animals in this, that once you make them distrust you, you'll never win their confidence again. And they don't trust us.'"

Kipling sighed. "He was quite right." He turned to Harry. "You are hardly alone in not having met and conversed with a real Afrikaaner Boer. South Africa is a very different place from the North-West Frontier. There, as you know, the intrepid political will come to know many of the tribesmen, not perfectly at all, but at least sufficiently to form an impression of character. Here, half the officers and men who have been wounded have never seen one of the enemy. But if it would please you we could go and view some?"

"How easy it must have been for those navigators of old like Bartolomeu Dias to think they had found the way around the southern tip of Africa, only to become becalmed in what is marked here as False Bay." Jolyon glanced up from the map spread across his knees. It showed the immediate region of Cape Town.

"Hardly becalmed, as you can see," Kipling shouted, leaning forward. "Dias named it the Cape of Storms, and he perished in such a tempest on his fourth voyage."

Without raised voice the noise of bursting surf from the great waves rolling onto the cliffs immediately below the train made it close to impossible to be heard. The rails hugged the shore of the bay and carried them from Cape Town to Simonstown. Sharing a look at the map, Harry could see the sharply hooked claw of steep and barren land that stretched southward to the Cape of Good Hope and Bellows Rock, where it divided the Atlantic from the Indian Ocean. The mainland ran about as far southward on the eastern extreme, so that the arm partly enclosed the waters of False Bay. In the hollow of its elbow nestled Simonstown. As the train rounded the corner of Glencairn, Simonstown's white houses appeared, clustered on the sea-beaten foot of a hill that swept upward to the silence of flying white clouds. And all the while, above the rattle of iron wheels on rails, everything reverberated to the assault of the rollers. Close in-shore half a dozen cruisers were lying sluggishly among the deep, moving waters. Above the tidy naval station the St. George's ensign floated from the shore flagstaff. The scene could not have been more removed from the dust, heat, and parched landscape of the veldt near Mafeking.

In the full glare and heat of afternoon, they climbed down from the carriage. The prisoners—some four hundred and fifty in number had been landed from *H.M.S. Penelope*, which sat at anchor in the bay—were encamped about a hundred yards out of the town. Jolyon was first to express any emotion at the initial sight of the prison camp. "Oh! I imagined there would be cells hewed from the rock or dungeons, or something…"

Harry couldn't tell whether his surprise expressed disappointment or relief. Just beyond the town the hillside took a gentler slope where a lawn of sea-grass fell into the sea. Some men swam in the energetic water calmed only a little by Simonstown's projecting bulk from the surf's excess.

Jolyon tapped Harry's arm. "It's… the place, charming!"

Enclosed inside a double fence, the prisoners were quartered in languid comfort. Kipling looked disconcerted as if now he was here he wished he might be somewhere else. Three faces pressed against the wires and stared.

"It's like being at Regent's Park Zoo," Jolyon said almost under his breath.

Harry knew exactly what he meant, like peering at a cage full of newly arrived exotic animals that had cost a great deal of money… and maybe a life or two. Appropriate to the thought, the hoarse braying of African penguins crowding parts of the beach could be heard in the gaps between the roar of successive waves breaking. Harry examined the fine, big men, stalwart and burned brown by the sun, stern looking, massive of jaw and forehead, molded after a grand pattern. These, then were the enemy, and while they did not bear any physical resemblance to those hillmen he'd spent time with on the North-West Frontier's mountains, they did share that air of large contentment worn by those who live much alone and out of doors; so different to the urban-bred European with his modern fussy comforts. Harry felt an affinity with men who counted a tent and a hard bed a benefit—like Richard and Edward: nomads at heart. He'd never thought of himself in that light, but now seeing the Boer prisoners he realized how very different the Harry Smythe-Vane of Benthenham College was to the man now looking on with a deep sympathy at his enemies.

They were lying on the grass, standing in little groups, sauntering up and down in the hot sunshine, playing cricket with ponderous energy, bathing and sporting in the clear apple-green water.

Kipling must have felt a similar emotion. "They're encamped on such a spot as people pay large sums for the privilege of pitching their tents," he said quietly. "Look at them, numerous enough to make themselves independent, the sun shining on their bodies, the sea breeze blowing. They have food and drink, and tobacco to smoke."

"And they are free to swim," Jolyon pointed out.

Harry counted twenty men. They splashed about, fooling around in the shallows, or swam farther out from the shore swimming powerfully for exercise. Where they bathed an eight-oar gig from H.M.S. *Powerful* swung on the swell, but Harry thought the boat's presence was not so much to prevent escape as to render assistance to tired swimmers, for even as they watched one lad reached out for the gunwale and a spare rower extended hands to clamp him safely.

Harry and Jolyon looked on with interest as Kipling engaged a few of the men who came to the fence. They were the face of the Old Testament, descendants of the Dutchmen who had defended themselves for fifty years against all the power of Spain when Spain was the greatest power in the world, raw-boned big men, hard-bitten farmers who had fought the numerous sub-tribes of the Xosa, Zulu, and Sotho to carve out their kraals. One who spoke English with an Afrikaaner accent thick enough to hack through addressed Kipling in a goading tone. "You, man. Can you tell us why we're here?"

The sun glinted off the writer's spectacles as he shook his head with some amusement at the offered truculence in the rhetorical demand. "It is because you have suffered the misfortune to be made captive after losing a fight to our troops."

"So, man, then you tell us why there is this war."

"Because you want to beat us out of Africa and we do not wish to go."

Muttering broke out among the others when one of their number translated, though Harry could see by their quick reactions that most of the prisoners understood English well enough.

"That's not the reason," the spokesman snapped back. "Now you've begun the war, we will drive you British into the sea. But if you had been content with what you had and left us to our own, we would not have interfered with you."

"Apart from our needing a port," another added forcefully."

"Aye, and having our independence recognized," shouted a third from the back of the little group.

The first speaker planted one fist on his hips and thrust the other out belligerently at Kipling, quite relaxed now as if debate were his natural element.

"I'll tell you what is the real cause of this war of yours. It's all those damned capitalists. They want to steal our country, the Unholy Trinity! You know who they are—Rhodes, Milner, and Chamberlain. They want to divide the Rand between them after we're all cowed, they think!" He spat on the grass at his feet. He was referring to Cecil Rhodes—with some good reason since the man had attempted to seize Boer lands before—Alfred Milner the Cape Governor, and Joseph Chamberlain the British government's Colonial Secretary whose policies lay behind every move made in South Africa. And Evan, Harry thought.

Kipling shook his head, as much in sorrow at the man's failure to understand the bigger picture as in exasperation. "But the gold mines of the Rand are the property of the shareholders. And many of them are foreigners, so whatever the outcome of the war, whatever government rules, the mines will still belong to the shareholders."

"What are we fighting for then?"

"Because you hate us." Kipling smiled broadly, which only seemed to irritate the man on the other side of the fence all the more. "Because you have armed yourself and attacked us, so naturally we feel it necessary to fight back."

"It's an evil thing to steal our country."

"My good man, we are only protecting ourselves and our interests. No one wants your country."

"Pah! The damned capitalists and the Jews do."

Kipling tried to reason one more time after taking a long breath. "If you had kept on friendly terms with us there wouldn't be this war. But you are determined to drive us out of South Africa—"

"We never wanted that!"

"You just said a moment ago that you would drive us into the sea, and that's what you want to do. You want a great Afrikaaner Republic with all of South Africa speaking Dutch, under your flag—"

"That's what we want!"

"Yaw, yaw," said the others, "and that's what we're going to have."

"Well there you are," Kipling said, spreading his arms wide. "That's the reason for the war."

The first speaker pressed close, his cheeks red with the effort of convincing his interlocutor. "No, no. You know it's the damned capitalists and Jews who have caused the war."

Jolyon wandered off toward the beach and Harry followed as the circular argument began a second revolution. After a while Kipling rejoined them. He sighed heavily. "Of course, they have a point about the 'capitalists,' as they call the gold mining companies. Gold is the root of this evil without any doubt. I wonder at the meaningful coincidence, but only this morning when breakfasting someone left behind an old copy of the *Newcastle Chronicle* dated December 5. Idly flipping through it, an article caught my eye. I tore it out and kept it. Here."

He pulled a news page from his shoulder bag.

"The correspondent made the point back then that sides might well be hard to take in this conflict. He was not at all enamored of what we are here to fight for and gives this pen picture of the precious *Uitlander* refugees whom he had seen."

Harry read with Jolyon peering over his shoulder.

It must be a great relief to the military commander in Natal to know that the 30,000 or 40,000 Uitlanders of Johannesburg had left that city before the outbreak of hostilities. Otherwise we should have had Cornishmen and Jew boys from the golden city whining and imploring our generals to come and save them. Nothing can exceed the contempt of the real Englishman for this veritable scum of the earth. It makes our blood boil to think that the pick of the British army is engaged in mortal combat to make things easy for the sharpers and swindlers who fatten on the illicit profits of the gold industry. On the other hand, one cannot help respecting the Boers, who are fighting for their hearths and homes. It will be one of General Buller's chief difficulties, when the troops draw near to Pretoria and Johannesburg, to know how to deal with the armed rabble who will crowd round him ready to offer advice and to seize on all lands and property within reach. Verily the lust for gold brings out the worst passions in the human race!

"Hmmm," was all Harry said as he handed Kipling the page back.

"Often times there are many more sides to a story, are there not? Shall we return?" He seemed to shake the Afrikaaner dust from his boots as he strode briskly back toward the town. As he went, Kipling spoke in a tone suggestive of composition. "So our prisoners blinked in the sun and listened to the boiling surf's organ-note, and brooded on the most beautiful picture I have ever seen: masses of bare rock towering into the bright sky, and an endless pageant of seas rolling grandly homeward from the south, from the infinite purple and blue of the Indian Ocean, grounding at the edge of the green lawn and showering snow upon the hot rocks." He gave them a twinkly smile. "And squatted in the ordure of their own misunderstanding."

Other than the eternal beat of the sea all was peace and quiet at the station, where a train waited for its scheduled return, twenty miles north to Cape Town. With the departure only due in ten minutes, the afternoon heat cooling pleasantly, the three men stood enjoying the clean ocean-driven breeze rather than board and endure a minute more than necessary of the stifling compartment. Kipling spoke as much to himself as to anyone, quietly murmuring a stanza that filled Harry with disquiet as he watched, fascinated by Jolyon's gentle swaying movement, balanced easily on the balls of his feet; a sight so precious against Kipling's words it made his throat clench painfully.

'Soldier, soldier come from the wars,
O then I know it's true I've lost my true love!'
'An' I tell you truth again—when you've lost the feel o' pain
You'd best take me for your true love.'

> *True love! New love!*
> *Best take 'im for a new love,*
> *The dead they cannot rise, an' you'd better dry your eyes,*
> *An' you'd best take 'im for your true love.*

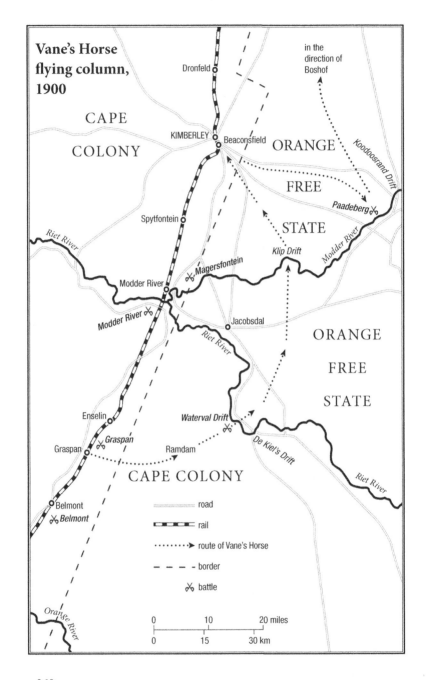

Vane's Horse
flying column,
1900

CAPE
COLONY

ORANGE

FREE

STATE

Dronfeld

in the
direction of
Boshof

KIMBERLEY Beaconsfield

Koodoosrand Drift

Paadeberg

Spytfontein

Klip Drift

Riet River

Modder River

Magersfontein

Modder River

Modder River

Jacobsdal

ORANGE

FREE

STATE

Riet River

Enselin

Waterval Drift

Graspan Graspan

Ramdam

De Kiel's Drift

Riet River

CAPE COLONY

Belmont
Belmont

Orange River

road

rail

route of Vane's Horse

border

battle

0	10	20 miles
0	15	30 km

CHAPTER 33 | *Orange Free State, February 1900*

THE EARTH SHUDDERED. An almost perfect dome of dirt, coarse veldt grass, and metal shrapnel erupted barely thirty feet in front of Harry—frightful forerunner of a field gun's dull boom. The range was so close that the cannon's report arrived a split-second after the shell's burst. His horse nearly threw him as it reared up on hind legs. Suddenly, an avenue of detonations, brown-gray trees of death, roiling like leaves in a wild wind, opened up around Vane's Horse. From the billowing smoke came a rain of soil and stones. Miraculously, no one fell.

Harry wheeled and took flight for the shelter of a small township of anthills just passed, surrounded by the rest of the flying column. He heard Jolyon shouting, urging Fletcher and Jarvis to rush the ammunition mules—and Neo, who was riding one of the animals—into the fire-shade of the sun-hardened sandcastles. Sergeant Travis yelled at Stevens and Norris to get their mounts into cover, and then ran after Harry as he climbed the nearest hill that towered up like the outpouring of a crazed Gothic architect. As they both attained the narrowed summit, scrambling for uneven hand and footholds, it was instinctive to press close to the hard extrusions of untold ant labor so as to avoid providing the Boer marksmen with easy targets. Harry prayed that no deadly snake had taken shelter in the convoluted fumaroles that riddled anthills. Below Jolyon's commands rang out faintly against the sprackle of Boer Mauser fire.

"How many, sir?"

Harry glanced around his spur at Travis. "I don't know." He raised his field glasses for a brief look, cursing that he hadn't dusted the lenses down, all too aware that if the foe spotted any reflected light, he'd be dead in seconds. Bullets whipped overhead with the weird sucking noise of near misses or zinged off the anthill spires in wicked spurts of sand. The coarse grains stung when they struck bare skin. As the old hands said, if you heard the bullet there was no point flinching because it had missed; you never hear the one that kills you.

"So much for the idea that Cronjé's troops have all retired to a laager somewhere between Jacobsdal and the Modder fucking river. What the flying shit are big guns doing here at Waterval Drift?"

Harry ignored the outburst. "Do you know it?"

"Not well. I had some distant family lived back there at Ramdam and I went fishing off the Drift with some neighbors once. That high ground to the north, why didn't they take a commanding position up there?"

Travis had a good point. Harry looked at the three long gray humps of barren rock rising from the grassy plain, the nearest protrusion only about fifteen hundred yards from the ford across the Riet River.

"A commanding position, but also a trap," Harry thought aloud. "I don't think they're supposed to contest the crossing. They're a rearguard waiting for contact with whatever we might send this way around their main camp at Jacobsdal, and a sloppy and unprepared one, it seems. I bet they'll pull back across the Drift if we attack."

"Attack!" Travis's tone voiced his doubt. "We're outnumbered. I'm still wondering how come we caught them on the hop? A few seconds more and we'd have ridden right in among the bastards."

"I know, but we must have surprised them. You're right we were almost on top of them before they got off a shot. Perhaps they anticipated a bigger force, just didn't spot us in time. They're better armed than I'd have thought, though. But not many men. Two quick-firing field pieces, French Creusots by the look, and crews, maybe less than twenty riflemen. No pom-poms, thank God."

At that moment, the unmistakeable sound of a pom-pom whumped once. Harry risked a second look around the rock-hard sandy turret he clung to and saw the ranging shot go in. The common shell blazed a trail and…

Smack on, Jo!

The dull thumping settled into a steady rhythm as Jolyon, with gunners Tonkins and Cowden, began to take a terrible toll on the Boers, who immediately hitched mules to their gun trains and began to pull back toward Waterval Drift, their route to safety across the Riet. Several figures giving covering fire vanished in puffs of blood and bone as a one-pounder pom-pom shell took them out. It was grim satisfaction to Harry that at last they had turned the weapon on the Boers, who had so far wreaked terrible execution among Tommies with their British made pom-pom guns.

"All praise to the pom-pom," Harry breathed.

"I'd rather praise the Afrikaaner Lord for throwing up antheaps when we needed them for cover. But it looks like you read the situation right."

"They're running for it all right. Come on."

The pom-pom below stuttered once and fell silent.

Brushing ants disturbed by their mountaineering from his khakis, Harry went across to the gunnery team, who were rushing through the post-firing procedure in a by-the-book way. Fletcher started hitching one of the mules to pull the lightweight gun train as Jarvis shut down the ammo wagon, cursing loudly at the stubborn mule supposed to tow it.

"Good shooting, lads."

"We need to refill the water canisters, Har— Major."

There was the slightest tremor detectible in Jolyon's voice, but probably, Harry thought, only by someone who knew him well. He glanced down to where Cowden was removing the lower barrel case plug to let the eleven pints of coolant water gush out as Tonkins busily oiled the interior of the barrel to prevent corrosion from the acrid propellant residue. Cowden stepped smartly back to avoid the draining water and a strong tang of the glycerine mixed in with it assailed Harry's nostrils and made him sneeze.

"Gets you that way, sir," said Tonkins with a tentative grin. The gunnies weren't yet used to Harry and trod warily of his untested temper.

"The damn thing was leaking, sir," Cowden spoke up defensively. "It's not a good screw."

"As the actress said to the bishop." Jarvis snorted at his own wit.

Harry hid a smile at the cheap music-hall joke. "Will that affect the firing rate?"

Jolyon nodded unhappily. "We might manage to tighten it up a bit more next time," he said pointedly at Cowden, who scowled.

"Can't help it if we was given a faulty unit… sir."

"Are they likely to return?" Jolyon jabbed an elbow in the direction of the Waterval Drift.

"No." A haze of dust raised by hooves and wheels well beyond the riverbank gave truth to Harry's assertion. The Boer unit was falling back toward Jacobsdal. He turned back in time to catch a look of relief pass momentarily across Jolyon's smoke-smeared face.

"Then I'll have time with Fletcher—he's good with his hands—"

"So they say." Now it was the turn of Norris to poke low fun. He approached from his watching position with a mean smirk on his face.

"—to sort something out," Jolyon continued doggedly. "But we used more water than I thought we would. We can refill the canisters at the river, so long as we're not going to come under fire."

"We'll be needing it again before long," Harry said quietly. He rounded on Norris. "You and Stevens ride ahead to the river. Be careful. Make sure those Boers are following the river's edge, which means they're headed for Jacobsdal and Magersfontein. That's where Cronjé's army is dug in holding General Methuen's divisions at bay."

Minutes later the small force followed in good order toward the drift and joined Stevens on the southern shore of the Riet. The river, about fifty yards across, meandered between several raised banks of shingle and at the deepest stretches reached no higher than the hock joint of Norris's horse. He turned in the saddle and waved them forward. The retreating Boers' field guns had left deep tracks in the damp sandy slope down to the water and through the shingle, and Tonkins leading the pom-pom gun mule took advantage of the compacted trail.

Harry glanced at Jolyon. He was showing nothing on his face that others would note, but Harry knew him well enough to see the telltale signs of nervousness mixed with exhilaration at his first taste of battle action.

"Why did they run off so quickly? I'd have thought they were supposed to prevent us crossing."

Harry shrugged. "They might be the rearguard and pulling back to the Jacobsdal laager or the redoubt at Magersfontein. Maybe Cronjé is concentrating his troops as Bobs brings the infantry up the rails."

They reined in beside Stevens to watch the gun carriage start to cross, with Sergeant Travis cursing at Fletcher in charge of the mule pulling the ammunition wagon. "Keep the fucking beast in line, can't you!"

"General French can't be more than a couple of hours behind us." Harry glanced back as if he might see a dust devil rising from the trailing cavalry regiments. "Stevens. Gallop back and inform the general that Waterval Drift is clear. We'll head north toward the Modder and keep checking to the west in case the Boers are making any moves toward Bloemfontcin."

Stevens nodded curtly, pulled his mount's head around and set off at a high pace, back the way they had come across the plain.

Harry spared no more than a second in watching the galloper's dust retreat toward Ramdam where General John French was gathering his cavalry force. They had much to do and had already come a long and dusty way since leaving De Aar, where he had outlined the strategy and the part Vane's Horse had to play in it.

That was three days in the past.

"Now we take the war to the Boers," Harry had begun. The constituent members of Vane's Horse were grouped around him beside a pen holding their mounts and pack animals a hundred yards from the junction sidings at De Aar. Neo stood guard a few yards away over a wigwam of the men's Lee-Enfield .303 rifles. The plain was a cloud of hot, whirling sand that shrouded near objects as closely as a fog, but instead of the damp coldness of a London pea souper, the Karoo radiated heat that sent the thermometer up to 135°F, even in the shade of the spreading Jackalberry tree to which the instrument was attached and under which Vane's Horse were gathered.

Stevens had to be dragged from the siding where he was admiring a stationary locomotive unit. "It's a GCR 3rd Class 4-4-0, one of the Neilson engines."

"Come on, Stevens. The major's waiting," they heard Travis say.

"It's just that they're putting everything on the Western railway, Trav! That loco is supposed to serve the suburban services to Salt River, Wynberg, and Simonstown."

"Enough!"

It was February 8, 1900. The depot was abustle with troops waiting for places on the armored trains running them up the line to Modder River where the stalled British force was dug in. They faced the army of General Piet Cronjé entrenched at Jacobsdal and Magersfontein, where the Freestaters and

Trasvaalers had brought the Highlanders under General Methuen's command to an ignominious halt in December.

"The plan is simple enough. On February 3, detachments of the Highland Brigade headed west and seized Koedoesberg. Not a strategic position. However, while we need to oust the Boers who seized the Cape Colony town, the main reason is to act as a feint . It's hoped it will take General Cronjé's eye off the build-up progressing at Modder River. And, more importantly…" he swept his gaze across the half-circle of men, "…off what we're about to do."

A shuffle of increased interest passed through Vane's Horse as Harry raised his water bottle and took a swig of the thoroughly boiled water. Drinking the waters of the Riet and Modder rivers, swollen with decaying corpses of horses, pack animals, and men, had decimated British ranks with enteric fever.

"The recently arrived battalions go up the rails to join the regiments bogged down since December. Sitting where he is, Cronjé prevents us getting through to Kimberley. Bobs wants the siege of Kimberley lifted as a matter of urgency so he needs the Boers dislodged from Magersfontein. To achieve this, General French will take the cavalry regiments on a wide sweep to the east across the Riet and Modder rivers. The high-speed flanking movement will threaten Cronjé's communications with Bloemfontein, which should spook him enough into making a retreat along the Modder toward the Orange capital. The gamble is that Cronjé won't accept a British cavalry assault alone on his siege lines will succeed. By the time he realizes French is actually maneuvering around him to reach Kimberley, it will be too late for him to do much about it—and more importantly, he will be on the run with the entire weight of our infantry regiments hard on his heels."

Harry paused for a moment to gulp some more water.

He and Jolyon had set out from Cape Town in the final days of January, bringing with them two gunnery corporals, Cowden and Tonkins, who Harry had part-persuaded and part-bullied free of the R.F.A. 14th Battery by waving Kitchener's order in the face of its commanding officer and citing "a need greater than yours… sir." They were reunited with Vane's Horse at the major De Aar junction. In Harry's absence Travis, Stevens, and Norris had recruited Fletcher and Jarvis, young Cape Colonists who cited patriotism and the desire to protect their families' farms as reason to join up, but who Harry thought just wanted relief from the boredom of helping out on the land. They were to look after the mules and small ammunition wagon containing the one-pounder pom-pom shells, belts, spares and repair kit, as well as the troop's rifle ammunition and food supplies.

"Our task is to blaze that trail ahead of General French's cavalry," Harry continued. "We'll move at speed but armed with the pom-pom gun here, so we will have some teeth if we encounter any enemy between here and the Riet River, and then on across the spit of land to the Modder River… which we're almost certain to do because Cronjé's lines of communication with Bloemfontein lie across our path. We'll keep in contact with the cavalry and sweep through north to Klip Drift on the Modder and then curve back in a northwesterly direction toward Kimberley. Our job's done when the cavalry engages the Boer siege lines. After that, it will be down to the generals as to what follows."

An hour later, with the horses, mules, wagons, and Jolyon's pom-pom, Vane's Horse rattled north aboard a train to Graspan where they alighted and prepared to set off in an easterly direction toward Ramdam and the Riet River. Elements of the 14th Brigade continued on to rendezvous with General Chermside's force at Enslin, seven miles farther on. At Graspan an air of organized chaos reigned as troops of the 11th Brigade sorted themselves into temporary tent lines ready for the infantry push planned to follow in the steps of General French and the cavalry dash for the Riet, Modder, and Kimberley. Though he'd not met him, Harry had some form with French, formerly the colonel in charge of cavalry in India. Alfred Winner's words of five years ago in the Café Royal came back to him: *Not bad to have the Army's Assistant Adjutant-General praise you…*

And so in the rush across the plain from Ramdam, they almost rode headlong into the remnant of Boer forces retreating toward Magersfontein through Jacobsdal.

Harry heard the faint shuffle as Jolyon elbowed his way on his belly up the sandy slope. Below the ridge on which they lay the ground sloped away before reaching the crumbled edge of a shallow cliff above the Modder River. The shallows of Klip Drift were clear in the muddy water, and so was the Boer laager on the river's north bank. It wasn't big. "Ten wagons in a triangle," Harry said. "And they command the crossing. What do you reckon?"

Jolyon raised his own field glasses and peered through them for a few seconds. "They've got the afternoon sun against them. If we place the gun just under this ridge, but with the muzzle in that dip over there so it's out of sight of the camp, and get a ranging shot, we could give them a headache before they know we're here."

Harry examined Jolyon's suggested disposition. "You're right. We'll open fire when the sun's just above the treeline. In the lengthening light they won't so easily see any dust we may kick up. I don't want them getting off a runner to Magersfontein. Then we can get the men up. Neo can hold the animals. French can't be far behind with the cavalry if they seized both drifts across the Riet."

Jolyon pressed his side against Harry after glancing back to see that they were hidden from the rest of Vane's Horse. The others, gathered in close formation behind a clump of stunted acacia trees, were keeping still and well out of sight of the enemy across the river until hearing from Harry as to the lie of the land.

Jolyon jabbed Harry with his elbow. "I know we're together, but I miss you. We never have the chance to be alone."

Harry's sigh reflected Jolyon's feeling. He swayed his head to the side until the brim of his bush hat brushed against Jolyon's head. They both turned in harmony and lips met, uncaring of dried, cracked skin. "Come, we've seen enough."

They rolled sideways to scrabble back from the ridge to a point where it was safe to stand in a half-crouch. As he turned Harry was sure he saw from the corner of his eye a movement behind them. He squinted into the low sun's glare. No more movement, but he was convinced someone had been looking up at him and Jolyon from down in the scree beyond which the rest of the troop waited. It might have been a head ducking down. Because he was unsure he didn't say anything to Jolyon.

"Let's get the gun set up."

Fifteen minutes later, Jolyon risked one final glance over the sandy ridge and gave Cowden the signal to fire the ranging shell. The thump and the gun's recoil shattered the silence. He and Harry scrutinized the scene before them through their glasses as a mushroom of sand and smoke plumed up some ten feet to the right of the laager and well back.

"Bring the range down one turn. Traverse left two degrees!"

Keeping crouched down, Jarvis staggered up from the ammo wagon under the weight of two pom-pom ammunition belts as Cowden slammed the control on the gun into automatic fire. Across the river Harry could just make out the panic among the Boers as they ran to their weapons positions between the closely drawn up jawbone wagons. Two men fell into their prepared foxholes, a comic tumble of arms and legs.

Pom-pom-pom-pom…

The explosive shells tracked left and right as Cowden ranged in on the perimeter of the laager. From across the river sharp cracks of Mauser fire answered. Harry ducked as bullets whipped into the ridge, but the light was against the Boers whereas it threw the Boer wagons into sharp relief and made of the laager an easy target. To his right Travis, Norris, Stevens, and Fletcher added to the noise with their Lee-Enfield rifles. The pom-pom gun fell silent. Tonkins immediately stripped the exhausted belt out and slapped in a fresh one he took from Jarvis. Within thirty seconds Cowden opened up again and poured lethal shot into the distant camp as Jolyon shouted instructions on aiming and range. Bright flashes of explosions lasted a second before smoke billowed out from each hit. Wagons flew to pieces under the onslaught. Men fell and shouts of pain echoed up. Looking back, Harry saw a dust cloud advancing on them.

"The cavalry's almost here. Give us cover," Harry yelled at the gun crew. "Travis, get everyone else down to the edge of the river. We have to get across while they're still in confusion."

Weaving to throw off the enemy's aim, Harry ran down the sandy slope and leapt over the rocky lip that formed the upper reaches of the riverbank. Half-sliding, half-jumping like a springbok, he made it to the thick scrub lining the river's shallow edge. Slapping feet and several thumps announced Travis, Norris, Stevens, and Fletcher. A second later, as Harry raised his rifle, another flurry of grit thrown up and Jolyon landed next to him.

"You should be back up there," Harry hissed.

"I want to be near you, if you're going to do crazy things like running into enemy fire."

A series of trumpet calls sounded and a moment later the growing thunder of hooves filled the air. Following the line of pom-pom tracery, the British cavalrymen hurtled over the lip to the side of where Vane's Horse lay crouched. In moments, cascades of water were flung up as hundreds of horsemen raced across the Klip Drift and were in among the Boers across the river. Harry led the way, wading up to his knees, following the horsemen into the fray. Behind, the pom-pom gun ceased firing to avoid hitting friendly troopers.

Jolyon was at his side as they raced up the shallow slope on the other side of the Modder. A bearded man took aim at Harry as he ran toward the nearest wagon. The Boer's finger tightened on the trigger. Harry threw himself sideways, hooked an arm around Jolyon's knee, and brought him down. The bullet zinged into the earth a foot away, having passed through air where Harry had been a second before. He rolled away from Jolyon, yelling at him to keep down, brought his rifle up over his spread body, and loosed three shots. He didn't know if he hit the Boer, but there was no answering fire.

It was all over within minutes of French's cavalry arriving. Survivors of the Boer contingent upped sticks and melted away into the darkening landscape of scrub and antheaps.

The General was impatient to be on his way but he was obliged to wait out the hours of darkness for the 6th, 7th, and 9th Infantry Divisions to catch up and take control of the river crossing thus ensuring that Piet Cronjé's lines of communication on the southern bank to Bloemfontein and any reinforcements were cut. Meanwhile, the cavalrymen were glad of the Boers' abandoned supplies in the laager. When Harry reported in shortly after midnight, French grunted a modicum of appreciation for the advance work. His square head move stiffly in line with his shoulders as though he didn't much like turning his neck, the face all downward planes, drooping eyebrows, and drooping mustache. "Major Vane. You were at that fracas at Chitral, were you not?"

Harry wasn't sure what that had to do with the action just ended, but agreed that he had indeed been present at the siege.

"Well done. Now I'm in a hurry. I gave my word to the Field Marshal that I would relieve Kimberley by…" he glanced at his timepiece, "…today, so no time left in which to accomplish that task. Here's what I need you to do for me…"

"We're to ride cover on the west," Harry informed his men, "and alert the general if the Boers try a break out northeast from Magersfontein and threaten our left flank as the cavalry approaches Kimberley. It'll be a dash and the pace of our mules will slow us down too much, so Tonkins, Cowden, and Neo you remain here with the ammo wagon and pom-pom gun. Fletcher and Jarvis, mount up and ride with us."

"Work on that water tap," Jolyon ordered his gunnery crew. "See if you can find a suitable spare among the Boer ordnance. I hate leaving it behind," he added to Harry.

French's cavalry set out from Klip Drift at 9:30 am on February 15 and were soon engaged by a substantial Boer force sent to block them. Vane's Horse rode into rifle fire coming from the river in the east while artillery shells rained from the hills in the northwest. In a short space of time faces running with sweat under the burning sun were streaked with sticky sand and cordite. The enemy were hidden behind the dust cloud thrown up by four thousand galloping hooves, but every few minutes Harry ordered a slower pace so they could all fire blindly from the saddle in the hope of keeping Boer heads down.

The route to Kimberley lay straight ahead through the crossfire. There was little choice left to French. Trumpet calls sounded and the men increased the already furious pace to a bold cavalry charge down the middle. As waves of horses galloped forward, the Boers poured down fire from the two sides. However the speed of the attack, screened by the massive cloud of dust the cavalry was throwing up, proved successful. The Boers panicked and abandoned the siege line. By that evening, General French relieved the town of Kimberley after some initial difficulty in convincing the defenders via heliograph that they weren't Boers.

"What a blasted place," Jolyon muttered. He walked his mount beside Harry's through what had once been streets and dwellings, offices and churches, now indistinguishable from the skeletal mineshaft workings amid blue hills of detritus. Ragged figures emerged from the dubious safety of shelters and warrens that resembled nothing more than the anthills of the plain. Here the inhabitants had hidden from unending bombardment.

General French, whether by intent or neglect, avoided Lieutenant Colonel Robert Kekewich, the local military authority and, with his officers gathered around him, went straight to see the political power of South Africa, Cecil Rhodes. In the general confusion, no one objected to a lowly subaltern accompanying Major Harry Vane and so Jolyon became one of those hastily introduced to the man who had sustained Kimberley throughout the siege. In spite of the filth and grimness of surroundings and personal attire and the sense of relief, Harry noted with an inwardly wry smile the way Rhodes held onto Jolyon's hand and the glitter of his regard.

"You can't really appreciate how things have been for those living here," Rhodes began, as much for the benefit of the gathered newsmen as for the military. "Imagine, daily, the warning signal from the conning tower, the clamor of bells and whistles, the sudden dash for shelter, and then the hum and roar, as loud and insistent as wind in a chimney, of the huge iron shells flying through the air, intent on death. Imagine waiting, hoping, praying that what the Boer gunner has sent hasn't got your name on it, and then the guilty relief at the noise of a falling building because if you can hear it, it isn't the one in which you are cowering, or the scream of some human creature who is nothing but a mass of steaming offal when you come up five seconds later.

"Think of this repeated sometimes as much as sixty or seventy times a day, night being the only quiet blessing. Can you wonder that men fear to walk upright, that they are listless and—in spite of the joy of the salvation you have brought—dispirited? And all this fear and horror has been borne on empty stomachs but for the scant quantity of horseflesh rationed each day. To the horrors of partial starvation the constant fear of a violent death were added. Mothers have seen their babies die because there was no milk or other suitable nourishment. A man may live on horse and mule flesh, but a baby cannot."

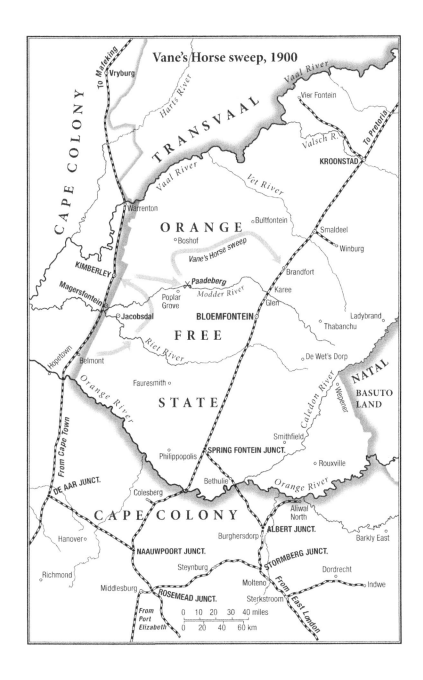

Vane's Horse sweep, 1900

CHAPTER 34 | *Paardeberg, February 1900*

THERE WAS TO be no rest for the cavalry. General Kitchener, in overall command because Roberts had been struck down by a fever, arrived on the following day to order French south and east again at the best speed the exhausted horses could make. Cronjé's main force had abandoned Jacobsdal when threatened by the British 7th Division and slipped behind French's dash to Kimberley. Now the Boers were headed east along the north bank of the Modder River, falling back on Bloemfontein, the Orange Free State's capital. The cavalry was to cut off the Boers' escape and prevent them joining Christian de Wet's kommandos, who were gathered to the south of the Modder.

At the Paardeberg Drift, where Cronjé had to cross the river to make conjunction with de Wet and to continue on toward Bloemfontein, the Boers became trapped between three British forces. Following his path along the north bank was the Royal Canadian Regiment of Infantry, which had snapped at the enemy's feet all the way. Bearing down from Kimberley was French's cavalry. Across the Modder the British 6th Division, coming along the south bank from Klip Drift, faced him.

Before reaching the Paardeberg Drift, Vane's Horse wheeled to their right in order to collect Tonkins, Cowden, Neo, and reclaim the pom-pom gun. Then the column made the best possible speed, following the churned up trail left by the retreating Boers and their ox-wagons.

"Must be thousands of them," Travis said, "Transvaalers and Freestaters, with their women and children, I'll be bound."

"With all their worldly possessions," Norris added, eager for booty.

The road rolled over a bare yet beautiful plain, turned from brown and dry into endless stretches of purple and scarlet flowers of the Karoo by a sudden downpour. Still shaking the damp from their clothes, which the sun rapidly dried out, they rode around the long hump of Paardeberg Hill. At its eastern end the plain opcncd up into a cityscape of anthills to the north. And up against the crossing, the Boers fought desperately against the combined fire of Canadian rifles and shells from French's mounted artillery. In no time, Jolyon had his crew pouring one-pounder shells into the battlefield. With every impact, hundreds a minute, river sand and smoke rose like hellish trees, shock-white at the point of impact, instantly turning to a thick churning brown and gray. They cast a pall over the Modder's sharp curve upriver of the crossing now closed to the Boers.

For ten days the Battle of Paardeberg raged, the British denied a speedy victory by the Boers' ferocious defense. Prevented from crossing at Paardeberg, Cronjé retreated eastward along the north bank and formed a massive laager close to the next crossing, the Koodesrand Drift. British and Canadian casualties were heavy, but on February 27, the reduced and exhausted Boers surrendered.

Vane's Horse was not present at this juncture because French had ordered the flying column away from the battle five days before. "You are to make a wide sweep to the north, Major Vane, and then turn east to reach the Midland railway line at Brandfort," French informed him sternly. "I want to ensure no scattered remnants of Cronjé's army sneak away toward the open veldt deeper into the Orange Free State trying to make their way to join Kruger's forces in Transvaal. You'll need to travel fast and light so you can't take the pom-pom gun with you."

Harry flinched in sympathy at Jolyon's evident horror.

"I'll requisition it, the wagon, and your two gunnery men."

Travis went to draw sufficient dry rations to last them for three weeks, after which they would have to live off the land. The harried commissary sergeant only gave way when presented with General French's writ, but of water he had none to spare. In the hurry to get under way Jolyon and Neo had only just sufficient time to boil water drawn from a well by the river—water of a dark and strange color. As it steamed in the billycan over a fire of mule dung Jolyon sat and watched the swollen carcasses of horses and men float down the brown stream from the Boer laager a mile above.

Leaving Tonkins and Cowden behind, Travis, Stevens, Norris, Fletcher and Jarvis rode off with Harry and a disconsolate Jolyon, who took Neo as pillion behind him. They learned of Cronjé's surrender some days after the event when a galloper sent after the troop caught up with them.

"Now you'll have to keep all your eyes peeled," he warned, before turning his mount's head around and putting it to speed for his return.

Before the vile tasting river water had given out in the midst of the dry, grassy veldt they came across a farmhouse with its pleasant fields, grove of trees, and spring offering sweet fresh water. In the following days and weeks, more farmsteads gave up drinking water from bore wells, but always the farm was derelict, windows broken, rooms gutted, and stock destroyed.

Jarvis took a bullet in the shoulder at the third farm they came upon. Harry blamed himself for their lack of caution in approaching the buildings, lulled by the abandoned landscape.

"You couldn't have known," said Jolyon.

"Of course I should have."

Fletcher crab-crawled to his fallen comrade's side.

"Fuck, that hurts!"

"Try and keep him quiet," Harry hissed, as he tugged the head of his horse around. "Give me cover!"

Hurriedly dismounted, Travis, Stevens, and Norris opened up a rapid fire on the farmhouse. They were answered, but briefly, as Harry rode at a gallop to the right and Jolyon to the left.

"How many?" Harry shouted.

"I can only make out two," Travis yelled back as Harry disappeared around the side of the one-story cabin.

Rifles barked, a fusillade of shots rang out across the veldt. Travis leapt to his feet, remounted and rode like the wind straight at the closed door, firing from his hip as he went.

"Like a fuckin' cowboy in one of them Wild West circus shows," Norris crowed.

More cautiously, he and Stevens led their mounts forward. Travis sprang from the saddle and kicked the door in, loosing two shots into the resulting void as he did. Shouts came from within.

"Yaw, we surrender, man. Don't shoot!"

Travis gave a hoarse laugh at the sight of two rumpled Afrikaaners, hands held wide, and Harry peering through a broken side window, the barrel of his smoking rifle pointed at one Boer, while young Jolyon aimed at the other from a second opening. The floorboards around their boots were splintered by bullets.

"Bastards shot me." Jarvis moaned.

Fletcher tutted. "It's not that bad." Jarvis made much of getting to his feet, one hand raised to his shoulder. Under his fingers a dark stain showed where the Mauser bullet had torn the khaki shirt and sliced across his skin. Fletcher went to gentle their horses and lead them toward the farmhouse. "You're lucky, mate. Them bastards use dum-dums. Taken your arm off at the joint if it'd gone an inch to the right," he added cheerfully.

"Jo— Lieutenant, keep them covered. Praat jy Engels?"

"Ja, man. Bloedige English is nodig in hierdie land, now you try and take it from us," the elder of the two spat out with a jeer.

"Then throw your weapons down. Well out in front of you, and then don't move another inch, or we drop you. Verstaan?"

The younger man laughed sourly.

While Jolyon kept them in his sights, Harry ran around to join Travis in the doorway. He gestured the two men out. "Stevens, Norris, get their hands tied behind their backs."

"You want me to shoot 'em, sir?"

"Hey, man, you can't! The Geneva Convention forbids—"

Harry sighed and cut off the Boer's shout. "We're not *always* in the habit of killing prisoners, Norris." He glared until he saw a look of resignation in the lad's eyes. "Just bind them up securely." He looked at the captives. "Where are your horses? Boers without a ride… that's not usual."

After a moment's sullen silence, the elder of the two nodded back over his shoulder. "Over to that copse there."

"Thank God for that," Travis said. "They'd have slowed us down something terrible on foot."

"Still think we should do 'em."

No one heeded Norris's grumbling.

"Wat is die klein swat kaffer doen?" The younger Boer dipped his head at Neo.

"I take off your manhood, Boere Fokker!" Neo snapped back. "Jy maak meer geraas as 'n seekoei."

Both Boers guffawed, but let Travis poke them into movement.

"What he say?" Norris wanted to know.

"He said they make more noise than a hippopotamus," Travis said.

The older of the Boers pointed at Neo. "Don't worry, kaffer. When Piet Cronjé gets his hands on you, you won't sound so brave."

Harry rounded on the man, eyes narrowed to suspicious slits. "What are you doing out here?"

The Boer clammed up and stared defiantly at Harry.

A cold smile played over Harry's lips. "You're deserters, no?"

"Ons is nie drosters… no desert!"

"Spies then. Maybe I will let Norris shoot you as spies. Meantime, your General Cronjé surrendered days ago. Fletch, go bring their horses over." He lifted his chin. "Your cause is lost, my friend. Now you'll come with us."

In the chill night air Vane's Horse commandos were glad of Neo's skill with building a smokeless fire that gave out heat without sending up telltale flames. They'd had the first hot food in three days—jerk flavored by herbs Neo had collected, stewed in Liebig stock from one of the few cans in their supplies. Bivouacked in a shallow curving donga, Harry hoped the fire-glow was hidden sufficiently to avoid detection and so afford them a night undisturbed by Boers. They were around, but as yet none had detected the presence of the British unit. He could barely make out the hunched shape of Fletcher against the sprinkle of stars, keeping the first watch on the low kopje above the ditch.

The rest of the men lay slumped on spread ground sheets, enjoying the fire's warmth in various poses of relaxation. Travis and Stevens smoked their pipes quietly, outdoing each other in quietly traded insults. Jolyon and Harry stared at the covered glow of the hot ashes, lost in their own thoughts. Harry suspected they were much the same—a sense of frustration that in this promiscuous company they ever needed to be cautious of letting slip any suggestion of their desire to be in each other's arms. Norris busied himself cleaning his revolver. Harry was uneasy at the looks he often caught Norris giving Jolyon, as if the Cockney was trying to remember where he'd seen the face before.

Jarvis, sore from the bullet graze to his shoulder and actually pissed at its being such an inconsequential wound, was tasked with keeping an eye on the two prisoners. They had learned that the elder—a bluff and squat presence, his face largely hidden behind a biblically patriarchal beard—was Emile de Klerk, and his young companion was Jan Ritman. Jarvis released his irritation by constantly probing them with questions intended to annoy, getting his own back for shooting him.

From up on his lookout rock Fletcher muttered, "This damned flat country," his voice loud enough for those below to hear him. "A man stands up he's near the tallest object around."

It was true. Somewhere thirty miles to the east of Boshof and twelve south of Bultfontein on the extensive grasslands there was a good likelihood of running into either a Boer kommando or rumps of Piet Cronjé's army falling back north from their defeat at Paardeberg Drift. At reasonable treatment and not the threat of torture, De Klerk and Ritman had finally admitted as much, that they had been dispatched at the first contact with the British forces on the Modder to carry the news of Cronjé's intentions to Jo'burg.

"What'll we do wiv 'em?" Norris grumped in continual repetition. "We ain't got the food."

"I know, lance corporal."

Jolyon smiled privately. He knew that Harry employed the brevet ranks to remind the men that—while they were in essence a bunch of irregulars—they were under British Army orders. It was too easy running about the veldt in the assorted, non-regulation attire that helped them to blend in with the country to ignore discipline. On the other hand, back in Cape Town both he and Harry had overhead one newspaper reporter who was watching a British mounted patrol ride past say, "They're decked out like Christmas trees, men and horses alike!" Harry could agree. As he said, "The Boer's military effectiveness isn't measured by the gleam on his buttons or the shine on his boots but by his skill with a rifle and his agility on a horse. We have to be the same."

"I still think they're a bloody nuisance… sir."

"You think I should have let you execute them?"

Norris recoiled in mock horror. "The thought never crossed me mind, sir."

"Good. I hope we can hand them over at Brandfort… as long as our advance has reached there by the time we do."

"Bleedin' month yet then," Norris griped.

To everyone's surprise, de Klerk and Ritman had not posed much of a problem. There didn't even seem to be a need to manacle them, although Harry insisted on their hands being tied firmly around the saddle horns of their horses on the move and covered by at least one gun in camp, with only a light binding around their wrists. Their acquiescence, it gradually became clear, was not from apathy but from a God-given certainty that their captors would soon all be imprisoned in turn or dead at the hands of a kommando. And this was not a fanciful wish considering the numbers of Boers likely to be retreating from the Modder to Transvaal. Two groups of stragglers had been spotted the day before, but at too great a distance to pose a threat and in too great a number to risk firing on, but at Harry's request Jolyon kept a record of their passage.

In this area of the Orange Free State there was not the easily found cover Harry had been used to up near Mafeking. Very few scattered copses of trees—rarely higher than a man seated on a horse—broke the flat grassy horizon, disturbed only by a distant range of low hill to the north and the small city of anthills where Harry called a halt for the night. The lone kopje on which Fletcher sat was barely eight feet at its highest point.

Neo sat cross-legged nearest to the fire, occasionally tapping a piece of super-heated wood to keep it all loose. At each light love-tap on his shoulder from Jolyon's boot he slumped forward in play.

Harry smiled to himself and felt the shift in the position of Jolyon's shoulder against his own as Jolyon stretched a languid foot out to nudge the boy again. The two had become fast friends, much to Harry's surprise. Neo called him Jo Jo Angrish. Harry was certain Jolyon would not have known any black Africans in England, and the few servants at headquarters in Cape Town made little impression amid the all-white military bustle. He assumed—unfairly as it turned out—that Jolyon's initial aloofness toward Neo indicated a disapproval of the Barolong boy's presence in the little unit, an adverse reaction to the effusive greeting Harry received from Neo when they arrived at De Aar Junction. Once Harry managed to untangle Neo's arms from around his waist, Jolyon only nodded his own greeting, but it was merely his natural politeness… and, Harry suspected, a shyness engendered by his first social interaction with an African: in Vane's Horse every man was forced to live on top of his comrades. It wasn't long before Neo favored Jo Jo Angrish's back to hang onto as they rode.

Norris was staring across the glow at Jolyon again. Harry noted that the expression on his narrow face wasn't a pleasant one.

"What exactly are you staring at?"

Harry was sure Jolyon knew of the scrutiny, but he'd never reacted to it before.

Norris raised his eyebrows in surprise. "Nuthin'." He added "sir" as an afterthought. "Just you remind me of someone."

"Will you stop jabbing at them," Travis suddenly complained to Jarvis. "Your constant droning is driving me bonkers."

"I was only asking how many Tommies they killed already."

"More than you, man," Ritman spoke up.

"That's where you're wrong. I don't shoot my own side."

The snide return didn't faze the Boer. He went on as though Jarvis hadn't spoken. "The Right is on our side. Why, when we were retiring from Jacobsdal we had to cross a great open plain above the river to the drift, never even an anthill for cover, and you had put twelve great cannons—I counted them—and Maxims as well, to shoot us as we went. But not one shot was fired. That was God's hand stopped them firing."

"Yes, after that we knew," de Klerk joined in, his voice a deep bass emerging from a mouth hidden beneath the overgrowth of mustaches and beard. "We knew we would win," he jeered.

Jarvis spluttered indignantly. "Of course the bloody guns didn't bloody fire, you stupid Afrikaaner git. I heard you'd raised the white flag!"

"Yes, but only for armistice," Ritman answered calmly, as though instructing a stupid child. "Not to give in. We are not going to give in. It was a retirement because your cavalry were so slow. We shouldn't be shot at for that."

"The guns were stopped by the hand of God," de Klerk insisted. "And so should they be, man. What are you doing here? This isn't your country. We don't want to live under your flag. We are free. You are not free."

At this, even Stevens roused himself. "What do you mean, 'not free,' huh?"

The Boers as one dipped heads at where Neo poked the fire, but it was Emile de Klerk who spoke.

"Well, is it right that a dirty kaffer should be on the sidewalk—without a pass too? That's what they do in your British Colonies. You make them equal! Like those coloreds you bring from India. Ugh! Free? You're not a bit of it. We know how to treat kaffers in this country. Fancy letting the black filth parade along the sidewalks."

Harry felt Jolyon's body tense where it pressed unobtrusively yet companionably against him.

Stevens, under normal circumstances a relaxed character, sat up angrily. "What the fuck do you know about it, you fuckin' South Sea Coconut?"

Jan Ritman returned the sudden aggression with an aggravatingly calm certainty. "Educate a kaffer. That's you English all over." He raised a hand to indicate Neo's form hunched over the fire trying to be invisible under the Afrikaaner's vituperation. "No, we educate 'em with a stick. That's what the kaffer understands. They were put here by the God'a'mighty to work for us. We'll stand no damned nonsense from the black stinkers. We keep them in their proper place—*ughnn!*"

Jolyon's boot took the Boer clean under his jaw in a move so fast neither Harry nor the others saw it coming. Ritman's head snapped back and his seated form stretched out from the force of the kick to fall back heavily on the rising slope of the donga's side. His hands, bound lightly at the wrist, flew up in tandem like an Indian fakir's supplication.

"Jo!" Harry was on his feet in a second, hands stretched out to restrain Jolyon, but too late to prevent him diving after the fallen Boer. His fists pummeled the man's chest and face. Ritman instinctively rolled over and folded his arms to protect his head.

De Klerk scrabbled back away from the fury. "Hey, man! That's really bad. Stop it now."

Harry grabbed Jolyon's shoulders and pulled him back up. He was spitting for a fight and bent over in Harry's grasp, panting heavily. "You filthy bastard. You think your God gives you the right… *pah!*"

Ritman groaned at the kick Jolyon aimed at his ribs. All the others, including de Klerk, were on their feet, alarmed at the sudden violence and nervous of the Boers' reactions, even though they were disarmed and their wrists bound.

Harry caught the look Norris was throwing in his direction; suddenly uncomfortably aware of how tightly he had Jolyon held in his arms. The lance corporal framed the slightest of insightful smiles on his thin lips.

"Sorry?" Harry's concentration wavered. It was two days after the incident in the donga and he was straining to resolve the distant dark specks seen through his field glasses. The heat haze across the plain set everything aquiver and made it difficult to determine whether what had alerted him was in fact men or just grazing beasts. He was vaguely aware of the presence at his side but didn't take his scrutiny from the view ahead. "What did you say?"

"I said I've remembered where I know Lieutenant Langrish-Smith from, sir."

They looked like antelope, but at the distance he couldn't be absolutely sure. Harry lowered the binoculars and slowly turned to Norris. He raised an eyebrow in query. "What?"

"I seen him before… sir."

"In Cape Town?"

Norris's chuckle mocked the question.

"Nah, sir, not Cape Town. Nor on the ship out, for I don't think we was on the same boat. It was London, sir."

"And what's that to me?" Harry had a sinking feeling that he knew what might be coming. They were stood in a slight dip some distance from where the rest of Vane's Horse and the two prisoners rested from the midday heat under the partial shade of a couple of acacia trees.

"It was *where* in London, what counts." Norris cocked his head to one side, eyes wide in innocent amusement.

Harry drew in a short breath. "Norris, if you have something to report, say it, man. Otherwise… shove it!"

"Is it Boers out there?"

"No. Antelope. What's your point?"

"The right honorable Jolyon Langrish-Smith. It was in Kings Cross I saw him once. With that cove who went with the writer chappie. You know the one I mean?"

Harry stared at the man with an icy calm and waited him out.

"The poof writer, Oscar. I seen you're sweet on him, the lieutenant, I mean."

"We've known each other's families, if *that* is what you mean." Even as he uttered the words, he knew Norris wasn't buying.

"He was with that Lord Alfred Douglas—Bosie, the rent-boys called him."

"And what were you doing in Kings Cross?" A mistake…

Norris's grin broadened into a triumphant smile. "So you do know what I'm on about, then. I live in Kings Cross. Not the best of London, I know, but I calls it home. Even if it is next door to one of them boy knocking shops. And I seen your Jo-Jo go in there with that Bosie."

"Get back to the camp, Norris. Now!"

"Oh, I will indeed, sir. When we come to an… arrangement? It's not like I want a lot. Just something to keep me going for when this is all over and we're back home. A little something to set me up wiv a market stall and some stock to make a living out of."

"You sniveling snake—"

"Oh come on, sir. Purleese! A career officer like you and Mr. Langrish-Smith… You don't need the Field Marshal's staff to find out what the Hero of Chitral is really like, do you, sir. Yes I know all about it. Made it my business. You see, I seen you and him when you think no one's looking. Saw you up on that ridge at the Modder that day, cuddling up. And I know. I know what you want to do with each other. Don't get me wrong, it's nuthin' to me what you want to do to each other, sir, different strokes for different folks, I always say. But I don't think the top brass, the Red-Caps, I don't see 'em as being as understanding as what I am. Course, I might be wrong, I mean I don't move in exalted circles like what you do, sir. P'raps up there, among refined folk like you, sir, it's all good and dandy to go poking young lads, like Oscar and Bosie liked to do. Like your little lieutenant liked doing. So don't deny it. After all, I'm not asking fer much. An' then your secret's safe wiv me. No one else need know you got a soft spot for the lieutenant."

"You fucking bastard!"

They both turned at expletives enunciated in clear Etonian tones. The antelope-grazed short grass on the bank behind had muffled Jolyon's soft footfalls.

"The hair's different, isn't it? Not the long bangs you used to have, Norris. But I heard your last words and it came back to me." He looked up at Harry, eyes wide in appeal. "He was there. The night Bosie dragged me to that awful place. He pretended Oscar was there and wanted to see me, but it was all a lie. A wicked lie. And this piece of offal was one of the boys Bosie wanted me to… to… have sex with. I only caught a glimpse of his face for a second. It's why I couldn't place him, until his own words gave him away just now."

"Not how I heard it, pretty boy." Norris fixed Jolyon with a self-satisfied gaze. "Bosie the man, he told me you needed a damn good rogering and that's why you was coming with him that night. Begging fer a hard fuck up the ass!"

Jolyon swung away in mute disgust.

Harry tried to seize the initiative. "So you're a whore, not just an innocent Kings Cross bystander boasting a high moral stance?"

The sarcasm went over Norris's head. "Thank you fer that, Major Vane. But so what? It's not my reputation on the line. You remember what happened to Oscar's boys. I mean that Taylor cove, he was sent down, serve him fucking right too, but all the boys what gave evidence they got off scot-free, didn't they? But not Mr. Wilde. He went down. Two years and hard labor. Near like to kill him, it did. Like it will you and him. But it don't need to go so far as that, does it?" His voice rose up to a wheedling whine.

Jolyon shook his head in impotent rage. "After everything... I just don't believe this!"

Harry blew out a coughing laugh. "What do you want, Kruger Rands?"

This time, Harry's bite didn't miss the mark.

"No need for that, sir, sarcasm doesn't suit you. An officer and a gentleman's word, that'll do." Norris sounded almost reasonable. "Give me a written IOU for three hundred pounds to be goin' on wiv—"

When they came, the shots rang out so close together it sounded as if a single rifle had been fired.

Three bodies hit the ground as one. Instinctively, Harry fell partly over Jolyon to protect him. He rolled aside, raised his head, only to duck down as more shots came from a nearby ridge. Not antelope then.

"Oh shit!" Norris moaned.

Jolyon crawled sideways and laid a hand on Norris, who groaned loudly. "He's hit, Harry!"

"Keep down, Jo. How bad?"

Jolyon held out a blood-covered hand. "Chest, but I don't know what the damage is." When Norris squirmed and tried to turn over, Jolyon held him down. A pink froth issued from between the blackmailer's fluttering lips.

"We must regroup with the others." Harry raised his head cautiously. "I count six, with extra horses, and they were running some antelope in front of them, cunning devils."

"I don't think Norris can crawl and we can't leave him here."

Just then they heard the report of rifles from behind.

"Well timed, Travis! He's giving us some cover. C'mon, Jo. We can come back and get Norris when we've driven these bandits off."

Another ragged volley broke out and scattered the oncoming horsemen.

Harry sprang to his feet and grabbed Jolyon's shoulder to raise him up. But Jolyon suddenly turned back, reached down and hoisted the inert form of Norris up over his shoulder. "Go!" he gasped. "I've got him."

Norris gave a shout of pain.

"No, Jo! You'll never make it with that weight."

Jolyon ignored Harry's entreaty. He lurched into motion. Harry snorted in exasperation, but he spun around, loosed six shots at the Boers.

"Over that crest. There's some cover on the other side of the bank."

The air overhead hummed in both directions as Travis directed more rifle fire at the enemy to distract them from aiming at his comrades.

Harry braced himself to help Jolyon, who was bent almost double under Norris's inert weight. The wounded man's screams rent the air with every step Jolyon took. To reach safety meant climbing out of the slight dip across which they now lurched. The wicked sting of bullets striking the ground was renewed as they came into the Boers' sights again. At the same time friendly covering fire died out instantly to avoid the risk of hitting the two rescuers when they staggered up the far side of the second dip.

Harry half-dragged Jolyon after him, desperately afraid for his lover, as he planted one foot after the other, gasping with the extreme effort under his human burden. Yet more shots cracked out and the ground around their feet erupted in spits of dirt. A spray of bullets narrowly missed Harry and spranged loudly off a tree trunk, showering his head with shards of timber and bark.

And then they were down among the acacias. Harry saw that Jarvis had his rifle firmly aimed at the two prisoners, while Travis, Stevens, Fletcher, and Neo—crouched behind some fallen boughs—were returning the Boers' fire in ferocious volleys now there was no risk of hitting their own.

"Shoot the horses!" Travis commanded, and immediately one of the Boers' mounts screamed and collapsed, hurling its rider forward to disappear in the high grass. Jolyon tried lowering Norris to the ground, but ended up dumping him on his side. He wasted no more time on the man who had just been blackmailing them, checked the magazine on his rifle, and joined the rest at the firing line. In the distance, one rider catapulted dead back off his horse, and the others turned and began to ride off, with one hauling the dismounted but apparently unharmed Dutchman up behind him.

"Opportunists," Travis spat out.

"Patriots, you mean," Jan Ritman growled, beginning to stand.

Jarvis lashed out with his rifle butt and caught the farm boy a blow on the side of his head. He slumped down, cursing in Afrikaans.

Fletcher flicked his rifle safety on and bent down to see to Norris.

Harry wiped a grimy brow. "The heat haze must have thrown their aim off. Better check that wound and get some sulphur on it," he ordered. "If Norris survives they can patch him up when we get to Bloemfontein."

"Not really, Major." Fletcher glanced up and shook his head. He pointed to two gaping holes high up on Norris's back. "He's dead."

"Christ alive." The high color caused by his exertions drained from Jolyon's cheeks.

"I reckon he saved your life, mate… I mean Lieutenant. For once—leastways for you, sir—it's as well they were dum-dum bullets. Spread on impact. Looks like they struck his ribs, otherwise they'd have passed right through the flesh and into your back as well."

On the ground, in a surprising gesture Jan Ritman raised his bound hands and took off his bush hat as a mark of respect. Emile de Klerk shook his head and then followed suit, managing to make the sign of the cross with his tied wrists.

Jolyon slowly raised his eyes to meet Harry's steady gaze. The unspoken exchange was as clear as if it had been voiced: it was a grisly justice.

Sergeant Travis broke the sudden silence. "You did your best, sir. That was a brave thing to do, try to bring him in like that under fire."

CHAPTER 35 | *Bloemfontein, March to early June 1900*

IN THE VELDT'S SUMMER HEAT a body decomposes rapidly. They buried Norris with ceremonial economy. The grave, as deep as Jan Ritman and Emile de Klerk could dig it in the time permitted them, lay in the shade of a kopje, wiping the backs of their hands over sweat-grimed foreheads. Harry placed his feelings on hold, for what point was there in recrimination? He could sense the relief and the horror emanating from Jolyon just the same as his own would if he allowed it. To the others Jolyon's was a natural reaction to the sudden death of a comrade, and one the young officer had done his best to rescue. If theirs was an official mission and not one performed by a bunch of irregulars, Mr. Langrish-Smith might even deserve a Victoria Cross for his bravery in the face of the enemy.

Ironically, it was Emile de Klerk who offered to say some words over the grave, for to British shame the Boer was the only one among the company able to quote passages of the Bible and Common Prayer, even in English translation. As de Klerk spoke, Jolyon held Neo in front of himself like a shield, hands on both of the black boy's shoulders, but in reality presenting him as a challenge to the Boers by placing him in the front row to make the point that it was his right to be there. Wisely, for once, Ritman kept his prejudices to himself.

When de Klerk was finished, they mounted and rode on toward the east.

"I'm tired, Jo." Harry spoke quietly as they walked their horses in between spurts of faster cantering. Fletcher was out at point; Travis, Stevens, and Jarvis had the two prisoners coraled between them, the Dutchmen's horse bridles tethered in line behind the sergeant. Jolyon and Harry trailed the others by some twenty paces. Neo's face was squashed against Jolyon's back and he breathed quiet snores. "I'm tired of looking over my shoulder, of peering to the left, the right, all around. I'm tired of the saddle."

"I thought you loved this life."

Harry's wry smile pressed his lips into a thin line. "If you had said that of me to my old school friends Richard and Edward Rainbow and particularly Alfred Winner you would have raised a guffaw of disbelief. They regarded me as a sybarite, not so very far removed from your one-time *Yellow Book* acquaintances, the aesthetes of the avant-garde. They saw me as a nattily dressed youth, something of a prig, truth to be told, certainly not a roughneck horseman, bearded, dirty, unbathed in days, riding the veldt, shooting from the hip like some cowboy from Buffalo Bill's Wild West Show."

If Harry hoped the recent events and his mention of Jolyon's former dissolute companions might loosen his tongue and give voice to the final block between them—the real truth of those days Norris had so horridly recaptured—he was to be disappointed.

They both looked ahead alertly as Fletcher's horse gave an excited whinny. Harry relaxed fractionally as the raised voice came back on the breeze. "She can smell water. I think there's a spring ahead, maybe another farmhouse."

Harry sighed. "I don't suppose my old friends would think of me now in the way they did, after what we've all been through, together and apart, but the truth is that I feel I've done enough for the Army." He glanced sideways. Begrimed and dusty, smudged and worn, just like Harry, Jolyon did not return Harry's look. At least they were too accustomed to their unwashed smell to notice that aspect. "I want to spend time with you, Jo." *In fact, the rest of my life, whatever that might be.* He looked ahead again. "But is that what you want?"

Jolyon didn't answer immediately.

They rode in a bubble of quiet that Harry felt even a breath might burst. He'd hoped that being together in the cauldron of conflict out on the harsh veldt would spark an epiphany and that all things would become clear. Yet the opposite seemed to be the case. Jo had been... not aloof exactly, but not forthcoming either. Now Norris had burst on them like an evil revenant determined to sunder the fragile relationship and his terrifyingly convenient death had thrown Jo, Harry was sure, as much as it had done him.

Jolyon considered his reply to the loaded question. When he spoke, it was in a low, serious tone. "I'm not that aesthete you saw when you returned from

India that first time. Nor am I what Norris tried to imply. I thought Oscar wanted me to be there. I hadn't understood fully what it was all about."

"But you recognized Norris…"

"He… he confused me, saying he knew me. I don't know." He licked cracked lips. "I hope Fletcher's right about a spring. There were, you know…" he looked in appeal at Harry, "two boys at school, but that was… not dirty. Not like Lord Alfred Douglas." He made the name sound like three dark curses. Harry bit back any words he might have wanted to utter.

"You changed me, Harry. You made me grow up. I went to Woolwich for you and nothing was more on my mind than passing out with a good score and getting on the first ship bound for the Cape. I thought the change would sweep all the rotten bits of the past away and now Norris has brought it back. I thought before if we didn't speak of it, it would fade away, and that if we did, well… you would never want me any more. Soiled goods…"

A missed heartbeat caused Harry to gasp involuntarily. Then he huffed out the breath he'd been holding, hardly aware of it. "I only think it would be good for you to let go of it, and to do that you need to drive out whatever ails you in your heart by telling me everything. I want you to be free, and I can see you are not. For me not knowing—perhaps inventing—is far far worse than anything you might confess. That I promise."

"I'm not ready, not yet, the Oscar business, and all that went with it."

Harry checked ahead at the rest of Vane's Horse, all concentrating their scrutiny toward the low hills rising up on the horizon. He reached out to grip Jolyon's arm and stared earnestly at the vision of grubby peasanthood riding beside him. "Jo, you could never hurt me more than you did that day at the Café Royal when you denied knowing me, and I forgave you that because I saw you were troubled, though I didn't know then by what precisely. Since that day, the worst I might have thought could never stop the feelings of deepest regard I've come to hold for you. You allowed me to heal you… at least, I flatter myself that I did help—"

"Oh, but you did!"

"I love you, Jo, and that's all there is to it."

The smile that suffused Jolyon's face warmed Harry as nothing else could do. He released his arm in case one of those riding ahead should look around. After Norris, Harry didn't want anything else to shift the world from its axis.

"That's all there is to it," Jolyon echoed. "So very simple, really." He swallowed so his barely visible Adam's apple bobbed up and down. "If I've never said it, if you've never understood it from my paltry moods… in my funny way I adore you, Haldane Smythe-Vane."

A loud yawn broke into their reverie. Neo straightened up, glanced about blearily with a toothy smile, and then turned his other cheek to Jolyon's back and was asleep as quickly as he'd woken.

"If you're now tired of 'all this,' then so am I," Jolyon declared. "I want what you want. I want us to be together. But I'm torn about it. Oh, not like that," he added hastily. "I mean about where. Where can we be together and not also have to look over our shoulders, peer to the left, the right, all around, waiting for someone to denounce what we are, what we have become? Oscars…?"

"We are not Oscars, Jo. Never! I don't know, though. But I'll think of something."

A week later, without further incident, Vane's Horse came across the rail tracks—or what was left of them. In their retreat north toward Johannesburg and Pretoria the Boers had dismantled the ironwork, which lay bent and twisted amid the scattered link-fastenings, wooden ties, and the line of aggregate ballast.

"We must be north of Brandfort," Harry suggested to Travis.

"Makes sense."

They turned their horses' heads south and rode along, following the destruction and the torn down telegraph poles. After about three miles they came upon the first evidence of the British advance, a vertical skein of smoke in the still air. Two miles father on a unit of sapper-engineers was hard at work repairing the track. Beyond the working party smoke and steam issued from a stationary locomotive. "Oh my, that's a badly battered Neilson GCR 1st Class 4-4-0TT," said Stevens as he fondly patted the piston rod cover. Three high-sided, armored and loopholed cars sat behind its squat shape. Lounging around on the gentle embankment were two companies of infantry.

"Don't they just look like a straggle of holidaymakers enjoying the beach at Brighton," Travis said.

Harry smiled. "You must have been knee high to a grasshopper when you were last in Brighton."

"Thigh high, anyway, but I'll bet nothing's changed when a spot of summer sun shines on the shingly sand. Packed in, like this lot."

More sappers were busily erecting new telegraph poles and stringing the wire. The captain in charge of the work gangs and the fusileers was bent over a rickety table where his telegraphist was hammering out a message. He had connected the key to the repaired line via a temporarily strung wire. It flapped in the breeze with the snapping sound of a flag line. Harry dismounted and walked over.

"Brandfort is ten miles farther on, Major Vane," the captain informed after Harry introduced himself. "I suppose you won't know that Bloemfontein fell without any fighting on March 13. How long have you been out on patrol?"

"Since a few days before the surrender of General Cronjé. That was the last I heard from a galloper sent after us with the news."

"In which case you will be happy to hear that The Natal Field Force under General Buller broke through at Ladysmith on the same day Cronjé surrendered at Paardeberg, February 27. Ladysmith was officially relieved the day after." Eyeing Jan Ritman and Emile de Klerk, he added, "There is a temporary prisoner of war camp at Brandfort. You'll be able to drop your Boers off there. I'll telegraph ahead so they'll be ready for you."

Harry thanked him and then added, pointing over at the lounging Tommies, "I'd keep them alive on their feet. We crossed the tracks of several Boer units retreating north. No knowing when they might regroup and become a nuisance."

It was strange to be reunited with Rudyard Kipling in Bloemfontein. "Lord Roberts," he told Harry, as he shook hands in turn with Jolyon, "has commissioned my services along with those of three colleagues—proper correspondents," he paused to huff a laugh of modesty "...to put together a newspaper for the troops. It's for their morale. You see we reached Bloemfontein with men who have done an extraordinary amount of marching and fighting while suffering exposure and privation. Some of the troops, particularly the Guards, walked more than thirty miles in one of the three days' continual marching. Many fought at Jacobsdal, Paardeberg, and Driefontein, and all this when reduced to less than half rations. Now, without so much as a meager rest, the troops must press on north to take Pretoria and end this war. This is the humble task the Field Marshal has set us, to provide the men with something uplifting to read. Do come and have a look."

Production of *The Friend* took place in the office of the former *Friend of the Free State*. To Harry the cramped square-shaped editors' room had the appearance of having been arranged out of a dust-heap, and stocked with machinery, type, and furniture that had originally been bought from a merchant of second-hand goods and left to itself for years of frequent dust storms. Incongruously, the clapboard walls were covered in a wallpaper of floral extravagance, which nevertheless in spite of its florid decoration was the color of dust.

"I am not the only pressganged writer in Bloemfontein," Kipling said. I'm to request an interview with another luminary of the pen but also the scalpel, if you would care to accompany me."

Intrigued, Harry and Jolyon walked with Kipling through tree-lined streets to the Longman hospital, actually a country club commandeered by the British Army. There they were taken to see to Dr. Arthur Conan Doyle who had exchanged his sleuthing stories of Sherlock Holmes for ministering to the wounded and sick of Paardeburg and the skirmishes since. After introductions and the usual courtesies, which included a slightly abashed Harry confessing his admiration for the great detective's stories, the doctor offered to show them around the establishment.

"It isn't only the shrapnel and the torn limb we treat here," Conan Doyle said before the entrance to the hospital. "In some ways far worse are the dreadful microbes of enteric which entered the blood of thousands of the soldiers, who found no other water to drink than that of the pestilential Modder River. It carried along and absorbed the corpses of men and horses as well as the sewage of the camps of both the Boers and our own. The enteric fever has carried off far more men than the shells of the enemy."

A sad memory of young men carousing on the deck of the *Dunottar Castle* flooded his thoughts, so bright in their pride at going to war to give the Boer a good kicking, now so many dead, not of glorious wounds earned in service of their Queen but of a killer fever.

Even though the hour was early the air of the wards reeked pungently of strong tobacco. Conan Doyle spoke to all the patients, and had a kind word for everyone, and those who were able greeted him with gratitude. To Harry's surprise, there were also several Boer patients and their one cry was, "We've had as much as we want. If we could only get back to our farms."

"Most of those to whom I have spoken," Conan Doyle said, "tell me that they never wanted to fight us, never hoped to beat us, and are heartily sick of the whole business. There are three other field hospitals nearby and it's the same story there. Boers and Englishmen lie side by side, sharing pipes and papers and talk with each other. Truly, animosity ceases at the hospital door," he added with a wondering shake of his head. "When it comes to the medical profession, our oath makes of us impartial angels. And many nationalities are now wrapped up in this business. The medical corpsmen are unspoken heroes in their efforts. Why, I have heard that across in Natal an Indian lawyer called Gandhi, whom some in Johannesburg have labeled 'troublemaker,' organized more than a thousand of his countrymen living there as ambulance workers to carry the wounded sometimes as much as twenty miles to a field hospital."

As they left, Kipling shook his head sadly. "Astonishing, isn't it, that in the final analysis what all this death and destruction comes down to is gold and diamonds."

One of those who lusted after gold and diamonds, who had done more than anyone to forge the British Empire in Africa—and even named a vast territory in his likeness—interposed his will in a move that was to transform the lives of Harry Smythe-Vane and Jolyon Langrish-Smith. It began inconspicuously with a summons on May 11. Harry grumbled that he'd hoped to have the coming weekend free of duties at last. "No doubt the general will pile a load of work on my shoulders and you can guarantee it'll need to be finished yesterday."

"Can't keep General French waiting," Jolyon said breezily.

"I know. He's a tendency to irritation if held up. I think it's being a cavalryman, all rush and dash."

"Then you know what it's like!"

At the cavalry lines, Harry found General John French in a typical distemper.

"Damned Roberts! Man has no feeling for horsemen. God only knows what Buller would make of it. Speaks highly of you by the way; Redvers, I mean, though I've no doubt Roberts would approve of you, having served in India.

Man's obsessed with his 'Indian Wallahs,' as he calls the officers who served out there with him. He tells me…" and French placed hands on hips, tucked in his chin, and imitated Bobs's growly tone. " 'The fighting at Poplar Grove has proved that the future lies with mounted infantry.' Redvers would throw a fit if he heard it. Mounted infantry indeed! Even the Germans consider the mounted infantry too poor at riding to fight effectively.

"Now, you didn't come to listen to me going on about the Field Marshal's dotty ideas. You were a political in India, weren't you, Major?"

"I was, sir." Harry kept his puzzlement to himself.

"And you impressed General Lockhart with your cartographic and topographic abilities, I know." French paused out of respect for Harry's Gilgit-Chitral expedition chief. The news of his death on March 18 was fresh in the minds of all who he had touched. General William Lockhart died in harness as Commander-in-Chief, India in Calcutta, but it was as the courageous supporter of Harry's crazy scheme to free Arshan's brother Firuz from the clutches of the evil Baktash-al Ghulam Ali that Harry most mourned Lockhart's passing.

"He recorded that you got on well with the natives," French continued, "so you are the ideal man for the job."

"I am, sir?"

"The war here is all but over. With Kimberley back in our hands, Colonel Mahon is bound to have the siege of Mafeking raised in no time, and Roberts and Kitchener will rapidly sweep up the Midland line to Johannesburg and Pretoria. At least, as soon as the quacks get this fever epidemic under control, they will. The Boers are finished and Kruger knows it. It would mean resigning your commission," he went on, confusing Harry with the non sequitur. "No need for you to rush that, though. I can arrange a six-month leave period, which ought to be sufficient to complete the task, and then you can make up your mind as to whether to resign your commission or stay in harness. How does that sound?"

"What did you say?" Jolyon couldn't contain his excited curiosity.

"I thought about it for a second and said 'Yes!' It's the answer, Jo. Of course, I insisted on having as an assistant mapper a certain Lieutenant Langrish-Smith, which does mean you're also on a six-month period of leave before a final decision on your future military career. It would be a great honor to aid in the completion of the longest railway line in the world."

"When do we start?"

"Just as soon as I've seen to the disbandment of Vane's Horse and the suitable settlement of the men."

"Fancy that, Mr. Rhodes asking for you."

Of Vane's Horse, only Neo and Sergeant Travis accompanied Harry and Jolyon. Stevens said he would join one of the irregular infantry companies continuing north up the Midland Railway with Roberts and Kitchener toward Jo'burg and Pretoria. "I'm going to get myself a train driver's job when this malarkey is all over," he said, glowing at the thought of driving one of the locomotives he so admired. Jarvis wanted to go back to his family's farm to the south of De Aar. Fletcher thought he'd make his way to join the Natal Field Army. Harry planned to take Neo along with them as far as Mafeking and his Barolong tribal land.

Jolyon expressed disappointment that he and Harry would not be alone during the great adventure that lay ahead of them, but accepted Harry's explanation that an expedition through the heart of equatorial Africa required porters. "You must have read of Stanley's travails, and he had a small army of whites as well as black porters. It will be tough enough as it is for just the three of us."

The remnants of Vane's Horse left Bloemfontein four days after Harry's meeting with French, intending to reach Kimberley by May 16. The route took them past the battle sites of Poplar Grove and Paardeberg. War's dismal aftermath lingered. Carcases of horses and oxen still lined the road, though most had been transformed to skeletal shapes after the aasvögels, the foulest of the vulture tribe, had picked them clean. At Paardeberg Jolyon followed Harry over to what was left of the deserted Boer laager, marked from a distance by abandoned wrecks of their large jawbone ox-wagons, themselves with their cloth coverings burned away so they resembled animal skeletons. The scene was eerie. The river, deep down between steep terraced banks flowed through the level plain. On the left side was the British position, well entrenched, with a few kopjes guarding one flank about two thousand yards from the bank. On the right the enemy's position extended farther down the banks of the river and up to the very edge of the British side.

The water was very low. The horses splashed through easily and they picked their way through the extensive ground cover on the steep banks, careful that a hoof should not misstep into one of many small pits or trenches dug there. These were not trenches like those of the British infantry or the long sangars the Boers made out on the veldt, but simple little holes dug in the banks, with room enough for a couple of men. In many cases it was evident that they were now also graves, for where the Boers were shot in them the trenches were simply filled in and the bodies thus rudely buried. On both banks, cemeteries marked where Canadian, English, Scots, Irish, Welsh, and Boers had fought, died, and been hurriedly buried.

With a chill shudder, Jolyon leaned close against Harry. After a moment, in the enveloping silence, Harry threw an arm around Jolyon's shoulder, grateful for the contact. "Look, everywhere—spent shells and shrapnel cases and cartridges," Jolyon said in an awed voice. He cast his doleful gaze over the littered soft ground bordering the river. There were many pathetic things: garments and personal belongings, children's toys and utensils all made by the loving hands of men and women.

The dread shadow of war lay as a shroud over the land and Harry felt the awful press of its futility.

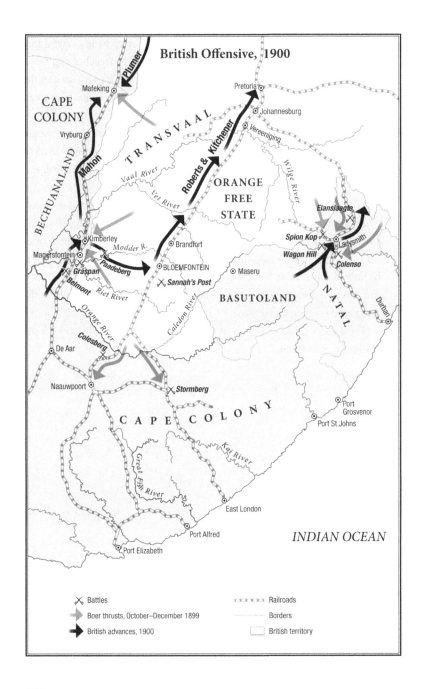

British Offensive, 1900

CAPE COLONY

Mafeking

Plumer

Vryburg

BECHUANALAND

Mahon

T R A N S V A A L

Vaal River

Vet River

Pretoria

Johannesburg

Vereeniging

Roberts & Kitchener

ORANGE FREE STATE

Wilge River

Elandslaagte

Spion Kop

Ladysmith

Wagon Hill

Colenso

Kimberley

Modder R.

Magersfontein

Graspan

Paadeberg

Belmont

Riet River

Brandfort

BLOEMFONTEIN

Sannah's Post

Maseru

BASUTOLAND

Caledon River

N A T A L

Durban

Orange River

Colesberg

De Aar

Naauwpoort

Stormberg

C A P E   C O L O N Y

Port Grosvenor

Port St. Johns

Kei River

Great Fish River

East London

Port Alfred

Port Elizabeth

INDIAN OCEAN

Battles

Boer thrusts, October–December 1899

British advances, 1900

Railroads

Borders

British territory

CHAPTER 36 | *Kimberley, May 16, 1900*

"I SAW LITTLE POINT remaining in Cape Town when my presence here in Kimberley would force Joe Chamberlain and Alfred Milner to dedicate resources to the defense of the city. I owe it to the citizens who live in a place I effectively founded. Politicians and generals only see what they call strategic assets and that would have meant gallivanting up the central Midland line to batter Kruger into submission at Pretoria instead of putting the interests of the diamond and gold mines first. In that I was successful."

Cecil Rhodes, former prime minister of Cape Colony, creator of Rhodesia, preened and settled back comfortably. He had requested Harry and Jolyon's presence at his residence for the day after Harry had announced himself on May 16 to the secretariat of the British South Africa Company, the public corporation founded by Rhodes with a royal charter in 1889. There, one of the staff recommended a nearby rest house that had opened again for business.

It was predictable that Neo's presence should spark an argument with the Indian gentleman who called himself the hotelier of Kimberley's Most Superb Rest House For Discerning Gentlesirs the minute Harry tried to secure accommodation for him. In spite of putting on his best military air, Harry failed to sway the Indian from his apartheid. Coloreds, as the Afrikaaners called the many immigrants from the subcontinent, seemed to want the blacks put as firmly in their place as did the Dutchmen. Eventually, where wielding the might of the Raj failed, some heavy breathing on the part of Travis caused the man to cave to the extent of permitting Neo the use of a former servant's room under the eaves.

In the month and a half since French's cavalry raised the siege, Kimberley had changed beyond recognition. A mining community, it would never be beautiful, Harry thought as they made their way to Rhodes's expansive house, but the speed of repairs was no doubt a reflection of its inordinate wealth.

"And celebrations are due for the news received on the telegraph just now," Rhodes said with a flourish. "Colonel Mahon and his two thousand mounted volunteers from the Imperial Light Horse and our own Kimberly Light Horse, who have fought their way from Barkly West since the fourth, made junction yesterday with Colonel Plumer." He saw their lack of comprehension. "I suppose you've been kept too busy in the southern theater to be aware of operations elsewhere. Plumer raised a mounted force in Rhodesia and kept the Boers on their toes farther to the north. A while back, he attempted to break through the cordon strangling Mafeking, but they were too many and he too few. But now the combined forces of Plumer and Mahon drove off the Dutchmen and lifted the siege of Mafeking in the early hours of this morning."

"They broke through today?" Harry sat forward, roused by the moment.

"That they did, Major Vane." Rhodes raised his glass in triumphant salute.

Harry and Jolyon followed the gesture, all broad smiles. Harry wondered how Stephe Baden-Powell was feeling.

"I understand the wires have burned all morning and already there is enormous excitement in London. They are hailing Baden-Powell a hero for withstanding the enemy for an astonishing two hundred and seventeen days. Now I can press the yeomanry Roberts and Kitchener left us to ensure the rails between here and Mafeking are in good repair. We need the railway functioning immediately! According to reliable information, no damage was done to the track up to Bulawayo. I've no doubt there will be parties of Boers on the move in the region around Mafeking and there will be a considerable amount of mopping up to be done, but I am eager to continue an undertaking stalled by war, one that will come to be regarded as the most important enterprise in all of Africa. Which brings me to why I asked you here to dine with me, gentlemen."

Harry sipped at his Scotch in a big glass crammed with the luxury of ice cubes, which he rattled appreciatively. A low, wide table of solid teak standing on the back of four carved elephants separated Harry from his host and Jolyon, who was seated on the sofa close beside Rhodes. At the tinkle of ice, Rhodes thrust out his chin and smiled broadly.

"Ah, that was a priority as soon as we had sufficient power to spare, to get the refrigeration units working at full blast." He chuckled. "And the wine, it's to your liking?"

Jolyon raised his glass of yellow-green Sauvignon Blanc in a glass so cold it dripped condensation. "Very fine, sir. Thank you."

"Fortunately, Boer depredations failed to substantially halt the production of wines in the Colony. And I'm fortunate that their shells deliverd only superficial damage to the house." Rhodes waved a hand at the room as he sipped his chilled boiled water flavored with lemon. "My doctor forbids alcohol, damn him."

Not only the town, but Rhodes' Kimberley residence—modest, as he called it—had been given a very recent facelift and gleamed with freshly applied paint and floor polish like a socialite lady after the repair of her maquillage. "I shall be returning to Cape Town shortly—after the horrors of the siege I need the peace of Groote Schuur to heal my soul."

Harry was pretty certain the real reason Rhodes wanted to get back to Cape Town was to ensure his voice was heard in the political corridors of power, and his demands met.

"But before that I am anxious to explain what it is I am asking of you, Major Vane."

Harry had made it clear there was no need for the double-barreled name. Rhodes was insistent, however, on using their ranks, even though for this occasion neither wore uniform. "An iron road to connect the red parts on the map of Africa from north to south, I understand."

Rhodes chuckled throatily. "I certainly wish to avail myself of your skills, Major Vane." He turned to Jolyon who he had insisted share the sofa with him. "And yours, Lieutenant Langrish-Smith." He emphasized this with a firm pat of Jolyon's thigh. "But I don't expect you to construct my railway with your bare hands. I'll come to that."

He turned his attention back to Harry. "I knew your brother Evan briefly at Oxford, and of course I'm aware of his work in London at the right hand of Joe Chamberlain to ensure Britain gains total control of Africa from the Cape to Cairo. Which is why it is appropriate that I am talking with you now, Major Vane, and your charming assistant." He turned a warm smile on Jolyon and squeezed his thigh above the knee. Jolyon flicked a guarded look across the low table at Harry. "General French was kind enough to telegraph me your army record, which details intrepid expeditions of the North-West Frontier's most inhospitable regions and no less than two tours of duty suffering the deprivations of Saharan heat. May I show you something?"

Rhodes stood and walked across the ornate room. As Harry followed, he felt Jolyon's tap on his arm and inclined his head the better to hear the whisper.

"He seems inordinately fond of touching my legs, Harry."

"They are extremely elegant legs, Jo."

A glower of frustration flickered across Jolyon's features at the unhelpful remark. "Is he, you know…?"

"One of us?"

Jolyon nodded.

Ahead of them Rhodes rounded a freestanding wooden construction of shelves above cupboards. Exotic potted plants shared shelf space with several books and items of tribal African sculpture.

"I've heard gossip to the effect." Harry looked as amused as Jolyon did not.

The secular rood screen separated the reception area's palatial expanse from what appeared to be an informal office. A large desk dominated its center. Ritual masks were arranged in groups on the white walls. A tall easel held a huge map of the African continent, with British territories, protectorates, and those lands held—so Rhodes must suppose—temporarily by the Boers but which Britain intended to take very shortly.

"It's been my dream…" he turned back to glare intently at his guests, "and in spite of what you may have heard whispered, not only *my* dream alone, that there should be a rail link between Cairo in the north and Cape Town in the south of this great continent." With two sweeps of a hand, Rhodes indicated all the areas marked in imperial red. "As you can see, there is but a small section between our southern and northern extremities which the Germans claim, a stretch of some seven hundred miles where the Union Jack does not fly— though four hundred of those are lake. However, the German authorities are entirely excited at the prospect of a railway linking markets from top to bottom and joining with their own planned route running from the Great Lakes to the coast at Dar es Salaam.

"Well before this conflict began I concluded an arrangement with the German East Africa authorities. It gave me leave to carry a telegraph line through German territory on condition that we lay down at my own cost a separate line solely for the telegraphic traffic of German East Africa. As of now, the telegraphic connection between the Cape and Cairo is nearly completed, to join with the system installed under General Kitchener and south of Khartoum as laid by the orders of his successor, Governor-General Wingate." He smiled wryly. "I should point out that Germany's territory is neither colonized, civilized, nor much occupied."

"What is it you want of us, Mr. Rhodes? To survey and mark the route, to undertake supervision of the engineering, to lay the bedding and ties…?"

Harry smiled to show he was teasing.

Rhodes clapped a hand on his shoulder and the other on Jolyon's. "A report. My shareholders, such as they are, will want to see the lie of the land, have a feel for the natives on the route and how they will react, even line up as workers. It may look daunting, but almost half of the total is already constructed. You will be familiar with General Kitchener's efforts in Egypt and the Sudan. There was a time when I thought I would have to raise my own force to deal with the Mahdi and his fanatic Dervishes, but Lord Kitchener did that for me. Once the Khalifa's power had been swept away, the line pushed south with dispatch. Thousands of the Dervishes who escaped unhurt from the slaughter of Omdurman are shoveling dirt at a beggarly pittance per day, and glad to get it.

"From Khartoum it seemed sensible to follow the Nile valley through Fashoda, but the area is pestilential, so it is being deflected to the west, toward a place called Wau."

He turned again to the map, this time indicating the South African section. "You know the line from the Cape to Kimberley, which continues in a northerly direction to Mafeking and then into Rhodesia to Bulawayo. We opened the section to Bulawayo three years ago to much celebration and the attendances of eminent men from England and America as well as the Cape, the Free State, and Transvaal. At the time, one of those men, the explorer Stanley, posed the question, "Why stop there?" And since then, we have commenced to drive the next section north across the Zambesi River to… here."

Harry leaned in close and saw under Rhodes's fingertip a dot marked Kapiri Mposhi.

"There is a well-used track between there and Abercorn on the border with German territory, and I anticipate it will also suffice to carry a railway. This damn war has caused much delay, but in truth from Abercorn there is no topographical mapping farther to the north, and that places the project in limbo until some understanding is reached—which is where you come in, Major Vane, Lieutenant Langrish-Smith. Intrepid explorers! Think! You will be tracing the steps of no less a man than Dr. Livingstone along the eastern shore of Lake Tanganikya through Buganda to the place where he met Stanley, Ujiji on the shores of the lake. From there, Lake Albert is in easy reach from which the White Nile wends its way north toward Khartoum.

"It has been relatively easy to string the telegraph lines. Wires take no heed of inclines that would defeat a locomotive, nor do they greatly disrupt tribal life, and so the route for the railway must necessarily deviate from that of the wire, and this is what needs to be determined. And which way to proceed north of Lake Victoria is open to question, though common sense suggests following the course Burton and Speke marked out to the northeastern end of Lake Albert and then take a line parallel with the White Nile but on higher ground than the swampy and flood-prone valley. Eventually the way must curve westward and cross the White Nile to arrive at the town of Wau in Equatoria, which I'm given to understand from the written words of Emin Paşa is located on the Nilotic plain hundreds of miles from anywhere. It may be a miserable place, but it is currently intended to be the terminus of the line coming south from Khartoum.

"There it is, gentlemen. We have the records of Burton and Speke, Livingstone and Stanley on the lands of Buganda and the Bunyoro kingdom amid the Great Lakes, but little else to go by. And while all of those men have been wonderful explorers, they were not surveying a route for a railway. And before you remonstrate, Major Vane, I am not expecting a construction expert's technical drawings, but the common sense view and expertise of one who has mapped the majestic Pamirs, the Karakorams, the Hindu Kush, and lived to tell the tale… and come back with sensible maps a technical man may follow up with his sappers and engineers."

"May I pose a question?"

"By all means, Major Vane."

Harry received the distinct impression that Rhodes did not welcome questions, which he probably considered a waste of his time, but he plowed on nonetheless. "The Sirdar, General Kitchener, in all his frantic endeavors to bring the Khalifa and Mahdism to an end, built rails at a pace, but even he decided against linking Aswan to Wadi Halfa and instead relied on river transport for that section. What is your feeling about that?"

Rhodes paused, and then led the way back around the shelving. "I have been advised on several occasions that river transport is the sensible answer for that stretch, but I am driven by the notion that if it is to be a Cape to Cairo Railway, it must have trains running the full length... on rails! However, that is not your concern since I already have engineers looking into the difficulties of the region. Your responsibility to this great enterprise will end at Wau. I need to be confident that the southern works can go ahead urgently, safely, and sensibly. Since the majority of funding is coming from my own resources, I need to be confident that this scheme is feasible." He turned before resuming the sofa and patting the cushion beside him for Jolyon to reoccupy the place close beside him. "Can you give me that, Major Vane?"

❧ ✶ ❧

"He needs it, too."

Harry was driven by ignoble amusement to question the precise nature of what Jolyon meant by what Rhodes needed, but the presence of Travis prevented the facetious remark that came to mind. Instead, he said, "He does?"

Jolyon glanced up from a copy of the *Cape Times*, the half-smile in his eyes communicating a silent understanding of where Harry had been about to go. Harry was seated across from him with Travis, both engrossed in a sheaf of maps Rhodes had provided when they took their leave the day before. Rhodes had also assured Harry that arrangements were in place for the British South Africa Company agents at Kapiri Mposhi and Abercorn to furnish the expedition with sufficient funds to hire onward porterage. The three men of the V.C.C.R.S. (Vane's Cape-to-Cairo Rail Survey, a designation jokingly supplied by Travis after a few beers) were seated in the stuffy lounge of Kimberley's Most Superb Rest House on cane chairs softened for Discerning Gentlesirs' behinds by thin antelope-hide cushions. Having drawn the line at having a native kaffer loose in his ground-floor rooms, the Indian hotelier banished Neo to the back veranda, where the boy curled up and dropped happily asleep.

Harry smiled at Jolyon. "What does he need?"

"Confidence. The notion of his rail connection to Cairo is clearly no secret, and not everyone is convinced of its benefits. Here, an American correspondent who claims to know much about '*railroad* construction,' compares Rhodes's projected undertaking to the Trans-Siberian Railway, of which he says: 'This is being built under the compulsion of an impulse, or an instinct, which it is impossible to justify on financial, political, or military grounds. The sacrifices which the construction entails will never be repaid and I could name a score of other methods of investing money within the Empire that would pay handsomely, pay far better than this transcontinental railway can ever hope to do.'

"He goes on to say… where is it? Ah, yes: 'If the Cape to Cairo line is not urgently wanted in order to expedite communication between London and the extremities of Africa for imperial or military reasons, it is still less wanted from the point of view of a dividend-earning investment. There is at this moment no through traffic of any kind between the Cape and Cairo. The two ends of the African Continent have absolutely nothing in common, except that they are both African, and that both are at present under the shelter of the British flag. To build the line would cost fifty million dollars…'"

Jolyin looked up, with a schoolmasterly expression. "Which the editor adds in a note is equivalent to ten million pounds."

He returned his eyes to the paper. "Er… to which our man adds it could cost at least that, possibly twice as much. He goes on, 'It is extremely doubtful whether it would earn a dividend or could even be worked except at a loss. And yet, notwithstanding all these obvious and indisputable considerations, it is by no means impossible that the Cape to Cairo line may be in working order in 1909.' January 20, 1909 is the date Mr. Rhodes gave to the writer to be present at the laying of the last rail," Jolyon finished.

"Then we had better get going." Harry dipped his head at the papers spread over the table in front of him. "You know there really isn't much known about the terrain much farther than a hundred miles above Bulawayo. We'll have a our work cut out if Mr. Rhodes is to see his last rail laid in a little under nine years."

Jolyon narrowed his eyes in a skeptical expression. "We may have a splendid time scouting our way north through trackless jungle, but our American gentleman here is doubtful that the same will be said of the railway line." He bent his head to the paper again. "He adds, a trifle condescendingly I think: 'It is difficult to explain why the keenly practical and stolidly unimaginative Briton should be bending his energies and lavishing his resources in order to construct a line from Cape to Cairo, except that the first and dominating cause is the fact that the idea has fascinated the imagination of Mr. Rhodes; and the second and hardly less potent reason is the fact that the Cape and Cairo both begin with the letter C. Possibly this second reason ought to have precedence over the first, for who knows how much of the fascination which has caught Mr. Rhodes's fancy was due to Apt Alliteration's Artful Aid?'

"Ha ha. The man has wit." Jolyon tossed the paper aside.

"And a florid, pompous tongue," Harry said.

"Like all Americans. Those I have known in the Cape are not quiet in their despising of our Empire." Travis glanced up from his calculations at the dismissive clearing of Harry's throat.

"The Americans have laid a great deal of track across their many wildernesses, Travis, so I'm sure they know about such things. I'm just saying that Jolyon's American correspondent prefers to direct ridicule at the dreams of greater men." Harry frowned thoughtfully. "Which is odd when you think that it was American enterprise which spanned the Atbara for Kitchener's railway to proceed south toward Khartoum. When the job was put out to tender, British bridge-builders said the construction would take two years, when Wingate, after he took over, wanted it done right then before the July floods! So the job went to an American company to build the seven spans needed, and within thirty-seven days of the receipt of the order, the Atbara Bridge left New York Harbor for its destination.

"You see if there is the will there is always the means and the way."

CHAPTER 37 | *Mafeking, 8–15 June, 1900*

GENERAL FRENCH'S prediction of a swift end to the war seemed to be realized when British forces stormed Johannesburg on May 31 and entered Kruger's Transvaal capital of Pretoria five days later. With Bloemfontein and Pretoria in Roberts and Kitchener's hands the Boers were finished and the war won, as far as everyone on the British side was concerned. The Cape government renamed the Orange Free State the Orange River Colony. There were those voices, though, raised in caution: the Republican Dutch farmers were a mobile force and had never been much given to defending towns.

Colonel Mahon's small mounted force of volunteers may have burst through the Boer siege and freed Mafeking, but it did not mean the way was open for the survey team to set off for the town as the first stop on the way to Bulawayo, and from there to cross the Zambesi at the Victoria Falls. In the intervening two weeks between the relief of Mafeking and the fall of Pretoria, contingents of Boers, small and large, were on the move after the chain of defeats and Harry bowed to the wisdom of the captain in charge of the small force charged with Kimberley's security. He advised Harry that it would be asking for trouble to send any but armored trains up the line to Mafeking in the immediate aftermath of its relief, and he had no soldiers to spare until the task of protecting the sapper-engineers repairing damage to the rails and telegraph poles was finished.

The delay may have caused Rhodes to fret, but for the small team there was much to be done before the V.C.C.R.S. could depart anyway. Harry had several more discussions with Rhodes, while Travis and Jolyon busied themselves drawing up lists of goods and supplies that would be required at each stage. The bulk of weapons, supplies, camping gear, and porters to carry it all, as well as a few pack animals and mounts would not be required until reaching Abercorn, according to Rhodes. He referred to his British South Africa Company simply as *The Company*. Travis cut it down further to a derogatory *Bee-Sac*, though never in the great man's presence. "I will have representatives of The Company organize a great deal of that for you," Rhodes assured Harry.

All in all, the preparations kept them three weeks in Kimberley, and so it was the seventh of June before everyone took places on the first real passenger train departing for Mafeking at the crack of dawn. Thanks to a lack of Boer interference and the Cape Government Railways' rapid reinstatement of the line and rolling stock from a war footing, the first part of the journey from Kimberley to Mafeking was undertaken in the relative comfort of a European-style train. Harry greatly approved of these. In contrast to the British railway car with its transverse eight-seater compartments accessible from the platform only through doors on either side, the corridor on the South African cars gave access to all the six-seater compartments for the length of the train. This freedom of movement meant passengers might take advantage of the "comfort" facilities as well as a buffet car—not that this one was stocked much beyond a few snacks.

A few hours out from Kimberley, Jolyon complained that V.C.C.R.S. was too much of a mouthful and voted for renaming the expedition Vane's Survey Team, or even more simply V.S. The motion was swiftly carried, even though out of modesty Harry abstained.

From Kimberley the 226 miles to Mafeking took a little under eleven hours, the train managing an average of 20 mph, often slowed on the steeper inclines, of which there were few in evidence to the eye but up which the locomotive nevertheless labored. After passing through Warrenton the valley broadened out into a prairie dotted with anthills and low, flat kopjes, but not a real hill in sight. It was terrain familiar to Harry and Travis on the return from Mafeking the previous year. The track crossed the Vaal River and then turned slightly west-of-north to Vryburg, a name that brought back unpleasant memories for that first encounter with the devastating power of the pom-pom gun.

As the train approached Mafeking the effects of such a long and unremitting siege were manifested in the abrupt change from a moderately fertile landscape populated by pleasant copses of trees into a region marked by utter devastation. Neo leaned from the window to stare in horrified fascination at modern war's destructive power. The clusters of stately trees that once graced the widespread streets of the settlement were reduced to stumps by artillery fire and, as it turned out, the inhabitants' desperate need for more and more wood to shore up collapsed buildings. Mafeking was a treelees town. Battle-scarred, ungainly barricades, yet to be torn down, stretched across those thoroughfares which had been exposed to the enemy's fire. At frequent intervals in the streets were visible the numerous shelter-pits, dug as protections against the enemy's shell and rifle fire. By their continuous use these holes had taken on the appearance of a permanent character.

The town exhibited all the signs of its brutal treatment. Apart from along the railway line and around the station where they had been renewed, telegraph poles and lamp posts were bent and twisted, some lying completely broken on the roadside. Weeds covered the roads and paths, and everywhere the neglect and demolishment of seven months' siege was in evidence. Where order reigned before hostilities, now all was confusion. Great furrows in the roadways marked the passage of the many shells which had come into the town. Everywhere the travelers looked, the walls of the houses were riddled with bullet holes or wide, ragged gaps punched out by the projectiles of the Boers' leviathan 94-pounder.

"The Boers nicknamed that damned great Creusot siege gun Grietje, which we adapted to Creechy or Old Creaky."

Baden-Powell looked remarkably sprightly for the man who had organized resistance to the besieging Boers for more than seven months.

As there was no suitable accommodation in Mafeking, the military conductor informed the few passengers that the train would have to suffice as hotel, and to Harry's surprise—who had anticipated his former companion at Simla to be engaged in operations outside the township—that was where Baden-Powell found them.

The colonel's first announcement tempered Harry's pleasure somewhat.

"I had a telegram from Mr. Rhodes to expect you. He treats the wire as if it were his own, which I suppose to a degree it actually is. He seems to think the military are here at his own beck and call. Nevertheless, it's very good to see you again, Harry. Unfortunately, no matter how much Mr. Rhodes wants to reach Cairo next month, I'm afraid you won't be going on to Bulawayo for a bit. You see there is suspected kommando activity to the northwest of town."

"Dammit, Stephe. I'd hoped the Boers would be swept away from the western Transvaal."

"It can't be helped, my dear chap, though I'm confident we'll get you under way again soon because—between you and me—I don't believe much in these phantom kommando units. I'm pretty sure we've rounded up most of the culprits, but Roberts and Kitchener insist that the speed of their advance left many Boers in their rear so there could be a resurgence."

After introductions to the other members of the V.S., Baden-Powell took Harry aside. They strolled along the length of the train and Harry heard Travis telling Neo to sort out something to cook on. A natural scavenger, he knew Neo would find something to use for the purpose.

"You may not have heard," Baden-Powell began as soon as they were out of earshot, "but along with lifting the siege—though bringing us no desperately needed sustenance, I might add—came the news that our Commander-in-Chief Lord Roberts is replacing Garnet Wolseley at the War Office. Those two never got on well. You know how Wolseley has always derided Bobs, calling him 'the Little Hindoo'—"

"I heard the joke, that he always favored the officers who served under him in India."

"Quite, and a delight you and I avoided. Well, I fear that as one of the 'Garnet Ring,' as the Roberts star rises in the firmament Wolseley's preferment of me will become a liability rather than an asset. In fact, it's already begun in a way. Tasked with the mopping up and restoration of order along the Colony-Transvaal border, I thought I would be given the help of Colonel Mahon's relief column. The men and officers were detached from Archibald Hunter's Natal Field Army. Do you know the general?"

"Indeed, I served with Hunter on the Nile campaign—at Atbara and in the advance on Omdurman."

"Ah, of course, where you dashed off to from Simla. It was natural for me to assume after the Relief I would come under Hunter's command and requested that Mahon's eleven hundred mounted rifles help me in garrisoning Mafeking and to undertake the pacification program in the western Transvaal. But Hunter refused and took Mahon back, so here am I, with a bare eight hundred and fifty men, of which only five hundred are fit and equipped to be a mobile force."

"With such slender resources I can see why there is the uncertainty you spoke of," Harry said with genuine sympathy.

Baden-Powell gave vent to one of his mock-Chinee Wun-Hi laughs Harry remembered from his role in *The Geisha* at Simla. And in the same voice went on, "Ah-so, Hally, yet with so small column I stirr confiscate over thousand lifles fom wicked Boer men, and put two hundred fifty behind bars for not co-oplating."

Wun-Hi abruptly vanished and the careworn appearance of a malnourished and overworked man replaced the humor. "We've also had to disarm large numbers of Africans who went marauding after the Relief. One can't really blame them. They too have suffered terribly, but we can't have armed tribesmen threatening the new and fragile peace, any more than I can allow vengeful Dutchmen to ride the veldt angry at having their farms confiscated for their part in the kommando raids. It's also vital we establish a framework of local government and policing, otherwise so-called pacified areas might well rise up again. The week before your train arrived, Harry, I have Roberts telling me to leave all that and use Colonel Mahon's force to crack down on marauding Boer units that I don't believe exist. At least, not in the concentration he seems obsessed with. And—note—with a force of men already removed from me by his subordinate, General Hunter."

"I know the frustration of mixed signals from command," Harry said in an attempt to be soothing. "But you can take some comfort from the brouhaha in all the British press about the Relief and your role in it, Stephe. You're labeled a hero."

"It's gratifying all right." Baden-Powell gave Harry a look of guarded pride mixed with pure exasperation. "But I tell you this: beware undiluted praise from those who don't know what they're talking about. As we speak, professional envy is beginning to drip corrosively and my reputation may well be destroyed through doing something which quite simply had to be done. There will be those lining up for the chance to sling mud, to say I trapped myself here rather than take war to the enemy.

"Anyway, you don't want to listen to me ranting on. I envy you the task Cecil Rhodes has set you, Harry. I loved my short time running around Matebeleland four years ago. Whatever travails uncivilized regions may throw up in your path, it's a far cleaner environment than the murky politics of the red-capped top brass. By the way, I wanted to say earlier that your comely Mr. Langrish-Smith is the epitome of what young British men should be."

Harry thanked him, as if Jolyon's attractiveness was Baden-Powell's gift.

On the dusty ground outside the first car, which the survey team had commandeered, they found Travis crouched over an upturned bucket that had been converted into a crude brazier, and the smell of cooking meat floated up amid a swirl of blue smoke. "That's all taken care of, Colonel, Major," he said, pointing at the locomotive's lounging crew. Evidently restocking the fuel tender and topping off the water tanks was done and the locomotive sat quietly issuing trickles of steam from pressure vents along the boiler.

Travis grinned up at Baden-Powel from under the brim of his bush hat. "Would you care for some sausages, Colonel?"

"Did you bring them with you?"

"Well, let's just say I liberated them yesterday from the rest house refrigerator unit and they've been in the buffet car's cool box on our ride up."

Baden-Powell moistened his lips and bit at the lower one. "I really feel I shouldn't, considering everyone else is still on quarter rations, but…" He sniffed loudly at the aroma.

Travis forked a stack of brown-blackened sausages onto a large tin plate and led the way up the steps and into the car. Travis and Jolyon took seats beside the window. Harry sat next to Jolyon with Baden-Powell opposite him. "Best keep out of sight," he muttered, although Harry reckoned no one could see the chief guzzling hot food through the grime-coated window.

"Come on in and get some," Harry said to Neo, who hovered uncertainly in the compartment doorway.

"Here." Jolyon waved him past the small pullout table Travis produced from under the bench seat for the plate and offered the boy a knee to perch on.

The sausages still sizzled and popped enticingly. In a second everyone dug in, shuffling the hot bangers from hand to hand to avoid getting too badly burned.

Baden-Powell made no comment about having a black boy so close in their presence, and as he chewed with evident enjoyment, he nodded amiably at Neo. "I'm sure I remember you. You were one of my Barolong scouts at the beginning."

Neo acknowledged that he was and that the Colonel-Master had given him a chit recommending him.

"And we ran into him on a patrol a few miles south of the siege line."

Baden-Powell's eyebrows shot up. "You were here?"

"Yes. That was back in November last year. Buller wanted to know how large Cronjé's army was, so we came snooping, and Neo joined my little force. Been with us since. Until now. Now it's time for him to rejoin his tribesmen and make a new life for himself."

"Those boys did me good service, slipping through the lines and liaising with their tribesmen to ensure we had a supply of cattle rustled off the Boers. And then it became too dangerous and most managed to get away."

For a while there was silence, broken by the sounds of chewing and swallowing and Baden-Powell's sighs of pleasure. He cleared his throat. "We made good use of the young white boys in the Mafeking Cadet Corps as well. Acted as runners to carry messages around the town, they did, and to the outlying posts, always at risk to their lives over the open ground. Sergeant-Major Warner Goodyear was their commander…well, he still is. Just thirteen, fourteen now. Most of them were eleven, twelve. They got to be skilled as gunnery lookouts to warn the townspeople when the siege artillery was aimed at a particular section of the town. Lord Edward Cecil looked after them— never could get on with that man, Prime Minister's son or not. His manner was not warm enough toward the boys. They needed encouragement and a tough manly love, not aloofness. Still, he organized donkeys for them to get around, until we ran out of food and the poor beasts went to the kitchen pot."

After devouring half of his third sausage, Baden-Powell said around a mouthful, "These are the most gloriously… delicious things I've eaten since… well since the last of the oxen got roasted up, and that must be two months ago, or longer, I can't remember." He swallowed the last morsel.

"Take the last one, Colonel," Jolyon urged.

Baden-Powell looked left and right at the others, and then picked it up between greasy fingers. "The starvation has been bad. The men became gaunt, the women haggard and careworn, and nothing has changed a great deal yet for the better since the Relief. Once we get some order into the countryside around, there will be some crops to raise and harvest again, but really the supplies must come up the railways now. After defense, my primary concern was for the rations. I became a quartermaster as well as an innovative chef. I had to provide for the native population as well as the white, amid many complaints on that score, especially from Captain Ryan, my Chief Commissariat Officer.

"Between the incessant shelling and the ever-present fear of maiming and the malaria and enteric dysentery the only thing to keep moral up was a full stomach, and that became increasingly hard to provide. When the mules and horses we had within the stockade became enfeebled beyond the point of usefulness, we slaughtered them. When a horse was killed, nothing was wasted. Its mane and tail were cut off and used in the hospital for stuffing mattresses and pillows. The shoes went to the foundry for making shells. After the hair was scalded off the hide, it was boiled with the head and feet for half the day, chopped up, and served as brawn."

The gruesome details seemed to have no effect on the colonel's appetite.

"The flesh was removed from the bones and ground in a great mincing machine. The intestines were scraped and the meat crammed in, portioned with a butcher's twist, and each man received a sausage as his ration. The bones were boiled up into a thick soup to be dealt out at the various soup kitchens; and afterward they were pounded into powder with which we adulterated the dwindling supply of flour. I could wish we had more horses to supplement the Africans' meager diet. They had to subsist on a porridge made out of the husks of animal forage oats. There were always locusts and termites, as well as stray dogs that ended up in the pot. But as you have seen out there, the garrison is famished, and what supplies are coming in must be eked out to ensure the mobile police column is fed sufficiently to be able to operate."

Harry couldn't sleep. Had the siege had killed off sound? He heard nothing of Africa's eternal night chorus: no trilling crickets, no barking of bush dog strays, no nightjars calling in the trees because there were no trees, and no one was abroad. He lay on his back, full length along one of the bench seats, and stared up at the curved compartment roof. A remark of Jolyon's ran around in his head about the kinds of tribes they might encounter in the central regions of Africa, and not wanting to meet any cannibal tribes like those Stanley ran into only twelve years ago.

"That was along the Ituri River in the Congo Free State," Harry had pointed out.

"I read about it, his journey up the river to rescue that Emin Paşa chap."

"We won't be going anywhere near there." Harry paused for a moment, a sour recollection of a short novel he'd read. "The Ituri Forest really is the

415

pestilential soul of the continent. You only have to read Joseph Conrad's *Heart of Darkness* to discover that. *Blackwood's Magazine* printed it in three parts back in the spring last year and it made me shudder. I thought I'd run into some pretty frightful customs in the mountains of the North-West Frontier, but nothing so… evil."

Now he was contemplating information Richard Rainbow had telegraphed in response to Harry's, written in haste at Kimberley to inform of their plans and that at some point in the near future, God and Africa willing, he would appear in Khartoum with Jolyon. (The Cape to Cairo telegraph line Rhodes had said was almost completed was still not operating, so Harry and Richard's communications went via the Atlantic cable and a Mediterranean connection to Cairo and thence to Khartoum.) He added that since the railway would almost certainly not follow the course of the existing telegraph wires, this might be the last communication he could send. Among hopes for a successful expedition Richard wrote: *Ensure circle north to edge Abyssinian highlands to reach Wau. Avoid Equatoria region Bahr-el-Ghazal. Tribes unreliable. To date no pressure to send commissioner or troops, too much else to be done other regions Sudan.*

Richard pointed to the writing of trader-explorer Georg August Schweinfurth, and Harry found a copy of his book in Rhodes's extensive library on African matters. It related Schweinfurth's travels through the Bahr-el-Ghazal, the watershed between the Congo and Nile rivers, some twenty years earlier. There he encountered the Asante, a tribe who killed their captives for the pot. Richard's caution and Schweinfurth's revelation he'd kept to himself. Why arouse the others' concerns when he had no intention of cutting a straight line from the northern tip of Lake Albert, across the White Nile to Wau, which would lead them through territory these Asante claimed for their own? The plan was to head due north from Buganda's capital of Mengo to the Abyssinian foothills, and then go west to Wau, as Richard advised.

Gruesome thoughts of cannibals ensured sleep's banishment. He was missing Jolyon. Harry swung his legs down and stood up. He stretched and then exited his compartment and walked quietly along the car's corridor. Through the almost closed door of one compartment there came a noise to cut across the night's deep silence: Travis, flung carelessly along a bench, fast asleep, snoring.

He wanted Jolyon. They had been very careful, but managed to spend a couple of hours in each other's arms in the late-night privacy of the Kimberley rest house when Jolyon came creeping along to Harry's bedroom. On the train it was just too risky. But even a quiet talk this evening was not possible because when he looked in Jolyon's compartment it was empty.

He reached the end of the car and went out onto the open-air platform. After a moment's pause he cocked an ear—voices, so quiet it could have been his imagination. No, definitely voices, and one could be in Jolyon's cadences. He stepped down to the ground and walked quietly back along the line of three cars. At the end, the train crew had shunted an armored open boxcar into place. It was to house a squad of soldiers when the train left for Bulawayo—a precaution Baden-Powell had insisted on. He had promised at least five riflemen to go with them for the first hundred miles in case they should run into any "South African Republicans."

Before reaching the end of the loopholed truck, Harry heard a cry, more of a sob, and Jolyon's muted voice, and then footsteps running away. He rounded the corner and immediately saw a dark figure in a forlorn slump against the end of the truck by the link-and-pin coupler.

"Jo!"

Harry drew close. Jolyon slowly turned to look at him.

"I couldn't find you. Was that Neo?"

He made out a nod of the head in the dark.

"He doesn't want to leave us."

Harry moved close and Jolyon laid his head on Harry's shoulder.

"But this is his home, Jo. He must seek his tribal elders and make a new life for himself now."

"I told him, Harry, but he wants to go with us."

"Why did he cry out?"

Jolyon snaked a hand around Harry's waist and gripped hard. "Because I said he had to go, now, that we can't take him with us." A bleak silence ensued, broken when Jolyon made a gulping noise. "He started crying. I've never seen Neo shed a tear before."

"I think he's soft on you."

He felt the jolt of Jolyon's body and the gripping hand clenched tighter. Jo raised his head. "Oh that's bollocks, as Travis would say. Why do you say it?"

"Because I think he is." Harry gripped Jolyon's shoulder. "Be honest, he's had more time clinging to you one way or another than I have these past weeks."

Jolyon stiffened, straightened his posture, and his timbre deepened. "Don't tell me you're jealous. Anyway, wasn't it you told me in Cape Town it wouldn't be easy for us—to be together. There was me at Woolwich, fondly imagining us rampaging over the veldt, just the two of us, picking off the Boers and making camp at night, cuddled up in each other's arms. I knew really it was a silly dream, but I'd hoped for more times than we've had." He looked up angrily, his eyes glinting palely in the light of the newly risen moon. "You don't really think I've been up to anything with Neo? Well, I haven't. Haven't even thought of it until you just brought it up."

He shrugged off Harry's hand and made to walk off.

"Jo, please, I didn't—"

"I told Neo firmly he had to find his own way now we're at peace. And I'm tired, so I'll go and lie down."

"Jo…"

Harry followed as far as the corner of the boxcar. Jolyon's silhouette retreated, darker than the dark backdrop.

PART SIX

Assuaging a rabid hunger, 1900–1901

"We penetrated deeper and deeper into the heart of darkness."

— Joseph Conrad

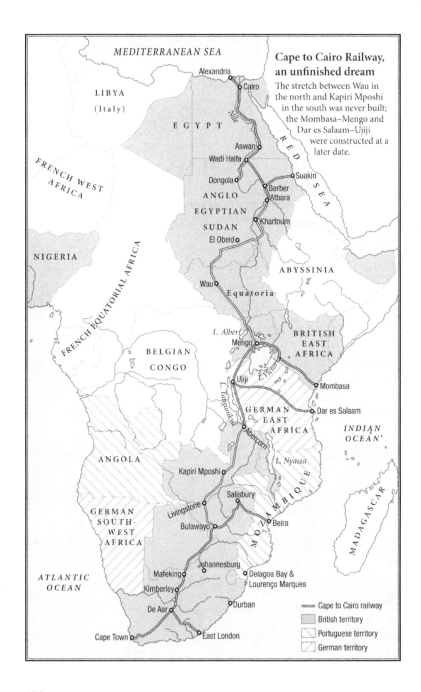

Cape to Cairo Railway, an unfinished dream

The stretch between Wau in the north and Kapiri Mposhi in the south was never built; the Mombasa–Mengo and Dar es Salaam–Ujiji were constructed at a later date.

MEDITERRANEAN SEA

Alexandria
Cairo

LIBYA
(Italy)

EGYPT

FRENCH WEST AFRICA

Nile

RED SEA

Aswan
Wadi Halfa

Dongola
Suakin
Berber
Atbara

ANGLO
EGYPTIAN
SUDAN

Khartoum

El Obeid

NIGERIA

FRENCH EQUATORIAL AFRICA

ABYSSINIA

Wau

Equatoria

L. Albert

BELGIAN CONGO

Mengo

BRITISH EAST AFRICA

L. Victoria

Ujiji

Mombasa

L. Tanganyika

GERMAN EAST AFRICA

Dar es Salaam

INDIAN OCEAN

Abercorn

L. Nyassa

MADAGASCAR

ANGOLA

Kapiri Mposhi

Salisbury

MOZAMBIQUE

Livingstone

Beira

GERMAN SOUTH-WEST AFRICA

Bulawayo

Johannesburg

Mafeking

Delagoa Bay & Lourenço Marques

ATLANTIC OCEAN

Kimberley

Durban

De Aar

Cape Town

East London

Cape to Cairo railway
British territory
Portuguese territory
German territory

CHAPTER 38 | *Rhodesia, June 1900*

SURVEY DIARY, FRIDAY JUNE 15, 1900

In addition to the official survey report, I have decided to keep a general diary of our progress for my own purposes. It will be a report I'd prefer to keep private since I may note personal matters.

We left Mafeking shortly after sun-up. There are three other passengers on this first run, a commercial traveler and two Company officials who came up in a train two days prior. Stephe is happy that the risk of vengeful Dutch farm boys molesting us is sufficiently reduced to let us go on to Bulawayo. Nevertheless, behind our three-car train he insisted on adding an armored truck and a detachment of five men of the Kimberley Horse. They were aggrieved at being dismounted and obliged to endure daytime temperatures in what is effectively a metal-sided cattle truck. Happily, their torment lasted only four hours and a hundred miles. They and the truck were uncoupled at Mahalapye. The station is no more than a third-class car and a goods van standing on three lengths of rail; the township, little better, a scattering of low-grade huts on a stream the color of the brown landscape through which it flows toward the Limpopo River. The cavalrymen can return home with the next transport headed south.

I estimate that at an average of 23 mph, the 490-mile journey to Bulawayo will take a day and a half, allowing for several stops on the way. It is likely to be uneventful, as we will be drawing well away from the Transvaal border. There is luxury again—a corridor train, and no less than four compartments to ourselves. We three intrepid explorers could spread out during the day, but Jo and I don't wish to be separated, and Travis seems content in our company. It is odd to be without the presence of Neo and I am sorry at his going, but I am convinced it was best for him to remain behind with his own tribe. The adjacent compartment is dedicated to our baggage, and while that is not yet of expedition dimensions it is still considerable, weighted down with surveying equipment like theodolite and elevation rods, marked distance chains, and a couple of plane tables. How Alfred Winner would laugh if he knew that it includes two fold-up bathtubs.

As I write, the day is well advanced. For some hours we trundled calmly across a plain of Karoo-like scrub, passing native kraals but nothing in the way of European farmsteads. At one point Travis waved at the barren terrain. He has a theory and explained it to us.

"Look at the hills over there. You see the elevated land, how it's jagged and cut up. That's the effect of ages of torrential rainfall, yet here in this flat valley there's no water. It's barren, but I'll bet you the soil is fertile. The dongas and bigger watercourses are dry, but the fact of them tells you how much water is washed away and wasted every year. All any colonists have to do is build small stone dams every few hundred yards to provide as many reservoirs as they will need. Turn the desert into a paradise."

In staring out the dust-smeared compartment window (closed for the fact of the dust and the prevailing stink of the locomotive's fire-grate discharge), Jo was dismissive and sounded disappointed. "I thought it would be, well, a lot rougher than this. It's not by any means Hyde Park, but it's all a lot tidier than I imagined."

"Jo, I'm sorry there are no Impi warriors painted white in dried mud brandishing their assegais and beating their leopard-hide shields," I told him. "It's more than twenty years since the battles of Isandlwana and Rorke's Drift. The situation is very different."

At that Travis told me off. "We're a long way north of Natal and Zululand now, *Major*."

"It was a figure of speech, *Sergeant*, a metaphor in fact."

Jo's reading hasn't taken in much of African politics. "The Matebele were Zulus who fled Natal to escape the clutches of despotic King Shaka at the beginning of last century," I explained. "They settled the region we're now passing through, between the Limpopo and Zambesi rivers, which is Southern Rhodesia."

"Yeah, and we kicked that old fucking bastard King Lobengula's ass back in '94 and that was the end of Matebele power."

Travis has a fine choice of pejorative adjectives.

"Which is why, with your water, this plateau can be prosperously settled. It seems to me," I said, "that the Company may have annexed the place to dig valuable minerals out of the ground, but they brought a framework of law, and soon farmers rushing to grab decent land will make the running in Rhodesia."

I nudged Jo, who is seated next to me. "Patience. We still have a long long way to go. I know Rhodes says Northern Rhodesia is rapidly becoming as settled as the southern half under Company governance, but there are uncivilized territories ahead of us where few, if any, white men have penetrated."

"Yeah, like along Lake Tanganikya in German East Africa and to the north of Buganda toward Lake Albert and farther north into Equatoria."

Travis often sounds a sour tone for no apparent reason, which has the effect of making me opposingly mellifluous. "But in between those regions the kingdom of Buganda on Lake Victoria is a Crown Protectorate, and I'm sure we'll find a welcome there."

"I shall be put out, to say the least, if I'm not to have a Speke-Burton-Livingstone adventure," Jo said. He knocked up the brim of his bush hat and wiped his brow. His elegant profile fills me with unexpressed longing. I think he's forgiven me for implying that he and Neo might have had an… attachment.

Travis grunted disapproval at Jo's flippant comment. "It will be adventurous enough if we take more than the minimum of riding and pack animals. The forests of German Africa, Buganda, around the lakes, and the swamps of Equatoria are rife with sleeping sickness."

Jolyon shuddered in distaste. "Sleeping sickness? That sounds gruesome."

"If you catch it, it's usually fatal, and the suspect is the bastard tsetse fly. The damn things follow cattle, oxen, and all beasts of burden, so the less there are on the hoof, the less the chance of us getting bitten."

"Is there no cure?"

Travis shrugged.

"I never went as far south as Fashoda in the Sudan," I said, "but those who did and were unfortunate in catching the disease eventually succumbed and died even after British medical treatment at Khartoum. Best is prevention, which is why we have long-sleeved clothing and why we'll sleep under nets—"

"Which will save us from being stung to death by fucking mosquitos at the same time," Travis added.

"You seem to know a lot about it, Travis," Jo observed.

"Har... don't think of me only as a dispossessed Cape Colony farmer." He gave us both a penetrating look as if about to say something of import, and then relaxed. "I'll tell you about it some time."

Survey diary, Friday June 15, afternoon

Travis and Jo doze in the close heat. The breeze is coming from a different direction now, so the compartment's window has been lowered, but does nothing to alleviate the temperature. The even-natured terrain and brand-new rails make for a very smooth ride, which adds to the soporific atmosphere.

The landscape looks to be kind to railway engineers, much more so than I suspect it will be once we reach beyond Rhodesia. I'm reminded of reading an article by the explorer Henry Stanley. On his way as an invited guest to see the newly opened terminus at Bulawayo just before the war, he observed that all of South Africa "seems to have been created for iron road making. It offers few difficulties and Hyde Park is extremely uneven when compared with it." Which is funny; that's what Jo complained of earlier. "And yet we have climbed some thousands of feet above sea level but at such a slow rate it's not noticeable," Stanley added.

I must have spoken some of this aloud for Jolyon opened his eyes and smiled thinly. "Are we there yet?"

The train stops briefly at halts of no more than corrugated-iron cottages, or parked railway cars, temporary accommodation for the guards and signalmen. Although the recently laid tracks have yet to encourage new settlements, at each stop crowds of natives materialize from the scrub and flock around, begging for bread, meat, or leftovers.

Survey diary, Saturday June 16, early morning

There is sufficient glow in the east to write by. We passed through Palapye in Bechuanaland during the hours of darkness, and the fact of a native township of considerable size was apparent only from the extensive flickering of rush lights winking like fireflies across the plain. Shortly after pulling away from the inadequate station the heavens unleashed a mighty electrical storm and it only relinquished its hold an hour past. It was a noisy and alarming experience. Electrical energy loves nothing so much as iron and in such a flat landscape a locomotive of iron running along iron rails acts like a magnet for every explosive discharge. At our last stop, still in the dark, I asked the driver how we survived continual strikes of killing lightning.

"You may have noticed, sir, how I slowed to a walking pace," he told me. "That's so the copper ribbon sweeps we throw out to either side don't bounce too much against the ballast at the side of the track. The lightning seems attracted to the high smoke stack on the boiler and from there it crackles its way to earth—and that is really where it desires to be—through the ribbons to the stones below, and is therefore mostly harmless to us."

I confess to having no idea what he's talking about, but grateful that he does know the correct remedy.

The passing landscape has begun to change and the ubiquitous thorn trees of Bechuanaland have given way to leafier woods resembling dwarf oaks, though still few trees are better than fifteen feet tall. The woods here clothe the broad plain between cultivated regions. It's a refreshing change for the eye grown weary of Bechuanaland's flat scrub savannah and the short indigenous trees of the regions bordering the Orange River Colony and Transvaal.

The sun has risen and it seems I spoke too soon. To my surprise Bulawayo is approached not through the anticipated beginnings of tropical jungle but across a reddish plain that supports a return of the tedious thorn bush. But after the storm, the monotonous burnt grass tussocks dotting the ground like large curled-up hedgehogs are now smothered in a carpet of green. Beyond and to our right, the whaleback shaped kopjes of the Matapos Hills may be seen. Travis on returning from the water closet nodded at them.

"That's where the black despot Lobengula fought the Bee-Sac militia back in 1893. Can't really blame the bugger. He fell for Rhodes's blandishments and when he realized it wasn't the hand of friendship the white man was holding out but his cock ready to sodomize the king, he took to the hills with his Matabele warriors. Of course, the poor man hadn't understood that Bee-Sac had the Maxim gun. Matabeleland became Rhodesia. The magic of rapidly expended bullets."

"I didn't peg you for a philosopher, Travis," Jo responded sourly. There are days when he never wakes well and the storm did keep us all from sleep… but I think it was Travis's use of the word *sodomize* made him flinch.

≈✦≈

Survey diary, Saturday June 16, morning

I write a little later, after getting over the shock… I'll come to it in its own time.

We all thought the train was slowing for Bulawayo, but it seemed not. Jo was idly wiping an oily cloth over the metal parts of his revolver when the brakes made a grinding noise on the rails. He swiftly holstered the weapon and shoved the window down—shut again against the storm—and leaned out. Steam and smoke wafted past his face as the train came to a stop, and he sneezed. "The engineers are getting off."

The military orderly acting as conductor bustled up to the compartment door and informed me that the three-man engineer crewmen get their breakfast here. "Then it's only an hour to Bulawayo."

Time to stretch legs and get some morning-dew fresh air.

Matapos Hills station is no more than a long grass hut built parallel to the rails with a low veranda supported on rough-hewn tree trunks. Above the awning a hand-painted board announces that it is the Matapos General Store and Rest House. Several piles of miscellaneous goods, fruit, and vegetables of indeterminate nature are scattered to one side of the three rickety tables where the train's crew and the three other passengers waited for their gari porridge, eggs, bacon, and tea. I have not acquired the taste for gari—a tasteless mess made from the root of the cassava plant—in the way some Europeans have.

Jolyon stayed in the car to nap, offering the storm as an excuse for his slothfulness. I wasn't hungry and Travis said he'd see if there was some decent tea in a bit. We strolled away from the hut and I pressed him to tell me more about the history he'd hinted at yesterday. It is an interesting tale indeed and I've tried to write it down as well as I remember him telling it.

"I was a farmer just the last few years, up until the bleeding Dutchmen got big ideas, though maybe I should do as they do and blame the greed of Uitlanders scrambling after gold and diamonds," he started. "When I first came out to the Cape I was little more than a wee bairn really and earning whatever I could, wrangling farm horses and the like. After a bit I joined up with the Cape Mounted Riflemen, one of their youngest, and that's how I met John Harrison Clark. He was a likeable rogue, born a South African in Port Elizabeth, I think. Hard as nails, tough as an old boot, fine shot, and he'd take visiting parties out hunting in the Little Karoo.

426

"Summat happened—they say he shot a man, he swore it was an accident, but he was made outlaw and vamoosed up north in 1887. He traveled to Mozambique and along the Zambesi into what's now Northern Rhodesia. After a while, he sent messages back to his old comrades in the Riflemen, asking for volunteers. None wanted it, but I did, so I followed his route and found him well settled in the land of the Mashukulumbwe. The sub-tribes in that ungoverned land, the Baila, Batonga, and Senga, proclaimed Clark Changa-Changa, which means fuck-knows, probably 'boss man,' but it was in praise for his organizing an army from among the more warlike Senga and then protecting the people from the Portuguese slave-traders who plagued the forest worse than the tsetse fly.

"Before long I was busy issuing trading licenses to merchants, ensuring they paid their dues in return, and strong-arming those who hesitated, if you know what I mean. I got a few scratches in fights with the Arabs and the half-breed Chikunda-Portuguese slaver gangs who didn't always agree that the region was under Changa-Changa's dominion. By then he called himself King of the Senga, Chief of the Mashukulumbwe, and the tribes thought he was a god because he halved their illnesses. No miracle. Clark insisted they boil their water before drinking the foul stuff. At first none of them could see the point in wasting time and fuel on such a daft ritual, but when the fevers reduced and the dysentery almost vanished, every man, woman, and child was ready to bow down.

"And he brought the Chikunda under his thumb by marrying Chief Mpuka's daughter and making himself their king as well, so lessening slavery even further. And the man is still up there, ruling the land and collecting his hut tax from the locals in return for protecting them from the slavers. I made enough under Changa-Changa to return to the Colony and buy me some farmland. Last I heard before the war was that Rhodes and Bee-Sac were in a bitter contest with Clark over who is really in charge, so I hope that won't cause us any problems. But it could do."

He fished around in his coat pocket and produced tobacco wallet, pipe, and began to fill and tamp it. "So that's how come I know the region pretty damned well."

"And why you were eager to accompany us, Travis. In which case I am fortunate that you chose to join Vane's Horse in the first place."

"Maybe so." He put a vesta to the pipe bowl and sucked at the mouthpiece. After stoking his pipe, he went to sit with the engineers.

I walked around the back of the grass hut, smoked a quiet cigarette, and absorbed some of the countryside's peace after the train's continuous rush and the locomotive's endless huffing and puffing and clanking. I stared up at the low and—considering their blood-soaked recent history—curiously uninteresting Matapos Hills in their overlapping confusion. I imagined storming them against the massed warrior army of Lobengula. I was lost in my thoughts when suddenly a distant altercation jerked me from my reverie. I turned and ran toward the train, aware that whatever alerted me had gone unheard by the loudly chattering rest house staff and their breakfasting guests.

As I neared the steps to the car's end platform, Jo pushed through the sliding door from the car's corridor as if chased by a great cat. He was agitated. His eyes went wide as he saw me grip the handrail and start to leap up the steps. And then another noise stopped me in my tracks. "What's wrong? I heard a—"

Jo started to shrug, raised an arm in resignation, and was pushed aside by a bundle of black skin, blushed lips, white teeth, and even whiter wide eyes.

I heard myself shout. And then Neo was in turn shoved aside by the irate conductor. "This is your boy," he spluttered. "Hiding away in the baggage wagon. That's where I found him. Damn stowaway!"

Neo gave a small wail, glanced at Jo, and then flung himself down the steps and into my arms. "Take me with you, Major Harry," he sobbed. "I sorry, but there no home for me in Mahikeng, no more. You now my home."

I stared up helplessly at Jolyon.

What is it? I seem to collect waifs and strays when I'm not rescuing them.

"I could always shoot him," Jo said, pulling his revolver from its holster. The grin belied the intent of his words, and in any case had no impact on Neo, who knew perfectly well that Jo Jo Angrish would never harm him. No longer his responsibility, Jolyon relaxed and obviously found the situation humorous.

What to do? Not much. I know I sighed, but at the same time I stroked the top of Neo's head. "Hush, you damned rascal."

"I work hard, Major Harry, promise."

"We'll all have to. I hope you know what's ahead. When's this damned train getting under way again?"

"I'll go and chivvy them up," the conductor said. He pushed his way down the steps past me, and a gleeful, bouncing Neo.

≈☆≈

Survey diary, Saturday June 16, afternoon

Finally, at a little before 12:30 a.m., Bulawayo finally appeared ahead as a few gleams of corrugated zinc roofs, the ridges of its houses scarcely higher than the surrounding thorn bush. I consulted one of my maps marked with distances. "We are now 1,360 miles from Cape Town and approximately 5,000 miles from Cairo," I pronounced.

"Still a long way to go," Jolyon observed sardonically.

"It would sound more encouraging if we looked at it as land travel, for that's a mere 1,300 miles, the rest being by the Great Lakes and the Nile… but that isn't the point, is it? Rhodes wants to lay his iron road the entire way."

"But we only have to explore the route as far as Wau."

I acknowledged Jo's point. "Which is about 3,000 land miles."

"It's still a long way."

"You wanted adventure, and we won't get anywhere sitting here. Time to get off and discover how long we'll be stuck in Bulawayo before we can take a train on to the end of the line at Kapiri Mposhi. That will give us another six to seven hundred miles without the need for wearing out our safari boots."

Survey diary, Tuesday June 19

It is 11 a.m. This is the first train since the weekend to leave Bulawayo for Victoria Falls. The Zambesi River marks the boundary between Southern and Northern Rhodesia. As for Bulawayo, I can only conclude that the railway's arrival will soon encourage the growth of this crude one-story shanty town, to turn into a fine city such as those which exist farther to the south.

The train was supposed to leave at 6:30 a.m. but only got under way at 7:15. Our accommodation is far less comfortable than the connection from Mafeking. The four of us occupy uncomfortable, barely carpentered slatted benches, roughly fitted on either side of a central aisle, in an open-topped truck. White engineers and native workers headed for the work camp at Victoria Falls are crammed into every seat of the three "first-class cars." The tight fit makes it hard to write and keep prying eyes from the pages of my notebook. Many more locals cling on by hand and foot to any precarious support they can find, and they are legion on the second- and third-class trucks—the ones trailing behind us piled high with construction materials.

Travis hired three Ndebele men as porters in Bulawayo. These three also lean over the low side, chattering happily with neighboring laborers in their Sindebele tongue. Travis took them on because—while drinking in a bar—he heard disturbing comments among the engineers that suggest Rhodes might have been economical with the truth as to the progress of construction. He fears we may have to heft our baggage without the assistance of a train. We will see soon enough.

4:50 p.m. A few minutes ago Travis pointed ahead and to our right. We near the river and the location of the gigantic falls is apparent at a distance. A wide curtain of mist rises like a white blade against a deep blue sky. It seems to erupt from a crack in the vast plain, which here is so devoid of vegetation it resembles a builder-god's workyard. The rail track has taken some astonishing diversions and double-backs to avoid steeply rising land, an indication of what to look out for when we reach the jungles and unmapped regions.

An engineer squashed in across the aisle from me became very vocal as we approached Victoria Falls, not so much a place of habitation as a work camp. He'd heard Jolyon expressing some excitement at the thought of crossing the Zambesi, and decided to put us right. "The bridge spanning the gorge, it won't be constructed for some time yet, gents, maybe a couple of years." To my dismay, he went on to prove Travis's pessimism well founded. "Across the gorge, on the Northern Rhodesia side, engineers are cutting and embanking, and laying the ballast bed in our direction from the settlement of Kalomo to Livingstone, which sits just over the river."

"You mean there are no rails, yet, no trains on the other side?"

He shook his head. "No ties or rails yet, though they're going at a rapid pace."

I consulted the map burned in my memory. "But Kalomo is a stretch of no more than seventy miles. Is there no transport for the hundred and forty miles from Kalomo to Kapiri Mposhi?"

The engineer wiped a grimy hand across his sweaty face. "Like it used to be, sir, a traction caravan if you're lucky or trekker's ox wagon train, or shanks's pony."

Indeed, Rhodes misled me as to the advanced state of his cherished line. I had no idea what the engineer meant by "traction caravan" and forbore to ask him, not wishing to appear completely green. Even when we get to Kapiri

Mposha that's not quite half way to Abercorn and the frontier with German Africa. I am beginning to have fond memories of the Indian railways I so castigated for their ponderous, boring journeys. At least they drew together all parts of the huge subcontinent.

Survey Diary, Thursday June 21

I'm confident Buffalo Bill Cody of the Wild West would be at home in Victoria Falls for it smacks more of frontier life than anywhere I have so far visited. Even Neo, now accustomed to a degree of European comfort, is happy to be on the move again after two nights spent under blankets on a hard wooden floor of the only building that approaches the name of rest house. Lying with ear to the boards I could hear termites feasting on the timber supports below.

Huge bastions of concrete and iron are materializing on either side of the terrifying gorge into which the Zambesi drops for 355 feet. The vast cataract—Mosi-oa-Tunya, the Smoke that Thunders—is so close everyone is drenched in its eternal spray and it's hard to be heard over the monstrous roar of water flowing with deceptive slowness into the abyss. The humidity and airborne mist creates a little tropical forest climate of its own all around the vertical cliffs.

The instruction Rhodes gave his engineers to *build the bridge across the Zambesi where the trains, as they pass, will catch the spray of the Falls* is being adhered to. Of the bridge, though, nothing. How do we get to the other side? Travis, when he came this way years ago, crossed the Zambesi well toward the east, where the river is once again somnambulant.

4:30 p.m. Now we are headed for Livingstone, I can write of our utterly terrifying and yet exhilarating experience. Jolyon, Travis, and Neo were as appalled as I when the senior engineer on duty explained the way across the steaming trench to the other side was via a treacherous cableway. The various cables were spider-web thin, or so it seemed at a distance, in truth thicker than a man's thigh, and the engineer assured me its construction was sufficient to take the weight of a locomotive. "Don't you worry, gents," he said with great cheer, "I have to get an engine over there soon, ready for the Livingstone-Kalomo section. The worst can happen in that little cab we have strung on the line… well, you think you're damp here but out in the middle it's more like swimming. It'll drench you."

It did.

The land opposite the promontory of the southern cliff (actually western because of the way the river twists here) is the identical height, thus avoiding the sensation of sinking or climbing that would have made the aerial passage so much worse. And once we were accustomed to the motion, the short journey became a joy. Surreptitiously, out of sight of the rest of the party, Jo snaked his hand into mine, and his grip matched in force the majesty of the view. From far away beyond the town of Livingstone, comes the great river, stretching out its mouth like a snake parting its jaws to ingest an antelope ten times its size. It seemed to approach right into our fragile car before gracefully curling over the cliff, which for eons it has been gradually cutting back.

Across the river, a short section of track to the town of Livingstone supports handcars. And here we crouch, the bedraggled members of V.S., soaked through, even a little chilled in spite of the day's heat. With a practiced push-pull motion, the Ndebele driver speeds his pump trolley along the track almost faster than a train. Our three porters, clustered on the end of the flatbed with the baggage, sing along joyously to the lead of the driver.

There is a Company administrator at Livingstone who should be able to speed us on the next leg. I had planned on reaching Kapiri Mposha tomorrow, but now I must accept it may not be until Sunday, which is June 24. I hope Travis and I have allowed sufficient contingency for unforeseen occurrences, but I am confident that with luck and British spirit, we will reach Wau by the middle of October 1900.

CHAPTER 39 | *Western Equatoria, Saturday November 10, 1900*

SURVEY DIARY, MONDAY NOVEMBER 5, 1900

It seems like an impossible age since V.S. left Livingstone, still bright with the sense of adventure. I am unwell again, damn it! I know the encroaching headaches and droopiness of spirit from before. The fever yet grows in my blood. One of the servants must not have boiled the drinking water long enough. I once thought we would reach our destination before October ended, yet here we are, encamped in the jungle in the middle of nowhere with a long way ahead yet.

I must try to summarize events. Keeping the topographical survey reports to date prevented me always detailing my more private thoughts, but the fever is blurring my perceptions. Neo will go gathering his herbs, look for the sweet wormwood that cured me in… when was it? Yes, August, before Mengo. And before then…

Sitting astride a henna-stained mule, whose silvery trappings shone in the morning sun, was Major Smythe-Vane, closely followed on a somewhat lesser decorated mule by his young assistant, Lieutenant Langrish-Smith. Both were attired in the Englishman's typical African dress of Norfolk jacket over collarless khaki shirt, matching knickerbockers and flat-topped bush hat with one brim tacked up. Immediately to their rear were the personal servants, Somalis from the coast with their braided waistcoats and white full-length robes. Then came stalwart Sudanese soldiers in dark hooded coats, with their blankets, water bottles, ammunition, belts, and guns and Zanzibari porters bearing iron-bound boxes of ammunition to which were fastened axes and shovels. Behind came a few donkeys laden with sacks of rice, other dry goods, and trade goods in the form of coiled brass wire and cheap Birmingham trade rifles with powder and shot. Four large-horned African goats followed these. With few beasts of burden because of the tsetse fly that invariably accompanied them, porters carrying an immense weight of weaponry and trade goods were as inclined as ever to desert and steal, unless stern discipline was maintained and...

The dream recurs... It wasn't at all like that. We never had Somalis or Zanzibaris for porterage, did we? The steeds came later, anyway. It was just a romantic daydream. The noble steed I remember lurched continuously, hiccupped brutally, and resorted to frequent steam-powered shrieks. It belched incompletely burned gas like an elephant breaking methane wind. The couplings between the trucks bearing us and the fuel and water tender in front clanked fitfully. Ahead a huge Burrel & Sons steam traction engine thumped over a small stream, abruptly clawed its way up the next rise, and dragged the extended caravan of wagons behind it. At either side of the well-worn track, screeching birds fled colorfully in all directions.

"Things have changed a lot around here," I remember Travis saying. He sounded regretful, as if the smoke-irrupting transport monster had stripped Africa of all its romance. I was happy for being on our traction caravan.

Our open-bed truck in which we were uncomfortably seated followed the tender into the dip. There was a spine-jarring thump and then it bucked up like a bad fairground ride. We hapless passengers fell against each other, unbalanced by the incline's sudden change. The traction steam engine's massive rear wheels threw up great divots of grassy mud that mostly passed overhead to bombard the porters in the following truck. Then the engine driver's native assistant twisted around from his shot-gun position, able for a moment to see over the bulk of the tender because of the train's undulant motion, a cheerful grin plastered over his broad face. "Good fun ride, no!" he cried out.

"It's not what I expected," Jo muttered for the hundredth time. We hung on to each other—legitimately—after being hurled together by the savage ride.

"Better than slogging through this heavy bush like in the old days," Travis admonished him for the hundredth time, making it sound as if Africa's enchantment had never been so sprightly anyway.

Livingstone to Kalomo to Lusaka to Kapiri Mposha to Abercorn. It's become a blur now. On which leg did Neo stand at the front of the truck, leaning over the low bulwark unheedful of the muck—wet in the dips, dry as charnel dust on the ridges—flying up in chunks from the engine and tender wheels? I can see his hands in a death grip on its edge, his body gracefully swaying against the frequent and violent lurches. His head is thrust forward with the excitement of a retriever waiting its master's command to fetch. Often, Jo reaches out to steady him, his Jo Jo Angrish.

The plume of reddish-brown dust thrown up by the caravan's passage hangs in the hot air behind, casting an ochreous mist over the forest. A minute after cresting the last rise from the stream just crossed, a series of covered wagons hauled by sixteen long-horned oxen passes by going in the opposite direction.

"It's busier in the trackless wastes of Africa than Piccadilly Circus on a Saturday evening," Jo grumbles. His sarcasm is tinged with a touch of awe at the weight of traffic on the road between wherever we are and wherever we are due next. The truth is that numerous tracks criss-cross this region of Africa. "No wonder they need our railway!" he shouts above the chugging Burrell.

I must check the official report for some dates. The fever is starting to make my hand shake. I know the signs. Soon it will overwhelm me, and trap us here in this dark jungle—the one dear Richard warned me as if at the commencement of a Grimm brothers' fairy tale never, ever to enter. And there have been worrying signs. Jo is certain that he saw in a pile of refuse left at the abandonment of a native camp what appeared to be the skeletal remains of a human hand and a foot. But there was no choice but to come this way. No choice. The iron road cannot swim lakes or climb impossible inclines.

I have some dates here now… We left Kapiri Mposha on Monday June 25. The Rhodes passport secured us reasonable accommodation at nights in the small rest houses, some private ventures, others official local government residences run under the auspices of the Company.

On Wednesday 27, I see, we ran into a bunch of Batonga warriors, armed to the teeth with spears and well cared for Lee-Metford rifles. In this stretch of country the Company's remit falters. We are short of Chisenga, between Kapiri Mposha and Abercorn and within the boundaries of Changa-Changa's kingdom.

Thank God for Travis. We were brought before the self-proclaimed king of the Mashukulumbwe, John Harrison Clark. He is a tall, raw-boned man, comfortably dressed in a native robe and wearing a dark-red fez on his head. Only the wide khaki bush pants protruding from under the robe's hem spoil the man's cultivated oriental appearance, that and the cuffs breaking over spit-polished black toecaps, and his barely tanned and very English face. In the trim of his mustache, Clark resembles any Company administrator. He was seated in a large armless cane chair, which was draped in two leopard skins. He stood from his throne immediately the minute we were thrust into his presence. He greeted Travis warmly.

He is at war with the Company. Clark argues with some fairness that it is down to his endeavors that the Arab and Portuguese slavers have been brought to book and some civilization delivered to the region, and not that of Rhodes and Co. They accuse Clark of passing himself off as a representative of the organization to secure personally lucrative labor and mining concessions with the local chiefs. This naturally arouses great anger in the Rhodesian capital of Salisbury and distresses some tribal chiefs who feel caught in the middle. He also taxes travelers and traders on "his" road, but Travis and Clark are truly old friends. I see I haven't mentioned this incident in the official survey report.

We were set free along with our traction engine, crew, caravan, and goods, and given an honorary detachment of Batonga to get us safely to Abercorn, where we arrived… yes, on Saturday June 30.

The natives call Abercorn (named after the first chairman of the British South Africa Company) Mbala. Now began the real exploration. The town sits about twenty-five miles from the southern tip of Lake Tanganikya, and about the same from the border with German East Africa.

I see it took two weeks before the expedition was ready to carry on into German territory. There was much to do. Robert Coryndon, resident Commissioner for the northern region had to secure permission from the German authorities at Dar es Salaam for us to traverse their country, even though they take little note of it. Travis had to recruit a corps of porters and secure provisions and extra equipment in addition to the survey apparatus brought from Kimberley before we could safely proceed into the real wilderness. As our ordnance expert, I put Jo in charge of the dynamite. I envisage we will need to blow out top surfaces to discover the geology of any hills in our way. Cuttings might be made inexpensively through limestone or shale, but basalt or granite would require a detour as we saw in the journey from Bulawayo to Victoria Falls, or cost a great deal in time and money to cut through.

Coryndon offered local wisdom. "Don't take too large a party. The natives get restless at small armies moving about. They think they are slavers; still plenty about because the Germans have done damn all in their territory. Avoid the shore of Tanganikya. The telegraph to Buganda runs along the eastern lakeshore because it's easy to get to in case of repairs from small boats off the scheduled steamers, but it's too mountainous for a railway line. Instead, strike out in a northeasterly direction from Abercorn and then swing around parallel with the lake on the higher plateau. You have no idea how important this plan of Mr. Rhodes is to us. It will change everything, and Abercorn will become a major hub, with connections north and south and east to the Indian Ocean. So I wish you all good luck, gentlemen!"

Coryndon received a German pass on Friday July 13. We set off on the Sunday after the colonists said prayers for us in church.

The fever progresses steadily. I must speed my writing, though my mind grows fuzzy. It's hard to merge the details of the official record with my memory. I must ask Jo to help.

There were no roads to speak of, some native tracks to follow if they traveled in the right direction. The landscape on the plateau above the lake is a mixture of dense forest, open woodland with thick undergrowth of shrubs and grasses, and riverside wetlands. Everywhere, small streams amble toward the lake, some twenty miles to the west of our line of march; crocodiles laze in the swamps and larger rivers, vicious serpents teem in every habitat. But we shot plenty of edible game to brighten the monotonous expedition fare, though that also meant we took care not to startle the variety of preying felines.

What should I write of this journey? After a few days it all becomes a blur of similarity. We trekked native paths because in the main they represented the most level way. Jo and I measured relative heights, marked the blank maps as carefully as possible, and made copious notes for the engineers who would follow our trail. We noted the presence of villages and the nature of the inhabitants. Behind us, the line of porters trailed back half a mile and slowly caught up at dusk as we made camp: fires lit; food rations heated; our two four-man pup tents raised; mosquito nets arrayed. Then, as now, Travis occupied one tent. Jo and I shared, and Neo insisted on lying down outside the flap of ours. For the first time since… it seemed like forever… Jo and I lay in each other's arms beneath the enveloping net and made love to the backdrop of the jungle's nonstop shrieking, whistling, squawking, growling, and rustling.

I wondered if Travis had drawn conclusions about our relationship, that it might be more than professional…? If he has it must be that he doesn't care, but he might not have noticed as we have been very careful.

On the second Sunday since leaving Abercorn, we took an early halt and spit-roasted two fine bucks Travis bagged earlier. With yams and rehydrated peas, it made a fine meal—almost a traditional Sunday roast.

A week later—Sunday August 5—having followed a slowly descending route closer to the lake, we came to Ujiji. Here Richard Burton and John Hanning Speke first reached the shores of Lake Tanganikya. Here Henry Morton Stanley finally found David Livingstone, whom the world thought to be dead. The lakeside town appears to be thriving from the passing steamer trade, the ships plying between British Buganda and British Northern Rhodesia; nothing in fact to do with the Germans. We remained two days at Ujiji, and after reprovisioning—to Jo's disgust with a lot of stinky dried lake fish—we left on the morning of Tuesday August 7.

Mengo, capital of Buganda, lay approximately 530 miles across a gently rising dome of lightly forested country in a direction a little east of north. It's good railway terrain. At a point well west of the southern shore of Lake Victoria, long shallow valleys run in precisely the right direction, finally issuing into well kept agricultural land leading all the way to Mengo.

At the small village of Lwanda, about 140 miles short of Mengo, a dengue fever struck me down on August 28, a Tuesday I think. If Churchill were here, he'd make it Wednesday.

That was all I remember.

It seems that for the next five days I lay exhausted and wasted, alternating between extremes of temperature. Jo nursed me day and night, while Neo scurried about the many village agricultural patches for herbs he believed would calm the delirium and soothe the skin rash. His remedy was effective and it broke on the third day. By August 28 I was able to continue, though Travis had some porters rig a litter for me, to be pulled behind a mule, and so we made it to Mengo in moderately good order on Thursday September 6, 1900.

To reach Wau by the end of October still seemed possible!

❧ ✦ ☙

The habitations of Mengo cluster on rolling hills, a place made pleasant by its elevation above the regions abutting the bays leading off Lake Victoria, which are more infested with mosquitos. In the center, standing on the tallest hill, is the Lubiri, or palace of the Kabaka, the King of Buganda. Christianity—Anglican and Catholic—have made great inroads here and there are cathedrals and small churches to serve the needs of the population. It has been a British Protectorate for seven years, but not without bloodshed. Kabaka Mwanga II feared the increasing influence Christian missionaries were having over his power base. One snippet of recent history amused Jo greatly: Mwanga was particularly incensed when the pageboys of his harem, fired by missionary zeal, refused his "rightful" sexual advances.

"It wasn't so funny for the Christians," I told him with a failed attempt at sternness, as I pulled from memory details I'd read in Rhodes' library. "The king began a reign of terror. He executed three of his ministers who had converted, as well as the first archbishop of British East Africa, James Hannington, on his arrival in Buganda. Many more martyrs went before the blade, all because Christians did not approve of his having sex with his pages."

"What happened to him in the end?"

"Oh, he's still alive in exile on the Seychelles. He granted powers to the British East Africa Company and then changed his mind and declared war on Britain in July three years ago. The Company militia defeated him in battle at the end of the month and he fled into German territory. Not the end of the man. He returned with a rebel army and was again defeated at the beginning of '98. He was sent to the Seychelles only last year."

"Such recent history. But how terrible for the boys, to be forced against their will to satisfy a despot's lust."

"If the act is forced it cannot be pleasurable. The man was insatiable. In spite of taking his pleasures between the thighs of his pageboys, he had sixteen wives and fathered ten children, seven of them boys, no doubt intended for the harem."

Today, the real power in Buganda is an old African hand, the British Commissioner Sir Harry H. Johnston. He controls a bureau of British administrators that increases in numbers every month. Yet in truth only the immediate vicinity of Mengo is known and overseen by these bureaucrats. To the north and west, as we soon discovered, British East Africa is no more civilized or developed than its German counterpart.

It's good for Vane's Survey team that Sir Harry is an ardent supporter of Cape-to-Cairo. In no time he helped arrange replacement porters for the Ndebele who wish to return home to Abercorn. The new men are largely of the Dinka people, who inhabit the regions of southwestern Sudan and southward into the Great Lakes region. Four of the men spoke English to some degree and had the advantage of being detached to us from the Mengo "police" force. I made Mabior, the most practiced in English, to be the sergeant, with Jok, Dut, and Garang his corporals.

When I told Sir Harry of my intention to follow the telegraph wire north from Mengo toward the Abyssinian foothills he tried to dissuade me. "Lake Kyoga is likely to defeat your intentions, Major Vane," he said. "To be frank, I have very little hard information regarding the swamp regions, other than that supplied by Rhodes' telegraphic engineers, and even they had to zigzag around to place their termite-resistant poles and string their wires to reach the foothills. And they still haven't gone much farther as yet."

Still—I see I wrote in the official report—we must try.

And we did try. We left Mengo on Jolyon's twenty-fifth birthday, Thursday September 20… and returned three weeks later, defeated by the unanticipated and many-fretted shores of Lake Kyoga (really the flooded Nile Valley), its five major tributaries, and innumerable smaller streams, all insect-infested, which feed the lake. To the east, the Victoria Nile runs in a northerly direction from Lake Victoria to Kyoga, and its pestilential valley denies further access in that direction. Even if there were a way across, an enormous quagmire spreads around the eastern extremity of Kyoga's waters, making a swing to the north and the Abyssinian foothills impossible. Treacherous riverine Kyogo drains from east to west, effectively blocking the way north. The entire region is either a boggy morass—the habitat of Nile crocodiles, aquatic constrictors, and deadly poisonous snakes—or densely forested low ridges between the valleys.

"Where the telegraph may go, we cannot," Travis said on October 6. Weary surveyors, no surveying done, and dispirited porters, we turned our heads south toward Mengo. It was the following day that Mabior came to me.

"Massa, we must go Karuma. The village has bridge. Cross Nile there. Way to Sudan."

I nodded and thanked him. I suspected an ulterior motive for the advice, which wasn't too hard to uncover. Mabior, Jok, Dut, and Garang are of a tribe of Dinka that inhabits the fertile grasslands to the southeast of Wau. Normally cattle-herders and farmers, these four, like many others, migrated to Buganda after a famine drove them to seek a fortune elsewhere. Now they wished to return and—conveniently—their homeland lies close to the route where the Cape-to-Cairo line will one day run on its way to Khartoum after leaving the Nile Valley. On that score, when Mabior understood the purpose of our survey and that we needed to reach the railhead at Wau, he gave me a puzzled look and said, "I know not steam engine run on iron rails like you say at Wau."

I pointed out he had been away from the place for some time and the rails were being laid as we spoke, south from Khartoum, then west past El Obeid and through Babanusa, there to turn south for Wau.

Back in Mengo on Wednesday October 10.
"This is young Ballantyne," Sir Harry said of the tall, thin man he introduced to me. "Your man mentioned Karuma, and Johnstone, here, has spent time up there. Tell Major Vane what you know."

Ballantyne coughed nervously. He had the habit of never quite looking at the person he was addressing. "Your Dinka man is correct. The only practicable route open to you for laying railways tracks is to take the long ridge that runs almost north from Mengo. It makes a dogleg around the western end of Lake Kyoga and the Nile, which twists sharply due north for several miles before turning again west to cut through the plateau, and so into Lake Albert. After the river has made that second turn and where it flows rapidly through the gorge the villagers of Karuma have built a rickety bridge… of sorts," he added apologetically. "It should be easy to construct a proper iron bridge to cross the Nile at that point."

"And from there?"

"You can't really go north to Gulu and after that into the White Nile valley. It won't be possible to lay rails through the low-lying and swampy Sudd. For great stretches it's impossible to tell marshland from the river, so choked does it become with a muck of reeds and water grasses the locals call *ward-i-nil*."

"I know it," I told them. "I've seen great rafts of it floating down the lower Nile."

441

"That's where it comes from."

"So where should we go, then?"

Ballantyne looked uneasy. "For the stated reasons, you can't get to Wau by going north on the eastern side of the Nile, so after crossing at Karuma, the only way lies to the west to where the Albert Nile is surely bridgeable at a place called Pakwach, which is about twenty miles from where the river leaves Lake Albert. After that I know only what fragmented records offer. Hardly any white men have ventured there, but the only suitable route between the Nile swamps on one side and the dense jungle of the Congo basin on the other is generally northwest, which will eventually get you to Wau."

Ballantyne petered out with the slightest of Pontius Pilate shrugs.

"Asante territory?"

Ballantyne nodded.

The Dinkas visibly paled when they understood we would not be following the Nile but skirting the Congo's forests. "But Sah," Jok said, eyes so wide his dark pupils looked like unhatched tadpoles in spawn. "Asante like human flesh."

"Is it so true?"

All four men nodded. Garang added that he had accompanied a white trader's expedition and they entered a village where the white man was received by the king, who handed over to him a bound slave. " 'Kill him for your evening meal. He is tender and fat, and you must be hungry,' king tell trader man."

Little consolation in this story that the slave was intended as the white man's dinner and not the explorer slain to satisfy the king's hunger. Richard warned me, but there is no alternative it seems, and surely a railway will rapidly bring civilization to a benighted area? This I recorded in the official report.

Sir Harry was concerned enough to provide two Winchester 1897 pump action shot guns and several boxes of the larger 2¾-inch cartridges. "They were confiscated off two American game hunters who decided they could dodge the license tax," he told me. "The five-shell magazine is a fast reload for rapid-speed firing. You might need them."

Prophetic words in more ways than one.

On Sunday October 14 I sent my last telegrams, to Rhodes and to Richard (I only hope Richard's will find him), apprising them of our intention, and the following day V.S. set out for Karuma, surveying the potential route as we went. We made good time, crossing the Victoria Nile over a surprisingly well-made

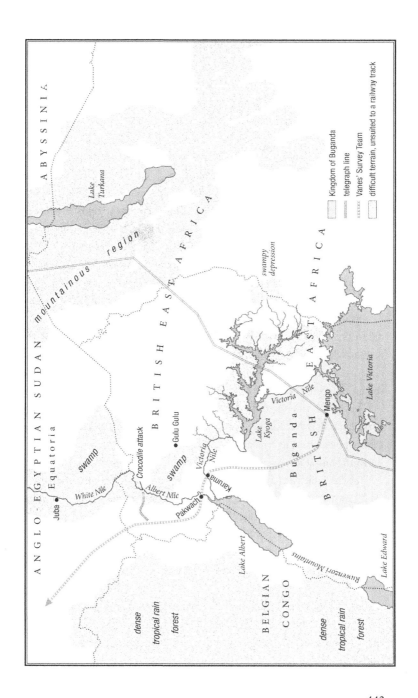

rope and timber bridge, and crossed the Albert Nile nine days after leaving Mengo. After a successful week's march and surveying, Jo, Travis, Mabior, and Dut turned aside with me to see what conditions along the Nile's banks were like. Jok and Garang were to lead the porters on along the line of march and then halt after ten miles, where we would catch up with them.

After some hours on our seemingly tireless mules, the lightly wooded land gradually sloped down. Underfoot it became boggy as the grasses grew taller until they nearly obscured the way forward.

"It's beautiful," Jo said, breaking a long period of quiet.

Scores of birds of all kinds clattered out from among the reeds. Eventually we came across a body of water, which appeared to have a current, but it was clearly little more than a braid of the Nile. The bank at least was stable and we all dismounted. Dut took the mules' halters and Jo ran forward, eager to dip his hand in the proper White Nile. I had turned to say something to Travis when Mabior, who was a few steps behind Jo, gave a shout of fright.

Instinctively, Jo sprang back and ducked at the same time, and it was well he did so. On the instant, a dark object lashed past within an inch of his head. My first thought was that a giant snake had attacked him. He gasped with horror as he recovered and swung around to confront a huge crocodile at the edge of the stream and a little below the bank.

"Jolyon!" I know I screamed out his name, helpless at a distance to do anything in that dreadful moment. Even as Travis and I burst into action, the giant reptile tensed, its triangular jaws gaped hugely, and the beast rushed up the short bank at Jo.

The crocodile's first assault had been a strike with its tail and had it not been for his own uncanny sixth sense and Mabior's timely warning cry, the monster would have swept my lover into the river.

The great lizard shot up the bank at an alarming speed for its monstrous size. Jo staggered back and managed to bring his Lee-Enfield up and loose a shot, which had no more effect than if he'd hurled a gnat at the armor-plated beast.

Instinct took over. I grabbed the shotgun from Travis's grip, dashed the few yards to Jo's side, who was trying to get off another shot while staggering sideways in a doomed attempt to avoid the creature's crushing teeth, and almost without knowing I'd done it, raised the barrel and gave the crocodile five pumps straight down its gaping gullet. I had enough time to notice with a shudder the maw's satiny pink prettiness, horridly at odds with its ghastly purpose. The animal rolled over onto its back and slipped down into the water. Then, horrifyingly, it turned and struggled to regain the bank.

There was no time to eject and bang in a second magazine, and anyway that was in Travis's possession, as the scaly leviathan once again opened what must have been aching jaws, but no less lethal for that. Then Mabior ran up and, placed the muzzle of his Winchester within a foot of its eye, fired: *one-two!* With a fire-hose hiss, the creature rolled over again, dead. It sank below the turgid stream, only to surface a few feet out. Almost too shocked to breathe, I leaned on Jo, who was, in fairness, the one in need of my support. The scaly beast floated with the sluggish current, rotating slowly, eventually becoming tangled in the *ward-i-nil* on the bank some twenty yards away.

Mabior gave a loud shout in his own Dinka, which Dut answered, while he struggled with the frightened mules. He then shouted two or three words, and turning to Jo with a wide smile said. "Get crocodile, good eating," and proceeded on his way toward the stranded croc without further concern.

We dined well in the evening, and the steaks were indeed, tasty. "I've said it before," Travis managed between bites, "that some bush-meat is very good. I've no doubt before we're through you'll have acquired a taste for snake. Some varieties are better flavored than chicken. Better to eat your crocodile than to be eaten by it." He gave a hoarse bark of a laugh somewhat at variance with his more normally taciturn appearance.

Jolyon joined in. What had been a terrifying experience suddenly seemed funny now he was safe. At the very thought of my near loss, I couldn't find it in the least amusing, but I smiled gamely.

"Still, Jolyon, it's been a good lesson on setting your eyes to the watch at all times," Travis said, rather pompously. "I've seen along the Zambesi and Luangwa rivers crocodiles carry off the native women when they're washing, and almost invariably the beasts sweep them into the river with a blow of their tails. Once in the water the hapless victim is carried off, drowned, and eaten at leisure."

CHAPTER 40 | *Western Equatoria, November 13 to 16, 1900*

IT WAS THE FIRST DAY Harry felt equal to the task of resuming his diary, sixteen days since the crocodile attack and the recognition of Mr. Ballantyne's assertion that a railway line would never run close to the Nile in Equatoria. Neo's herbal remedies had finally brought the fever temperature down to a bearable level, but for a throbbing headache.

"You were delirious, Harry," Jolyon said. "I was so worried to see you in such a state. I never think of you being unwell, even after that bout before we got to Mengo. But this was so much worse."

Harry started to sit up and then frowned. "I sense there's something wrong. I could hear raised voices earlier?"

Jolyon shuffled his feet. "Hmmm, a week ago, when we halted and made camp to wait for you to recover, some of the Dinkas went foraging and came back with horror tales. Travis and I went to see what the fuss was about and…"

"What?"

"A tree. There was this heap of refuse. Another empty native encampment, too small to be an abandoned habitation. Garang said it was an Asante raiding party's bivouac." Jolyon paused and swallowed, his gaze fixed on the tent's apex as though he was unwilling to engage Harry directly. He gulped again. "I saw fragments of human bones strewn among the detritus. It's hard to mistake the bones of a human arm, wrist, and hand. In any case, it got worse under this big spreading ebony tree. All around were shriveled human feet and hands, hanging on its branches. A lot of the porters took off soon after. They were so frightened. Travis tried threatening them, but his rifle was not as terrifying as the Asante."

Harry struggled upright on the camp bed. Instantly Jolyon was at his side, kneeling on the ground sheet to help support him.

"But we still have men enough, surely? We near the end of our march, so there are less supplies to carry."

"Oh, Harry, I wish it were so. Two days ago, while you were still insensate, the drums began to sound, distant, but insistent. In the morning the rest were gone, and with them most of the remaining supplies. Fortunately, they were too confused to take all the mules and I'd had the foresight to secure the guns and ammunition boxes in Travis's tent. To make sure they wouldn't be touched, I slept in the tent with him while Neo looked after you." A glimmer of a smile lightened Jolyon's troubled expression. "I wasn't jealous. You were in no condition to bother him."

Harry snorted. "I won't risk accusing you in turn of impropriety with Travis." He chuckled but the wet-sounding laugh pained his chest. "Mabior?"

"At least he and the other three have stayed loyal. I think that Winchester pump-action has given Mabior the courage to stay with us… for now anyway."

Over the next two days Harry laid on his bed, slowly recovering, but he felt too weak to stay on his feet for very long. At nights he lay with Jolyon, listening to the incessant drums. In the days he leaned on Jolyon and staggered about for a few minutes to gather strength. On Thursday November 15, he read through the diary entries he'd written up as the fever had made itself felt. A sudden disturbance caused him to drop the pencil he was using to amend some entries. He stuck his head out from the tent. The sight that met his eyes was a proper fright.

A group of about fifteen warriors stood at the edge of the clearing in uncanny silence. Barefoot and naked except for a variety of cloths and feathers to cover their loins, each man carried two long spears in his right hand and a half-man-height oval shield marked by painted, embossed devices in the other. Some wore headdresses formed of a band of animal hide or cloth from which grass stalks and more feathers extruded. Others went bareheaded, but with their hair piled up into astonishing creations, dyed a vibrant red.

They looked frightening and serious.

Obviously terrified in spite of hefting their rifles, the four Dinkas huddled behind Travis and Jolyon. Harry looked, but couldn't see either of the Winchester shotguns and presumed they were out of the way in Travis's tent, in front of which stood Neo, his Lee-Enfield aimed at the Asante. For surely that's who their visitors were.

One of the natives, overdressed in comparison to his fellows, stepped forward and spoke in rapid angry sounding phrases. He was unarmed and made a lot of clattering noises with every stabbing movement of his arms from the small hollow gourds and bones strung around his scrawny neck. A fantastic plumage formed of ostrich feathers sat on his head.

"Witch doctor," Travis said over his shoulder.

Harry straightened and walked slowly up behind Jolyon. "Do we know what they want?"

Garang stuttered a translation. "Witch doctor want… he say…"

"Go on," Harry urged.

"He want Neo. Nice plump boy, he say."

Neo, who had sidled over to join his comrades, instinctively shrank against Jolyon's side.

"Tell him he can't have the boy."

Jok began to shake badly so that his rifle barrel drooped toward the ground. He looked around at Harry, eyes wide with terror. "They want eat him, massah."

"Maybe more," Mabior broke in. "Asante men like sex with young boy. With prisoner they eat after they fuck."

"Tell him he can't have Neo, or anyone. Tell him."

Garang broke into a staccato burst of speech. The witch doctor stepped back as though slapped across the face, then turned to the men behind him, who began to beat the spears against their shields.

"This is turning ugly." Travis half turned his head without taking his eyes off the natives and Harry caught his humorless grin.

"He say you cannot pass through Asante lands unless pay toll." Garang indicated scowling Neo. "His chief want nice plump boy here."

"Fire over their heads." Harry wasn't at all sure this was the best course of action, but the warriors were definitely working themselves up to a frenzied state and he feared anything might happen.

"Guns up!" Travis shouted. He raised his rifle and took a high aim. The others followed suit, even Jok.

"Fire!"

With parade ground precision, six shots rang out simultaneously, followed a second later by Neo's discharge. Above the natives' heads, a shower of leaves exploded in a great burst, but before any fell, the Asante had vanished into the forest as though they had never been in the clearing.

An hour later as the tropical night fell with its non-existent dusk the drums started up, louder, more visceral in rhythm.

"They won't attack during the hours off darkness," Travis said.

"You're very confident of that."

"My experience says African tribesmen don't like prowling about in the night, Harry." He grinned mirthlessly. "But it'd be good to keep a watch, if Jo will spell me."

"I can take a turn."

Jolyon and Travis both turned on Harry. "No, you need to gain strength," Jolyon said.

Travis added his voice. "He's right. I'd get the boys to help, but I think they'll be too frightened to be any use. Better they huddle up and get some sleep."

Travis offered to take the first watch and wake Jolyon a bit after midnight and that meant he and Harry were free for a while to cuddle like the Dinkas , only in the privacy of the pup tent. "I think we'll have to detour around this bunch," Harry said. "The Asante heartland is much farther into the Congo basin so if we cut off to the north a bit we might avoid them."

A scratching at the tent flap announced Neo.

"You're shaking," Jolyon said. "Come in. You'll be safe here with us."

Harry sighed. *And I was feeling well enough tonight to engage in some foreplay, at least. Ah well…*

In the morning, events occurred in a blur. Harry woke to find himself alone in the tent. Then he heard Jolyon asking Travis if he had seen Neo.

"Not since I woke up…" Travis paused, presumably to check his watch. "Not since half an hour. He was tending the fire, and then… I don't know."

There was fear in Jolyon's voice. "Where the hell is he? Have any of you seen him?"

Harry rubbed his bleary eyes and stooped out from the opening to see the four Dinkas all shaking their wooly heads. "Damn! I'll guarantee he's gone to pick more herbs for me."

Travis exhaled angrily. "I expressly told the silly bugger to stay in our perimeter unless one of us went with him."

Guilt weighed heavily on Harry's shoulders. He knew Neo would do anything for him; even wander in a dangerous forest to gather medicinal herbs to ensure his full recovery. He cursed the weakness of his limbs. Travis's sudden bellow drove a spike through his head.

"Don't be a fool!"

Harry lurched across the small clearing toward Travis in time to see the heel of Jolyon's boot disappear between the dense foliage around the faint track.

"Shit!" Travis thwacked a hand against his thigh in frustration.

"We must go after him… them."

Travis swung around. "You're in no condition. Stay put, and keep our Dinkas happy. The last thing we need is for them to run off."

That Travis was throwing orders around like some commanding officer didn't even register with Harry. Everything screamed at him to leap into action and run after Jolyon.

Travis stepped up and placed both hands on his shoulders in an attempt to reason. "Major… *Harry*… Save your energy for the moment. If we're to get out of this alive, we will need the support of Mabior and the three other Dinkas."

Harry raised his eyes, stared a moment at Travis, and then nodded. "You're right. Go!"

Travis snatched a water bottle from where it hung on the front of his tent, slung it around his neck, along with a bag containing loaded .303 magazines, and with a grim nod at Harry, dashed off after Jolyon. Harry went and made sure Mabior and his three corporals were sufficiently calm enough to organize a perimeter patrol. "Stay in sight of one another. Don't leave the camp under any circumstances."

"No, sah. No." Mabior answered firmly, and then started making his dispositions.

Harry returned to the tent. He ducked through the flap and sought the billycan holding a little less than a pint of Neo's foul-tasting herbal tea. He dosed himself with half the liquid and grimaced, but now was not the time for weakness of any kind. He went back out and saw Dut facing out into the surrounding bush, rifle at the ready. Harry threw himself down to do as many press-ups as he could manage.

The day dragged by. At some point in the afternoon there came the faint crack of rifle fire, several shots in quick succession; then silence. What did the fusillade portend? Harry had never felt so impotent. The thought of Jolyon—and Neo too—out there on his own, tracking savages, made his skin crawl. It felt like the day would never end.

And then Garang gave a shout and a minute later, sweaty, grimy, and gasping for breath, Travis appeared.

"Water, man. Get me some water."

One of the Dinkas rushed up with a full water bottle and Travis upended it, gulped furiously, and then wiped the back of his hand across his parched lips.

"Hoo, that's better. Harry…"

"Where are they? Travis, did you see anything?"

"Yeah. I don't know about Neo, but I couldn't do much. There were just too many of them. I nearly caught up with Jo, but the bastards had laid an ambush, and he ran straight into it not that far ahead of where I was. Two of the fuckers dropped on him from a branch, bore him to the ground, and more rushed up to bind him. I fired at them, but I couldn't risk hitting him, so it wasn't very effective. When more came running down the path past the ambuscade toward me, I had to get away. I was outnumbered. I must've run near ten miles flat out."

Harry dropped his head into his cupped palms, as though cutting the light to his eyes would prevent them seeing the horror of the situation. When he finally looked up, Travis's chest had stopped heaving. He regarded Harry bleakly.

"I know what Jolyon means to you."

Harry ignored the implication in the words. "We'll have to rescue him and… Neo. You didn't see any sign…? I thought not. Any idea where they would have gone?"

No mirth accompanied the thin-lipped smile. "Not far from where they jumped Jolyon, I'd hazard. I saw several young boys and two women among the reinforcements, which means their village can't be much farther along that path from where I was. The proximity is why we've heard the drums at night, as well."

"So what are we waiting for?"

"Hold up. It's about an hour to nightfall." He called Garang over. "Do the Asante make attacks at night?"

The Dinka shook his head. "No, sah. Afeared of witches in night. Many witches."

Travis regarded Harry with a flinty expression. "As I expected." He rounded on the Dinkas. "Are you afraid of witches?"

Garang stood in uncertainty, but his three comrades laughed and Mabior spoke up for them. "No, Dinka not 'fraid witches, Travis-sah. My ox-self frighten off any witch."

Harry recalled a trader at Mengo telling him that adolescent Dinka boys were given an ox as a part of their initiation into adulthood, and the boy named his ox by its color, which then became his adult name, or ox name. This snippet of information slipped through Harry's mind in a flash of understanding. It did nothing to calm his terror.

"So we wait for night." Travis patted Harry's shoulder in an attempt at reassurance. "Dut and Jok can stay here and guard our things. Mabior and Garang with us. Then we'll track them down and check out the village under cover of darkness."

"But what if they... before we can get there?" Harry couldn't bring himself to voice the horror.

With an apologetic shuffle, Garang stepped up. "Sah, Asante like..." he struggled for the right word, "*season* food before cook."

The last dose of Neo's herbal concoction threatened to rise up Harry's gorge. "Season?"

Garang made the universal hand gestures to indicate sexual penetration.

A deep welling darkness engulfed Harry. He struggled to fight against the need to throw up.

Travis removed his bush hat so he could mop his brow. "We'll go quarter of an hour before dark. Get to the village as fast as we can, and armed to the teeth."

A few deep breaths went some way to recovery and Harry nodded slowly. "I still have several sticks of dynamite left. I'll go count them." He made the statement to occupy his mind. He knew very well how much of the explosive was left.

An early three-quarter moon revealed a landscape of light forest, low shrubs and grasses, and occasional denser clusters of trees covering regularly rolling hills. For some days after crossing the Albert Nile, the survey team's route had taken them across terrain folded into many shallow parallel valleys running toward the northwest. The higher ground they had followed was ideal for the planned railway. Harry, Travis, Garang, and Mabior now moved silently along the faint track that ran along the top of one such ridge.

Mabior and Travis carried the Winchester shotguns, with Lee-Enfields slung over their shoulders. Both white men had holstered revolvers, and in a bag at Harry's hip six sticks of dynamite were packed in cotton wool, along with a box of vestas for lighting the fuses he'd trimmed to only an inch in length. He'd also had the presence of mind to bring along the Very pistol—intended to be a means of locating a lost individual or party off on a side reconnaissance, but so far unused—and two red flares.

Travis had little difficulty in retracing his steps. As he'd pointed out, the Asante wouldn't site their village in a valley because of flooding; simply keeping on the track would bring them to its perimeter. But in the event, the sound of the drums acted like a beacon, and soon the glow of distant fires could be seen flickering through the undergrowth. Since leaving camp, a measure of calm had tempered Harry's determination. He still didn't feel on top of the world after the fever, but the thought of Jolyon and Neo's predicament blew all weakness away. Travis had been relieved to see his chief recover purpose again.

The four men crept nearer, two to either side of the track, keeping close to the jungle foliage. Harry, on the left, held out his hand. He sensed Mabior steal up behind him, and across the way Travis and Garang halted. Ahead, the path gradually widened and passed between two timber posts of a strange construction. Beyond, several circular huts with steep conical roofs of thatch were visible before the flank of the surrounding jungle cut off Harry's view of the rest of the habitation. From what he could see of the center it was a large cleared area populated by several of the Asante warriors, who appeared to be sauntering about, engaging others in conversation and laughter.

Around the edge of the open area, young men pattered away on tall, narrow drums while women and young boys fed fuel to several large braziers. Their glow glinted off the smooth, oiled skin of a sentry who stood close to one of the entry pylons. The Asante watchman was more occupied by the goings on in the village than keeping an eye out for intruders. Harry could see no perimeter wall or other defense, other than a low picket designed to keep domestic animals in and wild beasts out. He presumed the tribe's fierce reputation was defense enough against human incursion.

"You're the tactical expert," Travis whispered to Harry. "What do you reckon?"

"We need to get closer. Can you take the guard?"

Travis nodded. Moonlight briefly glinted off his knife as he eased it from its sheath. They all watched not daring to breathe as the man stepped forward as stealthy as a panther preparing to launch, although the drums covered any sound he might make. Closer, closer, and then in a swift move, Travis wrapped a hand around the sentry's forehead, pulled it back viciously, and before the man could utter more than a low gurgling choke, sliced the blade across his throat. The Asante slumped. Travis lowered his body quietly to the grassy ground. He signaled.

Harry started forward, followed by the two Dinkas, and crouched down beside the warm corpse. Closer in he could see that the pylons were no more than three saplings tied at the top into tall triangles, but it was the festoons of human skulls that gave them their odd shape from a distance. The stink of decomposing flesh indicated that some of the grisly adornments were newly detached from their owners' shoulders. That thought and the reality of Jolyon's plight drove Harry to want to rush forward instantly and start firing.

Travis's calm voice returned some sense. "What do you reckon?" he repeated.

Harry cast his gaze over the nearer huts and saw how closely they were built to the thick foliage behind. We'd get a better view from over there, from between the second and third hut."

It took ten minutes to work through the thicker undergrowth away from the path they had been following. At the back of the huts, the picket fence was taller, but still no barrier, and a minute later, the four were gathered in a tight cluster between two of the round hovels. Here the ground was largely cleared of growth, and the position afforded Harry a clear view of the proceedings…

And what he saw stole his breath clean away.

CHAPTER 41 | *Western Equatoria, November 16, 1900*

UNEVEN FIRELIGHT FROM the several braziers cast a hellish glow over the crowded clearing. Some sixty feet away Jolyon and Neo were held naked and upright in the grip of four tall Asante warriors, two to each captive. Two more young men stood behind the prisoners, feet splayed and hips gyrating. Hands held their kilts aside to reveal long erections pressed to the presented backsides of their victims.

Garang twisted his head away from the scene toward Harry. In the firelight, his face looked cut from obsidian. His terrified eyes engaged Harry.

"See, sah, they will season food first."

Any reaction Harry might have made was doused by the sudden shrill screams of terror from beyond where Jolyon and Neo were held.

Travis nudged Harry's elbow. "Holy shit, aren't those two of our Dinka porters? The ones who fled?"

Mabior groaned and shuddered.

Two powerful warriors, naked but for bangles on their wrists and around their necks dragged one of the Dinkas forward into the full glare of the nearest brazier, which Harry could now make out was little more than a crude pit of fiercely burning charcoal surrounded by a ring of stones that supported a worked metal griddle. The Dinka wailed continuously in terror and his comrade's sobs alternated with loud cries for mercy at the two holding him. Another powerful warrior, naked and massively aroused, shuffled up behind the doomed porter, grabbed his hips and with a shout of triumph thrust into his ass. The Dinka cried out anew. His whole body shuddered with the force of the fucking the big man standing behind was administering.

Harry watched the unfolding drama with abhorrence. The pace of drumming increased and women's shill ululations splintered the night air as the old witch doctor made his appearance. He came forward at a shambling gait that set his fantastic headdress to whipping and dancing like a coil of snakes. In one hand a large curved blade caught the golden glimmers of the glowing braziers, and this knife he waved at the unfortunate Dinka while he chanted shamanic incantations in a loud, high-pitched voice.

The booming drums increased in pace to a frenzied pitch, the black sirens of death reached an ear-shattering crescendo. The witch doctor raised his arm high and then with shocking suddenness brought it down and stabbed the Dinka in the chest with the big knife. At the same time an acolyte cut the poor man's throat. Another held out a bowl to catch the spray of jugular blood. The Asante who had seasoned the victim pulled loose. His huge cock wagged as he turned away from the gore-fest.

In seconds, women rushed up and got to work butchering the porter. First his head was lopped off and taken away by the witch doctor. In the shadows at the edge of the village, Harry, Travis, Garang, and Mabior watched in mute horror as their former porter's arms were skilfully detached and then, with powerful and accurate blows, his legs removed from the torso. His genitals were separated for special treatment. His hands and feet were cleaved from the limbs and discarded, the arms and legs jointed and coated with fat, and then popped onto the griddle to cook.

Harry shook his head in stomach-churning disgust. That this was to be Jolyon's fate was too much to contemplate. Resoluteness gripped his mind like a red-hot ring and fed strength to his fever-weakened frame. "Sergeant," he said to Mabior. "We need a diversion. You have the shotgun. Get at least a quarter way around edge and get in a good position to fire across the clearing. That way you will avoid hitting any of us. Here, take this as well." He pulled the Very pistol and flares from his equipment bag and handed them to Mabior. "When you're ready, fire one flare and then wait on my signal…" he waved a stick of dynamite, "…to open up with the Winchester."

Mabior nodded his understanding, as Harry laid out the six sticks out carefully in a line on the hard mud ground, ready for use as grenadoes.

Neo's two guards pushed the Barolong boy down and forward onto his hands and knees, and the young tormentor behind hitched up his loincloth ready to penetrate the forcibly offered asshole. Jo struggled against his captors. One caught him a vicious backhand across the cheek.

"Go!" Harry hissed at Mabior, and in a rustle of grass the Dinka was gone.

Harry and Travis continued to watch helplessly as more of the murdered Dinka porter was dismembered and prepared for cooking. To the side, another Asante had lined up to take his turn in seasoning the second Dinka. In the space of only a few minutes, the dissection of his comrade was complete and the stench of broiling meat filled the clearing along with a cloud of blue-hazed smoke.

Come on, Mabior, come on, come on…

"I don't think the Dinkas are the main event tonight," Travis said.

Harry feared the same, especially when some natives danced up to Jolyon, who hung partly insensible between his captors, and started to sniff his naked form and handle his cock and balls. They laughed uproariously.

"We'll get your sweetheart back, Harry, don't worry."

For a second an entirely different feeling of chill washed over Harry at Travis's words. In shock he flicked Travis a wide-eyed glance. The man never took his eyes off the abominations playing out before them. But he spoke as if he'd seen the look.

"I've known for an age, Harry, my man. Even with Vane's Horse. That wee little cunt Norris tried to involve me in his blackmail, you see. Now of course I could've thought he was just lying, but you'd have to be blind or incredibly innocent—and I'm saying most are when it comes to *unusual* sex—not to see the looks the boy keeps giving you, and you him."

"Unusual…" The word came out like a confused sigh.

"Well, it's not normal, is it? I mean the most of men prefer to fuck a woman. But what's it to me? After you've spent years among the tribes in upper Rhodesia, you tend to lose the objective of what's normal and what's not. I wouldn't have stayed with you if I didn't think you were a decent man, Major Vane. What you do in bed is your business. Now mine is to help you free those boys and get the hell out of here."

Harry took a deep breath, swallowed his shocked astonishment along with a bubble of utterly inappropriate humor at Travis. "You are full of surprises."

Travis gave him a wide, toothy grin that reminded Harry of an attacking shark he'd once seen in a book engraving.

They both heard the *ffrup!* The flare hurtled up into the sky, nothing more than a thin line of pale gray underlit pink from the fires. Its unfamiliar sound alerted none of the Asante, who were too busily engaged in the process of readying the second Dinka for the witch doctor's evil attentions. A second passed and then high above the trees a fricative firework *thrump* was accompanied by a bloom of brilliant red. In a second the entire village was cast in a suitably infernal light. In the same instant the drums fell silent and chatter ceased. The flare's sibilant hiss reached all ears clearly over the sizzling of grilling flesh.

And then a great hubbub broke out as a single gasp, immediately followed by screams and shouts of terror.

"Let's go!" Harry snapped a vesta alight between finger and thumb, held it to the fuse of the first stick, and in one clean action, hurled the dynamite up and out. His aim was as true as any cricketer's bowl down the pitch at Benthenham. "Haven't played in years, but not lost my touch," he crowed.

In the falling flare light the stick flew, tumbling end-over-end, in a trajectory that took it into the heart of the central cooking brazier. Harry had the second and third sticks lit and thrown before the first deafening explosion blasted metal shrapnel, burning coals, butchered Dinka limbs, and the body parts of two Asante cooks apart. One stick to the left landed among huts there, the third flew well to the side so it blew up in between two huts well beyond where Jolyon and Neo were held, and well away from where Mabior must be concealed.

And then the Dinka wasn't hiding anymore. Muzzle flashes from his pump-action shotgun showed brightly in the shadow of the hut where he'd secreted himself. *One-two-three; pump-pump-pump...* The gun's effective range of twenty-two yards was more than enough to fill the center of the clearing with a mist of pellets. Those Asante at closer range simply sprouted endless ruptures and a mist of blood merged with the smoke of the blasted cooking fire. Two warriors who were unfortunate enough to be only five yards from Mabior's position were torn apart and hurled back several yards as if they'd been jerked off their feet by a tug-'o-war team.

A fourth orange explosion blossomed against which silhouetted Asante died. In the blink of an eye chaos reigned among the natives, who shrieked in fear or pain and began to run for cover from a devil they did not understand. Some fell down in terror. The witch doctor came apart at the seams from a point-blank discharge of Mabior's shotgun. Abandoning their grisly task, women fled in all directions like headless chickens, adding to the confusion.

Travis moved first. He raised the shotgun in one hand and his Lee-Enfield in the other. Harry grabbed up the two remaining sticks of dynamite, thrust them back in his bag, and followed him with Garang on his heels. Across the clearing, Mabior emerged, shotgun now slung over his shoulder and firing with his rifle.

Harry left the Dinkas to drive the Asante out into the surrounding jungle, now dark from the setting moon and extinguished flare, and dashed to where Jolyon's startled guards still held him. Incredibly, the Asante youth who had Neo sprawled on the ground was fucking him in such wild abandon he was unaware of his imminent fate. Travis put a .303 shell through his head at closing range. Bone, brains, and blood exploded as Travis reached Neo and dragged him out from under the carnage of his dead rapist.

Even as Travis took out the Asante "seasoner," Harry fired at one of Jolyon's terrified captors. The man clutched his chest and dropped to his knees, dead before his corpse hit the ground. The other turned to flee only to take a .303 shell in the back. The close-range power-punch of the metal-jacketed bullet opened him up all along his spine.

Travis hauled a sobbing Neo to his feet, but even in his state, he still had the wherewithal to snatch up the dead fucker's clothing to wrap around his Jo Jo Angrish, now in Harry's arms. In his turn, Travis snatched the loin covering of the man shot by Harry for Neo to strap around his waist.

Jolyon pulled himself together and hugged Harry. Then he stepped back and saw that Harry was barely able to stand. "It's the fever. Harry you have to hold up." Roles swiftly reversed, it was Jolyon having to help his lover.

"Go, go, go!" Travis yelled.

They turned and begin to traverse the camp, aimed at the grisly pylons and the hopeful safety of the jungle path. Harry in his somewhat weakened state struggled as Jolyon tugged him along. Travis waved Neo and the Dinkas on to hurry after Harry and Jolyon. He nodded encouragement at Garang who had the surviving porter in his grip. The poor fellow was hyperventilating. Seasoned he may have been, but he'd escaped the griddle after all. Travis urged them all on while he turned to provide cover for Mabior to catch up.

Harry and Jolyon staggered up to the pylons and—uncaring of the gruesome burden of withered hands, feet, dripping heads, and stripped skulls—leaned against the nearest frame.

"I'll be all right in a moment, Jo." Harry protested. "Just need to catch my breath." He turned and took in the havoc they had created in such a short space of time.

Travis and Mabior, now both firing bursts from the pump-action shotguns, removing and slapping in new magazines, backed toward the roadway between the last two huts. Across the clearing two more men collapsed under the lethal hail of pellets. Travis punched the air as a signal and Mabior obeyed, turned and dashed to where Harry and Jolyon waited. As Travis drew level with the huts, three huge Asante warriors, bearing shields and spears, leapt out through the right-hand hut's entryway.

Harry's shouted warning coincided with Travis firing the shotgun, but he hadn't the time to aim and only managed to wing one of his foes before they were on him. In a flash and a curse, Jolyon let go Harry's arm, snatched up Harry's rifle, and turned back.

No, Jo! Get the hell out." Harry's shout fell on deaf ears. He grabbed Neo before the boy could follow.

Jolyon dived into the fight. He shot one attacker, chambered the next round only to get a dull click. Magazine out. He quickly flipped the weapon barrel over butt and wielded it as a club.

"Sergeant, you four form up on the track ready," Harry snapped out at Mabior, nodding at Neo, Garang, and the rescued porter. And then he ran toward the village where Travis fought with the Asante to wrest the spear from his grip, while Jolyon was down on one knee fending off the other Asante with his reversed rifle. Harry took aim, praying that Jolyon would not stand up. He squeezed the trigger. The Lee-Enfield barked, the vicious recoil almost knocked Harry from his footing, but in a microsecond the Asante's head burst like a heat-exploded watermelon, a detonation of blood and brains. He was about to go to help Travis when a howl came from behind. He whipped around to see more Asante leap from either side of the track and block the escape route. The warriors all crouched ready to attack.

Torn between two courses of action, Harry glimpsed Travis stagger as his opponent dealt him a hefty blow to the head with the shaft of his spear. The attack gave Jolyon a precious moment to close the distance and come up behind the Asante, and with a tremendous swing he struck the back of the native's head such a blow the rifle stock sheared. The Asante went down as if poleaxed.

"Go help the others," Jolyon said in a ragged voice. "I'll get Travis."

On the path Garang was shooting into the mass of warriors all chanting and waving spears and shields. Even as Harry rushed up, two Asante fighters went down, their place immediately taken by two more warriors. One drew his arm back and loosed his javelin, but a gutful of shotgun pellets spoiled the man's aim and the spear's blade buried itself in the trodden ground of the path a foot in front of Neo. The Barolong immediately ran forward, grasped the weapon's shaft, pulled it free, hefted it for balance, and threw it back. It struck a warrior in the throat. The spear's point punched clean through skin, flesh, and bone to emerge from the back of the man's neck, and the sheer force of Neo's throw impaled the man behind.

Suddenly, it was over. With a rapid-fire burst from Mabior's shotgun knocking three more Asante off their feet in a welter of blood, the rest took to their heels and in seconds the forest was silent but for the fading sounds of foliage being brushed aside in the passage of panic.

At the sound of heavy footfalls, Harry swung around to see Jolyon's slight frame buckling under the weight of unconscious Travis slung over his shoulder. Blood poured from a gash on Jolyon's upper arm. Partly silhouetted against the dying embers of the various village fires, partly illuminated by the carpet of stars overhead, Harry was filled with gratitude and love. Jolyon's near-naked form glistened with sweat from the exertion. Every fine muscle bulged with the effort. He looked magnificent and so far removed from the louche, dissolute youth of the Café Royal it was hard to believe both were of the same species.

In a moment he was back in Harry's arms as he took some of Travis's weight. "You must stop making a habit of this, Jo."

Travis groaned and shook his head. Between them they got the man onto his own feet.

"Let's get out of here before those… fuckers decide to come back," Harry said.

"Language, *Major*. Never heard you profane before." Travis managed a grin. "It's fortunate I'm so tender looking. Don't think I'd have survived if the bastards had been determined to kill me, but they obviously wanted me alive to serve up braised on a banana leaf."

CHAPTER 42 | *Tonj, Western Equatoria, November 17–28, 1900*

IF HARRY THOUGHT Vane's Survey was done with the cannibals, the cries of terror rising up from distant fields dashed his hopes. He stared at the great cloud of dust rising up from the tree-dotted brown grassland that stretched away to the south. With a clenched jaw, he handed the field glasses to Jolyon, and sighed in deep misgiving as to what the portent heralded. Almost a hundred miles lay between Tonj and the Asante village. On regaining the camp Neo and Jolyon had wasted no time in dressing and then everyone gathered anything of value, especially spare weapons and boxes of ammunition, as much as nine men and four mules—the only ones not stolen by the fleeing porters—could carry.

Harry recorded that the team left the survey trail in the early hours of Saturday November 16, carrying over 5,000 rounds of .303 ammunition. By dawn, following Mabior and Garang's lead in a northerly direction, they managed almost five miles. They marched against the grain of the landscape, across parallel, forested ridges and damp jungle valleys. Everyone kept a wary eye out for crocodiles in the swampier bottoms. There was no sign of pursuit.

For eight days the reduced team trudged north at best walking speed through a landscape of rolling hills in which the rain forest flora gave way to more arid species set amid sun-burnt grasses. They were entering the great sub-Saharan savannah that stretched from the West African coast to the Horn of Africa and the Red Sea. It could still surprise when water came close to the surface and the slopes became thickly wooded, before again giving way to semi-arid conditions. In many respects, Jolyon remarked, the land was similar to the Cape Colony's Great Karoo.

Mabior guided the team to the small farming community of Tonj in the heartland of the Bongo people, where they arrived on the first day of December, exhausted from the trek, but relieved to have escaped the undoubtedly enraged Asante.

And yet the dust cloud thrown up by hundreds of tramping feet was an early warning of imminent attack. As scores of frightened Bongo men and boys streamed in from the fields, Harry had the uncomfortable vision of the Asante warriors driving the farmers before them without remorse, as butchers drove sheep to the shambles.

"It is common here, sah," Garang said. "Bongo been cut down by Asante many years now."

Harry sighed. *Wish I'd known that. I'd have kept us going.* And immediately he felt unworthy for thinking it.

Tonj was not a village in any sense a white man would understand. Its round clay huts with their conical thatched roofs stood so far apart from each other that it took an hour to walk from one end to the other (a lot less across the much narrower width). Each home stood in its own vegetable patch, with acres of grassland between it and its neighbor.

The Bongo were not cattle herders, like the main Dinka tribes, but farmed cereals, kept bees for the honey they sold, and some families worked in forestry. Here and there around Tonj great piles of cut and stacked timber rose up like small castles. It was these Harry scrutinized.

"You're thinking," said Jolyon.

"I'm thinking I wish to God we had your pom-pom gun, is what I'm thinking."

"Mabior says the Bongo will fade away to the north," Travis said. "They'll lie low and hope the raiders get bored and go home."

"But that won't stop the raids, will it? Anyway, we know it's us they're after, and I have a gut feeling they'll keep on our trail until they run us down. No. We must encourage the Bongo to stand up to these man-eaters. I can't believe that Khartoum can't spare a company of Sudanese to station down here. General Hunter had them well trained and they behaved very bravely at Omdurman. In the meantime… see all that timber. We must persuade the elders to convince the men to build a stronghold."

Harry's expression turned thoughtful. "You remember on the train to Bulawayo I jokingly referred to the Zulu assault at Rorke's Drift?"

Travis frowned. "If I'm thinking what you're thinking… Lieutenant Chard had a lot more soldiers than we have, men trained with modern weapons. Didn't he have a hundred and forty British regulars. We're three with four— no five, Dinkas. And they're terrified of the Asante. To be honest, so am I."

"Facing about four thousand highly disciplined Zulu warriors who believed they were fighting for their freedom," Harry argued.

Jolyon did a rapid computation. "Odds of about twenty-eight to one."

"What do you estimate the Asante numbers to be? Theirs is a village, not a nation on a war footing."

Travis thought about it. "Hard to say, but looking at the dust they're kicking up I guess at about two-fifty, maybe three hundred?"

"Thirty-seven to one," Jolyon piped up. "Not that different, really."

Harry nodded sagely. "It sounds bad, but we're facing a ragged war band. All they want is to attack, stock up on prisoners, and retire to their woodlands where they happily anticipate an unholy feast of human flesh. They are not trained and motivated Zulu impis. And at Rorke's Drift the men only had single-shot Martini-Henry rifles. We've got fifteen modern Lee-Enfields and, thanks to keeping hold of four mules, enough ammunition for extended concentrated fire." He turned to Travis. "How long will it take to select nine men from among the Bongos?"

"Nine? Surely you mean seven? Plus us. As you said, we have fifteen rifles."

"We have the two Winchesters that did such excellent close-up work at the village. Mabior and I will take those, which gives us two more armed men on the firing line. At least we won't be facing gunfire, and those long spears don't look as savage as the Zulu assegai, but I've no doubt they're quite as lethal." Then he addressed Jolyon. "How long to get the men Travis selects trained up enough to aim a rifle and fire when ordered?"

Travis pointed at the approaching dust cloud. "That long."

It was hoped that the hastily erected defenses would stiffen the resolve of the men and older boys of the village who Travis and Mabior had exhorted to stay and fight to save their homes, but Harry hadn't anticipated another benefit it gave the defenders. A wooden wall as tall as a man's shoulder standing in their way baffled the Asante. Their ragged advance halted several hundred yards away in evident confusion. Amid the milling men, some brandished shields and spears at the defenders, but the gestures looked decidedly hesitant.

Harry prayed that the Asante weren't strong on strategic thinking because a swift reconnaissance of the barrier would immediately reveal that what faced them was the timber bulwark's strongest section. To the north of the small stronghold—it enclosed only the center of the village, some sixteen huts—only wagons, handcarts, and other domestic material bridged the gaps between five huts. Harry knew the few Bongo directed to defend it would not withstand a concerted attack.

The hold-up bought more precious time for the survey team to marshal their scant fusiliers. Mabior and his corporals' experience in the Bugandan police force helped in distributing the basic knowledge required to load magazines, sight, aim, and blank fire the rifles. They were a great help too in communicating with the villagers, Bongo only differing from Dinka in unimportant aspects. It also gave Harry and Jolyon the chance to assess what they were up against in terms of numbers.

"Not as bad as we feared, Harry," Jolyon claimed after their individual counts. "I made it one-eighty, maybe two hundred."

"I split the difference: one-ninety."

"Odds of ten to one, then with fifteen rifles and the two shotguns." Jolyon grinned gamely. "Not a problem! What's the plan?"

Harry gathered the Dinkas around Jolyon and Travis and started to explain. His strategy was simple: in effect a copy of what Chard had achieved at Rorke's Drift (and among others at that action received a VC for his effort). There, the lieutenant had three ranks of rifles, kneeling, weapons loaded. At the signal, the first rank stood, aimed, fired a volley, dropped to their knees to reload while the second rank stood, fired, knelt again for the third rank to take its turn. By that time the front rank was loaded and ready again. In this repetitious manner the infantrymen kept up a continuous barrage of murderous fire that slaughtered the attacking Zulus by the score.

"I wish we had a couple of Maxims, but we don't. And we don't have enough men to form three ranks some twenty-four men wide, like Chard had, but we're facing many less foes and we enjoy the advantage of technology—the Lee-Enfield is a different and much faster weapon than the Martini-Henry in use in 1879."

In the hands of a skilled soldier, the Martini-Henry was capable of firing 12 rounds per minute, whereas Harry anticipated the much more advanced Lee-Enfields wielded by the survey team could manage as much as 20 rounds per minute, perhaps 25. That gave a theoretical 300 rounds every minute. The ammunition stock stood at 5,020 cartridges, which would result in just over sixteen minutes of volley fire.

"I don't expect to achieve such a high frequency from an untried and insufficiently practiced body of men. To be effective this action has to be disciplined, every man must fire together, so that means the best rifleman can only shoot at the speed of the poorest. Still—jams aside, and the Enfield is most reliable—the average rounds per minute and the sheer coverage should be sufficient to keep the Asante dancing. The resulting extended firing time might be as much as twenty minutes to half an hour."

He let his eyes settle on each man in turn, mouth set in a grimly determined line. "If that isn't long enough to convince the surviving enemy to turn and flee, every man and boy in Tonj will be as good as dead anyway."

The point was well made. The five Dinkas, including the rescued porter in his borrowed clothes, shivered. Jolyon instinctively placed a hand on Neo's shoulder in mutual sympathy.

"Each man selected for the firing line beside us will get three pre-loaded 10-round magazines, so a single magazine load should last between 20 and 25 seconds. At that point the front rank will kneel, eject the empty magazine, slap in a new one, and prepare to stand again when the rear rank has fired off their volley of ten shots. We'll keep up the alternating fire by rank for as long as needed."

As the others immediately began their appointed tasks Harry drew Jolyon aside. "If we should fail this day, do as I intend and make sure you save your last revolver bullet—"

"I know, Harry, and I won't let them take me alive again, I promise. But it's not going to come to that."

A smile came to Harry's lips and, suddenly uncaring of onlookers, he took Jolyon in his arms and hugged him as if it might be the last time. Then they parted with resolute expressions, and not a touch of fear for the uncertainty of what lay ahead.

❧ ★ ☙

Survey diary, Wednesday November 28, 1900

Winston always said bad things happened to him on Wednesdays. I hope fervently that Woden preserves misfortune alone for Churchills. The natives out there were growing restless, and just before midday it looked as if the Asante war council—no doubt occasioned by finding their prey armed and fearsome behind a barricade—was breaking up. As far as I could determine, not a single warrior had been dispatched to explore the area around Tonj. So far, so good. All the enemy's preparations suggested a narrow and concerted frontal assault. This is what I hoped for and intended to encourage as much as I could. I wanted them all concentrated on our rifles.

Beside each rifleman knelt a magazine loader within easy reach of the shared out ammunition. I smiled to see Neo snuggled up against Jolyon, two magazines in his hands ready. My decision not to give the boy a rifle of his own annoyed him. "You're not quite tall enough to sight over the top of the parapet," Jolyon pointed out, coming to my defense. Teaching the fourteen young Tonj boys the proper way to load the magazines had cost the most of our limited preparation time, but their precision would be crucial in avoiding jams. Behind our low palisade my dispositions were made and we were as ready as could be in the short time given us.

Jolyon commanded the front rank of eight riflemen from the center. I'd placed our best shots there, the Dinkas (excluding Mabior) and two of the Tonj men who had shown the most aptitude (all those Bongos we chose had seen some service in the black Sudanese regiments up north). I wanted to ensure that one of the ranks would be capable of firing synchronously and at a fast rate, then the second rank with a rifle less could afford to work the bolt actions at a slower speed if need be. In each case, I would call the order to stand and aim, shout the first command to fire, and then Jo and Travis in turn would command the firing pace to match their slowest shooter. At the instant of ejecting the tenth cartridge, the rank would drop to the knees and change the empty magazine for a full one.

To Mabior I handed one of the Winchester pump-action shotguns and a box of cartridges. He took position at the right end of the firing line, while I took the other gun on the left end. We had an empty ammunition box each to stand up on so that we could risk the enemy's spears in order to reach easily over the palisade and cut down any Asante who attempted to clamber up it.

To our immediate flanks some fifty of the bravest villagers stood, eyes peering at their dreaded foe over the rough wall. They wielded medium-length jabbing spears used for hunting wild pig and antelope. Unlike the spearmen, the riflemen were kneeling out of sight of the enemy so the firing line would appear to present an easy point of assault. We didn't have to wait long. The constant rumbling sound of scores of Asante throats chanting gradually gathered momentum, seemed to shuffle like an orchestra tuning up into a single voice, and then grew into a resounding roar. Unlike the Zulus who beat spears against shields in complex, disciplined rhythms to inspire fear in their foes, these Asante simply banged away as individuals so it made a clattering sound like a hundred wooden clogs beating on pavement.

They began to move, an ebony and ochre wave of humanity, slowly materializing from the brown dust of their progress. I checked to see that all the riflemen were still crouched down out of sight of the rapidly approaching warriors. I wanted their chief to see me clearly, and all his men; I wanted them to see the white man who had come and stolen away their prisoners and left some of them dead; I needed every Asante to want the pride of killing the white man and to converge on our narrow killing line. I needed them to charge straight onto the muzzles of our guns. The chief, dressed in his war finery and surrounded by his ministers, was as fat as an African headman is expected to be to show his wealth, yet he danced along merrily enough for all the weight he carried.

Still out of range of thrown spears, I made the most of my visibility, standing well clear of the parapet. I taunted my foes with broad gestures and laughed larger than life as almost every Asante threw challenges back. The line that began the advance on a broad front now rapidly contracted as each individual set on killing me arrowed in. I noticed the chief had issued some battle orders: older boys and young men formed the front ranks, while after a slight separation came adults and veterans. Whether the youngsters were sent to the slaughter first to test the opposing strength or whether it was the pride of youth to make their first kills, I neither knew nor cared. It would make no difference once the rifles started their execution.

My orders had been to wait for the classic "whites of their eyes" moment to unleash our fire in order to preserve the maximum of surprise, but I soon perceived a flaw in the plan. As the enemy closed to within a hundred and fifty yards and increased the pace of their charge to a run, I saw the villagers supposed to fend the enemy off our flanks begin to show dismay. Eyes rolled, mouths gasped, spears drooped. They set up a miserable wailing at the sight of the dreaded cannibals rushing toward them, their sharp-filed incisors glinting evilly in the sunshine. If I didn't do something instantly, we'd lose them to panic.

I shouted out above the roar of the approaching crest. "Jo! We have to go early. Prepare!"

Jo gave a curt nod.

"Front rank, stand—Aim—Fire!

Crack… Crack… Crack!

With commendable efficiency the front rank unleashed its rounds so that the eight rifles sounded with only a fractional rolling in the discharge.

The effect couldn't have been more satisfying. Before Jo's men had dropped back down and Travis's taken up firing at a slower pace and with more ragged effect, at least a score of Asante lay dead or writhing on the ground. I lit and threw the last two sticks of dynamite into the advancing horde and bodies flew amid the eruptions of flame and smoke. Men were forced to leap over the fallen, still eager to reach the timber wall standing in their way. As importantly, the sudden collapse of so many of the enemy had a visible effect on the villagers. Heartened by the destruction of their foes, they all rallied and began stabbing out with their spears in defiance, a challenge which grew with each wave of the young Asante that stumbled and fell under the inexorable hail of lead.

But still they came on, warriors dashing to take the place of the dead and wounded. Instinctively—since I discerned no order—the native throng hurled their spears at us. I shouted out for all riflemen to take cover. One shower of lethal weapons would be it, for they could not relinquish their stabbing spears. I too ducked down but a split second late, for one blade sliced across the soft meat between my left shoulder and neck. I must have cried out because Jo started up. I managed to wave him down, as the last spears slammed home into the wood or flew overhead. A few screams from down the line indicated injuries among the villager corps, but in the main I think we withstood the only real blow the Asante could deliver at a distance.

It seemed sheer madness on their part to continue, but they came on. Pain shocked me back to my feet. The neck wound stung like mad, but it wasn't incapacitating me. By the time the ragged advance reached scant yards from our defensive perimeter, the forward Asante were suffering appallingly. Our .303 bullets tore holes in bared chests, shattered heads, cut to shreds limbs, as if we had the pair of Maxim machine guns I'd wished for striking them down. A haze of scarlet mist mingled with the thick dust.

And then they were among us. The spearheads were of a narrow leaf shape borne on thin but whippy shafts. Suddenly there seemed to be a thicket of the damned things. But the strategy had worked: almost all the Asante were clumped thickly before the firing line and not assaulting the weaker sections of the line where the Bongo would have been hard-pressed otherwise. I gave the order to form one line and fix bayonets—which had been unattached to avoid accidental stabbings—and then ordered independent rapid fire. The disciplined simultaneous cracks instantly turned into a rolling crepitation.

I heard the roar of Mabior's gun and three warriors slapped to the ground as if someone had roped their legs and whipped them out from under. The scattering shot caused carnage at point-blank range. Two huge brutes who had shown the sense to crawl up to the wall under cover of their own men, leapt up just below where Jo was standing. I spotted the movement, which he could not while he concentrated on firing over their heads at natives farther off. One thrust his spear up at Jo, but his aim was thrown in a jostle from behind, which also disturbed the other. I whipped up my Winchester and pumped out two shots. The first took Jo's assailant in the legs just as he prepared to thrust up again. The second hit his comrade, who had recovered his balance ready to stab. He was not much above six yards from the Winchester's snub muzzle and the velocity and cone of the pellets were concentrated. His torso exploded in a hundred wounds and his blood fountained over the nearest attackers amid bone fragments blasted from his collapsing torso. Another thunderous blast came from Mabior's gun and a headless corpse half turned, jostled again, and evacuated bright red arterial blood from the severed jugulars before it fell down among trampling feet.

But these were heels we were seeing. The native war band had had enough. Cheers rang out all along the line. I ordered the resumption of firing by rank, and more Asante dropped, even as they hopped around or jumped over their fallen fellow cannibals. I saw Jo, having started his sequence of commands, was not firing in line with his men. Instead he had the concentration of someone with a bead on a distant figure. I scanned the battlefield and spotted the fat chief, who stood amid the carnage berating his fleeing warriors.

The discharge of Jo's rifle sounded louder to my ears than all the others. The black mountain jerked once, twice, thrice, as Jo's bullets drilled into him with the precision expected of a Woolwich graduate. He went down in a cloud of dust. His entourage turned and fled with the rest. Within minutes the dust cloud of their passage, much lessened than on the approach, settled among the scattered trees.

The chittering of birds started up, soon joined by the cheers of the victorious villagers of Tonj, unbelieving of their achievement, but evidently very joyous of the fact. When I checked my watch I was surprised to see we had been fighting for almost twenty minutes, when it felt as if the action passed in a flash.

I write under the fussing administration of my dearest Jolyon. For a young man who didn't know a needle from a thread, who claimed to prefer a slim volume of unreadable poetry (though probably only holding onto it as a symbol) to an explosives manual, he makes a neat stitch—*ouch!*—where it's needed—in this case about six to close the wound. It's painful but thankfully clean after a dose of alcohol (brandy, which I took internally as well as externally) that sent the pain factor through the thatched roof I sit under. I make this entry before the light finally fades on this extraordinary day.

Travis took up the unenviable task of supervising collection of the dead and seeing to their burning. There are no wounded because in their righteous range, the Bongo ensured any man still alive was dead before his corpse went into the flames. Sixty-three were counted, about thirty percent of those who came to pillage, plunder, and… feed. Without a chief and after such a cull, I am sure that Tonj will now be free of the pestilence, but I have assured the village headman that I shall do all I can to see a company of Sudanese soldiers garrisoned here against any possible future aggression.

As Jo stitches and bandages, I ponder on the Asante's crazed charge, even after they started to take serious casualties. I conclude that these Asante—at least of this part of the tribe—had never encountered white men or their weapons before, and they couldn't absorb what was happening to them. They hadn't the knowledge to make a connection between the pointed rifles—which we did not hurl at them as if they were spears—and the appalling consequence a puff of smoke from a barrel had on their bodies.

CHAPTER 43 | *December 1900 to January 1901*

TEN PAINFUL HOURS reacquainting himself with the vagaries of the humped beast he thought never to ride again—he'd even avoided lurching upright on a damned camel in India—gave Harry ample time to curse Cecil Rhodes and recall Mabior's puzzled expression back in Mengo when he'd told the Dinka sergeant about the iron road the survey team would travel on from Wau to Khartoum.

"On the other hand," he said to an exhausted Jolyon unaccustomed to the swaying ride, "we should count ourselves lucky, I suppose."

A sick grin told its own story. "You call this lucky? It's all right for you. You spent months riding blasted 'ships of the desert' with Wolseley. How much longer do you think?"

Harry pointed to a smudge on the horizon. A veil of smoke. Wau, at last.

The team had been preparing to move out with the four mules on the Saturday following the defeat of the Asante when, amid much noise and excitement, a large caravan of camels entered Tonj. Camels were not a regular sight in the savannah lands, neither were Baqqara traders, so the villagers were agog to see what could be bartered and sold. Harry was less impressed at first, but he overcame his distrust of Baqqara, the mounted cow-herder-warriors who played such a big part in the Mahdist armies he'd fought. But Omar Mohamed Salih's family were unusual in being merchants, for whom horses were of little use when it came to carrying weights for great distances at reasonable speeds across the desert.

Salih confirmed Harry's worst fear: "No iron rails nor iron caravans at Wau. It is projected," he said with an air of disdain. "The Sirdar's engineers make maps and drawings. South of El Obeid many men have smoothed the intended path through the desert. This is good for me. It makes fast travel, even a whole day shorter to the White Nile."

Harry's dejection showed. Salih gave him an unctuous smile, spotting an opportunity.

"You have four fine mules."

"Yes?" Harry sensed the deal.

I am now for Wau, thence to Babanusa and El Obeid, and then along the Nile to Omdurman. I can offer your party camels and shelter in return for the mules to trade at Wau, where they need them, and… perhaps a further consideration…?"

And so the deal was struck. Harry signed a paper to give Omar Mohamed Salih two hundred British Pounds to be drawn on the Bank of Egypt in Khartoum on arrival. It was the financial establishment Rhodes had specified for funds on completion and Harry thought the mogul well deserved to fork them out. To Mabior, Jok, Dut, Garang, and the rescued Dinka porter he gave the Lee-Enfield rifles they had so valiantly borne in battle, along with remaining ammunition and the few Birmingham trade rifles, the sale of which should set them up reasonably when they finally reached their tribal homes. There were many tearful farewells, and more tears expended for those Dinkas who didn't survive the expedition.

The caravan covered the seventy miles between Tonj and Wau in less than eleven hours of non-stop riding, but at about half the camels' possible speed in consideration of Jolyon, Travis, and Neo who had never ridden one before. Harry was as ungrateful. He'd forgotten how awkward the motion was. Salih promised much greater speed after Wau.

They entered the town on Monday December 3 and took accommodation at a caravanserai of dubious cleanliness, while their Baqqara host spent days in negotiations with various merchants. Harry, to his amazed delight, found the town boasted a telegraph office and after much shilly-shallying persuaded the operator to send a short telegram to Richard in (he hoped) Khartoum and a terse one to Cape Town for Rhodes, with a promise to organize all the survey reports as soon as he reached Khartoum. Otherwise, it was a time of impatience in the anti-climax after the recent events.

They all kicked their heels and grumbled. Travis announced his intention of going home to England. "It's time I found a wife and settled down. I'm no longer for being a veldt farmer."

Jolyon and Harry, after shaking Neo off to find his own amusement, went for long walks around the town and found quiet spots at the edge where, under the shade of acacias and a young baobab tree, they took their ease with each other.

"I thought I'd nearly lost you when that great brute reared up with his spears," Harry breathed in Jolyon's ear.

"And you? I saw that damned blade pierce you. From where I stood it looked like it had gone clean through your head. I almost died of fright for you."

"And still I'm here."

"And you are." Jolyon beamed and blinked tears from his soft lashes at the same time. "There hasn't been time to thank you."

"For what?"

"Everything, Harry. For saving me from being eaten, even from… well…"

He trailed off, and Harry knew Jo was thinking of poor Neo, who didn't escape the rape, the "seasoning." He shuddered at the memory and held Jo tighter.

After a while he said, "You have a far away look. What are you thinking?"

Jolyon smiled warmly. "I was thinking how nice, I'm finally going to meet your old school chum you go on about, Richard. I expect you'll be happy to see him, won't you?"

I ought to tell him all about Richard and me, the past… but this isn't the time.

"I shall be, and seeing Edward again."

"His brother."

Harry bit his lower lip and then fixed Jolyon with a steady gaze. "They aren't brothers at all. It's a complicated story for another day, but suffice it to say that Richard and Edward are lovers… like you and me."

"Blimey!" Jolyon's face was a picture. "So we're not alone?"

"No. We are not alone, Jo. More, young Gregory Hartley… he…"

"As well!"

"Mmm, he has a lover too, a rather handsome young Ja'alin, a black Arab boy." Jolyon frowned. "Did you know this when he was in London?"

Harry looked suitably guilty. "I did, but I couldn't exactly introduce him to you by saying, 'Jo this is Gregory, he has a male lover,' could I?"

Jolyon spent some minutes digesting these revelations with an expression fading in and out of almost-giggles and calmer smiles. Then he said, "You could have told me in private… Oh well, no, I suppose it wasn't your secret to divulge. I forgive you, I think. What are we going to do when we reach Khartoum?"

Harry sniffed and flicked an irritating sand fly from his eyelashes. "Apart from making love on a comfortable mattress, I don't know… yet. Why don't we wait until we do get there?"

"Sounds like a plan… the first part as well."

Jolyon's sexy grin went straight to Harry's loins.

For much of the way the horizon ran in a flat line barely visible between the expanse of land and copper sky. The track, compacted by the passage of camel, mule, and horse hooves, was of the same bright orange-red laterite that covered the savannah. Against it, the ochre-yellow grass tussocks barely showed, and only the scattering of dark green scrub bushes and mimosa made any contrast. A monotonous landscape and without any shade, unforgivingly hot in the day. For two hours with the sun directly overhead, the drivers halted their camels, bade them kneel, and everyone sheltered under robes raised up on the sticks used to tap their mounts' necks to give directions.

Even with these pauses, Omar Mohamed Salih assured Harry that speed was of the essence, that the caravan would cover the 775 miles to Omdurman in twelve to thirteen days. "It be less if we hasten on the smooth road the engineers have left. The camels can march seven or eight of your miles each hour and can go eighteen hours at a stretch, but we will ride for less so they carrying more burdens."

And at that rate they made it to Babanusa on Tuesday, El Obeid on Sunday 16, and the Nile on Friday 21 December. It was getting dark when the weary travelers entered the outskirts of Omdurman on Sunday 23 December. Harry immediately located his old army headquarters offices to find them hardly manned. "Everything has been relocated to barracks over the river," the subaltern on duty informed him. But he had a telephone and a directory, and Harry thought Richard Rainbow's voice on the other end of the line was as sweet as a glass of Cotswold Hills spring water.

Predictably, turning up in company with Travis, Neo, and Jolyon, Richard and Harry's reunion was more guarded than it might have been. After introductions and promises of tall tales to come, Travis insisted on going off to find accommodation for himself until such time as he organized his transfer to Cairo. Eventually, Edward suggested he give Jolyon and Neo a guided tour of the Condominium colony, and suddenly they were alone.

"How wonderful!" Richard began. "You arrive just in the nick of time to celebrate Christmas with us. In spite of the fevers you mentioned, you look fit as a fiddle, hardly aged a day since our first march into the Sudan deserts."

Harry snorted. "You look younger than ever, and I feel every one of my thirty-four years. The only saving grace is that Jolyon is catching me up!"

"Oh, I feel my age, but Ed says you're only as old as you feel, and he's a sprightly twenty-one... apparently. And it's good to have Gregory around as well, keeps one feeling young having young friends."

"Gregory and Zaki are here in Khartoum as well?"

"We're all here. In fact even Yussuf and his extended family are expected any minute from Suakin. The railway makes getting about so much faster than it used to be. So you being here completes the party splendidly, my dear Harry. And... with the handsome Jolyon Langrish-Smith you have spoken of..."

The sentence trailed off, an inferred assumption pretending to be a question.

Harry looked both abashed and delighted at the implication in Richard's tone. He simply nodded.

"Do 'heart' and 'home' come into the equation?"

"Yes, Richard. They do."

"Then this will be a Christmas to remember." He reached out, pulled Harry into his embrace. "I'm so happy for you. For both of you. I hope he knows how lucky he is?"

"I hope so too! By the way... I haven't ever told Jo about us. I will," he added hastily at the look of remonstrance on Richard's face. "Soon. Promise."

They broke apart. Richard leaned on a chair back. "For the festive season most of those of us in the employ of the Condominium Government of the Sudan haul ourselves to the leafy-green, airy spaces of Khartoum and put aside the drudgeries of the wastelands for a week or so. Gregory and Zaki arrived two days before you, and it is there we're all going for the festive celebrations. My Lord Langdale has a very spacious palace fit for an eastern potentate—at least, we tease him it is. Anyway, there are rooms aplenty and… a relaxed atmosphere for those of us whose loves are… less conventional.

"By the way, you have been out of news contact for some time, so I don't suppose you know that your friend Churchill got himself elected as the Conservative Member of Parliament for Oldham in October?"

"There was a general election?"

"There was, and everyone made a huge fuss of him, the fêted hero for escaping the Boers."

"What day were the results given?"

Richard frowned as he thought back. "Er, October 24, I'm sure."

Harry's eyes went wide in joyous amusement as he mentally checked his diary. "Hah! That was a Wednesday. Good old Winston, though a little less of the 'old,' I think!"

Puzzlement wrinkled Richard's brow over the relevance of the day, but he let it pass. "Mind you, he received a lot of help from Jo Chamberlain to get the seat, a sort of Cape Colony old school tie. And speaking of which, when Ed gets back and you launch by request into descriptions of your adventures in darkest Africa, we will demand the earlier chapters dealing with the war in South Africa."

As if he'd heard Richard speak his name, footsteps on the stone floor of the Rainbow residence announced the return of Edward with Jolyon and a bubbling Neo in tow. "Apart from the few days *chez* Greggers," Edward was saying, "you and Harry will absolutely reside with us until such time as you… Ah!" He smiled at Richard. "I was just telling Jolly here, that he and Harry are welcome to stay with us until they find a place of their own." He raised his eyebrows in query. "You are going to stay in Khartoum?"

Harry focused his eyes on Jolyon. "What do *you* say… *Jolly*?"

Hiding a knowing smirk, Jolyon turned the question back on Harry with a shrug. "I have only London to return to England for, nothing else. You're the one with family to think about."

"Is there gainful employment?"

Richard and Edward spoke at the same time. "The old man would love an officer of your experience on his staff." They laughed at their telepathic communication. "And I'm sure an experienced gunnery officer like Jolly, will be most welcome too," Edward added.

"By 'old man,' I presume you refer to the Sirdar. Then after the New Year I shall apply myself to Sir Reginald Wingate and sell my soul and Jo… Jolly's to the old man."

"I think that deserves a toast," Edward said, ringing a small bell on the sideboard. "Did you tell Harry that my old friend Yussuf is due later this evening from Suakin, and bringing his ever expanding family with him? You remember him, Harry. Met him at Rissington."

Harry agreed he had. And then Edward and Richard busied themselves ordering cocktails from the serving boy who entered at the summons.

"So… *Jolly*?" Harry spoke quietly with an amused grin.

"I don't mind, actually, Harry. I don't know why but when Edward says it, it sounds, well… sexy."

The teasing smile did its execution as sublimely as an Asante spear. Harry clutched his heart in both hands. And then he grabbed the back of Jolyon's head, pulled him in hard, and kissed his mouth fiercely. Behind, them Neo grinned broadly while Richard and Edward clapped enthusiastically.

The Christmas festivities passed in a haze of good fellowship and—after the long privations of the survey—in unbridled luxury at Gregory and Zaki's palatial home set in its broad, landscaped gardens. On Christmas Eve they joined the Sirdar's staff officers and embassy guests for a celebratory dinner in honor of the Queen, who was, according to her custom, spending Christmas at Osborne House on the Isle of Wight.

"I understand Her Majesty is suffering the effects of her great age," Sir Francis Reginald Wingate informed Harry after offering him a post on his staff as a district commissioner (*We'll sort out which in the New Year, when you have decided to stay out here*). "It's the rheumatism in her legs makes her near-lame, and she has difficulty signing state papers for the cataracts in her eyes. Ah…" He looked beyond Harry's shoulder. "You must excuse me, Major Vane, I'd far more enjoy hearing about your exploits in the dark heart, but I fear the French ambassador has a greater claim on my time. Come see me… oh, sometime toward the end of January, Give yourself a chance to become acclimatized."

"Harry, it is good to see you again."

He'd had little chance for a private conversation with Gregory since he and

Jolyon had been speedily settled into a suite of rooms across a wide hallway from Richard and Edward, who vacated their own pleasant bungalow for the comforts of the Langdale mansion for the holiday. After a massive and very traditional Christmas luncheon, the party went to sprawl in the garden on divans set out under shade trees and Gregory came to settle next to Harry.

"I've been concerned for you ever since the last communication from Mengo. I understand you encountered several adventures on route, but nevertheless, here you are, safe and sound. And Jolyon too." He narrowed his eyes in a conspiratorial squint. "And happy?"

"I am, as I can see you are with Zaki."

Life in the Sudan appeared to be dealing kindly with Gregory Hartley, Lord Langdale and absentee member of the House of Lords.

"On that score, your brother Evan is a godsend in looking after my interests in the Upper House. Which is to say really that he doesn't bother me with it." Gregory gave one of his cheerful laughs that had once captivated and almost unseated Harry.

"Major Vane," Zaki said as he approached with new glasses of well-chilled champagne for Harry and Gregory (Jolyon was chatting with Edward).

"Harry, please."

Zaki smiled as he handed over the glasses. "Gregory has spoken of you to me, and how kind you were to him while he languished in your country."

Harry almost choked on his first sip. "I wouldn't call it 'languishing' exactly."

Zaki grinned to show he was teasing. "I must go and make sure your young Neo is properly introduced to Yussuf." To Harry's surprise, Zaki suddenly leaned down and hugged him around the neck and then swept off. Harry grinned at Gregory and at the antics where, like an excited puppy in the midst of his litter, Neo jumped into the group swelling around Zaki and Yussuf.

When they had a moment apart from the party, Harry satisfied Jolyon's natural curiosity about Yussuf. He told him of the black Sudanese man's dalliance with Edward Rainbow in the deep desert of Kordofan, held as slaves by Sheik el Bakhat.

"I think if I had learned of that a year or so ago, I would have shuddered at the thought of white men consorting with black." Jolyon scowled at his prejudice, and then cracked a smile. "But I think recent events have altered me in many ways, so long as the color conjunction is by consent of both parties."

Harry laughed. "I don't think Edward and Yussuf's relationship was one of Asante and white captive, Jo! Hmm, have you seen Neo?"

They both looked over to where Neo, Harry noted with amusement, was playing a great deal of attention to Yussuf's eldest daughter, a comely girl of about fourteen. She expressed her father's bubbly humor and enjoyed her mother's beautiful looks. For her part, in the broken English that was their *lingua franca*, she was evidently thrilled at Neo's lurid descriptions of their adventures.

"I think I'd better go and act the chaperone." Jolyon winked and walked off to leave Harry to his thoughts.

He sighed inwardly with a satisfaction he realized he hadn't felt in a very long time. This was not the wellbeing arising from a job well done, a mountain climbed, an enemy defeated, an Empire saved; it stemmed from a sensation of coming home which he attributed to being among friends of like minds, even if of widespread ethnic and social backgrounds. It was a satisfaction of being close to Richard and yet comfortable with the clasp of friendship, held in the radiance of his love for Jolyon. And young Neo's evident infatuation with Yussuf's daughter only added to the glow. He looked across the crowded garden to where an animated Richard held court, his hand casually resting lightly on Edward's broad shoulder. Memories flooded Harry's vision: of long days at Benthenham College; of a hayloft at Hadlicote Hall; of the Camel Corps and their dreadful march across the Bayuda Desert, battling Dervishes all the way; of the discovery that Edward had been captured by Mahdist fanatics, that beloved Richard had found his brother only to lose him again; of Richard frantically learning Arabic and his determination to search the sandy wastes for his "brother," his lover.

There was a quiet step and a presence at his shoulder. He didn't need to look to see who it might be. He felt Jolyon's fingers secretly find his own and gently entangle them. Harry turned his head, a happy smile on his lips.

At a steady two and a half miles an hour the Nile flowed past the boardwalk. Harry and Jolyon sat with bared feet swinging idly above a crocodile's reach from the water. Not that many of the basking reptiles came close to the busy shores between Khartoum and Omdurman. It was a grand view there on the sharp projecting tip at the northwest of Khartoum. The two Niles mingled their waters and curved around the half-moon of Tuti Island, ironically a pleasing blue on the left for the White Nile and a sludgy brown on the right for the Blue Nile. Away to the north the Mahdi's Tomb raised the ragged edges of its war-damaged cracked boiled egg of a dome above the stew of new buildings and the bulk of the Khalifa's palace.

"Last time I was here everything over there was a shambles. The Lyddite shells fired into the town from the gunboats did terrible damage."

"They rebuild quickly... oh, look!" Jolyon pointed back over the low hump of Tuti Island to where a moving trail of white smoke, partly hidden between the serpentine curves of the Blue Nile Bridge, marked the passage of a train chugging across the river on its way north to Atbara. "Do you think that's Travis's train?"

"Might be. I never bothered to check the timetable, but I'll bet there's a lot to be done to get the schedules working properly. I felt guilty leaving him at the station, but it wouldn't have been practical for us to hang around for days saying goodbye."

"At least Rhodes had the good grace to apologize for sending us on a wild goose chase to find rails that have yet to exist."

Harry smiled magnanimously. "We gave him what he needed."

"We did."

"Now it's up to him and his shareholders to make the Cape to Cairo railway a reality."

For some minutes neither spoke, content to press shoulders and bump feet.

"Shall I accept Wingate's offer of work, and shall we remain here in the Sudan?"

There was little hesitation. "Oh yes, Harry. Let's do. Isn't it funny? If you'd asked me that a year ago I would have shuddered. London's my home, my hearth, my beating heart, I thought. I couldn't possibly live anywhere else—"

"With all the ordure, animal and human, clogging the gutters and walkways and streets, with fogs so clotted a man might expire after inhaling a few lungfuls of the pestilential stuff while sidestepping the desiccated bodies of unwanted infants or blind-drunken madams of the night sprawled under foot?"

"With all that, yes. It's not the point. I'm not Gregory. I can understand he was out of his depth in London, but he was born to this country, this life. I was not. And yet, for all its alienness , it has one huge advantage—amid no doubt many minor ones—and that is one I've now seen. Richard and Edward, Gregory and Zaki—they feel free to be as they wish to be, and no man raises a word against them with accusations of… well, you know…"

"Unnatural practices," Harry breathed the words, and then louder, "No native, anyway. Not surprisingly, expatriates tend to be more censorious, though I allow there is something about the freedom of the warmth and the wide-open spaces that promotes a freer attitude to life, whatever your credo. It's the freedom given by not being shut up all the while in cluttered rooms warmed by coal fires so the front scorches while the back freezes. I've always held that miserable English parlor fires are responsible for the pinched-in, narrow-minded Englishman. And perhaps a life lived more on the edge out here means people are not as oppressed by social convention." He reached out and ruffled Jolyon's clipped hair. "So London has lost its appeal?"

"There was a time when I thought the city was my entire world. It gave me everything I needed. You see, I did my best as a military cadet at Eton, but the smart uniform didn't fool me into wanting a career in the Army. Truth is, it was just dressing up… I was so young, Harry. I mean we all were, but in here…" He tapped the side of his head, "I was a child. And while I played my part at cricket on Mespots, the rougher field sports were not my forte. I wanted something more refined, the finer things in life, even as I knew how much my father disapproved of what he called the artifartists."

He fell silent, and much as Harry didn't want to interrupt the flow of words he saw Jolyon formulating, he had to ask, "Mespots?"

"Oh, one of the school's playing fields. Because it was stuck between two streams it was named Mesopotamia. We boys shortened it to Mespots." He gave Harry a wan smile—a tucked in dimple—but his narrowed eyes suggested the inner tension that exhibited itself in the increased swaying of his legs. "Look, with the perspective of these past years I see what I felt then in a different light. I'm ashamed now of how I reacted when the cholera took my father and mother." He fixed his gaze on Harry, as if anticipating criticism. "Of course their deaths, particularly the loss of my mother, was a terrible shock, but at the same time I was relieved because with Father gone I knew I would no longer be bound to the Army for the rest of my life."

"And yet here you are… or have been."

Jolyon's smile turned rueful. "That's because of you. I don't know why you believed in me. God knows, but I gave you no cause."

So much water under the bridge—wasn't that what Richard said as he drove me to the station at Bourton all those years ago? He peered down into the very stuff of life swirling its way beneath his toes to irrigate the valleys of distant Egypt. "It was my responsibility. At least that's how I felt at first, but then…" The deep breath Harry took shuddered a little as he exhaled. "You became very dear to me and then more. I loved you." He paused for a moment. "You healed me."

Jolyon raised his eyebrows in surprise. "*I* healed *you*?"

"Yes."

"You never said anything quite like that before." He twisted around to stare back over the river at the train's tell-tale smoke trail, now fading above the roofs of North Khartoum's new buildings. "My God, but I've been blind! It was Richard," Jolyon whispered, realization setting in. His head snapped around. "It *was* Richard, wasn't it, who hurt you so badly?"

After a moment, Harry sighed again. "It wasn't his fault. I should never have come between him and Edward, but… at first I didn't know how they felt for each other, and then suddenly Edward wasn't there. He ran off and Richard turned to me in his misery. I thought his sadness was natural in one brother for the brother he'd just lost, perhaps forever. I didn't know… their feelings. How could I have done? They were supposed to be twin brothers, and therefore how could they…?"

"Be lovers?"

"Mmm."

"But they're pretend brothers and—"

"Lovers, then and now."

It was Jolyon's turn to consider what Harry had said, and left unsaid. "So I was, what? A consolation?"

The word stabbed a dagger point into Harry's heart. That Jo should harbor that possibility after the past four or more years they had shared appalled him. He covered his alarm by turning to wrap both arms around Jolyon's slight frame in a vicious hug, as much intended to hurt as reassure. "No! Never." He lifted his hands to grasp Jolyon's head on either side behind the ears and buried his fingers in the soft hair. For a while both were lost for words, and then, muffled by his lips pressed against the flesh of Jolyon's neck, Harry murmured, "When I saw you at the Café Royal I'd already been through the period of consoling my wounded heart."

He straightened and leaned against Jolyon's shoulder. Under the Nilotic sun's disk, the embodiment of Ra, of life's daily journey, Harry poured out the story of William Maplethorpe and of Arshan, of the guilt he suffered in abandoning Arshan, even though he always knew deep down that fulfilment didn't lie in the Persian boy's embrace.

"I had passed beyond any ricochet from the loss of Richard by the time you and I met again in London. It's hard to explain how I felt when I saw you lounging there beside that slug Bosie. I couldn't divorce the image of Jolyon Langrish-Smith, Eton cadet, so smart in his uniform, so proud, so upright, bright as the polished brass buttons on his tunic, cheerful, elegant… oh…"

"I was a child." Jolyon whispered the repetition.

"Yes, and yet that's what I still saw that day at the Café Royal, the handsome youth superimposed over the child and a sneery veneer—which I knew, knew, knew wasn't natural—doubly superimposed over the youth. The charming twelve-year-old was still there, somewhere hidden… no, suppressed, pushed under by the urge to be a part of Wilde's indolent, louche, and dissolute set."

A loud, brash horn underlined the venom of Harry's final words. The fussy steamer sounded again. It passed by where they sat on the point, towing a string of flat barges laden with building materials. They looked like a line of ugly ducklings paddling to keep up with mother duck. Harry fell silent. He could feel nervous shivers running up and down Jolyon beside him.

"Bosie kept on at me, if I wanted to be the sort of fellow Oscar liked and would promote, I had to do *certain* things (the hidden undercurrent was always there). Bosie… he wanted to turn me into a rent-boy and learn from the boy-whores in that place in Kings Cross he sometimes frequented with Oscar; like poor Norris." He suddenly directed a fierce gaze at Harry. "I don't really blame him, Oscar I mean. You see it was his nature and he wasn't really a cruel person. Vain, yes, but nasty wasn't a word in his vocabulary. I truly believe Oscar loved one or two of those wretched messenger boys, in his way. But Bosie *was* cruel. He liked to use working-class lads for sex. Laborers, grooms, messenger boys, and layabouts he could boss about and overawe with his noble title, sneery-haughty speech, and swaggering manner. Then he cast them aside, always chasing after new sensations, and he made Oscar into something he wasn't."

"Did he use you?"

"Oscar? No— yes. In a way. He once asked me to lie back so he could undress me, arouse me, and use his mouth on my..." Jolyon waved a pointed finger over his crotch. "But he never expected anything in return. The one time Bosie tried to make me do it to him I refused and ran off."

The steamer's horn sounded again, more distantly as it passed beyond the bulk of Tuti Island.

"It was all very quick, you know—that time. I'd left Eton, lost my parents, was cast adrift by the delays of probate. I must have been ripe for seduction by Oscar's brilliant aura and the glittering, aesthetic society his intellectual gravity attracted into orbit around him."

"But the true aim of the seduction was physical, not intellectual."

"Oh, I was soon aware of murmurings. There was innuendo. And soon the suggestion of sexual liberation moved from the philosophical to the licentious and to practical experiment. And the slyest tongue of all belonged to Lord Alfred Douglas. But then... well, it was all very quick. Bosie vanished for a week and I had Oscar all to myself. He took me to see the opening of the play. You know, because you were there too—"

"You cut me dead."

"I did, of course I did, representative of the philistines. The Prince of Wales was there too. It was his box. I was excited! The future King and Emperor speaking to me like an equal, and Oscar was so charming and kind. And then Bosie returned, determined to drag me into the sex acts he liked to perform with the lowlives he set Oscar up with. But I resisted him. I wasn't, after all, a poor telegraph messenger boy. That night Norris saw me... oh... my body did yearn for adventure, but my heart revolted at what I was supposed to do. I'd allowed myself be fooled, dazzled by surface things. I'd seen only the beauty of Oscar's Salome, not the slime at its core. I was naïve. Norris may have seen me dragged in, he never saw me run out minutes later. Then came the trials."

Jolyon's voice quieted with the last sentence, and he sat thoughtfully, staring down at the sluggish water sighing against the pilings on its way to Egypt, toward Cairo and Alexandria 1,857 miles away by river traffic.

"Everything was suddenly too much. I can see it now; then I could not. The death of my parents, the stultifying life with my guardian aunt from which I was desperate to escape, the scintillating talk, the excitement of being among all those artists, the crucible of their creation, it swept me away and took me out of the trajectory to which by nature I suppose I should have adhered—a dull Army cadet, to follow in my father's boots." He gave Harry a sly wink. "That's what I saw when you spotted me in the Café Royal: my dull future assured by my dull godfather. Saint Harry— no, Saint Haldane— he is going to rescue me from the hard-fought-for joys of creative freedom. I called you a philistine, I remember, because where I saw the glories of brilliant minds I knew you saw Sodom and Gomorrah."

"I saw debauchery and depravity clothed in a too easily assumed brilliance."

"I'm not even sure I understood what Sodom represented! The court trials shattered my dreams. They painted everything I desperately wanted to be a part of in the colors of lechery and cheap corruption. My party balloon burst."

"And I led you into your dull military future."

It was Jolyon's turn to impulsively encircle Harry's waist and fling his head on his shoulder. "No! Don't sound sad, Harry. Oh, I suppose at first, once I started to take notice of my surroundings again, I thought I was allowing myself to drift like one of those fairground automatons into your influence. But that changed. In fact I saw the light on the road to Damascus."

"I wasn't aware you'd ever been in Syria."

Jolyon snorted a stifled laugh at the sardonic tone. "No, silly. Of course I haven't. Do you remember the day Mr. Alma-Tadema came to call for me and you had a look like thunder on your brow at his intrusion into your carefully constructed Jo-Jo convalescent home?"

"I, thunder? Yes, I do remember. I wondered what such a famous artist could want with you."

"Nothing like that, I can assure you. No, I think he saw something similar to what you did and wanted to whisk me away from what he perceived as a decadent influence. I met him once or twice long before you turned up in London. He talked to me, a mere boy, I talked back and he was amusing, jolly in fact. He made me laugh, which in turn made him chortle. When he called at the Albany that day it was because he wanted to show me one of his paintings. Lord Leighton had purchased it, and with others it hung in the domed Silk Room at Leighton House. What an extraordinary place! And that's where I met my Damascus, in the Arab Room. The Damascene tiles are glorious. I don't know why, but they acted like a physick on me. It was as though the color, pattern, and light poured into me as I looked up, dizzied by the angle I had to hold my head to view them.

"When I came out onto Holland Park I walked in a daze along Kensington High Street, hardly paying attention to Mr. Alma-Tadema. I felt cleansed, and…" With an odd shyness, Jolyon sought Harry's hand and squeezed it. "And for some unfathomable reason I saw you in a new light—someone who truly cared for me. From that moment I began to think that I wanted to please you, and in so doing it would please me too."

He gave Harry's cheek a lightly caressing kiss.

"And here we are."

"Yes, Jo. Here we are."

Abruptly, Harry threw his head back and broke out into loud laughter. In the next second he was on his feet. He reached down, grabbed Jolyon's hands and dragged him up onto the pathway. Jolyon's eyes went wide in expectation as Harry's arms slid under his armpits, grasped his back, and swung him in a tight circle so rapidly that his bare feet rose up from the centripetal force. Face to face they spun around, faster and faster until the rivers, Omdurman, and Khartoum became a giddying blur cocooning Harry and Jolyon in mutual passion.

The Belgian Ambassador, taking his routine late afternoon constitutional with his poodle in the riverside parkland, glanced across from his path at the sounds of unaccustomed merriment. There, at the end of the point, silhouetted against the lowering sun, the astonishing sight of two grown men whirling like Dervishes met his squinting eyes. And they were laughing joyously, as if there could never be another care in the world.

Saturday January 26, 1901

We are a happy party in spite of camel-sore bottoms and the sad news from England. It arrived on the telegraph late on Tuesday, two days before we started out for Gedaref. Our Queen, the Empress of India, Victoria Regina, is dead. Long live King Edward VII. The Sirdar informed the colony in all due solemnity, for she has reigned over the growth of the greatest Empire the world has ever known. And yet, what empire ever lasted? Even the Roman, so apparently enduring, began its long descent into ignominy almost the moment Augustus relinquished his rule to death. Victoria made it into the new century, and now we enter the Edwardian era of great optimism and hope, of a world where the philosopher-seers tell us scientific, medical, and technological advances will bring us to the utopia they predict. Sadly, I am minded that humankind, like the veldt leopard, does not change spots over much.

And so in South Africa the conflict we thought finished when Field Marshal Bobs captured Pretoria, still drags on, turned now to the kind of fight the Boers most relish: guerrilla warfare, and it's left to General Kitchener to bring them to heel. Well, he's nothing if not dogged.

"Would you care to accompany me to Gedaref?" Gregory asked us a week ago. "At this time of year I go to lay flowers on my father's grave and make sure the little church there is being looked after. In a day or so we'll have another special guest to go with us. Abu el-Khatim is son of the lord of El Obeid. He honors the memory of my father for saving his life when a wound in Abu's left arm became gangrenous. He had to amputate it, but Abu lived. He called my father Mudil, the name he took when he was trapped in El Obeid."

"Your father was a doctor?"

Gregory laughed, and squeezed Jolyon's shoulder. "No, just a translator like me, but he imitated a surgeon well enough, it seems."

So we prepared for the journey. "It is not as Gregory and I found it in September '98," Zaki told Jolyon. "In so short time there is the telegraph along the Blue Nile and lines to Gedaref, Kassala, to the Red Sea, up to Suakin. Now a military road joins town and village, so we may ride in comfort and pass nights at government rest houses. All in two years."

"This is very good news indeed," Jolyon retorted. "I think I've had enough of sleeping on hard ground."

Wearing his hat as the Sudan's Governor-General, Sirdar Wingate gave his bleassing to this Gedaref trip. He suggested (that is he ordered) me to continue to Kassala. "Take the time to improve your knowledge of the region," he said, indicating that I might well administer the district soon, a half-military, half-civilian role, with a score of troops and a small battery of field guns that Jolyon is pleased to have at his potential future command.

What has made it all the more enjoyable is that we are a large party: Gregory and Zaki; Richard and Edward; myself and Jolyon; but also Yussuf and his family in easy companionship with the Baqqara Abu. Neo rides with them, learning Arabic from Yussuf's eldest daughter Abina. I suspect he will be happy finally to part from Jo-Jo Angrish and me and continue with Yussuf to Suakin. I hope when the day comes, Jo and I will be invited to the nuptial ceremonies.

Richard is most solicitous of me… as he has always been. I am warmed by his presence, the very fact of him, and that we bear each other an affection beyond passing, yet one that warms for its comradeship now and not the burning passion that once beset me. We had not long parted company with the Blue Nile and begun the two hundred and fifty-mile ride across country to Gedaref, which is expected to take us four days of not over-exerted riding, when Richard maneuvered his camel close beside mine. Jolyon was several yards ahead deep in conversation with Zaki, with whom he gets on as well as he does with Neo.

"I've thought about Jolyon a lot since you arrived, and of the hints you have let slip over time," Richard began. "Isn't life strange? In a good way, as often as not. Do you recall the Christmas after Edward disappeared when you invited me to spend it with you at Hadlicote?"

I laughed easily at the memory. How would I ever forget the haystack days when Richard and I became lovers? And I know from his wry expression that he knew I would never forget it.

"We were standing in that damned huge drawing room of your parents," he went on. "It was crowded and good cheer ruled, and I asked you, 'Who is the strikingly good looking man of military bearing?' You looked across the room and said, 'Colonel Langrish-Smith, a friend of my father. His boy Jolyon is my godson.' You were a bit sniffy about it, Harry. 'The child is attractive enough as tadpoles go when they are of the age of… oh, what is he now? Seven,' you said. 'I have only seen him squalling at his christening and here at Christmas last year. They obviously left the brat behind in London this year.' And so you dismissed your future. But then, who could possibly have known the future? As I said, isn't life strange?"

Gazing ahead, contemplating Richard's words I wondered whether I should feel jealous to see the three young men—Zaki like a dark filling in the white sandwich of Gregory and Jolyon on either side—holding each other like a loving triumvirate and thinking nothing of it, for the sight is common among friends in Egypt and the Sudan. But I didn't. I felt blessed in my friends and in the love of my life, and that he is now among friends who care about him too.

We rode on in companionable silence for half a mile and then I sensed

Richard's inscrutable gaze taking me in. "What?" I said with a smile pushing at my lips.

"I see the way you look at him, and he at you, and I know the feeling that emanates from such quiet contemplation. You have at last found a home for your heart, Harry. You once told me that I had completed my trek while you were yet still on yours. Now I'm sure that aspect of your life is complete and it is the rock on which to build the foundation for the rest of your lives." Richard nodded his head adamantly. "Out here, my dearest Haldane—don't pout, I'm entitled—you and Jolyon will flower."

When Jo dropped back to ride on my other flank, Richard smiled and pulled ahead to leave us alone. I saw us all—Richard, Edward, Gregory, Zaki, Jo and I, riding through the gathering dusk into the east. The sun's red light cast our shadows as long rippling shapes far ahead of us across the uneven sand as we rode into our new life—our new adventure.

There is a beautiful herald of spring in Afghanistan, when the purple crown of the istalif iris pushes up through the snow—a symbol of eternal hope. Jolyon reaches out his hand and entwines his fingers with mine. Forever, I turn my head to gaze into his beautiful eyes, a happy smile on my lips.

My iris.

Author's note

The Yellow Book, published in London between 1894–1897, was a cultural journal associated with the Aesthetic and Decadence Movements. Aubrey Beardsely was its first art editor. The yellow cover had associations with illicit French literature (pornographic books in Paris were wrapped in yellow paper to indicate their sexually lascivious content). The publication lent its name to the "Yellow Nineties" and the "Yellow Aesthetic." Wydham's Theatre actually opened on November 18, 1899, but it served this story's purposes to bring that event forward by almost a year. The figure given for construction of the Cape to Cairo railway in 1900 of £10 million is based on the exchange rate at the time of 5 US$ to the British pound. Luxor was generally referred to as Thebes in the late 19th century, but it seemed sensible to use its modern appellation, which actually derives from the Arabic *al-quṣūr*, which in turn was borrowed from the Latin *castrum*, a fortified camp, which was how the Romans treated the ancient Pharaonic temple precinct. Harry's daydream at the start of Chapter 39 is a rewritten borrowing from British illustrator, writer, and African explorer Herbert Ward's description of the brave start to Henry Morton Stanley's Emin Pasha Relief Expedition of 1886–1889. While many of the characters in the book are fictitious, there are several who are based on their real historical presence in the locations mentioned at those times. I may sometimes have treated them in a cavalier fashion, but not, I hope, completely against their natures. In alphabetical order:

Allan Aynesworth
George Alexander
Lawrence Alma-Tadema
Col. Robert Stephenson Smyth
   Baden-Powell
Aubrey Vincent Beardsely
Sir Henry Maximilian "Max" Beerbohm
Gen. Sir Bindon Blood
General Sir Redvers Henry Buller
Joseph Chamberlain
Winston Leonard Spencer-Churchill
Aleister (Edward Alexander) Crowley
Lord Alfred "Bosie" Douglas
Col. Algernon Durand
Sir Henry Mortimer Durand
Arthur Conan Doyle

Gen. John French
Mahatma Gandhi
Joseph Rudyard Kipling
Gen. Horatio Herbert Kitchener
Col. William Lockhart
Gen. Sir Charles Metcalfe MacGregor
John Walter Edward Doulas-
   Scott-Montagu
Alexander Edward Murray, 8th Earl
   of Dunmore (Viscount Fincastle)
Field Marshal Frederick
   Sleigh "Bobs" Roberts
Major George Scott Robertson
Cecil John Rhodes
Oscar Fingal O'Flahertie Wills Wilde
Francis Edward Younghusband

GLOSSARY

amir: commander (*also* emir)

bacha bazi: dancing boys, *lit.* "playing with children"

beg: chief or ruler

boosa: hay or fodder

brevet: in the military context, it means a commissioned officer has been granted a higher rank title as a reward for gallantry or meritorious conduct, but without receiving the authority that goes with the rank. Officers were often brevetted by their commanding officers in the field to replace wounded or killed officers of the same rank when there was no time to seek approval from the War Office in London.

chota peg: a *peg* is an old Anglo-Saxon measure of alcohol, *chota* is Hindu for "small"; an Anglo-Indian afternoon short of usually whisky (1oz or 30ml) taken with soda water.

cornet lowest officer rank in the British army, equivalent to a second lieutenant (subaltern), abolished in 1871, except in the Blues and Royals and Queen's Royal Hussars, where it is still used.

daguerreotypist: Alfred Winner's description of photographers. In 1839 Frenchman Louis Daguerre introduced the first photographic process, called after him the daguerreotype. By the mid-1860s, less expensive processes began to replace it, but the term daguerreotypist persisted for some time after.

dharamasala: resthouse or waystation for pilgrims in India.

dhoolie: lightweight covered litter or palanquin, also *palkee*

Eton Fives: a game similar to squash, but for four players in doubles, in which a small hard ball is kept in play using gloved hands in a three-sided, double-level court. Fives never moved beyond the precincts of British public schools. Other variants are Rugby and Wessex Fives.

donga: Afrikaans for ditch or dry watercourse, see also *khor* and *nullah*

drift: a river crossing, or ford in South Africa; a place where the river runs slowly enough (drifts) and is shallow enough for men and horses to cross from one bank to the other.

fatwa: legal ruling

felucca: A small, single lateen-sail Nile boat, with only the prow covered, capable of carrying up to usually twelve people. Generally used for ferrying passengers across the river and for transporting lightweight goods, such as food supplies.

firangi: foreigner

ghazal: Urdu or Persian love lyric

hammam: Turkish-style steam bath house

hircarrah: *lit.* "all-doer," runner, messenger, journalist, political, spy, usually spelled *harkara* today.

haveli: courtyard house, traditional mansion

havildar: non-commissioned native sepoy rank equivalent to sergeant in the British Army of India.

Impi: a regiment of Zulu warriors who were armed with a throwing spear, short stabbing spear (*assegai*), and knobkerrie (*iwisa*) club.

jemadar: the lowest rank of native sepoy junior commissioned officer in the British Army of India.

jezail: a matchlock musket used by the tribesmen of Afghanistan and the Hindu Kush region, heavy, slow to load, and clumsy in use, but very accurate thanks to its extremely long barrel. Usually heavily decorated.

jezailchi: Afghan infantryman armed with a jezail

jirga: a council of Pashtun elders convened to settle disputes

juwan: a young man, youth

kafila: a caravan

kaffer: the derogatory word used by Boers (Dutch Afrikaaners) to describe black Africans.

kafir: a catch-all Arabic word (*kāfir*) for those not of the Islamic faith, which translates as "non-believer" or "one who conceals the truth." It means precisely the same as **infidel**, which is a Christian word derived from the Latin *infidelis*, meaning "not faithful."

kahwa: the Turkish spelling of **qahwah**, Arabic for coffee (and by extension a coffee house). *Qahwah* originally meant "wine," so coffee became the wine of the Muslims, to whom real wine was forbidden. Not to be confused with some definitions which state that *kahwa* is a form of Kashmiri green tea.

khan: Pashtun tribal chief

khedive: Egyptian ruler, viceroy of the Ottoman sultan in the 19th century.

khor: a dry watercourse in the Sudan, see also *nullah* and *donga*

khutba: a sermon delivered at Friday prayers

kopje: Afrikaans, a small hill, generally in a flat area

Krupp gun: a heavy breech-loading piece of field artillery manufactured by the German steel-making Krupp family. The guns came in a variety of types and caliber, from a 6cm (2.4 ins) mountain gun to the massive 24cm (9.5 ins) naval gun, and with ranges from 2,500 meters (2,700 yards) to 6,000 (6,500 yards). They were considered to be the finest weapons of their time.

kumbukht: rascal, useless person, idiot, unlucky person

lakh: a hundred thousand (used with rupees)

Lee-Enfield: bolt-action, magazine-fed, repeating rifle , main firearm used by the military forces of the British Empire and Commonwealth during the first half of the 20th century. It was the British Army's standard rifle from its official adoption in 1895 until 1957. It replaced the Lee-Metford rifle.

Liebig: a concentrated meat extract produced from carcasses and named after its developer, the German chemist Justus von Liebig. Its value lay in its near-imperishability and that it quickly made a nourishing broth when small amounts were added to hot water. In 1899, the product was trademarked as Oxo.

lyddite: an explosive material made from the chemical compound picric acid, which was the first high explosive considered able to withstand the shock of being fired in conventional artillery without blowing up on firing. The French first started manufacturing the compound with guncotton under the name *melinite*. In 1888, Britain began manufacture at Lydd, Kent, hence its name. Its first British use was at the Battle of Omdurman.

maidan: open space used for army drill or parades

malang: mendicant fakir or dervish

malik: petty chief, village headman

Martini-Henry: a lever-actuated breech-loading single-shot rifle which replaced the Snider-Enfield when it entered service in 1871. The rifle, and its cavalry carbine versions, had a thirty-year service period, and in the right hands could fire 12 rounds per minute compared to—at the best in the hands of untrained natives—one ball per minute from old muzzle-loaded musket. The Martini-Henry was gradually replaced by the **Lee-Enfield** bolt-action, magazine-fed rifle in 1895.

Maxim-Nordenfelt: (later Vickers) gun, nicknamed the Pom-Pom gun, was designed in the 1860s as an enlarged version of the Maxim machine gun. It made a light, wheeled field artillery piece firing a nominally one-pounder explosive shell. It became an anti-aircraft gun in World War I.

munshi: Indian private secretary

namak haram: *lit*. "bad to your salt" – an ungrateful person or disloyal

narghile: *see* "shisha"

nullah: a ditch or dry watercourse in India, see also *khor* and *donga*

Pashtu: language of the Pashtun people

pishkhidmat: personal servant of a sardar or king

pom-pom gun: *see* "Maxim-Nordenfelt"

pundit: "one who knows," native agent, usually employed in intelligence-gathering, surveying and mapping

pustin: Afghan sheepskin coat

qala: typical Afghan fortified village on the plains and low hills usually surrounded by nine-to- twelve-foot-high (3–4 meters) mud walls. Each dwelling is interconnected with the others to form what appears as a single structure and the walls are an integral part of the structure itself.

rahdari: protection money, a toll levied by Afghan mountain tribes to keep roads safe

sangar: shallow trench and low mud wall to protect against jezail fire, or an emergency fortification constructed with bushes, similar to the Egyptian *zareba*

sardar: chief, commander, or nobleman

sepoy: Indian infantryman

shir maheh: Afghan freshwater fish similar to trout

shisha, sheesha: also sometimes called a hubble-bubble, is a water pipe in Arabic-speaking countries in which the tobacco smoke is drawn through a vessel of water before being inhaled by the smoker. **Narghile(es)** the same as used in the Indian subcontinent.

sowar: Indian cavalryman

subaltern: term for British junior commissioned officer under the rank of captain, being the various grades of lieutenant,

Sirdar: the rank assigned to the commander-in-chief of British armed forces in the Anglo-Egyptian army in the late 19th and early 20th centuries. There were five sirdars, three appear in the novel: Sir Evelyn Wood (1883–85);

Lord Francis Grenfell (1885–92); **Herbert Kitchener** (1892–99); **Reginald Wingate** (1899–1916); Sir Charles Watson Spinks (1916–37)

syce: Indian groom, stable hand

talib: religious Muslim student or proselytizer

takht: throne

telegram, telegraph: modes of communication which have been made extinct first by the telephone, fax, then by email and cell phones. The sender wrote out a message in almost the form used today for texting. This was sent from a telegraph office, or later the post office, in a similar way to the old fax machines.

ward-i-nil: *lit*. Nile Flower, which grows abundantly in Equatoria and along the length of the Nile. The fibrous roots, stems, and the fleshy leaves make large rafts which often break free. Before the dams were constructed, whole islands would drift from Upper Egypt downstream and even out to sea.

zareba: (also **zeriba**, **zareeba**, or **zeribah**), an African term for a temporary military enclosure, the sides constructed of thorny brush wood, strengthened with wire, behind which a force may camp comparatively safe from sudden surprise. The term came into prominent use during the Anglo-Egyptian campaign of 1884. The protection is also used against wild animals.

zenana: harem, women's quarters

Books 1 and 2 of THE EMPIRE TRILOGY
A Life Apart was M/M Romance Book of the Month, March 2013

"What a magnificent treasure Kean has created. The heroic lovers are certainly two of most unique and memorable characters and this is the most remarkable book I have read." Goodreads

"Gregory's Story is a wonderful story full of emotion, bravery, love, hardship and faithfulness. Loved having the Rainbow "brothers" continue and play such a vital role. Loved the other gay fellows that fleshed out the book." Goodreads

Set against the turmoil of religious uprising in Egypt and the Sudan toward the end of the 19th century, the books follow the fortunes of "brothers" Richard and Edward Rainbow from their teenage years to maturity, when their experience comes to the aid of orphaned Gregory Hilliard. In both novels, Harry Smythe-Vane features, but in the third of the trilogy, *Harry's Great Trek*, he gets to tell his own adventurous story. Taken together, the three books add up to a tumultuous tale of the heyday of the British Empire, the greatest the world has ever known.

"A masterful, unforgettable celebration of the human heart...It is by far the most powerful thing of beauty I have had the honour to enjoy in recent memory."
Goesta Struve-Dencher

"The most fascinating story I have ever read. I was totally captivated. It's erotic, sometimes explicit, it has romance but it's not M/M Romance. It's Gay Fiction with a Scifi twist." Goodreads

Embark on an erotic journey through time. From Ancient Sumer, Egypt and Rome through Renaissance Italy, modern Europe, Africa, and the Americas to the future above Earth, witness a kaleidoscope of human lives felixitated by this most enchanting being, named Felix.

Goodreads M/M Romance Book of the Month, July 2012

Books available in paperback and Kindle from Amazon, and other eBook formats from good bookshops and online retailers

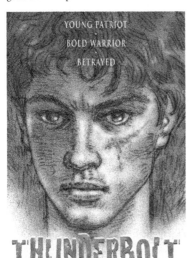

"Roger Kean has created a most captivating young man in hero Malco and a spectacular adventure of a war within a war in this historical rare gem. Roger Kean is a genius." Goodreads

"All in all, a fun romp around the Western Mediterranean during the 3rd century BCE with more than a hint of m/m romance." Goodreads

When Hannibal launches his army on a daring campaign to invade Rome, his cousin, teenager Malco, is proud to take part in the glorious endeavor. Through his eyes and the loves of his life—Juba, Numidian warrior, Trebon, eternal friend—this violent tale unfolds across the rich tapestry of history, of political intrigue, and brutal bloody war.

Made in United States
North Haven, CT
03 July 2025

70327395R00274